I0763473

THE DATA COLLECTORS TRILOGY (COMPLETE SERIES)

DANIELLE PALLI

THE DATA COLLECTORS TRILOGY (COMPLETE SERIES)

ISBN: 978-1-7367982-3-2 (Print version)

LCCN: 2023903486

This is a work of fiction. While several places are based in fact, the characters in this book are products of my imagination and used fictitiously. Any resemblance to actual persons, living or dead, business establishments or locales is entirely coincidental.

THE DATA COLLECTORS

Published by: Skinny Leopard Media, Sarasota, FL

ISBN: 978-0989989381 (Print version)

LCCN: 2020911339

BREACH OF CONTRACT

ISBN: 978-0990335283 (Print version)

LCCN: 2020923555

BETWEEN THE LAYERS

ISBN: 978-1736798263

LCCN: 2021917469

DEDICATION

I wondered if The Data Collectors would ever see the light of day. The story had played out in my head in fragments for the better part of seven years… maybe more. I'm not certain anymore. All I know is that all of a sudden, the characters began haunting me. I had had enough imaginary conversations with them and dreamt about them so often that if one of them knocked on my door in person, I wouldn't have batted an eye.

Finally, in 2020, The Data Collectors, the first book in the series, was published. The next two, Breach of Contract and Between the Layers, soon followed. I could have easily gone down the rabbit hole and written a dozen more books in this world… I still might.

But the trilogy wouldn't have been possible without the support of a few key people…
Thank you, Cindy Readnower of Skinny Leopard Media, for editing, formatting, publishing and offering all manner of marketing support and guidance over the years. Thank you, Graham Mack, for co-narrating and mastering the audiobook versions of this series, and offering invaluable audio support as I sought to hone my skills in the voiceover world. Thank you Joan Peters, who not only designed all the original covers for the trilogy, but even provided me with my one and

only painting lesson. I still have my amateur work hanging on my wall as a reminder of her patience and friendship. Sincere thanks go out to my friends, family and colleagues who were my beta readers, reviewers and cheerleaders.

I especially give enormous thanks to my partner in love and life, John Palli, for his never-ending support and belief in me, even when I didn't believe in myself. At varying times, he has been a beta reader, technical expert, researcher, and even a character stand-in when I needed to physically block out a scene.

Finally, I need to send a heartfelt thank you to the cat who started it all – Ms. Katrina, the spark behind this entire story. I hope there is a special place in the afterlife for kitties who inspire the building of worlds.
I am grateful.

Danielle

CONTENTS

THE DATA COLLECTORS

BREACH OF CONTRACT

BETWEEN THE LAYERS

THE DATA COLLECTORS

SECTION ONE

"If human laws are universal laws, then consider why anyone would kill another—fear, greed, power or hate. Often a combination of those traits. So, ask yourself who might exhibit those traits?"

DRAMATIS PERSONAE

Roman Aurelius: Human male (Section 0), wavy black hair, green eyes, tall and slender.

Cepheus Baruch: Royal male (Section 1, Section 3), stringy gray hair, yellow eyes, tall and lanky, shapeshifter (lizard/human).

Tanager Blackletter: Erde male (Section 1), curly blonde hair, brown eyes, average height and weight.

Drake Cushing: Human male (Section 0), black hair, blue eyes, medium height and stocky.

Bryce Cushing: Human male (Section 0), brown hair, blue eyes, medium height and build.

Dr. Archibald Ennis: Human male (Section 0), bald, brown eyes, tall and thin.

Fatima Fortunata: Human female (Section 0), purple hair, gray eyes, short and Rubenesque.

The Fortunata Family (Human): Keti (aunt), Tai (brother), Mama Fatima (mother), father, extended members, varied hair and eye colors.

Lucene ("Lucy") Jones: Earth-born female (Section 0), blonde or brown hair, hazel eyes, average height and weight, toned body.

Kunz Malaya: Male (Section 5), monarch, blue/gray fur and matching eyes, small, bulky stature, shapeshifter (wolf/human-like).

Reverend Isabella Simone: Human female (Section 0), spiritual advisor, white hair, violet eyes, tall and thin.

Jim Sparks: Erde male (Section 1), sandy hair, hazel eyes, short and slender.

Bagheera: Male cat (Section 0), black shorthair with yellow eyes, very handsome.

Fredo: Lesser Royal male (Section 3), red body and black eyes, large and thick, salamander-like with no noticeable shapeshifting abilities.

Ginny: Human female (Section 0), red hair and pale gray eyes, short and plump.

Hamish: Royal male (Section 3), brown hair and gold eyes, short and slightly overweight, shapeshifter (lizard / human-like).

Ivan (the Tinkerer): Human male (Section 0), red hair and green eyes, medium height and stocky.

Morphinae: Vitruvian (Section 2), shapeshifter, (varied gender, species, coloring), Balance-Keeper. Often prefers doll-like and butterfly-like lifeforms.

Odessa: Vitruvian (Section 2), shapeshifter (varied gender, species, coloring), prefers mermaid-like form the most.

Sabrina: Royal female (Section 3), black hair and yellow eyes, tall with average build, shapeshifter (lizard / human-like form).

Director Sutton: Human male (Section 0), light brown hair and hazel eyes, average height and slightly overweight.

LOCALES / SPECIAL GROUPS

The Assembly: Intergalactic gathering for the Intergalactic Peace Project (IPP).

Balance-Keepers: Special interest group in Section 2, Vitruvians. Will intervene to ensure all forces remain in balance.

Data Collector: Specialized team from Section 1, collecting data on Earth to save species.

Erde: Planet in Section 1, known for setting up preserves to rescue and protect humans.

Erdelings: Species from the Erde planet in Section 1.

Intergalactic Peace Project (IPP): Formed to create and maintain peace among intergalactic species.

International Registry of Alien Residency (IRAR): Created by the United Commonwealth (UC) to record and track aliens living on Earth.

Peace-Keepers: Nickname given to all inhabitants of Section 2, in particular, those living on Erde.

Royals: Nickname given to all inhabitants of Section 3, no specific planet-base, nomads.

Section 0: Earth and planets from common and neighboring galaxies.

Section 1: Erde and planets from common and neighboring galaxies.

Section 2: Vitruvia and planets from common and neighboring galaxies.

Section 3: Royal landscape and planets from common and neighboring galaxies. Galaxy boundaries change regularly.

Section 4: Limited communication with neighboring species, located in a section of the universe with multiple black holes.

Section 5: Silva and Trappist solar system as well as planets from common and nearby galaxies.

United Commonwealth (UC): Earth subdivision of the IPP to keep and maintain peace.

Terrestrial Academy of Research and Awareness (TARA): A leading university in Achel where the Data Collectors are trained.

Vitruvia: Planet in Section 2 known for its renegade band of Balance-Keepers.

Vitruvians: Species from the Vitruvia planet in Section 2.

PROLOGUE: THE STORM

25 YEARS AGO. 20 YEARS BEFORE THE ASSEMBLY.

"Forget the paddles, idiot!" Drake yelled to his younger brother above the wind and thunder as the downpour from the squall beat on them mercilessly. "Just hang on!"

The storm rolled in so quickly that the boys had no time to react. The waves were choppy, tossing their wooden fishing boat up and down as if it were a small coin that someone was flicking up in the air and then catching as it landed.

The sky was black, and visibility past the end of the boat near non-existent. With each toss of the boat more water splashed inside. The older boy tried to reach one hand to grab at a life jacket that slid past him, but he hadn't been quick enough, and it lodged itself under a downturned bucket at the front of the boat.

Bryce gripped the seat beneath him with both hands at his older brother's instructions. "What are you going to do?" He yelled over his shoulder as the sharp rain pelted him in the face.

"I'm going for the lifejackets!" Drake wiped the drenched hair from his eyes and tried to stand before the tossing of the boat landed him with a hard thud onto the wooden seat.

"Let me try! I'm closer." The younger boy lifted slightly out of his seat and cautiously reached an arm out in front, feeling around the wet floor until he touched what he thought must be the strap of one of the vests. "I've got it," he began to say, before the next wave overtook them, knocking him off the boat and into the frigid water. A loud thunderclap erupted, followed by an electrically-lit sky.

"Bryce!" the older boy screamed. The sky went black again. Moments after, the boat lurched onto its side, sending him into the lake before landing on top of him, cracking the side of his head in the process.

Bryce resurfaced, gasping for air and flailing his arms frantically. He circled his arms over the top of the downturned boat and hugged it for life. "Drake! Where the hell are you?"

A crack of lightning lit up the sky once more, just long enough for Bryce to see a head surface from the water. "Drake! Over here!" he yelled. "Swim this way!"

As instructed, the head began to move toward the boat, and it was only when it was several feet in front of him that the young boy could tell that this wasn't his brother.

Staring back at him was a blue face with black eyes that looked more like large buttons. Its skin had the texture of a crocheted plush toy, and its hair was stringy like indigo yarn. Just when the boy had convinced himself that it was the head of an abandoned toy that somehow ended up in the water…it blinked.

Bryce began to scream as the blue figure slowly drew itself out of the stormy seas, suspended in the air. It turned to look at him. The creature's chest was bare, and he wore ragged blue jeans that seemed like an afterthought. His body had the same pattern as his face. Otherwise, he had two arms and two legs and was almost human.

"I don't know what the fuck you are," the boy yelled at the figure, "but you gotta help me find my brother!"

The figure stared at the boy intently, as if doing mental calculations. Bryce fell silent, somehow understanding that his fate was at the mercy of this blue creature. From the scowl on the creature's face, Bryce feared that it would sooner kill him than help his brother.

The creature came to a decision, stretching one hand out over the water. Moments later, Drake's body floated to the surface. Bryce began to scream again, his words incoherent as tears flooded his face. The button eyes followed the scream as the boy's eyes grew wide in fear. The creature outstretched his other arm and Bryce found himself being lifted out of the water, hovering several feet above the waves.

As quickly as it had begun, the storm faded, and the night rolled in. Bryce felt himself being carried like a cat by the scruff of its neck, across the water alongside his brother, finally being deposited gently onto the nearest mangrove island. He struggled to balance among the meandering root system of the red mangroves that served as their floor. His brother lay limp along the small patch of wet sand. The creature stood over Drake, once again lost in thought. A moment later he flipped Drake on his back and touched a finger to his chest. With a jolt, the older brother's chest rose, his upper body lifted in midair, and then fell back to the ground. Water poured from his mouth as he choked air back into his lungs. He turned with eyes glazed over to look at his savior.

"Drake!" His brother called, stumbling toward him. At the sound of his name, Drake sat upright, shivering. Bryce knelt beside him, throwing his soggy arms around him in an embrace. "I thought you were dead!" he cried.

"He was," said the blue creature's deep voice.

"Who…what the hell are you?" Bryce croaked out as the creature turned his back on the boys and began to walk into the lake.

"Morphinae," the blue creature announced over his shoulder. "I am Vitruvian."

This meant nothing to Bryce, but as the creature began to descend into the lake, he remembered. "Thank you!" he called. Morphinae nodded slightly at the acknowledgement.

"Wait!" Drake found his voice. "You can't just leave us here, Bluehead! No one knows we're here, and we have no food or water."

"You should have known better," Morphinae chastised, his eyes growing dark. "Being at sea in weather such as this with no provisions." Once again, he began calculating thoughts. His button eyes turned momentarily to Bryce, and something in his heart softened. *But,* he thought, *the boy did say 'thank you.' Humans hardly ever did that.* Finally, he answered, "I will see that you have help." With that, he descended into the lake.

"Cepheus, please help us." Seven-year-old Lucene Jones concentrated as hard as she could, scrunching up her face until it hurt. She sat strapped into the back seat of her parent's green utility vehicle, hugging a plush, black, cat toy for comfort. The rain poured down violently, pelting the hard top, making it sound as if the rain and thunder were coming from inside the vehicle. Lucene's mother, Dora Jones, kept gripping the center armrest with both hands, twisting her body uncomfortably to check on Lucene in the back seat.

"I'm going to pull over at this next rest stop," her father, Xan, yelled above the storm, white-knuckled hands gripping the steering wheel. Dora nodded in agreement.

"Don't worry, Lucene," her mother comforted, "Daddy's going to pull the car over until the rain passes. It'll be okay." Her mother's words did not match her feelings. She, too, was afraid. Lucene could feel it. "Why don't you work on one of your meditations? It will help calm you down."

Lucene nodded. She had been doing that very thing. She imagined an open red door in front of her. Through it, was the storm. She watched the storm at a distance as she moved further and further from the door. With her mind's eye, she slammed it shut, drowning out the thunder and lightning trapped behind it. It was silent.

"Please, Cepheus," Lucene tried again, this time whispering aloud, "Could you please help us? We're really scared."

From lightyears away, Cepheus replied, "I will try."

Lucene took comfort in that and was just beginning to relax a little when she felt the car jolt. Her mother screamed as the SUV swerved off the road and began tumbling over and over, leaving Lucene hanging from her seat belt. She felt pieces of glass shatter around her, some of them embedding into her skin as the rain poured into the car. The last thing she remembered was a painful shock running through her before everything went black.

Cepheus felt the energy of a lightning bolt shoot through him, awakening him from his meditation with a sudden start. He looked down at his arms in surprise but noticed no visible signs of any trauma.

He tried once again to mentally connect with Lucene first, and then her parents, to no avail. He uncrossed his legs and stood clumsily, taking a moment to lean over and place his hands on his knees as if to both stretch his limbs and catch his breath. A tear rolled down his otherwise expressionless face.

He left the meditation room, softly closing the door behind him.

"Well?" Tanager asked eagerly, noticing his older friend and mentor's blank expression. "What happened?" The young man paused from the ornate wood sculpture he was carving.

"Nothing…nothing," Cepheus whispered, hanging his head. "They are gone. She is lost."

CHAPTER 1
THE HOSPITAL ROOM
25 YEARS AGO. 20 YEARS BEFORE THE ASSEMBLY.

"Well, Ms. Fortunata, it appears that you were well-named," Dr. Archibald Ennis peered over his clipboard at the plump girl squirming in the hospital bed who was attempting in vain to unravel herself from an ill-fitting robe and a tangle of bedsheets. "We just let your parents know that you're going home today. Bet you're glad about that!"

Fatima Fortunata let out a giggle, "I sure am!"

Dr. Ennis smiled back, "They'll be up in a few minutes. You just sit tight."

Fatima wasn't sure she knew how to sit tight, or loose for that matter, her facial expression turning to one of deep contemplation as she gave it some thought.

Dr. Ennis passed by the second hospital bed and paused for a moment to look at the less fortunate Lucene. He tried to smile encouragingly during his quick retreat out the door.

Young Lucene let out a sigh. *When were her parents coming to get her?* she wondered, feeling a sudden bitterness in the pit of her stomach. She looked down at the strange, new fern patterns on her arms. According to the doctors, who were unaware of Lucene's keen sense of hearing while they were discussing her condition at the nurse's station with some Child

Services something-or-other, she had been struck by lightning. They were watching for signs of numbness or tingling in her arms, dizziness, and headaches. So far, she exhibited none of these symptoms and the doctors were somewhat baffled.

"What happened to your arms?" Fatima asked, now standing at Lucene's bedside, barefoot.

"Lightning," Lucene answered. "It hit me and left these patterns on my arms."

"Does it hurt?" Fatima looked concerned.

"Nah," Lucene replied. "But I think it might be permanent."

"Cool!" Fatima squealed, enthusiastically. She thought about this some more. "I read in my comic book—not the one I have over there," she shook her head as she waved her hand at the book that lay face down on the end table beside her bed. "But the one I have at home, where this guy got struck by lightning and then had supernatural powers!"

"What are sup-ah-nat-ah powers?" Lucene wrinkled her nose, sitting up with interest.

"No, silly!" Fatima let out a giggle. "Sup-er-nat-ur-al...like, being able to fly, or super strength or the ability to read minds."

"Oh," Lucene was doubtful of this ability, but was willing to give it a try. "Okay, let's see...without actually *telling* me, think of your age, and I'll try to guess by reading your mind."

Fatima clapped her hands. "Oh, goody! You're fun! The last time I was in here, the girl didn't want to play or even talk to me." She furrowed her brows and thought of her age with all of her might.

Lucene closed her eyes and pretended her forehead was a movie screen, and she was watching it to see what would appear. She turned her head slightly to the left, and then right, and smiled.

"You'll be nine in a few days. Your birthday is Thursday," Lucene blurted out, not really sure where that information came from.

Fatima's eyes flew open wide. "Oh my gosh! You *are* supernatural. How did you *do* that?"

"I dunno," Lucene confessed. Though there was something familiar about the experiment, but her head felt a little fuzzy, and she was having trouble remembering much of anything. "I just saw you blowing out a cake with people standing around you…like a party or something. There were nine candles on the cake."

"That's amazing," Fatima gushed, "but where did Thursday come from?"

"I heard a song in my head, one I don't remember ever hearing. It was talking about Thursday's child, so I figured it had to be this Thursday."

Fatima's eyes grew wide with admiration. "Wow!" A nurse walked by the room, pushing a meal cart, pausing to scowl at Fatima. She pressed a finger to her lips to encourage Fatima to be quiet.

"Okay, let me try," Fatima whispered, checking to make sure that the nurse had passed. "You think of your age, K?" Without asking permission, Fatima climbed up on the edge of Lucene's bed. Lucene bent her knees, hugging them close to her to make extra room.

"Okay," Lucene thought of her age as clearly as she could.

"Eight?"

"No."

"Nine, like me?"

"No."

"You can't be ten. You're too little. You're not ten, are you?"

"I'm seven."

"That was my next guess." Fatima snapped her fingers.

"How come you're in here?" Lucene wanted to know.

"I have an arrhythmia," Fatima declared as a point of pride, dramatically waving her hands in the air for emphasis. "My heart beats funny, but not in the normal way that abnormal hearts beat. It's *mysterious* and very rare. My mom says it's because I'm so musical."

"You seem awfully happy about it," Lucene seemed doubtful.

"I'm always happy," Fatima answered with a shrug, as if that explained everything. And, in some way, it did.

"Fatima!" An older version of Fatima bounced in the room, bringing a boatload of energy and smiles with her.

"Hi, Mom!" Fatima climbed off the bed. Lucene watched as Fatima's mom wrapped her in a big hug. She wished her mom would hurry up and get here. Her heart sank a little. Something about the feeling told her that this was never going to happen. She choked back a tear as Fatima introduced her, "This is Lucene! She's my new friend. And, she's got superpowers!"

"Does she?" Fatima's mom played along, her eyes growing wide. "How wonderful!" She put out a hand and gently shook Lucene's. "It's nice to meet you, Lucene."

Lucene felt a warm glow rise from where the woman touched her hand to all the way up her arm. She smiled back. It was almost as if the woman had hugged her too.

Glancing down at the girl's arms, Fatima's mother became aware of the dark tree-like brown patterns on them but thought it impolite to mention them. To Fatima, she said, "Your father is pulling up the car and the nurse will be up in a minute so we can check out."

"Okay, lemme just get my stuff." Fatima went to grab her kid-sized, hot pink suitcase while her mother dashed to the nurse's station to confirm that someone would be along shortly. Fatima's suitcase rolled loudly across the white hospital floor as she passed Lucene's bed. "Here," Fatima paused and handed her a business card. "This is my calling card."

"You have a card?" Lucene seemed surprised. "I thought only grown-ups had those."

"I'm in the advanced classes," Fatima said matter-of-factly and without boast, as if this explained why a nearly nine-year-old would need a business card. "It has my full name on it, see?" She pointed. "If you ever end up in Florida, you can come visit me!" Fatima gave her new friend a hug. "See you soon, Lucene!" She waved as she met her mother at the door.

"Take care, Lucene," Fatima's mother called. "I'm sure your parents will be along in no time to collect you."

Perhaps Fatima was more supernatural than she realized, since Lucene was in New York and saw no reason why she would ever end up in Florida. She certainly did not expect to see her new friend anytime soon—at least not by her definition of "soon."

Lucene looked down at the calling card as if it carried with it some luck. *Fatima Fortunata,* the top line read. Beneath it: *Parrish, Florida.*

CHAPTER 2
THE ASSEMBLY
FIVE YEARS AGO.

Lucene sat in the assembly room where more than 215 Earth representatives from the United States gathered for the Intergalactic Peace Project's (aka, the IPP) annual conference, sponsored this year by the United Commonwealth (aka, the UC). Above their heads, they were surrounded by a series of large flat screens, each one reflecting the representatives from Earth along with those of neighboring planets in their own gathering places. Some were in giant lecture halls, like the one Lucene was in, while others could be found in large outdoor coliseums. The agenda was lengthy and a solid four hours was planned for today's first meeting. From the look of it, there were nine planets in attendance, three fewer than last time. This was cause for concern.

She tugged nervously at the hem of her blouse. It scratched at her skin and felt almost as uncomfortable as her restrictive polyester pants and close-toed foot crushers, falsely advertised as shoes. Business attire never felt quite right to her. It was as if she were expected to wear a Halloween costume for 48 weeks of the year. *We can easily communicate with beings from other solar systems,* she thought, *but we can't seem to master 'business casual.'*

For the thousandth time, she fumbled with the translation headset wrapped tightly over the top of her head and snaking down the side of her face. It kept getting tangled in her blonde locks in spite of her repeated attempts to smooth her already abnormally straight hair. Somehow, she managed to set off a loud screech from the headset that had everyone in the assembly eyeing her with at least a minor level of annoyance. Lucene hated technology, more specifically, anything that she considered an unnatural wave-like connection to something else, such as wireless fidelity or virtual keyboards. In her mind, they were too easy to intercept and even corrupt. She got by with her headset by reminding herself that she could unplug it at any time.

"Sorry," she called, not realizing her microphone volume was still set on "max." A few executives jumped, tugging their headphones from their ears at the sudden vocal interruption. Lucene quickly set herself to "mute." Her boss, Drake Cushing, turned his head casually in her direction, grinned slightly out of one corner of his mouth, and then shook his head. Lucene let out an embarrassed sigh and slunk back in her seat. This was her first invitation to attend the conference and now she feared, it might be her last.

The other scribes around her did not seem to notice the eruption, too busy typing rapidly on the hologram keypads in front of them, their words projected onto the front of drop-screen visors that fell over their eyes. The visors, themselves, were attached to their translation headsets, making the group appear more android-like than human. Only they could see what they were typing. There were also a few archaic laptops, and a couple of daring early adopters of Mind-to-Text technology who sat in deep concentration as their thoughts were translated onto the visor in front of them. The latter was not yet perfected, and the scribes could be heard mumbling "delete" and "replace" under their breath.

Then there was Lucene, the only person in the room with a pad of paper and a pen. Recording and photographic devices were not permitted, except by an official member of the council, and Lucene was not, resigning herself to a mid-level government position. A few of the other scribes looked over her shoulder, perplexed. One young, sharp-nosed, auburn-haired woman leaned over and whispered into the ear of the man sitting beside her. She pointed at Lucene's notepad and stifled back a laugh.

"Who let Lucy, the teenage blogger, in?" she asked, reading Lucene's nametag as she spoke. The man beside her shifted uncomfortably in his seat and chuckled nervously. Lucene was tired of being mistaken for a teenager. She was, after all, 27. It's just that her body seemed to think she was still only 17. The woman eyed the tree-like lightning marks on Lucene's arms. Lucene pulled at the edges of her three-quarter-sleeve blouse in a futile attempt to cover them fully. Most of the time, she forgot they were there, except when someone paid special attention to them.

"Well," Lucene responded pleasantly, "Your information can be hacked from a million miles away. Mine, someone would have to physically take from me." The sharp-nosed woman looked surprised at being heard from such a distance. "And," Lucene continued, "It still wouldn't matter, because no one would be able to read my shorthand anyway."

"To each her own," the woman mumbled, sitting back with a complacent grin. She snapped her visor back in place and adjusted her headphones. Lucene choked back a response, secretly wishing the woman's virtual keyboard would suddenly display all the letters inside out, making her notes illegible.

"May I have your attention please," the facilitator on the central large monitor announced. "The gathering shall now commence. Please make yourself ready." There were short pauses between the facilitator's comments as the universal translator found the closest match to English or Spanish. During these meetings, Lucene occasionally liked to slip her headphones off and listen to whichever planet advisor was leading the session. Their native tongue, while mostly incomprehensible to her, was beautiful and fascinating. Though today, with the new headphones, she dared not, in case she accidentally caused another disturbance.

Today's speaker was from Trappist, a planet about 40 lightyears away. She watched as his bulky form projected outward from the screen, making it appear as if he were standing in the room with them. The likeness was so real he could have passed for a live person had he not been hovering in midair with a translucent glow around him.

While he had two eyes, a nose, two ears and two hands, that's where the similarities between he and Earthlings ended. Section 5 inhabitants moved on four limbs, two of which were retractable depending on whether the limb's owner opted to walk on two legs or run like a wolf on all four. Underneath his silver uniform, wrinkled gray-blue fur was the other obvious differentiator.

"For those who do not know me, my name is Kunz Malaya. I am the monarch of Silva, from the Western region of Trappist in Section 5. I am honored to be with all of you today. We will open with the setting of intentions."

For the next five minutes, Kunz read through the IPP creed to uphold peace at all costs, to be compassionate to brother and sister planets and to make open communication a priority—all things that sounded wonderful to Lucene when she first arrived. But, like others, the more she saw of war, hypocrisy, of planets fighting in the same way that countries on Earth fought, of death and disease, the less enthusiastic she became about her role recording and collecting all of this data. In fact, at this moment, she wanted nothing more than to go home, climb into bed, and bury her head under the covers.

"Today, we open our discussion with the most pressing cause for concern," Kunz frowned. "For this, we invite Cepheus Baruch of the planet Erde in Section 1 to take the floor."

One of the tall screens moved out from the wall as Cepheus's hologram stood in front of them, high in the air. He wore a plaid sweater vest over a long sleeved, cream-colored dress shirt and long black dress slacks, which told her that he was not only trying to appeal to the Earth audience, but more specifically, those in the Northern regions of the planet. "Thank you, Monarch. And, good morning, Assembly," he said. Chills ran through her when Cepheus began to speak. There was something familiar about his deep voice, though she couldn't determine why. The most human-like, those living in Section 1, had almost all of the same features with two exceptions. One, they had the capacity to heal from injury much more quickly, and two, their life expectancy was more than double that of a human. Consequently, they aged much more slowly than humans. It was rumored that Cepheus Baruch was born among the Royals in Section 3, giving him the unique ability to transform into lizard form in self-defense, and even grow back arms and legs if they were somehow removed. In her eight years working for the United Commonwealth, she'd never seen anything of the sort of those from Section 1 or 3, and thought the whole thing was a silly legend.

As she observed the speaker, Lucene felt a gentle warmth start at her heart and move outward toward her arms, legs and face, followed by a gentle buzzing through her entire being. She sat upright and began to smile, as if she had just re-discovered a long-lost friend, but caught herself. After all, she didn't know this man, did she? She'd only heard about him through past conferences. Lucene refocused her attention to the meeting at hand.

"What the heck?" the sharp-nosed woman behind her protested. "My keyboard is not projecting properly. It's like it's reflecting upside down and backwards. How can I possibly take notes on this?" Lucene withheld a smile. Really, she hadn't meant to do that...mostly not.

"Here, let me see," the man sitting beside her whispered. "Maybe it's something with the settings." She reluctantly unclipped her visor and handed it to him. He, in turn, temporarily replaced his visor with hers. "Hmm...looks fine to me." She snatched it back as he was still removing it.

"It is not fine, but I will have to type without looking and hope for the best." The man shrugged, returning his attention to the meeting.

"As most of you know," Cepheus began solemnly, "Erde has a special interest in supporting the inhabitants of Earth and their mission to re-create an environmentally sustainable world." Many nodded; others remained expressionless. "Unfortunately, there have been some disturbing patterns of late."

"Please share with us what you mean by 'disturbing,'" Kunz encouraged.

"We've noticed within the past 200 years, the depletion of Earth's natural resources, unusual weather patterns leaving disastrous conditions behind, the decreased availability of water, increased pollution, subjection to toxic elements—including damaging rays from the sun, and ill health of all species on Earth."

A murmur from the crowds ensued, mostly from Earth representatives, some present in the room and several others from their remote locations, their grim faces clearly visible on their screens.

"Order and dignity, please," Kunz addressed the crowd. "Cepheus, please continue."

"About 30 years ago, before the IPP was in existence, the people of Erde decided to try and intervene on the Earth's behalf by sending representatives to collect data on the existing conditions in an effort to discover a solution."

"Data Collectors who pretended to be humans, moving in secret among us," Drake Cushing interjected loudly from his seat.

"Please...Drake," Kunz intervened, reading Drake's nametag for reference. "Cepheus has the floor. We will hear responses momentarily."

"My apologies, Monarch." Drake slid his headset off in frustration and ran his hand through his thick, wavy hair, before putting his headphones back in place. He crossed one leg over the other, resting his ankle on his thigh. He tapped his upturned shoe with a stylus pen, in obvious annoyance. Lucene was surprised. Usually, her boss was exceptionally calm. She didn't understand this current state of agitation.

"It is true," Cepheus continued, "We did move in secret because we had no idea how humans would respond to our presence on their planet. And, as you well know, in the interest of, as you would say, 'transparency,' we informed the IPP of our Data Collectors as soon as a division was formed. They have since been entered into the International Registry of Alien Residency."

"And what happened after they were added to the IRAR?" the monarch asked, sympathetically.

"They began to die off. More specifically, someone or several people began to kill them off." Lucene could have sworn that Cepheus shot her a direct look of warning as he spoke. A wave of panic swallowed her.

You must protect yourself, Lucene. Cepheus's voice spoke to her, but not through the translation headphones. She heard his voice from inside her head. Lucene stared back at Cepheus's hologram, astonished. *How did he do that? More importantly, how did he know her birth name?* She'd been going by 'Lucy' since she was a child. Cepheus quickly averted his gaze.

The crowd erupted with holograms appearing all over the room as other realms tried to take the floor.

"Order and dignity, please!" Kunz exclaimed, and one by one began to mute both the audio and hologram visuals for the screens around the room. "Cepheus, please continue. You have about one minute to finish your presentation before I must give the floor to someone else."

"Thank you, Monarch. The fear is more than just the safety of Earth and the safety of our people, our Data Collectors. We believe that a group from one of the neighboring sections is involved in this slaughter, beings who do not wish to see Earth survive."

"Insanity!" Someone from Section 3 proclaimed. "To come here and be accused by the so-called Peace-keepers!"

"I'm not accusing any specific Sections or planets," Cepheus explained to no avail.

I didn't hear him accuse anyone; Lucene found herself defending this man she didn't know. She went through the filing system in her brain to try and remember. *Ah,* she thought, *the Royals*. The Royals were nomads —a very aggressive group that was constantly seeking to take over uninhabited planets to claim as their own. Many of the other Sections nicknamed them the "Royals" as an insult to their narcissistic and elitist ways. Somehow, they took it as a compliment. So, the name stuck. They had a tenuous relationship with the IPP, at best.

"Requesting the floor next, Monarch," Drake Cushing stood. Cepheus bowed and stepped back, his hologram fading as he did so.

The monarch acknowledged Drake's deference to the order of things and granted him the floor next. Drake stood and quickly made his way to the circular platform at the front of the room.

"Thank you, Monarch," Drake nodded to the facilitator, as was customary. To the crowd, he said, "Cepheus Baruch claims that the Data Collectors came here 30 years ago in the efforts of 'helping' the Earth by deceptively posing as humans to collect information about us." There was a murmur from the crowd. "But isn't it true that your planet has at least a dozen, quote, unquote, 'preservation' areas designed to support human life where you've absconded with members of the human race against their will?"

"No," Cepheus answered from his station on Erde, his hologram resurfacing above them. "Our preservation areas were set up by the Terrestrial Academy of Research and Awareness to provide a safe place for humans should the Earth prove unsustainable."

Lucene had heard of TARA, but she always thought it was more like an intergalactic university that welcomed many species to meet and study there. *Preservations?* This was new information to her.

"Ah, yes. TARA," Drake mocked, looking up at him. "Does TARA's 'research' include human experimentation in the interest of 'science'?"

"Absolutely not!" Cepheus was flustered. From behind Cepheus, other attendees in his group shook their heads in anger at the accusation. Over his shoulder, a younger man with a mop of curly hair peered at Lucene, curiously. She caught his gaze, momentarily, before averting her eyes. In a room of this size, she reasoned, and with so many neighboring planets in attendance, it's ridiculous to think that either of these men were looking directly at her. *Must be like a painting in a museum, where the eyes seem to follow you.*

"And, isn't it more accurate," Drake paused for emphasis, "that your Data Collectors were killed by humans in self-defense when they refused to return to your planet with you?"

"No, that is untrue."

"So, there are no humans currently living on Erde then?"

There was a pause. "There are..." Cepheus answered, honestly. "But they came with us of their own free will."

There was a loud uproar from all audiences and Cepheus's protests went unheard.

"Order and dignity, please!" Kunz protested, and the crowds slowly settled down.

"I don't recall anyone from Section 1 notifying the IPP of humans being relocated to another planet, do you?" Drake addressed the crowd, waving his arm and surveying the room for the answer he already knew. This was news. "You say you come in peace," Drake yelled above the crowd, which was getting louder by the minute. "But isn't it true that Erde is keenly interested in occupying Earth and moving the humans out...indefinitely?"

"No," Cepheus's eyes became flooded as if injected with a yellow die, and his nose began to shift, taking on an almost beak-like appearance. He closed his eyes and took a few deep breaths. Lucene felt herself become agitated on his behalf. She surveyed the growing unrest in the lecture hall, as many attendees were now on their feet and protesting upward at Cepheus's hologram. *Moving humans out? Was this related to the files Drake recently asked her to procure from the International Registry?* She was pulled back from her thoughts.

"For this reason, I move that Erde and all planets in Section 1 be banned from the IPP and be entered into investigation!" Drake demanded.

"Let us explain," the curly-haired man appearing behind Cepheus, jumped to his feet.

"You, sir," Drake addressed him. "Do not have the floor. Be silent!"

The commotion continued as Kunz Malaya tried in vain to calm the heated discussions in the forum. In all of his time as monarch and an IPP member, he'd never seen this level of contention before, and wondered what he was missing?

Lucene surveyed the scribes surrounding her, all feverishly typing their observations. She folded her notepad and tucked her pen away. "Excuse me," she said to the people who occupied the seats beside her. They leaned back into their chairs to let her pass. Once in the aisle, she made one final glance back at Cepheus's hologram who looked back at her with a nod, before returning to the chaos. She made her way out into the hallway and toward the building's exit.

"Excuse me, Lucy," a burly security guard stopped her. "Aren't you forgetting something?" Lucene looked down at her notepad.

"Ah, sorry. My brain doesn't seem to be working right today," she joked nervously.

"Happens to the best of us," the guard smiled.

No information of any kind left the building without permission. Written, audio and visual content was carefully curated and approved before any of it reached the media and the outside world. She'd have to leave her notes in her lock box in the resource room. Lucene quickly made her way down the hall past the IPP offices to the opaque glass doors at the end. She paused in front of them as a translucent red light passed over her form. "Welcome, Lucy," the computer greeted her, and the door automatically slid open. She slipped over the threshold and made her way to her lock box as the door closed behind her.

Lucene never did return to the IPP summit that day. In fact, she never returned to the United Commonwealth building ever again. After locking up her notes, she darted past security and out onto the streets of Manhattan. She breathed a sigh of relief as she exited the property, as if she had somehow been held prisoner there and someone might stop her at any time and prevent her from leaving. She began walking toward her apartment, mentally making her escape plan.

Escape from what? she asked herself. She didn't really know, but somehow Cepheus's warning echoed in her head. *You must protect yourself, Lucene.*

Moments later, she caught the unusual scent of sulfur. She jolted in panic as one might experience during a hypnagogic jerk, just before falling asleep. Then, an explosion shocked the ground. Lucene turned to see smoke billowing out of the Commonwealth building, followed by crowds of people fighting their way through the doors on the first floor. On the upper levels, government employees shuffled onto emergency escape hatches that sprang into place once the upper windows had been triggered, sliding one by one down toward the street below. Lucene stood motionless as sirens sounded and ambulances and military trucks pulled up to the scene.

"Stand back," a police officer waved an arm in front of her and the onlookers that had gathered around Lucene without her noticing. The police began roping off the area with many of Lucene's colleagues on one side, and her on the other. Through the smoke, she saw her boss rushing from the building, a handkerchief held over his face. Even from this distance, she could see that he was limping slightly.

Under normal circumstances, she would have stayed to make sure those she knew were safe, and to offer her testimony to investigators. But somehow, she knew that the best course of action was simply to blend in with the mounting crowds...and then disappear.

CHAPTER 3
THE TERRESTRIAL ACADEMY OF RESEARCH AND AWARENESS (TARA)

ONE YEAR AGO. FOUR YEARS AFTER THE ASSEMBLY.

Students of the Terrestrial Academy of Research and Awareness, or TARA, as it was known, behaved much like students on Earth. And, save for a few refugees from neighboring planets, most looked like humans, as well.

The academy was founded as a way to educate students about Earth and other alien species and their cultures. One of its advanced training tracks was specifically targeted toward Earth studies and included those who would eventually work on one of the many Human preserves on Erde. They would be teaching humans the skills to evolve as a species in order to adapt to varied climates while protecting them until it could be determined if Earth would continue to be habitable for humans, or if other arrangements needed to be made. In return, humans living on preserves, shared as much as they could with TARA to ensure the success of the mission.

Other tracks included environmental research and development, in which TARA scientists examined collected data about the ecology and resource partitioning on Earth and created systems for the restoration of the Earth's natural balance...assuming they could convince key world leaders to adopt them.

Last, and arguably the most enviable track, was that of the Data Collectors—the ones who would make the yearlong journey to Earth on special assignment to collect information in their specialty, be it oceanic, freshwater, flora, fauna, substrate, human behavior, weather conditions and the like. Upon arrival, many Data Collectors opted to remain on Earth and report back throughout their lifespan.

But when the IPP was formed just over four years ago, Data Collectors began disappearing in large numbers. Many others had been found dead under questionable circumstances. Travels to Earth had been halted, but given the three-year commitment required for proper training, it was decided that classes should continue...for now.

A mild-mannered professor wandered through the long hallway toward Cepheus's office, passing dozens of students ranging from the very young to very old, and each dressed in a variety of garb…if at all. Not wanting to stifle anyone's free will, no major restrictions were put on dress code at the academy. That respect for personal choice had always been a distinguishing quality of those living on Erde and that culture was particularly evident at the school. The one complaint had been when several students decided to attend class garment-less, which disturbed the sensibilities of more conservative students and professors who were simply worried about hygiene. A compromise had been reached, and those students agreed to at least wear a bathrobe or a toga-like coverup while in class. Being a more empathic planet, conflicts were generally resolved quickly, and Erde enjoyed the distinction of having planet-wide peace for more than 100 years, so much so, that they became known as the Peace-Keepers to neighboring planets within the galaxy.

The professor knocked softly on the office door. "Cepheus, my friend, may I enter?" He pushed the door open just enough to peer around the corner at the tall man hunched over his work desk at the far end of the room. His features were shrouded by the black-hooded cape he'd taken to wearing.

"Yes, of course, Tanager," Cepheus replied, almost in a whisper. "Come in."

Cepheus's dimly lit office was something to behold, resembling a cross between an overstuffed library and an inventor's workshop. The room was filled wall-to-wall and ceiling-to-floor with books, electronic devices, blueprints, and scientific models. Contraptions hung from the ceilings and cluttered the tabletops. The windowsill above his desk housed an array of green plants, all competing for sunlight.

"Your students missed you today," Tanager offered, resting his brown, vegetable leather briefcase on top of a pile of books stacked haphazardly next to the desk where his mentor sat. "I'm afraid I'm not nearly as knowledgeable about Earth Agroecology as you are."

Cepheus turned his head, briefly regarding the younger man standing before him who was clad in a retro-style tan tweed jacket with matching slacks, and nodded. There was a glaze in Cepheus's eyes, as if he didn't understand what was being said, but preferred to be polite. His nimble fingers returned to their task of unraveling a series of tangled wires that were connected to an indeterminate metal contraption with wings that sat motionless on his desk.

"We received some news today," Tanager continued, "about Lucene."

Cepheus stopped working and looked over his shoulder. "Lucene?" he repeated, quickly sifting through the files of information in his mind, trying to match a memory to his immediate sadness at the sound of her name. "I thought she was dead...twice."

"No, my friend," Tanager continued, "she is very much alive, and she needs our help."

"Lucene needs our help," Cepheus repeated in a low voice. "What can we do?"

"According to one of our Data Collectors, she has resurfaced in Florida."

"Not dead?"

"No," Tanager confirmed.

"The car accident?"

"She survived."

"The assembly?"

"She survived."

"Then," Cepheus finally concluded. "We must go and retrieve her."

"I wish it were that simple." Tanager sat on the edge of the desk with one foot firmly on the floor. "With the Earth being such a hostile environment, I don't feel safe sending any of our new recruits under those conditions. Plus, it will take us two years round trip to bring her home, and we believe your parents..."

"My parents *are* dead," Cepheus interrupted, not without a hint of anger.

"I'm sorry, the *Royals*. We believe they already have a head start on the technology and are capable of travelling to Earth and back much more quickly than we do. If they find her before we get to her, I'm afraid..."

"They will torture her," Cepheus finished. "As they did the others...as they did me."

"Yes," Tanager was concerned. "They have no idea how her skills work, and may damage her in the process, or worse."

"I will go for her," Cepheus announced.

"Are you certain? I would go with you, of course, particularly since you are still under...Watch."

There was a long pause as Cepheus regarded a box of metal gears on his desk, presumably to operate a clock or similar mechanism. He stared at them intently. "If the universe operates like a clock, the planets being a system of gears all working together to keep the proper time, what will happen if one of those planets stop turning? How would the rest of the universe survive?" He began pulling the small gears out of the box, one by one, and lining them up on the floor at his feet—the only available space left in the room.

"Cepheus?" The man did not respond to Tanager; he was busy frenetically rearranging the gears just so. Tanager let out a sigh. "I believe it's time for your medication." Without another word, Tanager put an air syringe up to Cepheus's ear and depressed the plunger, delivering an antipsychotic serum via a fast-paced puff. The slender man's eyes opened wide for a moment, in surprise, before his body began to topple forward. Tanager caught him and guided the man as carefully as he could, to the floor.

He could hear the sounds of students in the hallway just outside the office. Tanager quickly lunged for the door, closing it just as a few students passed by and looked in his direction. Revisiting the man lying on the floor, Tanager removed his own jacket, balled it up, and tucked it under Cepheus's head like a pillow.

CHAPTER 4
THE MAN IN THE BLACK FEDORA

FRIDAY AFTERNOON. FIVE YEARS AFTER THE ASSEMBLY.

It wasn't often that Lucene went grocery shopping in the middle of the day on a Friday. Come to think of it, it wasn't often that Lucene went grocery shopping at all. But there she was, loading up her green, box-shaped motor vehicle on a rainy afternoon, trying to unlatch the tailgate with one hand while attempting to balance her produce-filled cloth bags with the other. She wasn't having much luck.

"God, damn it!" She cursed as several apples, an orange and two Spanish onions rolled out of the bag she'd propped against her thigh that headed straight into a puddle. As she leaned down to retrieve them, her shopping cart began rolling away with her small leather backpack in tow.

Abandoning the fallen spoils, she ran after the cart, though not before the tailgate had a chance to coax her along by smacking her bottom. Lucene let out a few more expletives, cursing the rain, her matted wet pixie cut, and the melted hair mousse that burned her eyes as it ran down her forehead.

"May I be of some assistance?" Tanager asked, catching the shopping cart midflight and spinning it around with one hand. He was standing next to a lamppost holding a bright red umbrella with his other hand.

She could barely make out his round features beneath the black hat he wore and the upturned collar of his gray trench coat.

"I'm okay, thanks." Lucene gave a gracious nod, snatched the cart, and proceeded to roll it back to her car. Hunching her shoulders as the rain grew heavier, it pummeled her neck and back. Water had now successfully soaked its way through her long-sleeved gray cotton t-shirt and jeans. For once, she was grateful that she'd remembered to wear a bra.

"At least allow me to shield you from the rain while you collect your groceries," he was persistent, sheltering her with the red umbrella as he fell into a quick step beside her. He wasn't much taller than Lucene and struggled not to accidentally poke her with the point of one of the umbrella's metal ribs. To his own discomfort, he endured the rain making a loud patter as it rudely smacked the rim of his fedora. He had a strange energy about him. Lucene could almost feel it, as if their skin were touching even though there was more than a foot of space between them.

"Um, okay, but I don't want to be a bother," she answered nervously, slinging her backpack over one shoulder and giving the cart a shove, watching as it sailed into the cart return, clanging against other carts in its path. She bent over the puddle and scooped up the fallen fruits and vegetables, decided they were still "good enough" and tossed them haphazardly into a cargo bin in the back of her car and slammed the tailgate shut. Tanager waited patiently as Lucene awkwardly fumbled with the tailgate lock. "Well, that's that. Thanks so much..." The man didn't respond. "Uh...good day to you, sir," she tried to dismiss him a second time.

"It was my pleasure," he tipped his soggy hat, and continued to cover her head with the umbrella until she was safely in the driver's seat. She felt her heart speed up, just a little. She sucked in a deep breath and held it, momentarily.

Lucene didn't like to think she was the kind of woman who thought the worst of people, but it wasn't every day that strange men went out of their way to help her. Other women, yes, but she never felt herself the sort who would warrant that kind of attention unless the intentions were bad ones. She kept a sidelong glance at the stranger standing outside of her car as she revved the engine. The green monster gave a pathetic shudder as the engine died. "Come on, Kermit," she pleaded with her car. "Not today." She revved it again…and again…nothing. "God, damn it," she hung her head with a sigh.

She watched as this strange man in the black fedora gave a slight knock on the driver's side window. She let out another deep sigh and strong-armed the window handle, rotating it just enough to produce a small opening between the top of the windowpane and the roof.

"If I may suggest," he offered, pressing his lips up toward the open space, as if it were a microphone. "My car is just over there." He pointed to a small blue compact car sitting in the otherwise empty lot. "Perhaps I could give you a lift? You can get your perishables home, and we could have a look at what's troubling your vehicle after the rain has stopped. What do you think?"

"While I appreciate the offer," Lucene bit the corner of her lip, "you should get out of the rain and quit worrying about me. I'll just phone my roommate and ask her to pop around the corner and pick me up." She fished through her backpack as if searching for something.

"Very well," Tanager conceded, mouthing the word 'pop' as if it confused him. She tried not to look too relieved. "I'll just wait in my car over there until you've made your call, just to make certain you have assistance on the way. You can," he paused a moment to think, "give me a wave as an all clear that help is on the way." He puffed his chest up and smiled, as if satisfied with his choice of words.

"Sounds like a plan," Lucene smiled, uncomfortably. He paused again, as if processing what she said, before flashing a smile and darting off to the warmth of his dry little car. Lucene picked up the closest item that looked like a phone, a small black notepad, and held it to her ear, pretending to have a conversation.

She glanced over at the man waiting patiently in his car, his fingers rhythmically tapping the wheel as if he were listening to music. From what she could see, he appeared to be clean-shaven with a small, nondescript nose and a medium complexion. His eyes were masked by the hat, but she could make out a tangle of curly blonde hair creeping down from the edge of it, the color hers used to be before she died it an unobtrusive brown and chopped it off. He looked relatively normal, but that didn't mean anything. It was then that she noticed his mouth was moving. *Was he singing?* She grinned in spite of herself.

A sudden flash of lightning, followed closely by a loud thunderclap, jolted her out of her momentary distraction. She dropped the notepad and tried to start Kermit, still dead. Lucene quickly weighed the options. She could run the 50 yards back into the grocery store and ask to use their phone, if only she could actually remember her home phone number. After all, she never phoned herself, or anyone, for that matter. She could ditch the groceries and walk four miles back home, or she could let the strange man in the black fedora give her a lift.

A wave of electrostatic flashes streaked across the sky overhead as lightning struck the ground in several places at once, the boom of thunder in her ears indicating that the storm was now directly overhead. The sky grew black, as if nightfall had arrived early. The lights of the supermarket went out in synchronicity. Such was par for the course in the "lightning capital of the world." Ironic that she chose to live in Florida, considering how much she hated thunderstorms. It was almost as much as she hated the cold. That was why she moved to Florida in the first place, wasn't it? She couldn't quite remember. No, that wasn't it. *You must protect yourself, Lucene.* The words came back to her as if she were hearing them for the first time. But, several years later, and she still couldn't figure out what exactly it was she was supposed to be protecting herself from, although, invisible forces seemed to loom over her in her mind's eye. Still, everything had been completely normal since her arrival in Florida. Well, almost normal.

The heavens picked that moment to finally open the floodgates, as a torrent of drops beat loudly on the top of her car. She shivered uncomfortably as fear overtook her, and that sinking feeling in the pit of her stomach returned. She gazed down at the brown patterns on her arm. Were they glowing? No, it couldn't be!

At that moment, she spotted a shadow out of the corner of her eye, and then it was gone. She tried to dismiss it as a side effect from the lightning strike, but if she had to be honest with herself, she suspected she was being followed. It happened many times, too, over the past few weeks to mean nothing. Of the two potential threats, at least she could see one of them. And what she could see, she reasoned, she could do something about.

Lucene reluctantly rolled down her window just enough to call over to Tanager, who was still sitting in his car singing to himself. He stopped singing abruptly at her beckoning. "Not having much luck, I'm afraid! If it wouldn't be a terrible bother, I'd like to take you up on the offer for a lift."

"It is not a bother at all," he called back. Moments later, the headlights on his car came to life as he made a U-turn and pulled up beside her.

Lucene quickly jumped from her car and ran to unlock the tailgate.

"Please, allow me," he offered. Tanager opened the passenger seat of his car and motioned for her to climb inside. "I will retrieve your groceries, madam." Lucene somewhat reluctantly took a seat, allowing him to close the door after her. She glanced over her shoulder as he, one by one, snagged her grocery bags and settled them into the trunk. "Close," he commanded of her car, but the tailgate remained open. "Close," he commanded again.

Curious, Lucene thought. She moved to roll down her window but couldn't find the controls. She motioned to him through the window, symbolically turning a key. He nodded in understanding, locking up her green monster, and snatching her keys from the latch.

"Here you are," he handed them to her as he sank into the driver's side. "I should have assumed it required a key turn."

Lucene forced a smile, taking the keys with one hand while keeping the other on the door handle, mentally making a plan in case she needed to make a hasty exit. *Weren't grocery stores the number one place where women got attacked by rapists?* Alarmingly, she wasn't entirely sure how to open this car door. There were no visible latches.

"You're very kind, Mr...." It was only then that Lucene noticed the rental sticker on the windshield. She felt the color draining from her face. *It's not even his car, registered in his name. He could be anyone, from anywhere.*

"Tanager," he smiled warmly, displaying a mouthful of perfectly aligned teeth. He put out his hand, cordially.

"It's nice to meet you, Mr. Tanager," Lucene reached across her chest with her right hand. He looked as if he were about to kiss it, so she quickly gave his hand an abrupt shake. She jumped slightly, as a static electric shock ran up her arm. She released his hand and returned to clutching the car door handle. "My name is Lucene." Even after five years, it felt strange using her given name: but for some reason, she no longer felt safe using the nickname she'd grown accustomed to for many years. Plus, changing her name gave her the illusion that she could somehow shed her past just as easily as she had discarded the name 'Lucy.'

"Loo-seen," he repeated the name slowly, as if saying it for the first time. "What a beautiful name," he declared, his brown eyes lighting up as if he were a small child who was just handed a big cone full of cotton candy. He tapped the steering wheel and started the engine. "Oh," he said as he released the break, "Tanager is my first name."

"Unusual," Lucene crinkled her eyebrows and pursed her lips as if trying to figure something out.

"I could say the same about 'Lucene.'" Tanager glanced in her direction as he left the near-empty lot and turned down the main strip that crossed in front of the deserted shopping center. "In my case, my family loved birds. My mother's name was Wren, and I suppose she thought she was being clever."

Lucene smiled (for real this time), letting her shoulders relax ever so slightly away from her ears. *He didn't feel like a rapist,* she thought.

"Where am I going," he asked.

"Just over there," she pointed. "Turn right at the next stop sign. I'm a few miles down."

She contemplated whether or not to point out someone else's neighborhood and walk the remainder of the way, but she already knew Tanager just well enough to suspect that he'd insist on helping her carry her bags inside. Besides, she didn't want to contend with the rain, or the lightning, or the strange shadows she kept seeing. Instead, she directed him down the small, winding street, past a series of horse and dairy farms and cottages surrounded by tangles of palmetto, magnolia, banyan and oak trees, some of which were at least a hundred years old.

Several turns later, they concluded their journey. "Make a left here and follow the dirt road to the little yellow house at the end," she instructed. "The one with the bright red door." When they arrived, the driveway was empty.

As anticipated, not only did Tanager insist on carrying her bags of groceries inside, but also in running around to the passenger's side in the rain and putting out his hand to assist her climbing out of the car. He handed Lucene his red umbrella. "Go on ahead," he told her. "I will catch you...I mean...catch up."

Just then, the rain stopped. Lucene folded the umbrella and shook it slightly before handing it back to him. "Thanks," she said. "I'll open the window for us. Give me a second."

Tanager mouthed the words, "Give me a second" to himself. *Odd,* he thought, but assumed that he should simply wait a moment and then follow her through the window.

She darted across the cobblestone pathway, bypassing the front door and heading around to the side of the house. Tanager watched her, curious. Lucene fumbled with her keychain, and then inserted a small copper key into the window frame and slid it open. The window was just low enough where she could easily step over the ledge and plant a muddy shoe on the table that sat inside, just below the window.

"Hey, Chica," a short, Rubenesque, woman with wavy lavender hair that was long on one side and short on the other, greeted her from inside. "Why didn't you just ring the bell?" She instinctively reached for Lucene's coat as the soggy roommate took a seat on their living room couch and tugged at her muddy shoes. She'd attend to the man she'd left holding her groceries in a moment, not wanting to leave dirty footprints all over the floor.

"I didn't see your car in the drive and assumed you left for work early."

"Nah, Ivan's still trying to fix the compressor something-or-other for me. I swapped shifts with another cook and am not due in for another couple of hours. Agh!" She jumped, pointing wide-eyed at Tanager, who was skulking at the window.

"So sorry, madam," he said, apologetically. "Uh…where would you like your groceries?"

"Oh! Fatima," she explained to her roommate. "This is Tanager. Tanager, come around to the front door, and Fatima will let you in. Oh, wait…here, hand me those." She motioned to the bags of groceries still in his arms. Lucene took one and handed it to Fatima, and then grabbed the others and placed them on the nearby kitchen table. She once again motioned for him to go around to the front door. Tanager thought it best not to question why she had climbed through the side window in the first place.

"What happened?" her lavender-haired friend called as Lucene headed through the kitchen to the main entryway. "It looks like your hair was replaced by a clump of soggy beach grass. Didn't think it was even supposed to rain today!"

"It wasn't," Lucene mumbled at her luck as she began unpacking the groceries and laying them out on the counter. From outside, a second band of rain passed over the house and a thunderclap made them jump slightly.

Fatima peered over her shoulder. "Hey, where are the onions?"

"They'll be along in a moment," Lucene answered with a nod toward the door. Fatima obliged, flinging the door open, enthusiastically. Tanager had just enough time to run back to the car for the remaining goods, and now stood with cloth bags hanging on his arms like sandbags weighing down a boat. Fatima let out a high-pitched giggle that seemed to start out low, from the depths of her heart and gradually go up the scale as it made its way out and into the air.

"Here, let me help," Fatima relieved Tanager of the bags of produce he was attempting to juggle and laid them, one by one, on the table. She gave Lucene a wink. "I didn't know we were expecting visitors!" The man in the fedora paused to smile and tip his hat to her. Then, seeming to remember something, he pulled the hat from his head and held it to his heart, sending a small puddle of rainwater splashing to the floor. A tumble of curls fell around his face as he regarded the lavender-haired, gray-eyed woman who was only a few inches shorter than he, but considerably heavier.

At that moment, in the far end of the living room, an all-black cat peered its golden eyes around the corner of a doorway. Seeing a stranger, he quickly retreated back into the bedroom, his tail twitching nervously.

"Okay, formal introductions are in order. Tanager, this is my roommate, Fatima." To Fatima she offered, "Tanager rescued me from the grocery store when Kermit flaked out again." Lucene surveyed the pile of groceries on the table, bypassing the fruit in favor of a cinnamon roll she plucked from a pastry bag.

"Fah-tee-mah," Tanager emphasized the name as if committing it to memory and bowed his head slightly. "Another lovely name."

"Well, he certainly is quite the charmer, isn't he?" Fatima chortled, the laugh pulling up from her belly and resonating outward through her pursed, upturned lips.

"Oh no," Tanager answered seriously, "I don't practice magic, only science."

"I see," Fatima answered, shooting a wide-eyed glance at Lucene. "Well, kind sir, may I offer you some water or a cup of coffee while you're here?"

Lucene shook her head in caution, munching absentmindedly on a roll, as if on autopilot, but Fatima dismissed her. Tanager caught Lucene's glance and offered a practiced reply, "No, thank you. I'll just be on my way."

"Uh, thanks again for your help." Lucene started toward the kitchen door, stopping short of actually touching it.

"Surely, you will return to have dinner with us tomorrow night?" Fatima was persistent, ignoring a "what do you think you're doing, are you crazy?" glance from her friend and refusing to open the front door without an answer. "I'll be making..." she glanced with disdain at the Spanish onions, "something other than a red onion chutney and goat cheese tartlets, I guess."

"What? Didn't I get the right onions?" Lucene protested. This is why she rarely got grocery duty.

"No, these are Spanish onions. It's okay."

"What's the difference?"

Tanager interrupted the banter, "I beg your pardon. I must be going. As for dinner, I don't think I should..." He regarded Lucene's contorted face before she realized he was watching. She quickly replaced it with a smirk, leaning on the counter in what she hoped would appear to be a casual manner.

"You most certainly should. It's the least we can do for rescuing my friend from the grocery store. Ivan from next door is joining us, too," Fatima motioned toward their neighbor's house.

"Very well, then," he relented. "What shall I bring?"

"Just bring yourself and your scientific...disposition at 6 p.m." Fatima hastened him along before Lucene could protest again. "You know your way out of the neighborhood, yes?"

"I believe I can manage," Tanager snatched his hat and quickly placed it on his head. "Now, about your car..."

"No worries, I'll call for a tow after the rain stops. Thanks."

Tanager didn't know what a 'tow' was but nodded politely. "Until tomorrow night," he tipped his hat, and was gone. Fatima closed the door behind him.

"What the hell, Fatima?" Lucene slapped her leg in exasperation. "We don't know anything about him, and you invited him back into our home."

"Well, you trusted him enough to let him give you a ride in the first place," Fatima replied, as she dug through the grocery bag, unpacking an assortment of vegetables, lentils and other bulk food items. "Besides, you need to have a little more faith in people. He seems nice, and he certainly seems quite taken with you."

"I only let him give me a ride because I was low on options, and I saw this...never mind." Lucene was too frustrated to argue. "So, assuming Ivan the Tinkerer gets your car finished in time, is there any chance you can give me a quick ride back to the store before your shift tonight? Kermit seems to fix himself after a rest, and I'm hoping he'll do better once he's had a chance to dry out a bit."

"Sure, but I will never understand how a 35-year-old car will magically spring back to life, every time after it stops working. I swear that it somehow keeps running because it doesn't want you to *feel* bad." Fatima put the last of the groceries in the refrigerator while Lucene tossed the cloth bags into the adjacent laundry room. Lucene couldn't explain it either, but up until today, she'd been lucky, and the green monster hadn't left her stranded.

"Ya know, I could take a wee look at Kermit fer ya," a voice called from the window. Both ladies jumped at the unexpected voice behind them, remembering too late that the side window was still open with rainwater running across the sill and down the walls. On the other side, a red-haired bulky man with a mustache and goatee grinned, placing his oil-stained hands on the sill. He didn't seem to notice the rainwater.

"That's okay, Ivan, but thank you," Lucene declined.

"She doesn't trust anyone messing with her vehicle, and she won't buy a new one because she doesn't trust cars with computers in them."

"Ah," Ivan nodded in a way that really suggested that he had no idea at all what she meant, but was just being agreeable.

"That's not true, Ivan." Lucene explained. "I trust you. It's technology I don't trust."

"Wanna come in?" Fatima invited.

"Nah, I gotta git back to the shop. Just wanted to let ya know yer car's ready. I left it in the drive." Ivan was very proud of his work, and Fatima listened intently as he filled her in on the step-by-step process from diagnosis to completion. He clearly wasn't in that much of a hurry after all.

Lucene instinctively grabbed a small glass and spoon in order to mix herself an absinthe cocktail, before she remembered that she still had to go back and get her car that evening. She opted for soda instead.

Within the next hour, the rain let up and Fatima inched her petite yellow car up to Lucene's beat-up monster. Lucene hopped inside and revved the engine up, first try.

"Figures," Fatima called over the rumble of the engine. "Hey, listen. My shift doesn't end until 2 a.m., but I'll keep my phone on in case you have any more problems. I'll just have to call you when I'm on break. Do you remember how the landline works?"

Lucence wrinkled her nose and made a face. "Yes, I remember how phones work, smart-ass." She reached for the car door, neglecting to mention to Fatima that while she knew how to work a phone, she couldn't for the life of her remember where it was in the house. The kitchen? Living room? She never saw a use for it and wasn't always the most observant of people. "I'm heading home anyway," Lucene continued. "I can make dinner for us if you want and leave you a platter in the fridge."

"No thanks, Chica!" Fatima laughed, knowing full well Lucene's inability to find her way around the kitchen. "I'll get something at work. You just get home safe." Fatima waited just long enough to see that Lucene was safely on the road before taking off. As she looked in the rearview mirror, she commented to herself, "Her and her freaky car karma."

CHAPTER 5
ROMAN MEETS FATIMA
FRIDAY EVENING. FIVE YEARS AFTER THE ASSEMBLY.

It was 9:15 p.m. on a Friday evening, and Roman wasn't having any fun at all. He pushed his way past a crowd of twenty-something-year-olds congregating around the house band at the entranceway to the Crab Shack on the Pier bar and grill. It wasn't so much that he hated crowds as much as he abhorred what he would call a "lack of decorum." He detested it in himself as much as those around him. But then, his emotions were a little irregular as of late. By the time he'd elbowed his way up to the bar, he had decided that this night's research would likely be a bust. Not only that, but he was certain his blood sugar levels were dropping. Nothing he ever had to worry about where he came from.

"Gin and ginger beer," he told the bartender as he clumsily inserted himself between an awkward man and woman who were occupying two bar stools at the edge of the counter. He smiled apologetically at the woman for accidentally nudging her elbow. They were attempting to have an intimate conversation while yelling above the noise. From his best estimate, it was their first date, maybe not even a date. They likely met two hours earlier and were trying to determine where, if anywhere, their "relationship" might go. If Roman had to venture a guess, it would have been nowhere. "And," Roman added. "A bar menu please, I'm famished."

"Excuse me," the overly confident and equally overweight man on the barstool snorted. "If you hadn't noticed, the lady and I are trying to have a conversation. Do you mind?"

The woman blushed. "It's okay," she told Roman in a nasal voice that was accompanied by a thick Northern accent. She twirled a lock of her bleached hair around one finger and smiled sheepishly. "It's crowded, and hard to get the bartender's attention."

The man glared impatiently at the interruption, the color in his face rising as he gripped his beer.

By then, the bartender laid Roman's drink down. He thanked her, plunked a twenty on the bar, tucked the menu under his arm, grabbed his drink, and started to walk away...but he couldn't quite bring himself to. This was just the sort of situation that would aid in his research. And, he was feeling much more brazen these days.

"Actually," he turned to the now-crimson man. "I did notice."

"What are you talkin' about?"

"I had noticed that you were trying to have a conversation."

"Yeah? So, you're just an asshole for no reason?" He laughed and nudged the pear-shaped woman who twirled her hair faster as she attempted to shrink into her stool.

"If you'd really like to know," Roman answered, matter-of-factly, "this woman has been politely trying to figure out how to get away from you for the past twenty minutes or so." The woman hunched her shoulders in a further attempt to condense herself. "She was trying to give you the benefit of the doubt, figuring you were nervous by the way you keep tapping your thick fingers on the bar and clearing your throat for no reason. But the truth of the matter is, you're just an unhappy man with anger issues, and when you get right down to it, she's not attracted to you at all. In fact, from what I've observed here tonight, she'd be much more interested in someone like me."

"You've got a lot of nerve!" He struggled to slide off his bar stool. The woman perked up, holding back a smile as she looked up at Roman, hopefully.

"Oh, don't worry. I'm not the least bit interested in your lady friend."

The woman looked crestfallen. "I just wanted to be straight with you to save you both an entirely uncomfortable evening."

The angry man clenched his fist, jerking his head in the blonde woman's direction, "Is that true?"

She snatched her purse and cradled it in her arms, uncomfortably. "Kinda," she admitted.

The man shot a spiteful glare at Roman.

"Sir, I can see that I've made you angry. However, I was just saving you both considerable time and unpleasantness."

"What are you, some kind of relationship expert?"

"Well, I do consider myself well educated when it comes to matters of the heart."

Without further comment, aside from a grunt, the angry man grabbed his sunglasses and pushed his way to the door, leaving his lady friend to close out the tab.

"Well," the woman offered, motioning to the bartender for a check, "thanks for saving me, anyway." Roman was about to walk away when she stopped him. "Hey, hang on a second. Uh, what's your name?"

"Roman," he paused as he quickly rotated through his mental rolodex of human behavior before offering his hand to shake hers, remembering that kissing someone's hand is generally frowned upon except in more personal settings. "And you?"

"Marcy," she answered before continuing. "Mind if I ask you something, Roman?" "I don't mind at all," he flashed a wide smile of perfect teeth.

"What's wrong with me?"

"Whatever do you mean?"

"Well, you seemed to size that guy up right away, and my lack of interest. So, I'm guessing you are pretty observant."

"Yes, very." He set down his drink and menu and leaned his tall frame casually into the side of the bar, resting an arm on the counter. He wasn't being conceited. Roman was matter of fact about most things. As the bartender plunked the woman's tab onto the counter, he took a moment to mouth the words, "The ahi tuna, please," as he pointed to the menu. She nodded and kept moving.

"Well, what I mean is..." Marcy tried again, "what's wrong with me that a jerk like that would like me, but someone like you wouldn't find me interesting? I'm a nice person, and I like to think I'm somewhat attractive."

"You're beautiful," he answered in earnest. A few passer-byes stopped to look at her, then him, trying to determine if he were making a joke. Roman was, after all, considered handsome by most cultural standards: black wavy hair that nearly reached his shoulders, bright green eyes and a pale complexion that only made his eyes more striking. Conversely, it wasn't that Marcy was entirely unattractive, but she certainly didn't fit the norm. She had large arms with little definition and equally large breasts that looked as if they'd pop out of her tank top at any moment. The rest of her frame seemed out of proportion. Her perfume and makeup were as extreme as her suntan, all of which appeared to have been quite heavily sprayed on.

"Well, thank you," she blushed. "But what is it about me that has me ending up with people who take me for granted, or someone – like that guy – who seems rude and angry all the time?"

Roman considered the question more carefully, noticing that a few people surrounding them were straining to hear his response. Marcy had a look on her face. *What was it?* Fear, he realized, and knew at that moment that he could either crush or raise her spirits. The first option, he also realized, would in no way be to her benefit. Even in his cranky state and with his newfound penchant for saying exactly what was on his mind he relented, sitting on the now unoccupied stool next to her.

"From what I have observed," he chose his words carefully, "you have a kind heart, so much so that you'd likely sit for hours listening to an unpleasant man talk at you rather than hurt his feelings." Marcy turned redder and gazed at the floor, crumbling her lips together, embarrassed. "However, I have also intuited that you attempt to dress and behave in ways that you think will make others happy with you instead of being the kind of person who you are happy with. Love yourself, and you will find love."

Her eyes lit up, as if suddenly struck by an idea. "You know, you're right!" Marcy quickly fumbled with her purse, slid off her bar stool and tugged at her bunched-up skirt until it untangled and hung just above her knees. At that moment, the bartender set a small plate of ahi tuna with avocado and wonton crisps in front of him. Marcy rested a hand on Roman's arm as he was about to take a bite of his food. "Thank you, Roman. What you've said makes a lot of sense, and I appreciate your honesty. Enjoy the rest of your evening." She slid a few bills under a coaster for the bartender before making her exit.

"You, as well, lovely Marcy."

By this time, Roman had drawn a crowd of female admirers along with a couple of men, each one asking him relationship questions.

Finally, he took a bite of his tuna appetizer. His eyes lit up, and he smiled brightly. Suddenly, his evening had gotten better.

"Excuse me!" He called to the woman behind the counter. "Who made this exquisite dish?"

"Uh, I dunno." She turned to a server who had stepped behind the bar. "Hey, Sally, who's working the line tonight?"

"Why?" Sally looked up from the ice maker suspiciously. "Something wrong?"

"Not at all," Roman gushed. By then, he'd already devoured half of his plate while a woman with her hair piled up on her head, held in place with several strategically placed pins, rested her hand impatiently on his arm.

"What about me?" She demanded, batting long eyelashes at him. This, Roman found annoying. He was through playing one-part counselor and one-part matchmaker. He was busy eating, after all.

"Okay, last one," he announced, gazing at his team of admirers. "One second," he told the woman. To the bartender, he asked, "May I have another order of this, please? Thank you." He pointed to his dish. "And, could you give my compliments to the chef? This is the most amazing food I've ever eaten." The bartender was too busy to roll her eyes, but her extended pause spoke volumes. But the more she brought him, the better the tips, so she nodded politely and grabbed a passing server to put the order in.

"Are you a food connoisseur?" A small-framed man with spiked salt and pepper hair asked with a smile.

"No," Roman admitted. "I just really like food." To the woman who refused to let go of his left arm, he said, "I would offer that it is in your best interest to develop a strong sense of independence." He promptly relieved his arm of her grip and turned back to his gin and ginger beverage.

"What's that supposed to mean?" She pouted. "I'll never find someone?"

Unlike Marcy, it was evident to Roman that anything short of a harsh dose of reality would not get past this woman's emotional wall. "It means that your need to find someone may be scaring off your potential prey. Ease up a little. I think I speak for most men when I say…" He leaned in flirtatiously, as if sharing a secret with her. "Confidence and an independent spirit are *very* attractive."

"Oh," her face became suddenly flushed. "Okay, thank you."

"No problem at all, and good luck."

He snagged his drink and shouldered his way to a small, unoccupied pub table in the far corner of the room, hating not being able to savor his food on account of the perpetual interruptions. "Ah, well," he thought. Another should be along shortly. He drained his drink. He assumed his height worked to his advantage, as he towered over the crowd; and yet, when he attempted to alert the bartender as to his new location, his flailing arms went unnoticed.

"I hear the sashimi is awesome," a voice from below Roman spoke. He turned, and dropped his gaze toward Fatima, who was holding up a second plate of the tuna sashimi. She set it down on his pub table.

For the first time this week, Roman was in love.

"Are you the chef?" he asked her.

"'Chef' is such a strong word for a place like this," Fatima snickered. "How about 'cook'?"

"I would call you 'amazing'."

For the second time that evening, several onlookers dressed in designer garb and purses worth more than the average person's monthly rent seemed perplexed, horrified even. But when they gazed at Roman lovingly, it was clear to see that he wasn't telling a woman what she wanted to hear; he was speaking from his heart. Perhaps that's what made him so attractive.

Fatima let out a full-bellied laugh.

"What a delightful laugh," Roman leaned an elbow on the pub table and rested his head in his hand.

"Another charmer!" She smiled until her cheeks hurt. Unlike Tanager, Roman was completely versed in Earth culture, in addition to his vast studies in psychology, anthropology and sociology, he was fully equipped with metaphors and terminology across many continents. So much so, that he was contemplating writing a book about it when he got back home and entitling it, *How to Behave Like a Human in 30 Days or Less,* as a guide for his fellow Erdelings.

"I have been told I am charming, yes." He answered without the slightest hint of modesty. "What is your name, amazing cook."

"Fatima," she, once again, let out that infectious laugh that rolled up her toes in a wave.

Fatima? He was astonished but tried not to show it. Could this be *his* Fatima? The one he had been searching for?

"Hey, hang on a sec," she broke the awkward pause. Fatima disappeared through the crowd, navigating her large frame effortlessly as Roman attempted to follow her with his eyes, hoping she hadn't gotten too far and was planning on coming back.

A moment later, he saw a bottle of wine floating high in the air as Fatima reemerged carrying the bottle and a glass.

"Try this," she instructed. "It's a limited-edition chardonnay and I know you'll like it with this particular dish." She poured Roman a glass and waited for him to take a sip, followed by a taste of the tuna and avocado.

"Even better than the last order," he complimented, trying to memorize her face.

Fatima's cheeks blushed crimson as she kicked the base of the pub table nervously with her toe. She was not generally shy, but it wasn't often she was given such high praise from such an attractive admirer.

"Well, I gotta get back to the kitchen," she motioned a thumb over her shoulder. "I just had to meet the man who gave my food such rave reviews."

As she turned to leave, Roman touched her arm lightly. "I'm Roman, by the way," he told her hastily.

"Well, it was very nice to meet you, Roman."

With that, Roman watched as his lavender-haired beauty with the mesmerizing gray eyes darted through the swinging door that led to the kitchen. He savored the wine and sashimi for the next half hour with a stupid grin plastered on his face. He was oblivious to the loud music, dancing and noise from the bar goers around him. Someone might have accidentally elbowed him in the ribs a couple of times, but he couldn't be sure, and he certainly didn't care.

Roman was confused. TARA had placed him in charge of studying love and the reproduction habits of the human population several years ago. Yet, today he admitted to himself that his emotions have been getting the better of him, and he didn't know why. Had he been human for too long? Was his genetic coding changing, or is this just a result of conditioning? He'd have to make a note of this in his report and have himself screened on his next TARA medical check-in.

Surely, what he was currently feeling could be labeled "infatuation," couldn't it? This was an emotion he was becoming all too familiar with lately. Consequently, he had outlined the timeline of emotions that proved to be fairly consistent: the initial stages of "puppy love," infatuation, and "crushes" only lasted about two or three months, longer for the unrequited. After the hormonal rush wore off, love sometimes developed, but only after that initial grace period. He was certain that "love at first sight" was a myth. Even more implausible is that he began to feel love before he'd even met Fatima. He picked up the loving energy she put in her food. He knew from his research that emotions are vibrations, and it made sense that he'd feel love...but *in love*? Impossible.

For the first time, he did what he swore he'd never do. He took a pen from his shirt pocket and scribbled his first name and number on a paper coaster. So, there was no confusion, he wrote at the top, *For the cook called Fatima.* He took his place by the swinging door that led to the kitchen as a classic country band took the stage, opening with their local hit, "Love Hit Me Like a Truck."

The best way to describe Roman's behavior at that moment was to say that he was doing a great job of skulking. As he skulked by the kitchen door, occasionally peering through the tiny circular window, a few of the servers became nervous.

"Can I help you?" A beefy man who matched Roman's height but outweighed him by about 80 pounds of pure muscle, asked in a low voice, resting a meaty hand on his shoulder. Roman glanced at the security badge attached to his black t-shirt.

"Yes," Roman answered, gratefully, completely missing the obvious. "Would you mind delivering this note to the cook who calls herself Fatima?" He pushed the note into the beefy man's chest.

"If I pass this on, will you be on your way?" The beefy man enquired.

"Oh, definitely. And, I would be most grateful..."

The man snatched the note from him. "Goodnight then." He made his way into the kitchen, stopping once through the doors to shoot a warning glance through the window on the off-chance Roman decided to follow. Roman reluctantly pulled himself away from the door, and after giving himself a harsh talking to, decided to call it a night.

He meandered quickly through the bustling crowd, keeping his head low to avoid eye contact, particularly with anyone he'd met earlier in the evening. Once outside, the unusually thick air enveloped him in a shroud of sticky heat. He spotted a few couples hastily making their way to their cars. He paused beside his small, black electric vehicle and glanced back at the restaurant, where people were packed in like sardines in a can. Not a single person wanted to sit out by the dock with the temperatures rising, not falling, as the sun went down. "And still they're denying that climate change is real," he muttered angrily to himself as he got into his car. Instead, the "Powers That Be" blamed the abnormal weather patterns on the Urban Island Affect and, of course, an act of God. He drove home in silence.

Once Roman had reached his small condo, he kicked his shoes off by the door. He then stopped at the small efficiency kitchen and pulled a single ice cube from the freezer, walked across the room to the adjacent living room, and deposited it in the planter of a Moth orchid that was blooming beside the window. "Sorry," he apologized to the orchid, closing the shade that remained partially open while he was gone. "I should have done that this morning."

The room resembled a minimalistic hotel room with stain resistant gray upholstery covering a small couch and chaise lounge. Against the wall, sat an espresso-colored TV stand and 32" flatscreen that the stand seemed to swallow.

He flopped on the couch and reached into the drawer of a small coffee table that was wedged between the chaise and the couch. Roman pulled out a notepad and pen. He wanted to get his notes from the evening down before he forgot anything. Instead, he started sketching aimlessly on the page. It wasn't until he got to the eyes that he realized what he'd done. He held the notepad away from him and smiled at the round face and lopsided hair…Fatima.

It was only then that he noticed the phone in his shirt pocket was vibrating: one missed call.

"Hi," he listened to Fatima's voicemail message. "I hope this won't sound too forward, but I'm having a couple of friends over for dinner tomorrow night at 6ish. Wanna come? Here's the address..."

Roman snatched his pen and scribbled down the address. Perhaps the evening wasn't so bad after all.

CHAPTER 6
IVAN THE TINKERER
FRIDAY EVENING. FIVE YEARS AFTER THE ASSEMBLY.

To Ivan's credit, he never asked a lot of questions. It wasn't that he didn't care, as much as he thought it best he did not know. If he didn't know, then he couldn't be held responsible for sharing. He liked to dance a fine line that few can manage—that of being morally neutral. Less inclined to label anything as inherently good or bad, he preferred to make decisions based on practicality, and its benefit to the whole.

Somewhat reclusive, his neighbors had taken to referring to him as "Ivan the Tinkerer," as he spent most of his time in a small commercial garage behind his house, rumored to have more inventions in the works than Da Vinci or Edison ever had.

As with many inventors, it all started quite by accident. As a teenager, he noticed he had un-customarily thick auburn hair that coiled tightly and grew faster than a kudzu plant, an unfortunate reality that required he shave almost daily. His first invention was his home-crafted laser hair removal system that left a noticeable scar under his chin. He now alternates between a goatee and a beard because it's easier than explaining. After a series of fails: an electromagnetic weight reducer that provided first-degree burns, a voice-activated drone equipped with a flashlight and miniature toolkit that mistakenly propelled a ratchet handle whenever he said, "screwdriver, flat head," and a gas, spring-foot propeller intended for home use that would eliminate the need for a footstool that was largely functional, but required a considerable amount of balance. He finally made it big at the age of 37 when he introduced the world's first portable, 3-D printed, micro-tool car repair kit. Sale of said invention to people who could actually market it, netted him a comfortable retirement and the luxury of spending his days doing what he liked best—creating tools to make the world a safer and more efficient place.

Late into the evening, Ivan was busy working on an engine that didn't really exist. Hunched over a laptop that rested precariously on the edge of a table saw, he typed in a code with his two meaty index fingers. The computer would beep, he'd scratch his head and wipe his fingers on his hole-ridden t-shirt as if he were cleaning his hands of the formula, hit delete and try again. Meanwhile, a car engine—a real one—sat helplessly on the garage floor awaiting its fate. A hollow knock on one of the doors brought him out of his quandary. Remembering their agreement, he retreated to the back of the garage, opening a small side door to greet his guests.

"Good evening," Tanager smiled in his affable way. "You must be Ivan."

"I am at that," Ivan bellowed. "Cepheus! Good to finally meet ya. Come on in!"

"Thank you, but I am Tanager. I believe my friend, Cepheus, said that you were expecting us?"

Ivan's intellectual capacities made it difficult for him to connect to the average person, particularly in social settings. As a result, two years ago he'd taken to posting to a private inventor's blog where likeminded tinkerers could share ideas and ask for advice without, he had hoped, giving away too many trade secrets. Maker197 showed up in their invitation-only chatroom one day, and a friendship was formed. It was only when Cepheus requested room and board for a few days that the two learned one another's names, and this was after more than a year of online communication.

Cepheus and a colleague would be in Ivan's neck of the woods and both needed a place to stay. They could pay handsomely for room and board if Ivan could be counted on for discretion, as Cepheus claimed to be working on a special project and didn't want competitors to know he was in town. To Cepheus's surprise, Ivan offered to put them up for a few days in the two spare guest rooms in his home, but he didn't want money. He wanted mathematics.

"Ah, yeah." Ivan shook Tanager's hand heartily. "Good to meet ya, friend of Cepheus."

Tanager waited for Ivan to ask where Cepheus was, and a long awkward silence ensued while one person waited for the other to speak. Ivan leaned against a wooden table, looped his thumbs in the belt buckles of his jeans, and stared expectantly. Finally, Tanager broke the silence.

"So...Cepheus is just getting a few things out of the car and will be along momentarily."

"Ah good, I have the rooms all ready for ya both."

"Thank you..." Tanager paused cautiously, "there's just one thing I should tell you first, so that you're not caught off guard..."

Cepheus didn't wait for the invitation, he peered his head around the door like a tentative cat, as if to gauge the safety of his arrival. Even in his relatively normal state, he still had sharp, vampire-like features: a pointy chin and ears, and sallow eyes. The gray patch of hair on his head was thin at best. He blinked nervously at Ivan like a frightened animal.

Tanager cautiously waited for Ivan's reaction, but Ivan seemed oblivious. "Cepheus, old boy! Nice to finally meet ya. Git over here!" Cepheus floated over to his friend who gave him a bear hug and slapped him on the back. He returned the sentiment with a soft pat on Ivan's back. "Let me get ya situated. I'll help ya with yer bags."

"Thank you, my friend," Cepheus answered in his deep, resonant voice that didn't seem to match his lanky frame. "We have traveled light."

Tanager was puzzled. It had only been a few years since non-humans had been allowed to freely travel to the United States, and only those representing foreign relations were permitted to live here as temporary residents. And yet, Ivan showed no visible reaction to Cepheus's rather unique appearance. Perhaps he was premature in asking Cepheus to wait in the vessel until Tanager thought it appropriate that he could be present.

"I have some news for you," Cepheus whispered excitedly to Ivan, as the tinkerer hoisted a bag from the back of their vehicle before Cepheus could protest.

"I cannah wait to hear it," Ivan smiled back.

"I think I may have the solution to your battery algorithm quandary." Cepheus's eyes lit up.

"God bless ya, I've been fighting with the voltage and timing all evening. If yev got a solution, I swear I'll build ye yer own damn guest-house next time ya visit."

Tanager followed soundlessly behind the two men who were busy chattering in hushed voices like schoolchildren sharing secrets. While he was happy to see Cepheus returning to his normal self, he questioned their anonymity, his trust in a virtual stranger, and Lucene's safety. The thoughts weighed heavily on his mind as he allowed Ivan to escort them into his home. How much had Cepheus actually shared with this human? He turned pale as he soon found out.

"Just one question, if ya don't mind," Ivan asked Cepheus as he put the bags down in the hallway. "Did ya manage to conceal yer spacecraft at the preserve properly, or do I need to do recon?"

CHAPTER 7
SABRINA AND HAMISH
FRIDAY EVENING. FIVE YEARS AFTER THE ASSEMBLY.

Sabrina was used to getting her way—always. And Hamish secretly worried about the consequences the first time that did not happen. When she was sweet—which wasn't very often—she was very sweet. But when she was angry, venom poured out of her eyes. Literally. Still, after 58 years of marriage, he felt an odd sense of duty to her. It wasn't love, exactly, was it? No…maybe? He wasn't sure.

Sabrina felt out of place in her surroundings and he knew she hated that. She often wore ill-fitting pantsuits or black dresses and red lipstick, along with equally red nails in an attempt to pass as more human-like. However, her flat nose and gray-toned skin were difficult to cover up with makeup. She contemplated cosmetic surgery and pigment injections for the trip, but decided against it, since she found herself to be exceptionally gorgeous under normal circumstances. None dared to disagree with her.

"Ham!" His wife's voice jolted him to attention, rattling his nerves.

"Yes, my love?"

"We're going to need to have another baby."

"If you say so, my love."

"Right away!" She pulled him into the bedroom suite. "Twice as evolved and it's a shame we still have to do things the primitive way."

Hamish and Sabrina were among the last of the Royals. Somehow, they evolved slightly faster than almost any other species in the universe, while aging approximately 68% more slowly than Earthlings and 18% more slowly than the rest of the known multiverse. It was no myth that they could regrow organs and limbs if not mortally wounded or suffering an incurable disease (there weren't many), and they could adopt their lizard features to protect their outer form when under attack. This included rugged leathery skin and venom that flowed from their nails at will, if they scratched you. They weren't always particularly fond of this form, mind you, but it was functional during wartime, and... unfortunately...involuntary when under duress.

Sabrina pulled Hamish close to her in a tight embrace.

Hamish gave her an obligatory peck on the lips. Hamish was much shorter and wider than his wife, looking more like a plump iguana stuffed into a three-piece suit.

"Why did you kiss me?" she demanded. "I didn't tell you to do that."

"I was being affectionate," Hamish explained. "I thought you'd like it."

"My dear stupid husband, this isn't about affection. It's about survival. Haven't you noticed that of all the species across the universe, humans are the only ones who have *devolved*?"

"And yet their populations are three times that of our Royals, in spite of our evolution."

"So are fruit flies, but what's the value in them? I can't wait until we can clean the slate and try again."

"We've tried before. What makes you think it will work this time?"

"Because this time, we'll have a genetically born Data Collector to help us."

"And why would she be inclined to do that?"

"You saw what happened to Cepheus," she reasoned. Hamish nodded, solemnly. "Then you know how persuasive I can be."

Not forty-five minutes later, the Royals were ready for the evening's dinner party in the hotel's banquet hall. Sabrina surrounded herself with fellow Royals, along with neighboring species that she deemed acceptable, running the only five-star casino hotel she knew of in the area that was both maintained by, and catered to, Royals. The general population was unaware, as it was managed by humans who were paid exceptionally well to keep their mouths closed. It only took one leaker to the local paper to mysteriously die by accidentally getting run through a commercial dishwasher, several times, before, even more unwittingly, becoming locked in the walk-in freezer overnight, for the rest of the staff to catch on.

Yes, employees were carefully vetted and often included underground aliens doing their best to blend with the human population in the event they needed to act as the public face of the casino to answer any odd rumors that might be floating about. Rumors, for instance, that thanks to illusive architecture, the hotel was sectioned off so that Earth guests stayed on one side, and aliens on the other - the two sides never to meet. The outside world must never know that the aliens who frequented the place were as illegal as the money they gambled.

The currency at the Royal casino was the Earth dollar. While Sabrina detested humans, she still loved their money. It was considered of special value in the universal marketplace because once humans went extinct, their money would cease production and become valuable antiques. She already had plans to create a money-lined room in her palace when she returned home.

Sabrina and Hamish waltzed through an alien banquet hall, followed by Fredo, their personal bodyguard. Fredo was a formidable beast with a bright red salamander-shaped body and arms and legs as large as tree trunks. He wore what could only be described as a form-fitting black wetsuit that kept his skin moist and his body cool.

Guests looked up from their one-armed bandits, roulette wheels and card tables as they passed, most choosing to wear cocktail dresses and suits from the world they were visiting, though many were noticeably from the wrong time period.

A chestnut-haired woman, donning what could best be described as a black and white gothic cocktail uniform, carried a large box filled with candies and cigarettes. She presented it to Hamish as he passed, who politely declined. Fredo intercepted, not so politely, telling her to kneel before her sovereign.

"That won't be necessary..." Hamish began, but it was too late. She'd already kneeled, dramatically balancing the box of goodies on her thigh, uncomfortably.

"You don't approach the sovereigns, and you don't speak unless spoken to," Fredo spat, swiping his arm and tossing the remnants of her box all over the floor.

Sabrina smirked at first, until she noticed a few disapproving glances from her guests. "Fredo! That was uncalled for." She leaned over the woman, taking her by the chin and lifting upward until the maiden had no choice but to stand. "Forgive me, my dear. My serf is often protective of his ambassadors. I would love a box of your delightful cigarettes." The girl, along with several staff members who heard the commotion, rushed to her side, helping to gather up the contents of her box before she sheepishly presented it to the queen. Sabrina selected one.

"Matches?" the girl inquired and winced in Fredo's direction.

"Not necessary, thank you," Sabrina announced, swiping a nail across the tip of the cigarette. A small ember quickly began. She puffed for a moment. "Most acceptable." They continued down the aisle as a quiet sign that guests should collect their things and follow the procession. Dinner would begin shortly.

CHAPTER 8
LUCENE MEETS CEPHEUS
FRIDAY AT MIDNIGHT, OR THEREABOUTS. FIVE YEARS AFTER THE ASSEMBLY.

Something that went bump in the night startled Lucene from an incredibly unproductive nightmare about being kidnapped by aliens for special powers she did not possess. She sat up quickly as her eyes struggled to adjust to the blackness, vaguely aware that the nightlight was offering no assistance. She threw the blankets off and planted her feet on the carpet. She tugged at her pinstriped pajama top, adjusting her matching pants as she stood.

"Bagheera," Lucene called out to their black house cat. "Whatcha doin', kitty?"

The room went silent as she fumbled for the light switch. As the bulb flickered to life, she let out a scream.

A cloaked figure the size of a full-grown man crouched atop her dresser. His face was partially shielded by the black cape, and he peered over his shoulder with lizard-yellow eyes and an Ibis-beaked nose. His skin was a pale yellow with a green hue.

"Mrow?" A sound murmured from under his cape.

Lucene's heart was pounding loudly in her ears as she put a downturned palm out in front of her. "Please, do not hurt my cat," she implored the beast.

The beaked figure glanced down at his cloak. As it fell away from his arm, Bagheera could be seen cradled in the beast's arm as the figure pet him gently with his opposite hand. "I want the cat," Cepheus answered simply. The beast leapt gracefully to the floor and headed toward the bedroom door, Bagheera still nestled in one arm.

"No!" Lucene spoke firmly, picking up the nearest weapon she could find: a weighted brass hand mirror. The beast looked at his reflection in the mirror as if mesmerized by his own image.

"But I want the cat," he paused. "And I want that reflective glass, too." He moved toward her.

"Stop!" Lucene commanded. The beast obeyed, shrinking backward like a chastised animal. "I don't know who you are…"

"Cepheus."

"I'm sorry, what?" Lucene asked.

"I am called Cepheus, and I want the c—"

"Yes, I understand…uh…Cepheus. You want the cat; but you may not have the cat." He crinkled his face in discontent. "However," she held out the brass mirror, "you may have the mirror."

Bagheera wiggled out of his captor's arm and leapt to the ground just as Cepheus snatched the mirror from Lucene's grasp, but instead of running to safety, as was his typical behavior around strangers, Bagheera stood by the man's dirty leather boots, grooming.

Cepheus gazed at his reflection and murmured, "I would never hurt the cat."

The intruder blocked the entrance to Lucene's bedroom, and she had little confidence in her ability to pry the window open in a timely enough manner to leap to her escape.

"Cepheus," her voice crackled, nervously. "Who are you and why are you in my house?"

The beaked man's eyes rolled slightly, and he swayed his head back and forth as if he were trying to sift through files in his brain and remember something. In her own way, Lucene was doing the same. *Why was that name so familiar*? She tapped the side of her head with her palm as if to knock things in her brain back into place.

A sudden knock at the door made Lucene jump. Under normal circumstances, she would have screamed for help at the top of her voice, but as she looked down, she noticed Bagheera was purring as he rubbed up against the man's boot.

Instead she asked, "May I answer the door, please?"

Cepheus seemed confused. "The door did not ask you a question." The knock repeated, more insistent.

"Lucene," a voice called from outside.

"Tanager?" She answered carefully, afraid to make a sudden move. "I will be right there!" To Cepheus, she asked, "Would you please let me through to open the door?"

"Let you through what?" he asked, leaning over to show Bagheera his reflection in the mirror, smiling broadly, revealing a row of saw-like teeth.

"Cepheus," she tried again, calmly. "Please walk forward three steps." He took exactly three steps forward and Bagheera followed him. The mirror caught light from the lamp and reflected a bright beam on the carpet. The cat began chasing the light, pawing at it in vain. Cepheus let out a gleeful snort, baring sharp teeth once again.

Lucene took the opportunity to rush through the bedroom door. A soft light from a lamp in the living room left on when Fatima was working late partially filled the room, giving more light-bouncing opportunities for her cat. "Bagheera," she called as she ran to the kitchen door, in an ineffective attempt to get her cat to follow her. She didn't expect that he would, as he never had in the past.

She stood in front of the red door, reaching her hand out, but unable to open it.

Tanager could feel her energy on the other side of the door. "Lucene, please let me in."

"I can't," she answered helplessly. "The door's locked and I have to get out." She ran to the window and quickly unlatched it. She had one leg on the side table, and the other over the sill, when Tanager came around the corner and stopped her.

"I can help," he reassured.

"Let me out, there's a strange…being…"

"Cepheus, I know," he answered. "Let me in."

Lucene pulled her leg back, glancing nervously over her shoulder toward her bedroom. Cepheus was still playing with Bagheera, waving the mirror around as the cat pounced on stray light beams. Tanager gently nudged his way past her as he climbed through the window, tipping his hat in an apologetic gesture for his brashness. He glanced momentarily at her very thin pajama set, which did little to hide the details of her form. He tried not to notice. Lucene leapt from the table and followed him.

"Cepheus," he commanded. "Please stop whatever it is you are doing and come out here, please."

Lucene pulled her shoulders back, trying to make sense of what was happening.

Cepheus peered around the bedroom door, grinning sheepishly like a small child. He walked out of the bedroom, clenching the new beloved mirror to his chest with Bagheera right at his heels. He smiled down at the black feline.

"I want the cat," he explained to Tanager.

"Yes, I know you do, my friend," Tanager answered calmly as he removed his fedora and placed it on the dining room table. He began peeling his brown leather gloves off. "But please be careful. If her cat were injured in some way, Lucene would be very upset." Cepheus recoiled as Tanager came closer.

"I would never hurt the cat," Cepheus dropped his gaze in shame, "or Lucene."

Lucene was startled at the sound of her name as it passed his lips. There was something familiar about his voice. *Where had she heard it before?*

"I know you would never intentionally hurt anyone," Tanager set the gloves on the table beside the fedora, walked around the dining area until he was within arm's reach of Cepheus. "Now, as I was saying..." Before Cepheus could react, he placed a small cylindrical tube inside one of his ears and released a puff of air from a vacuum seal. Cepheus's eyes rolled backward, and his lean body lurched forward. Tanager put out an arm to catch him, struggling slightly with Cepheus's tall frame. Lucene jumped at his side, helping as Tanager guided Cepheus over to the couch where the faint beast promptly collapsed in a heap. Tanager did his best to adjust the beast's limbs so that his arms and legs weren't sprawled in every direction. "He'll come round in a few minutes, you'll see."

"Well, that's reassuring." Lucene threw her hands in the air. "What the hell is going on?" she demanded. "And who are you people, really?"

"Are you sure you don't already know?" Tanager stood up, looking intently into her eyes. His gaze made her uncomfortable, but there was something soothing about it too. She still felt anxious about tonight's activities, but no longer threatened by either of the men. *What kind of weird hypnosis is this?*

"Know what? You're not making any sense." As if on autopilot, Lucene made her way into the kitchen and pulled a bag of pork rinds from the pantry. Among her many eccentricities, Lucene was also a nervous eater. She began munching on a rind as Tanager looked at the bag distastefully. "Life was completely normal until you showed up yesterday, and now...him!" She pointed at the slumped over Cepheus before licking her fingertips. Bagheera now sat at his feet, watching expectantly.

"Normal?" he questioned. "I am curious as to your definition of normal."

"What's that supposed to mean?" Lucene demanded.

"For example," Tanager offered. "Is it normal that you have the worst diet of anyone I have ever seen and yet, you have the body mass of an athlete?"

"My diet is just fine. Besides, I exercise. And, how would you even know what my diet is like, or my body mass, for that matter? I don't even know what my body mass is!"

"No? Fatima exercises...daily...and she's still a good 20 pounds heavier than you. She eats better, too."

"Again, how would you know that? Have you been stalking us? Is that what you were doing outside the grocery store the other day?" Now thirsty from munching on the pork rinds, she reached in the refrigerator for a can of ginger beer, annoyed at what she perceived as a distinct invasion of privacy.

"Well, no," Tanager answered calmly. "Stalking implies that I am obsessed with you and am a threat."

"Aren't you?" Lucene squinted her eyes at him, not really believing it herself.

"No. It might be better if you sat down," Tanager suggested, pulling a chair out from under the dining room table. Lucene sat, taking the pork rinds and ginger beer with her. Tanager took a seat across the table. "We've been watching you for several weeks now, trying to find the right time, and the best way to make our introductions."

"'We'...meaning you and the lurking vampire over there," Lucene gestured toward Cepheus before snatching a napkin from the dispenser on the table, resulting in several sticking together with orange pork rind smudges. She fought to no avail with the napkin holder.

"I really wanted to reveal this in a more delicate way...," he paused, with minor annoyance, as he helped steady the dispenser for her, "but we appear to be short on time."

"You're going to tell me that you and Cepheus aren't from this planet." Tanager was surprised. "Yeah, that much I figured out." Lucene let out a snort and took a sip of her soda. "And you came all this way to give me nutritional guidance." Lucene's snarky side was always unleashed when she felt defensive or misunderstood in some way.

"Yes, and we knew your parents. Do you remember?"

Lucene's breath caught in her chest. "What do you know about my parents?"

A moan from the couch interrupted their conversation. Cepheus sat upright, rubbing his head. "How long have I been in the other state?" he asked Tanager.

"Oh, about 30 minutes or so. I came looking for you as soon as you disappeared."

"Oy," Lucene jumped at the sound of a resonant voice coming from the window. "Everything okay in here?" Ivan popped his head through the open window.

"Yes, my friend," Cepheus answered, struggling to his feet. "I apologize for my episode. I'm okay now."

"Wait," Lucene looked at Ivan. "You know these two?"

"Er, well, yes and no," Ivan struggled for the right words, and then decided that answer was sufficient.

"Ivan agreed to help us solve a problem with our vessel. He is quite brilliant," Tanager offered.

"Right," Lucene squinted her eyes again. Something in her brain connected with something in Tanager's brain. "Because you need to leave Earth and return to Erde." She took a sip of her drink, absentmindedly.

Tanager paused. "What makes you think we are from Erde?"

"What?" She looked up, as if distracted. "I have no idea where you are from," Lucene answered, with no recollection as to what she had just blurted out. "What I want to know, is what you know about my parents." Tanager gave her a sideways, confused-puppy stare before exchanging questioning glances with Cepheus.

"What?" Lucene demanded. "Why the looks?"

"Um…beggin' your pardon," Ivan called from the window, but can someone open the door so I can join you? Unless this is a private conversation."

"It's not," Lucene answered. "But these gentlemen were just leaving." Tanager started to protest. "You cannot be here when Fatima gets home from work," she told him. "And furthermore, you cannot tell her anything about this."

"Aye," Ivan agreed. "Don't know what all happened here, but her heart is weak, and she should nah be stressed. Why don't ye two come back to my place and leave the ladies be." With that, Ivan vanished from the window.

"Okay," Tanager reluctantly agreed. "But we need to continue this conversation...very soon."

Cepheus leaned over to give Bagheera a final scratch behind the ear. To Lucene, he said, "My memory is foggy, but I hope I didn't do anything…inappropriate." Lucene could feel the sorrow in his heart. He continued to stare at her as if she were a long-lost daughter that he hadn't seen in a very long time. He wanted to hug her and tell her everything, but he knew the timing wasn't right. Instead, he smiled at her with a sense of pride. In spite of everything, here she was…alive and well. She was resilient, just like her parents.

"Not at all," she replied gently, shaking him from his reverie. "And if it makes you feel any better, my memory is a little foggy too."

"I don't understand how that would make me feel better," he answered in earnest, fumbling between clarity and confusion. Lucene was too tired to explain the expression.

Tanager unlocked the door and Cepheus made his exit, Ivan on the other side, carefully taking his arm as an assist. To Lucene, Tanager asked, "Are you okay to..."

"Lock up?" she answered, somewhat embarrassed. "Er. Would it be a horrible bother to ask you to bolt the door from the inside and..." She motioned toward the window.

"Of course not, I mean, no bother at all." He tried to focus on her face, not the rest of her. She felt a strange buzzing across her skin as he passed in close proximity to her. She noticed it briefly in the car ride the day prior, but now, it seemed to be getting stronger.

It was only after he'd climbed through the window and she'd secured the latch, that she realized he'd left his hat and gloves behind. The sound of an unhappy car motor could be heard coming from down the street. Fatima. Lucene quickly snatched the gloves, stuffing them into the hat and tucking them under her arm. She then grabbed the rinds and soda before retreating into her bedroom and shutting the door. After depositing everything she held onto her dresser, she quickly shut off the light and felt her way to her bed. It was only after she was snuggled beneath the covers that she realized she'd forgotten something.

From behind the door, she could hear Fatima fumbling with the lock. Once inside, she heard her friend say, "Oh, Bagheera? Did your mom forget to take you into her room before bed?"

Damn it! Lucene thought.

"That's okay, kitty," Fatima cooed. "You can come sleep in my room tonight."

CHAPTER 9

THE INTERNATIONAL REGISTRY OF ALIEN RESIDENCY

FIVE YEARS AGO. SEVERAL WEEKS BEFORE THE ASSEMBLY.

"Lucy Jones, come in," Drake Cushing invited Lucene into his office. "Shut the door behind you, if you wouldn't mind." He looked her over from head to toe, admiring the shape of her legs and the way her flared, knee-length skirt moved when she walked. Her white blouse, however, was buttoned up to the neck…disappointing.

Lucene blushed at the attention, not considering the possibility that his gaze was borderline inappropriate. In fact, in her mind, this was the beginning of a recurring fantasy she had in her head about her boss.

"Don't just stand there like a lemming, sit down," he directed her toward a chair across from the desk where he sat.

And the fantasy was gone.

She sat, crossing her legs modestly at the ankles and resting a notepad in her lap, tapping her pen nervously against it. He smiled his usual toothy grin. Standing up, he moved over to the front of the desk, sitting on the edge of it with his legs extended and hands supporting his weight by grasping the top of the desk on each side of his hips. His new authoritative position was unnervingly close to Lucene, who was forced to look up at him to meet his gaze. After what seemed like an uncomfortably long silence, he spoke. "I have a new assignment for you," he announced, suddenly.

"Oh," Lucene was surprised. The past three years had been tedious, to say the least. She was beginning to think she'd be stuck in the file room forever if she didn't do something about it.

"I don't think we've been utilizing you to your full potential. I admit, part of that was my fault. I always thought you received special treatment because of your *situation*," he glanced at her arms. She crossed them, nervously covering up the burnt-in scars. By "special treatment," Drake was referring to the fact that she went to college with a partial need-based scholarship. When added on to a modest academic scholarship, she had enough to get through her undergraduate degree but just barely. As an orphan being shuffled from one house to another, she took it upon herself to move out on her own by special government permission, as soon as she'd turned 17. The following year, she'd applied to a state university and qualified for assistance.

"But I went back and looked at your file."

"Why?" Lucene was legitimately curious.

"No particular reason," he cleared his throat, and stood up, doing a three-quarter turn before changing his mind about something and sitting back down. "Well, that's not exactly true. I happened to notice other newer employees moving out of that file room, but not you. I confess, I thought it was a competence issue, but then..." He moved to his desk drawer, pulling out a file that had about four pages in it, at best. "I looked at your resume. Top of your class, you then worked your way through grad school, and in the past three years you haven't taken a single sick day and have received nothing but stellar performance reviews. Which makes me wonder, why on Earth did you never ask for a promotion or to be moved to a department with opportunity for growth?"

Lucene gave the question some serious consideration. "I don't know," she answered quietly. It was the truth.

"Well, I noticed," he dropped the file on his desk with a sense of smug satisfaction. "And, if you're willing, of course, I'd like to give you a test assignment."

Lucene nodded with a sense of excitement and apprehension. She was flattered to have received the attention of her department's director, but the thought of leaving the file room suddenly felt rather terrifying. "Of course," she practically whispered.

"Good," he answered. "I should warn you that you'll be dealing with some sensitive information. I trust you will keep it to yourself?"

Lucene nodded. *Who would she tell?*

"Is that a 'yes,' " he paused impatiently.

She nodded again before adding, "Yes."

"Good, that's what I thought." He went back to his desk. "First, I need you to retrieve some files for me. The file numbers are…" Lucene opened her notepad, ready to take down the numbers. "No, don't write them down, just remember them."

He has a lot of unwarranted faith in my memory, she thought.

"IRAR4—"

"Wait," Lucene interrupted. "I don't have clearance to access files from the International Registry."

"I know," he leaned uncomfortably close, looking into the distance as if making a decision before turning his gaze back toward her. "Neither do I." Lucene returned a questioning expression. "There are forces at work here that require us to break the rules for the greater good. I need someone I can trust. I trust you, Lucy." He smiled broadly. He could tell from her facial expression that that trust was not shared.

He walked back to his desk and took a seat opposite her, planting his forearms on his desk and leaning in as if letting her in on a special secret. "I have a story to tell you," he spoke quietly, forcing her to sit on the edge of her seat and lean in to hear him.

"When I was a young boy, I almost drowned during a storm."

"Really?" Lucene was intrigued.

"It's true. My younger brother, Bryce, you may remember him from the office holiday party last year..." Lucene remembered. Bryce was the complete opposite of his older brother. Where Drake oozed confidence, and always showed up for every special occasion dressing in a tailored suit with an attractive, well-proportioned fashion model on his arm, Bryce preferred to live in his brother's shadow. He wore understated brown dress slacks and an ivory shirt to every company event. If there were more than a dozen people in the room, he became nervous, and would hug the least occupied corner. With a watered-down drink in his hand, his equally understated wife of six years always stood beside him. Drake got him a job in the cyber-security department several years back, and he was likely to remain there for the foreseeable future.

"Well, we were foolish enough to plan a fishing excursion despite all warnings against it due to inclement weather," Drake continued, raising his voice slightly when he noticed Lucene's mind wandering, as if visualizing the entire event. He snapped his fingers in front of her eyes, jolting her back into the room. "Our parents were out of town and we thought we knew everything." Drake went on to share his story about the storm, and how an alien being named Morphinae flew up from the waters to rescue him. Lucene's eyes widened. "I know, it sounds preposterous," he laughed, gauging her reaction.

"I believe you," Lucene responded, astonished that she, unequivocally, did.

"Well, I was supposed to die that day, but didn't. And I was saved by an alien being. Who would have thought it?" He didn't wait for an answer. "Soon after that I realized my purpose in life. There are beings on this Earth, some who are here to help us, like Morphinae, and others who mean to harm us. It is my mission to help navigate the murky waters of intergalactic negotiations to create unity, while also protecting Earth from being exploited. Doing that requires that we sometimes break the rules. Do you understand what I'm saying?"

Lucene nodded, although she wasn't completely certain that she did. All she knew is that at that moment, she wanted to both prove to herself her value and not let her boss down. For some reason, she needed his approval. Still, something felt very wrong about this. "I'm just not sure..." she began.

"You can't spend the rest of your life hiding behind the safety of books and file cabinets, Lucy." *That hurt,* she thought. "Now, I know you'll find a way. Those numbers are..."

Lucene watched the numbers scroll across her mind as she committed them to memory. She nodded, and quietly left the room.

CHAPTER 10
CLASS
FOUR YEARS AGO. ONE YEAR AFTER THE ASSEMBLY.

"I'd like you to take a deep inhale through your nose. Feel the air as it moves to the back of your throat, and then down into your belly, to about two inches below your navel," the meditation instructor said, in a flowing, melodic voice. "Pause your breath, and then exhale slowly." The instructor sat tall, her neck long and back straight. She wore a pair of brightly colored palazzo pants and a short-sleeved yellow tunic, accenting her dark skin and elegant white hair wrapped in box braids. If you looked closely, you would notice a serene smile on her face.

Fatima shifted uncomfortably on her meditation bolster and squeezed her eyelids tightly together, taking uneven breaths.

It was all Fatima's idea. She was convinced that Lucene was bottling up unwanted emotions and was certain that trying a meditation class would help slough all that stuff off. And, it was her turn to pick a class.

In an effort to expand their horizons, also at Fatima's suggestion, the two friends embarked on a monthly ritual of trying something new for the month and then seeing what would stick. They had already attempted sailing lessons, stand up paddle boarding, bocce ball on the beach and lute making classes. So far, bocce ball was winning.

Lucene sank into meditation easily, somehow. All of this felt familiar. She could hear the instructor's voice in the distance as she continued,

"For this meditation, we are seeking to explore a situation from the past that may be preventing us from moving forward into the future."

It was a small class, only nine people in attendance. They were meeting in a small temple that turned out to be a short distance from Fatima's cottage, the class led by the church's priestess, Reverend Isabella. One man started to drift off to sleep but caught himself as he began to slump forward. He snorted slightly, looking around to make sure no one had noticed, and resumed his practice. Another woman sat with clenched fists, slowly releasing them as the meditation continued.

"You are walking down a long hallway, and at the end of it, is a door," Isabella continued. "Walk slowly toward it." Lucene felt uneasy but made her way toward the door. It was a Rembrandt-style, rustic, red arched door. "Behind that door, is the past stressor that we will work with today." The instructor reminded everyone to approach whatever arose from the perspective of an outside observer. Lucene's face became flushed. "Put your hand on the knob or handle…and slowly open it."

The door swung open and Lucene let out a scream.

"Oh my gosh, what happened?" Fatima tried to rush to her friend's aid, only to realize that her right leg had fallen asleep and she couldn't stand up. She pounded on her leg and winced through the feeling of pins and needles. There was a murmur from the class, as Isabella knelt down beside Lucene and took her by the shoulders, rubbing them gently to bring her back to the present. "It's okay," she told her. "You are safe." Lucene nodded, embarrassed.

Isabella called for a five-minute break. The class stood, stretched and moved about the room whispering, with occasional glances in Lucene's direction. Lucene stood, doing a forward bend and wrapping her arms around the back of her legs to stretch, then rolled up to a standing position and rotated her head from side to side to loosen up her neck. "I'm okay now," she told the teacher with a confidence she didn't really feel. "But I think I will step outside for a moment."

Isabella nodded slowly, understanding, but said nothing.

"I'm fine," Lucene reiterated, even though she hadn't been asked a question. She stepped out into the parking lot. The sun shone brightly on her face.

"Wait up," Fatima called, limping slightly after her friend. "What the heck happened back there?"

Lucene wasn't entirely sure herself. "I don't know. I got to the door, and it was red."

"Red!" Fatima interrupted. "Couldn't you have imagined a green door or a blue door?"

"I couldn't help it. It wanted to be red. Anyway, I opened it, and suddenly I was flooded with images, and sounds and emotions...so much emotion…that I just couldn't take it," Lucene began trembling. Fatima wrapped her arms around her friend in a sideways bear hug, pinning the top of her arms to her side. "I could feel all the pain and joy in the world, at the same time. It was just too much," she explained, feebly attempting to hug her friend back, but managing only to tap Fatima's forearms with her free hands. "Sorry to embarrass you."

Fatima let out a giggle that made her entire body quiver like a Jell-O Jiggler. "Oh my gosh," she laughed. "As if that were possible. Don't worry, my friend," she released her bear hug and looked Lucene in the eyes. "I have no shame."

Lucene wiped a tear from her cheek.

"Excuse me," Isabella approached, her palazzo pants swaying gently in the breeze. "I'm sorry to interrupt, but I feel compelled to speak with you." Lucene and Fatima stepped back to allow her to join their circle. "As you know, I am priestess of this sanctuary." Lucene and Fatima introduced themselves in return, waiting for the pitch inviting them to become a member of her church. They both hated being recruited, as neither of them considered themselves to be particularly religious.

She handed Lucene her card. "I am in need of an assistant to help me manage the sanctuary. If you are seeking a job, please contact me, or just stop in. The door is always open *for you*."

"You don't even know me, and you're offering me a job?" Lucene was surprised, partially because she had just made quite the spectacle of herself, and even more so because she happened to be in need of some type of income.

"Anyone with that much empathy is clearly called for a higher purpose." With that, she went back into class. "We'll be continuing class in a moment, perhaps just a simple breathing meditation instead, I hope you both will join us."

"Sure," Lucene answered, "we'll be right there."

"You sure?" Fatima asked.

"Yeah, as long as there are no more red doors, I'll be fine."

"I was right about one thing," Fatima bragged as she followed Lucene back inside.

"Yeah, what's that?"

"You sure do have a lot of pent up emotions to slough off."

CHAPTER 11
JOURNEY TO EARTH
ONE YEAR AGO. FOUR YEARS AFTER THE ASSEMBLY.

"We will be entering the Deep Zone soon," Cepheus informed Tanager, who was in the fitness room running—no, more like taking a brisk jog—on the moving belt. He loathed exercise, in spite of knowing its necessity for health, and was constantly measuring exactly how much of it he needed to be at peak performance without going above that ratio at all. "Make yourself ready."

"Thanks," Tanager replied, working on his colloquialisms as much as possible before their visit to Earth. "I'll suit up." He slowed his pace and stepped down, the belt crawling to a stop as soon as he did so. "Do I have time to hit the showers?"

"Hit the—" Cepheus paused for a moment, and then nodded, "yes."

Within a short time, Tanager had changed and was strapping himself into a navigation chair beside Cepheus.

The Deep Zone was an ocean-like pocket in space where extreme pressure could prove hazardous to both themselves and their vessel. To compensate, the vessel had collapsible external walls that were vented to add an extra layer of protection, while still letting interstellar gases pass through without harming the ship. As an added precaution, travelers wore more traditional suits with built-in oxygen masks that were fastened into their seats. Fortunately, this was a small zone, which meant they would be able to resume normal flight functions within the hour.

"Are you nervous?" Tanager asked his colleague. His voice sounded like a faraway broadcast as the sound traveled from the intercom in his suit to the headset in Cepheus's.

"Why should I be nervous?" He sucked in a deep breath.

"About meeting Lucene. She'll be about 31."

"32," Cepheus corrected.

"Yes, 32. She'll be about 32 when we get there, and you haven't spoken with her in more than 25 years."

"That's not entirely true. You're forgetting the assembly."

"Ah, yes," Tanager remembered.

"She may not have remembered because of the lightning strike, but I know a part of her recognized me."

The two traveled in silence for the next ten minutes, each routinely running monitor checks to make certain that all of the contractable sections of the ship remained intact. "But, yes," Cepheus said.

"What?"

"Yes, I am nervous." They continued in silence for a few minutes more. "What about you?"

"What about me?" Tanager asked.

"Are you nervous?"

"Why should *I* be nervous?"

"Because we learned at an early age that you were both of the same vibration, and that it was very likely that you'd make a good pair."

"Don't be nonsensical."

"Silly."

"What?"

"I believe the word you were looking for was 'silly.' Don't be silly."

"Exactly, *thanks* you…I mean, thank you." Tanager pointed toward a clear window view of an approaching ringed planet. Cepheus nodded and smiled. "I have no reason to be nervous," Tanager finally answered. "Firstly, she's many years younger than I."

"What does that matter?"

"Nothing where we come from. I recognize that we typically live twice as long as Earthlings, but it will matter to her."

"Why should it? If you don't tell her your age, she'd never know."

"Well, that would be misleading, wouldn't it?"

"Perhaps so," Cepheus agreed.

"Secondly, we're from two different planets—two vastly different experiences."

"That might change."

"And thirdly," Tanager persisted. "Who is to say we'd even feel that way about one another?"

"Same vibration," Cepheus pointed out.

"All that means is that we're inclined to have similar interests and values. That doesn't mean anything. And fourthly…"

"There's a fourthly?" Cepheus was surprised. Tanager nodded.

"And fourthly, our biggest concern is getting her to safety. That needs to be our focus."

"This is true," Cepheus acknowledged somberly. The two continued on their journey, taking a moment to admire the surplus of stars popping up as they neared the Deep Zone's end. A good half hour passed before Tanager spoke again.

"Yes."

"Yes, what?" Cepheus asked. "I've forgotten the question."

"I am a little nervous."

CHAPTER 12
THE GATHERING
SATURDAY EVENING. FIVE YEARS AFTER THE ASSEMBLY.

Fatima buzzed through the kitchen like a hummingbird, singing to herself. How she managed to move with such ease while wearing an ankle-length brown corset dress, high-heeled boots and with clock charm bracelets running up and down her arms, Lucene had no idea. If Lucene was not mistaken, the tune was "Some Enchanted Evening." She watched as her friend swiftly diced up onions on the cutting board, Fatima's lavender hair pulled back on one side in a tight bun as she gazed softly at the board in front of her and smiled, not really seeing it. Lucene had witnessed this look many times before, and it could only mean one thing—Fatima was in love— again.

"You seem extra cheerful today," Lucene commented, casually pushing the dining room chairs in so they lined up neatly around the table, all while doing a cursory check to make sure there was no evidence of last night's encounter. Fatima smiled softly and nodded but did not reply. "Anything I can do to help?" Lucene offered, uncertainly, peering down at her rather loose-fitting teal maxi dress, wondering if she were over or underdressed. Having no sense of style, she really wasn't sure.

The two did not entertain very often, and when they did, it was usually when Fatima's very large family descended on them unannounced. In those instances, Lucene had nothing to do but watch in wonder as both men and women coordinated a large-scale meal with minimal bickering as to whether the soup needed more garlic, or the rice could use a pinch more saffron.

"Hmm..." Fatima thought for a moment. "You could set the table. We need five places. Oh, and maybe put on some music, something fun."

After a quick mental headcount, Lucene came up with only four names: Fatima, Ivan, Tanager, and, of course, herself. She knew that Cepheus's appearance would inspire too many questions and he would not be in attendance. "Fatima?" Lucene adopted *that* tone of voice. "Why do we need *five* places?"

"Oh," Fatima waved her hand as if the matter were of small consequence. "Because I met someone." She let out a twitter and, quite literally, jiggled up and down like a small child who just learned that she was going to Disney World.

"Fatima, you *didn't*, once again, invite a total stranger into our home!"

"I did!" She twittered again, grabbing Lucene's shoulders for emphasis. "And, he's *wonderful*. Don't worry."

But Lucene did worry. Still, she bit her tongue. She knew better than to try to reason with her friend. And yet, she cringed every time Fatima met someone new, or rather, every time she fell in love, which was pretty much the same thing. She hated having these confrontations with Fatima. Voicing her opinion in the past would always result in an argument. It was the only time Fatima would lift her nose like a dog sniffing the air, reminding Lucene just who the house really belonged to. Still, her concern escalated. Fatima didn't typically invite them home until they had been around for a while, which didn't happen often. Perhaps it had been unwise of her to allow Tanager to give her a ride home. It sent the wrong message that it was okay to trust strangers.

"So..." Fatima coaxed. "How about that music?"

"Oh, right." Lucene scurried to the living room and inspected their growing music collection. Fatima's music was mainly housed on a digital sound bar about the size of a small brick that sat inconspicuously beneath a television, which was, admittedly, not much bigger. Beneath the TV lived a vintage portable DVD/CD player, amplifier, and a cabinet which held Lucene's outdated CD collection. She flipped through them haphazardly, as they were in no particular order, before settling on one with minimal scratches and adding it to their media player. Cole Porter's "Begin the Beguine" filled the room.

"Ooh, I love this one," Fatima cooed. "Can you turn it up?" She hummed along gently from the kitchen.

The two friends may not have had much in common, but they both shared an eclectic taste in music, which included a particular fondness for songs ranging from the 1920s through the 1940s. Fatima preferred to stream her music online, but knowing Lucene's distrust for computers and advanced technology, she humored her friend's insistence on playing only CDs, drawing the line at cassettes and vinyl records.

The doorbell let out a bird-like tweet signaling an arrival. Fatima quickly wiped her hands on her apron. "Here!" She held a wooden spoon over a large pot of homemade curry lentil soup. "Stir!" She commanded. Lucene quickly obeyed, grabbing the spoon dutifully while Fatima answered the door.

There stood Ivan and Tanager. Tanager was dressed in a double-breasted gray suit, button-down vest, and crisp white shirt that looked more in line with the time period of the music they were listening to than with today's era. He carried with him a bottle of a 15-year-old tawny port. Ivan, on the other hand, wore a black Earth Day t-shirt and the only pair of jeans he owned without holes in them. He polished the look off with penny loafers, placing flat washers where the pennies should have been.

"We happened to arrive at the same time," Ivan explained awkwardly after seeing the laser-eyed warning Lucene shot from her place at the stove. He understood enough to know that it was best to keep Cepheus hidden and pretend that he and Tanager hadn't met before this evening. It wasn't much of a stretch, as the gentleman had really only known each other for the past 24 hours.

"Well, since you two have already met," Fatima smiled graciously, " come on in. It's nice to see you both again."

Tanager offered up the port. "I wasn't sure what to bring," he apologized, but I thought this might be a good digestif? The woman working at the store recommended it." Fatima accepted the gift, eyeing the bottle approvingly.

"Perfect," she whispered, and meant it wholeheartedly. Still smiling, she set it on the counter. "Please, make yourselves comfortable." Fatima relieved Lucene of the spoon at just the right time, as Lucene began stirring the pot so fast, they would have been eating pureed lentil baby food in a few more minutes.

"Yes," Lucene jumped in. "Nice to see you again. Can I take your jacket for you?" While Lucene helped Tanager with his suit jacket, Ivan followed Fatima to the kitchen, scratching nervously behind his ear.

"So, uh...while not exactly a dinner gift, I did bring something fer ya." Ivan reached into his back pocket and pulled out a tiny plastic case and popped it open. Inside, was what looked like a phone memory chip. He held it up for her to see. Fatima politely moved in for a closer look.

"I see," she replied politely…but she really didn't. "Thank you."

"Aww, ye don't even know what it is yet, cuz I have nah told ya." He smiled sheepishly, well, more like a bearded goat, actually.

"What is it?" Fatima asked. Having finished with the soup, she moved to the Spanish onion tortes in the oven. She shooed Ivan away from the oven door, and he backed up to the refrigerator, still holding the tiny black disk between his meaty thumb and forefinger.

"Well, let's say your car was a homing pigeon…"

"Interesting," Fatima offered, engrossed in removing the torte from the oven and testing for doneness. "Would you mind putting down a trivet for me?" She motioned an eye toward the still unset table. Ivan rushed to comply, putting the small device back in its case, and tucking it into his pocket.

Lucene wrapped Tanager's jacket around the back of one of the dining room chairs, and then darted around Ivan in a quest for dinner plates.

"May I be of assistance?" Tanager offered, helpfully.

"Sure," Lucene answered, pausing to look him in the eyes as if searching for information. She still needed to ask him what he knew about her parents, but had to find the right time.

"No," Fatima jumped in. Lucene took a step back, jarred from her thoughts. "You're our guest. Just be comfortable and Ivan can help Lucene set the table for the five of us." Ivan tilted his head slightly, unsure whether to be offended at not being considered a guest or flattered that she was comfortable enough with him to put him to work. He decided on the latter. After all, he did know where the silverware was kept, and had the table set for five in no time. He had just begun to wonder who the fifth-place setting was for, when the doorbell rang.

"Salad!" Fatima exclaimed as she ran for the door. Both men looked like confused puppies, but to Lucene, it was perfectly clear. When Fatima cooked, she went into militant mode.

"Excuse me," Lucene nudged Ivan out of the way. As expected, an Asian kale salad with peanut dressing sat inside the refrigerator, waiting for its debut. Lucene grabbed the covered glass bowl, quickly setting it on the table before rummaging for tongs in the utensil drawer. According to her best estimation, dinner would be in exactly five to seven minutes, just enough time to greet the final guest, make sure everyone had a beverage, and then serve the torte, soup and salad together. Not one to believe in serving courses, as that just complicated things, Fatima preferred to set the feast out all at once. Ivan had learned the hard way that it was best to start with the hot foods while they were still hot, then move on to what was already cold, lest he receive an icy stare from the chef.

"My lovely Fatima!" Roman stood in the doorway, dressed in a button-down black poplin shirt with white buttons and a pair of black jeans and matching shoes. His wavy black hair was tied back. Fatima's smile matched Roman's and then some, revealing two deep-set dimples and blushing cheeks. Her gaze fell on the carnations in his hand. They were frosted purple! "These are for you," he offered. "They match the highlights in your hair."

"Who's that?" Ivan asked Lucene, with visible uncertainty from the kitchen.

"Not sure," Lucene answered honestly. "She's only just met him."

"I don't like him," Ivan decided. "There's something about him that rubs me the wrong way."

"Rubs you *how*?" Tanager was confused.

"It's an expression." Ivan and Lucene answered in unison.

Fatima seemed to have momentarily forgotten all about dinner, and everyone else in the room, for that matter. "Thank you," she answered, attempting to tuck a strand of hair behind her ear nervously, only to remember that it was rolled up in a bun. "They're beautiful. Please, come in." Fatima stepped aside. "Roman, this is my friend and roommate, Lucene." Lucene offered a hand politely. Roman outstretched a pale, thin hand and took it, hesitantly. "Nice to meet you," she said.

"Any friend of Fatima's is, no doubt, a friend of mine," he gushed, kissing Lucene's hand in a grand gesture. Fatima blushed once more. Lucene smiled politely, and then retreated to the kitchen sink to wash her hands.

"This is my neighbor, Ivan," Fatima continued, ignoring Lucene's departure. Ivan scowled momentarily, before conceding to offer his hand. "Aye," he added. "And longtime friend and Praetorian. Don't kiss me hand," he advised. Roman shook it, cautiously. Ivan noted the softness of Roman's palm and handshake, adding it to his mental list of why he did not trust him. Fatima did not seem to notice. "And this is Lucene's friend, Tanager from..."

"Out of town," he offered.

"I am pleased to make your acquaintance," Tanager followed suit by presenting an outstretched hand in friendship. Relieved, Roman shook it without incident.

"Drinks!" Fatima launched back into military mode and softly added, "While I just go and put these in some water."

"Please," Lucene suggested. "Have a seat while I get the wine and water." As expected, Tanager insisted on helping, and was tasked with setting out five water glasses, and filling them with cooled lemon water from the refrigerator while Lucene opened a Rioja Reserve that Fatima had settled on just for this evening. "I'll get the wine glasses," Ivan declared before adding, as he glanced toward Roman, "since I know where they are."

Lucene was only two minutes off, as dinner was served exactly nine minutes after the arrival of the last guest. It was mostly uneventful, with a few praises to the chef and compliments on the wine. Lucene sat at one end of the table, Roman at the other, with Tanager seated to her right, Ivan to her left, and Fatima sandwiched between her two admirers, across from Tanager.

"So, how is it that you two met?" Roman inquired, eyeing Lucene and Tanager back and forth.

"Tanager rescued me from the grocery after my car broke down in the rain," Lucene answered, simply.

"The Fates are amazing women, aren't they?" Roman remarked, shooting an admiring glance at Fatima. "And, how long ago was that?"

Tanager retrieved his pocket watch. "About 29 hours ago," he answered, snapping it closed, and placing it back in his pocket.

"Really?" Roman was taken aback. "I would have guessed that you'd known each other for years. Interesting."

"And how did ye two meet?" Ivan rested his elbow on the table, motioning toward Fatima before she nudged him to remove the offending elbow.

"I was at the bar at the restaurant where Fatima works." He paused to take a forkful of the torte before continuing. "I wasn't having any fun at all until I tried the most exquisite ahi tuna made by this lovely lady."

Ivan sat back and shot Fatima a self-explanatory look. *Really?* the glance said. *At the bar where you work?*

"The Fates," Fatima shrugged her shoulder and sipped her soup.

"And what brought ye to the Crab Shack that fateful evening," Ivan inquired. "Searching for a soulmate, were ya?"

"Not at all," Roman answered, turning his gaze back to Fatima and clasping her hand gently at the table. Fatima did not chastise him for putting *his* elbow on the table, and shyly clasped his hand in return. "It just worked out that way." Ivan swallowed a bit of salad with some difficulty. Lucene was beginning to share Ivan's sentiment, but not out of jealousy. It was due more to his over-the-top overtures to someone he met just the evening prior. It was as if he were a child in a man's body, experiencing puppy love for the first time. Tanager sipped his wine in silence, observing with as little judgement as possible.

"If you must know," Roman continued, as if relenting to divulge private information under duress, "I was there for my research."

"Research?" Tanager's eyes perked up, intrigued.

"Yes," Roman continued. "While I can't go into detail at this juncture, I can tell you that I am an anthropology professor currently conducting research for a white paper I'm writing on relationships in the modern era."

"How fascinating," Fatima all but batted her eyes at Roman. "Let us know how we can help with that research," she fawned. Realizing that her statement may have been interpreted more seductively than she had intended, her cheeks returned to a flushed crimson.

Ivan's also flared red, but for a very different reason.

At that moment, "It's Time to Say Goodnight" began playing from the sound bar. It was unclear whether Tanager found it to be the perfect diversion in order to diffuse a potentially volatile situation, or whether he simply liked dancing. Whichever the case, he quickly turned to Fatima and asked, "As host of this evening, would you honor me with the first dance?"

"Well, sir," she answered, brushing her napkin to the side. "I would be delighted." Fatima took the hand he offered and accompanied him to the living room, where they began waltzing in the small open area in front of the couch. Fatima, among her other talents, was an enormously good dancer, and followed easily as Tanager led her around the floor.

"Can I ask you a question?" He whispered, leaning in.

"Sure," she smiled warmly. "Ask me anything."

"I couldn't help but notice that Lucene seems to have an aversion to doors. Any idea why?"

"Oh, only red doors," Fatima answered matter-of-factly. "That's why she goes through the window and avoids the front door," she motioned toward the kitchen.

"I see. Actually, no, no, I don't see. Why red doors?"

"She won't tell me. I've offered to paint the front door a dark blue, but she would have none of it."

"Why not?"

"Because she said she would always know that it was a red door posing as a blue door." Tanager simply nodded, as if this logic made perfect sense, and the two continued their dance.

"There's more," Fatima whispered. "She doesn't like computers or things with computers in them."

"Really?" Tanager was curious. "Did she say why?"

"I dunno," Fatima shook her head. "But I suspect that she thinks someone is trying to follow her. She's been weird like that since she moved in with me five years ago. I try not to pry."

Tanager's expression changed, as if a lightbulb just went off in his head. He pushed the thought away and replaced his look of surprise with a warm smile. Fatima smiled in return.

Roman admired Fatima from the kitchen, resting his chin in his hand on the table, with a half-upturned smile plastered across his face. "I wonder what they're talking about," he mused. "Me, I hope." It was only then that he noticed Lucene awkwardly pushing a stray piece of kale around her plate. "Um, Lucene, would you care to dance?"

"I would, except that I really don't know how to do…that," she motioned toward Fatima and Tanager, who were floating around the room like Fred and Ginger.

"Not to worry," Roman answered, "I have a solution. Follow me."

Lucene reluctantly followed Roman to the makeshift dance floor while Ivan decided it might be a good time to pop open the port.

"Now," Roman instructed, circling an arm around her waist. "Step on my toes."

"Excuse me?" Lucene gave Roman a sideways look. A good deal taller than Lucene, she ended up peering at his nostrils.

"Step on my toes," he tried again. "Then you don't have to worry about a misstep. Don't worry," he reassured. "I don't mind."

Lucene stepped carefully on his feet. He winced. "Sorry," she moved away.

"No, it's…fine."

Lucene wasn't so sure it was fine. He awkwardly lifted one weighted foot at a time as they hobbled in a misshapen square pattern.

From the kitchen, Ivan noticed a carpetbag sitting at the end of the long countertop, the one Fatima carried with her everywhere. He glanced at the two couples on the dance floor, but each seemed preoccupied. He once again removed the tiny case from his pocket, and reached into Fatima's bag, poking around until he'd found what he was looking for.

Moments later, the song ended, and another began, "Moonlight in Vermont."

Fatima smiled as she crossed paths with the other couple, stopping abruptly. "Lucene, let me show you how it's done. May I cut in?" Lucene gratefully stepped down from Roman's toes and allowed her friend to cut in. Roman circled his arm around her thick waist, and the two moved with surprising ease. His lean frame stood more than a foot above her. As far as couples go, many tend to resemble each other, but these two were like watching a plantain and an acorn squash dance.

"May I teach you?" Tanager spoke softly over Lucene's shoulder. She shivered.

"Well, you can try, but I've got no rhythm," Lucene laughed awkwardly as she turned to face him.

"I don't believe that's true," Tanager answered, thoughtfully. She expected verbal instruction, but instead, he simple began stepping and she followed. It was as if there were a magnet between them and she naturally followed where he led. Before she knew it, she too was moving with ease around the room. They kept dancing, long after the music stopped.

Lucene glanced up to see Roman, Fatima and Ivan off to the side of the room, watching the two in earnest.

"Well," Fatima offered. "One, I didn't know you could dance, Lucene. You've been holding out on me. And two, you both realize this isn't the 18th century and you're allowed to actually hold hands when you dance?"

It was only then that Lucene realized that Tanager had not actually had his arm around her waist, nor did they have their arms up in a traditional couple's dance. But the energy between them was so strong that she was sure they had been touching. Tanager searched Lucene's face for some sign of recognition but found none. Instead, she pulled away and headed back to the kitchen. She glanced down at her arms, noticing that the branch-like lightning patterns had a glow about them. Lucene quickly crossed her arms awkwardly in front of her. "How about pouring me some of that port, Ivan?"

Roman arrived home with an ear-to-ear grin that he just couldn't shake. It wasn't often that one found the woman of their dreams, and yet, he had. Nothing could spoil this moment.

He stopped abruptly when he reached his bedroom, eyeing all the pictures on the wall. There was a brief swirling in his head—like when you awaken from a dream and it takes you a moment to remember who and where you are.

"Stupid man," Roman hit himself in the forehead. He had been so distracted by love that he forgot all about his mission—Lucene. There were pictures of her, and others, tacked up all over the walls. He'd followed her from New York to Florida. Yes, his research for TARA was important, but Lucene's safety was supposed to be his primary concern.

What's more, is that he was almost fooled by this Tanager…almost. *Why hadn't he realized it sooner? He's got to be working for them.*

He slipped the lapel camera from his shirt, pulled a portable computer out from the bedroom dresser drawer and set it on the carpet. Plugging it in, he then retrieved photos—mostly of Tanager and Lucene dancing, but also of the entire evening. The camera had been set to auto-capture regularly. From another drawer, he drew out a mini-printer, hooking the cable to the computer and laying them side-by-side on the floor.

After he'd printed what he felt were the most relevant photos, he searched for pins or sticky putty to post them to the wall. *Where did he put them?* He searched the bathroom, catching a glimpse of himself in the mirror. He paused; it was almost as if he were looking at a stranger. He didn't recognize himself.

Roman opened a drawer and found it filled with prescription bottles. "I see what's happening here," he looked up and told his reflection. "The Royals know I'm here, and they're trying to torture me too."

CHAPTER 13
ALL MEN ARE CRAZY
SUNDAY MORNING. FIVE YEARS AFTER THE ASSEMBLY.

"He told you what?"

"That he's an alien," Fatima grinned gleefully from the corner of the couch, where she sat nestled, hugging a throw pillow to her chest.

"When did he have time to tell you that?" Lucene stood behind the couch, before being summoned back to the kitchen by a teakettle whistling on the stove. "Sometime between the 'let's have port' and 'pass the creme brûlée?'"

"Relax," Fatima called after her. "It was at the end of the evening, after the boys had left and you were clearing the dishes. Hee! How fun is that?"

"I'm not sure why you find this so amusing." Lucene returned to the living room, handing Fatima a cup of tea. While cooking was not her thing, tea, she could manage.

"What? It's not like it's the first time I dated someone who claimed to be from another planet," Fatima reflected. "Besides, you of all people should know that there are some aliens taking up residence on Earth."

"Yeah," Lucene agreed, "but there's so much controversy around them that most keep a low profile and don't advertise it, particularly beings who look so much like us that we wouldn't know the difference without checking the International Registry. Why would he be that open about it?" Lucene thought back to her recent encounter with Cepheus. Previously, her only interaction with other life forms, to her knowledge, was when she was working with the UC, and that was merely as an observer. And even then, they were tuning in from their home planet, not Earth. Somewhere, in the corners of her brain, a memory surfaced. It had something to do with Cepheus and his connection to the IPP.

"Look, I'm not saying I believe him," Fatima interrupted the thought and it vanished as quickly as it arose. "Just that I don't care if he *thinks* he is. He's sweet." Fatima sighed, wistfully.

"But, that's crazy."

"All men are crazy," Fatima reasoned. "At least this one's not suicidal. I once had a boyfriend, this was way before you moved here, who threatened to chain himself to the underside of a delivery truck and let himself get dragged to death if I didn't go back to him after we broke up."

"What did you do?"

"I felt bad, so we dated for another year."

"Oh, Fatima." Lucene shook her head, taking a seat beside her friend.

"The way I see it," Fatima paused to take a sip of the tea, nodding with approval at its preparation. "We all choose our life experience, our reality, if you will. If he chooses a life experience where he's an alien, then who am I to argue?"

"But what if *his* life experience can potentially cause harm to *your* reality?

"Oh, he's harmless," Fatima waved her hand in the air, "even if he is a bit paranoid."

"Paranoid? What do you mean 'paranoid'?"

"Well…he thinks he's one of the last Data Collectors left on the planet."

"What?" Lucene's eyes widened. Synapses in her brain began to reconfigure and connect as memories from five years ago began to flash like camera bulbs behind her eyes.

"You know, the story that was in the news a couple years back about aliens from Erde hiding among us collecting information about us to report back."

"No, I know who they're supposed to be. I'm just surprised he claimed to *be* one." *A little odd that he would surface at the same time as Cepheus and Tanager. Did the men secretly know each other, but pretend not to for some reason?*

"What's wrong?" Fatima looked concerned. "Your face just turned white as a ghost. Does this have something to do with your time in New York? I know you don't like to talk about it but..."

"I just want you to be careful."

"Awww, that's why I love you, my friend. I will be careful."

"So, what's he collecting data on?" Lucene asked. "Don't they have a specific area of expertise?"

Fatima giggled, settling back on the couch. "Oh, you're going to love this, he's studying the nuances of romantic relationships. He wasn't lying when he said he was writing a white paper last night at dinner. And, get this, he told me he didn't believe in love at first sight until he saw me."

"That's very...sweet," Lucene was unconvinced. "And where's lover boy today?"

"Said he had to meet another of his friends from back home today, some guy named Jim, Jim Sparks. What a funny name. He lives on a boat."

"Another Data Collector. So, there's two of them?"

"Yeah, but they have to be careful since they tend to be a target for hate groups. Come to think of it, maybe I shouldn't have told you?" Fatima looked concerned.

"Fatima, who would I tell? I'm practically a hermit."

"Reverend Isabella or, I dunno, maybe your new boyfriend, Tanager?" she teased.

"He's not my...oh, never mind." Lucene stood. "Speaking of Reverend Isabella, I've got to run some errands and get to work. I promised I'd get there early to help set up for the new moon celebration she's having tonight."

"I don't understand you, Lucene." Fatima eyed her friend curiously. "You have a master's degree and had a great job with the UC that had tremendous potential for growth. Why on Earth, no pun intended given our recent conversation, would you take on an entry level administrative job at a local church that pays minimum wage and offers no hope of advancement? I don't get it."

"No, you don't," Lucene answered. "And, I'm afraid I can't explain it to you. I'm sorry."

"Hmmm…maybe it's not just limited to men. Maybe we're all crazy."

"Perhaps," Lucene acknowledged, as she made her way back to her bedroom to grab a pair of shoes. "But not everyone's brain got fried by lightning, either. I can't explain to you what I can't remember."

"True," Fatima acknowledged. "But you remembered me." She smiled as Lucene resurfaced from her bedroom, moments later.

"How could I forget?" Lucene pinched her friend's cheek, playfully.

"Hey, don't wait up. I'm heading to a family reunion today and won't be back until late. If you change your mind and want to join us, the number is on the fridge."

"Thanks," Lucene answered awkwardly. To say that Fatima's family was fun loving was an understatement, and yet she still couldn't handle the energy of being around that many people in one location. "I will." In the meantime, she made a mental note to ask Tanager about Roman and investigate this Jim Sparks.

She couldn't explain it to Fatima because she couldn't quite understand it herself. Lucene looked down at her arms. People viewed them with odd fascination, as if she had intricate henna work tattooed on her arms. But to her, their patterns unlocked a secret somehow. Except that ever since she got them, she couldn't remember what it was. She barely remembered the car accident that killed her parents. Nor did she remember the lightning strike or much that happened in the first seven years of her life. But she did remember meeting Fatima in the hospital room as a child and was grateful for the only true friendship she'd had for most of her adult life.

Lucene pulled Kermit into a new age shop and pulled out her list. Reverend Isabella had sent her in to pick up Peruvian resin and a hand drum she was having repaired. The woman behind the counter greeted her with a smile. "Hi, Lucy," she beamed. In spite of Lucene's many requests to be called by her complete name, the shop owner never seemed to remember. Lucene cringed, but said nothing. She gave a polite smile back. "I've got Reverend Isabella's drum right here," she pulled it out from underneath the counter.

"Thanks." Lucene picked up a bag of resin from a wall display and placed it on the counter. "We need this, too."

"So weird," the woman continued, carefully unwrapping the drum that she had rolled in cloth for protection "You can see that it's smooth again." She ran her hand over it for emphasis. "But how on Earth did it get punctured like that? It's like someone jabbed a knife through it."

"I couldn't say," Lucene answered. "How much do I owe you?" After completing the transaction, Lucene left the store and climbed into her vehicle with the resin and drum placed carefully in the passenger's seat.

It wasn't as if she didn't like people, but she didn't trust inquisitive ones who can't remember your name even after you've been a customer for more than four years. The less she knew, Lucene reasoned, the better.

She had no idea how the drum got damaged in the first place, but since Reverend Isabella didn't ask her a lot of questions, she gave her boss and mentor the same respect. In truth, Reverend Isabella had been the one person who had been able to help her with her "glitches," like the one she'd experienced the first day in her meditation class. Since then, her mentor had made a point of inviting her to every meditation, yoga and tai chi class held at the sanctuary. She periodically suggested things for Lucene to be mindful of, encouraging her to practice this while tending to her tasks of gardening, cleaning or providing info to attendees.

Things like, "When trimming the shrubs in the garden, be sure to thank them for providing oxygen to the air we breathe and for protecting us from the harsh sun. Let them know that you are trimming them so they may continue being a source of health and beauty to all who visit us." Or when a Northern Mockingbird randomly flew through an open window into the main hall, she'd say, "Ask them what message they have for you, and be sure to thank them. Guide them to the window if they've gotten lost and give them space to leave unharmed."

And when that backfired, like when the shrubs and birds became too chatty, instead of calling her crazy, Reverend Isabella taught her to mentally separate herself from the chatter. Since she quickly learned that red doors were a source of stress, Lucene was taught to shut the red door, leaving the sounds behind it until she was ready to address them. Lucene didn't understand her phobia, or the flashes of insight that would hit her like a thousand radio waves tuning in to different channels—all at the same time, but she was grateful to have someone treat it as a gift to be trained instead of a mental illness to be eradicated.

So, while she may have been making only minimum wage at a little sanctuary in Parrish, the benefits she received working there were profound. Plus, she felt safe being hidden away from normal day-to-day interactions. This is why she stayed, but she couldn't quite articulate this to Fatima. She wasn't sure if she would ever be able to.

CHAPTER 14
FAMILY
30 YEARS AGO. 25 YEARS BEFORE THE ASSEMBLY.

"Tanager!" Two small boys, spouting a mess of curly orange hair on their heads, ran up, each wrapping their arms around one of his legs as Tanager pretended to struggle as he walked through the door.

"Boys," a tall woman with bright auburn hair called, cradling a small child as she reached the door. "Let him be," she laughed.

"Tanager! Tanager!" One of the boys tugged at his pant leg. "Guess what I'm going to be when I am as big as you are?" he asked. Without waiting for an answer, he spat out, "a Data Collector!" He smiled a wide, crooked smile.

Tanager mussed his hair. "Well, that is a noble occupation." The other boy would not be overshadowed by his twin.

"And I'm going to be a professor, just like you and my dad," he proclaimed proudly.

"That's enough, boys," the red-haired woman intervened. "Go and help your dad with the samphire stew." She leaned over to touch her forehead to Tanager's in a warm greeting. "So nice to see you again, friend."

"You as well, Petrichor. And this must be the lovely Tallulah." He went to stroke the baby's fine hair with his hand, but the child caught one of his fingers and held on with pure fascination, giggling gleefully. "The grip of a tigress," he complimented, "what a strong soul."

"She takes after her mother," Cepheus's wife smiled. "Come in. Dinner will be ready in just a moment." Tanager followed Petrichor through their living room. While he'd been in their home a number of times, he was still in awe of it. There were two built-in waterfalls on each side of the room that flowed gently into a pond that poured under the walkway where he now stood. Live vines hung from the ceilings with bright yellow, orange and red flowers growing from them. "Be careful of the Walleyes," she warned, glancing at her feet. "They appear to be agitated today." As if on cue, several fish leapt across Tanager's feet before disappearing under the water.

Dinner was held at a small round table in their kitchen. Unlike the living room, the kitchen was simple with stations for growing hydroponic herbs and vegetables, a station for prepping food, one for cooking and another for assembly. Behind the stations were walk-in units with foods stored at varied temperatures. The assembly line ended, and the kitchen table began, making the layout as efficient as possible. Adjacent to the kitchen was a formal dining area used to entertain dignitaries, colleagues, friends and distant relatives. But Tanager wasn't considered merely a friend and colleague. He was an honorary member of their immediate family, and despite a considerable age gap, Cepheus regarded Tanager as his brother. And so, he sat at the informal table in their kitchen, as a sign of high respect.

One of the boys ran around the table, laying out platters while the other filled glasses with water. This boy had a tentacled creature stuck to his shoulder, its suction arms wrapped around the boy's arm and a bulbous one-eyed head peering at Tanager curiously. It tapped the edge of its tentacle like a dog wagging its tail.

"Cephi," his mother scolded. "Get Merla out of the kitchen and back in the water. She has no business being at the dinner table!" The boy reluctantly took his five-legged pet into the living room and released her into the pond. "Wash your hands," she commanded, once he'd returned.

As was custom, everyone took their place once dinner was ready. Cepheus went around the table with a stew cart, passing out food and bread to the boys, then his wife, then Tanager. Baby Tallulah sat in a safety chair next to Petrichor, being bottle-fed by a mechanical system attached to the chair. Once everyone's plate was filled, he filled his own and took a seat. Petrichor reached for a bottle of homemade pomegranate and blackberry wine, pouring it into an empty cup and passing it to Tanager who accepted with a smile, before doing the same for herself and her husband. Pretrichor was the best wine maker in their village. During one particularly poor growing season, her vineyard thrived while many others failed to produce a single crop. It was Cepheus's belief that his wife had literally loved the vineyard back to life.

They held hands in a moment of silence, each giving thanks to the spirit of their choice before the boys dug into their food with gusto.

"I have news," Cepheus proclaimed, eagerly.

Tanager quickly swallowed a mouthful of stew before answering, "What news?"

"Dora and Xan have finally made contact."

"Really?" Tanager seemed surprised. "After hearing nothing for two years, I was worried something had happened to them."

"As was I," Cepheus nodded. "And something did happen, something wonderful!"

"Well, don't keep me in suspense."

"They had a baby, a girl," Petrichor announced, reaching over and touching Tallulah's cheek and smiling.

"On Earth? That is good news!"

"There's more," Cepheus said.

"What?"

"The child has abilities."

"Abilities?" Tanager questioned.

"Without any genetic altering, she was inherently born with all of the same abilities as our Data Collectors."

"Astonishing! A natural empath born of two genetically enhanced Data Collectors."

"Her skills have to be developed, of course," Cepheus explained in-between sips of wine. "But now that Dora and Xan have resumed communication, I can begin mentoring her remotely."

"Wonderful news. But did they say why they dropped communication?"

"Let's just say it was unsafe for them for a time," he sent a knowing glance in his boys' direction, and Tanager understood.

Tanager redirected the conversation, "This calls for a tribute." He raised his glass in a toast, and Cepheus and Petrichor joined in. "We send blessings to the beautiful family that is Dora, Xan and…what is the child's name?"

"Lucene," Cepheus supplied. Tanager suddenly got chills down his spine but didn't know why the name had significance. He shook it off and smiled.

The children had all been put to bed, and Cepheus, Tanager and Petrichor were sitting in the living room watching the Walleyes jump as they sipped an after-dinner cocktail. Merla was acting strangely, Petrichor noted, as their octopus-like pet climbed the vines of one of the walls.

"Strange," Petrichor noted to Cepheus. "She's never done that before."

Moments later, there was a loud explosion as the walls of the living room caved in, sending water, debris and bloody Walleyes flying mid-air, smacking down on what was left of the stone walkway that had bisected the living room.

Petrichor had barely yelled, "The children!" when there was a second explosion at the back of the house. Her face contorted in horror. Royal soldiers poured in, several grabbing Cepheus before he could react and dragging him outside. He called to his wife, peering over his shoulder just seconds before witnessing a soldier grab Petrichor and break her neck with a single twist. Her head lying limply to one side, he tossed her body into the pond as easily as one might throw pellets to a fish. Cepheus began screaming, only to be silenced by another soldier striking him on the back of the head with his fist.

For Tanager, everything appeared in slow motion as he watched Cepheus being dragged away, unconscious with blood running down his face. Petrichor floated, face down, to the surface of the pond. The rooms where the children slept were now piles of rubble and smoke, and with the roof of the house now gone, he could see the dark sky and stars above. It was a humid night, and the air was sticky. Instinctively, he sought to run after his friend, only to feel a soldier grab and slam his body to the ground, wrapping his arms behind his back and tying them together. His face was pressed into what was left of the stone floor. Moments later, he was being dragged, semi-conscious, across the ground, rolling over grass, dirt and rubble, cutting his body and the side of his face. He felt pain and was no longer able to open one eye. Tanager was about to lose consciousness before he was suddenly flipped over and a bright light blinded him.

Fredo loomed over him, dressed in a soldier's uniform that appeared two sizes too small. "Sovereign Sabrina and Sovereign Hamish did not appreciate the Peace-Keeper's interference with their son decades ago, any more than they appreciate them ruining trade negotiations now." He kicked Tanager in the ribs. Tanager let out a groan but could not react beyond that. "Take a message back to the Peace-Keepers in charge of TARA. Tell them that if they do not pull their Data Collectors from Earth immediately, the Royals will react swiftly and families of Erde will meet the same fate as this one experienced here tonight."

The lights faded and Tanager lost consciousness.

CHAPTER 15
THE VESSEL
SUNDAY MORNING. FIVE YEARS AFTER THE ASSEMBLY.

Not long after Fatima left to visit her relatives, there was a knock at the window. Tanager stood peering in from outside. Curious, Lucene unlocked it and slid the glass panel open.

"Can I show you something?" Tanager asked, tipping his hat to her. Lucene didn't know whether the hat was a disguise or if he had an old-fashioned notion that men should always wear a hat when outdoors and remove it when inside.

"That depends. Is it obscene?" She answered, flatly.

"No, why would it be?" Said Tanager, missing the joke.

"No reason. What did you want me to see?"

"Please, follow me." He held out his hand to help Lucene through the window.

"I'm good," she waved away his hand. "I'm a pro at this." Tanager stepped aside, giving her space to climb down. He continued to be confused by her choice in words. Lucene closed the window, locking it behind her and tucking the little key in her pocket. "Okay, I'm ready."

Tanager led the way silently, heading toward Ivan's house. But, instead of going to the front of the house, as Lucene had expected, he took her the back way, where Fatima's cottage and Ivan's shed shared a connected lawn shrouded by oak and red cedar trees.

She'd never seen the inside of Ivan's workshop, but having heard strange sounds emanating from it at all hours of the night, Lucene was curious. Tanager gave a knock on the door. After hearing a few odd whirs and clicks, the door slid open.

Cepheus's eyes lit up in both surprise and joy at Lucene's arrival. "Lucene," he smiled. "It's nice to see you." Lucene beamed back, noticing a gentle warmth in the center of her chest. "He is a genius," Cepheus continued, nodding toward Ivan, as if he'd waited all morning to share this information with her.

Cepheus motioned toward the workbench with what looked like a small compressor connected to an even smaller computer. Behind them, the computer projected what appeared to be the engine room of a large craft. Had it been real, it would have engulfed the entire shed. The workshop, itself, was filled from wall to wall and ceiling to floor with tools and gadgets—the larger items mounted neatly to the wall, the smaller bits of hardware stored in stackable containers on shelves.

Ivan was too engrossed in problem-solving to do more than grunt at Lucene before returning to work. "Cepheus, you've got thinner fingers than me. See if you can thread this wire."

"Of course," Cepheus's eyes grew wide, half in acknowledgement of suddenly realizing Ivan's solution and half to indicate his support. Everyone watched curiously as Cepheus delicately threaded the wire, reconnecting it to an adaptor.

"Ivan is helping us get home faster," Tanager whispered over Lucene's shoulder. She shuddered ever so slightly at his close proximity but did not back away. "Perhaps you will decide to come with us," he said in a manner that was half-joking and half-serious.

Ivan briefly glanced up from his project, but said nothing.

"And, why would I do that?"

Cepheus nodded at Tanager and resumed working with Ivan. It was almost time to begin welding.

"Why don't you and I take a short walk?" Tanager suggested.

"Probably safer," Ivan agreed, handing Cepheus a spare welding mask.

Lucene nodded. She'd witnessed the after-effects of Ivan's experiments gone wrong numerous times and was happy to keep her distance. "There's a short trail behind the house. That do?"

There was a pause as Tanager translated the meaning of 'that do.' "That will be perfect."

They walked in silence for several minutes before Tanager offered, carefully, "I'm trying to share this info with you as gently as possible."

"Well, spit it out," Lucene replied, somewhat impatiently, after a long pause. "I'm sure it will be fine." *There it was again, that stupid energy between them. What was that?*

"Spit it o—," Tanager paused. "Oh, speak quickly and hold nothing back. I see."

"First time to Earth?" Lucene chided.

"First time to any planet, actually."

"Well, you've got me beat."

He eyed her curiously. "The way you speak is fascinating." She felt her cheeks getting warm and quickly diverted her eyes. He fought back a small grin. "I think I understand contractions now, but my slang is obviously outdated. You would be excellent if you ever decided to teach a class on Earth communication back home."

"Let's not get ahead of ourselves," Lucene said. *Damn it! There I go again.* Before now, she hadn't realized that nearly everything that came out of her mouth was an idiom. Tanager interrupted her thoughts.

"I don't think it's wise for me to 'spit it out.' It may be too much all at once."

"Well, what can you tell me? Maybe you could start by telling me what you know about my parents?"

Tanager paused. "Do you not remember them at all?"

"Did *your* parents never tell you that it's rude to answer a question with a question?"

Tanager let out a sigh. She was proving more challenging than he expected. "It was Cepheus who met your parents first…a very long time ago…on Erde."

There was a long pause while Lucene struggled to connect the dots. "Are you suggesting that they were not born on Earth, or that they were on Erde…for some reason?"

"Your parents were born on Erde. Cepheus met them at the Terrestrial

Academy of Research and Awareness...where your parents were training to become Data Collectors." He paused for the information to sink in. "Are you familiar with what that means?"

She and Fatima had just discussed this. "I remember...What was their assignment?" She vaguely remembered that her dad loved plants and thought it might have something to do with horticulture.

"Well, it...changed after you were born."

"Oh," Lucene frowned, thinking she'd interrupted their work.

"No," he touched her shoulder. "You were...are...a good interruption." He smiled. "Your parents," he reminisced, "were the kindest people, and they adored you."

"Wait," Lucene commanded. Tanager stopped in his tracks. "No, not literally." 'Literally' didn't help much, but he was beginning to understand the communication patterns in her mind the more time he spent with her. "How could you know them? You've got to be at least five years younger than I...maybe more. Were you a baby?"

"Actually, I knew them very well. As it so happens, I'm actually older than you."

"Really, how old are you?"

"I'm about 56 years in your timeline."

"But you look half that. How is that possible?"

"It's just that our environment is more ideal than Earth's. Our physical systems are more evolved than yours. Therefore, we heal faster and do not age pre-maturely."

"Pre-maturely? So, we should be living longer?"

"Under the right conditions, both in the internal physiological environment and the external environment, your average lifespan would be double what is currently is. Were it not for your medical breakthroughs, some of which we contributed to, your species would definitely not have fared as well."

"I see. I mean," Lucene clarified, "I understand."

"Thank you," he laughed. "I've started a list of common expressions and am cataloging them. It's a long list."

"I'll bet," Lucene answered. "Oh, there's another!"

Lucene wanted to know more about her parents and was about to ask.

"I would love to tell you lots of stories about your parents, perhaps on the long journey back home?"

"You are a tease...there's another. I'm afraid I can't stop myself." *What the hell is wrong with you, Lucene?* she thought to herself. He was making her nervous in a *he's much more attractive and interesting than I first thought* kind of way.

"It is okay. That's how I learn. 'I'll bet,'" he smiled at picking up the term. "Cepheus knew at least 99% of all Earth expressions, regardless of culture. Unfortunately, he lost much of it after the...incident."

Her attention was suddenly brought back to the present in an abrupt, and sorrowful, way. For this, she didn't need to ask. While Lucene couldn't make out the details, she could feel that Cepheus had suffered extreme physical and emotional pain...and betrayal. She could also feel how sorrowful that made Tanager, and now, her as well.

"They will hurt you, too," Tanager read her thoughts.

"Hey, stay out of my head," Lucene whined. "I mean, is that it?" She pointed to the side of her head. "Could you actually read what I'm thinking if you wanted to?"

"I'm sorry," he apologized. "We are on a similar wavelength. I pick up mostly emotions, but occasionally, words and phrases too. But, don't worry, your brain puts out natural blockers for anything private. It would be very difficult for me to see anything you didn't want me to."

"But not impossible."

"No, not impossible. Though, if I sense resistance, I will try to be polite."

"Well, that's reassuring," she answered, for once without sarcasm. *Did he know he was making her nervous? Stop it brain. Stop it!* "So, who's trying to hurt me and why?"

Tanager paused for a moment before answering. "In addition to rigorous training at the Terrestrial Academy of Research and Awareness, TARA for short, Data Collectors voluntarily participated in a DNA splicing program. When given certain biological attributes, they were 90% more likely to respond to intuitive training. Each Data Collector on Earth was paired with one of the trainers on Erde. Instead of transmitting information over the air waves, they could do so telepathically."

"Neat trick," Lucene admired.

"No trick," Tanager replied. "It had to be the right combination of biology, training and emotional predisposition toward compassion."

"In other words, soulless jerks need not apply." Tanager looked at her, quizzically. "Never mind," she said. "So, my parents had the right combination. But I've never been sliced and diced, nor given any special genes. I've never trained at your academy, and I'm not known for being the most touchy-feely of people."

"No," he agreed solemnly. "You are probably the last person anyone would mistake as having special skills."

"Gee, thanks."

"That is a good thing. It is probably what kept you safe for this long."

"Not helping."

"My concern is..." He took her by the shoulders and looked into her eyes. She shivered slightly but didn't resist. "Your parents discovered early on that you had all the signs of someone who had received the DNA splicing, except that you hadn't, but you were born to two people who had. You are the only natural born Data Collector, and from that, we can hypothesize that there exists within you the potential for great power, with training...of course. Some dangerous people can't seem to decide if they should fear you or use you."

By this time, they had looped the nature trail and were back at the shed in time for Ivan to say, happily, "I think we're on to something!"

Cepheus curled his long-nailed fingers lovingly around the compressor they had been working with. "Ivan has figured out a way to get us home in half the time it has taken us to get here."

"How?" Tanager asked, skeptically.

"Well," Ivan scratched his head. "Are ye familiar with virtual machines?"

"Yes."

"And machine learning?"

"Yes!" Tanager grew increasingly more excited.

"So, let's pretend the vessel has one engine with hardware abstractions that convince it that it really has two engines. It will do the trial and error all on its own until it actually figures out the engine efficiencies to make it react as if there are actually two engines at work instead of just one."

Tanager's eyes lit up. Cepheus began to bounce up and down like an excited cat.

"Ahem," Lucene interrupted. "Can you explain this to those of us who haven't a clue what you're talking about?" She could feel their excitement but understood little else.

"Aye," Ivan said. "We won't know fer sure until we actually install this contraption in the physical vessel. But, if it works, it means they'll have enough power to get back to Erde in six months instead of a year."

"Six months?" Lucene muttered. She couldn't even manage six hours on a plane without getting claustrophobic. She couldn't imagine committing to a journey that took that long. Besides, she wasn't entirely convinced that Tanager and Cepheus could be trusted yet. It took more than two days to get to know someone. It had taken her a good four and a half years before she learned to trust Ivan. And then there was a faded memory that wanted to come out, like an itch that she just couldn't seem to scratch.

"You don't have to decide tonight," Tanager reassured her, feeling her apprehension.

"But, very soon," Cepheus added.

Lucene started to turn away, the doors to the shed about to close behind her before she doubled back. The sensor on the doors triggered and they slid back open. Tanager was the only one who looked up while the other men re-focused their attention on their experiment.

"I am helping out at the local sanctuary. There's a new moon celebration tonight. I don't suppose you'd care to join me?"

"I would be delighted," Tanager replied, nodding a head toward the two hard at work behind him. "I am useless to these gents anyway. It is best if I'm out of the way."

"Okay," Lucene answered. "So, I can come pick you up in Kermit."

"Kermit?"

"My car," she explained.

"Your car has a name?"

"Why wouldn't it have a name?"

"Didn't you say it was rude to answer a question with a question," he teased.

Lucene rolled her eyes. "As I was saying, I can pick you up. Where are you staying?"

"Just over there," he pointed to the house.

"You're staying with Ivan? Both of you?" *How had she not noticed that?* "Never mind, in that case, can you meet me by the window. Say, 6 p.m."

"Certainly," he smiled. "By the window at six." Lucene began to walk away. "Wait...please." Lucene turned around. "You feel far more emotionally stable than one would expect considering the information I just gave you. Why?"

"Maybe once you've spent more time in my head, you'll understand," Lucene smirked. "It all makes perfect sense to me. I've never felt like I belonged on this Earth. Never!"

CHAPTER 16
THE UNDESIRABLES
FIVE YEARS AGO. TWO MONTHS AFTER THE ASSEMBLY.

"Roman Aurelius," the imposing man formed his question more like a statement. "I'm Director Sutton and in charge of the American division of the International Peace Project." Director Sutton stood over Roman who was seated in a straight-backed chair that was too low to the ground for his long legs. His knees knocked the bottom of the folding table in front of him. The room was painted a dull gray and mostly bare except for two chairs, a desk and a "Peace for All" Assembly poster advertising the next IPP event in Dubai next year. Somehow, Roman wasn't feeling the love that the IPP claimed to espouse. After an indignant body scan and rude questioning, they had yet to offer him so much as a glass of water...and he was parched.

"It's nice to meet you, Director Sutton." Roman folded his arms and tilted his head in a way that would suggest otherwise. "What can I answer for the IPP today that I wasn't able to answer last week, or two weeks before that?"

Director Sutton waved away the two men who were standing at the door. The last to exit closed the door behind him. Sutton pulled up a chair and sat across from Roman, removing the rather thick Manila envelope that he had tucked under his arm. He laid it on the desk. Roman let out a deep sigh as the bulky man opened it to page one, eyeing the director's unsavory wardrobe —a pinstriped shirt so tight that the buttons threatened to pop at any moment, with gaps between them that revealed a yellowing undershirt from too many washes without bleach to cover up the sweat stains. There was no doubt in Roman's mind that Director Sutton was a bachelor, and likely to remain so for quite a while.

"Roman Aurelius," he said again. "That your real name?"

"Yes, no relation to Marcus," Roman smiled. Director Sutton didn't get the joke.

"It says here you were a high school anthropology teacher until a year ago when you were let go."

"No, not let go," he corrected. "I am currently on a sabbatical."

"That's not what it says here."

"Well, your report is wrong. Likely someone at the administrative office at school clicked the wrong box on the computer screen. I can phone the principal if you like?"

"That won't be necessary," Director Sutton nodded as he read further, as if whatever followed in the report explained what he needed to know.

"You seem to have an insatiable interest in aliens," he continued, flipping through the pages of his report.

"Well, as I've stated many times before, it is part of my research. And that is the definition of a sabbatical: to take a year to continue studies in one's field of expertise in order to remain current on developing trends."

"I know what a sabbatical means, Mr. Aurelius. But, why aliens?"

"What could be more interesting to an anthropologist than learning how humans will adapt to the integration of beings from other planets coming to live on Earth?"

"Integration may be a strong word," Director Sutton sucked at his teeth, distastefully.

"You don't like the idea of non-humans populating the Earth?" Roman asked.

"We're not here to talk about me, Mr. Aurelius. We're here to talk about the fact that you have an entire collection of photos, documents, and in some cases, interviews of aliens who are voluntarily listed in our International Registry. How did you even find these aliens, Mr. Aurelius?"

"Behavior patterns," he answered simply.

"Behavior patterns," Director Sutton repeated.

"Exactly."

"Care to share what those might be?"

"Actually, I'd rather not."

"Why not?"

"I don't know if you are aware of this, Director Sutton, but non-humans aren't exactly safe in our world. If you look at what happened with the Data Collectors ever since they alerted us to their presence decades ago..."

"I'm glad you brought them up," Director Sutton pulled a series of photos from his file and began tossing them on the table. "Recognize any of these 'non-humans,' as you like to call them?"

Roman turned white. They weren't just any photos of Data Collectors, they were photos of deceased Data Collectors, ones he's spoken with and they had been murdered in various graphic ways.

"What's the matter, Mr. Aurelius?" Director Sutton appeared suspicious.

"What do you mean, what's the matter?" Roman coughed back a gag reaction and fought off tears. "Why would you show me these? That's horrible!" He pushed his chair back and hugged his knees to his chest, heels resting on the edge of his seat.

"Take it easy, Mr. Aurelius," Director Sutton patted the table. "Can I get you a glass of water? Maybe some coffee?"

"Water would be nice," Roman brushed back a tear, slightly embarrassed. The director opened the interview room and poked his head out, motioning to one of his assistants and mouthing the word 'water.' A moment later, a cup of cold water arrived. Roman unfolded himself and accepted the cup of water, sipping it slowly. Finally, he asked, "Do I need a lawyer?"

"As of right now, Mr. Aurelius, we have no reason to suspect that you are actually involved in their deaths. However, you seem to have a knack for finding them. Are there any more aliens out there that we should be aware of?"

"No, the IPP confiscated all of my research—a year's worth of information that I painstakingly gathered, I might add."

"I'm sorry about that, Mr. Aurelius." He didn't really seem sorry. "But it doesn't reflect well on the American division of the IPP that beings from other planets are showing up dead in remarkably high numbers. If you can help us locate any remaining Data Collectors or have any insight as to who is killing them off, we would be very appreciative."

Roman paused for a moment before answering, "Director Sutton, I am unaware of any other Data Collectors or alien beings in our midst."

"Well, just answer me this. You're an expert in human behavior. Who would want them dead?"

"That's just it, Director Sutton, we're not dealing with strictly human behavior."

"Any theories?"

"If human laws are universal laws, then consider why anyone would kill another—fear, greed, power or hate. Often a combination of those traits. So, ask yourself who might exhibit those traits?"

"Why don't you just tell me?" Director Sutton tilted his head impatiently.

"Well, from an everyday human perspective, if aliens inhabit our Earth, humans may fear that aliens will overthrow us. Or, at the very least, take our jobs, use up our resources, create overcrowding and try to change our culture. For religious zealots, aliens go against every belief 75% of the world has held dear for centuries, the fact that there is life on other planets. Furthermore, the existence of alien life on other planets where they are thriving, means that they are likely much more advanced that we are."

"So, you think humans are targeting aliens. But you just said we were dealing with 'universal laws.' That suggests to me that you also think aliens are involved." Director Sutton leaned back in his chair and smirked, proud of his deduction.

"Yes," Roman nodded. "I also believe that aliens will target both humans and non-humans if it is to their benefit."

"Why?" Sutton leaned so far forward that Roman could smell his breath. Coffee and bologna were not a pleasant combination. "In this case, what's their motive?"

"This has been going on for nearly 30 years now, probably even much longer than that. Why are you asking me questions you already know the answers to, Director Sutton?"

"You just let me ask the questions." The Director shifted, visibly annoyed. "What reason would one alien group have for killing another?"

Roman rubbed his forehead with one hand in an attempt to stave off a mounting headache. "Let's pretend that Earth is a well-sought-after tropical island that several people want to buy. One bidder might simply wait in the hopes that the owner can no longer afford it and buy it out from under him when the owner is ready to give up. Another bidder might make life difficult for the owner, perhaps even making threats if he refuses to sell. Meanwhile, you have a special interest, a close relative, who would much rather lend the owner money and teach him how to sustain his island and rebuild it to its former glory. That's what we are, also, most likely dealing with here."

"So, assuming these bidders are actually aliens from different planets who want to take over Earth, are you suggesting that one of these bidders is trying to snuff out the competition?"

"In a manner of speaking."

"And what about the fact that humans are still very much living here?"

"A necessary casualty in their mind, I'm afraid." Roman placed his fingers on the table and began drumming them rhythmically. "But you knew all this, Director Sutton."

"But I needed to know how much you knew."

"That's everything. You may kill me or arrest me now."

"I have no interest in harming you, Mr. Aurelius," Director Sutton replied. "But I can't promise we won't be watching you. It's easiest if you willingly share any information you come across from now on. Understood?" Director Sutton stood.

"I understand."

Roman left the IPP satellite station more rattled than he had in the past. Some of the people in those photos he had spoken to recently, and he had a gnawing feeling in his belly. What if he had led someone directly to them and gotten them killed? As he walked into a local bodega, he had another fear: What if he were in danger too?

He surveyed the market with caution, noting a security mirror in the upper corner of one wall, and a camera on the other just next to the TV situated behind the checkout counter. What if they were filming him at this very moment? Roman grabbed a bottle of kombucha and a bag of green bean chips and stood impatiently in line while some woman rifled through her oversized backpack looking for exact change. He eyed her purchases in disgust—beef sticks, potato chips, donuts and a large bottle of lemonade. *What is it with Earthlings? They put the worst foods in their bodies and wonder why they become ill?* Although, he thought, she seemed to be awfully fit for someone who indulged in high calorie foods. He wondered…

"We accept credit cards, too," the cashier offered helpfully.

"No, thanks. Don't trust them," Lucene answered. Roman tilted his head. *What a peculiar thing to say,* he thought. "Aha," she proclaimed, proudly producing a nickel. By then, a long line had formed behind Roman. The cashier sighed, accepting the coin.

Just then, a news report came on, and everyone paused to look up at the TV screen.

"Think you'd recognize an alien? Think again. Our latest report uncovers the truth. There may be more foreign visitors on Earth than you believe. Moira Sugg brings us this developing story after this…"

"Damn undesirables," an overweight man behind Roman sputtered. "They should all go back to where they came from." There were a few mutters from people behind him, some nodding in agreement, while others folded their arms and looked around uncomfortably. "Hell," he continued, "they don't even speak English."

Lucene turned to look past Roman, at the man standing behind them. "Has it ever occurred to you that less than 20% of the Earth speaks English? And, it's commonly thought that Earth languages are considered primitive in the multiverse, with our planet being one of the few remaining whose linguistics haven't evolved over time."

The man paused for a moment. "Alien lover," he mumbled and turned his gaze toward the ground.

Lucene completed her purchase, regretting having called attention to herself, and made a hasty exit. Roman quickly laid his cash on the counter. "Keep the change," he told the cashier, gathering up his purchase and following Lucene out the door. He watched as she hopped into her old utility vehicle, annoyed that he couldn't trigger his lapel camera. The tiny camera kept beeping at him, needing a firmware update. He would have to return in the hopes that she would pass this way again.

SECTION TWO

"Stay calm and remember, you are in control of what experiences you let in."

CHAPTER 17
THE FORTUNATA FAMILY
THREE YEARS AGO. TWO YEARS AFTER THE ASSEMBLY.

Lucene wandered into the kitchen still wearing a baby blue bathrobe and white comfy slippers. Her hair was a short, disheveled dust mop on her head. As she reached into the refrigerator for a morning ginger beer and a pastry, she could hear Fatima snoring from the room next door. She smiled to herself, as Fatima's nasal sounds were as boisterous as she was—they would make an elephant-like "ah" sound on the inhale and an enthusiastic cockatiel-like whistle on the exhale. She was her own one-woman zoo.

She was just about to settle on the couch with the morning paper when she heard a commotion at the door. "Shit," she muttered to herself. "Not today."

"Hullo-oh!" one of Fatima's aunts rapped on the door. There was a sound of chattering people behind her. "We're heee-rr-e!"

As Lucene ran to Fatima's room and began banging on her bedroom door, she witnessed Fatima's younger brother Tai peering through the side window with a wave and a wide-eyed grin. Other faces soon followed, smiling broadly and clearly oblivious to the fact that Lucene was still in her night clothes. She waved back, weakly, as Fatima threw open her door still in a long white nightgown with earplugs in and an eye mask drawn upward and hanging awkwardly on her forehead.

Fatima's reaction was distinctly different. Her face grew into a wide smile.

"Hi!" She waved enthusiastically at her brother and extended family through the window, motioning them to come to the front door.

Lucene took it as her opportunity to retreat into her room.

"Don't hide in there forever," Fatima ordered to Lucene as she threw open the door for her family.

Inside her bedroom, Lucene closed the door and stared at Bagheera. "I know, right?" She gave the cat a scratch behind the ear before he retreated under the bed. "You got extra room under there?" she joked.

Had she actually been paying the kind of rent she should be paying for room and board, instead of the meager amount that Fatima requested to cover monthly utilities, she would have complained a long time ago about boundaries. It wasn't that she didn't like them, per say, she just couldn't manage that much energy from that many people at once, particularly without so much as a phone call warning that they were coming.

Lucene threw on a white t-shirt and blue jeans while mentally preparing herself for the onslaught of smiles and questions. "One hour," she repeated to her image in the mirror as she brushed her teeth. "We agreed to one hour." That was deal she made with Fatima for events such as this one.

"You're my best friend," Fatima would tell her. "I want them to get to know you." When she saw Lucene's reluctance, she would add. "Okay, how about this? One hour. If you can socialize and mingle for just one hour, then you can make some excuse about having to get ready for work or something, and you won't hear a peep out of me."

Lucene plastered a smile on her face as she threw open the door.

"Ah, there she is!" Fatima's mother gushed, running toward the young woman and wrapping her in a tight, bear-like embrace. She had to admit, Mama Fatima had an unconditionally loving energy. She hugged her back, and actually kinda liked it. After an eternity, she finally released her grip.

"Hey, hey" Fatima's brother Tai gave her a one-armed bro hug, back-pack slung over his opposite shoulder. She suspected Tai might actually have a small crush on her and overcompensated by being aloof. "Whassup, Lucene?" *Oh, you know, Tai,* Lucene thought to herself, *the usual. I hate crowds. Computers are tracking us. Red doors give me the willies, and I'm certain I'm being watched. Other than that, just dandy."*

"Not much," Lucene answered. "How about you?"

"Same," he nodded his head and punched her playfully in the arm. "Wanna see the new virtual keyboard I bought? It's so cool. Nobody has these yet…but I know a guy." He reached into his backpack. *No, no, no,* Lucene thought, followed by, *they've been around for years, just not to the public.*

"Sure," she forced a smile. *One hour…*

The loudness and banter continued as one-by-one, each family member took turns hugging her. Some part of Lucene enjoyed the inclusion and appreciated that none of them seemed to be remotely mean-spirited or judgmental. The worst that could be said about them was that they lacked boundaries, both physically and culturally.

"Seeing anyone yet?" Fatima's very large, heavily made-up Aunt Keti nudged Lucene in the arm.

"Not yet," she answered. It had been the same answer for as long as she'd known them, and she suspected they thought this was strange.

"Yeah, neither is Fatima at the moment," Aunt Keti frowned, as if this was news to Lucene. Then, she had a thought. "Hey, you two aren't a couple, are you? I mean, we don't care if you are. I was just wondering."

"No, Auntie Keti," Lucene replied. "We are not."

She leaned in closer. "You would tell me if you were, right?"

"You'd be the first to know," Lucene whispered back.

"Good." Keti was satisfied. Then she noticed Lucene's lightning-scarred arms. Her face fell, sympathetically. "That doesn't hurt, right?"

"Not at all," Lucene answered, not for the first time since her meeting Aunt Keti nearly two years ago.

"Ah, well," she grabbed Lucene's chin with her hand and squeezed, her nails leaving an imprint on Lucene's jaw. "You're still beautiful."

"Thank you," Lucene attempted to reply, fish faced. *For the record, the lightning marks don't hurt, but your eagle grasp does!*

"Quit hogging Lucene's attention, Auntie," Tai complained. "I wanna show her my cool new tech."

Keti pinched his cheek and wrinkled her nose at him. "Such a smart boy," she praised her nephew.

One hour...

"Hey, Fatima, where do you keep the turmeric?" Fatima's father rifled through the kitchen pantry. "I always forget."

"I don't have powder, only fresh. Check the veggie drawer in the fridge," Fatima called back, turning the oven on before they'd even decided on what they were making.

*One...two...three...*Lucene counted twelve people, including herself, spread out between the living room and kitchen area. This was ten more people than was comfortable.

"Okay, so then, where's the grater?" her dad yelled back.

"Check this out," Tai tried to put the visor over her head so she could try the virtual keyboard herself.

"No!" She said so loudly, pushing it away, that Tai turned pale and the family all stopped talking. The room was suddenly silent.

"I'm super clumsy," Lucene offered. "It looks expensive and I don't want to break it."

"Aww," Tai smiled, knowingly. "It's okay, you won't." The entire family let out a relaxed sigh and went back to their chattering.

"Hey, Lucy?" Fatima came to her rescue. "It's getting late. Don't you have to feed Bagheera and get to work?"

"Oh, geez," Lucene looked at the clock in mock surprise. "Thanks for reminding me."

"You have to work on a Sunday," Aunt Keti lamented. "That doesn't seem right."

"Lucy is the assistant director at our local sanctuary, very important spiritual work."

"Ohhhh," their eyes grew wide in admiration.

"We understand," Mama Fatima said. The family nodded in approval. "It was nice to get to see you, if only for a little bit."

Fatima shot her friend a wink before Lucene escaped to the sanctity of her bedroom. Bagheera eyeballed her quizzically from under the bed.

"I made it, Bagheera," she reached down and rubbed his ear. "One hour."

CHAPTER 18
MR. CUSHING AND THE ROYALS

SUNDAY AFTERNOON. FIVE YEARS AFTER THE ASSEMBLY.

"What do you have for us?" Sabrina demanded. Fredo gripped Drake's shoulders and squeezed until the man winced and began slumping to one side.

"Easy boy," Drake spat through clenched teeth. Fredo's grip remained fast.

"Fredo, let him go," Hamish ordered, sounding more ambivalent about the whole ordeal than usual.

A look of disgust crossed Sabrina's face. She enjoyed watching someone else's pain, even more so if she was watching someone else inflict it. She rubbed her belly, instinctively. Hamish used to be fun, she remembered. Now, he was a bore.

The four stood in the enormous abandoned warehouse, completely out of place in the surroundings. The sovereigns were dressed to the nines, while the rotted reinforcements that held the ceiling in place threatened to cave at any moment. Sounds of water slapping the dock could be heard outside.

"I encourage you to be…uuughh…nice to me, Sovereign," Drake groaned. There's a good chance I have access to something you want." By now, Lucene's former boss was hunched over to the point where he could almost rest his head on one knee.

"You found her?" She nodded to Fredo. "Release him!" Fredo obeyed, disappointed.

Hamish raised an eyebrow as the two—Royal and serf—exchanged glances but said nothing.

"I believe I have found her," Drake rubbed his shoulder. "But I have to be sure."

"Well, where is she?" Sabrina demanded.

"Somewhere safe," Drake lied. "Somewhere secret."

"I see," Sabrina began circling him like a shark. "You're not going to try and change the nature of our deal, are you?" The veins on her back turned a murky green as her skin began yellowing. She momentarily cursed him in her native tongue. Drake's pain turned to amusement.

"Now, my sovereign. Why would I change our deal when you have been so…hospitable?" He glanced over his shoulder at the large salamander who was busy picking at his teeth with a nail.

Fredo hoped he could soon expire this human in a slow and painful way. He didn't like him. He was fake, and he didn't like fake. He could appreciate his female master's power and danger because it was true to who she was. He could even stomach the fact that his male master was weak and somewhat feeble. It was who *he* was. But he had a difficult time with anyone who pretended to be something they were not. He would call him a chameleon, and chameleons were so afraid of their world that they always changed color to fit their surroundings. Fredo did not doubt that this human would turn on his masters anytime it suited him.

They had enlisted Drake Cushing's help long before that fateful Assembly explosion. Or, rather, Drake solicited his services as a negotiator between the Royals and the Vitruvians. The proposed plan was to help them divide Earth up between the two species. On the surface, it was a fair deal that would only be enacted if and when Earth was no longer habitable by humans. He'd be well paid for his time and, with any luck, he'd have long since died of old age before the deal could be actualized. At least, this was what the Royals and the Vitruvians were told in negotiations. In truth, he had no qualms about selling Earth out to the highest bidder as long as he was offered protection and a comfortable life. Thus far, the Royals were taking the lead, and his side deal included the delivery of one woman with very special skills who could help ensure the Royals gain control of the planet sooner, rather than later.

"The plan is the same as it has always been, Sovereign." He took a seat on an old whiskey crate, careful to make certain it could support his weight.

Sabrina leaned against a wooden beam. "I just need to be sure you'll keep your end of the bargain."

As instructed, Drake met Fredo back at the abandoned warehouse at the designated time. It was a half a mile from the Sovereign Casino. Fredo opened the limo door for Drake and motioned for him to get in. Fredo didn't even try to hide the contemptuous sneer on his face, slamming the passenger door a split second before Drake managed to pull his leg safely inside. In spite of Fredo's actions, Drake's expression remained calm.

"Thank you, Fredo," Drake smiled politely after the salamander stuffed himself, rather uncomfortably, behind the driver's seat. Fredo adjusted the mirrors so that he wouldn't have to look at the annoying Earthling in the back seat, and the two road to the casino in silence.

Fredo pulled up alongside another two-dozen identically designed limos lined up at the service entrance to the casino. There were no service trucks that evening. The 54 IPP representatives popped out from their limos. They were all that remained of the original 215 representatives, just five years prior. Following the assembly explosion, many retired, some disappeared, others resigned, and a large number fell victim to mysterious onsets of heart attacks, strokes and brain tumors, though most had no history of illness.

"Drake Cummings, old buddy. How the hell are you?" A portly man about 25 years his senior, who outweighed him by as many pounds, sidled alongside Drake and slapped him on the back.

"Good to see you, Max," Drake forced a smile, despite the remorse in his chest and sourness in his stomach. While they rarely agreed on political matters, Drake considered him a friend.

As the group gathered, several wolf-like beings from the Trappist region wandered by in pack formation, each shifting their bodies upright and standing on two legs as they passed through the side door.

"Do you believe this shit?" Max nudged his friend. "Aliens crawling all over this place like fire ants and nobody on the outside knows about it. Ridiculous!"

"I know what you mean," Drake agreed. "If the media got wind of this, we'd have a shit-storm on our hands."

Fredo's security team began a formation around the IPP officials. "This way," one instructed, leading them to an unmarked gray door that slid open as he approached. One by one, the delegates shuffled through.

They were led through a dark and narrow hallway, taking several twists and turns before arriving at their conference room. It was ornate with plush, red, swivel chairs surrounding a long dining table that took up almost the entire room. Silk tapestries hung from the wall and two large, teardrop-shaped crystal chandeliers hung above the table.

"Must have set these guys back a pretty penny," Max nodded at the tapestries. "Each one of them must go for $75,000 a pop."

As the delegates took their seats, a female attendant from the casino's waitstaff quickly ran around the room pouring what appeared to be wine into the crystal stemmed glasses at each seat.

"Now, this is my idea of a meeting," another joked.

"Oh, I don't drink," one woman protested, blocking her glass. "Maybe just some water?"

"It's the non-intoxicating kind, madam," the attendant explained. The woman nodded and took a polite sip. It tasted like wine...but, wasn't.

"Nice to know we're outsourcing to other planets now. And to think, we used to complain about all the jobs going to China!" yet another man joked.

From a mile away, Sabrina and Hamish watched the room from a remote viewer with growing annoyance.

"Not what one would expect from members of the International Peace Project, is it?" Hamish asked his wife.

"Indeed not," she agreed. She looked distastefully at a fat man placing his entire meaty hand over a plate of hors d'oeuvres being offered. "Don't these fools recognize how powerful we are? I control the weather. If I had wanted to, I could have wiped out this little petri dish of a planet long ago!"

"Patience, my dear," Hamish put a hand over his wife's as if to console her. "Just a few minutes more." Sabrina pulled her hand away in irritation without taking her eyes away from the viewer.

At long last, all delegates of the IPP were at the table, greedily filling up on libations and small servings of filet mignon and shrimp bites.

Drake quickly surveyed the room, as if memorizing it and everyone in it. Satisfied, he nodded to one of the attendants. Drake stood while Max was waxing eloquently about which planets had the best soil for starting a vineyard. "Excuse me, Max, I need to step out. Be back in a moment." Max nodded and gnawed on a bit of shrimp. For a split second, he thought about asking his friend to go with him, but that wasn't part of the deal. And, who knows what the repercussions of that might be? The attendant stepped away from the door, allowing Drake to pass.

His palms were sweating as he made his way down the hallway. The humid air smacked him in the face as he exited the building. Without a word, Fredo opened the door for him and they were on the road moments later.

In the distance, he heard the explosion, but didn't turn around. He couldn't. It was as if he was frozen in place. Drake could see the flames in the reflection of the rearview mirror as he realized that at least half of the casino was now gone.

"That seemed awfully large for such a small room," Drake choked to Fredo.

The sound of fire trucks and ambulances drowned out Fredo's reply, so he'd waited until they'd turned off onto a side road and were a safe distance from the main highway. Fredo tried again, "Sovereign doesn't have a need to return to the casino again, so there was no reason to leave it standing."

"You mean...but there must be thousands of people in there!" Drake felt sick to his stomach.

"Yes, they're dead. But, congratulations. You get to live. It's your lucky day."

CHAPTER 19
NEW MOON CELEBRATION
SUNDAY EVENING. FIVE YEARS AFTER THE ASSEMBLY.

Tanager was already waiting for Lucene when she climbed out of the window. He was wearing his usual fedora and long jacket even though it was at least 85 degrees out. The sun was setting, and he stood partially hidden behind a large oak tree in the yard, just a few feet from the window. Were it not for the sudden feeling that she was being watched, she might not have noticed him at all.

But he noticed her, watching her expertly climb through the window while wearing a flowery, knee-length sundress, both with admiration at her agility and her...well, just everything. From the ground, she tugged her dress into place and smoothed her hair. She had it combed straight with a simple hair clip in the shape of a dragonfly, which pulled several locks of hair away from her face.

Lucene headed toward the driveway, beckoning him with a quick nod.

She climbed into Kermit, pulling her dress away from the door before slamming it closed, realizing only then that instead of getting in the passenger's seat, Tanager stood politely by the side of the house.

She made a laborious effort to roll down the driver's side window. "Hop in," she finally called. He glanced furtively in each direction before coming toward her, making her instantly regret having spoken so loudly.

Tanager looped around the front of the SUV. "Open," he instructed, staring at the door. The door didn't move. He tried again before looking quizzically at Lucene. "Turn key, remember?" she smirked, leaning across the passenger seat to release the lever from inside.

"Ah, yes," he recalled, pulling on the door's handle and clambering inside. "I assume 'hop in' is just a figurative term?"

"Yeah, just figurative," she confirmed. After a long and awkward silence, she felt the need to make small talk. "So, since you're new around here, I don't suppose you've ever been to a New Moon Celebration before, have you?"

"No, this would be my very first." He wrinkled his brow, puzzled.

"You have no idea what it is, do you?"

"Not in the slightest."

"But you know what a moon is, right?"

"Naturally."

"Well, a new moon is said to be symbolic of new beginnings. Plus, this one is extra special because it will become the blue harvest moon."

"Why is that special? Does your moon actually turn blue?"

"Not exactly. It sometimes gives the illusion of turning blue, and... well...a blue moon is so rare, hence the expression, 'once in a blue moon.' " She searched his blank expression for recognition. "Never mind," she continued. "It's when there's a second full moon within a single month. On top of that, the harvest is symbolic of reaping the rewards of all a person's hard work. So, this celebration is where we ask for all the blessings we want related to all the goals we have set throughout the year up until now. We start at the new moon and let it build all the way until the moon is full."

"Fascinating. Who do you ask?"

"Well...God...the Universe...your higher self on a different plane... pretty much whatever you believe in."

"And what do you believe in, Lucene?"

Lucene paused for a moment. "Good question," she stared at the road uncomfortably and continued driving.

"Where is this celebration taking place?"

"Ah," Lucene answered. "There's an open field behind the sanctuary where I work. The minister, Reverend Isabella, will open the ceremony by having me and a couple other helpers pass out wish paper and pens for participants to write down their wishes. We then collect them for her. She'll lead a meditation where we focus on what we wrote. The papers go into a burning bowl, anointed with oils. The bowl is set on fire, and Reverend Isabella uses a feather to fan the flames up to the heavens."

"But what if a person's God of choice is an Earth spirit living in the ground. How will the prayers reach them?"

"It's symbolic," Lucene re-iterated. "Besides, the ashes are then sprinkled over the field, so I'm sure Earth spirits are included."

Tanager nodded. That answer was deemed acceptable.

"And, now I have another question for you," Lucene glanced in Tanager's direction.

"Yes?"

"What's with the fedora and the jacket all the time? Are you in disguise?"

"Apparently not." He looked down at his garb. It hadn't escaped his attention that he didn't quite mesh with his new surroundings, but hadn't quite figured out how to remedy the situation just yet.

"Well, if you're trying to be less conspicuous, you would have done better to wear shorts and a t-shirt. To kind of blend in."

"Then, I probably shouldn't confess that I'm wearing a crisp, armed shirt with fancy pants under my coat."

"Armed shirt with fancy pants?" Lucene laughed. "Oh, I think you mean a long-sleeved shirt with dress slacks. Aren't you hot?"

"Sweltering."

"Tell you what," Lucene offered. "Let's stop in 'the Closet' at the sanctuary before we hit the ceremony. We're early and have a few minutes to spare. We have a large assortment of clothes in varied sizes that people have donated. I'm certain we can dredge something up for you to help you fit in." She pulled into the parking lot as Tanager deciphered 'dredge' in the context of the conversation. "Follow me," she instructed, leading the way to the back of the sanctuary.

The Closet, as it turned out, was a small, faux wood-paneled room. Two sides of it were lined with clothes racks, men's clothing on one side, women's on the other. The wall closest to the door held simple shelving filled with shoes, separated by their intended gender and further segmented by size. Next to the open door, two curtains hung in concealing circles. The center of the room, however, was not nearly so well organized. A long table sat with a variety of ties, hats, scarves, and even a few pieces of woven and metal jewelry.

Tanager surveyed the room with interest. Lucene sensed his question. "It's for people who need everyday clothes or clothes for a job interview but can't afford it. How about this?" Lucene held up a Hawaiian shirt, peppered with palm trees.

"That seems very...obvious...to me," Tanager answered carefully.

"Nah, people will just think you're a tourist."

Tanager's eyes suddenly lit up as he spotted a gray fishing hat with a piece of aqua ornamental bait stitched to the side. He tried it on, happily.

"Oh, that's definitely you," Reverend Isabella popped her head into the room. She was stunning with a blue-green, multi-hued, full-length robe and beaded headdress.

Lucene and Tanager looked up, somewhat startled at the interruption.

"Lucene, tell me, who is your new friend?" She peered at him closely. "Or, should I say, old friend?"

"Reverend Isabella," Lucene replied quickly. "This is a friend of mine from New York, Tanager. Tanager, this is Reverend Isabella. She founded this sanctuary and is the head minister."

Isabella resisted a laugh as Tanager tipped his fishing hat to her. She put out a hand and, to Lucene's relief, Tanager shook it instead of kissing it. "It's nice to meet you." She couldn't help but notice that his hat was completely out of place with the rest of his attire.

"Tanager is here on business and completely forgot to pack casual wear. We thought perhaps he could pick out a couple of pieces here, and in exchange, he could donate one of his suits to the sanctuary."

"Given the cost of your threads," Isabella eyed him again. "I'd say the sanctuary is getting the better end of the deal. I'm sure it will make someone in need very happy."

"I sincerely hope it does," Tanager answered. Until that moment, he hadn't considered that by swapping clothes, he might actually be helping an Earthling. The thought made him smile.

"It's not much," she pointed to one of the curtains, "but you can change there. I hope you will join us for the ceremony."

"We'll be there," Lucene confirmed. "I'll be out front to help in about 15 minutes, if that's okay with you."

"Perfect," Isabella winked, before she seemed to, quite literally, float out of the room.

Within no time, Tanager had settled on one pair of shorts, one pair of cargo pants, two casual shirts, one sun cap and, although he really didn't need it, one fishing hat. He opted to wear the cargo pants, a Hawaiian shirt and a "Salt Life" cap. Lucene managed to talk him out of the fishing hat, explaining that it might be out of place for this event. He kept it anyway.

In exchange, he left his dress shirt, slacks, suit jacket and trench coat folded neatly on the center table. "Is it okay if I keep the fedora? I've grown somewhat attached to it."

"Of course," Lucene smiled. She had grown rather fond of him wearing it. "I promise you that what you have left is more than enough."

"Once I return home, I will ask Ivan to donate the rest of my clothing as well."

"That is very thoughtful of you." Lucene tilted her head and smiled at him with admiration. Remembering herself, "We'd better get going. Why don't I drop the rest of your things in the car first?"

Lucene planned on depositing Tanager at a nearby lawn chair while she helped Reverend Isabella, but in true Tanager fashion, he had to be of service. She handed him some crinkled wish paper, which he distributed to attendees strewn out across the field, some in chairs and others on blankets. She followed up with pencils.

"Hey, I like your shirt," a man commented to Tanager, who looked down and beamed proudly at the man. "I used to have one just like it, until the missus made me get rid of it," he nodded toward his wife. Her faced flushed with embarrassment as she elbowed her husband in the ribs.

"He has too many, and I must say it suits you better than it did him." Her husband grunted. Tanager didn't put the connection together and simply tipped his cap to her as a thank you. With that, they continued their task.

"Well, fancy meeting you here!" a boisterous voice came at them from behind, startling Lucene. There, Roman hovered over them, dressed in his usual, all-black, goth-like jeans and t-shirt. He grinned at her in a way that made her uncomfortable.

What exactly did he know about her that she didn't already know about herself?

"Roman, it is nice to see you again," Tanager shook his hand in earnest. Lucene found it interesting. Her tendency was to distrust until proven otherwise; whereas, Tanager, on the other hand, seemed completely neutral, a blank slate until someone showed their worth, or lack of it.

"A fine celebration, isn't it?" Roman spewed enthusiasm. "The only thing that would make it better is if my lovely Fatima were here."

Lucene searched his face for insincerity through his flowery words. She found none.

Moments later, Reverend Isabella addressed the crowd. All fell silent and settled in for one of her meditations. Lucene motioned for Tanager to take a seat beside her on a blanket that was offered by a family sitting nearby. "We brought extra, just in case," they smiled.

Lucene instinctively sat cross-legged on the ground, resting her palms lightly in her lap, left over right and closing her eyes. Tanager could feel her energy shift immediately…surprising. He assumed the same pose, his left knee lightly touching her right, and the familiar energy between them was back again. Lucene opened one eye to glance at her knee, just to make sure they were actually touching…they were. After the dinner last night, she had to be sure. Tanager smiled lightly to himself.

Roman knelt behind them, sitting on his heels and holding his arms out with palms raised and thumb and forefinger pressed into a mudra. Several people looked on with interest, but mostly to wonder how he planned to hold his arms up for that long, and then sank back into their own meditation.

Reverend Isabella began with a protection prayer, blessing the land

and all those who were on it, asking that all learn to walk gently on Mother Earth. Lucene's mind sank. Images floated up from her subconscious, along with the words, "experimentation" and "preserves." Suddenly, she was back in New York, watching as the IPP summit went up in smoke. More images surfaced, flooding in faster than she could filter them. She opened her mouth, about to let out a scream.

Tanager wrapped an arm around her and touched the palm of his hand to the side of her face, pulling her toward him. Roman watched with interest, expecting him to kiss her. Instead, he did something very odd. He pressed his forehead to hers, and in a moment, she calmed down. She couldn't bring herself to open her eyes. Tanager knowingly pulled away and returned to the meditation.

Some time later, Reverend Isabella summoned people to come up, in groups, to drop their wish paper into the fire. Lucene took that as her cue, jumping up to help guide small groups, making sure small children didn't get too close to the flames. Roman gave her a knowing look as he tossed his paper into the fire, except that she still didn't know what it was she was supposed to know.

After the ceremony, people began to gather up their belongings and head home. Tanager was pulled away momentarily by Reverend Isabella who asked for his assistance in gathering ceremony materials. He obliged without question.

As Lucene moved to help them, Roman took her by the elbow. "Walk with me for a moment, won't you?"

Confused, Lucene fell into step beside him, taking two paces to his single, long stride. She looked up at him, questioningly. "I know you like him," he said, not looking at her.

"Who?" He nodded over his shoulder. "Oh, you mean Tanager…well, I suppose he's alright."

"Just be careful. He's not who you think he is."

"What do you mean?"

"I mean, I think he is a traitor and is secretly working for them."

"Who's *them*?" She asked, more confused than ever.

"The Royals," he stopped, nodding, as if this should have meaning to her.

"I literally have no idea what you're talking about." She stared him in the eyes as if demanding meaning. Roman was taken aback. She really didn't remember.

"He's dangerous," his expression turned dark. "I thought he was here to help our planet...as I...I mean, as others who came here before us were; but I am concerned that the stories are true."

"And, what stories would those be, Roman?" Lucene bristled a little at the accusation.

"His only interest is in helping the Royals wipe out civilization as we know it and re-populate the Earth…and he needs you to do it."

CHAPTER 20
MR. SPARKS
MONDAY MORNING AT THE DOCKS. FIVE YEARS AFTER THE ASSEMBLY.

It took little time for Lucene to find him. Somehow, she'd settled on the most unobtrusive boat along the docks, watching as a frazzled little man climbed aboard, seemingly having a conversation with himself.

"Jim Sparks?" Lucene asked.

"Uh, y-y-yeah," the man answered, trying to arrange his dirty, unkempt hair without much luck. He looked around nervously, giving his unshaven chin a scratch. "Do I know y-y-you?"

"I don't think so, but I'm not sure. My name is Lu—"

Jim's eyes grew wide as he spotted the tree-like patterns on Lucene's uncovered arms. "C-c climb aboard…q-q-quickly." Jim motioned for her to hurry. Lucene obeyed, even though all common sense would have told her getting into a strange man's boat was a bad idea. She'd already done a lot of uncommon sense things lately. Why should this be any different? From across the marina, a pear-shaped woman with frizzy, red, curly hair glared at her from her tiny houseboat, her eyes peering suspiciously over the romance novel she was reading. Jim waved to her in reassurance.

"Hmph," the woman muttered, returning to her book.

"Surprised to see y-y-ou, Lucene. Er, make yourself c-c-comfortable," he offered, once she was inside.

Lucene looked around the boat, littered with pieces of unwashed, tattered clothing on the seats, a few dishes and utensils with food still stuck to them on the dinette, and a smell worse than Red Tide. The man, himself, would have passed for homeless had she not, in fact, been standing in his home.

Lucene politely lifted an unwashed t-shirt from a chair with her forefinger and thumb, gently placing it to one side, and half-sat on the edge of the seat, conscious that she may need to check herself for lice after the visit. Jim leaned against the pantry door, apologetically.

"Sorry," he apologized. "I haven't had time to c-c-clean yet this week...been a little busy." The tiny sailboat looked as if more than a week had gone by since it had received a little tender loving care...more like 52 weeks.

"Mr. Sparks," Lucene was confused. "You seem to know *me*. Do I know *you*?"

"Good, good...good question," he stammered. He ran his hands through hair and then tapped his fingers together as he searched for the right words.

"How should I put this," he tapped his head. "They're gonna k-k-kill you." He finally blurted out. Lucene was taken aback. Once again, she was getting a 'danger' alert. She knew she should have been afraid of this stranger, but he gave off a similar recognizable energy as Tanager and Cepheus, albeit much weaker and more...frazzled, somehow. She continued with caution.

"Wait. What? Who?" Lucene searched his face for meaning. He held his head. "Who is going to kill me?"

"My head hurts," Jim responded.

Instinctively, Lucene went to him. Jim flinched slightly as Lucene touched three fingers to his head. For a moment, she could feel his pain and his fear. *The Royals,* she heard him think. Jim wiped a few painful tears from his eyes, using the hem of his t-shirt. He reached into his pocket and pulled out a prescription bottle and popped a pill, chewing it up, crumpling his face at the apparent bitterness.

"I'm sorry you're in pain. But you must tell me, how are the Royals involved in this?" she asked, backing away.

"Ah, you got that," he nodded. "We always knew you were special."

"About the Royals?" she asked again.

"A nasty bunch," he shook his head. "They c-c-came here eons ago to repopulate Earth—and other places—by setting up their nurseries. 'Cept things didn't go as planned, and now they want to k-k-kill everybody and try again."

"Everybody, or just me?" Lucene persisted. She knew the Royals were banned from the IPP because of shady practices, but this part was new.

"Well, you're special. They want what you have…gee, my head hurts. They want what you have…what I have…had. They tried to take it from me, but I wouldn't give it to them. But you…" His eyes grew wide. "You're more than special. C-c-an't let them get you."

Lucene began to see images in her head, bright lights, sounds, pain, surgeries—many, many surgeries. She began to scream.

"No, no…" Jim clasped his dirty hands over her mouth. "Mustn't do that." He looked around nervously. She mentally shut a red door with the sounds, sights and pain trapped behind it.

"Everything okay in there?" the red-haired woman croaked, peering her head down from the top deck of the sailboat, suspiciously. With no way to get from her houseboat to Jim's sailboat at such speed, it could only be assumed that she'd been listening in for some time.

"Y-y-yeah," Jim called to her. "Thanks, Ginny. My…er…niece saw a roach and got sc-c-cared."

"Don't doubt that. Your place is filthy!" She coughed. What she did doubt, however, was that Lucene was his niece.

"Y-y-you c-c-can go now, Ginny!" Jim called up to her, visibly annoyed.

"Hmmph," she said again and began shuffling toward the exit ramp. She decided that she had no interest in meeting, what she presumed, was the "other" woman anyway. "If you want me, you know where to find me!" she called. Under her breath, she swore, "Niece, my ass!"

"Y-y-you should go," Jim told Lucene. "It isn't safe. Ginny's a sweet gal with a big mouth."

"Just one more thing…do you know a fellow by the name of Roman?

He's very tall with dark hair and a light complexion. He claims to be... one of us," she said, carefully.

Mr. Sparks shook his head fervently. "Nah, I never heard that name before...not ever. I'd be c-c-c-areful if I was you."

"Thank you, Mr. Sparks. And, I hope your head feels better."

A weird calm overcame the man. "Thanks, it already does. Always knew y-y-you were special."

"Hang on," Lucene paused. "Let me at least give you an address where you can find me. Perhaps we can meet again soon. I have a friend who I believe might be able to help you...with your headaches."

"Naw," he shook his head. "Don't give me your address. Okay, maybe." He nodded. "Y-y-yeah. No...no." He debated with himself for the next minute, nodding and then shaking his head.

"Do you have a piece of paper, by chance?" She interrupted him, looking around with uncertainty.

"Jest think it, and I'll see if I c-c-can retrieve it."

Just think it? She was getting used to her connection with Tanager, but hadn't considered its wider application, and she certainly wasn't trained on how to use it yet.

"I'll try," she nodded, thinking the address as hard as she could. Mr. Sparks winced a little, and then gave up with a sigh. "I'm sorry, Mr. Sparks. I'm not sure how to direct my thoughts like that."

"It's ok-k-kay. Y-y-y-ou'll git it back soon." He leaned in. "Y-y-y-ou jest whisper the address to me. I'll remember."

Lucene wasn't terribly sure about that, but she obeyed. "900 Prosperous Lane. It's..."

"That's enough," Mr. Sparks waved his hand. "I know where y-y-you are."

Lucene nodded. "I'll be going now." As she began to climb the stairs, he stopped her.

"Oh, y-y-yeah. Y-y-y-ou might want to watch out for mermaids and blue butterflies too. They c-c-claim to be here to help; but, I'm none too sure about them." Lucene gave a confused nod and quickly made her exit.

Monday Afternoon

Jim Sparks was quite shaken by Lucene's visit earlier in the day. He instinctively reached for his pain medication and chewed an extra pill. He retreated to his bed: a small mattress located in a cubby hole toward the back of the boat. As he felt the boat listlessly drifting back and forth, up and down, he remembered his homeland. So much time had passed since he left Erde that he struggled with certain details. But there were some things he could remember vividly...its lush green landscapes, unspoiled waters...and their language. He loved that their native tongue was so melodic. Neighbors from visiting planets always commented that they didn't have to speak the language in order to understand its sentiment. And, if exposed to it long enough, they were able to easily speak it —even without formal training. He'd spoken next to nothing but English since he'd arrived on Earth. Jim smiled blissfully to himself as he floated off to sleep, mumbling a few blessings to himself in his old language.

He didn't hear that someone had boarded the boat and was making their way toward him. In his mind, he was already elsewhere.

CHAPTER 21
MR. CUSHING AND THE MERMAID
MONDAY AFTERNOON AT THE DOCKS. FIVE YEARS AFTER THE ASSEMBLY.

"You've been a bad boy, Mr. Cushing."

Drake Cushing's gaze shifted downward toward his sneakers. There, just beyond the dock where he stood, the greenish-blue torso of a woman waded in the marina, her lower half obscured beneath the water's surface. Her indigo hair was cropped short and matted against her head. Her face had natural streams of blue-and-gray, flowing stripes across it making her the perfect camouflage if she had been standing in front of the Northern Lights, and tiny gills could be detected on each side of her neck. Everything else about her features looked perfectly human from this vantage point, and she did nothing to hide her breasts as she bobbed up and down in the water.

"Odessa, how lovely to see you," Drake flashed her his toothiest grin, the fake one he always used to imply friendliness when he didn't really mean it. He continued his walk along the dock. She swam alongside him, a splash of fins thrashing behind her. He pretended not to notice. He had an appointment to keep. Finally, Odessa grew impatient and splashed him with her tail, just enough to wet his jeans, but preserve his shirt and suit jacket. "What can I do for you this morning?" Drake scowled, stopping abruptly and wiping a water droplet from his eye.

"There's a nasty rumor going around that you're double-dealing, Mr. Cushing." Odessa smiled flirtatiously, waving her arms back and forth to keep her afloat. "My superiors don't like it."

Odessa was the reason people still believed in mermaids. She wasn't one but looked every bit the part. In reality, she was an informant for the Vitruvians from Section 2 and was supposed to report any and all suspicious activity that might affect the wellbeing of her people. As with all Vitruvians, she had the ability to shift into different forms, sometimes human-like, but more often what Earthlings would describe as "animals." She discovered she was partial to the water and spent most of her time as close to the marina as possible, only coming on land when her job required it.

"I don't know what you've heard, but I can assure you, Odessa, my intentions are honorable." He squatted down to look her in the eyes, but not before surveying his surroundings. While it may have been becoming slightly more acceptable for species from other planets to take up residence on Earth when on special government assignment, it certainly wasn't common, and it certainly wasn't appreciated. "I'm simply fulfilling my role as Chief Negotiator between your people and the Royals, as both parties have asked of me. Please don't interfere."

"When have I ever interfered, Mr. Cushing?" Odessa pouted, her feelings hurt. "I have no allegiance to anyone whatsoever…I'm just doing my job."

"Well, you can tell the Vitruvians that everything is going according to plan."

"Morphinae might disagree with you."

"And how is our little blue butterfly these days?" Drake did nothing to hide his contempt.

"That's a fine way to talk about someone who saved your life."

"You know something?" Drake ignored the comment. "Your people have a strange way of getting what they want. They won't overtly kill anyone, but if the Royals decide to decimate the human population, well, that's just fine. Everyone will divide the spoils and the Vitruvians walk away with the self-righteous illusion that they are a peaceful people."

"Tsk tsk," Odessa clucked at him. "And here I thought you'd understand, being American and all. We put our people first. Sure, we'll defend ourselves should the Royals prove to be less than honorable; but we do our best to mind our own business."

"Like what you're doing now, you mean?" He motioned his hand wildly into the air. "Look, I prefer not to be seen in public talking to a mermaid."

"I'm not a mermaid!" Odessa squealed. She quickly softened her expression, however, when she saw Drake's amused expression. She had fallen right into his trap.

"Odessa, it's been a pleasure," Drake lied. "But tell the Vitruvians they have nothing to worry about. The deal is going down according to plan." With that, he waved a hand in dismissal and stood. Odessa made a gesture with her face that was probably derogatory on her planet, but one that was completely lost on him. She did a few backstrokes before disappearing beneath the water.

Drake pulled a handkerchief from the back pocket of his jeans and wiped his brow. It was getting easier with each attempt, but he still found this whole business nerve-wracking. After a few cursory glances around him, he made his way just past a tiny white houseboat in the marina. He took a seat on a nearby bench, as planned, and pulled out his cell phone to send a simple text. "I'm here."

Moments later, Mr. Sparks' Ginny showed up, disguised with a scarf around her head and thick sunglasses. Her frizzled red hair poked out from under the scarf.

"Hi Ginny," a neighboring boater waved as she walked by. She began to wave back before remembering that she was supposed to be in disguise. Ginny quickly ducked her head, grabbing her scarf with both hands under her chin and tugging it tightly. Drake watched with a curious expression, as she walked past the bench where he sat, looked over her shoulder and kept going. She made it to a lamppost several feet away before she turned and shuffled back over to him.

"You Cushing?" She whispered gruffly.

"I am." Drake flashed her a grin. "You must be the lovely Ginny."

She let out a hoarse laugh, followed by a cough. She sat down next to Drake, who instinctively slid away from her as he caught of whiff of heavy cigarette smoke. His eyes began to water slightly before he once again made use of his handkerchief.

"Now, you promise me that Jim's gonna be okay, right?"

"Of course, Ginny. I'm so glad you phoned me. The family has been worried sick."

"I kinda had a feeling it might be something like this," she shook her head. "Poor, Jim. He's a sweet man, but a little touched in the head…ooh, sorry. I didn't mean that."

"It's quite alright," Drake reassured her. "Mental illness can be so unpredictable. He up and disappeared one day, and if it weren't for you, we wouldn't have found him. Now, which boat is his?" Ginny cleared her throat, awkwardly. Drake nodded, understanding. "Of course," he pulled a folded cashier's check from his shirt pocket. "Three thousand dollars as a finder's fee and our family's gratitude."

Ginny's eyes lit up like a dog spotting a squirrel. She took it gingerly, trying not to appear too eager. "I wouldn't even ask for it. It's just that I can really use the money right now."

"I completely understand."

"And, he'll be okay?"

"I assure you, Ginny, Jim is going to get the best care from top doctors. When he does, I have no doubt he'll be back to visit you. I hear he's a little sweet on you," Drake teased, nudging her arm.

"Aw, g'on," Ginny's cheeks turned red. She tucked the check in her bra strap under her blouse. "Not too sure 'bout that. Had a young thing stop by earlier." Her eyes lit up. "Hey, he claimed she was his niece, but that can't be right, can it? Seein' how the family's still looking for him?"

"That is curious," Drake agreed, trying to suppress his own curiosity. "Did you happen to meet this…niece?"

"Naw, he tried to keep me away…probably some young floozy. "

"Could you describe her for me?"

"Well..." Ginny tapped the cashier's check, subconsciously. Drake took the hint.

"I don't have much," he informed her, reaching for his wallet. "But I could give you an additional $100 cash for your troubles." He pulled out a crisp bill.

"Aw," Ginny snatched the bill from his fingertips and tucked it behind the other, unoccupied bra strap. "I wouldn't ask for it, 'cept…you know. I'm a little light on cash these days."

"Times are hard, all around," Drake frowned, sympathetically. "I'm grateful for your help."

"Well," she thought for a moment. "Her hair was kinda short and brown."

"Yes?"

"Mmm…couldn't see her eyes, but she had a normal-ish shaped face."

"Yes?" Drake grew impatient."

"Wore jeans and a green t-shirt…nothing unusual about that."

"Anything else?" Drake clenched his teeth.

"Oh," her eyes suddenly lit up. "There was one thing!"

"Yes?"

"She had these weird tattoos on her arms. Looked like tree branches." Drake's surprised micro-expression was lost on Ginny. He quickly recovered.

"You didn't happen to catch her name, by chance, did you?"

"Well, it was hard to get with Jim's stuttering, but it sounded like 'Lucy.' "

"You've been very helpful, Ginny, thank you." Drake stood. "If you remember anything else, you know how to reach me. I promise to pay you for your efforts."

Suddenly, her eyes lit up. "Ooh! I remember she lives off Prosperous Lane." Ginny hugged herself proudly and leaned back on the bench. "They didn't think I could hear, but I have ears as sharp as an owl's. Say, who do you think she was?"

"No idea," Drake answered. "But I will certainly report it to the family. Could be a drug dealer. Who knows?"

"Probably that," Ginny furrowed her lips.

"Now, where can I find Mr. Sparks?"

"It's the tattered white sailboat over there, next to my houseboat. Mine's the one with the yellow flowerpot on the deck."

"Thank you, Ginny," he answered, watching as she struggled to stand. "To avoid Jim getting embarrassed, would you mind keeping our talk to yourself?"

"Nobody will hear a peep out of me, I swear," Ginny promised, eyes wide.

"Well, that's just fine. Good day, Ginny."

"G'day, Mr. Cushing."

CHAPTER 22
SANCTUARY
MONDAY EVENING. FIVE YEARS AFTER THE ASSEMBLY.

Between Mr. Sparks telling her that the Royals were trying to kill her, an unusual visit from Tanager and Cepheus who, for all she knew, *could* have been the Royals, and Fatima's new alien romance, she needed to clear her head. She made her way to the Singing River Sanctuary, but not before leaving a note in Ivan's mailbox to meet her in the serenity garden at the church as soon as possible, but not to tell anyone where he was going and who he was going to see. She signed it, "Kermit's mom" in the hopes that he would, for once, actually check his mail on time and, that he would realize it was she who made the request.

A series of ivy-draped trellises surrounded the gardens with a fountain composed of planets orbiting the sun. At its base was a circle of people, animals, and mythical creatures standing together in unity collecting water that flowed from each of the planets into the pool of water at the bottom. Around the fountain were four stone benches etched with names: Stillness, Quietude, Tranquility and Peace. Branching out from the center were four shell pathways. Between each was a variety of native plants: Beautyberry, Fire Bushes, Oyster plants and Muhly grass.

Lucene sat on the Quietude bench, in hopes that it would calm her racing mind. She assessed what she knew so far. In a matter of days, she had met four strange men, all of whom seemed out of place with their surroundings and, based on their behavior and wild claims, possibly psychotic. One claimed she, herself, was born from alien parents. And all four seemed to think she was special, and, as such, was in great danger.

She knew she had irrational fears: being tracked or controlled via phones, car computers, laptops and other GPS systems. Red doors scared the Bejesus out of her, and it didn't matter if they were attached to a house, a car, or something else. She had wild gaps in her memory and, if she were being honest with herself, the real reason that she didn't tell Fatima about her life in New York wasn't so much about privacy as it was that she simply didn't have the full picture. She remembered pieces of it: the car accident, certain days working at the UC, the awesome falafel food truck near Times Square. Furthermore, if she were being even *more* honest with herself, she could swear that the tree-like tattoos on her arm were starting to change shape.

"Lucene, I didn't expect to see you today, particularly after staying late to help out with the celebration on Sunday." Lucene lurched a moment in her seat, before realizing who it was. Today, Isabella wore her long white hair in tight braids with a large-brimmed straw hat covering her head. For once, instead of her usual flowing attire, she was actually wearing green linen pants with a matching button-down shirt. In her hands, she carried pruning shears, gloves and a bucket.

"Hi, Reverend Isabella," Lucene greeted her quietly. Maybe Quietude was working.

"Lucene, I've told you before. You don't need to call me 'Reverend' outside of ceremony. Isabella is just fine." She sat on the Peace bench and crossed her legs, revealing tan sandals with laces that crisscrossed up to her calves. "If I may inquire, what brings you here today, on your day off?"

"Well..." Lucene thought for a moment. "Fatima's family is in town, and they have very, well, boisterous personalities."

"Yes, I can see that." Reverend Isabella smiled.

"I thought, since the sanctuary rooms are not in use at the moment... perhaps I could stay in one of them for a few days. You could take it out of my pay, of course."

"Of course, you are welcome to sleep here as long as you need. I have no intention of taking it out of what little I pay you as it is," she laughed. "If anything, your staying here will give me some relief if we have walk-ins needing refuge."

"Thank you, Isabella," Lucene responded, sincerely.

Isabella rose to go, but before she did, she looked down at Lucene and said, "However, in the future, it is completely acceptable to answer a question with, 'I would rather not say.' There's no need to fabricate a story." Lucene blushed and nodded. Isabella continued, "Let me try this again. If I may inquire, what brings you here today on your day off?" Her violet eyes looked straight into Lucene's.

"Uh...I'd rather not...say?"

"Exactly," Reverend Isabella answered, and started down one of the pathways, carefully lifting her feet to avoid bits of broken shell from collecting in her sandals. "The kitchen is open to you should you need to store anything in the refrigerator or make yourself something for dinner. I lock up at 9 p.m., but you can let yourself in and out with your key at any time."

"Thank you, Isabella." Lucene stared into the fountain. "You are wonderful."

"Yes," Isabella smiled. "I know I am, as are we all."

Lucene had just about given up on Ivan showing when she suddenly spotted a mop of red hair cutting through the dark and heard the shuffling of feet from around the corner. She gave him a wave but remained quiet. Timed lights resembling multi-colored fireflies lit up the bushes as the sun went down.

"Aye, Lucene," Ivan gave an awkward wave as he approached. "Turns out I can enter a church without getting struck by lightning," he laughed at his own joke, but then coughed when he caught sight of Lucene's lightning-stricken arms. "Er, sorry. That went different in me head."

Lucene smiled. "It's okay, Ivan. I get the joke."

Ivan stood at the fountain and scratched under his chin. "So, uh, I got yer note."

Lucene nodded. After waiting through a long pause for a question that didn't come, she continued.

"I'm really worried, and I wasn't sure who to talk to."

"Whew!" Ivan let out a sigh. "I'm so glad ye said that. I've been worried, too." He kicked the base of the fountain with his toe absent-mindedly before catching Lucene's questioning look. He pulled his foot back and blushed. He really didn't know how to behave in churches, or anywhere where social norms were expected to be kept.

"You have?" Lucene asked.

"Aye! This Roman fella shows up outa nowhere and tries to hooch up to Fatima. I don't trust him, I tell ya."

"Ivan, that's not at all what I'm talking about."

"It's not?" He tugged at his earlobe. "Then, what?"

"How well do you know Tanager and Cepheus?" she asked.

"Well, Tanager I only jest met, but Cepheus and I have been corresponding for over a year now."

"Corresponding?"

"Aye. In an online technology board."

"But, how long have you known him…in person?"

Ivan calculated on his fingers and looked upward as if trying to remember. "Since…er, Friday evening."

"So…three nights ago, the same night Cepheus wigged out and showed up in my bedroom trying to steal my cat."

"Aye. I thought that was weird me-self, but Tanager explained it to me."

"And that explanation would be?"

"He went through a bad trauma…lost his wife and kids, and that jest broke him. Random triggers set him off and he can't seem to adjust his human-like state with his lizard one…poor fella."

"And it doesn't concern you, having him in your house in such a fragile state?"

"Nah. Everybody's been through something." Somehow, that answer seemed very reasonable to Ivan, but not at all acceptable to Lucene. Surprising, given her random outbursts and aversions to red doors and computers.

There was another long silence. Ivan stared into the fountain, almost mesmerized, as if he were trying to figure out the mechanics of how it worked.

"They think I'm an alien, you know?" Lucene said, matter-of-factly.

"Hmm..." Ivan answered, and after a pause added, "That makes sense."

"It does?"

"Aye. You're as eccentric as the lot of 'em, so it stands to reason yer having trouble adjusting to life on this planet. Did it never occur to you that maybe ye didn't belong here? Originally, I mean. Of course, ye belong here, but—," he stumbled over his words.

"I get it," Lucene held up her hand. "And, I guess so. I knew I didn't quite fit in but..., why would someone want to kill me?" She looked at the ground, contemplating this.

"Say what now? Kill ye?"

"I went to meet a Mr. Sparks after Roman mentioned to Fatima that he needed to speak with him about research."

"I knew it would git back to that guy. I tell ye, I don't trust him!"

"Ivan, focus!" Lucene commanded.

"Sorry."

"The point is, this Mr. Sparks was obviously traumatized. He said he'd been tortured, and if I had to guess, there's more to Cepheus's story than Tanager led on. I think he was tortured as well."

"Tortured, by who?"

"The Royals."

"Who the hell are they?"

Lucene tapped the side of her head. "I feel as if I should know...from my time working with the IPP, but I can't remember."

"Ye worked for the IPP," Ivan stated, not questioned. "Seems there's a lot we don't know about ye, eh?" Lucene did not respond. "But why would someone want to hurt ye? Ye seem pretty harmless to me."

"I don't know, but I can't risk putting Fatima in danger. The sanctuary rooms here are empty at the moment. I figure I can hide here for a few days until I sort things out."

"Who's gonna look after ye though...ye should call the police."

"And tell them what? That I may be an unregistered alien, but I'm not sure. And, oh, by the way, people I don't know are out to get me?"

"Hmm, well. When ye put it like that…" Ivan thought a moment. "Ye should confide in Tanager and Cepheus. So far, they seem to know more about ye than ye know about yerself." He nodded, as if that settled it. Lucene paused for a moment.

"Okay," she agreed.

"Really?" Ivan was surprised. "I didn't expect ye to agree with me so readily. I didn't think ye trusted them."

"I don't," Lucene confessed. "Well, not entirely, I don't."

"Then, why would you do it?"

"Because I trust you, Ivan." Ivan blushed a little. "Can you please let them know I'm here, and definitely let Fatima know that I'll be gone for a couple of days, but don't tell her where."

"Aye. I don't know where Tanager is at the moment, but I will let Cepheus know. I'll also give a knock on Fatima's door."

"Thanks, Ivan. You're a good friend." She gave him a hug.

Ivan blushed again as he bear-hugged her back. "Well, ye just stay safe."

With that, Ivan made his exit, being careful that no one was watching him. At least, he *thought* no one was watching.

After Ivan left, Lucene quickly unlocked the back door to the church and, just as quickly, locked it behind her. She made her way down a narrow hallway, passing a small bathroom and pausing at the kitchen to grab the turkey and Swiss cheese sandwich she had stored in one of the large industrial refrigerators. She grabbed the sandwich, tucked an aluminum bottle of water under one arm and made her way toward the main congregation arena.

From her vantage point, she was greeted by a nearly ceiling-high stone wall in the shape of a half moon, ornately colored by a mural depicting scenes from the natural world. There were strategically placed wall fountains dripping into a narrow pool that wrapped around the wall. The only break in the wall was a compact passageway with a small cobblestone path that led to the seating area and lectern.

Lucene passed along the pathway, marked at each side by two tall areca palms and towering stone-like seats that descended into the floor. When viewed from the front entrance, the room looked more like a sunken indoor Grecian garden with a five-tier coliseum seating area that formed a half-moon around a small, octagon-shaped platform. The slightly raised platform was encased by four tall cream-colored columns and was accessible by two small steps at one side.

"A most unusual church you've got here, Lucy," Drake observed, standing in front of the main double doors holding what appeared to be a Canterbury picnic basket.

Lucene almost dropped her dinner, peering closely at Drake in case she'd made a mistake. After all, she hadn't seen the man in over five years, not since the assembly.

"I like what you've done with your hair," he motioned toward his own neck to reference her short pixie cut. "Though, I think you look better with long blonde hair, not that you asked. Just a personal preference."

"What are you doing here?" Lucene was confused. A knot in her stomach began to form, but she couldn't tell whether it was apprehension or just nerves. After all, he was her longest-standing crush and, to her annoyance, she still found him attractive.

"Is that the way you greet your old boss?" He smiled. She didn't react. "Fair enough," he nodded. "The truth is, I'm worried about you."

"Why?" she answered.

"Because you are in danger." She winced and began to protest. "It's okay, I know. I came to Florida because of an emergency meeting with the IPP. We're trying to prevent the Erdlings from abducting humans and taking them back to Section 3. What I didn't realize at the time was that this human was...is...you." Lucene didn't answer and didn't move. "Could we sit and talk for a moment?"

"Sure," she answered finally, motioning to a seat in the coliseum.

"A most unusual church" Drake repeated absently, gazing at the seats surrounding him.

"Oh, this is no ordinary church," Lucene explained, as if it needed explanation.

"I can see that," Drake agreed, tapping one of the seats with his foot, surprised that it felt as if it had some give to it.

Lucene spoke. "Bioplastic seats made to look like stone but far easier to work with and much more comfortable. Give it a try." Drake set the basket down, stepped up to the first row and took a seat. Surprised that he sank ever so slightly, as he did. He leaned back and stretched his feet out. "See?" Lucene beamed with pride, "next generation memory foam seat cushions and backs."

"Interesting," was all he said. Lucene handed him the basket, her sandwich and water container before climbing up to take a seat next to him, leaving a space between them. "What have you got there," he asked, referencing the sandwich.

"It's a clean meat turkey sandwich," she opened the container. "Want half?"

"Clean..." He was confused.

"Clean meat," she explained. "It's grown from the cells of animals, but no animals are harmed in the making of it. Isabella frowns on actual meat in her sanctuary."

"Uh, what's her feelings on cheese and wine?" he asked, taking half of the sandwich.

"Is it cruelty free, organic cheese?"

"Said so on the label."

"Then, she is a fan of both."

"Excellent." Drake lifted the flaps on the basket. "This is five years overdue, I think," he smiled at her. Lucene's cheeks flooded with pink. "I hope a New Zealand red Zin is okay with you?"

"Maybe just one glass," Lucene conceded. "I've got to keep my wits about me."

Drake poured two glasses and offered Lucene one. "Thanks," she said. The weird sourness in her stomach returned. Stupid nerves.

"A toast," Drake announced, holding up his glass. "It's taken us five years to finally enjoy a drink together," he joked. Lucene politely tapped his glass, not sure how to take the comment. After all, he had never in the past, suggested that an after-work drink was an option. Perhaps because he was her boss at the time?

"Earth to Lucy," Drake snapped his fingers in her face. She flinched in surprise.

"Sorry, I was just wondering what you know about these people who are after me, how you found me, and how you plan to help."

He took a bite of his sandwich. "Tastes like turkey," he exclaimed, happily.

"Well, what did you expect a turkey sandwich to taste like?"

"The way you described it…tofu."

"Surprise," she joked.

He reached back into the basket and drew out a small ready-made plate of diced gruyere and sliced gouda. She plucked a slice of gruyere and took a bite. Drake set the plate down.

"None for you?" she asked.

"Truth be told, lactose intolerant. But you enjoy it. Now, about your questions, do you remember our last conversation before you… eh…disappeared?"

"Not sure," Lucene confessed. "My memory's been a little foggy lately."

"At the time, I told you that there were forces at work, three, to be exact. The Earth, as we know it, is changing, and there needs to be an intervention. Ringing any bells?"

Lucene ate another bite of cheese. "What kind of intervention?"

"We humans are killing our own kind, destroying the planet, and creating our own famine and disease in the process," he continued, ignoring the question. "Really, if left to our own devices, we will be the only species in history to make *ourselves* go extinct! Isn't that insane?"

"Sounds…like it." Lucene cautiously responded. She gnawed at another piece of cheese slowly, feeling a little sluggish. "What three forces are you talking about?"

"Have you been approached by someone named Cepheus Baruch offering to take you back to Erde in Section 1 for your protection?" Lucene stopped chewing. "I can tell from your facial expression, that I am correct. You may not remember him from the last Assembly you attended, but I can assure you, he cannot be trusted."

"Why not?"

"Why not?!" Drake seemed perturbed by the very question and

sucked in his breath for a moment. "For one thing, because they have been abducting humans for years under the guise of creating safe havens for us. When, in reality, all they've been doing is human experimentation for their own research."

"That's one," Lucene took a sip of wine, groggily.

"Then, there are the Vitruvians from Section 2. They claim non-interference and will do nothing to help protect us against ourselves. But their so-called renegade band of 'Balance-Keepers' are all about balance when the chips are in their favor. Their idea of 'out of balance' really means, 'what's not in our best interest.' "

"That's two." Lucene went back for what was now her third slice of cheese, not realizing that she'd allowed her half of the turkey sandwich to fall to the floor.

"The Royals. They are what we humans should have become, evolved in every way, physically and intellectually."

"The ones trying to kill me?"

"Kill you?!" Drake laughed. "My silly, naive, Lucy. They are the only ones trying to actually help you."

"How?"

He peered at her closely, gently removing her wine glass from her grasp before she dropped it on the floor. "By fixing you."

"Fixing me?"

"Yes," he whispered, "Don't you get it? Your poor family was a product of Section 1's experiments. Surely you sense that…pardon me for being indelicate…you're not quite right in the head."

Lucene nodded, groggily and yawned. "How are they planning to fix me?"

"By helping you use your slightly altered brain in an intellectually superior way."

"But what about emotionally and spiritually?" Lucene was going for sarcasm, but still wasn't sure where those words came from, since she never considered herself as possessing deep empathy nor a spiritual nature.

"A species cannot flourish being touch-feely. There are too many predators out there just waiting to wipe us out. We're finally seeing evidence of that now. And as far as spiritually, why pray to a god when you can become one?"

Lucene wasn't sure how she suddenly went from silly and naive to a god. She also wasn't certain when the room started revolving. "So, what would you, in your infinite wisdom, recommend?"

"There are negotiations in place with planets from nearby solar systems to help us restore our planet. Since many representatives from these neighboring friends have taken up residence in Florida, we decided to hold the meeting here."

For once, Darke paused to gauge Lucene's reaction. Finally, she answered. "There's just one problem with all of this," she finally blurted out.

"What's that?" Drake clenched his jaw.

"My damaged brain doesn't believe you," Lucene slurred her words as her mouth went numb. She spit a piece of chewed cheese into her napkin, since swallowing it was not an option, and let out a cough.

Drake started laughing. "Easy there," he caught her by the shoulders. "I'm surprised by your constitution, though, I guess I shouldn't be. Between the sleeping meds I added to the wine and the cheese, you've guzzled and eaten enough to down a horse."

Lucene tried to form an unseemly response, but the words wouldn't come.

"Okay, she's ready," Drake announced. Two human-sized red salamanders emerged from the shadows with a gurney in tow, and one easily lifted a drowsy Lucene to her feet. She put up a pitiful attempt at resisting, but her legs were turning to jelly. "Imagine my surprise," he told her, as they laid her on the gurney and began strapping her into place, "when I learned that Lucy Jones' parents were listed in the alien International Registry that you so nicely procured for me back in New York." Lucene, vaguely conscious, recalled the files he'd asked her to find that day in his office five years ago.

"My parents?" Lucene fought to remain awake.

"But not you." He looked down at her. "You weren't listed because you were born here. By the time I'd made the connection, you had already run away. Do you know how many Lucy Jones there are in this country, let alone the world? It took forever to find you. And to think," he said finally, before everything faded to black. "You were right under my nose for three years."

Drake nodded for the guards to take her away as he carefully packed up the picnic basket, pausing only to take a bite of his sandwich. "Clean meat," he laughed. "Who would have thought?"

"Who are you?" Isabella demanded at the surprise guest in her sanctuary.

Drake turned to see the striking dark-skinned woman with snow-white hair standing in the doorway. It was at that moment she caught a glimpse of a gurney and two red salamanders disappearing down the back hallway pushing something. She couldn't quite see what it was.

"I was just leaving," Drake replied, reaching into his pocket and pulling out a small pistol. He shot Isabella through the chest before she could react. She fell to the floor in a heap. He raised his arm and set its sights for a head shot.

"Mr. Cushing." One of the guards came running back in. "Ambassador Hamish and Ambassador Sabrina are on the line. They want to know if you have the girl, and when they can collect her. They are rather insistent."

He looked at the lifeless body on the floor. Blood was beginning to pool from under her shirt and spill out onto the floor.

"Okay." He put his gun away and dropped his sandwich on the floor, trampling on it on his way out. After all, he'd be long gone before anyone could match any prints or DNA to him.

CHAPTER 23
SPARE PARTS
MONDAY EVENING. FIVE YEARS AFTER THE ASSEMBLY.

"Cepheus, we've got a situation here, and I need yerr h—"

Ivan stopped mid-sentence as he witnessed his friend perched on his work table pulling an assortment of washers, wing nuts, screws and the old pair of pliers out of containers that were lined up on shelves or hanging on the wall…neatly labeled, he noted to himself with disappointment. He had planned on filling Cepheus in about his talk with Lucene at the sanctuary moments ago, but this episode clearly needed his immediate attention. Cepheus paused to analyze a small brass gear before tucking it in the jacket pocket of his long black coat.

"Ye okay, buddy?" Ivan asked, at which time, Cepheus hissed at him, accidentally hitting his head on a hanging mason jar light that shined over the workstation. He didn't seem to notice.

Cepheus, still hunkering over the table like a wild animal eating prey it had caught, continued to tear through tools and accessories, exhibiting an odd sense of pure joy at each trinket he discovered. Ivan, not usually given to unnecessary worry, watched his friend with a mix of concern and odd fascination.

"I want this shiny grabber," Cepheus announced, holding up a small adjustable wrench, proud of his find.

"Sure thing," Ivan answered. "Whatever ye need."

Cepheus nodded, as if that answer was expected and acceptable. At that moment, he hopped off the table and darted out the back door.

"Where are ye—" Ivan began, following Cepheus out of the shed and down the trail in the dark, stopping at a large tree stump—the remains of an Oak that had fallen during the last major storm. Ivan repurposed it as his favorite "think" spot, often sitting there for an eternity until he'd solved a major problem.

He watched as his friend reached his hand into a small hole that an animal had made along its side, uncertain whether that "animal" had been Cepheus. "Don't know that I'd reach in there, could be brown recluses and—"

He was hissed at again and fell silent as Cepheus carefully tucked his new treasures safely into the hole like an oversized ferret. He then grabbed a handful of dirt and haphazardly tossed it over the hole in a poor attempt to cover it back up.

Without acknowledging Ivan, he darted back to the shed. Ivan pulled out a pocket flashlight and followed him back, more slowly this time, as the darkness seemed to fall rather rapidly over the sky.

As he approached the shed, he saw car lights in the distance. He recognized them as Fatima's. *One disaster at a time,* he thought. He would phone her after he'd gotten Cepheus under control. It was then that he remembered the medicine that Tanager had given him should Cepheus have an episode.

He ran back in the shed. Cepheus had moved onto the engine that they'd been working on and began to plug and unplug wires.

"No, no, no!" Ivan swatted his friend's hands away. "Don't do that!" Cepheus's eyes grew wide as he instinctively shoved Ivan away. He was deceptively strong for a thin and wiry frame, and his push sent Ivan reeling overtop of a custom motorcycle he'd built, sending him crashing to the concrete with the bike on top of him, enough to pin him painfully to the ground, but not enough to puncture any organs he might need in the future. Fortunately, he'd had enough mishaps to remember to tuck his chin, so his head missed smacking against the floor. There was a pause before the pain in his spine connected to his mouth. "Ow," he whined.

Like a cat who'd been shooed away from the pantry, Cepheus promptly went back to exploring the workstation again, oblivious to Ivan's discomfort or that he'd caused it.

Just then, Ivan's cell phone rang. With some difficulty, he managed to slide a hand under the bike and into his pocket to retrieve it.

CHAPTER 24
ODESSA AND TANAGER
MONDAY EVENING. FIVE YEARS AFTER THE ASSEMBLY.

Tanager may have arrived here with some misconceptions about current Earth attire, lingo and customs, but he was observant and a quick study. Plus, he had Lucene to guide him. By the time he'd reached the marina, he was wearing a pair of bone-colored weekender shorts, a coral, mesh-lined fishing shirt and river sandals. His curly locks were stuffed under the "Salt Life" cap he took from the Closet. Sadly, since his borrowed threads belonged to a much taller and bulkier man, nothing fit quite right. Conversely, the sandals were Ivan's, and at least one size too small. Consequently, he still stuck out.

He searched the water using night vision binoculars, but so far, the only things he spotted were clumps of eelgrass, several needlefish and assorted marine debris.

"Well, would you look at that getup," a voice from the water called. Tanager lowered his binoculars, only to find that Odessa was at the edge of the dock, right at his feet. "Looking for me?"

"As a matter of fact, I was," Tanager answered, seriously. Odessa floated on her back, with her breasts bobbing up and down like two buoys in the water. Tanager politely looked away. "Could you float a little…lower? That's very distracting."

"Get you a little hot and bothered, does it?"

"Hot? No. But it does bother me...a little." Odessa smiled and lowered herself in the water, treading so that only her head and shoulders were visible.

"Thank you."

"Didn't do it for you," Odessa smirked. My nipples were getting a little chilly." Tanager remained silent. "So, what brings you here? Did you miss me?" She winked.

"It is always nice to see you..."

"Oh my God, you are such a bore!" Odessa whined. "Always nice to see you," she mocked. "Blah blah blah. Tanager, if you're ever to truly understand Earth culture, you're going to need to learn how to be far less Goddamned polite!"

"I will take it under advisement, thank you," he replied as she rolled her eyes. "We're running out of time," he admonished. "I need you to tell me where the Royals are, and if they have located our Earth-born Data Collector yet."

"Hold the phone. *You* may be running out of time. Whereas, *I* on the other hand, have all the time in the world." Tanager let the phone reference go for now, with a mental note to research the expression later.

"Odessa, I know you love this world. So do we. But if Sabrina and Hamish fulfill their mission, this Earth will be recycled. And, I promise you, it won't come back as something you will love, and it won't be a place where anyone outside of the Royals will be invited." Odessa seemed to be considering this for a moment, her face crumpling in what could only be described as despair. "All living beings on this Earth will die, and this will only be the beginning."

"But I cannot interfere." For the first time ever, Odessa seemed to be choking back something that felt like a sincere emotion. "I can only report what I observe and deliver messages as instructed."

"Then, surely you can tell me..."

"To *my* people, not yours."

Tanager tapped the tip of his sandal on the dock and hung his head, willing a brilliant idea to pop into it. In what instance would her people allow her to divulge such important information? Suddenly, he looked up. "Morphinae is a Vitruvian, is...ze...not?" Tanager struggled with Earth's gender-neutral pronouns, finding language here incredibly difficult. *Was it ze and zir?* He decided on the masculine pronouns, since male was Morphinae's most common form. Odessa became indignant. "Morphinae is a renegade...a maverick. He is a Balance-Keeper, but who the hell knows how he measures what balance is?"

"Can you tell Morphinae what you know?"

"I suppose. But what would be the point of that?"

"Will you call on Morphinae, please? I know he will listen to you. Tell Morphinae, and then maybe I can convince him to tell me what I need to know."

"And why would I do that?" Odessa asked, seeking validation.

"Because I know that this is your home more than Section 2 ever was."

Odessa thought for a moment, and then tilted back her head, letting out what could only be referred to as a siren call...a melodic sound that can be adjusted to reach only certain frequencies. To Tanager, and to many, it was a beautiful sound. On Earth, however, it seemed that only animals had the ability to hear and appreciate it.

It took several minutes, but eventually, Morphinae floated in as a butterfly and transformed into his masculine self.

"Well, don't you look handsome?" Odessa flirted.

"I chose this form when I saw whose company you were keeping," Morphinae flashed a glance at Tanager. "I sense he is uncomfortable with the female form."

"Is that true, Tanager?" Odessa winked. "Do women make you uncomfortable?"

"Please, Odessa, there is no time." Tanager answered. Odessa shrugged. A small fishing boat could be seen approaching the dock. "This might not be the best place to talk. Is there someplace more private we can go?"

"Absolutely." Odessa winked. With that, she used her arms to hoist herself onto the dock as her fins transformed into legs. And yes, she was completely naked. "Follow me," she said, unabashed. A moment later, she turned and held her finger to her lips for silence before shapeshifting into a blue-green butterfly. She nodded for Morphinae to do the same. Tanager, with no such capabilities, merely struggled to follow their errant path. Eventually, the three had relocated to a small storage unit inside a large abandoned warehouse. The two Vitruvians resumed their former appearances. This time, however, Odessa was wearing a strange grass-like skirt. Tanager eyed it curiously.

"Oh, it's attached," she confirmed. "You can touch it if you want," she licked her lips. Tanager's face flushed.

"I don't have time for…" Morphinae began to complain.

"Fine. Fine. Fine." Odessa sighed. She pointed an upturned palm toward Tanager. "Speak," she commanded.

Just as Tanager was about to explain to Morphinae why he was summoned, voices could be heard echoing in the distance…but very much in the same warehouse as they were.

Odessa's eyes grew wide in mock amazement, as if to say, "Well, would you look at that?"

The voices belonged to none other than Hamish and Sabrina. And they were talking…not quietly…about Lucene. The three listened with interest.

"Do you really believe he has her?" Hamish asked, tiredly.

"If he doesn't, he will very soon. I'm out of patience, and we need to get out of here tonight, before the entire SWAT team arrives…or, whatever it is they are calling them these days."

"I suppose it didn't help that you blew up a casino," Hamish responded, nonchalantly.

"Shut up, you idiot," she pointed a clawed finger at her husband's throat. "I don't need a lecture from you about how bad my temper is, and you shouldn't anger me in my…" She caught herself. "You shouldn't anger me."

"But where are they leaving from?" Tanager whispered. Odessa pressed her fingers to Tanager's mouth and shook his head as a sign to be quiet. Just then, Tanager's watch gave off a warning chime, along with an accompanying red light.

"What was that?" Sabrina looked up.

"Nice going," Odessa whispered, and she and Morphinae transformed back into butterflies and headed for the rafters. Tanager frantically silenced his watch and hid behind what looked like a few cobweb-covered bourbon barrels…and hoped for the best.

Moments later, Hamish replied, "I'm sure it's nothing, but we should take cover, just in case."

'Cover' turned out to be the very storage unit where Tanager was hiding. "I cannot believe we've been reduced to hiding like vermin," Sabrina complained. They were just about to shut the door when Odessa appeared, this time wearing a blue-green suit that was clearly another shapeshifting maneuver. It appeared as if she actually were wearing clothes.

"Knock, knock." She smiled, standing at the entryway. "Sorry if I startled you just now, Sovereigns."

"What do *you* want?" Sabrina clutched her clothing as if trying to hide her embarrassment.

"My superiors were just alerting me to confirm that your meeting with them will commence as scheduled tomorrow?"

"Yes, of course," Sabrina nodded.

"Excellent," Odessa turned to go.

"How did she know we were here?" Sabrina asked her husband.

"She's one of the observers. No doubt she notices everything. Good thing we're leaving tonight."

Tanager remained motionless until he was fairly certain they had left. Still, he knew that running would appear suspicious. Instead, after darting out of the storage room, he sauntered over to the docks as if he owned the place. It was only when at a safe distance that he picked up speed. The alert he received meant that Cepheus was undergoing trauma again. But what kind, he couldn't determine.

CHAPTER 25

NEWS STORY

MONDAY EVENING. FIVE YEARS AFTER THE ASSEMBLY.

Fatima and Roman were at the cottage, snuggled on the living room couch under a blanket, with two glasses of wine and an assorted cheese plate and grapes sitting on the end table. Occasionally, Roman would reach for a grape and offer it to Fatima who playfully let him feed it to her.

Roman clicked the remote and the TV sprang to life. He was about to switch to movie streaming when a "breaking news story" graphic popped up on the screen. What followed was a location shot of a small church with crime tape wrapped around the building and investigators shooting photos and taking notes.

"Hold on," Fatima stopped him. "That's Lucene's church. Turn that up!" she commanded. He obeyed, and the two watched a young reporter give details about the scene behind her.

"This just in! We've learned that Reverend Isabella Simone of the Singing River Sanctuary in Parrish has been shot. She was rushed to a nearby hospital where she is in stable condition. No word yet as to what happened. We'll bring you continuing coverage on this developing story."

"Oh, my gosh," Fatima whined. "Lucene spends a lot of time there, even when she's not working. I hope she wasn't there!" Fatima unwrapped herself from the blanket and leapt to her feet.

"Can you call her cell phone?" Roman sat up, concerned.

"No, she doesn't carry one."

"Who on this planet doesn't carry a cell phone?" Roman was shocked.

"*She* doesn't. She says they're too easy to track. We have to call the police."

"And more breaking news..." the television interrupted again. The news anchor had a momentary look of glee at her good fortune, being there for not one, but two, important stories. She quickly recovered, touching her ear as if receiving information from an ear mic. "We've just learned that a man was found dead on his boat at the Port Hammond marina. He's been identified as 53-year-old Jim Sparks. Further details are being withheld as his death has been ruled as suspicious."

Fatima's face turned pale. Roman tossed the blanket aside and stood. "It's not what you think," Roman explained waving his hands as he spoke.

"Jim Sparks," she whispered. "Dead."

"I know, but that had nothing to do with me. I'm as shocked as you are." For once, the trusting Fatima appeared unconvinced.

"We have to call the police," she backed away, slowly. When she'd reached the kitchen, she bolted for the door. She'd gotten as far as unlatching it and turning the knob.

"Stop!" Roman commanded. "Or, I'll shoot." Fatima paused, glancing over her shoulder, her heart rate beginning to escalate. Roman stood in the living room, a gun pointed at her chest. "Please, close the door."

Fatima obeyed.

"I didn't kill Jim Sparks," he claimed.

"I'm having a hard time believing you when you have a gun pointed at me," Fatima's eyes welled up. Her hands were shaking. Roman instinctively moved toward her to comfort her before catching himself.

"If they found Jim Sparks, they can find me. We need to leave. It isn't safe here."

"Again…gun," she pointed out.

He slowly pointed the gun toward the ceiling, holding it with two hands at the ready. "I was afraid you'd run away. If they find you first, they will torture you to get to me."

"Who are *they*?" Fatima whined.

"I'll explain on the way. Just get your cat and I'll tell you where to drive us."

"My cat," she repeated, confused. "You mean, car?"

"No, cat. There's a good chance we won't be coming back for a while. I'm pretty sure you don't want to leave him behind. Now, I'm going to put the gun down if you promise not to run away."

Suddenly, Fatima choked out a laugh.

"What's so funny?" he wanted to know.

"Put the gun down, silly. I'll get Bagheera." She made her way toward Lucene's bedroom—the cat's favorite hangout. "I don't know of any murderer who'd be concerned about killing me but saving my cat."

CHAPTER 26
REVELATION
MONDAY EVENING. FIVE YEARS AFTER THE ASSEMBLY.

"We need to call the police, not hide out in your apartment," Fatima tugged her arm free from Roman's grasp as he pulled her inside and shut the door. She set her large, paisley, beach bag on the carpet, and Bagheera leapt to his freedom, instantly beginning to sniff around his new surroundings.

"No police," Roman barked back, running to the living room window and peaking around the red blackout drapes to make sure they weren't followed. "I've already told you; they'd like nothing more than to see all of my kind destroyed."

"Well, we can't just stay here and do noth—" Fatima stopped, mid-sentence as her eyes fell on the far wall in the next room, partially revealed through the open bedroom door. Roman glanced over her shoulder. As he caught wind of what she saw, he rushed to the door to close it, but she'd already made her way inside. "What is this?" She stared, mesmerized by the wall-to-wall photographs and notes strung all over it like a giant collage—photographs of her going to work, of Lucene and Tanager dancing, of Fatima talking to Ivan in the yard, a calendar noting arrival and departure times, and a US map with thumbtacks all over it.

"It's part of my research," Roman explained hastily, slipping past Fatima and guiding her out of the room, closing the door behind them.

"But there are pictures of…me…on that wall," Fatima's voice trembled softly as her eyes began to well up. She slumped against the wall and put her hand to her heart. "Is that all I am…research?"

Roman's spirit crumbled as he choked back tears. "Of course not, my love." He rushed to hug her, only to discover her struggling to stand. He wrapped his long arms around her plump waist, supporting her as they made their way across the room where she sank into the couch.

"I'm okay. I'm okay," Fatima waved a hand to dismiss him. "Just need to catch my breath." She was surprised by the episode, as she hadn't had one since…she tried to remember. It had to have been about five years, not since Lucene had come to live with her. That much she knew.

"Meeting you was a happy accident," Roman gushed, pulling her attention back. "You saved me, Far." He knelt in front of her, enfolding her hands into his.

Fatima tensed up, pulling her hands away as Roman searched her eyes, questioningly. "Far? Is that supposed to be some sort of nickname for me?"

"But—." He backed away slowly, mouthing the words 'Fatima' then 'Far,' as if trying to figure something out. There was a space in his memory that was blank, and he struggled desperately to remember as one might struggle to remember a once-vivid dream. He backed into the living room wall, sliding down it like a rag doll until he had come to his knees. Wrapping his arms around his legs, he laid his head in his lap and began rocking like a small, scared child. "Far!" he cried as he rocked. "How could I forget you?"

Fatima struggled to her feet, looking helplessly from side-to-side, wondering which disaster to deal with first, her missing friend or the broken man at her feet. Who could she call for help? More importantly…*who* could she call who would actually believe her?

Remembering her fallen purse, she rushed to it, fumbling nervously for her phone. She hit a speed dial number, waiting impatiently, eyeing the fallen man on the floor who was still very much in his own world.

"Alo, Fatima," Ivan answered, his voice sounding strange.

"H...Hi," Fatima choked back. "Ivan, I need your help."

"What's wrong?" Ivan voiced concern. "Are ye hurt?"

"No, it's Roman." Fatima swore she could feel Ivan cringe on the other end of the phone line. "He's had a breakdown and is acting strange."

"Seems to be goin' 'round," Ivan answered. "Got me hands full with a similar situation me self." Fatima could hear strange rustling sounds over the phone.

"Is everybody going crazy? Never mind…it gets worse. Lucene's in trouble."

"I know that, but how do you?"

"Wait...what?"

"I just spoke with her at the church…Crap, I wasn't supposed to tell you that!"

"What? When?"

"I dunno, maybe about 30 minutes or so. Why?"

Fatima let out several uncharacteristic expletives. "Well, you must have just missed the shooting."

"What?!"

"Never mind, Lucene's not there. At least, I don't think she is. I don't know where she is. Just get here and we'll figure it out."

"Aye, where are you now?" Ivan asked.

"I'm at Roman's apartment." Another cringe. Fatima rambled off the building number and street. Ivan made a mental note of it, repeating it in his head to make it stick.

"Ye may want to wait out front, if he's acting kookie."

"No, I'm okay, and I think we should lay low. Please be careful and… thank you." Ivan felt a little pang of feeling in the center of his chest, near his heart…just a little.

"Aye…be there in a jiff." There was doubt in his voice.

Ivan did his best to use his upper body to push the bike off of him, succeeding only in moving the handlebars so that one was now poking into his rib cage. It was at that moment that Cepheus reached into one of the drawers and pulled out a plastic syringe.

"Oh, shit," Ivan mumbled. "Man...wait!" Too late. Cepheus had already run back outside, presumably to the tree trunk to hide his latest find. Ivan waited for what seemed like an eternity, but Cepheus eventually came back.

"Cepheus, ol' friend. I need you to git over here and help me." Cepheus ignored him. Ivan felt a numbness start to overtake the lower half of his body as the weight of the bike began cutting off circulation. "Cepheus," he tried again, a little louder, but hopefully not loud enough to inspire another violent reaction. "Lucene and Fatima need us." Cepheus, who had been pawing through a box of metal fasteners, suddenly looked up."

"Lucene...in trouble?" Ivan could almost see a gray cloud over his friend's head, as if a storm were beginning to clear and sunlight was about to come through. "I thought she was dead."

"Why would you think that?" Ivan's eyes grew wide, wondering if he'd somehow been involved with Lucene's current disappearance. "Never mind, I need you to focus. Put down the toys and help me!"

"Of course." Cepheus said, quietly, stepping down off the table with catlike grace and brushing off his dark pants, as if to brush off cobwebs. Suddenly, realizing his friend was pinned under the motorcycle, he quickly reached down and lifted it off him with one hand. With the other, he offered his hand and hoisted Ivan awkwardly to his feet.

"Thanks, man." Ivan struggled for a moment to stand upright and took a few cautious steps to make sure everything was still in working order.

"Are you okay?" Cepheus asked. "I hope I didn't do anything...inappropriate."

"Ye were a hot mess, ye were," Ivan blurted out. Diplomacy was not his strong suit. "But that doesn't matter right now. We've got to get going, and fast. Follow me."

The two rushed to Ivan's van, nicknamed the "mongrel" because of its unique build and functionality. It sat in the covered car port next to the driveway. Cepheus instinctively climbed in the back while Ivan settled into the driver's seat up front. Ivan wasted no time in backing down the drive and heading out. As they passed Fatima's house, there was a roaring explosion as the cottage burst into flames. Remnants from the explosion floated around the mongrel. Startled, both Ivan and Cepheus jumped in their seats. A moment later, there were two more explosions. Peering in the rearview mirror, Ivan saw both his and Fatima's home and his workshop on fire. Instinctively, he hit the gas pedal and didn't look back again. Ivan's heart raced when it sank in that had they wasted even half a minute more, they would be dead.

"Tell me the truth, Cepheus. I won't be mad..."

"It was not me, my friend." Cepheus answered, reading his thoughts. His mind now returning to clarity for the first time without requiring medication. "It was they."

"They, who?" Ivan asked over his shoulder, as he turned the corner and headed toward the highway.

"The Royals."

There was a loud knock at the door. Fatima quickly eyed the peephole, seeing a thick red beard staring back at her. She opened the door and Ivan and Cepheus rushed in.

"Yer not hurt, are ya?" Ivan took Fatima by the shoulders, concerned.

"No, I'm fine. It's him I'm worried about." She gave a confused once-over at the lanky man who accompanied her neighbor. "Your eyes are very yellow," she said, almost transfixed.

"And your hair," Cepheus answered in a deep voice, "is very purple."

"It's good that we're both so observant," Fatima whispered back in something between a joke and surprise. Ivan wrapped an arm around her, concerned.

"He's not from around here," Ivan said.

"So, I gathered," Fatima whispered back, sinking into Ivan's chest for support.

Cepheus went over to the crumpled man, cautiously. He sank down next to Roman, who picked his head up and looked at Cepheus, his eyes suddenly widening with recognition. "You are one of them?" He wiped his tears with his sleeve. Fatima and Ivan watched the scene with a mixture of amazement and concern.

"I am," Cepheus answered. "You've been searching for us for quite some time, haven't you?" Roman nodded. Bagheera came out from behind the curtain where he had been hiding and began rubbing up against Cepheus's leg. He reached out to scratch behind the cat's ear, but did not turn his attention from Roman. Cepheus hung his head for a moment, as if listening to something, and then nodded back in understanding. "Was he sick for very long?"

"Two years," Roman sobbed, looking at Fatima as if to apologize. Fatima smiled back, weakly, a mix of understanding and disappointment. "I heard about the Data Collectors during the televised report of the newly formed IPP many years ago, when Section 1 first revealed their presence on Earth. I thought that if they cared that much about the planet, and had the technology to help us..."

"That we might have had the resources to save your beloved?" Cepheus acknowledged.

"Yes," Roman answered. "Maybe even take us back with you? To your planet?" Roman looked at Fatima pleadingly. "I didn't remember any of this until now. I swear to you, lovely Fatima, I didn't intend to hurt you."

"I know," Fatima pulled away from Ivan and rushed to Roman's side, kneeling down and touching a hand to his shoulder. "Who was he?" Ivan pretended not to care.

"He was a monk, originally from the outermost region of Macar. It's billions of lightyears from here. His people lived on a small planet—very primitive. They relied on their sovereign for everything: food, shelter, healing, protection. And then, Far was born."

Roman went on to explain that when Far was a boy, he demonstrated the unique power of transporting himself over great distances to avoid danger. He was also a prophet, and that made their sovereign uncomfortable. Far was nothing but a skinny, frail little thing with blonde hair and pale green eyes. "There was nothing intimidating about him, and yet—"

"They tried to kill him," Fatima filled the gap. Roman nodded.

"Yes. His family told him to run...to run to the farthest place he could. That's how he found his way to Earth. I met him thirteen years ago, when he was an adult."

"Kinda funny, when you think about it," Fatima wiped a tear from her eye. "You tried to suppress your pain so much that you ended up dating a fat woman with lavender hair and gray eyes…the absolute opposite of Far." She laughed a little, though she wasn't really happy.

"Oh, sweet Fatima," Roman touched her hand. "You are beautiful and wonderful. And, I do have love for you. I just…forgot…everything for a while. I'm so sorry."

"Oye," Ivan's eyes widened, being pulled away from the story. "We needs to warn Tanager 'bout not coming back to the house!"

"What happened to the house?" Fatima asked.

"The Royals happened," Ivan answered, still not completely certain who they were.

There was another knock at the door.

"Where is Cepheus?" Tanager demanded, storming in, syringe in hand, as Ivan opened the door, quickly shutting it after him. Seeing Cepheus, Tanager immediately rushed to his friend's side, leaning down and holding the syringe to Cepheus's neck. Ivan grabbed his arm and shook his head.

"He doesn't need it," he nodded to Cepheus. Having left Roman to Fatima's care, Cepheus was now sitting cross-legged on the floor, eyes closed as if in deep meditation.

"You mean he recovered? On his own?" Ivan nodded again. Tanager let out a relieved smile, mixed with hope.

"How?" Fatima began, pausing a moment to take in Tanager's new wardrobe.

"Tracking device," Tanager explained impatiently. "Cepheus, while my mentor and the brightest man I know, is still under Watch. Unfortunately, I'm not as intuitive as he, so..."

"So you..."

"Know him," he finished her sentence, pointing. "Yes."

"Will all of you please begin speakin' English? Yer making me head hurt," Ivan complained. "What in the hell is 'under watch'?"

"Where is Lucene?" Tanager demanded, finally taking a moment to survey the room.

"We don't know," Fatima answered. "She was last seen at the church where she works, but there was a shooting and she is missing."

Tanager's face turned white and he held back the tremors he felt in his hands and heart. He turned back to Cepheus. "I know where the Royals are. They're hiding in an abandoned warehouse at the marina. Can you sense if Lucene is near there?" Cepheus lifted his chin slightly, to acknowledge the question, but did not open his eyes.

"Why would he know where she is?" Fatima questioned, pointing to the yellow-eyed Cepheus on the floor.

"Because he's her mentor," Tanager answered. "She doesn't remember, but he trained her as a small child."

This didn't seem to clarify things for her.

"He's psychic," Tanager said. That seemed the easiest explanation. Fatima nodded. Tanager lamented the fact that he was supposed to have a similar vibration as Lucene, and yet he couldn't connect with her. Truth be told, neither one of them had been trained properly.

"You mean, I was right?" Roman looked hopeful. "She's the one?"

"The one," Tanager agreed.

"One what?" Fatima asked.

"She's not from here, and she's very…special."

"You mean she's an," Fatima couldn't believe she was saying this, "*alien*?"

"Yes, and she's not safe here. We need to take her home."

"But this is her home!" Fatima's chest began to rise, as Ivan motioned with his hands to lower her voice, pointing to Cepheus. She turned to Ivan, "So, we're just all okay with this?"

"I was wrong, Fatima," Roman struggled to his feet. "My mind wasn't right. They're not experimenting on humans. They are attempting to genetically modify Data Collectors to accurately gather and report information back home. Somehow, that got switched up in my head."

"Genetically modify!" Fatima was incredulous. "How is that better?"

"Fatima, please." Tanager pointed to Cepheus again. "First we need to find her."

Fatima nodded and bit her lip.

The group waited in silence for what seemed like hours. In reality, it was closer to 20 minutes.

Cepheus's eyes popped open. "I know where she is."

CHAPTER 27
THE RED DOOR
RIGHT NOW. FIVE YEARS AFTER THE ASSEMBLY.

"We've been so stupid," Hamish exclaimed, rubbing his forehead tiredly. "For the longest time, we assumed that if we simply learned the special gene-splicing cocktail added to the Data Collector's DNA, we could replicate the process and transmute our own Royal army."

Lucene struggled with the restraints that had her strapped to the hospital gurney. "I don't know what you're talking about," Lucene panicked. "You've got the wrong girl."

Lucene let out a yelp as an attendant, dressed in a long gray lab coat, thrust a needle haphazardly into Lucene's arm.

"Don't lie to us, you stupid creature." Sabrina stuck her face right above Lucene's, spitting a little as she spoke.

"Don't you know who you are, my dear?" Hamish asked in a deceptively calm and collected voice. "What you are capable of?"

As Lucene stared at the harsh fluorescent lights above her head, the world around her began to fade.

"Begin the process," Hamish ordered to the two female attendants in the room. "We haven't much time."

Lucene dreamed as she'd never dreamed before. She found herself floating back to the house she lived in when her parents were still alive. She was five, and it was one of many training sessions that they would have together.

Her father sat across from her on the floor, his legs folded under him, cross-legged. His eyes were closed, in a state of deep meditation. Lucene did her best to mimic his movements. She rested her hands solemnly in her lap as she also sat cross-legged with her eyes closed. She had no innate flexibility, and her thighs popped up off the floor like winged butterflies. She felt jittery and found it difficult to sit still.

"Stop fidgeting, Lucene, and concentrate," her father said gently.

Lucene let out a frustrated sigh and tried again. Her brow furrowed in deep concentration.

From across the room, Lucene's mother watched with interest. She sat at a high-top table in the kitchen, nervously folding and unfolding the same dinner napkins over and over.

Both Lucene and her father sat there for some minutes before his eyes popped open with excitement.

"A green elephant," he proclaimed.

Lucene smiled proudly. "Yes!" she answered, thinking back to a plush toy her dad had won for her at the state fair a few months back. "A green elephant!"

"Very good, Lucene. Your powers of transmitting messages are —"

"You thought I was going to picture a yellow sunflower in my head." Lucene giggled just thinking about the giant sunflower mural on the wall in her bedroom. It made her happy every time she saw it.

"But—" her father began.

"And mom is worried that they will soon discover who I am and take me away." Her face fell. Dora stopped folding and shot her husband a concerned look. He simply nodded.

"Very good, Lucene. But how did you manage to both transmit an image while also receiving what I was thinking, and what your mother was thinking, at the same time."

"I'm not sure," Lucene furrowed her brows once again. "I was thinking really hard about the green elephant, when it turned into a sunflower. You were handing a flower to me. Then, I saw strange looking lizard people trying to take me away. Mommy stared through the window. She wanted to help, but she couldn't move. They popped into my head so fast, that I didn't have time to stop them."

Lucene's mother came into the room to join them, sitting down next to her, running a hand through the girl's long hair. "Yes, that's right, Lucene. And what should you do if you ever see those lizard people?"

Lucene didn't even have to pause and take a deep breath. Without thinking, she answered, "Run."

Lucene awoke with a throbbing headache that made her sick to her stomach. Bright lights blinded her as they flashed repeatedly in her face. Sounds reverberated in her ears as if someone had turned up the volume on every radio station on the planet, causing a cacophony of words, music and background noise. Random smells bombarded her olfactory system, and her tongue was heavy with the taste of metal. Her skin itched with the feeling of crawling bugs, though she was unable to sit up or move her arms or legs to swat them away. Her neck ached, and she realized that her head was somehow pinned against the gurney, too, making it impossible to get the kink out of her neck. Her pulse quickened, and she desperately fought the urge to do what one of the loud voices was urging her to do.

"Go ahead, scream," Sabrina admonished, bitterly.

From just a few miles away, a deep voice cut through the chaos. *Lucene, can you hear me?*

Cepheus? Lucene could barely hear him among the other noises. *If that's you, please send help!*

Focus on my voice, his thoughts transmitted. *Filter everything else out except for my voice.*

I don't know how, she thought.

Yes, you do, Cepheus responded. *Close your eyes if you need to. Remember your training. Now, more than ever, you must remember.*

Lucene clenched her eyelids tightly together as she flashed back to the training her parents had given her, from the time since she could first remember to the day the lightning struck and her parents were taken away forever. That was nearly five years of almost daily lessons in mentally sending and receiving messages, of picking up what others were sensing and feeling: humans, animals, plants, anything that lived and breathed. The memories flooded back with squall-like force. In addition to all the other sensations, it was almost unbearable. *I can't, too much noise!* Lucene's face and arms pulsed with heat as if they were on fire.

Focus on just my voice, Cepheus ordered, more forcefully now. *Silence everything else.*

Dizzy and on the verge of passing out, Lucene's world suddenly went quiet. She sucked in a deep breath. *Okay,* she answered, simply.

Very good, Cepheus answered. *Keep breathing...inhale in...exhale out.* This was familiar to Lucene, not just from working with her parents. His voice and very presence were familiar though. How? She returned her attention to the task at hand.

From outside her consciousness, Sabrina snapped, "What happened? What's wrong with her?" She nudged Lucene's arm, but got no response. It sounded to Lucene as if Sabrina were far away, speaking from the other end of a tunnel.

"Probably the same thing that happened to all the others, including our son," Hamish's lazy voice answered. "You've driven them mad."

"But she's supposed to be the 'gifted' one, born of two Data Collectors with the perfect DNA structure." She pushed one of Lucene's eyelids open quizzically and peered into the motionless hazel eye. "Do you think we can still take DNA samples even if she dies?"

From inside her mind, Lucene awaited more instructions.

Now, Cepheus continued. *I need you to imagine that someone has opened a window and there's a breeze gently blowing in. With it is a scent. What do you smell?*

She imagined the window; she could almost feel the breeze. Somehow, Lucene expected to smell one of Fatima's apple cinnamon pies baking in the oven or the scent of fresh cut flowers from the garden, but she didn't. Surprised, she transmitted, *I smell brackish water, disinfectant, and something loamy.*

Excellent, Lucene, Cepheus praised. *Now, keep your eyes closed, and imagine there's a radio in the room. Someone has just switched it on and has tuned into a single channel. Only let one channel in. Have you got it?*

Yes.

What do you hear?

I hear a woman with a grating voice. Sabrina. Her name is Sabrina. Lucene could feel the tension and fear emanating from Cepheus's energy. *Who is she?* Noises began to overtake her mind once more: cars, horns, voices, music, as if all the stations were on at once.

It does not matter. Stay focused. Filter the noises that do not matter. Only let the most important ones in.

I hear gulls, and water hitting the side of a dock…and the sounds of a motorized boat in the distance…I think I'm at the docks, Cepheus. Except...

Except what?

The birds are next to me. But all of the other sounds are below me. I think I am in the air.

We're coming for you, Lucene. Stay calm and remember, you are in control of what experiences you let in.

In that quiet space, Lucene was suddenly aware of a series of doors in front of her. A few opened on their own, letting in a swarm of sights, smells, tastes and sounds. In her mind's eye, she slammed them closed. She even closed the window and turned off the radio. In the silence, she asked herself, *Which door will tell me why Cepheus is so familiar to me?* Through the darkness, a red door appeared. She walked over and stopped cold. Her face felt flushed and her palms sweaty. She took a deep breath, then opened the door. Suddenly, she was transported back in time, and found herself sitting in the back seat of the family's SUV during a storm. Her mother peered nervously over her shoulder from the front passenger side as her father's hands gripped the steering wheel. She felt terror. She was crying out to someone for help. Who? *Cepheus.*

The memories returned, and it became clear how she knew him, why his voice was so familiar when he stood to speak at the IPP convention several years ago and when he first appeared in her home. He was her mentor. Her parents had taught her basic meditation and intuitive proficiencies, but she needed more than that. Beyond sending and receiving messages from a single source, she received insight from her entire surroundings and was even able to, in some small way, manipulate the experiences of those around her. This caused them concern, and they turned to TARA for guidance. Because of her potential power, they paired her with Cepheus, a well-respected scholar and skilled empath. It was hoped that she would grow to be capable of transmitting data about her surroundings back to Erde more regularly, and use her skills to make Earth a better place. Her parents would ensure that she was morally grounded and would not use her power in a dangerous manner.

How on Earth could I have forgotten all that? She wondered. Ah...she knew the answer. The lightning strike, losing her parents that evening, and the fear of being in danger, the perfect cocktail for forgetting. Then take into account being thrust into the foster care system and shuffled from one home to the next, it's no wonder this got locked away deep inside her...until today.

From the far corners of her consciousness, Lucene heard a knock at the door. Being careful to only open one door at a time, she shut the red door in her mind and waited. A dark gray door appeared.

"What do you want?" Sabrina's voice demanded in the distance.

Lucene mentally opened the door to see who was on the other side.

"They're closing in. It's time to move."

Drake. Even with her eyes closed, she could visualize the young man sauntering through the door to where she lay, confident in all circumstances. The only difference between her vision and reality was that she could actually see herself, lying on the gurney, pale and helpless. He peered down at her with disinterest, and yet, there was something else that went deeper. Regret?

"Well, who's fault is that?" Sabrina snapped.

"You can't have everything, Your Majesty," Drake sucked in his breath. "You can't blow up a casino holding all the remaining IPP members on Earth and expect there *not* to be an investigation."

"Fine," Sabrina waved her long fingers at the attendant. "Wrap her up. She's going with us."

"It won't work," Lucene whispered, her eyes snapping open. Sabrina peered down at her in surprise.

"What won't work, my dear?" Hamish asked, almost sorrowfully.

"Even if you figure out the recipe, it won't work on you."

"Why the hell not?" Sabrina pushed Hamish out of the way. "Is it species-specific?"

"Nope," Lucene answered groggily. "You have to have empathy, and you have to train it regularly. You are impatient, impulsive and lack even basic sympathy for others."

Sabrina's eyes turned yellow and her claylike nails began to rapidly grow as she transformed into her lizard state. "You stupid—" she raised an arm. Hamish caught it.

"Please, my darling," he reasoned. "If you destroy her in anger, then we've lost. She can't teach us empathy if she's dead."

Lucene was on a roll, as knowledge came pouring in and flowed right back out again. "You can't explain it verbally," she emphasized 'verbally' and smacked her lips together. "You communicate with your heart and your thoughts, in that order, over great distances."

"Can those messages be intercepted?" Sabrina demanded as they began rolling the gurney toward an upright pod-like structure—presumably a protective shell so that Lucene would "keep" for the long journey. They pulled the strap off her head and neck in preparation.

"Only if you're on the same frequency," Lucene groggily rolled her head to one side, happy that it now swung freely from side to side.

"And what frequency is that?" Sabrina spat.

"Love," Lucene answered. "That's why messages go back and forth between the Data Collectors and TARA without anyone noticing." Lucene smiled. "It's so simple when you think about it. The Peace-Keepers are like none other. Plans for restoration and peace right under your noses, but you couldn't sense it." Lucene snorted and began laughing drunkenly.

Once again, Sabrina raised an arm. Once again, Hamish intercepted.

"Earthlings are nothing but germs in a petri dish that I can wipe out by sending one tsunami. And what did Peace-Keepers learn about war and self-defense?" she bragged. "Nothing! That's why they were so easy to destroy, one by one. Couldn't even withstand a simple interrogation without dying or going insane." Sabrina paused for a moment, peering so close to Lucene that she could smell the lizard's acidic breath.

"Neither could your son," Lucene replied softly.

"What?"

"Cepheus. He's your son, isn't he? He was a Royal but he couldn't withstand your torture either, could he?"

"That wasn't my fault," a brief look of something like remorse crossed her face. "I hadn't realized that living among the Peace-Keepers for all of those years would have turned him into putty."

"Sovereigns," a soldier addressed them as he burst into the room. "Pardon my intrusion, but I believe we have visitors who could impede our departure. Do we destroy or imprison?"

"Kill them," Sabrina announced. "What good are Earthlings to us?"

"Not Earthlings," he answered. "Your son."

"Let me handle this, my dear," Hamish replied calmly. "You must prepare for departure."

"And trust you to do what needs to be done?" Sabrina barked. "Not on my life."

CHAPTER 28
THE RESCUE
NOW. FIVE YEARS AFTER THE ASSEMBLY.

"Let me come with you," Roman implored. He wiped his eyes with the sleeve of his ruffled shirt and stood. "I've spent several years researching the Data Collectors, the IPP and TARA. I probably know more about how the Royals operate than anyone."

"Then you know how powerful they are," Tanager reasoned.

As the group prepared to leave, Fatima quickly scooped Bagheera up. He protested as she placed him abruptly back into her carpetbag. "Sorry, kitty," she apologized, zipping it enough to prevent his escape and hanging it on her arm. "Hey," she called to the team, who were already following Tanager's lead out the door. "Don't you think we need to do something about *that* first?" She pushed the door to Roman's bedroom open, where his flowchart of images and information were clearly visible.

Ivan swallowed with some difficulty, bothered both by what he saw, and that Fatima clearly knew what was behind the bedroom door. He pushed that out of his mind for the time being.

"Not to worry, my fair Fatima," Roman was restored to his old bravado. "I have had to relocate quickly before." He ran into the room, took a long rope at the edge of the diagram in hand and pulled. The team watched with interest. Three seconds later, the entire diagram was up in flames.

"Let's go," he instructed, taking Fatima by the arm and motioning others toward the door.

"But," Fatima protested. "Fire?"

"Flame retardant walls. It will cause a lot of smoke and may cause someone to call the fire department, but it will fizzle out in a few minutes. I disabled the smoke alarms in here for that reason. But we need to leave. Now."

With that, Tanager ran out of the room with the team close at his heels as they made their way out the door and down the back staircase leading outside.

"Respectfully," Tanager pulled Roman and Ivan aside, "I suggest you use your knowledge to assist Ivan."

Ivan's ears perked at the mention of his name. "Aye," he answered. "The vessel?"

"Exactly," Tanager nodded, reaching his car, which was parked down a side lane behind the Mongrel, its front tires on the curb and its back end hanging precariously in the street. "We need to be prepared to head out as soon as Cepheus and I retrieve Lucene." To Fatima, he advised, "You should go home. You'll be safer there."

"What home?" Fatima snorted, unwilling to be dismissed. "I've been led to believe that I no longer have one."

Tanager looked surprised. "What do you mean? What happened?"

"The Royals happened," Ivan grumbled, still not entirely sure who they were. "They blew up their home and mine." Ivan rested a hand on Fatima's shoulder. "Perhaps you'd be safest with us."

Tanager nodded. "But, be careful. If you see anything suspicious, run. Between the IPP, the military, and the Royals, I have no idea who might try to intercept you." Had Tanager known that nearly all of the IPP members—minus Drake Cummings—had been killed in an explosion in the part of a casino that no one even knew existed, he may have felt a slightly less sense of urgency, but only slight.

"At the very least, I can stand guard," Fatima offered as she, Roman and Ivan headed toward the Mongrel. She followed Ivan's lead, as he motioned for them to climb in the back and strap themselves in.

As Cepheus got in alongside Tanager in their little blue car, a few pedestrians stopped to gape at his appearance. He pulled his hood a little further over his face before they remembered that it was impolite to stare.

"Are you certain you are ready for this, my friend?" Tanager was concerned.

"Yes, it's time I faced them."

"Where are we headed?" Roman asked after they'd driven out of town and were now venturing down several overgrown and isolated streets in the middle of nowhere.

"To a preserve..." Ivan began.

"Never mind, don't say it aloud," Roman admonished, hastily. "Can't be sure who's listening."

Under normal circumstances, Fatima would have assumed it was part of Roman's delusions. But now, there was a possibility that he was right.

Ivan continued down one path after another, moving further and further from civilization. Roman wasn't even sure some of where Ivan was driving was technically roads, but the Mongrel seemed to pass over the terrain with ease. It may have been his imagination, but he could have sworn the truck was adjusting in height and width so that its body remained just above any water and tall grass, and slipped easily between cypress trees.

"We're here," Ivan finally said as he managed to park his vehicle at the center of the marsh where they now sat. He reached under his seat and pulled out knee-high rubber hip boots. "Check under your seats. You've got some, too."

Sure enough, under each seat was a pair of one-size-fits-all boots.

"Why do you have so many of these in your car," Fatima wanted to know.

"Used to run eco-tourism trips some time ago," he explained.

"Really?" Fatima was surprised. "You've been my neighbor practically forever. How did I not know this?"

"There's lots ye don't know about me," he answered seriously. Opening the driver's seat door, he hung one foot out at a time as he slipped them into the boots before sloshing his way, calf-deep in water, toward the back. "There's just one problem about our current situation," he said.

"Only one?" Fatima chortled.

"What's the problem," Roman asked.

"These Royals, whoever they may be, blew up me lab. We'll have to get by with the tools I've got here." He opened the double doors where Roman and Fatima were stationed. They'd unfastened their seat belts and were already hastily pulling on spare boots that they'd found under the seats. It was a choice between those and flippers, and the boots seemed more appropriate.

"Anything else we can use to help us?" Roman inquired.

"Well, I've got this 3-D printed micro car repair kit that might be useful."

Cepheus and Tanager drove toward the docks. "I was just here," Tanager lamented.

"Was it my fault? Did you have to come after me because of an episode?" Cepheus felt ashamed.

"Not exactly. Er…do you remember having an episode?"

"I remember not being myself, and then something bringing me back. Perhaps if I had not gone away, you would have found her sooner."

"I'm certain it would have made no difference. After all, it was you who located her, and I don't have your powers of reception," Tanager offered, graciously.

Once they arrived, Tanager stopped their vehicle. He and Cepheus jumped out not bothering to confirm that it was in park or that the engine had been turned off.

The two headed toward the abandoned warehouse at the end of the marina. "When I heard the Royals, they hadn't located Lucene yet." Tanager continued, "I can't say what happened between the time I left and now, but I know for certain that I wouldn't have been equipped to face them without your help."

Cepheus detected movement, and signaled Tanager to be quiet. On the building's ground level, demolished soot and stone lay all around them along with broken wooden beams and debris. A single lightbulb cast a dim shadow over the area, doing little to help with visibility. The warehouse appeared empty this time around. Cepheus paused for a moment to listen.

"You might want to try the roof," a voice called from beneath the docks. Odessa swam up to one of the nearby pilings. "But you didn't hear it from me."

"Thank you," Tanager seemed surprised at her continued support, given her resolve to never interfere.

"Don't thank me," Odessa called before swimming off. "I don't want to see Earth destroyed. It's my home, too." With that, she made a swan-like dive and vanished beneath the water.

Tanager turned to find Cepheus already scaling the walls of the warehouse like a brown anole. He realized that he'd have to find another way up. Running back inside, he scoured the ground floor until he found an old stairwell. As quickly as he could, be began the long climb to the roof, cursing the fact that he hadn't spent more time on the treadmill.

Preferring to travel the old-fashioned way, the Royals' vessel sat on the roof in preparation for its launch into space. To the common observer, however, it would not appear to be a spacecraft they witnessed before them, but a rooftop green space. A small green patch of grass protruded from the metal rooftop which, when viewed from a distance, appeared to be no more than an environmentally friendly mound. The irony was not lost on Cepheus, who leapt gracefully from the ledge onto the roof. The irony, of course, was that the Royals would risk destroying all of Earth's natural resources in order to take control.

Hamish sensed his arrival before he saw him. "Cepheus," Hamish said, instinctively aware that the anole had slipped beside him. Hamish stood overlooking the horizon, clad in a three-piece gray suit with a blood-red tie and black patent leather shoes, looking as human as possible. In the back of his mind, Cepheus wondered exactly who they planned to meet, since they were planning their departure from Earth and the garments were completely unsuitable for travel. Were they stopping somewhere along the way?

Just behind him, Sabrina stood, regally decked out in a bright red, sequined dress and heels with long, matching colored fingernails. On her wrist, she wore a large, round watch. "Fredo, you've got two minutes to get here or we leave without you," she screamed into the watch's receiver. "And, you can rot on this mangy planet!"

"Cepheus," she acknowledged, turning her attention to the caped man before her. She pinched his face in her hands to get a closer look. "Finally!" He resisted the urge to snap her fingers, choosing, instead, to gently break his oblong face free from her eagle-like grasp. "But, you're too late to help us now. We already have the girl. You're useless to us."

Hamish opened his mouth to protest, looking at his son, sheepishly.

At that moment, Fredo emerged from the stairwell, dragging Tanager behind him like a rag doll. "Found this in the stairwell," he grunted, tossing Tanager to the ground before crossing his tree-trunk arms in front of him, exposing the talons on each hand.

Animal-like scratch marks were visible across Tanager's neck and face. Cepheus went to rescue his friend, but Hamish stopped him. "You're too late. There's nothing you can do once the poison has reached his heart. Which, by the look of it, already has." Tanager's complexion turned a sallow yellow as the veins in his neck gradually became an intense blue. His eyes began to glaze over.

"What are you?" Sabrina asked the crumpled man on the ground, "An Earth-loving Peace-Keeper?" Then, her eyes grew wide in recognition. "Wait! Don't tell me this is Tanager, the other famous foundling responsible for training the precious Data Collectors? Some leader you are… were." She spat on the ground beside him. "Fredo, let's go," she weighted her foot alongside the green patch and reached her hand down as if to grab a handful of grass. Instead, her fingers wrapped around a lever. She lifted back the hatch and began to descend into the craft with Tanager's assailant at her heels like an overgrown puppy. "Finish this, Hamish," she commanded, "or I will."

"You have to let Lucene go," Cepheus told his father, calmly, as soon as his mother and Fredo had gone. He fought back all emotions and came from a hollow space where feelings refused to live.

"I'm afraid it's not entirely up to me, son. You know as well as I do that I'm just a figurehead and that neither of us have the power that Sabrina seems to think we do. We answer to a higher source, and that source thinks that that girl is very important to us."

Cepheus nodded for a moment, gazing off into the distance. He wasn't planning his next move, he was tuning in. It was then that he realized Lucene was already on board and they were ready to depart.

"Then, you leave me no choice," Cepheus grabbed his father by the collar with both hands and attempted to hoist him off the roof and into the water below. His father fell haphazardly over the ledge before his instincts kicked in, and he caught himself on the wall with suction-like hands, his feet scrambling to kick off his shoes, to afford him a better grip. Cepheus lost no time. He deftly climbed into the ship's hatch, setting the lift to descend at full speed once inside, anticipating another battle below. He knew his father would survive the fall but hadn't expected him to recover so quickly. Unfortunately for him, he didn't have it in his heart to kill, even now. Equally unfortunate is that his parents had no such qualms.

As expected, Fredo pulled him from the lift before it touched the floor. With a tremendous swing of his arm, the bodyguard tossed Cepheus violently into a metal wall, recoiled his arm and moved to strike a second time. Cepheus dragged himself to his feet, sidestepping the attack, and planted a blow to the side of the salamander's absurdly large head. Fredo barely flinched. He swung his battering ram arm widely, knocking Cepheus to the ground. His target's head slammed against the wall for a second time. Using what little training he could remember, Cepheus swept his leg across Fredo's knees, toppling the soldier. The red salamander landed face-first on the ground with his arms in front of him bracing his fall, artfully ending up in what could best be described as the pushup position—a skill he'd learned in the military for following up a fall to avoid broken knees and ankles. Fredo leapt to his feet with a triumphant smile in time to see that Cepheus was gone; he'd already made his way to the bridge. "Lucene, where are you?" he called, now close enough to be within earshot.

There was a muffled cry down the hall. He followed it, finding Lucene still strapped to a gurney and Sabrina pressing her hands across her mouth to stifle her scream. Even with limited mobility, Lucene had one remaining option. She bit...hard. Sabrina let out a scream. "You little..." Her poison-tipped fingernails descended as she prepared to lash Lucene's throat. Cepheus grabbed her arm and dislocated it in one move. Sabrina wailed in pain and paused to relocate it as Fredo grabbed Cepheus from behind in a bear hug. As Cepheus struggled, he pushed his feet off the gurney, which toppled sideways, taking a strapped in Lucene with it. The side of her face hit the cool surface of the floor sending pain shooting through her skull. There she remained, lying sideways, hanging painfully off the gurney from the shackles that bound her to it. Fredo's grip across Cepheus's chest grew tighter and the wiry man struggled to breathe. His knees weakened as he became increasingly lightheaded. Fredo tossed the man back and forth, his legs flopping like a fish out of water, making it impossible for him to even kick his assailant in self-defense. Cepheus finally stopped struggling, both to catch his breath and to hopefully gain his freedom.

Suddenly, Fredo stopped, loosening his grip on Cepheus, who fell in a heap to the floor, gratefully swallowing the air around him. A trickle of blood dribbled from Fredo's mouth as he landed with thud on top of Cepheus. Once again, Cepheus, his frail-looking frame beaten, had gotten the wind knocked out of him. He squirmed out from under the massive Fredo. It was only then that he noticed an oversized fingernail protruding from Fredo's back. Hamish, in full reptilian form, stood solemnly at the beast's feet, sucking at his bloody finger, his suit tattered around him as his tail swung in agitation from side to side.

"What have you done?" Sabrina clasped her injured arm. "What have you done!" She fell to her knees, sobbing over Fredo's body.

Hamish stepped around them, removing a key from his jacket pocket and unlatching the shackles from Lucene's arms, legs and chest. He helped her slowly to her feet, trying not to bleed on her. She held onto his arm for support. Cepheus struggled to his feet and rushed to her side, eyeing his father questioningly.

"I'm sorry, my son. I was angry and felt betrayed when you left us. But what we did to you..." he said looking into Cepheus's yellow eyes and seeing a man perpetually stuck between the transformation of being half human and half lizard, one demolished by the loss of his family. "There is no excuse for what we did to you."

"You idiot!" screamed Sabrina, still sobbing over her lost Fredo. She raised her good arm and barked into her watch. "Emergency backup needed immediately, no restraint! I repeat—"

Hamish grabbed Sabrina's arm with one hand. He wrapped the other around her neck and shoved her into the wall. "Hush, my darling." To Cepheus, he admonished. "Best to go now, my son."

Cepheus bowed his head slightly, and guided Lucene back to the lift. He heard a loud choking noise, followed by silence. Hamish was saying something to those on the other end of receiver, something to the effect of, "False alarm, stand down." But he couldn't be sure. He didn't look back.

At the surface, Lucene spotted the tall blue figure of a woman with yarn-like hair standing over Tanager's body. "No!" she cried, breaking free from Cepheus's grasp and running over to kneel beside Tanager.

"He appears to be dead," Morphinae pronounced, without feeling. Having grown tired of his male and butterfly forms, Morphinae had now transmuted into a female figure.

"You are the blue butterfly Mr. Sparks talked about." Lucene wiped back tears. It was a statement, not a question.

"Yes," Morphinae cocked her head to one side, curiously.

"Can you save him?" Lucene asked.

"Perhaps." Morphinae regarded Tanager as if weighing the possibility. "But I don't understand why you need me."

"Will you help us?" Cepheus knelt on one knee and wrapped a protective arm around Lucene. "She's not ready yet, and I'm not powerful enough."

"I can only retain balance, and balance here appears to have been restored."

"The way you restored balance when you saved a young boy's life once? A boy who would come to not deserve it," Lucene spouted angrily, her eyes red from tears. Morphinae was taken aback and felt a pang of something. What was it? Guilt?

"Be careful," Cepheus warned. But Lucene could not be silenced.

"A boy whose influence led to thousands of people being killed, and a world that is now in danger of being destroyed, repurposed and repopulated out of greed. That same boy whose actions inevitably led to a very well-meaning and kind man lying dead at your feet. If you do not save this man, you have upset the balance. The universe needs more of the loving kindness that this man has to offer."

The gnawing in Morphinae's stomach grew stronger. It was a rare feeling, indeed. Morphinae relented, leaning over Tanager's stiff body, she touched a hand to his heart. His body jumped as if receiving a jolt from a defibrillator and returned to stillness. Morphinae tried again. Once again, his body jumped, but nothing more.

"We are too late," Cepheus mourned. He began twitching as his eyes began to roll back into his head.

"No, no, no," Lucene commanded. "Stay with me, Cepheus. You have to help me." He hugged her shoulders tighter and nodded, pulling himself back into the present. "I refuse to believe that we are too late," Lucene touched a hand to Tanager's heart. "Once more, please."

"Okay." Morphinae obliged, putting her hand on top of Lucene's. Instinctively, Cepheus did the same. "Come back to us," Lucene implored. She felt energy flow through her arms like a gentle wave of water, magnified by the combined intensions and energy of those around her. The branch-like strands of lightning that decorated her arms began to glow.

Tanager gasped for breath and color flooded his face. His chest heaved as he sucked in oxygen. Without thinking, Lucene grabbed his hand in hers, and held on tightly. Tanager turned his gaze toward hers and joked, "Well, she certainly is a charmer, isn't she?"

"Oh no," Lucene sniffed back, playing along. "I don't practice magic, only science." She leaned over and pressed her forehead to his for a moment before catching herself and backing away.

Tanager raised his gaze toward Morphinae. "Thank you, my friend."

"You don't need to thank me," Morphinae responded, coldly. "I am here only to restore and maintain balance, nothing more. I don't have any friends."

"Understood," Tanager acquiesced. "But should your position on such things change in the near future, we are here for you and indebted to you."

Morphinae nodded awkwardly, before rising up into the air as if attached to strings. Suddenly, her wings unfolded as she transformed herself into a little blue butterfly and fluttered away.

Cepheus helped Tanager to his feet. "We must go, quickly." The three helped each other to the stairwell as if they were a house of cards, each one holding the other up. They made a less-than quick descent, but finally reached the docks.

"You three look worse than a dried-up horseshoe crab on the beach after mating season." Odessa wrapped her arms around one of the dock's pilings, and swished her tail back and forth playfully, enjoying the show.

"Wonderful, I'm being insulted by a talking ship's figurehead," Lucene retorted. Just one month prior, she might have been taken aback by Odessa's mermaid-like appearance. But little surprised her these days.

"We might owe Odessa our gratitude for sending reinforcements," Tanager responded gracefully. The three moved as quickly as a water turtle toward their car.

"You mean, Morphinae? Nah, I had nothing to do with that." Odessa swam along beside them. "My job is only to report my findings to the Vitruvians. What they do with that information is entirely up to them."

"Of course," Tanager acknowledged, but did not stop.

"If you're heading out now," Odessa offered. "I might suggest an alternate form of transportation."

The three stopped. "What do you mean?" Cepheus asked quietly.

"You three are already a spectacle. Driving around in an easily identifiable car with angry Royals and the people they betrayed nipping at your heels might not be the way to go."

"What do you suggest?" Cepheus leaned in quietly, ignoring Odessa's obvious attempt to flash her breasts at him for attention. She did a few backstrokes, with her upper torso glistening under a strategically placed dock light.

"You might consider traveling by sea instead of land. I can't help you, of course, that would be interfering. However, if you happen to follow me without my knowing, well that cannot be helped, now can it?"

"How is it that you know where we're going?" Tanager asked, suspiciously.

"I know everything," she winked at him. "For example, if you happen to take that boat over there..." She motioned toward the dilapidated fishing boat that used to belong to Mr. Sparks, which was now wrapped in police tape. "How can I stop you? It doesn't appear to be in use at the moment. Cops have gone home for the evening, and I don't expect them to be back until first light."

Tanager lengthened his frame, standing tall with renewed energy. "Excellent." Then he turned to Cepheus and Lucene, still wearing his ridiculous fishing outfit. "Do either of you know how to sail a boat?"

"I can manage," Lucene acknowledged. "What say we follow the mermaid without her knowing it."

Odessa splashed beside them, annoyed. "I'm not a mermaid," she complained, letting out a sigh. "Off I go, unaware."

Hamish stepped over his wife's body, and then Fredo's with a surprising lack of feeling. He would figure out an excuse and how to dispose of the bodies later. For now, he knew it was time to leave.

Suddenly, something grabbed his ankle. He looked down to see Fredo staring up at him with wide black eyes. Hamish was just about to take his other heel and drive it into the salamander's face.

"Wait," Fredo gasped. "My Sovereign."

Hamish paused. It was the first time Fredo had addressed him as such, where he felt he actually meant it. It sounded almost like...respect.

"What do you have to say to me?" Hamish's tired face dropped into a deeper grimace.

"I understand if you want to kill me,"

"Well, then we agree on something," he lifted his foot.

"The baby," he gasped, coughing up blood.

"What baby?" Hamish's eyes suddenly grew wide. "You mean... Sabrina is...was...pregnant?"

"Yes," Fredo whispered.

Hamish turned to look at his wife's lifeless body on the floor.

"How is it that you knew this before me?" Terror crossed the salamander's face.

"It's not my baby, is it?" He pressed his heel into Fredo's throat. "Is… it?" *That explained Sabrina's urgency to make a baby,* Hamish thought to himself. *It was just a cover.*

"No," Fredo choked, defeated. He knew there was no chance of saving the child now–his child. It was his first and only feeling of humanity, and an emotion that felt like sorrow crept into his soul.

Hamish's first instinct was to leave them both—and the baby—to die. His thoughts returned to Cepheus. She had taken him from them. It was her fault. Now, there were no heirs to take his place. *Unless...*

Hamish picked up the receiver again. "Disregard previous orders," he feigned panic. "Send medical and military aid immediately! My dear Sabrina and I have just been attacked. So has my Royal guard. "

He leaned over Fredo's body. "Now," he grit his teeth. "If you want me to let you live, you need to hurt me enough to be convincing. Go ahead, take a swipe at me."

Fredo, his blood, spilling out over the floor and beginning to lose consciousness, obeyed, raising an arm up weakly. Hamish had to lean in so Fredo could reach. The salamander took a large swipe across Hamish's face. The Royal let out a yelp as blood trickled from his left eye.

Backup could be heard from the space craft's upper level as aid rushed to descend to their station. Moments before they arrived, Hamish gave one last order to Fredo, "You are never to speak of this incident—ever again."

CHAPTER 29
THE GRAND ESCAPE
NOW. FIVE YEARS AFTER THE ASSEMBLY.

"This is the end of the line," Odessa called. "I can't take you any further. But I suspect you know the way from here."

They docked their boat at the water's edge with little concern about securing it and climbed onto a narrow stretch of sandy shore not much wider than three feet before being engulfed by towering tupelo trees.

"Thank you, Odessa," Tanager's voice was warm and grateful.

"Didn't do it for you," she replied as she swam away. "This is my home, too."

Cepheus sniffed the air momentarily. "This way," he instructed. Tanager and Lucene struggled to keep up with Cepheus as he seemed to move his body in putty-like fashion, wiggling between low-lying overgrown foliage. It was when he reached the freshwater swamp and began nimbly dancing across cypress knees and clinging to trees without ever actually sticking a toe in the water, that his two followers stopped to assess their situation. Cepheus disappeared soon after.

It was then that they heard low voices in the distance.

"Hang on, I've got ye covered," Ivan suddenly appeared, sloshing through the water carrying two additional sets of hip boots and a caving helmet. "Put these on. I've got cottonmouths in here."

Tanager obeyed but looked confused.

"Venomous snakes," Lucene explained, putting on the lit helmet before also accepting the boots. "You don't need to be poisoned twice in one day."

"It's just up a ways." Ivan motioned.

After suiting up and following Ivan's lead, it wasn't long before the Mongrel was in view, floating effortlessly above the water. It was what lay beyond it that caused Lucene to suck in her breath. Her helmet light caught a glimpse of something protruding from the center of the swamp. It was a tall, moss-covered dome with branches sticking out of it from all directions. It blended with its surroundings with the exception of its placement. Somehow, she recognized what it was.

At that moment, the branches moved as a hatch at the top opened and Cepheus climbed out. There was little surprise on Lucene's part that he had found his way inside the craft with such speed. "Quickly, my friend," he called to Ivan.

Ivan sloshed on as fast as possible, artfully grabbing tree limbs attached to the outside of the space craft and making his way to the top. He was not as nimble as his taller, more slender friend, but it was clear he was comfortable climbing. He followed Cepheus down the hatch, inside.

"It isn't much," Tanager apologized, turning to Lucene from their watery, ground-level view, "but it is more modern than what you on Earth are used to—a bit more space and a few more comforts. Plus, we have the option of being in hibernation for at least part of the trip."

"And, how long did you say this trip would be?" Lucene asked, standing knee-deep in water.

"If Ivan was successful in creating a virtual engine to link to our actual engine, then we may be able to make it home in half the time it took us to get here, about six months."

"This is a lot to take in," Lucene was pale.

"It may provide solace to know that if your current space agency attempted the same trip, it would take them approximately 115 years to reach our planet, given their present technology."

"A little solace." Lucene agreed.

Tanager touched her shoulder, and that familiar, comforting energy flowed through her. "I understand your feelings. Unfortunately, you are not safe here. We are your best option for survival."

"And if I hate it there, can I come back?"

"I wish I could make that promise, but I cannot guarantee we have the resources to do so, not without risking more lives and spending an enormous amount of money to do it." He was empathetic to the deep, conflicting emotions that Lucene was feeling: sadness, doubt, fear, excitement and hope all rolled into one. "You haven't been alive here for some time now. You've been hiding for years without knowing why. What I can promise you is that the quality of life, your life, will be better with us. If we can safely get you home."

"You keep saying 'home' as if it's mine. But this is the only home I've ever known."

"And how has this home treated you?"

"Well, I have my friends: Fatima, and Ivan and Isabella." Tanager cringed at the mention of Isabella, though he wasn't sure why.

"Hey! Over here," Fatima waved from the side of the craft. Her large frame looked mouse-size by comparison. Roman was beside her and reached to steady her as she threatened to lose her footing.

At that moment, a helicopter could be heard in the distance.

"I don't mean to alarm ye," Ivan popped his head out from the top of the craft. "But, that's nah good." He was referring, of course, to the helicopter, which undoubtedly carried armed military personnel. "They don't take too kindly to aliens randomly stopping by and blowing houses up!" The irony of a team of soldiers waging war at the loss of members of the Intergalactic Peace Project was lost on them as the explosion, suspiciously, did not reach the news. "Best if we talk inside," he climbed to the top of the craft. "Roman, can you help Fatima climb aboard, and then the others?"

Roman, who had slipped back into a quiet funk of depression mixed with shame, found renewed energy at the thought of possible redemption, and of being useful. He offered his arm to Fatima. "May I?" he asked, sheepishly. Fatima gently took his arm, a funny scene given that they were sloshing in murky water and not about to waltz on a marble dance floor, as his gesture suggested. She began to climb the side of the craft and was more agile than Ivan had anticipated. "Jest go fer the handles that look like rounded branches. They are secure to hold onto and step on," he offered. Roman held his hand at Fatima's back, and once realizing she was a nimble climber, began to follow her.

"I used to use the rock-climbing wall at my gym all the time, back in the day," Fatima called to Roman, proudly.

"I can see that. Good going," Roman forced a smile.

"Shall we?" Tanager suggested, lifting an upturned hand toward the craft as an invitation. "This isn't a trap. You don't have to go with us if you don't want to."

"I know," Lucene looked into his eyes. She knew he wasn't lying to her. "You go first."

"But," Tanager was well versed in old customs that called for the male allowing the woman to take the lead.

"You almost died today, Tanager," Lucene reasoned. "Even with left-over sedatives in my system, I maintain that I could sooner catch you if you lose footing than the other way around."

Tanager hated to admit that she was right. "I will follow your suggestion, not because I am unable, but because time is of the essence."

Lucene giggled.

"What is funny?" Tanager asked.

"'Time is of the essence,'" she laughed. "The only slang you know from this side of the planet is nearly a century old."

"Really? They don't say that anymore?" He glanced over his shoulder as he climbed.

"Hardly ever," she assured him.

The entrance to the vessel was centrally located, planting the group, who had now formed a small circle around the ladder leading upward, right at the main control room. Fatima, Roman and Lucene looked around in wonder. Thick bucket seats with harnesses, four on each side of the craft, lined the walls facing outward. It almost appeared as if a human-sized suit were built into each one, just waiting to wrap around anyone who sat in them. Two had steering panels in front of them, while the others had an assortment of navigational gear. Additional display panels lined the walls above and below them, all within reach, even when seated. While the chairs faced light green metal walls at present, uneven paneling suggested that they opened up to reveal windows to the outside world. Ivan and Cepheus wasted no time. They had to finish testing the system, with Cepheus taking a seat at one of the controls and Ivan disappearing through a hatch in the floor leading to the engine room. Moments later, he and Cepheus were communicating over an intercom, barking commands back and forth.

"There is a surprising amount of greenery in here," Roman noticed. Hanging from the walls were a variety of air plants and vines.

"Yes, we find it helps keep us calm, even during stressful situations," Tanager answered. "They also help purify the air, and many of them are actually edible." To demonstrate, Tanager plucked a white flower from one of the vines and took a bite. He then picked a second one and offered it to Roman, who took a hesitant bite. Roman wrinkled his forehead in anticipation, but then relaxed. "Tastes like honey," he proclaimed, rather happily.

From where they stood, they could see the corners of four slightly partitioned-off rooms, with only one having a visible door. One corner appeared to be the sleep station; another, a small efficiency kitchen and dining station; the third, a fitness and bath area; and the fourth seemed more hidden away.

"What's through there?" Lucene asked.

"It's our study and meditation room," Tanager answered. "Let me show you."

"This is like the coolest tiny house I've ever seen!" Fatima nodded excitedly. "With real estate being at a premium, I think it's fabulous that you made space for a meditation room."

"While we use it ourselves, we constructed this one with Lucene in mind. It is the vessel's largest room, aside from the engine room." Tanager motioned for them to follow. He slid a wood-covered metal door to one side. Lucene felt herself emotionally pulled inside. It had the faint smell of wild ferns with soft lighting and a domed ceiling that gave the illusion of a sunrise or sunset, depending on what time of day you were in the room. "It adjusts the scene throughout the day so that we feel less confined on our journey. It also helps us keep ourselves adjusted to the days as we travel."

"Extraordinary," was all that Roman could say.

There were deep couches forming a circle, sitting on top of a soft grass floor. The walls were forest-like, giving the illusion of being outside, surrounded by trees, with the sounds of birds and cicadas in the distance. In one corner, a small waterfall began trickling quietly, on cue with people entering the room.

"Wait," Fatima pursed her lips, "don't you have to wear clunky space suits all the time and float around uncomfortably all the way home?"

"We have lightweight emergency suits in the event of unexpected climates or internal malfunctions," Tanager answered. "But for the most part, we are able to maintain an internal gravitational system and oxygen supply much like Earth. We are typically able to wear whatever garb we choose."

Lucene, who had been looking up at their internal sky the entire time, mesmerized, said to Tanager, "Okay."

"Okay, what?" Fatima asked.

"Okay," Lucene looked at Tanager, and he heard her thoughts. *I will go with you.* His facial expression was one of relief.

"I think that means she's agreed to go with them, my darl— Fatima," Roman answered, catching himself before calling her 'darling.' "

"Yeeeeesssss!!!" Ivan could be heard exclaiming from across the vessel.

"While I share in your excitement," Cepheus called back. We must leave now. I can feel them closing in."

Sure enough, from one of his monitors, he could tell the helicopters were getting closer, which meant the trucks and sea crafts could not be far behind. One monitor was also beginning to pick up voices in the distance.

"Gather, quickly," Tanager commanded. The group obeyed, circling up, once again in the center of the vessel.

"We have enough provisions and space for whomever wishes to join us, but you have to decide now."

"Fatima," Lucene implored. "You should come with us. They can fix your heart."

Fatima's eyes welled up. "I can't go," she almost whispered. "My family is here."

"But the military and police will never leave you alone," Roman warned. "It won't be long before they discover your connection to the Data Collectors, and they will arrest you for interrogation."

"But I have nothing to hide," Fatima answered. "Once they return home, what secrets will I have?"

"Unfortunately, they might not see it that way," Roman warned.

"Er," Ivan stepped up. "That's if they find us. I happen to own this land, all 125 acres of this preserve, and another 200 acres on the other coast. I can help Fatima hide, if necessary, and reunite her with her family at a time when it is safe."

Roman felt a faint pang of possessive jealousy, but pushed it aside as he knew he had no right to it. "I'm not sure it will ever be safe, but I support your decision, if you decide to stay."

"Thank you," Fatima answered. "I will stay. And, I trust Ivan to keep us safe."

Ivan's face lit up with the pride of a small child who just rode his bike without training wheels. "Aye, I will do me best."

"I assume that means that you will be staying, Ivan?"

"Aye," he nodded, simultaneously with Cepheus as if they'd already had this discussion. "I have technology that needs to get in the right hands in order for us to have a chance at surviving in this multiverse. We are far too behind."

"Yes," Cepheus acknowledged. "And remember, it came from you."

"Aye," Ivan nodded. "I feel funny taking credit, but I understand why."

"And you?" Cepheus put a hand on Roman's shoulder.

"You know I would give anything to come with you," Roman teared up. "For me to heal and maybe even to find Far someday."

"You are welcome with us, friend," Tanager reassured him.

"We need to git," Ivan announced. He gave Cepheus a bear hug, which caught him off guard for a moment, before he wrapped his arms gently around his friend in a return hug. "Ye too, bring it in," he hugged Tanager, who awkwardly hugged him back. It wasn't as if they didn't show physical affection on his planet, he just wasn't used to Earthlings being forthright about it. He followed suit, giving Roman a hesitant half-hug, half pat on the back. Roman did the same in return.

"You're okay," Ivan decided. Roman smiled weakly back.

"Thanks," he replied.

Finally, it was Lucene's turn. "I will miss you, Ivan." Lucene's eyes welled up as she embraced him fiercely.

"Right back atcha," he answered, circling his arms around her small frame.

Fatima followed Ivan's lead, hugging each of them, one at a time. At last, Fatima faced Lucene, both now crying feverishly. "I'm gonna miss you so much," Fatima cried. "You're my best friend. And, I should tell you I still think you're crazy for going, but I understand why you would. Just be careful, okay?"

"I'm going to miss you, too," Lucene wailed back as the two women wrapped arms around one another. "But I will be okay, and I will find a way to contact you. I promise." Fatima released her and nodded.

Suddenly, Lucene gasped. "Oh my god, what about Bagheera?"

"Safely in the Mongrel, don't worry. I wouldn't let anything happen to our fur baby." Lucene let out a sigh of relief.

"We need to go now," Ivan took Fatima's arm gently. The four remaining crew members watched as Ivan and Fatima climbed up the stairs and through the hatch. "Cepheus, I'll signal ye when we're a safe distance from the vessel."

Cepheus nodded. "Stay safe, my friend."

Once they had exited, Tanager moved quickly. "Please take your seats and pull on the lever to the right of your chair. Don't be alarmed. The suits embedded in the seats will wrap around you and conform to your shape. The harnesses should then trigger automatically." He motioned to them to take specific seats on the opposite side of the control room, with he and Cepheus on the other. The two obeyed, and Lucene and Roman were soon strapped in place and feeling as if layered in bubble wrap with a thin window to the world where oxygen flowed. "I won't have time to give further instructions until we're out of this atmosphere," he yelled so they could hear him through the suits, testing their harnesses to make sure they were secure. "For now, treat this like a roller coaster in one of your theme parks. Keep your head upright, your back against the seat and hold onto your armrests. It will be a bit intense at first, but the pressure won't last long. Once we are clear, I will give the okay to get up and move around."

With that, he strapped in beside Cepheus and turned on their audio gear. He took a deep breath.

"Are you ready, my friend?" Cepheus asked.

"Ready," Tanager confirmed.

As if on cue, a message came in over the ship's speakers. It was Ivan "We're clear! Go now and be safe!"

Ivan and Fatima were now in the Mongrel, traveling through the swamps at a low speed to avoid detection. "Even if they can see us," Ivan reasoned, "they won't have the vehicles to get into these close spaces." He maneuvered the vehicle through the swamp grass and trees, and Fatima could have sworn that the Mongrel was ever so slightly changing shape to match the terrain.

"Where are we headed?" Fatima asked.

"Well, once we exit the preserve, we need to ditch this vehicle. Which reminds me,"

"Yes?"

"Is yer car reliable enough to get us to the other coast?"

"My car? Of course, it is. You of all people should know since you're the only one who repairs it, silly," Fatima laughed. "But I don't see how it can help us. We left it back at Roman's apartment, remember?"

"Well, I have a wee confession."

"Ivan, what did you do?"

"Well, ye remember at dinner when I showed ye that little present I made for you?"

"Not at all," Fatima confessed.

Ivan let out a sigh. "Never mind. Can ye reach inside yer bag and fetch me yer phone?"

"Sure." Fatima reached behind the seat to retrieve it.

"Now, just follow my instructions exactly." Ivan began rambling off demands that began with, "Hit the numbers 1 and 5 while pressing and releasing the power button 3 times," and eventually ended with, "Okay, now re-start your phone and tell me what you see."

Fatima restarted the phone. "I see a map with a little blue dot on it. The dot is moving."

"Where is the dot headed?"

"Looks like it's headed toward the highway, not too far from here."

"Yeeeessss!" Ivan shouted. "Keep an eye on where that little dot goes, okay?"

"Sure. Why?"

"We've summoned yer car. With any luck, it will meet us somewhere where we can easily retrieve it."

"Seriously?" Fatima looked over Ivan, wearing his torn jeans, faded shirt and hip boots. He hadn't even bothered to take his spelunking helmet off. "You are full of surprises, Ivan."

"Aye," he smiled. "Looks can be deceiving. Didn't know I was such a great catch, didja?"

"So, I'm discovering." Fatima sank back into her seat. "Did you say we were going to some land you own on the other coast? Do you really have over 200 acres?"

"Well, it's more like 700 acres, in total." Fatima's eyes grew wide. "Figured I'd buy as much land as I could while I had the money to help prevent more developments and habitat loss."

Moments later, she heard a shuffling from the back of the Mongrel. Bagheera had long ago found his way out of the carpetbag and had been curled up in corner in the back of the vehicle. "I suppose we should pick up a sandbox somewhere soon."

The realization hit them both at the same time. "Too late," Ivan wrinkled his nose as the scent of cat urine wafted to the front of the vehicle.

"I suppose we had that coming," Fatima reasoned. "Stuffing the poor boy in the bag."

"Aye," Ivan's entire faced cringed at the aroma.

Just then, Fatima's phone began to ring. "It's my mom. She must have heard the news and is freaking out."

"Don't answer, and don't touch anything on yer phone, not until we git yer car."

"But she'll just keep calling. And, if I don't answer, soon, *everybody* in my family will be on high alert."

"As soon as we get to the other coast, we'll find a way to get a message to them. I promise."

Fatima nodded, and sank back in her seat.

CHAPTER 30
DRAKE AND MORPHINAE
TUESDAY EVENING. ONE DAY AFTER THE ESCAPE.

Things hadn't gone at all the way Drake had planned. He sat in a club chair in the corner of his hotel suite staring at the floor. A wall-mounted reading light hung over him as he poured himself yet another scotch. It was well after midnight, but he was still dressed in a dark blue suit with a matching tie and a crisp white shirt underneath from an earlier meeting with the Royals. He hadn't even bothered to take his leather shoes off. Behind him, the waves of the Gulf could be heard crashing against the shore, along with the faint sound of beachcombers drunkenly singing "Margaritaville" and laughing as if no one had thought of that before.

At 12:09 a.m., there was a knock at the balcony door. Not the front door, mind you, but the balcony door which was three stories from the ground level.

"Come in, Morphinae," Drake grunted.

Morphinae entered the room quietly via the balcony, and Drake did not even question how he managed the lock. This evening, Morphinae was dressed exactly as he remembered him as a boy: torn jeans, a blue crochet face and with button eyes.

"Do you know why I am here?" Morphinae asked, standing over the man.

"Why don't you tell me," Drake answered roughly, downing the last of his drink and looking up at Morphinae.

"I upset the balance when I saved you that day. I have to make amends."

"Killing me won't make amends," Drake laughed nervously. "Do you know how many people have been murdered or injured as a result of my actions?"

"Three thousand two hundred forty-eight," Morphinae said, blinking.

Drake hung his head. "Can you grant a man one final drink before taking your revenge?"

"Of course," Morphinae granted. "But I am only a Balance-Keeper. I seek no revenge."

"Right," Drake poured himself as tall a serving as his glass would allow and held up the bottle to offer Morphinae some as well. Morphinae shook his head, declining.

"If it helps, I will not kill you in any worse manner than the fate you would have suffered if you had drowned. In fact, if you prefer, I can drown you in the—"

"It's probably best if you don't tell me, and make it as quick as possible," Drake held up his hand.

"Of course. I will try not to make you suffer."

"Why are you being so nice to me?" Drake questioned. "I don't deserve it."

"I hold myself accountable as much as I do you," Morphinae explained. "After all, had I not saved you, none of this would have happened. I feel as much remorse as I sense that you too now feel."

"I tried not to care." Drake gulped his scotch. "I tried to be the hard businessman and consummate professional. But then I turned over the nicest employee, nicest woman, I have ever known to some of the worst people on the planet, strike that, in the universe." He brushed away what looked like a tear. "And in the end, I couldn't go with them, couldn't bear to watch what they might do to her. I am weak."

Morphinae nodded. "I understand. I am not prone to feelings, and yet I was moved too when she was almost taken by the Royals."

"Almost?" Drake gazed a drunken head up, with interest.

"Yes, the Peace-Keepers from TARA intervened just in time."

"Excellent. That's great," Drake answered, thinking. "Where is Lucene now?"

"She's with them, why does it matter?" Morphinae nodded, noting that Drake was nearly finished with his drink.

"Well, you are technically a Vitruvian, are you not?"

"Yes, but I am also a Balance-Keeper. We follow a special law. You know this."

"But, wouldn't it help you make amends for your actions if you and I worked together to bring Lucene to your people instead? I mean, who better to ensure that her powers are used in the fairest way possible than the Virtruvians? The bleeding-heart Peace-Keepers on Erde wouldn't even begin to know what do with that kind of power."

Morphinae's face dropped into a frown of disappointment and Drake could almost see a shadow pass before his eyes. He set down his empty glass. With no further hesitation, Morphinae spoke, "It's time."

CHAPTER 31

ISABELLA AND THE LONGHORN BEETLE

TUESDAY EVENING. ONE DAY AFTER THE ESCAPE.

"How are you feeling, Reverend Isabella?" the nurse asked the woman lying in a hospital bed in a private room. She was no longer being given oxygen, but an IV was still supplying her with necessary pain killers and healing remedies. Unlike the stark white walls and rampant smell of disinfectant in the old style of hospital care, this one had nature-green walls and sea-colored tile floors. The faint blend of cinnamon and clove could be detected in the air. There was a light drumming music playing over a portable sound system in the room.

"I am well, my dear Miranda." Isabella smiled at the young nurse. She thought to tell her she needn't call her "Reverend" outside of ceremony but decided against it. Knowing Miranda, she would continue to do so anyway, and chastise herself every time she forgot. So, she remained silent. "I was shot the other evening in my own sanctuary, and yet I am still alive to talk about it. I'm guessing the Universe isn't finished with me just yet."

Miranda smiled at her minister in gratitude. "Of course, it isn't," she answered. "We need you." With that, the nurse left, and Isabella settled in for a short meditation. As she began drifting off to the quiet sounds of the drums, she noticed something.

"Well, hello there," she glanced at the large yellow and black Longhorn beetle that was resting calmly on her arm. "I didn't see you until just now. A beetle is a sign of transformation. Will you now be taking me to a different realm?" The beetle gave no response, but instead of brushing it away, Isabella simply laid back and smiled, sinking into her meditation.

Oh, no, Odessa thought happily as she calmly rested on the older woman's arm. *You are right about transformation. But your friend Miranda is also correct. This world needs you.* She smiled in anticipation. *We are going to have so much fun together!*

BREACH OF CONTRACT

THE DATA COLLECTORS BOOK TWO

SECTION ONE

"Empathy is a heart thing, not a head thing. Everyone is affected by their environment, their internal and external ones. You put someone under stress, and they will react. It's that simple."

DRAMATIS PERSONAE

Roman Aurelius: Human male (Section 0), wavy black hair, green eyes, tall and slender.

The Baby: Born of Sabrina and Fredo (Section 3), now adopted by Hamish.

Cepheus Baruch: Royal male (Section 1, Section 3), stringy gray hair, yellow eyes, tall and lanky, shapeshifter (lizard/human).

Hysechia: Unknown origin, female (Section 1), striped black and white tiger with golden eyes, human-like features.

Petrichor Baruch: Erde-born female (Section 1), the late wife of Cepheus, long auburn hair, pale blue eyes.

Tanager Blackletter: Erde-born male (Section 1), curly blonde hair, brown eyes, average height and weight.

Bryce Cushing: Human male (Section 0), brown hair, blue eyes, medium height and build.

Clusaladek: Erde-Born male (Section 1), tall and thin, blonde hair, pale blue-gray eyes.

Commander Royce: Erde-born female (Section 1), walnut and gray hair, coal colored eyes, small and athletic frame with deep wrinkles.

Constable Melokuhle: Erie-born male (Section 1), bulky with dark skin, curly black hair and brown eyes.

Dallen: Vitruvian male (Section 2), non-shapeshifter, gold hair and blue eyes, tall with strong build.

Dr. Archibald Ennis: Human male (Section 0), bald, brown eyes, tall and thin.

Far: Macar-born male (Unsectioned by the IPP), blonde hair and green eyes, pale and thin.

Fatima Fortunata: Human female (Section 0), purple hair, gray eyes, short and Rubenesque.

Iris: Undetermined gender and species (Section 1), covered in black armor with little discernible features, average height and weight.

Lucene (Lucy) Jones: Earth-born female (Section 0), blonde or brown hair, hazel eyes, average height and weight, toned form.

Kunz Malaya: Trappist male (Section 5), monarch, blue/gray fur and matching eyes, small, bulky stature, shapeshifter (wolf/human-like).

Jasper Set: Demon male (Section 4), red eyes, bald, thin legs and barrel-like body, small wings.

Reverend Isabella Simone: Female (Section 0), spiritual advisor, white hair, violet eyes, tall and thin.

Bagheera: Male cat (Section 0), black short hair with yellow eyes, very handsome.

Fredo: Lesser Royal male (Section 3), red body and black eyes, large and thick, salamander-like with no noticeable shapeshifting abilities.

Hamish: Royal male (Section 3), brown hair and gold eyes, short and slightly overweight, shapeshifter (lizard/human-like).

Ivan (the Tinkerer): Human male (Section 0), red hair and green eyes, medium height and stocky.

Mallory: Erde-born male (Section 1), heavyset, dark hair with multi-colored eyes.

Mateo: Unknown origin (Section 1), short and heavy, little hair, long tail.

Marzipan: Unknown origin, male (Section 1), firefly and ladybug-like features, multicolored with wings.

Morphinae: Vitruvian (Section 2), shapeshifter (gender, species, coloring), Balance-Keeper, often prefers doll-like and butterfly-like forms.

Moksha: Royal (Section 3) assassin, black hair, yellow eyes, petite but athletic build.

Neroni: Erde-born female (Section 1), olive complexion, slightly heavyset, red-green hair and brown eyes.

Odessa: Vitruvian (Section 2), shapeshifter (gender, species, coloring), prefers mermaid-like form the most.

Renenet: Unknown origin, female (Section 5), red / brown fur and fire agate eyes, tall and broad, bulky stature, shapeshifter (lion / human-like).

Sabrina: Royal woman (Section 3), black hair and yellow eyes, tall with average shape, shapeshifter (lizard / human-like form).

Director Sutton: Human male (Section 0), light brown hair and hazel eyes, average height and slightly overweight.

Townspeople: Humans from other planets, Earth and beyond, includes Abe, Marcy, Mrs. Glazor and others.

Wilah: Erde-born female doctor (Section 1), tiny and thin, translucent glow.

Xeni: Unknown origin (Section 1), pink eyes, heart-shaped face, blue-black hair.

LOCALES / SPECIAL GROUPS

Achel: Main province on Erde.

The Assembly: Intergalactic gathering for the Intergalactic Peace Project (IPP).

Balance-Keepers: Special interest group in Section 2, Vitruvians. Will intervene to ensure all forces remain in balance.

Data Collectors: Specialized team from Section 1, collecting data on Earth to save species.

The Crosses: Preservation sites and residential homes on Erde comprised of four quadrants.

Erde: Planet in Section 1 known for setting up preserves to rescue and protect humans.

Erdelings: Species from the Erde planet in Section 1.

Global Environmental Agency (GEA): Earth organization for environmental concerns.

Intergalactic Peace Project (IPP): Formed to create and maintain peace among intergalactic species.

International Registry of Alien Residency (IRAR): Created by the United Commonwealth (UC) to record and track aliens living on Earth.

The Null: Crustacean-like species in Section 4 trying to destroy the universe in order to serve the mighty Segue.

Peace-Keepers: Nickname given to all inhabitants of Section 2, in particular, those living on Erde.

Planetary Defense League (PDL): Government entity on Erde for protection.

Royals: Nickname given to all inhabitants of Section 3, no specific planet-base, nomads.

Section 0: Earth and planets from common and neighboring galaxies.

Section 1: Erde and planets from common and neighboring galaxies.

Section 2: Vitruvia and planets from common and neighboring galaxies.

Section 3: Royal landscape and planets from common and neighboring galaxies. Galaxy boundaries change regularly.

Section 4: Home of the Null. Limited communication with neighboring species, located in a section of the universe with multiple black holes.

Section 5: Silva and Trappist solar system as well as planets from common and nearby galaxies.

Singulari: The Null people in Section 4. They bow to their God, Segue and refer to themselves as Singulari (which represents their religion).

United Commonwealth (UC): Earth subdivision of the IPP to keep and maintain peace.

Universal Marketplace: A place where money and goods are exchanged.

Terrestrial Academy of Research and Awareness (TARA): A major university in Achel where the Data Collectors are trained.

Vitruvia: Planet in Section 2 known for its renegade band of Balance-Keepers.

Vitruvians: Species from the Vitruvia planet in Section 2.

PRELUDE: THE STATE OF THE ASSEMBLY

Tanager Blackletter and Cepheus Baruch, professors of the Terrestrial Academy of Research and Awareness (TARA), are returning to Erde's home planet in Section 1. They are accompanied by Lucene Jones and Roman Aurelius from Earth after the Intergalactic Peace Project (IPP) banned all of Section 1, along with the Vitruvians in Section 2, and the Royals in Section 3, for allegedly breaking the rules of the IPP.

TARA sent their Data Collectors to Earth in an effort to save the human race. Still, their initiative fell under the scrutiny of some ill-intentioned people who would rather auction off Earth to the highest bidder. The Data Collectors are genetically modified Erdelings with an exceptional capacity for empathy and the ability to transmit information through thoughts and emotions instead of words.

Lucene Jones is an anomaly in that she was born of two Data Collectors and appears to have these skills naturally. The Royals discovered her through their surveillance of The Data Collectors and want her for the powers she could potentially bring to their military brigade. Meanwhile, the Vitruvians claim non-interference and yet, have made questionable alliances with a former member of the United Commonwealth (UC) on

Earth, Drake Cushing, in the hopes that they would assume control of Earth and hand-deliver Lucene. Their intentions for her were never made clear.

Now, there is to be a New Assembly, one where Erdelings and Vitruvians must form an uneasy alliance.

CHAPTER 1
CHATROOM
SEPTEMBER. FOUR MONTHS BEFORE THE NEW ASSEMBLY.

Kudzu48: Maker197 - private chat - urgent

Maker197: I am here.

Kudzu48: Authorities closing in on all inventors. Not safe. FortuneGirl getting questioned regularly. Having more health incidents as a result.

Maker197: How can I help?

Kudzu48: Prototype vessel nearly complete. Need coordinates.

Maker197: When will you launch?

Kudzu48: One week.

Maker197: Will send support to meet you at a mid-range locale and guide you the rest of the way.

Kudzu48: May need medical.

Maker197: I understand. Coordinates incoming…

Cepheus sent Ivan the coordinates to a way station halfway between Earth and Erde, then quickly logged off and cleared the channel.

"You look worried," Tanager observed. "What happened?" Tanager paused, holding steady the chisel he was using to hand engrave a piece of wood he'd shaped into a mermaid. He sat at the other end of

Cepheus's desk, on a small stool surrounded by a floor covered in blueprints, contraptions and possibly a bit of last night's dinner that had fallen there. Tanager had to shuffle the mess aside to fit in his stool.

Where Tanager's office was well-organized and minimalist, Cepheus's space was a mess, and chronically filled wall-to-wall and ceiling-to-floor with model prototypes for flying machines, automatic vegetable growers, manuals and hand tools. Tanager had simply come in to ask to borrow a chisel when he noticed his friend online and suspected he was in contact with Ivan on Earth. He decided to stick around and find out.

"The government is continuing to harass Ivan and Fatima. It is my fault." Cepheus hung his head solemnly, his eyes starting to roll back in his head as he half fell into a desk chair.

"No, no, no." Tanager leapt to his feet and grabbed his friend by the shoulders, dropping the carving and chisel on the desk in the process. "Get a hold of yourself. I can't deal with two of you having an episode on the same day."

Cepheus looked up, suddenly amused. "Get a hold of yourself," he smirked, revealing his vampire-like teeth. "*I can't deal*… You have spent much time with Lucene of late, haven't you?"

Tanager's face turned crimson. "People on the preserves talk that way, too, you know."

"I see," Cepheus acknowledged. The distraction was enough to keep him grounded.

"Tell me, how is the Earth government continuing to question Ivan and Fatima your fault?" Tanager released his friend's arms and returned to his stool, picking up the fallen carving to resume his work.

"It was I who reached out to Ivan in the first place. And…"

"Yes?"

"I gave him a bit of technology—"

"What kind of technology?"

"It was to help Earth catch up. They are still so far behind in their technological development. But it was enough to cause suspicion."

"What did you tell him?"

"You know the Vessel?"

"Of course, I know the Vessel. We recently spent seven months on the

Vessel—a month more than we planned thanks to the Royals tracking us." Agitated, Tanager accidentally cut too deeply into the wood and the edge of the mermaid's tail chipped off. He flung the tool and carving back onto the desk in disgust. "Sorry," Tanager apologized. "Please continue."

Cepheus shut down his personal computer, stashing it in a desk drawer, the only one that wasn't chock full of papers and trinkets that he thought he might someday have a use for. He had to push it down a little to get the drawer to close.

"Well...that."

"You showed him how to build his own?"

"Well," Cepheus continued, "not exactly the Vessel. Most of that Ivan figured out himself when we met. But a modified, clean-air transportation system. Ever since he presented his discovery to the Global Environmental Agency, authorities have become more aggressive."

"What will they do?"

"You know the Vessel?"

"Yes," Tanager grew more impatient. "We just covered this."

"That."

"So, he is building a vessel?"

"A slightly smaller one, yes." Tanager was afraid to ask. After a long pause, Cepheus shared, "Actually, it is already built...Ivan and Fatima are coming to Erde."

"Well, you are just lovely," Fatima complimented the lavender growing outside their home, checking the soil to make sure the outdoor sprinklers did their job the night before.

"Thank ye," Ivan joked, coming up behind her from the walkway and wrapping his arms around her in an embrace. "I just shaved this morning."

"I didn't mean you, silly." She leaned back into his hug.

It had been a year since the Vessel left, carrying Roman and Lucene off to a strange new world with Cepheus and Tanager. Fatima missed her friend dearly but took solace in the fact that Ivan still had a connection with Cepheus so she could check in on Lucene. That, and she continued the meditation practice that Reverend Isabella taught her, and lovingly sent Lucene intentional mental messages each evening. On more than one occasion, she could've sworn she heard her friend whisper back, "Thank you." But that couldn't be, could it?

Life had been as challenging as it was blissful. They hid out on a remote preserve that Ivan owned, waiting it out for several months until the media coverage and questioning from the military died down. Unfortunately, as soon as Ivan resurfaced in an attempt to share some of his new ecofriendly travel knowledge with like-minded people, he was singled out—along with several other scientists and futurists—as either being of alien origin or negotiating with alien beings. In truth, it was the usual scenario, fear of the unknown and fear of intellectuals spreading bad ideas to the masses. *Or,* as Ivan reasoned, *fear of spreading good ideas to the masses and empowering individuals and small businesses.* This, he reasoned, was more likely the case.

At the same time, Fatima's heart condition worsened following Lucene's departure. Ivan chalked it up to Fatima missing her best friend and did his best to be supportive. But deep down, they both suspected it was something more. Lucene had special gifts, that much Fatima knew, but how they affected Fatima's health? Well, on that, she was still unclear.

The one positive in all this is that seven months of seclusion had a way of bringing people together, and Fatima and Ivan's relationship blossomed into something more than friendship only months after their arrival.

"I sent a wee message to Cepheus jest now," he told her.

"Was he there?"

"Aye. I told him of our plans."

Fatima began tearing up. "I can't visit my family first, can I?"

"I don't think ye should. It jest is nah safe." He hugged her harder. "But we can git a message to them once we arrive."

"In six months!" Fatima protested.

"Let's see how the travel goes. Perhaps even a month sooner… And, on the plus side, you'll git to see Lucene again. Won't that be nice?"

"Yes," Fatima nodded, wiping away a tear. "That, it will."

CHAPTER 2
THE NULL AND JASPER
26 YEARS AGO. JUST AFTER THE CONTRACT WAS SIGNED.

The Null rarely spoke, and when they did, it typically sounded like the chirping of a spiny lobster trying to scare a predator when its resistance was low. The Null were always on the defensive, and when they were not, the group communicated in a cacophony of hissing, popping and volcano-like explosions. There was a loose hierarchy, but often one was always overtaking another. They thrived best under chaos.

An individual black hole dweller of the Null collective was unlike anything one would find anywhere else in the multiverse. A cross between an opaque sand flea and a jellyfish, they slithered across their world in a slow pace, with their frail crustacean-like spines the only thing that would help one hold its shape.

There were only two reasons for a black hole dweller to bother connecting with another black hole dweller. The first would be merely for survival. When their gelatinous bodies were connected, they moved in a blanket-like wave across their world, their venomous underbelly killing anything in its path. The second would be to destroy. The Null believed that their god, Segue, wanted this entire universe destroyed so that it could begin anew, like entropy and destruction, before order and regeneration. The collective in our universe also believed that other Null throughout the multiverse had been more successful than they had and that Segue must be angry with them. Therefore, the one agreement the black hole dwellers held dear was that they needed to destroy more quickly.

Jasper Set knew this, and he loved it. Jasper was convinced that no other demon in the multiverse loved chaos as much as he. The Null people were the epitome of chaos, of anger and fear, and of destruction. In a weird twist, he loved the Null as one might love their own parents. In fact, he was convinced that he was born out of their collective consciousness.

However, unlike his jellylike crustacean family, he was spawned from their imagination and what little they knew of the worlds they had already swallowed, in what was their ever-expanding black hole that they called "home." He had distinctly human features, if you could imagine a man walking around with skin that was so translucent that you could see all of his organs underneath. His eyes were red. His nose, toucan-like in length and form. His ears were long and pointed and rotated back and forth like that of a Great Dane following a sound. His chin was sharp enough to shuck a raw oyster. His chest was large and as round as a barrel, but his hips and legs were thin. It was difficult to imagine how he could move on those legs without the steady use of his small, bat-like wings for balance and propulsion. And yet, he flew through the air effortlessly. But when he stood, on the other hand, his back pitched forward over his feet as if balancing a plate on a stick.

Jasper traveled through the universe causing chaos for his own amusement. But he was getting bored. It was all getting too easy. Convincing the Null to leave the Royals alone until further instruction at the behest of Segue, of whom he represented; getting sentient life forms on planets to destroy each other in bloody wars in the name of religion; even causing stars to die out or grow larger, killing off planets through ice and fire. It was all him. The universe was his sandbox. But what was he to do now?

Jasper floated from galaxy to galaxy, checking in on worlds and occasionally giving one a nudge and batting them around a bit. Sometimes, he was so bored that he'd possess a human or two, but that was rare, and he often grew tired of that after only a few weeks. From his best estimation, there were only two things missing from his existence that could bring him "happiness," by his definition. One, to pierce the universe and cross the planes to the multiverse, perhaps meeting more of himself so they could compare notes. And two, to find a worthy adversary that would pose a challenge for him. Thanks to his recent contract with the Royals, he now had one such opponent in mind.

CHAPTER 3
THE CONTRACT
26 YEARS AGO. BEFORE THE ORIGINAL ASSEMBLY.

"Can't you do something about this?" Sabrina barked at Hamish, overlooking what remained of a once-lush and vibrant planet. They hadn't loved it enough to give it a proper name, settling on the Training Grounds because here was where most lesser Royals were shipped to for military discipline.

Sabrina and Hamish were the sovereigns assigned to the Training Grounds and were given a small palace at the highest part of the now-desert landscape, where they could oversee much of their domain. The palace, by contrast, was filled with ornate furnishings from across the universe, exotic animals, and every manner of fruit tree and plant that they had gathered on their travels. With little regard for how these exotics would adapt in this varied climate, parts of the palace appeared almost jungle-like, with servants on constant alert so that invasive flora would not overtake the rest, and that violent fauna would not render another species extinct—possibly killing a few of the lesser Royals in the process. For all of Sabrina's complaints about the ignorance of humans about such matters, she wasn't much better.

"My dear," Hamish answered in his usual tired voice, "we have a visitor."

The visitor didn't wait to be properly escorted into the room. Instead, he swirled around Sabrina like a slow-moving tornado, eyeing her from every angle with excited curiosity.

"What are you doing? Why aren't you kneeling before your sovereign?

Jasper Set flew in so closely that his large nose poked the edge of hers. He laughed as she pulled away in disgust. "I don't kneel," he laughed. "To be clear. You ans-s-s-s-wer to me and not the other way around." He elongated the "s" with a snake-like tongue.

Sabrina was about to protest when Hamish interrupted, "My dear, this is the demon known as Jasper Set. He is of the Null people. You asked for him, remember?"

Sabrina spun in a circle one more time as she tried to follow Jasper's twirling, becoming dizzy, as her long cream-colored, Victorianesque gown tangled around her legs. It was only when Hamish reached out to grab her elbow, preventing her from tumbling over, that Jasper stopped whirling. Her eyes grew yellow.

"Careful, princes-s-s-s," Jasper warned.

Sabrina didn't like snakes any more than she liked the impertinence of someone confusing her for a princess versus the sovereign that she was. Jasper knew this, and it amused him to no end.

Sabrina's anger was eclipsed by another emotion, one that Hamish hadn't recalled ever seeing on her face before and was taken aback—fear. "Yes, of course," she acknowledged. She couldn't bring herself to bow, but Sabrina did manage to tip her head awkwardly.

Jasper crossed his arms in front of him, his right elbow resting on his lower hand while his fingers curled around his mouth as if stifling a laugh. He was hoping for more of a challenge, but quickly realized that this was not going to be the case.

"Tell me, princes-s-s-s. What is the reason that you summoned me?" Jasper already knew the answer, but he enjoyed watching others squirm in discomfort.

"Yes, well," Sabrina motioned toward Hamish's throne at the helm of the room, even though it pained her to do so. The Royals typically bowed to no one in this universe, but she knew this demon's power and the violent nature of the Null. Unlike her people, while violent, they had a sense of self-preservation. But the Null had no concern over minor incidents such as death. In fact, it was a great honor for them to be able to die for their Segue.

She clapped her hands and a team of servants arrived with food and libation. They began laying them out on a long table opposite the thrones as a second band of servants carried in a series of pedestals which they quickly arranged, equidistant from one another, around the table.

Jasper smiled, folding his wings between his shoulder blades and hobbling on what resembled two long egret legs, slightly thicker, but not nearly supportive enough for his large torso. When he reached the thrones he grinned widely, looking directly into Sabrina's eyes as he plopped his rear-end into the cushion of her throne. She sucked in a breath, watching as he slung one leg over the arm of the chair. "Nice," he complimented. "Is this real gold?" He felt the arms of the throne. Jasper didn't need to ask. He knew the answer.

Sabrina glared at Hamish with eyes that were clearly fighting back a rare combination of rage, fear and helplessness. She folded her arms in front of her, her own fingernails digging into her biceps until they almost started to bleed.

Hamish cleared his throat, coming to his wife's rescue. "If I may, my esteemed counselor," he knelt on one knee before Jasper, bringing his eyes in direct line with Jasper's crotch, another facet of this entire scene that made Jasper's insides boil over with mirth. At that moment, he was convinced that he was the most content of all the demons in the multiverse.

Fredo watched from the doorway in obvious disgust, his wetsuit-like uniform bulging in the arms and legs as his muscles twitched involuntarily. Why Sovereign Sabrina chose this weakling of lesser Royal to join the ranks with her many years ago, he would never understand. The Training Grounds deserved a stronger male lead, such as—. He rubbed his large forehead and suppressed the thought. It wasn't his place.

"As you know," Hamish spoke quietly, "our Training Grounds are no longer adequate for our species. The climate is shifting, our population is growing, and resources are meager. We must move again."

"Oh," Jasper answered with interest. "Where to?"

"We were thinking, of, well, Earth."

"Earth?" Jasper tapped a pointed finger on his forehead. "There's something off about that equation." He snapped his fingers. "I know what it is! Earth already *has* a prime sentient species living on it, humans. Hmmm, if only there were something we could do."

Sabrina found her tongue. "We deserve that planet, not them." Hamish shot her a warning glance, and she, for once, fell silent.

"I see, and where do you suggest we place these humans?"

At the bottom of the deepest ocean, where the lot can drown, Sabrina thought. Jasper smiled at her. She turned a ghostly white as she realized that he could read her thoughts.

"It is not our concern what you do with them," Hamish responded as if he were talking about moving a piece of furniture instead of an entire species of living, breathing people. "We just need the space. You understand."

"I *do* understand," Jasper sat upright, planting his feet on the floor and tapping his fingertips together. "Up, up, up." He motioned for Hamish to stand, which he did with some effort. Jasper paused for what seemed like an eternity. "But you have a Royal army that, when combined with other military reserves from Section 3, could easily take over one measly little planet. What do you need me for?" He leaned an elbow on the arm of the throne, resting his chin on his upturned palm.

Hamish cleared his throat. "Well, there is the little matter of the Null."

"My family?" Jasper feigned surprise. "Whatever do you mean?" Sabrina began grinding her teeth in annoyance. *Really? You really don't know what he means?* Jasper paused once again, turning a deliberate head in Sabrina's direction. "I was talking to him," he pointed at Hamish. Sabrina, once again, fell silent. It was hard enough for her to keep from running at the mouth; silencing her thoughts was near impossible.

Hamish played along. "You know, the Null seek to destroy this entire universe—the multiverse, even—if such a thing truly exists. We also know that you have the Null wrapped around your finger."

"Yes, well." Jasper rolled his eyes in fake humility, gesturing with his hands in the air as if he didn't understand it either. "My parents love me; what can I say?"

"Perhaps, your Excellence, you might consider, uh, re-directing your family, to another part of the universe for a while—a diversion of sorts."

"And thwart their holy duty of destroying the universe on behalf of the great Segue?" Jasper Set appeared shocked.

"Come now, Jasper," Hamish let his guard down and addressed Jasper informally. Jasper didn't seem to care. He was enjoying this. "You don't really believe that there's a god that wants to recycle the multiverse, do you?"

"Don't I, though?" Jasper paused before standing and only with the aid of his wings. After an eternity, he answered, "You're right, I don't." He began pacing the room, pausing at the long table filled with an assortment of meats and fish and a few leafy greens and fruit. He spotted a roach crawling across one of the pieces of meat and settled for that instead, popping it in his mouth and crunching heartily. He glanced up and smiled at Fredo happily. Fredo grimaced, but not in disgust. He also noticed the roach and had been eyeing it for himself. Jasper took a long nail and picked at his tooth to dislodge a bit of roach leg that was caught between them. "And, what's in it for me?"

"There's the girl?" Hamish offered, hesitantly.

Jasper tilted his head sideways, confused. *What girl?* He thought to himself. Sabrina noticed his expression and realized that he really didn't know. "The Earth-born Data Collector, of course." She smiled for the first time, feeling as if she had the upper hand.

"Uh, Data—what's that, now?"

Somehow, the Erdelings, Data Collectors and the entirety of Section 1 life forms had fallen outside the scope of his radar. *How was that possible?* "Surely, you've heard of the Peace-Keepers in Section 1?"

"The Peace... Bleh." He wrinkled his lips as if he just tasted something bitter. "Awful word, can't even bring myself to say it."

"Well, the Peace-Keepers," Sabrina emphasized the word, "are trying to save Earth. And, they're getting in our way." She went on to fill Jasper in on the abridged version of those living in Section 1 and the special, empathic powers of the genetically modified Data Collectors, including the story of how Lucene was a natural-born empath of two Data Collectors. Jasper listened with growing fascination. Sabrina ended with a promise of delivering said natural-born empath to him in exchange for Jasper re-directing the Null so that the Royals were no longer in the Null's impending firing line.

When she was finished, Jasper smiled. "But why, dear S-s-s-sabrina, do you think I need you to retrieve the girl? I'm all-powerful. I can just pluck her out of the air myself."

"We weren't sure of it until just this moment," Hamish put an arm around Sabrina's waist, and for once, she did not recoil from his touch. "You can try, but the fact that you didn't even know of either species' existence can only mean one thing."

"And what is that?" Jasper Set's expression grew dark. Hamish, Sabrina and their attendants all looked out the window at the storm clouds that had suddenly rolled in over their landscape.

"You can't touch goodness. They may not be perfect, mind you, but they're just good enough that you can't reach them."

"Well," Jasper frowned. "We shall s-s-s-see about that." With that, he rolled himself into a swirling tornado once more before vanishing beneath their very eyes.

"Now what?" Sabrina barked.

"Now," Hamish grinned out of the corner of his mouth, "we wait."

For the next three months, Jasper Set didn't sleep. He managed to determine roughly the universal coordinates for where Section 1 resided by a process of elimination. He sailed through Section 0, felt ill at the "mostly good" Section 2, gleefully paused to cause more havoc in Section 3 and took a week touring Section 5, which had annoying pockets of impenetrable provinces which he vowed to return to once he'd gotten Section 1 all sorted out. During this time, he avoided his own stomping grounds—Section 4. The Null, he decided, would never understand. But every time he thought he'd reached Erde's atmosphere, he seemed to be transported back to where he started that day. He'd even gone so far as to seek out Data Collectors living on Earth since, he reasoned, they might be more susceptible to influence while outside of their normal environment. The most Jasper had been able to do was occasionally plant a bad headache in the brains of those he suspected were Data Collectors, mixing up their memories temporarily. But they were only the ones who'd grown fearful and had since rejected their former career, preferring to blend in as humans for the remainder of their days. He couldn't permanently injure them, or influence their behavior, or even kill them. It wasn't as if he particularly wanted to, mind you. He was just irritated that he was unable to.

Finally, he returned to the Training Grounds, demanding an impromptu meeting with the sovereigns. Hamish and Sabrina were more than happy to oblige.

"I've decided to help you," Jasper oozed graciousness.

"Well, no surprise—" Sabrina began before Hamish overtook the conversation. It was rare for him to display these moments of strength, usually spurred out of desperation for their situation as they were becoming increasingly more desperate.

"Thank you, Your Eminence," Hamish answered. Not really sure exactly what to call Jasper, his title for the demon changed regularly. Jasper found this funny and enjoyed the variety of ways in which Hamish demonstrated deference.

"I took the liberty of drawing up a little contract," Jasper flew over to the long meeting table, knocking a chair out of the way and rolling a scroll across the top of the rectangular tabletop. Hamish and Sabrina eyed the contract cautiously. "I think you will find that I'm being very generous," he gushed. "What I'm offering is 30 years of protection from the Null rolling over the Royals—to include your nomadic adventures to varied sections of the universe, providing that I can reach you, of course."

"Of course," Hamish acknowledged. It was implied that Section 1 was one of those areas where Jasper's powers could not reach.

"In return," Jasper tapped a long finger on the contract for emphasis. "I want the girl you spoke about. When can she be delivered?"

"I'm afraid that will take some time," Hamish cleared his throat, uncomfortably.

"Why?" Jasper was legitimately curious. "You offered her. Do you have the all-powerful genetic freak for me, or not?"

"It's just that," Sabrina came to her husband's aid, "we haven't been able to locate her…exactly."

"What?!" Jasper's temper was triggered once again as he smashed the table in two, the contract spilling to the floor. He grabbed it and ripped it in half. Once again, it grew dark outside as a sudden storm began rolling in.

"We can get her for you," Hamish assured him. "We just need a little time."

"How much time?" Jasper demanded.

"We don't know exactly," Hamish answered honestly, "but certainly before thirty years is up."

Jasper Set paused before a bellowing laugh erupted from the depths of his being. "You expect me to honor the entirety of your contract without having any collateral in advance, and no promise of when the result might be delivered?"

"What choice do you have?" Sabrina questioned, curtly.

"What choice?" Jasper swooped in, so that his face was right overtop of Sabrina's. Unlike last time, she was prepared and didn't move. She didn't even blink. She just stared back at him with the same intense gaze. "I could have the Null kill you and your entire race right now. Holy Segue, I could even do it myself!"

"But where is the fun in that?" Sabrina asked, coyly. She may have been temperamental and sometimes scattered, but she wasn't stupid. She'd taken the last few months to research everything she could about Jasper Set, and now she knew his weaknesses. "What we're offering you," she glanced at Hamish, who eyed her with the closest resemblance that he could to admiration, "is a challenge. You can't reach Section 1 and the Peace-Keepers yourself, and we're offering to hand deliver their most powerful to you. How you deal with her once we do, is on you…unless you feel your power wouldn't be strong enough even if we, quite literally, gave her to you?"

Jasper Set took the bait. "I agree to your terms." He waved his hand and the table reconnected itself, the contract now once again intact, overtop of it. "And, for my own self-interest, I'm going to throw in a bonus."

"What kind of bonus?" Sabrina wanted to know.

"I can toy with the Earth, sending hurricanes and tsunamis, but nothing I do seems to dramatically impact these precious Peace—" He choked back the word when he felt bile in his throat. "—these precious Data Collectors," he complained. "But," he paused for emphasis, "if I give *you* the power, Sovereign," he gestured to Sabrina, "That might be different."

Her eyes lit up, greedily. "What sort of power?" she wanted to know.

"For the next thirty years, I give you the power to control the weather on Earth. I can't touch the Erdelings who reside there, but I'm a demon. I wonder if you can. Either way," he concluded. "I am certain that you will have fun trying."

CHAPTER 4
THE BABY
AUGUST. FIVE MONTHS BEFORE THE NEW ASSEMBLY.

"Permission to approach, my Sovereign." Fredo bowed at the door of Hamish's private office. He was half the size of his formidable former self, and the black uniform that clung to him wrinkled to match his shriveled skin, a product of losing too much weight too quickly after Hamish had nearly stabbed him to death almost one year ago.

"Granted," Hamish announced, tiredly, staring out the window of the now-barren landscape. They would need to find a new home soon; that much was certain. He was hoping it would be Earth, but now he feared that this option would be unlikely.

Fredo had come to terms with his sovereign's angry outburst, the one that caused Hamish to lash out and kill his wife, Sabrina, after no longer being able to bear witness to her cruelty, at least when it came to their son, Cepheus. In truth, he was filled with a new respect for his sovereign—Hamish was finally being true to himself and exhibited a strength Fredo did not expect. What surprised Fredo even more, however, was that Hamish had allowed the baby to live, particularly since it wasn't his own.

"The baby is awake," Fredo informed him quietly, remembering that he was not permitted to say the Child's name out loud, nor refer to its gender.

"And is it in good health?" Hamish asked, without turning his gaze.

Fredo paused. "It is."

"If there is nothing else, I permit you to leave now." The baby was not his. That much he knew. He suspected it was a product of an encounter between Fredo and Sabrina, but he refused to entertain the thought past that point. All he knew was that in his estimation, Sabrina had been responsible for driving their son away from them. And now, this Child, a child that was not born out of any relationship between he and his late wife, was a suitable replacement for what he had once lost. He would not make the same mistakes that she had made.

"There is one other matter, my Sovereign..." Fredo began to step forward so that his shoulder was in line with Hamish's, before Hamish shot him a warning glance. The red salamander retreated three paces back.

"What is it?" Hamish grew impatient.

"Moksha has been found."

"Alive?"

"Unfortunately, yes."

"Well, retrieve the traitor so that she can face execution."

"It is more complicated than that," Fredo explained cautiously.

"You are boring me, Fredo. Say what it is you have come to say."

"She is living on one of the preserves on Erde."

Hamish could feel his eyes beginning to water, and he fought to keep from transitioning into his warrior-like lizard state. He took a deep breath, something he wouldn't have attempted even one month ago, but it seemed to help him maintain control. "And they accepted her?"

"It would seem so, my Sovereign."

"Can we get her back?"

"It is not advisable to do so." Fredo's shoulders sunk forward in an uncharacteristically sullen way.

"Why not?"

"We have calculated the risk, and if we are to petition to re-enter as members of the Intergalactic Peace Project, attacking the Peace-Keepers to retrieve a soldier may be...misconstrued."

"Why? We are simply rescuing one of our own. Is not a rescue mission a worthy cause of war?"

"Not in this case, my Sovereign." Fredo framed his words carefully. "It seems that she has claimed sanctuary."

"Sanctuary!" Hamish's eyes and nostrils flared, and his nails began to ooze venom. He raised an arm at Fredo, who backed away, unwilling to fight back.

"Yes, my Sovereign…sanctuary. If we were to attack, it would not be perceived as a rescue mission, but vengeance."

Hamish took another deep breath. "What is our best course of action?"

"We have an unusual suggestion."

Hamish turned and took a seat on his council throne as if he'd suddenly remembered it was his. It was Sabrina's idea to have a throne in every room in the castle, in case they had to be "sovereign-ly" at a moment's notice.

Fredo took to one knee and bowed out of habit. "Get up, you idiot." Hamish barked. It was a grim reminder of Sabrina, one that caused him a mix of emotions. *Perhaps I should do away with bowing,* Hamish thought. *I might even burn all the thrones in the castle one day.* Fredo stood.

"What is the legion's formal proposal?" he finally asked.

"We could send in Far."

"Far? That worthless scrap of an insect? He's so frail he would likely break in half during the journey. I didn't even think he was still alive."

"He is doing better…just well enough. If we could send him to claim sanctuary on the same preserve as Moksha—"

"He could find out what information she's been spouting about us." Hamish reveled at the idea. "And, perhaps collect some data of his own." He laughed at his own joke. *The Data Collectors,* he thought, *are wasting time doing things the wrong way. Leading with the heart, not the head, can only end in destruction.*

"We've also been endowing him with some…misinformation," Fredo continued. "If they think he is a refugee, they will trust him."

"How can we be certain he won't turn on us as well?"

"Our methods have come a long way, my Sovereign." Fredo's eyes lit up as if he momentarily remembered his former glory. "We've been steadily programming his thoughts for a year now. I believe he is ready."

Far was a prophesier who escaped from his home planet of Macar when its leaders became too afraid of his power. It was surprising to them, given that he was a waif-like man with pale skin and a soft voice. His skills in fortune-telling and in-body astral travel were unlike anything anyone had seen. He landed on Earth for a while, but the atmosphere was too polluted for his frail form, and he developed cancer. Somehow, he accidentally propelled himself to Section 3 and was promptly arrested by the legion. They would have killed him right away if they didn't think that he could potentially be useful. For that reason, they did what they've never done before...they actually nursed a non-Royal back to health...sort of.

"What happens when he encounters Moksha," Hamish wanted to know. "Won't she become suspicious?"

"She left before his programming began. In fact, I'm certain she would have wanted to take him with her, but he was too weak, and she couldn't wait. If anything, she will be pleased to see him."

"Then make the boy ready."

"Yes, my Sovereign." Fredo awkwardly backed slowly away from Hamish, retreating through the chamber door before pausing.

"Is there something else?"

"I was just wondering, my Sovereign—"

"What is it?" Hamish began grinding his sharp teeth so much that you could hear the crunching.

"The baby—"

"What about the baby?"

"May I...hold it?"

"Absolutely not!" Hamish spat. "I will be along in a moment to feed it."

"Yes, my Sovereign."

CHAPTER 5
THE RETURN TO ERDE
MAY. EIGHT MONTHS BEFORE THE NEW ASSEMBLY.

"How is she?" Tanager asked, concerned, setting the Vessel on autopilot, removing his harness, and standing up for a stretch.

"She is okay. She's resting," Cepheus answered, shaking his head. "We tried to think of everything. If only we'd have had more time to prepare the Vessel before our return."

"Perhaps, but you and I made the journey without incident, and that took us a year. It's only been three months and Lucene is…not adjusting well."

"We were trained for this. She was not," Cepheus answered simply, motioning for Tanager to follow him into the meditation room. "Perhaps we can speak quietly in here."

The doors opened to reveal a mid-day landscape; the dome lights gave the illusion of a forest in the distance, complete with a slow running waterfall and a gentle stream. At the center of the room, Roman occupied one of the couches wearing his usual black jeans and a black t-shirt, now beginning to show signs of wear from constant use. His bare feet dug into the grass beneath them. He sat upright, with a blissful smile on his face and eyes closed in meditation. As soon as he heard the door open, he opened one eye. "Hello, gentleman," he said pleasantly.

"I'm sorry, Roman," Cepheus apologized. "Had we realized you were taking a moment of solitude we would have gone elsewhere."

"No apologies necessary," Roman shifted his weight slowly and stood. "I was about done anyway. And I would have put a note on the door if I required some alone time."

The notes were Lucene's idea. Cepheus and Tanager had no need for this when it was just the two of them traveling. If one entered the room while another was reading, meditating, studying or even pacing in circles for problem-solving purposes, the other just…adjusted. Neither of the men saw it as an intrusion, nor felt the deep need to be alone. For the humans, however, this was not the case, most especially with Lucene. She grew anxious if she went into the space to be alone and someone entered the room without realizing she was there. Roman, while he appreciated the solitude, was not as perturbed by four people sharing a relatively small space. If he didn't like the intrusion, he simply went someplace else. There were four quarters on the ship: the meditation area, the sleep station, the dining area, and the exercise and bathing station. And, if he really wanted an escape, the engine room was enormously large (by comparison), with plenty of little nooks and crevices to curl up and hide away.

But Lucene was hypersensitive, a trait they assumed was related to the fact that she was born of two genetically spliced Data Collectors. They were engineered for empathy, and in Lucene's case, she was born with a boatload of it as a result. Unfortunately, after two months of being on the Vessel, she complained, "I feel like a God-damned sardine in this place!" A meeting around the dining table was held. And, as they ate smoked fish and drank a sweet wine (except for Cepheus, who was the lead on duty at the time—he settled on water), it was decided that they would put a sign on the meditation room door, or any door, for that matter, when absolute privacy was needed. Most often, Lucene would put the sign over her sleep pod, which was odd since no one would disturb someone while sleeping, except in emergencies.

All was better for a short time, but now, in month three, she seemed to be unraveling again.

"Would you gents prefer to speak privately, or can anyone join?" Roman smiled pleasantly. He was not without issue, he realized, having spent the better part of a year obsessing over the Data Collectors so much that he eventually came to believe that he actually *was* from Erde, an alien sent to research relationships among Earthlings. In reality, he was a former anthropology professor who sank into a deep depression at the loss of his love, Far, a man who *was* an alien and left to find a cure for his own life-threatening disease. It had only been two months since Roman had come to his senses, and he vacillated between feelings of excitement at his journey to a new world and grief at his deep loss, and then to hope that he would one day find his beloved again, whole and healed. Recognizing his own fragile feelings, he was naturally sympathetic to those around him and understood that Lucene had seen more than her fair share of trauma.

"Actually, this matter concerns you as well, friend. Please, join us." Tanager answered. The three men took a seat on the circular deep-seated, wood-toned couches. Roman opted to cross his legs under him. Cepheus did the same, while Tanager slouched backward, stretching his legs onto the grass in front, crossing his ankles and arms in front of him as the couch all but swallowed him.

"I suspect that when we realized that one of the Royal ships may have spotted the Vessel near the way station, forcing our diversion from our original course home, we may have...unsettled Lucene," Cepheus offered quietly.

"Well, six months being stuck together in a relatively small space is an adjustment," Roman acknowledged. "Learning that the journey is delayed by an entire month, well, I can understand how that would set off any introvert."

"And how are you adapting to this news?" Tanager asked.

"I'm an odd duck," Roman answered. Tanager took a moment to mouth the words to himself *odd duck,* making a mental note to look it up later. "I was so crazed in *finding* you, and then, in my mind, *becoming* you, that, while a little confining at times, this is the first peace I have experienced in a very long time."

"I'm happy for you, friend," Cepheus touched his arm.

"I have you to thank, Cephi," Roman replied.

Cepheus cringed at Roman's recent use of this affectionate nickname. It reminded him of home, of his late wife and children, and how Petrichor used to call him that. He pushed that memory back into the corners of his mind and locked them away, for now. Recognizing that Roman knew not of the name or the images it conjured, he tried to integrate its new reference in his mind, replacing a bad memory with a good one.

"Are you okay?" Roman stopped suddenly.

"Of course," Cepheus smiled, pulling himself back from sinking. Tanager had noticed it as well and was at the ready in the event an anti-psychotic was needed. As far as mental and emotional stability went, he seemed to be the only balanced member of the crew, a responsibility that he did not take lightly. "So, the meditation I have taught you has been helpful?" Cepheus asked.

"Enormously," Roman placed his hands on his knees, elbows jutting outward.

"What I am having trouble understanding," Tanager interjected, "is why her training isn't helping her. Cepheus, you worked with her as a small child and have been teaching her almost daily since we've been on board. But, instead of becoming calmer, Lucene actually seems more agitated."

"Do you think she needs a break from all the mindfulness training? Maybe bake a pizza, crack open a few beers and chill?" Roman offered, helpfully.

"A break, maybe," Tanager agreed. "I'm afraid we're out of any pizza-like ingredients, and the closest we have to beer is flavored club soda... and, what are we chilling?"

Roman opened his mouth to speak, "Eh, never mind."

"There's a larger concern, I'm afraid," Cepheus spoke in a hushed voice. The two men leaned forward to hear him. "I was communicating with Dr. Ennis."

"Archibald Ennis? The doctor who first tended Lucene as a child, after the lightning strike? Is he still alive?" Tanager was surprised.

"Why would you be surprised? That was 25 years ago. He was a young man at the time. You know that humans live past 40 now, right?"

"Of course, I know that." Tanager uncrossed and re-crossed his arms, sulking a little.

"Wait," Roman interjected. "I remember him from my research. Wasn't he the cardiologist who was also a self-trained medical geneticist...I mean, I don't know about his credentialing, but he definitely did his research."

"The same," Cepheus nodded. "It was Lucene's odd reaction to the lightning strike that got his attention. That was the first of many anomalies he's seen at the hospital. Since then, he's become obsessed with people who should have died but didn't or should be incapacitated from an injury but aren't. The interesting twist is that he wasn't even Lucene's doctor. He was checking on young Fatima who happened to be in the same hospital room."

"How did you come to know Dr. Ennis?" Roman wanted to know.

"Chat room," Cepheus answered. Somehow, his vampire-like, lanky form and deep voice sounded odd saying that.

"For a scholar, you spend an awful lot of time online communicating with people from other planets. First, Ivan, and now, Dr. Ennis." Tanager was perplexed by this.

"I see no problem with this," Cepheus explained. "By the time a book is printed, it is likely out-of-date. But, if I check in with the experts, be it a Makerspace forum where I meet inventors, or a medical specialty group where I connect with Dr. Ennis, I'm learning."

"But, aren't you guys more evolved than Earth? What can you learn from us?" Roman eyed him with confusion. As a former anthropology professor with keen observation skills, sometimes he still missed the obvious. It was as if he had a hyper-focused awareness, but only about specific subject matters.

"We may be technologically advanced as a whole, but I would never be so conceited as to think that we have all the answers nor that another species has nothing of value to add."

"That's very big of you," Roman answered.

Big of you? Another one for Tanager to learn.

"So, what is it that Dr. Ennis told you?" Tanager wanted to know.

"It's not good, I'm afraid." Cepheus let out a deep sigh. "I'm not sure if it's accurate or not. We won't know until we get back home and do further testing."

"What is it?" Tanager twitched.

"You know how we genetically modified the Data Collectors,

including ourselves, to become empathic and be able to transmit messages across long distances without words?"

"Yes," Tanager answered impatiently. "Of course, I know that. I was there. Why are you asking rhetorical questions?"

"Well, we assumed that my being under Watch had to do with mental illness caused by my parents torturing me."

"Of course, it was."

"But what if it wasn't?"

"I don't understand."

"We also assumed that Lucene's behavior was a result of her parents dying when she was a child, being forced into the foster system, not being an Earthling, getting struck by lightning, and almost getting killed…several times."

"Did you hear yourself just now?" Tanager pointed at him for emphasis. "How could those things not be the reason for her current behavior?"

"They may be causing an exaggeration of symptoms, but —"

"But what?"

"What if her trauma…my trauma…were merely triggers for a deeper problem?"

"Such as? What deeper problem?" Tanager looked from Cepheus to Roman and back to Cepheus. Roman merely shrugged but was eager to hear his response. Roman was also wondering why they weren't just thinking at each other since it was their gift. But he then concluded to himself that they were probably speaking for his benefit. Either that or mentally transmitting messages was probably complex and took a lot of energy. He settled on it being a combination of both and thought he might ask them another time.

"According to Dr. Ennis, genetic splicing can backfire, and a traumatic event can trigger the foreign gene to mutate, potentially causing other illnesses, including…mental illness."

"What? No, I don't believe it!" Tanager shook his head feverishly. "By that logic, we should all be under Watch, but I don't have the same symptoms that you and Lucene have exhibited, and I went through the same trauma as you when—" Tanager stopped himself and winced. "I'm sorry, I didn't mean to bring it up."

"It is okay, I understand." Cepheus coughed uncomfortably, stuffing back an emotion.

Tanager was referring, of course, to the time the Royals broke into his home and killed Cepheus's entire family, and nearly killed both he and Tanager as well.

"I'm not saying it is for certain," Cepheus explained. "But it is something we must address with the terrestrial academy when we get home."

"I don't mean to throw a wrench in the works," Roman added. *Wrench in the works. I swear, these humans have a lot of idioms,* Tanager thought. "But I haven't been sliced and diced, but trauma sent me over the edge. How can he be sure it's related to genetic modification?"

"Numerous tests that he began after the assembly," Cepheus answered. "Many Data Collectors sought out Dr. Ennis for medical advice because he was among the few doctors they trusted. He's analyzed hundreds of blood and DNA samples and has recently started to notice some patterns. It may not be the case, but we have to at least consider the possibility that our process is potentially hazardous. It would be unethical not to."

"What about the students at TARA?" Roman asked. "Have any of them exhibited similar behaviors as those Data Collectors on Earth?"

"Good question," Cepheus answered. "I checked in with Dr. Wilah and my lead students, who are assuming our roles while we travel, and they've indicated that only a handful of students are exhibiting questionable behavior following a strange illness. But they assumed it was because they were physically unwell. Those students are currently being observed and are in quarantine until we can be sure that they are not contagious. But, on the whole, Erde is a peaceful planet, so the chances of a traumatic event setting them off are much rarer compared to Earth."

"Which brings us back to Lucene. What do you suggest we do about her current behavior?" Tanager picked at a stray thread on his pant knee nervously. He was worried about her.

"Yes," Lucene called from the entranceway. The men hadn't heard the door to the meditation room open. Lucene stood in her nightclothes, without concern over propriety or if any part of her pajamas were see-through. They weren't, but the top did cling rather tightly.

They just recently left the B-612 way station, scrounging what limited clothing and other supplies that they could. While Cepheus and Tanager had a limited wardrobe on board, the humans did not and procured what they could at the station. There wasn't much. Since the Royals were spotted nearby, TARA couldn't risk sending a relief vessel to bring more clothing and other provisions. They had to make do with what they already had on board and what they found on B-612.

Cepheus and Tanager drew their eyes to the floor, politely. Roman was indifferent. "So," she continued, "what *do* you suggest we do about Lucene's current behavior?"

"Ah, you are awake," Tanager stated the obvious. "How are you feeling?"

"Fine," Lucene crossed her arms in a way that suggested that she was not at all fine. "What does whatever you were talking about have to do with me?"

"I was just explaining a few things I recently learned about us and your parents. Perhaps you should sit down."

For the next month, Lucene's behaviors became increasingly worse. She vacillated between absurd delight, randomly laughing at everyday events out of context with anything remotely amusing, and extreme agitation, particularly if her personal space was surrounded by items she had arranged just so, and then someone unwittingly moved an object, such as a chair or dinner plate, without requesting permission first.

"What are you doing?" Lucene demanded one evening when Tanager took a red spoon out of a kitchen container so he could enjoy an afternoon snack. He looked down to see her sitting at the dining table with scraps of paper strewn all over it, pieces torn in odd shapes with unrecognizable symbols scratched across them. She laid her arms over them and leaned in as if she were a young child protecting her secret diary.

"I was taking a break from studying and thought I might have some leftover butternut porridge." He felt strange having to explain himself.

"Well, that's my fork," she eyeballed it. Tanager paused for a moment before slowly putting it back in its holster. He carefully reached in and pulled out a *blue* spoon that he held up carefully for approval.

"That's fine," she barked, returning her attention to the slips of paper before her. She began brushing them together as if brushing crumbs into a pile before sweeping them up and depositing them into a trash bin. The right side of her face twitched slightly in a tick that had only recently developed, and only showed up when she was particularly anxious.

He stood awkwardly in front of the cooling unit before reaching in to retrieve the leftover porridge, wondering exactly where he was going to eat it since Lucene had taken up the entire dining area with…whatever the hell it was she was working on.

"You can go now," she finally looked up, dismissing him with annoyance.

He had intended to heat up his food before eating it, but now thought better of it. He took the cold container and the approved blue spoon and made his way to the navigation room where Cepheus was finishing up routine checks. He took a seat next to his friend.

Cepheus eyed Tanager's food questioningly, and then nodded. "Lucene?" he asked.

"I'm afraid so," Tanager answered.

"Shall I go talk to her?"

"I don't think it's a good idea. She's got that twitch thing happening."

"Knock, knock," Roman tapped the wall in a jovial manner, even though there were no actual doors separating the navigation room from other areas of the Vessel. It was one central location.

"Yes, Roman. What is it?" Cepheus questioned.

"Any idea what this is?" he held up what once was a tattered fishing hat. The shiny ornamental bait that had been attached to the side was now poking through a hole at the center. It appeared as if someone had taken scissors and cut chunks off the rim. "I found it stuffed in one of the gears under the treadmill."

Tanager let out a sigh. He must have displeased Lucene…again. He had made every attempt to communicate more effectively with her, even suggesting a few "date nights" where he'd planned a special meal in the meditation room, under a starry dome with soft classical music playing. On those nights, Cepheus and Roman made themselves as scarce as possible, Roman spending extra time in the exercise area upping his strength-training routine while Cepheus took his time making the rounds in the engine room, often checking the same equipment two or three times. The plan almost always backfired, however, because there would always be something that set Lucene's mood into one of agitation. One evening, she went as far as to suggest that when they got back to Erde they should "see other people."

"My favorite hat," Tanager took it from Roman who gave him a perplexed look. *Really?* Roman didn't understand how that monstrosity could be anyone's favorite anything, but he felt bad for his friend.

The sound of a loud cackle interrupted the conversation. Lucene stood in the navigation room, barefoot, holding up a torque wrench. "Any idea how this ended up with the utensils?" She continued laughing hysterically.

Roman went to retrieve it from her, but she held it over her head. He wasn't sure whether she was trying to keep him from taking it from her, or if she were threatening to hit him with it. "No, it's mine. I found it."

"You found it in the kitchen?" Cepheus asked calmly. He was trying to connect with her empathically, but all he could sense was a turbulent swirl of emotions, and he couldn't seem to lock in on anything stable.

"Yes, but only after I was done with it in the engine room." Both Cepheus and Tanager exchanged a shared look of alarm.

"What *exactly* were you doing in the engine room?" Tanager made the mistake of gesturing with his hand as he spoke. Lucene took it as an attack and swung the wrench wildly. Roman grabbed her wrist and wrestled it from her fingers.

"Ow," she winced, rubbing her wrists. She stuck her tongue out at Roman, like a small child.

Cepheus didn't wait to witness the remainder of the scene play out. He snatched the tool from Roman and climbed through the passage to the engine room to assess the damage. "Safety measures," he spat at Tanager, who nodded at the cue.

"Can you handle this," Tanager asked Roman.

"Of course," Roman understood. They'd been through this scenario before, although this was the first time Lucene was in the engine room to their knowledge and had potentially put them in danger. Cepheus went to assess the damage, if there was any, while Tanager followed close at his heels in case there were unexpected occurrences such as a fire or a sudden lack of oxygen in the room.

"What are you supposed to handle?" Lucene let out the beginnings of a temper tantrum. "Me?"

Fortunately, this is where Roman's personality shined. He flashed a pearly white smile. "Lucene," he called her name in a sing-song voice, wagging a finger playfully at her as if she were in trouble. "What did you do?"

Lucene suddenly let out an uncontrollable giggle, like a small child, covering her mouth with her hands. Roman continued to smile, waiting patiently for her to calm down. Finally, she whispered, "Nothing," managing to get it out, breathlessly. "Hah! Did you see the look on their faces?!" She tapped Roman lightly on his chest, her eyes wild with glee. "I didn't do anything. I just wanted to see the look on their faces to think that I did."

"That was very naughty of you, Lucene," Roman played along. "But don't you think you've had enough fun for one evening?

Lucene's face dropped. "But I don't want to go to bed yet," she whined.

He wrapped an arm protectively around her. "I know, but I'll be heading to sleep myself after I let the gents in on your little joke. A good night's rest will do us all a world of good."

She grew serious. "Do you think they'll be mad?"

Roman reassured her, "I'm sure it will all be fine." He guided her to the dressing area, politely averting his eyes while he waited for her to privately shower, use the facilities, and change into a gown. While he did so, he sent a message from his watch, and a green light flashed to both Tanager and Cepheus's watch, indicating a perceived "all clear." Tanager and Cepheus continued to check all of the equipment that Lucene could have possibly tampered with, just in case, before returning to the navigation center.

"All done," Roman held out a robe for Lucene when she returned from the shower, once again wearing the same pair of tight-fitting polka dot pajamas. She smiled as she put her arms through the sleeves.

"Why can't Tanager be as nice to me as you?"

"Well, not everyone can be born with my charm and devilish good looks, now can they?" He opened the door to her sleep pod and gently nudged her back, guiding her inside.

"No," she smiled wistfully. "I guess they cannot."

Once she'd settled in for the night, Roman administered a light anti-psychotic airborne spray into her sleep pod. He also triggered the alert on the outside of her chamber that would send a signal to his watch if she got up in the middle of the night. It was his turn to keep an eye on her.

Frankly, they were all growing increasingly weary of this.

A meeting was called that night in the meditation room. It was decided that it would be in everyone's best interest if Lucene were placed in deep hibernation for the remainder of the journey. But, they decided, they had to get her to agree to it. The last thing they wanted was for her to be forced to make a decision that was against her will, out of their desperation. In a clear-minded state, she eventually agreed several days later. And, with much reluctance and sadness, Tanager set her sleep pod into a dormant state where Lucene would remain asleep until they'd reached Erde.

CHAPTER 6
THE WESTERN CROSS
SEPTEMBER. FOUR MONTHS BEFORE THE NEW ASSEMBLY.

"I don't understand," Roman complained, rubbing an eye like a small child being told he had to finish his peas. "I've taught anthropology on Earth for nearly two decades. What makes you think I am incapable of teaching it at TARA?"

They arrived at the Western Cross just moments earlier. The terrain was most comparable to New Mexico and Arizona—a desert landscape, except with more pockets of running water and greenery. The air smelled of sage and fresh berries. In the distance, a small village could be spotted, adobe-like housing surrounded by red rock that was layered with vibrant white, green and earthen minerals. It was beautiful in a way that was completely different from the central city of Achel. For a moment, Roman almost forgot to be annoyed.

"It's not that you are incapable," Tanager explained gently, adjusting the fedora he'd taken to wearing after Lucene destroyed his fishing hat. "It's just that your information is a little...incomplete."

They arrived at the center of the village. There were a few residents meandering through the cobblestone streets, many of whom stopped to greet Tanager. He tipped his hat awkwardly. They snickered a little but were polite enough not to say anything. Roman couldn't help but notice that these Earthlings were a little...different. Some looked as human as he did, while others were distinctly taller and leaner (if that were possible) by several feet. Others were much smaller and wider with heads that were disproportionately large, matched only by their even bigger eyes.

"I thought the preserves were to save members of the human race," Roman whispered, confused.

"These *are* members of the human race," Tanager explained as they made their way through town, passing a bakery, a cheese shop and a clean meat chop shop. "They're just not all from Earth."

Roman stopped walking. "Hang on," he said, motioning with one hand. Tanager paused, searching his database of Earth idioms and then nodded with a smile. "I thought Earth was it, and that that's why you were so keen on saving our population from extinction."

"Yes," Tanager acknowledged, taking a seat at an outdoor cafe and motioning for Roman to join him. "That was the original plan. I was as surprised as you were to return home to find that Earth was just one of many life-sustaining planets for the human race. Unfortunately, the people you are witnessing are facing the same perils as Earth, and they need our help." For once, Roman was speechless. "Really, Roman," Tanager chastised lightly, "Are you so self-centered as to think that you and Earthlings were our only potential concern?"

"Kinda," Roman admitted.

A large woman with curly hair that ran down to her ankles approached the table. "Tea to start?" she offered.

"Yes, thank you," Tanager answered. "And you?" he asked Roman.

"Got anything…stronger?" Roman asked.

She looked at Tanager, confused.

"Alcohol," Tanager explained. "Something in the gin variety, if you have it."

"Ah, of course," she smiled at Roman. "Perhaps you'd fancy a gin and rossenberry tonic?"

"What is rossenberry?" Roman looked at the woman and back at Tanager, confused.

"He's recently arrived from Earth," Tanager explained.

"Ah, I see." Her red eyes grew wide. "I've always wanted to go there. I've heard it's lovely in the winter…is it?"

"Is it what?" Roman was distracted.

"Is Earth lovely in the winter?" Roman likened this question to "I know a guy who lives in New York. Maybe you know him?" He was more interested in the gin and rossenberry tonic and knew of one sure way to get it. "It certainly is." He flashed a smile. She blushed a little. "Tell me, my dear...what is your name?"

"Marcy," she turned redder.

"Marcy," he smiled, calling up a memory. "I knew a Marcy on Earth. A lot like you, but her hair was a little lighter. Lovely woman." If Tanager knew how to roll his eyes, he would have. Instead, he sat and watched the exchange with the curiosity of a small puppy. "Tell me, Marcy. What *is* a rossenberry?"

"Oh, it's like your cranberries only sweeter and more aromatic."

"Well, that would be just fine."

"Marcy," Tanager asked. Marcy's face fell when she pulled her gaze from Roman. *Really,* Tanager thought, *I just don't get it.* "Could we have one of your succulent meat pies to go with it?"

"Ah, certainly," she smiled proudly. They were her specialty. "Back in a jiffy...as you Earthlings would say." She darted back into the cafe, leaving Roman and Tanager to return to light conversation and people-watching.

"Meat pies," Roman inquired. "Isn't that...wrong, here...somehow?"

"Clean meats," Tanager explained. "Same protein, vitamins and health benefits but healthier and without killing anything...more like growing a plant, really."

"Is it any good?" Roman wanted to know.

"Prepare to be amazed," Tanager boasted as Marcy set the plates before them, another male server right behind with the beverages.

"Made 'em fresh this morning," she waited, expectantly for Roman to take a bite.

"Delicious," Tanager offered. She ignored him, continuing to eye Roman attentively. He took a hesitant bite, and then his eyes grew wide.

"Amazing," he offered, as the server poured Tanager's tea. Roman kept chewing slowly until she'd walked away. "Okay," he leaned in to whisper, "it's not bad, I'll give you that, but it's not...."

"Bacon?" the young server offered with a smirk, winking at Roman.

"Exactly," Roman winked back. "Good, but not bacon." The server grabbed a tray and wandered off to help another patron.

"You remind me of a mermaid I once knew," Tanager said flatly.

"How so?" Roman asked.

"Never mind," Tanager took a bite of his pie, followed by a sip of tea. "We have to discuss your research."

Roman was sipping his gin when he caught sight of someone with a monk-like robe in his periphery, peering at Roman from in front of a bookstore window on the corner. Roman's face went paler than anyone thought possible.

"What is it...what's the matter?" Tanager looked at him, concerned.

"Far," Roman answered.

"What about him?" Tanager asked, but Roman was already on his feet, making his way toward the robed figure who had already disappeared into the bookshop.

"He's here."

"Uh...Cepheus," Tanager said aloud, to the air. A few passers-by looked at him quizzically but said nothing. "I'm still working on this mental communication thing. So far, I can only connect with Lucene. But, if you can hear me, I may be a few minutes late to the agricultural section. Roman's just run off." He trotted off in a slow-run toward the bookstore (Tanager was not the most athletic of individuals). "Will meet you in a while."

From several miles away, on an inspection visit to the rural areas of the Western Cross, Cepheus nodded to himself. *You're learning,* he praised, unconvinced that his friend could hear him. After all, while both men were genetically modified Data Collectors, Tanager's training was cut dramatically short when Cepheus went under Watch and Tanager suddenly had to replace his friend as lead instructor at TARA—and then later, when the men had to return to Earth to rescue Lucene, they had made progress during their long flight home and Tanager was very skilled. But there was still more that Cepheus needed to teach him.

Like someone learning a new language, Cepheus suggested Tanager refrain from using his communication watch unless absolutely necessary when they spoke. The pathways of empathic dialogue had to be cultivated, person to person. So, while they could pick up bits and pieces from random individuals, emotions and a few phrases, the connections between specific people had to be trained. This was a tricky agreement as Tanager was still responsible for monitoring the whereabouts of Cepheus and Roman—both of whom were under Watch until further psych-evaluation deemed them safe to society and themselves. The fact that Cepheus was still allowed to train Tanager and resume most of his day-to-day responsibilities at TARA was somewhat questionable. However, Erde was a small planet with limited resources, so inhabitants often had to find creative ways to fulfill many roles.

Cepheus felt as if he were mostly cured...maybe 80%? That was his unscientific findings. What he did know was that he hadn't had to have any antipsychotic medications since their long journey from Earth and that when he felt himself slipping, he was fairly good at recognizing the signs and bringing himself back.

"Cepheus, old boy, good to see you," a portly man in coveralls startled him out of his reverie. The man vaguely reminded him of Ivan, but without the accent and about twice the girth.

"Abe, it's nice to see you. I saw the work you've done at Tanager's new high-home...impressive."

"Well, thank you very much. It was not easy given Tanager's odd specs, but me and the missus are happy with the way it turned out." Abe was carrying several long wooden beams in his arms as if they were weightless. Behind him, a thick woman wearing jeans and a flannel shirt stood by an electric truck. When she saw Cepheus, she waved pleasantly. "Just making the rounds, are you?" Abe asked, quizzically.

"Yes," Cepheus answered. "Just...making the rounds."

"Any word on...you know...relocation?" From a distance, Abe's wife shot him an *oh no, you just didn't* look. "We love it here, but a few of the non-natives appear...restless."

"I wish I could be more optimistic, Abe," Cepheus admitted. He was torn. He didn't want to lie, but he also didn't want to give people false hope. "But thus far, none of the endangered planets appear to be ready for re-occupation just yet."

"I understand," Abe said. "Will you inform the village at the next town meeting, or shall I?"

"It's probably best if it comes from someone at TARA," Cepheus answered. "We have a young woman in the research department who's recently relocated from Earth. She could help validate what she's seen on her planet. Have you heard about Lucene?"

"Have not had the pleasure."

"Well, once she's out of quarantine, we'll be sure to bring her around to meet everyone."

Abe noticed his wife tapping her foot. "The missus is getting impatient. I best be going."

"Good to see you, friend."

"You too, champ."

With that, Abe stacked the beams onto the back of the truck as his wife climbed into the driver's seat. Moments later, the two drove off. Most non-laborers used public transport to get to neighboring towns, or they paid a premium to borrow common cars from a public lot if they wanted to go on a road trip. But for those who had jobs requiring the transporting of heavy materials, such as Abe and his wife, who owned a construction and remodeling business, the government made special exceptions provided they filed for a laborer's license.

Cepheus continued along the dirt path toward some of the local farms, pleased to inhale the fresh country air and flat planes. He could see the mountains in the distance. Like Earth, the rural regions of the Western Cross preserve had hundreds of miles of farmland for growing plant-based foods of every variety. They also had cows, oxen, deer, chickens and horses, but none were for slaughter. They milked the cows and ate the eggs from chickens, but only after asking them for permission first. The oxen and deer were subject to small skin cell scrapings periodically in order to grow clean meats. For their acts of service, these animals were treated like royalty, given as much food, space and comforts as an animal would want, which, admittedly, wasn't much.

A small cottage on a modest plot of land caught Cepheus's eye. *That is odd,* he thought to himself. *When was that built?* The cottage was painted a deep purple with Ivy vines on the roof flowing down the sides. The stained-glass windows had grape designs on them. *A vineyard,* he observed. He hadn't seen one in the Western Cross before and was puzzled. He wrapped his cape around him tighter as the wind picked up and made his way to the cottage.

He passed through the property gate and made his way to the front door, knocking lightly on it. There was no answer. He didn't want to be impolite, but curiosity got the better of him. Cepheus walked to the side of the house and attempted to peer through one of the grape-stained windows.

"You there," someone poked him in the ribs with a stick. He turned to witness a small but athletically built woman wearing what appeared to be burlap pants with a brown linen short-sleeved blouse. "Any reason you feel the need to be looking in my window?" She scowled at him, furrowing her eyebrows. The pupils in her yellow eyes began to stretch and grow.

Cepheus was taken aback. "Are you a..." he couldn't bring himself to say it.

"A Royal?" she finished. "By birth, yes. In spirit, no." She held the stick out as if she were dowsing for water. Once her aggression waned, she realized something. "Oh, so are you," she stated, not asked, momentary lowering the stick before remembering something and snapping it back up again, holding the tip of the branch against his throat. "Are you here to try and bring me back because I claimed sanctuary and..."

"No, no, no," Cepheus held up his thin hands in surrender and tried to explain. "I am one of the lead instructors at TARA and a former negotiator for the Intergalactic Peace Project. I am only here to check on the preserves and make sure everything is okay. TARA is partially funded by the statecraft, so I have to file quarterly reports."

"I see," she dropped the stick. "And what, may I ask, do you have to report on that requires you looking through my cottage window?"

"I apologize," Cepheus's eyes welled up in what she could only interpret as allergies or possibly...tears? "My wife...my late wife ... she was a winemaker. I was just surprised to see a vineyard in the Western Cross. She was the only person able to grow grapes in this region..." He observed the rows of blue, purple and pearlized grapes. "Until now, it would seem."

"Yeah," the woman answered. "The Eastern Cross would have been more ideal. But I just happen to like the landscape here."

Cepheus smiled. "My wife felt the same way."

"I'm sorry about your wife," she replied, taking a moment to untie her black hair, adjust it, and then tie it back up again, forming a tiny knot on her head. "I'm Moksha." She then saluted, like a Royal. Cepheus offered his hand in return. Moksha paused for a moment before lowering her arm and shaking his hand in return. "Old habit." She glanced awkwardly at the ground.

"I'm sorry to pry," Cepheus apologized. After an awkward pause, he asked, "Why are you here?"

"I could ask the same of you."

"I ran away from home as a child and ended up here."

"Same here...except, as you can see, I'm not a child." Cepheus could see that. As far as Royals were concerned, Moksha would have been considered quite beautiful among the nomads. "Not the normal Royal stomping grounds, is it?" She laughed awkwardly, breaking the momentary silence. "Maybe a short chat over a cup of wine?"

Normally, Cepheus would not drink while on duty, but he was intrigued. "Perhaps just one," he replied. She unlocked the cottage, something Cepheus found to be odd since no one on any of the preserves typically felt the need to "lock up." Lucene was the only other person he'd encountered who did that.

He followed her inside and was ushered to a small table in the kitchen. "Sorry," she apologized, "it's too small for a proper dining area."

"No, it's...just fine." Cepheus felt his eyes glazing over slightly.

"Hey, are you okay?" she asked, tapping him on the chin with her fingers, peering into his eyes.

"Yes, sorry." He regained composure. "I was just, remembering."

Her face fell, sympathetic. She remembered herself and reached for two clay wine cups, pouring a glass of rossenberry wine for them both. Moksha raised her cup in a tribute. "To new friends," she offered. He tapped his cup to hers and took a sip. It was just as he remembered.

"You seem very sympathetic for..."

"A Royal?" she finished. "I could say the same about you."

"Perhaps because I escaped while I was still very young," Cepheus explained. "When Erdelings took me in and gave me sanctuary, I couldn't have been more than a teenager…I can't remember exactly."

"Just a moment…" Moksha suddenly realized. "You are not Cepheus Baruch, are you?" Her eyes grew wide as if someone splashed her face with cold water.

"Unfortunately, yes."

"My Sovereign," she began to kneel before catching herself and then stood up again. After a moment of awkwardness, she flopped into a chair, embarrassed.

"Old habits are hard to break," Cepheus replied generously. "And, of course, you don't need to do that. I renounced the throne a long time ago."

A long pause ensued as they sipped their wine. Both seemed lost in thought, but for very different reasons. For Cepheus, Petrichor's wine had been earthier in flavor, somehow. Moksha's was a little thinner and sweeter, but equally good. Cepheus tried to connect with her using his thoughts, but of course, that wouldn't work. She was a Royal, not a Data Collector, untrained, and not known for compassion. And yet…

"What is it?" Moksha asked, fidgeting nervously with one of the small turquoise earrings that wrapped around her ear and dangled about an inch below her lobe.

"Forgive me for saying this," Cepheus began cautiously, "but you seem far too kind to be a Royal. What was your station?"

"This ought to be good for a laugh." She smiled. She had a nice smile, Cepheus noticed, and then caught himself. "I was…"

"Yes?"

"Um…an assassin?" She bit her lip.

"Is that a question?"

"No, that's it. I was an assassin."

"No," Cepheus laughed. "Tell me, really."

Moksha let out a sigh before guzzling the rest of the wine in her cup and refilling it moments later. She offered Cepheus a second glass, but he waved his hand away in decline.

"Okay, so you know how on Earth they have dog fights using pit bulls?"

"Unfortunately, yes."

"Well, you know how, no matter how much they try to train them to fight, there are ones who are peaceful and don't really want to hurt anyone or anything?"

"Yes?"

"Well, that was me." She furrowed her brows and dropped her gaze to the floor.

Cepheus let out a laugh.

"What's so funny?" Moksha demanded.

Cepheus smiled broadly. "It appears we have something in common."

Tanager flew through the bookstore doors with such force that several traditional magazines blew open and fell from the shelves. An older woman at the counter looked up in surprise. "Electronic or print?" she asked cautiously.

"Wha..." Tanager slowed down and thought for a moment. On the second floor, he spotted Roman darting between two columns of books. "Print," he answered. "Thank you!" He didn't wait for further instruction. After finding a spiral staircase, he bound up them, two at a time.

The older woman seemed perplexed but wasn't interested enough to pursue it further. She dropped her gaze back toward the electronic romance novel she was reading on a small device. The Navy SEAL from Earth had just met the half-android and half-human woman in a freak mishap on Mars and the bookstore attendant was dying to find out what happened next. After all, how could a wild seal and a person make such a relationship work? She didn't even think seals had legs...confusing.

Meanwhile, Tanager peered around a selection of intergalactic travel books. He witnessed Roman giving the frail man he had been chasing after an affectionate kiss and thought it best not to interrupt. Instead, he grabbed the first manual he could find, a heavy textbook outlining all the known galaxies by sections. Given the age of the book, he estimated that it was off by about 15 billion galaxies, ones that were housed in three newly discovered sections. He tried not to eavesdrop, but he really couldn't help it. After all, he was Roman's guardian while he was under Watch, was he not?

"My darling, how long have you been here?" Tanager heard Roman ask as Roman wrapped his arms around Far, hugging him to his chest. Had Roman not been overcome with emotion, he might have noticed Far's body bristle, just slightly, at the embrace before relaxing his body and lightly wrapping his arms around Roman's waist. For a moment, Far softened at the familiar feel of Roman's chest and the scent of his skin before remembering himself and regaining composure.

"About five minutes ago?"

"What? From where?"

"I escaped," he thought carefully for a moment, adopting a well-timed contorted look of pain as Roman gazed at him lovingly. "From the Royal Training Grounds. I have been a prisoner there since I fled Earth looking for a cure."

"My darling, I can't believe what has happened to you," Roman fought back a tear. You must be exhausted. Let me get you back to my high-home in the city."

"High-home?" Far used the question as an opportunity to pull away.

"Yes," Roman laughed. "Erde's term for an apartment or condo. It's on loan for now, but once I begin teaching at TARA, that's their Terrestrial Academy of Research and Awareness, I'll begin paying for it, a little at a time." Roman wrapped an arm around him. Let's get you home, so you can have a bath and something to eat, and time to rest and recharge.

"That would be…lovely," Far answered softly.

"I'm so glad you found me," Roman's heart opened wide with the belief that as soon as Far could escape, he returned to him as if his heart were a beacon. He wondered about Far's health as his survival projections had not been good several years ago on Earth. *Well,* he reasoned. *There's time for that discussion later.* "So glad you found me," he repeated.

"Yes," Far answered hesitantly, as the two men passed Tanager, who went unnoticed as they descended the spiral steps. "Me, as well."

CHAPTER 7
THE COSTUME SHOP
SEPTEMBER. FOUR MONTHS BEFORE THE NEW ASSEMBLY.

It was still early when Lucene ventured out of her little cottage at the Eastern Cross. Having just arrived three weeks earlier, she was only now permitted out of quarantine, but it was still requested that she not leave the Eastern Cross region until the beginning of October, just to be on the safe side. She'd gone through a strange battery of remote tests with Dr. Wilah, who was presently aboard a vessel heading to a way station between Erde and Earth, followed by a remote consultation with Dr. Ennis on Earth and an odd series of psychological questioning administered mainly by Cepheus. Tanager was included after it was deemed that she was mostly back to "normal."

She couldn't really explain why she'd gotten so temperamental around Tanager, but since he seemed to be an emotional trigger for her, they thought it best to give her a little time before the two resumed moderate communication. Cepheus explained to her that it had to do with some disconnect between the emotional centers of her brain and the logical ones, a bridge normally helped by meditation. But for some reason, in her case, it was as if her emotions suddenly enveloped her entire thought process, and until she'd actually worn herself out (time on the Vessel's treadmill seemed to help), there was no reasoning with her.

Once they'd awakened her from deep sleep and introduced her to

Erde and her new home, they anticipated aggravation by the change—reactions that did not come. She seemed to be calmer, more receptive to what was happening around her. So instead, in what would seem a counterintuitive approach, they requested she take a break from meditation and do, essentially, whatever she felt she needed to do in order to adapt, providing she stay within the Eastern Cross. At least, remain there until they could gauge her physical and emotional reactions to her environment, as well as the environment's reaction to her. Townspeople were alerted that there was a new inhabitant, something of which they had become quite accustomed to over that past few years.

For Lucene, this was her first taste of freedom in a long time. She was no longer running from some unseen and unknown aggressor, nor was she trapped on a small spaceship for months. She tried to remember the last time she was able to move about so freely without feeling apprehensive...five years old? Six? She really wasn't sure.

The truth was, she needed clothes and groceries. She'd managed to procure a few of the essentials at a local mart, though there was some confusion about what they considered fruits and vegetables versus what she believed. But they were kind, asking what part of Earth she had been from and trying diligently to match her request with what they knew of Earth and her preferences. She didn't have the heart to tell them that, the truth of the matter was, she was an unskilled cook. And, in the end, it made no difference what they gave her. Her goal became pretty simple, "Sell me foods that I can boil or pan fry in twenty minutes or less that are reasonably good for me."

The attendant at the grocery store nodded enthusiastically. "That," he told her with a smile, "we can do."

Now, as Lucene peered down at the threadbare one-size-fits-all dress that had been at the way station, the one that she was now wearing, she couldn't help but think that she needed...well...help.

She set her cloth bag of groceries on the sidewalk and pulled the watch Tanager had given her out of her pocket. She was still not comfortable wearing it, but she promised to keep it with her so they could track her if needed, and she could phone someone if she needed help. It also had this handy app that managed her money for her. She'd been given a small stipend from TARA and use of the cottage, provided she work with the students on whatever research projects they needed. In this case, *she* was the project. The agreement was for three months, and they could revisit that plan in the new year to discuss the next steps. Surprisingly, Lucene wasn't at all worried about what she would do about food and lodging after those months had passed. There was a strange sense of peace and the trust that Cepheus and Tanager would somehow make sure things were okay for her. Not unlike her friendships with Rev. Isabella, Fatima, and Ivan, this brought her contentment. And while she had grown to appreciate Roman and value his friendship, she didn't necessarily trust in his ability to be a source of support, even with his extensive knowledge of human behavior.

She opened the bank app…not a whole lot left until the next deposit, but perhaps enough for one or two new simple outfits? Across the street was a sign, Mallory's Costume Shop. Except, the window displayed a mix of contemporary Earth garb, pant suits and jackets, jeans, dress shirts and sweaters, along with an array of odd-looking garments that included triangle-shaped silver hats and striped unitards that looked like adult-sized onesies.

Lucene grabbed her groceries and made her way across the street. As she peered through the darkened window, she let out a disappointed sigh. The sign on the window said, "Closed." About to give up and head home, a hand reached toward the sign and flipped it to "Open." A face smiled from inside the window—difficult to make out with the glare from the sun. Suddenly, the lights sprang to life as the shape motioned a hand for her to come inside.

"Welcome! Welcome," said the very large and colorful man behind the counter. "Welcome to Mallory's Costume Shop, here to serve all your pre-made and custom wardrobe needs." He surveyed her dress, distastefully. "And, from the look of it, you have needs."

Normally, Lucene would have countered with a snarky comment, but she was won over by his exaggerated overtures. He wasn't finished with his assessment.

"Did you just step off a boat that had been lost at sea? What happened to you, child?"

"Close, but it was a spacecraft coming from Earth. This was all that they had for me to wear."

The man's eyes flew open wide to reveal pupils that sparkled like tiny cut gemstones. Prisms actually flowed from them, leaving reflections of light on the floor. He touched his hand to his mouth. "Oh, my goodness…tell me you're not Lucene, born of Xan and Dora…two Data Collectors." He gave an exuberant little bounce…very little. His large frame didn't allow for much movement.

"Okay, I'm not Lucene," she answered, flatly.

He paused for a moment, eyeing her deadpan expression before letting out a chortle and waving a hand at her. "Oh, you got me. And let me just say, it's an honor to serve you. I am Mallory, owner of this establishment." Lucene paused for a moment, mainly because she kept getting distracted by the array of glittering garments that were displayed on the wall. "What, were you expecting, a woman? Don't feel bad, so was my mother." He laughed again.

"No, I'm just…confused."

"Oh, aren't we all, dear?"

Lucene began wandering between the racks displaying clothing tightly packed together and separated by size. "You're a costume shop…?"

"Yes, we are a quick study, aren't we?"

"But some of this looks like stuff I would wear day-to-day."

"And where are we from?"

Lucene got his point. Earth clothes, at least some of them, were costumes to those on Erde. "So, if I wanted something basic, something everybody wears on Erde, what would I buy?"

"Well," Mallory leaned a hairy arm on the counter and rested his chin in his palm. "I would argue that I don't sell *basic*, but what I can tell you is that my store caters to a wide variety of styles, some more traditional and then also the non-traditional." He walked from behind the counter and eyed her up and down. "Casual or dressy?"

"Casual…something I can wear to TARA and blend in with students but could also wear day-to-day."

"Maybe something like Earth, so it's not too dramatic a switch, but something we also wear here…like your jeans and sweater variety?"

"Yes," Lucene smiled. "Exactly."

"Budget?"

"Cheap."

Mallory tsk-ed at her. Lucene wasn't entirely sure anyone had ever tsk-ed at her before. "Well, Mallory doesn't do cheap, but I believe we can find something suitable. But first, how about we put your grocery bag in my refrigerator, or those poor pomegranates are going to taste like ass by the time you get home."

"Oh." Lucene glanced down at her bag and the pomegranates sitting on top. "Sure, thanks."

"Follow me," Mallory slid a glittery prom gown aside that was hanging on the wall, revealing a plain brown door, opening to what was presumably the back room. There, he led her down a narrow hallway that he seemed to barely fit through. They passed another room, one with a row of sewing machines with chairs on alternate sides of a long table, spaced out in a zig-zag.

"That's the sewing room," he explained. "I have several workers who help me with custom fittings and designs. I find when I space the chairs out, it enables them to converse with one another without straining their necks while giving them room to work, helps morale and productivity."

"I see," Lucene answered. But, she really didn't. They passed another room, where the edge of a bed and a long, ornate dresser could be seen. "Do you live here, too?"

"Yup. The shop is my life. Couldn't see myself anywhere else." At the end of the hallway, and by contrast to the large bedroom, was a tiny efficiency kitchen that appeared to have been constructed in the 1930s, complete with a small monitor-top refrigerator, tub sink and porcelain gas-range stove. Even the backsplash was covered in a floral print wallpaper. Mallory popped open the refrigerator which revealed a few paper cartons of what appeared to be last night's take-out, along with a glass bottle of carbonated water. Having pulled one of the metal shelves out and laying it, lopsided, in the sink, he pushed the cartons aside enabling him to shove the entire grocery bag in and shut the door without pressing too much to get it all to fit inside. "Voila!" He seemed proud of himself. "Now, on to more important things. Follow me."

Instead of going back through the hallway, he led the way into his bedroom, which alarmed Lucene until she realized that there was yet another door that opened directly back into the shop. The two emerged behind the counter as another patron walked through the front doors.

"Ah, Mrs. Glazor, how nice to see you again," Mallory gushed. The woman was wearing a wide-brimmed hat, boatneck dress and white gloves. Her smile turned to a look of pity as she surveyed Lucene behind the counter.

"My latest project," Mallory held a hand up as if letting Mrs. Glazor in on a secret. He winked and she smiled back with a nod. "I have your garments right here." Hanging in front of the door from which they'd just emerged was a long white satin gown.

"Just beautiful," the Glazor woman gushed. "What do I owe you?"

"Well, let's see." Mallory plunked a few keys on a retro cash register that had a strange brass handle on the side. "Custom dress…fittings…fabric…oh, let's just say, an even 4,000 units."

Lucene's face dropped. She wasn't sure what the dollar equivalent to a unit was, but since her account had about 3,925 less of them, she was pretty sure she couldn't afford whatever Mallory had to sell.

"A bargain, if you ask me," Ms. Glazor smiled gleefully. She plugged a few numbers into her watch, and the cash register lit up. Apparently, it only looked retro. Mallory cranked the handle, which quickly caused the woman's watch to light up. It was, presumably, to send her a receipt. "Thank you, Mallory. You will be hearing from me again…probably for…mmm…baby clothes!" She winked at him. "Ta ta!"

Lucene felt like she'd stumbled into a 1940s American sitcom, and she couldn't get out. After Mrs. Glazor left, Mallory's face turned sour. "Horrible woman," he confessed before turning his attention back to Lucene.

"Arms out," he ordered, pulling out a vinyl tape measure. Lucene was confused until Mallory demonstrated by outstretching his arms, parallel to the floor, in a T shape. She followed as Mallory measured her from wrist to shoulder and across her back. "Skinny thing," he commented.

"Listen, Mallory," Lucene began. "While I appreciate your help, I'm realizing now that I probably don't have enough money to pay for whatever clothing you can provide for me."

Mallory stopped and glared at her, offended. "Did I ask you for money?"

"Well, not yet, but…"

"Well, don't shoot me down before you hear my offer!" He let out a boisterous laugh. "I'm not going to design you a custom dress, so relax. I'm just getting a sense of your overall size to fit you for something ready-to-wear. For example..." He moved across the floor and flipped through the clothing racks, beginning with pants. "I'm thinking...this." He thrust his hand out and shook the denim jeans, indicating Lucene should take them. She did. "And this." He handed her a second pair of dress-casual pants. "And this." He'd moved over to a shelf full of sweaters, pulling out a simple solid blue, short-sleeved cotton one. "And finally...this." It was a long-sleeved burgundy cardigan coupled with a button-down white blouse, which Lucene would never have given a second glance to, but on third glance, she decided, it wasn't half bad.

"Okay," she acquiesced. "Should I try them on?"

He paused for far too long, as if she were a small child uttering her first words, giggling to himself. "No, child. You can try them on at home. I assure you; these are a perfect fit for you."

She laid them on the counter and surveyed the selection...pretty neutral and basic. Lucene was okay with this. "How much?"

"Don't be gauche," he chastised. Lucene was confused. How come when Mrs. Glazor asked, it was perfectly acceptable. But when she asked, it was gauche? "Let's see," he thought a moment. Lucene did too. She had about 40 units she was willing to spend, leaving her just enough for emergency food until her next deposit. *Please be less than 40 units. In fact, 35 would be ideal.* "How about 35 units...oh, my word, I can't believe I just said that. Yes, 35 units. Take it now before I change my mind."

"I'll take it," Lucene announced enthusiastically, pulling her watch from her pocket. She held it up and plunked a few buttons as she'd done for the grocer. The cash register lit up...success.

As Mallory was putting her selections in a paper-like bag, she spotted a mannequin in the corner. She wandered over to it. It was wearing a black-flared skirt with a striped sweater. Something about it intrigued her. "That's from our French designs," Mallory explained. "One of my clothiers works part time in the French district and loves the style."

Maybe next time, Lucene thought. "Just for future reference...how much is it for the sweater and skirt?"

Mallory thought for a moment. "Well, it's a package deal." He walked over to the mannequin. "It's the only one we have in stock, so you'd have to wear the display. Fortunately, she's as waif-like as you are, and the fabric is clingy, so it will adjust to your shape. But you can't get the top and skirt without these..." For a large man, he moved easily throughout the aisle. He stopped at an accessory shelf, pulling down a red beret and matching scarf. Without asking, he plunked the beret sideways on her head and wrapped the cravat around her neck. That, along with her worn-out dress, was a sight to behold. "There you go," he said, pleased.

"I've given you everything I can afford. I don't suppose you do layaway?"

"Laya—" this sent Mallory into a tizzy. "There you go, being gauche again. Tell you what, you agree to burn that awful dress you're wearing when you get home, and you can have the entire ensemble for 20 units, payable in...say, one month? Oh," he added. "And I want the pomegranates from your grocery bag."

"It's a deal!"

Mallory packaged up Lucene's new wardrobe and gathered her grocery bag from the refrigerator. She carried the clothing bag on one arm, groceries on the other. It was a bit of a struggle, but she didn't have far to go. Mallory considered offering to lend her a hand cart but then thought better of it. *For an itty-bitty thing, she has the muscle tone. She'll be fine,* he reasoned.

"Thank you, Mallory. It has been a pleasure."

"The pleasure's all mine." Mallory opened the shop door for her as she exited. Then he added, "You are an accomplished young woman, I can tell."

"Really," she seemed unconvinced. "But I haven't done anything yet."

"Oh," he nodded in understanding. "But you will."

CHAPTER 8
ALLIANCE
OCTOBER. THREE MONTHS BEFORE THE NEW ASSEMBLY.

"Commander Royce, it's an honor to finally meet you," the Vitruvian representative bowed his head politely to the head of Erde's Planetary Defense League or PDL for short.

"Likewise, Representative Dallen," Commander Royce acknowledged, offering a slight bow in return.

Neither was what the other expected. Dallen had bright golden hair and equally brilliant blue eyes, uncustomary attributes for most Vitruvians. Had they been any less striking and embellished, he could have passed for a human. Commander Royce, by contrast, was a small, athletically built woman with walnut hair that had thin gray streaks in it and coal-colored eyes decorated by several deep-set wrinkles on her face.

"Please be seated," Commander Royce motioned toward one of the throne-like, high-backed chairs that wrapped around a large round meeting table. The League's Negotiation Room was ornate with flowing red and gray tapestries that hung from the walls, along with potted vines blooming with orange, red and yellow Cosmos flowers. There were no windows, but the glass domed ceiling revealed the cloudy sky, which was constructed so that they could see out but no one flying overhead could see in. Dallen took a seat and was quickly offered a glass of water from one of the commander's attendants, who set the beverage next to him on the table. Dallen didn't seem to notice. Instead, his eyes lit up when the Negotiation Room doors opened.

In walked Lucene wearing a yellow sundress and brown ankle boots that were completely out of place for her surroundings. Had her new friend Mallory seen her selection, which were left-over remnants from her wardrobe on the Vessel, he would have cringed. Yet, she couldn't quite bring herself to wear her newly acquired clothing out in public—yet. *Little by little,* she reminded herself. *There are only so many changes a person can adapt to at once, aren't there?* Plus, her appearance was, in some small way, a point of protest, though Lucene wasn't entirely sure what she was protesting.

It had now been eight months since she left Earth with her traveling companions, Cepheus, Tanager and Roman, after being rescued from the Royals. She'd only been on Erde for one month and still felt completely out of place in her new home. Her hair was a visible testament to her adaptation, with several inches of blonde hair growing in and replacing the brown bottom half that had been dyed to conceal her identity. To Dallen, however, she was stunning. He wouldn't have even noticed Cepheus, dressed in a pair of black pants and a tan button-down shirt or Tanager, wearing a dull brown suit jacket and matching slacks, had Commander Royce not acknowledged them.

"Welcome, scholars," she announced with pride, motioning for them to take a seat, eyeing Lucene's wardrobe curiously.

"Our apologies for the delay, Commander Royce," Tanager pulled out a chair for Lucene, who took a seat first before Tanager settled into the chair next to her. Dallen eyed this gesture with great interest. He was not familiar with this Earth custom and even more confused as to why it would be practiced on Erde.

"We came directly from class and ran into a small situation on our way," Cepheus added, taking a seat beside Dallen.

"Nothing serious, I hope." The Commander glanced between the three newcomers. Lucene shifted nervously in her seat, knowing full well that she was, at least in part, the reason for the delay. The small cottage she had been offered at the Eastern Cross was a preserve where the landscape was most like the terrain she left on Earth—the West Coast of Florida. It had palm-like trees and was near the ocean. Even the seabirds resembled seagulls and sandpipers, but it was still obvious that she was on a different planet surrounded by people she didn't know and couldn't easily escape from.

She hadn't realized before her journey how much her friend Fatima had protected her when she grew anxious, from too many people and too much energy. Even as housemates, Fatima could sense when Lucene needed a break and would either offer to retreat to her own room or simply suggest that everyone take a "silence break," where no one spoke, and the house was quiet until that time that Lucene felt like talking again. She realized now, more than ever, how much she had under-appreciated her friend.

"Nothing serious," Tanager assured her, sending Cepheus a knowing look.

"Good," the Commander paused as an attendant set cool water beside each of them. "Then, may I present Representative Dallen from Vitruvia." Dallen nodded his head and gave a slight wave of his hand, a customary greeting, when all were seated. There was a strange chill in the air. "And may I also present two lead professors and well-respected Earth scholars, Cepheus Baruch and Tanager Blackletter." They nodded in return, cautiously. There was a brief but awkward pause before Tanager realized that it was his turn to speak.

"Oh, and…Commander Royce and Representative Dallen," Tanager offered, "may I please present Lucene Jones. Lucene has recently arrived from Earth…seven months of travel on the Vessel and only one month on Erde."

Why does it sound as if he's making excuses for me? Lucene wondered to herself.

"Hi," Lucene waved, splaying her fingers in what was not at all customary. Dallen couldn't take his eyes off her, smiling at her odd mannerisms. She began nervously tapping her fingers on her lap under the table, fidgeting uncomfortably. Tanager reached under the table and took her hand in his and held it discreetly out of view from the other attendees. She squeezed it, appreciatively, in return, and settled into her seat.

Cepheus smiled with a somewhat exaggerated sense of pride, adding, "Our instructor in training, Roman Aurelius—also from Earth—

was supposed to be joining this discussion today, but he appears to be absent." His deep voice made the situation sound graver than he intended and didn't match his smile.

"Absent?" Commander Royce was concerned.

Tanager intervened. "Since he is new here also, we suspect he's either gotten lost or hasn't adapted to our system of time yet," he laughed heartily to cover up his own awkwardness at the situation. "But Lucene, as they say on Earth, stepped up to the plate, and is standing in on Mr. Aurelius's behalf." Tanager couldn't help but smile at his correct use of the idiom. He still found Earth slang fascinating.

"We are deeply grateful," Commander Royce acknowledged. "Thank you for being present."

"Sure," Lucene bit the side of her lip and shifted in her seat. She really didn't think she stepped up to the plate at all. In fact, she threw what some might call a mini-tantrum at having to stand in for Roman because he was off with who knows who doing who knows what. Cepheus and Tanager finally convinced her to drag herself out of bed and at least throw on a dress and comb her hair and join them.

Commander Royce feigned more confidence than she actually felt. She had been in charge of the PDL for the past forty years, overseeing the Erde military divisions for both local (within the Erde atmosphere) and non-local (outside planets) protection, as well as heading up Erde's membership to the IPP. Compared to Earth, Erde was a much smaller planet, roughly the size of the United States, Canada and Mexico combined. It had enjoyed planet-wide peace for more than a hundred years, leaving her with little to do on the local front. As for the non-local department, Erde was overlooked by many species living in Sections 2, 3, 4 and 5, so the army would "train and maintain" but had little to do in terms of establishing new defense tactics. Thus far, membership with the Intergalactic Peace Project (IPP) had taken up the bulk of her attention, establishing the Data Collector training with TARA, working with the IPP to help other planets reach their level of peace, and helping Earth recover and evolve given its current climate.

It was only within the last year that it came to light that there were other Earth-like planets in need of support. And, in all likelihood, there were many more. This put a strain on their resources. To make matters worse, their efforts in helping Earth did not go unnoticed by those that would harm them. In fact, their Data Collection work had become so successful that it put them on the radar of those living in far regions of the universe. With their general location known, Erde was no longer as safe as it once was, and she considered her efforts with TARA and the IPP to be both her greatest triumph and her worst failure.

"Representative Dallen," Commander Royce shared, "has graciously offered to meet with us on behalf of the Vitruvian people. He is sympathetic to our current situation, and their people would like to help. We will, of course, be conducting more comprehensive meetings with our Defense League and its leadership, but I thought it beneficial for him to meet with you regarding what next steps TARA might take on the Data Collection initiative. Representative Dallen, I turn the conversation over to you." With that, Commander Royce took a seat.

Dallen stood, knowing full well what everyone in the room was thinking, feeling the full weight of their distrust in spite of their amicable gestures. He indulged in one more glance in Lucene's direction before standing and addressing the group as a whole. His garb was almost as striking as his features, wearing a white tunic with a gold-striped ribbon that ran from his left shoulder, across his chest and down to his right hip. His pants were made of a thick silver material that appeared to have bits of metal in them, possibly for protection.

"I know," he began, "that you are well aware of the previous agreement Vitruvia had with the Royals, something which my people have come to regret."

Tanager shifted uncomfortably in his seat but said nothing. Cepheus's eyes bored into the middle-aged man's head as if trying to pry information loose from it, but Dallen was well guarded. Lucene, on the other hand, didn't feel much of anything, for once. Instead, she was distracted by Dallen's shiny golden hair that seemed to catch light like sun on a mirror—enhanced by the fact that the sun was actually shining through the dome at that moment and bouncing off his head—causing a prism-like effect on the curtains.

"At that time," he continued, "our goal was to not interfere with anything pertaining to Earth or surrounding planets, but merely to be available should Earth become...shall we say, *available*? If that happened, naturally, we felt it would be safer in our hands than the Royals."

"Then," Commander Royce interrupted, "why make an arrangement with the Royals at all? To the outside observer, this gives the impression that your people were siding with them. And they are not known to be the most compassionate of species."

"We know that now, Commander," he dismissed the comment with a flick of his wrist and repeated softly, "we know that now. We assumed that the Royals would no doubt take a large portion of Earth and hoped that we could salvage what remained. We promise you; we had no intention of hurting Earthlings nor forcing them out."

"Then, what would you have done with them?" Tanager asked pointedly.

"Well…we would wait and see."

Tanager was not prone to anger, and yet he felt his unoccupied hand beginning to make a fist under the table. Lucene noticed the unusual reaction and gave his other hand, the one she had been holding, a squeeze. It was her turn to be supportive. He felt it and took a deep breath.

"Wait and see what? Wait and see if Earthlings died and then take over the space like new landlords?" Tanager asked. Lucene was surprised. Tanager was usually much more cautious with his words.

"We meant no harm," Dallen explained calmly. "We just don't believe in interfering. We simply act according to what is, it is our culture. It is our way."

"We understand and respect that, Representative Dallen," Commander Royce interjected, shooting a warning glance at Tanager. "Perhaps you could share with our scholars why it is that Virtruvia is offering to work with the Erde people at this time?"

"Quite simply," Dallen explained, "we have since learned that not only did the Royals breach our contract, but they made a separate deal with the Null—the Singulari worshippers in Section 4."

"The void dwellers?" Cepheus sat upright. "They are real?"

"Unfortunately, yes. And, as violent as the Royals are, the Singulari make the nomads in Section 3 look like small children at play in a sandbox."

Lucene suddenly had that mental glitch, the one where she was on the verge of remembering something important from her past but couldn't. It was that all-too-familiar feeling of an itch she couldn't scratch. It had to do with her brief time on the Royal ship when they tried to kidnap her. *Aha!* Suddenly, she sat upright, causing everyone to turn and look at her in surprise.

"What is it?" Tanager asked, releasing her hand and giving her back a light rub for encouragement, another gesture that confused Dallen...and bothered him a little. *Why?*

"I was heavily sedated, mind you," Lucene fought to remember. "But they were dressed for a meeting—Hamish and Sabrina. They were taking me and going to meet someone...I think they were going to hand me over to them. But then, when you rescued me," she touched Tanager and Cepheus each on the arm, "well, I guess they couldn't keep up their end of the bargain."

Cepheus fell silent for a moment. Until then, it hadn't occurred to him that when Hamish, his father, had killed Sabrina, his mother, and let him go, he was doing more than freeing him and helping Lucene. His actions likely sealed his death, and that of the Royals, as a species. It was a far greater sacrifice than he had appreciated at the time.

"I don't know the current state of the alliance between the Royals and the Null," Dallen confessed, "but I do know that they are both very dangerous. If Vitruvia and Erde work together and share our resources, perhaps we can get you re-instated into the IPP and enlist the help of all species living in Sections 0, Sections 2, and even Silva and the surrounding planets in Section 5. We can save Earth...and each other."

Tanager thought a moment. He knew his empathic skills were not as advanced as Cepheus's, nor as rich in potential as Lucene's, but he couldn't escape the gnawing sensation in his belly. "So, it is now in your best interest to help Earth...as a bargaining chip to get us to work with you and share our knowledge," he answered sourly. "Lucky Earthlings."

Commander Royce was about to object, but Dallen quickly flicked his wrist again and smiled. "I understand your hesitation and your lack of trust," he acknowledged. "Believe me, your reaction is much more temperate than that which I've faced from your military personnel thus far." There was a long pause. It felt as if all the air had been sucked out of the room.

Lucene took a sip of her water. *Just say it,* she thought. *Just say that you recognize that Vitruvia has made many mistakes. That they may not be as compassionate as the Peace-Keepers, but they are honest and speak the truth.*

Dallen looked up with a start, eyes focusing directly on Lucene's until she dropped her gaze uncomfortably. He returned his attention to the group. "I recognize that Vitruvia has made many mistakes," he began. *What the—?* Lucene thought. "We may not be as compassionate as your people, but we are honest. I speak the truth."

Close enough, Lucene thought, wondering if she passed those thoughts on to him to share or if he reached into her head and grabbed them. If the latter, she didn't like it.

Tanager looked at Cepheus, and the room fell silent as the two seemed to have a split-second private conversation without either of them opening their mouths. As the elder of the two, Cepheus spoke, "We understand, and we appreciate your honesty. What do you need from us?"

"Wonderful," Commander Royce smiled broadly, breathing for what appeared to be the first time all day. "What are our next steps?"

"Well," Dallen grinned, glancing around the room, taking an extra moment when he zeroed in on Lucene. "As a start, I would love a tour of the Academy. In particular, I've heard wonderful things about your Makerspace."

CHAPTER 9
THE WITCHES OF FRANCE
OCTOBER. THREE MONTHS BEFORE THE NEW ASSEMBLY.

"Come here often?" Odessa asked Reverend Isabella, sliding next to her as the older woman was peering closely at a rare heliographic photograph preserved beneath shatter-proof glass and hanging on a wall at the Parrish museum. They were running a special exhibit on the witches of France throughout history.

"Tell me, Odessa," Isabella answered, never taking her eyes from the image. "Is there anything that you *won't* hit on?"

Odessa thought for a moment. "Earthworms," she finally replied. She stood beside Isabella, wearing a red flared skirt with black stockings, a yellow blouse, and her head covered in butterfly barrettes. Her usual Northern Lights blue-green skin was now a shade of pale peach, something the shapeshifter had most likely adopted to avoid drawing attention to the fact that she was not human. On this, she had an internal battle. She loved the attention but knew it could be risky. Therefore, she constantly had this, "look at me, no, don't look at me" angst about her.

"Earthworms," Isabella responded curtly, trying to understand how this was where Odessa drew the line.

"Well, yes," Odessa explained. "They eat dead organic matter which is gross. And have you seen their castings?"

"Enough." Isabella held up her hand. "Forget that I asked." Isabella stood regally in a brown and yellow tunic top with matching palazzo pants.

Odessa stretched to peer over Isabella's shoulder. "Ah," she nodded. "One of the first photographs ever." She thought a moment. "Northern France, 1830."

"Yes," Isabella answered quietly, pushing back a memory.

"Wasn't that when the townspeople took it upon themselves to burn a witch, even though it was technically no longer a crime?" Odessa searched Isabella's face for a reaction.

"What is it that you want?"

Odessa sighed. "I want to enlist your help."

"*My* help," Isabella was surprised. "Doing what?"

"I'm not sure if you're aware of this, but six years ago, Vitruvians, Erdelings and Royals were all banned from the Intergalactic Peace Project."

"Believe me," Isabella instinctively held one hand over her belly, where she had been shot in her Sanctuary earlier in the year, by the double-dealing Drake Cushing. "I am aware."

"Well, I think you should petition to become a member of the new IPP."

"Me?" Isabella looked down at the small-framed Vitruvian. "I have absolutely no qualifications to join the Earth IPP."

"No," Odessa furrowed her lips as if considering this. "But," she placed a hand on Isabella's shoulder. "If I recommended you as a Vitruvian IPP member, well, I suppose that might make a difference. While *you* may find me distasteful, I am somewhat influential with my superiors despite being among the lower caste. What do you think, Bella?"

Isabella glanced over her right shoulder, eyeing the hand before shrugging it away. "It's Reverend Isabella."

Odessa removed her hand, appearing hurt at the snub. "Why don't you like me?" Odessa whined. "I helped heal you." She stood, pouting.

Isabella let out a sigh. "I don't dislike you," she finally conceded. "I just disapprove of you wantonly throwing your sexuality around when so many of us have worked so hard for so long on this planet to make ourselves be seen beyond our gender."

Odessa thought for a moment. "Yes," she nodded "and, some longer than others."

"What is that supposed to mean?"

"Take a walk with me Bel—Reverend Isabella." She resisted the urge to circle her arm around Isabella's waist and lead her. She motioned for Isabella to follow her. She darted around several tourists taking flash photograhs before a security guard asked them to turn their flashes off. Isabella gracefully kept pace.

"See this?" She pointed at a timeline on the wall, set at the start of the exhibit. Her finger hovered above a date. "1245 in southern France. A woman convinced her inquisitor that she had no magical powers, and the inquisitor let her go."

"And?" Isabella eyed Odessa curiously.

"The inquisitor that year murdered 346 women and two men accused of being witches. This was the only person he let go, despite protests from many accusers."

"Fascinating," Isabella sounded unconvinced.

"And here," she pointed to another date, "1308 in Paris. A concubine was burned at the stake after being accused by a lord's wife of practicing sorcery."

"Ah, yes," Isabella replied thoughtfully. "Jealousy."

Odessa noticed a spark of recognition.

"And over here," Odessa took Isabella by the arm and tugged her.

"How much more of this is there?" Isabella wanted to know.

"Not much more," Odessa reassured her, dragging her to the opposite wall in the exhibit. "Here," she pointed. They stood before a large oil on canvas depicting the execution of witches by hanging in 1718 in a small village in southwestern France.

"Know what happened here?" She waited for Isabella's reply, holding her breath.

"Many of the women on trial were accused of seducing the men in the village by casting spells. In reality, most of them were raped against their will, and their accusers were the men trying to cover up their own crimes." Her violet eyes seemed to grow darker as she pinched her lips together. Odessa looked down and noticed both of Isabella's hands were balled into tight fists.

"Pretty awful," Odessa remarked.

Isabella looked at her young friend, incredulously. "Pretty awful?" She paused. "Is that how you would describe it? Pretty awful?" She gestured toward the painting. "This is exactly what I'm talking about when you throw yourself at everything on two legs—sometimes four—with no respect for your body or that people may only be interested in you because of your appearance. Many of us died trying to be seen as more than objects, being punished if men couldn't control themselves around us."

Odessa dropped her eyes, hurt. Then, she had a thought. "I hear what you're saying—I also notice that you referred to 'us' twice in that sentence."

Isabella seemed startled for a moment, as if piecing together Odessa's agenda—which was becoming clearer by the minute. She turned her back on Odessa and made her way toward the next exhibit room.

"Hold on." Odessa ran in front of her. "Hear me out." Isabella stopped. "I understand where you are coming from. But the flip-side of this argument is two-fold. First, I am not human. I am a shapeshifter. I can be male or female. I just prefer being female." Isabella threw her hands in the air, exasperated. "And second," she continued, "you fought for religious freedom and equality for more than 700 years. It is because of your efforts that women today—misguided by your estimation, or not—have the freedom to flaunt their sexuality if they choose to do so."

Isabella considered this for a moment. Odessa had a valid point. Who was she to judge how Odessa behaved? Then, as if it suddenly occurred to her, "What do you mean, 700 years?"

"Ah," Odessa smiled, happy that she and Isabella were finally on the same page. "Shall we return to the only photographic evidence we have in this exhibit of the 1830 version of Isabella?" This time, the two walked side-by-side, waiting impatiently as several other visitors gathered around the picture. One eyed Isabella curiously but said nothing.

Finally, the heliographic image was free. "Look here," Odessa leaned in close so that her breath almost clouded the glass. "The image is not super fabulous, but who does that beautiful creature about to be hanged look like?" There, stood the old Isabella. Her skin was lighter, and she appeared a bit heavier, but the resemblance was uncanny.

"How is it that you live so long and have escaped death so easily?" Odessa asked. "That's what I still haven't figured out."

"You are more clever than I gave you credit for."

Odessa perked up. "Why, thank you, Reverend Isabella!"

"Isabella is fine," the older woman said. "No need to call me Reverend outside of ceremony. I was just being irritable."

"Is it witchcraft?" Odessa continued, and the spark of admiration Isabella had for Odessa went out as quickly as it was lit.

"No," Isabella was adamant. "I no longer practice the occult, nor do I claim any one religion."

"Why'd you stop?" Odessa leaned against the wall, until a guard made her way toward Odessa and motioned her to move. "Sorry," Odessa mouthed and stepped away from the wall. "I'm kidding. I get it. But your skills are valuable to us."

"Who is *us*?"

"The Vitruvians, silly. And the Erdelings. You have great wisdom and negotiating powers."

"You can see how well my powers of negotiation worked there," Isabella joked. Then, after noticing several more visitors eyeing the two and the bits of conversation they overheard with odd fascination, she added, "Perhaps we should continue this conversation elsewhere."

Odessa nodded, and the two proceeded to exit through one of the museum's side doors that led to a small patio area, which was empty at present. There was a small fountain at the center depicting an image of a Native American man on horseback. They sat at the edge of the fountain. Odessa began to take her shoes off so she could dip her toes in the water, but Isabella shook her head. Odessa dropped her head like a small child being chastised. She had been away from the water for nearly six hours now, and she missed it.

"The point is," Odessa continued, "you learned through trial and error how to reach people who are unreachable. You understand the inner workings of politics and the human thought process better than anyone. And most of all, you have influence."

"Influence?"

"You think I don't know that your little Sanctuary is one of many that you set up here and throughout Europe? You have an underground following. They can help us on our mission."

"What mission would that be?"

"We need to save this planet, for one thing. And to do that, we need to keep the Royals and the Null people away from it."

"The Null people? The black hole dwellers in Section 4? I thought they were a myth."

"Afraid not," Odessa eyed the drops of water in the fountain lovingly. "And they are after more than just Earth. They'll go after all planets in Sections 0, 1 and 2. That includes Erde as well." She gauged Isabella's reaction.

Isabella nodded. *Lucene,* she thought. Isabella was almost positive that Lucene had been relocated to the sanctuary planet, but until that moment, hadn't been sure.

A long silence ensued. Finally, Isabella answered, "What would I need to do?"

CHAPTER 10
THE NEW CONTRACT
AUGUST. FIVE MONTHS BEFORE THE NEW ASSEMBLY.

Jasper Set rolled into the Royal palace in his usual, tornado-like fashion, pausing to purposefully knock down a few Cyrtostachys renda palms that Sabrina had collected on one of her final visits to Earth before her untimely death. He watched gleefully as they fell like a stack of dominoes until they, at last, reached what appeared to be a shrine with Sabrina's image molded in a ten-foot tungsten sculpture. The tree fronds slapped the late sovereign in the face as they found their final resting place. Despite all that Jasper knew of the multiverse, he still could not be certain what happened to a being after it died.

It is a myth that all demons are from the underworld and ruled by the devil and that there was simply heaven, hell, and purgatory. Jasper, for example, being of the Null, lived in the upper world. He didn't believe in the all-powerful Segue and wasn't too sure about the afterlife. This lack of understanding only served to infuriate him further.

"Jasper, your Excellence," Hamish bowed politely once the demon had swirled into the main meeting room. Hamish was in his usual place, standing by the long glass window, somberly overlooking the remains of his once-great city. Something he had done, almost constantly, for the past 25 years.

Likewise, Fredo stood guard, as he has always done. This time, however, he was saddened. He loved his former sovereign, and now his child was to be raised by Hamish, a Royal he was sworn to protect, even though he felt that Hamish did not entirely deserve his loyalty. Still, he knew that his child would enjoy a much better life as a leader versus a lesser Royal—a member of the military class, as he was. Yes, his child could one day come to have what he had imagined for himself—absolute power.

"What am I exc-c-c-cellent at?" Jasper asked.

"Well, it's just—"

Jasper let out a bellowing laugh. "Hah! I am jus-s-s-s-t kidding. I know all of the ways in which I am exc-c-c-cellent." Fredo stood behind Hamish, at the respectful distance, grinding his teeth so hard that it could be heard from the next room over and probably down the hall. "Fredo, my good man. Nic-c-c-ce to s-s-s-see you again. My, my...have you los-s-s-st weight?"

While many Earthlings like it when someone accuses them of losing weight (as if they were enormous to start with), for Fredo, this was the height of shame. He ground his teeth even more forcefully, refraining from a response.

"Hamish," Jasper admired, scanning the sovereign from head to toe. Hamish was dressed in a long purple robe laced with golden threads and diamonds. "You're looking as regal as ever in an unas-s-s-suming, 'how the hell did I get here' s-s-s-sort of way."

Hamish smiled knowingly. Twenty-five years had made him smarter, and he refused to fall into Jasper's trap. Jasper liked a show, so he was fully prepared to entertain the demon.

"And where is the lovely wife?" Jasper scanned the room, up and down, back and forth, even peeping beneath what used to be her throne, just in case.

"She's dead," Hamish said curtly, without feeling.

"Oh my," Jasper feigned surprise. "How did she die?"

Hamish thought momentarily to lie—after all, the confession could affect their original contract. Instead, in a moment of bravado that bubbled up from the ground and now coursed through his veins, he answered, "I strangled her to death in a fit of rage because she disgusted me."

A long pause ensued before Jasper let out another of his boisterous laughs.

"Frankly, my good man," Jasper confessed. "I didn't think you had it in you." Hamish was not sure how to respond, so he said nothing. "Can't s-s-s-say I'm s-s-s-surprised though. She was a feisty one, though, wasn't she?" Jasper thought a moment. "I think I will miss-s-s her."

Hamish did not share the sentiment. "The reason I asked you here…" Hamish began.

"Yes-s--s-s," Jasper floated over to Hamish, standing at an overly personal inch from his face, so that the spray from his "sss" covered parts of Hamish's face. It didn't help that his breath smelled like eggs that had been left out in the sun. Hamish stood adamant, refusing to react. "Why did you as-s-sk me here?"

"There's the matter of our contract," Hamish reminded him.

"Ah," Jasper put his hands behind his back, pacing back and forth with his spindly legs hovering in mid-air, his short wings doing the brunt of the work to keep him afloat. "What about our contract? You're not breaking our agreement, are you?"

"Certainly not," Hamish reassured. "It's just that, the original contract was between you, Sabrina and me. With her gone, I wanted to be sure it was still…valid."

Jasper thought about this. If the contract were null and void (forgive the pun), he could have his people roll right over the Royals—but then he'd never have the girl. On the other hand, five more years seemed like an eternity. And, if Hamish failed, as he had successfully done for the past 25 years, then the results would be the same. Why wait?

"This is tricky," Jasper acknowledged. "This could technically be cons-s-idered a breach of contract, wouldn't you s-s-say?"

Hamish felt his face grow hot as little beads of sweat formed around his brow. "I didn't anticipate losing one of our co-signers, Jasper. It's an unfortunate event, not a breach of contract."

"No," Jasper corrected. "An accidental drowning is an unfortunate event. Death by s-s-strangling is very much on purpos-s-se."

Hamish thought a moment. "What if I sweetened the deal by offering you a new and better contract?"

"Go on," Jasper leaned in with interest.

"We promised you a Data Collector with special powers, where, once identified, might prove to be useful to you. What if we upped the ante, so to speak?"

"How so?"

No prolonged "s" there, Hamish noticed. *Did he voluntarily turn it off and on for effect?*

"Not only can we give you the girl," Hamish continued, "but we can provide a beacon of light that will lead you to the entire Peace-Keeper planet, where all the empaths live. Now, instead of having one all-powerful minion to do your bidding, you could have dozens...thousands even." Honestly, Hamish had no idea how many, if any, were still left. According to Far's recent accounts from his visit, there weren't that many. Hamish decided to leave that part out. "The point is, we have someone living on Erde that can act as a lighthouse, guiding you toward them, something you simply cannot seem to do on your own."

"You're forgetting one important thing, Hamish," Jasper laughed. "Now that I know he's out there, what's to stop me from finding him on my own? Your beacon is not all goodness and light. I can find the planet without you...or should I say, *her*?"

Hamish was not a braggart, but he knew when he had the upper hand, and this was it. He smiled. Jasper really didn't know.

"*Her*, you say?"

"You are referring to Moksha, are you not?" Jasper was bluffing. But he was certain he was convincing.

"With all due respect, your Excellence," Hamish replied. "If you could have found her, you would have already. The fact that I'm still alive and that the Training Grounds are still here is proof that you still need me."

"I don't need anyone!" Jasper hissed, his face aglow with fire and anger as he once again shoved it in front of Hamish, touching nose-to-nose.

"The truth is," Hamish touched two fingers to Jasper's chest and pushed him away as if pushing away a helium balloon. Jasper floated backward. "Moksha is either too good, and you cannot see her, or the planet, as a whole, has so much positive energy that it's protecting her. Either way, in spite of your protests, you do need me. Agree to a new contract, and I will make sure you have the girl and a direct route to Erde and..." Hamish paused for dramatic effect.

"And what?" Jasper was impatient.

"A mole to help corrupt the lot of them."

"I don't unders-s-stand," Jasper began flitting around the room like an annoying fly trying to find its way out, buzzing by the windows, the upper corners of the ceiling and finally to the carefully arranged food table that was always made available to him when he visited. This time, he noticed to his delight, they added a plate full of crispy roasted roaches salted just the way he liked them. He couldn't resist pausing to crunch on a few, nervously.

"What if I told you that I had a plan to help you break down their resistance? Lose enough of that good energy for you to worm your way through the barriers that prevent you from penetrating their planet and wreaking havoc? What would that be worth to you?"

"And there it is-s-s," Jasper pointed a long finger in Hamish's direction. "It wasn't just that you were worried about my cons-s-sidering the first contract void. You want s-s-s-omething else. What is it?"

"It seems the Earthlings are more resilient than we first anticipated," Hamish confessed. "And my superiors are growing impatient with the Royal military clan."

"You want me to wipe out an entire s-s-species so that you can take over? Without giving them a s-s-s-porting chance? Where's the fun in that? Bes-s-sides, even if I were to agree to s-s-something so dramatic, the s-s-simplest thing would be to have my family roll over Earth. But then there'd be nothing left but a black hole. It would be us-s-seless-s to you."

"You misunderstand my intentions," Hamish explained. "I'm not asking you to roll over Earth. I'm asking you to roll over my superiors."

Fredo's spine arched as he listened in shock at what his Sovereign was suggesting. He was sworn to loyalty toward Hamish and was bound to protect him. But he was also loyal toward his people. What Hamish was suggesting was out-and-out mutiny. He couldn't allow this. He stared at Hamish with such force that Hamish could not help but feel it. But his Sovereign didn't seem fearful at all. Instead, he peered back gently, with those tired but knowing eyes—and smiled out of the corner of his mouth.

Fredo shrank. Of course, he would follow along with this for plan the baby. As the son of his Sovereign, his child would inherit the Earth and a better life than what he could provide as a ruler, not a warrior. But if he went to Hamish's superiors, something that was just not done by a member of his caste, not only would they be unlikely to listen, but he feared what his Sovereign might do to the baby. And at this point in his life, the child was the only thing Fredo could point to that actually had meaning to him.

"You devious son of a gun," Jasper bounced joyfully. The "sss" was gone again, Hamish noticed. "I give you credit, Hamish," Jasper continued. I didn't think you had it in you. But I do believe you may be worse than Sabrina. She couldn't contain herself, but you bottle up all that negativity and deceptiveness into a bulky little unassuming package of a lizard." Jasper floated over to Hamish and poked him in the chest in praise. "Now, I understand why Sabrina picked you. You were more alike than different."

"I know you mean that as a compliment," Hamish answered lazily. "But, you're wrong. That's not why she chose me."

Jasper furrowed his brows. He prided himself on understanding how other beings thought, but he seemed to be having a number of misfires today. Instead, he returned his attention to the conversation at hand.

"What did you have in mind?" Jasper asked.

"Keep the Null away from the Training Grounds and Earth but direct them to several nomadic hubs in the universe where the bulk of the Royal Almighty live. It will give me the time and space I need to occupy Earth and grow a new breed of Royals with myself at the helm."

"S-s-such poise, S-s-such grandeur." Jasper shook his head. "And in return, you deliver the girl you have been promis-s-sing, along with these other do-gooders for me to play with. S-s-s-eems like an unbalanced trade, if you ask me." He paused to search Hamish's face. "But wait, there's more, isn't there?" Jasper suddenly spouted, gleefully, like a gameshow host. "What is it?"

"The mole I spoke of isn't Moksha. His name is Far. In addition to the gift of prophecy, he can also transport himself between worlds. Can you imagine what would happen if you had Lucene's time-space manipulation and Far's multiverse-jumping skills?"

Jasper's eyes grew wide. The possibilities were endless. His mind began reeling. Where would he begin? First, he would follow the original plan to see what his doppelgängers in varied realms were doing. Then, they would devise a plan to grow their powers. What then? *Oh, well, I guess that will become more obvious when I match wits with my other selves.* But the larger question remained, how had he not been aware of a non-Peace— bleh, he still couldn't bring himself to even think the name... How had an anomaly of energy in the universe escaped his attention? Was the power of positive energy really strong enough to shield them? "How much time do you need to deliver Lucene and Far to me?" he choked on their names. *Funny,* he thought. *I can barely bring myself to say their names, either.*

"Not long," Hamish answered. "But to be clear, this new contract would be an amendment to the old one. We have five years remaining on that contract."

"That long?"

"You've waited 25 years, what is five more?"

"Done. I'll draft a new version..."

"That's not all," Hamish continued. "This means that the Null will no longer come after me or my military clan. They will steer clear of Section 0 and Section 3 indefinitely. And—"

"There's an *and?!"* Jasper was indignant.

"Imagine," Hamish reminded him. "No longer being bound to a single universe, discovering what else exists if not the Mighty Segue...having all the answers at your disposal, and powerful beings to support you."

Jasper sighed. *That would be nice.*

"And?" Jasper motioned for Hamish to continue.

"Do whatever you wish to the Peace-Keepers, but do not hurt my son Cepheus, unless absolutely necessary."

"Aww," Jasper mocked. "What a proud papa."

"And—"

"Seriously, if there are so many amendments to the contract, and these are supposed all-powerful beings, then why not keep them for yourself?" Jasper was growing increasingly suspicious.

"Because," Hamish was blunt. "I have neither the time, the patience, nor your skill to convince them to use their powers for my bidding. I see you as having no such obstacles."

Hamish had successfully appealed to Jasper's ego.

"Go on," Jasper smiled, proudly. "And?"

"I want Sabrina's name removed from the contract. And, in the event that anything happens to me, I want a new name added as my successor."

Fredo's eyes grew hopeful.

"Really?" Jasper looked back and forth between Hamish and his guard. "What name?"

"It will be in the contract," Hamish answered simply. "We don't say it aloud."

---

75 Years Ago. When the Training Grounds Were New.

"How many men are you currently training, Fredo?" A then-young Sabrina peered from the top of the open-air overlook where she watched the military practice drills below with a mixture of curiosity and boredom. Broken out into groups, some were practicing hand-to-hand combat while others were using primitive staffs and materials that could be procured in nature within a moment's notice. A few were learning remote weaponry using more advanced technology, which was incredibly dull to watch as it largely involved a group of rugged men and women gathered around holographic fish simulations.

"Currently, we have 132 men and women, my Sovereign. But we are expecting at least two dozen more recruits within the next month."

"I didn't ask you about the women, Fredo," Sabrina clarified. "How many men? More specifically, how many men who are mature enough to provide me with an heir?"

Fredo was taken aback. It had been only a few weeks since Sabrina lost her husband during a routine exploratory mission to a nearby planet. It was assumed that he contracted a rare disease in the unmarked territory, and he was dead within three days of becoming ill. His body had only been retrieved and buried on the Training Grounds one week prior.

Fredo approached his Sovereign cautiously. "At least fifty or more men would fit that criteria, my Sovereign." He stood beside her, shoulder-to-shoulder. This was generally too close for a lower-level Royal to stand when in the presence of a superior, but the line of questioning had him almost—hopeful. "But, why would someone of your caliber even entertain the idea of these unworthy lessers?"

"Not that it's any of your business, Fredo," she snapped back but then let out a coy smile. "Alright, I'll tell you anyway." She stepped away from the ledge and made her way gracefully along a stone path toward the palace, still under construction, with the main throne room and several meeting rooms not yet under shelter from the harsh weather. She motioned for him to follow. "If I don't find a replacement husband soon, then my parents will find one for me. And, I shudder to think who they'll expect me to spend the next 150 or more years with. No, I need to marry, and quickly, before they have a chance to interfere."

Fredo followed Sabrina like a lost puppy at her heels, even though he was more than a foot taller than her. "If you are in need of a husband, I would be honored to fill that role," Fredo boldly offered. "Protecting you would still be my primary concern, of course, but—"

"Stop!" Sabrina commanded. Fredo obeyed, his normally red face appearing pinker. She eyed him for what seemed like an eternity. In truth, she found Fredo to be all brute and no brain, and the last thing she needed was an emotionally overgrown child for a mate. Furthermore, she shuddered to think about the intellectual capacity of whatever spawned from their coupling. No, she decided to herself after pondering for several minutes while Fredo stood, motionless, beside her. Fredo might be good for an occasional rendezvous, but he wasn't Sovereign material. She also needed him to protect her with his life and emotions had a way of getting in the way of all that. "No," she told him, pausing while he let out a heavy sigh. "While I'm certain you would provide a mighty heir for me, you're much too valuable as my protector for me to ask such a sacrifice of you."

"But I wouldn't consider it—"

"No, Fredo." His face fell. She wasn't the sentimental sort, but she did need him to stay focused. "I am honored by your chivalry," she complimented. Softness was not her forte, and it felt forced. "But we must find someone more suitable."

Fredo shoved his feelings to a place in the back of his mind not likely to resurface anytime soon and nodded in understanding. "Very well, my Sovereign. What did you have in mind?"

"I'd like you to give me a tour of the Training Grounds and introduce me to the men. Don't tell them why I am there, though. Do you understand?"

"Yes, my Sovereign."

"We'll just tell them that I am there to see how training is progressing so I can make my report."

"I understand."

The two walked in silence down a long and winding dirt and rock staircase that had been cut into the side of the mountain. There were flimsy rails that had yet to be fastened properly. But since Sabrina and her late husband rarely felt the need to leave the palace grounds, and the only ones who typically used this entrance and exit were their guards, they were in no rush to fix this, as the palace was still under vast amounts of construction.

Fredo stopped to gather his chief guards, explaining that Sovereign Sabrina wanted to watch the troops and possibly ask some questions. They bowed, without question, offering to line their respective training teams up as Sabrina passed.

For the next several hours, Sabrina moved throughout the Training Grounds, soldiers snapping to attention upon her arrival. To avoid suspicion, she occasionally threw a question toward a female trainee, how long have they been there? Who was their family? What was their primary skill? That sort of thing. Along the way, she passed several soldiers who Fredo suspected would be suitable for her needs—handsome and skilled soldiers who would no doubt produce a fine heir, but she seemed disinterested.

"That's all for today," she finally told Fredo. "Escort me back to the palace."

"Of course, my—"

Sabrina stopped, mid-step. In the distance there was a young frumpy man carefully watering a sad looking palm tree protruding forlornly out from between some rocks. The man appeared to be...*singing* to it.

"Young man, what are you doing?"

Hamish put his small watering can down in surprise.

"Kneel before your Sovereign, you insolent boy!" Fredo yelled, about to deliver a physical assault. "Why aren't you with your troop?"

Sabrina touched Fredo's arm. "That's enough, Fredo. I can handle this." To the young man who appeared to be several years younger than she, she asked again. "What are you doing to that palm tree?"

"I'm giving it water. It was almost all dried out."

"Aren't there more suitable servants for this purpose?"

"One would think so, my Sovereign. But they must have missed this one. Another day and this Cyrtostachys renda might have died."

"A Cyrtosta—what?" She was confused.

"A Cyrtostachys renda palm. They are very regal, don't you think?" Sabrina thought for a moment. She'd never considered a plant to be regal, but she did concur that it was an attractive little tree.

"Why do you care what happens to this tree? It's just a plant. There are others."

"Not like this one," Hamish observed. "You see, this one is growing between the rocks when it shouldn't. It's resilient. And look at the way its root system has adapted by—"

"That's fine," Sabrina interrupted him. "What's your name, young soldier?"

"Hamish," he answered calmly, looking at her deeply as if he actually saw her. She tugged her blouse tightly to her chest with one hand. "Come with me, young man," she motioned.

"But, my Sovereign," Fredo whispered in protest. "I know this boy, he's among the worst of our fighters. And look at him. He's shaped like a plump pear!"

"Yes," Sabrina smiled. She couldn't articulate what it was about Hamish, exactly. Their language had no word for compassion, and yet she could feel the deep emotion he seemed to have for this silly little green thing growing in the dirt. "He's perfect."

Fredo looked at Hamish and back at Sabrina. Hamish was, admittedly, a little frightened. *Was she planning on killing him? Feeding him to one of her exotic pets?* He couldn't be sure, but he followed blindly. It was his duty.

"Meet us back at the palace, Fredo. This young soldier will escort me." She turned and remembered something. "Oh, and when you do return—bring the little tree with you."

CHAPTER 11
THE MAKERSPACE
OCTOBER. THREE MONTHS BEFORE THE NEW ASSEMBLY.

The Makerspace was something to behold. Unfortunately, a good portion of it was lost on Lucene. At that moment, she wished her friend and former neighbor Ivan were there to explain some of the equipment and technology to her. But she reminded herself, he and Fatima would be there soon. Of course, then her concerns about the Royals, the IPP and adjusting to her new life on Erde were replaced with another one, *would Ivan and Fatima make it there safely?* She trusted Ivan's mechanical abilities, but like it as not, the two left Earth in a hurry with the first working prototype Ivan had created…well, the second if you count his adaptations to the Vessel.

Dallen snapped his fingers in front of Lucene, interrupting her daydream. "Hello," he smiled broadly, "are you there?" She bit back a snarky reply, but only because she was immediately distracted by the people mover they were now boarding (at least, that's what she named it in her head). And Lucene had to watch her step, particularly since she was still wearing boots that were slightly too large for her. Tanager went to offer his hand, but Dallen had already taken Lucene's elbow and was escorting her onto the mover and promptly shouldering Tanager out of the way. Tanager clenched one of his fists, annoyed. Cepheus shook his head at his friend. *It's not worth it,* he thought. Tanager nodded and calmed down. After he, Cepheus, Lucene, and Dallen were safely inside the small open-aired elevator-like contraption, their guide, Renenet, closed the metal side gate and locked it. "I would advise that you hold onto the guardrails or take a seat," she said with authority. "This transporter moves in all directions."

Renenet was a broad woman with a large and muscular frame. Her hair looked like that of a lion's mane, her face the shape of a feline, complete with soft patches of fur, but with a human mouth and almond-shaped eyes that resembled fire agate. She was the director of the Makerspace, a responsibility she did not take lightly. After all, while Erdelings as a species were somewhat behind other populations when it came to military tactics and defense, discipline and containment centers, as well as gaps in their development of health and social services departments, when it came to technology, transportation, energy conservation, agriculture, and education, few could match them. TARA's Makerspace was so large and well-equipped that many businesses in Achel contributed to its growth and had a working agreement to pool resources with one another in exchange for the ability to rent out sections of the space as needed.

As Lucene and the others took a seat on one of the fold-down plastic-like chairs, Renenet hit a few levers and the transporter began to ascend. Both Lucene and Dallen craned their necks to peer over the railing of the glass box as it moved. Tanager smiled and kept glancing at Lucene to gauge her reaction.

Soon, they had an aerial view of the Makerspace. Renenet paused the transporter and waited, expectantly. Without thinking, Lucene and Dallen both stood in unison by the guardrails and peered down. From this view, the entire Makerspace looked like a Fibonacci nautilus shell, with each compartment representing a room dedicated to a specific purpose.

There was a Hot Room where people could be seen glass blowing and working with metals, a giant kiln in one corner. A few rooms down was a machining area. The next, someone could be spotted sanding a large piece of wood. Still, further down the spiral, robotics of varied shapes and sizes could be witnessed in various stages of development—some in disassembled chunks on a lab table, others skirting under the feet of those working there, and a few actually participating in helping their creators construct new versions of themselves. From their vantage point, it was as if they were watching a well-orchestrated ant farm at work.

"What's that?" Lucene pointed, seeing a shadow spiraling in circles from the central ground floor through the vein of the shell, stopping in what appeared to be a textile and sewing room.

"It is a transporter like this one," Renenet explained, "That one is slightly larger and better equipped to move machinery to and from the loading dock. All shared tools, such as your lathes, band saws, welders, routers and such, are kept on the ground floor near the commissary. They can be easily moved from their central location to anywhere in the Makerspace."

"Easily moved?" Dallen was surprised. "But some of those industrial machines must weigh at least sixteen thousand units!" To Lucene, he explained, "that's around a thousand pounds where you come from."

"Perhaps it's easier if I show you," Renenet offered. "Please take a seat."

Lucene and Dallen sat beside Cepheus and Tanager, who were watching the couple as if they were parents taking their kids to their first amusement park, or to see the ocean for the first time. Tanager even forgot for a moment, his growing dislike of Dallen.

The transporter began moving again at Renenet's command. But this time, instead of going straight down, like an elevator, it revolved 90 degrees and made its way toward a wide-mouth opening that looked like a cave. The group began a slow spiral, like blood moving through a vein. Each room they passed, larger than the last. "Here's a good place to stop," Renenet decided. The transporter spun to face the front of what appeared to be an auto-repair shop. There were vehicle stalls on each side, messy shelving cluttered with tubes hanging off the sides, hand drills, toolboxes and spare tires. Lucene even spotted the occasional odd-shaped car door and windowpane.

"Looks like Ivan's workshop," Lucene commented. "Is he here?" she joked.

Cepheus let out what Lucene had come to determine was a laugh, except it sounded more like a purr that got trapped in a cat's belly, never to quite make it out of its mouth.

"Not yet," Tanager smiled. "But no doubt he'll feel quite at home when he gets here." Cepheus nodded.

"Who is Ivan?" Dallen enquired.

"Ivan the Tinkerer," Lucene explained, "was my next-door neighbor back on Earth. He's invented all manner of contraptions, including transportation technology that got us home faster."

Tanager perked up slightly at Lucene's reference to Erde as "home." Maybe she was beginning to settle in, after all.

The transporter set off a beep, and those scurrying around the room paused to look up before resuming their work, disinterested in whomever it was in the transporter. One tall man in overalls, carrying a large plastic box, skipped across the conveyor at the center of the room and hurried out of the way. The transporter followed the conveyor track, until they had turned to face a large, saucer-shaped vehicle.

"I thought this was a car shop, but it's not, is it?" Lucene's face grew wide as she peered at a smaller prototype for the very Vessel that she, Roman, Tanager and Cepheus had arrived on not a month earlier.

"It's a multi-purpose transportation room," Renenet explained. "As you can see, this would be quite a large object to move under normal circumstances, but watch."

Renenent moved closer to the vessel and barked a series of voice commands. The transporter buzzed as two large metal arms forked out on each side of it, adapting their width to the size of the spacecraft. Meanwhile, the vessel began to move. The platform on which it sat lifted, and a thin square tile disconnected itself from the floor, allowing itself to be hooked onto their transporter and easily pulled onto the conveyor.

"How much does that weigh?" Dallen was surprised.

"It's a pretty compact prototype," Renenet dropped her mouth in a thoughtful frown. "Probably only around seven thousand pounds or one-hundred and twelve thousand units."

"And what powers this transporter?" Dallen questioned as Renenet finalized moving the vessel to the conveyor and pulling it as the transporter backed toward the vein in which they had come through.

Renenet squinted her eyes and let out what could best be described as a low growl. "That's proprietary," she murmured.

"But if I am to work with your people, I need to know what resources I—" he corrected himself, "we have at our disposal."

"All you need to know is that it works," Renenet shot an annoyed glance at Cepheus.

"Representative Dallen," Cepheus explained calmly. "We are happy to share any and all of our resources, technology and blueprints where necessary—after we are reinstated to the IPP and have solidified our agreement with the Vitruvians. Until then…you understand."

"Quite," Dallen answered curtly, pouting.

Tanager balled his fists again, but after witnessing a questioning look from Lucene, released them.

"Hey," a large man in orange overalls suddenly called. "Renni, where are you going with that?"

"Don't worry," she reassured him. "I'll bring it right back. I'm conducting a demonstration."

"Oh, okay," he scratched his head. "But wouldn't it be easier to use the…" Renenet shot him a warning glance, her eyes like daggers. "Er, never mind," he went back to minding his own business.

Dallen missed the exchange as he was busy surveying the room as if taking mental pictures of everything he saw. In fact, every once in a while, his eyes blinked rapidly like the shutter on a camera. More interesting was when he tilted his head to one side before a quick blink.

"Is something in your eye?" Lucene tilted her head in front of his face. He was annoyed at first, but then when he caught sight of her quizzical expression and pursed lips, he couldn't help but smile. She was exquisite. He didn't even mind that a few strands of her hair fell in her eye. Normally, that would be something he would have corrected by helpfully pushing it behind her ear. But somehow, *disheveled* was a good look for Lucene.

From the corner of the room, Lucene caught sight of a small woman with red hair and bright blue eyes. Unlike the others working nearby, she was clad in very Earth-like jeans and a simple green t-shirt. She wasn't working with heavy machinery, though. She appeared to be painting tiny miniatures of the larger prototypes on the main floor and putting them in a small model spread out on a long table in front of her. The only thing missing from the miniatures was a classic model train. The woman's eyes suddenly looked up, piercing their way past her to someone else... Tanager. Tanager momentarily returned the gaze.

"Who's that?" Lucene leaned in and whispered to him, cautiously.

"A mistake." Tanager clenched his teeth.

"Now's a good time to take a seat," Renenet advised, missing these exchanges. The transporter, now with a small vessel in tow, backed fully into the vein, but instead of continuing its spiral path, it began dropping. Lucene grabbed her stomach as it lurched.

"Sorry," Tanager touched her hand, suddenly remembering she was there. "I should have warned you. But the drop is quick."

"Good to know," Lucene felt a little queasy. From the look of it, so was Dallen. But Tanager didn't care about him.

Renenet explained that for general use, the spiral was adequate, but for large machinery that needed to be relocated to and from the docking area, the central unit was most efficient. The group watched as the doors to the loading dock opened, and they were suddenly in an outdoor covered space, surrounded by flying contraptions, land vehicles, a few dome-shaped boats and even sections of what appeared to be a part of the SpeedCircuit under reconstruction. When Lucene looked up, she witnessed several aircrafts being suspended from the ceiling, as if they were waiting in the queue to be tinkered with. "Before we go back, maybe Lucene would like to see the research and performance spaces," Tanager offered.

"Good idea," Cepheus nodded. "That will give her a sense of how the Makerspace and the rest of TARA are interconnected."

Renenet's face dropped. Clearly the performance space, which housed the music, theater and dance area, and the research space which included a library, chemistry lab, and medical lab, did not interest her nearly as much.

Apparently, it didn't interest Dallen much, either. He was about to protest and ask to return to some of the other more interesting spaces, such as the robotics or prototyping rooms until he saw Lucene's face light up. The Makerspace, while beautifully architected, was too much technology and far too many computers in one space. She was better than she had been now that she knew exactly who had been after her (the Royals) and that she was safe. Still, a music area with instruments and a dance floor went beyond just feeling safe. That sounded much more interesting.

He smiled at Lucene. "I think we should definitely see your performance area. I am rather fond of the theater." Dallen made a mental note of the rooms he planned to revisit at another time — a necessary detour, from his perspective.

Renenet deposited the vessel into a free space, and the tile sank into the floor. One of the ground-floor attendants dressed in denim pants and a rough burlap shirt was confused. Renenet let out a sigh, "Just a demonstration," she explained again. "I'll come back for it as soon as I'm done giving a tour."

"We give tours," the attendant was surprised.

"Apparently," Renenet mumbled under her breath, quickly recovering when Cepheus shot her a warning glance.

"Yes," he answered softly. "Commander Royce and the PDL requested we give Representative Dallen from Vitruvia a tour of our Makerspace."

"I see," the attendant turned to look at Dallen. He really didn't. Not sure how he was supposed to respond to dignitaries visiting, he did the only thing he could think of, he curtsied. Tanager was perplexed. *And I thought I was confused by extraterrestrial customs.*

Renenet guided the transporter down a long hallway, stopping at the main cafeteria and lounge on the ground floor of TARA's educational department. "I'm afraid that this is where I make my exit." Renenet seemed a little too happy to be relieved of her duties. Frankly, she had more important work to do.

"Thank you, Director Renenet," Dallen flashed a pearly white smile and bowed slightly. Renenet perked up for a moment and broke into a smile. At least she had been acknowledged by this visitor.

"Yes, thank you," Lucene chimed in. Renenet's smile dropped as she turned her gaze from Dallen to Lucene. She seemed almost... angry at Lucene, for some reason. *Don't you shoot those dagger eyes at me,* Lucene thought. Suddenly, Renenet relaxed her expression. "You're welcome," she answered, pleasantly enough before retreating with the transporter.

They had now been delivered to the entranceway in which they had arrived after having spent the last hour exploring the expansive performance and research spaces. Tanager paused to show Lucene the room where they would meet in the morning to begin their work, then the four retreated through the glass doors out into the world.

Cepheus was prepared to escort Dallen back to his temporary living quarters on Achel, while Tanager ensured that Lucene was comfortable finding her way home from the SpeedCircuit.

"May I have a moment?" Dallen asked Cepheus quietly.

"Of course," Cepheus stepped back as if Dallen had something confidential to share.

"No, not with you," Dallen explained, motioning toward Lucene. "May I have a moment to speak with Lucene?"

"Why are you asking me?" There was a long pause.

Finally, Dallen understood and broke the silence. "Lucene," he redirected his question, "may I speak with you for a moment?" He took long strides over to her. "Alone," he added as he sidled his way between Lucene and Tanager. Tanager didn't move as he watched and waited for Lucene's reply.

"Sure," she answered awkwardly, and Tanager reluctantly retreated to join Cepheus by an outdoor fountain, the two men engaging in a private mental conversation about the day's events. Occasionally, Cepheus had to fill in what Tanager missed through actual words, but they were purposefully cryptic, and few and far between.

"I would like to escort you to dinner tomorrow evening," Dallen announced.

Lucene searched his eyes for a moment. "Is that a question or a command?"

"It's more of a request," Dallen was taken aback. Lucene glanced in Tanager's direction, not quite sure how to respond. "Do you need his permission?"

"Of course not," Lucene shot back before catching herself. She couldn't be certain whether or not Dallen was being sarcastic or serious. "Dinner would be lovely," she finally answered calmly. This was different from how she felt on the inside. In fact, her stomach felt a bit like the lurch from when the transporter dropped them to the ground floor. Only this one felt worse. *What was that?* She asked herself. *Nerves,* she thought finally. After all, aside from the makeshift date nights Tanager attempted to clumsily plan for them aboard the Vessel, she really couldn't remember the last time she had been on a proper date. She searched her memory but gave up once she had retreated back more than a decade ago when she was still living in New York. *Surely, she dated…someone.*

Dallen snapped his fingers in front of her face. "Are you there?" he asked. Lucene was beginning to hate that. "So, I will see you tomorrow night then," he added, "that was a question."

"Yes," Lucene smiled uncertainly. "Tomorrow night."

CHAPTER 12
TEST RESULTS
OCTOBER. THREE MONTHS BEFORE THE NEW ASSEMBLY.

"Class," Tanager addressed his students, twenty-one in total, as they eyed Lucene with a mixture of curiosity and fascination. She pulled the sides of her cardigan sweater together uncomfortably, as if she had been standing there naked the entire time. *Why are they looking at me like that? And why did I let Mallory pick out this ridiculous outfit for me? I'm not cardigan material.* "As you have no doubt figured out, this is the Lucene you've waited more than a year to meet. Please make her feel welcome."

The students, all of varied age, size and skin tone lined up, one behind the other. One by one, they stepped in front of her, gave a polite bow and offered quietly, "Welcome, friend," before stating their name. Most were odd-sounding: Xeni, Cluseladek, Neroni, and so on. Lucene wasn't sure how to respond, so she gave a slight nod of her head in return, looking to Tanager for guidance. He nodded back, reassuring her that this was the appropriate response. So, she nodded her head in acknowledgment, one at a time, before the students returned to their seats. Except, they weren't seats, exactly. They were tall stools with the tops tilted at a sharp angle and adjustable to each student's height so that the class was half standing and half seated at the same time. There were no back supports, and she noted with some surprise that they all had remarkably good posture. There were two crescent moon-shaped lab tables, one in front of the other, facing the teacher's desk and what appeared to be a clear glass screen where she would have expected a chalkboard or whiteboard to be. Granted, it had been a while since she'd gone to college, but she suspected the technology was slightly more evolved than on Earth. From the side, the tables appeared to be comprised of stacked glass, as if they were a series of layered microscope slides. The tops of the desks were a neutral pearl, matching the chairs.

"Please open Lab Resource Test Book Number One. We will begin by reviewing the summary." Lucene watched as they tapped the table and text appeared in front of them, scrawled neatly before each student.

"Are you sure you're ready for this?" Tanager asked Lucene quietly, touching her shoulder lightly. Although they had begun to rebuild an empathic connection over the past month, he was still finding it challenging understanding her emotional state from moment to moment, as it still felt a little...queasy. That was the only word that he could think of to describe it.

"I'm ready," Lucene was determined. "The sooner we can figure this thing out—" She caught herself. "The sooner we can figure *me* out, the better." He smiled weakly. His motives for wanting to understand her better went well beyond his interest in her as a research subject for the Data Collectors, and he was self-aware enough to recognize that.

Both Lucene and the class had been prepped prior to this meeting. Each student in the class, along with both Tanager and Cepheus, had the genetic splicing that was designed to enhance empathy prior to training. There was a fresh batch of students, seventeen in all, who applied for the Data Collector training path, in spite of the violence that had been reported on Earth years prior. The new idea from the school's governing bodies was that perhaps the same training could be tailored to a different purpose, one that might be useful on Erde and in negotiations with neighboring planets. But following a review of Dr. Ennis's work back on Earth, there was now concern over the possibility of the genetic modification being dangerous to a student's mental health. Therefore, all new students were added to a future waitlist, or they opted to join a different learning path at TARA.

Of the students that remained, those that were now semi-seated in front of Lucene, all agreed to undergo voluntary psychological testing paid for by TARA.

"Everyone here has already gone through the screenings we're going to begin today with you, Lucene," Tanager explained. "And they repeat these screenings every four months, following subsequent training. Please, have a seat." Tanager directed her to one of two chairs in the room that actually looked like armchairs, situated next to his desk, side-by-side. Lucene sat, sinking into what was a remarkably comfortable cushion. Tanager sat beside her. "There are thirteen tests in all, designed to get a baseline marker as to where you are right now. Unfortunately, we didn't have the advantage of testing you at an early age, so our baseline is really somewhere in the middle. While these students," Tanager motioned to the class, "were tested as soon as splicing was complete. And, they were all adults at the time. Which is why you are particularly unique." *Not the only reason you are unique,* Tanager thought. Lucene looked up in surprise, blinking twice but saying nothing. *Did he say that last part,* she wondered. Tanager continued, "Genetically born with this mutation and having had it develop, admittedly with some rocky starts and stops, has us all curious about what we're going to find."

The class nodded eagerly, whispering to themselves. At least, Lucene thought they were whispering. Except, their mouths weren't moving. She was used to her, Cepheus and Tanager occasionally sharing thoughts and emotions, but it was disconcerting being in a class that seemed to be talking with one another in their heads. As if on cue, they all fell silent in uniform politeness so as not to make her uncomfortable. She looked up in surprise, and the young girl called Xeni smiled encouragingly at her, giving her a proud thumb's up. Lucene smiled back. It seemed as if Xeni was testing out her knowledge of Earth customs.

"We don't want to overwhelm you, so over the next week, I'll be having you meet with no more than three students at a time, specifically trained to administer a baseline test in a particular area. Then, you and I will meet to discuss the results before we all re-convene as a class." Tanager paused. "Does that sound okay with you?"

Lucene nodded.

"Good." Tanager was satisfied. "Do you remember the thirteen areas we'll be testing, or would you like a refresher?"

Lucene thought a moment, but only a handful of tests came to mind. *Stupid, fuzzy mind,* she thought, immediately looking around to see who else heard that, but no one reacted. It was as if they followed some code of ethics and realized that in her current state, it would be construed as an intrusion. "A refresher, please," she requested.

Tanager turned to address an exceptionally tall student at the back of the class. The young man was wearing a toga-like sheet, and his pale skin with bleached blonde hair, coupled with a commanding presence, gave him the appearance of an ancient Etruscan male that had stepped straight out of a history book. "Cluseladek." Tanager asked, "Since you consistently register high marks in memory, could you please remind everyone in the class what we're testing for—without looking at your book?" As he finished his last statement, the text that was scrawled across the desk in front of Cluseladek disappeared.

Cluseladek smiled proudly. He was up to the challenge. As if standing at a lecture, he addressed the class, being careful to strategically make eye contact with each person in the room several times. "I would be happy to, Professor Tanager," he answered.

Lucene giggled at the title. Tanager wrinkled his brow and shot her a *what was that for,* look. She suddenly had a flashback of Tanager back on Earth wearing a goofy fishing hat and Salt Life shirt and was having a difficult time seeing him as a professor. Then she had another thought, and her face dropped. She'd have to remember to have the costume shop re-create that stupid hat that he loved so much, the one she ripped apart in anger on their trek home.

Cluseladek interrupted her thoughts. "The thirteen tests we use are designed to assess our strength levels in the following areas: overall physical health, intelligence, memory, cognitive balance, telepathy, ethical mind control, telekinesis or psychokinesis, empathy levels, healing ability, precognition, psychometry and remote viewing."

"Holy crap," Lucene blurted out. Tanager turned slightly red, but the class laughed, clearly finding her lingo amusing. "I can do all that?"

"Well, not entirely," Tanager responded. "Most students have varying levels of skill in many of these areas, not necessarily all. We're not completely certain yet why, say one person excels in memory, as with Cluseladek, while another is an expert psychometrist, like Xeni, or has a proficiency in precognition with a minor strength in remote viewing, like Neroni."

Lucene tried to remember which one Neroni was, and then a slightly larger than average-sized woman with an olive complexion and red-green hair waved in her direction. Lucene nodded, noting with some level of surprise how striking Neroni's hair looked against her skin, something she would not have guessed. *Olive, red and green should not go together,* Lucene reasoned. *And yet, on her, somehow, they do.*

Tanager noticed that he'd once again lost Lucene's attention and raised his voice slightly. "Well done, Cluseladek," Tanager praised. "But you missed one."

"No, I didn't, Professor Tanager," the boy answered smugly. "The final test is the one that no one has successfully scored on and is still a working hypothesis."

"And, that would be?" Tanager raised an eyebrow.

"Time and space manipulation."

"Very good, Cluseladek. You may sit down." As he sat, the text from his book reemerged on his desk.

"Did you do that?" Lucene pointed to the desk. "How did you do that?"

"Easily," Tanager answered. "And I only have an average level of telekinetic powers; which, I might add, were all but useless on Earth. I'm still trying to figure out why." Tanager wrinkled his mouth and forehead at the puzzle.

For the remainder of class, Tanager reviewed each of the thirteen testing areas, what the tests involved and how they were administered and measured. He then divided students up into respective categories for Lucene's week-long process. They were beginning tomorrow with cognitive balance. Tanager, along with three students, would be conducting a series of assessments.

Lucene didn't have to ask why they were starting with a test that monitored mental health and screened for potential disorders first. She knew they had to make sure she wasn't batshit crazy before they continued.

Xeni didn't look like a person, exactly. More like an animated cartoon come to life. She had large pink eyes that were out of proportion with the rest of her face, a short blue-black pixie cut for hair, a heart-shaped face and a small mouth. She could best be described as boisterous. Much younger than Fatima, at least in demeanor, Xeni reminded Lucene of her best friend if Fatima were manic and perpetually overly caffeinated.

When Lucene arrived at the TARA psychology lab the next morning, it was Xeni who greeted her first. "Hi, Lucene! OMG, I'm super excited to be working with you today!"

It had come to Lucene's attention that Xeni was going to cycle through every Earth phrase she knew for practice. But, unlike Tanager, Xeni seemed slightly more current, but only by about a century. Though to be fair, Tanager was progressing the longer she and he spent time together…when they weren't arguing, of course. That was progressing too, she realized. Lucene also came to understand that most of their communicative misfires had more to do with some of the strange ways her brain had been interpreting their interactions. While not one to pile on the self-blame, she at least had enough self-awareness to recognize that she had been more off kilter than usual ever since the trek to Erde.

"It's nice to see you again…"

"Xeni," the young girl finished as Lucene was going through the class roster in her brain, trying to remember her name.

"Xeni," Lucene repeated back to her and nodded. She wasn't sure if she was supposed to nod after every interaction, but it seemed appropriate yesterday, so she maintained the custom.

Tanager looked up from the clipboard with information that he was sharing with Cluseladek. Except, the clipboard appeared to be that same translucent glass that made up the lab tables, and the information hovered above it as if the notes jumped off the page. They consisted of a series of charts and an odd language that was lost on Lucene.

Moments later, Neroni arrived, carting in a tray filled with a large metal canister and a plate of pastries. "I know we don't typically eat in class," she explained, "but today is a special occasion." She smiled at Lucene with a calm warmth. "We don't always have such an honored guest."

It was only at that moment that it sank in. Lucene wasn't just some

Earthling that came to visit. Not an experimental prototype to study. They legitimately valued her. She felt it like a wave running through her. It struck her with an unquestionable knowing. They appreciated her abilities and admired the life tragedies that she'd had to overcome. It was an odd feeling—being respected like that. Lucene fought back a tear—another surprise, as the last time she was moved to tears was the moment on Earth when she thought Tanager was dead. This was far less traumatic than that. *Perhaps I'm becoming more sensitive,* Lucene thought.

"Thank you, Neroni," Tanager acknowledged. "Lucene, please help yourself. Unfortunately, the coffee is non-hyper-inducing, and the pastries have no artificial sugar; but I think you might enjoy them anyway. We just couldn't give you any sedative or stimulant that might alter the results of today's tests."

"I see," Lucene replied. Back on Earth, caffeine and sugar were her go-to's, but after seven months on the Vessel with limited food supplies, her diet had since become better. This was the first time she realized that she didn't crave either of those things. "Thank you…"

"Neroni," the woman supplied. If Lucene had to guess, Neroni had a good fifteen years on Xeni. However, given that Erdelings age much slower than humans and matured at a different rate, that may have been closer to thirty years.

Tanager and all three of his students waited for Lucene to pour herself a beverage and snatch a pastry before they partook themselves.

"I should explain," Tanager said between bites of a swirled piece of bread that resembled a cinnamon bun. "Xeni, Cluseladek and Neroni are the senior students in class. In fact, when Cepheus and I traveled to Earth to retrieve you, we had no other qualified staff to be on the receiving end of our messages back home, nor anyone to substitute teach some of our classes. These three did a remarkable job of stepping into leadership roles and supporting us remotely. I'm very proud of them." Xeni moved her head and shoulders side-to-side as if doing a strange victory dance. Cluseladek raised his chin proudly and puffed his chest out like a peacock. Neroni, the most modest of the lot, merely smiled and lowered her eyes to the floor.

"Uh, good work…" Lucene responded awkwardly, once again

fighting back the odd tear. "If it weren't for you, I might not be here today. I mean, literally. I could be dead right now. So, thank you."

"'Aint nothin' but a chicken wing," Xeni chortled. Lucene made a mental note to discuss idioms with Xeni at some point in the future, before the young girl drove her crazy…well, crazi*er*.

Clusaladek and Tanager began unpacking instruments that had been tucked away inside the cabinets that lined the room. Xeni, eager to help, all but tripped Cluseladek as he turned to place something on a lab table, only to find the young girl underfoot. "Perhaps," he suggested thoughtfully, "you can help us by warming up the wave machine."

"Sure, I can do that," she responded enthusiastically.

Neroni took Lucene by the elbow and said quietly, "I know you're new here and still getting settled. I don't know if you need it or not, but I happened to stumble across an old dress in my closet this morning. It doesn't fit me anymore, but I suspect it might be perfect for you. I left it hanging in the public bath at the end of the hallway if you want to try it on."

"Oh, okay," Lucene replied. *That was nice of her.* "Thanks—I'll take a look." Neroni nodded before pushing the pastry cart into the corner of the room and out of the way.

For the next three hours, with a break after each hour, they ran tests. Some were simply asking her questions and taking notes. Others involved having her sit under what she could only describe as an old-fashioned hair drying seat, like the one you'd find in salons. Only, instead of heat, these tiny silver, pen-like cylinders were positioned all around her head as brain graphs registered colors and forms in holographic shapes in front of her, while the four testers in the room took notes. Occasionally, Tanager would point to something of interest, and they would nod. Lucene sucked in her breath, remembered she wasn't breathing, and then tried utilizing a relaxing mindfulness tool Cepheus had once taught her. She took a deep breath. *You are safe. Computers are not the enemy.* Lucene opened her eyes and smiled, an encouraging sign to Tanager that she was okay.

At one point, she was asked to meditate, as well as possible, with everything that was happening around her. She closed her eyes again and focused, and somehow, in her mind's eye, she could suddenly see

Tanager's surprised expression looking down at her as if her eyes were open. She could also see the reason for his surprise. Even with her eyes closed, the hologram in front of her, coming from her mind, was an exact moving replica of what was happening in the room around her, registering in her brain.

After an exhausting regimen filled with more questions, more brain scans, interpreting drawings, creating some rudimentary drawings herself, and some other odd balance-type exercises, they concluded for the day.

"Thank you, everyone. I think that's enough for today," Tanager announced. To Lucene, he asked, "We covered a lot of ground. Are you okay?"

Lucene nodded, but she was tired. She'd heard the expression "bone-tired" before but never understood it until this moment. She could feel exhaustion all the way deep into her body.

"Professor Tanager," Xeni chirped, "if Lucene is tired, I can accompany her home."

"Thank you, Xeni. But that won't be necessary." Neroni adopted a knowing smirk as she glanced from her professor to Lucene but said nothing.

"Have a good rest of the day, everyone," Neroni waved, as she and Cluseladek made their exit. "C'mon Xeni," she tugged at the young girl's sleeve. "Maybe the three of us can stop at the common area for dinner before heading home. My husband is watching the kids today, so I have time to be social. What do you say?" Both she and Cluseladek agreed and after saying final goodbyes to Lucene, they left.

"So," Lucene asked, after everyone had left. "Tell me the truth. Am I crazy?"

Tanager's heart sank a little. "Of course not," he replied softly. "Why would you think that?"

"Oh, I dunno, maybe because I killed your fishing hat on the Vessel and have periodically been snarky and horrid to you ever since." She found her eyes getting a little red as she fought back tears. *What the heck was up with all of this emotion lately?*

A stray piece of hair fell from where Lucene had it pulled back, falling over one eye. Lucene blinked as it tickled her eyelid. Without thinking, Tanager brushed it behind her ear. "You have been under a great deal of stress. The test today indicates heavy trauma, but nothing that would lead us to conclude that you are anything but...normal."

She let out a sigh of relief. Somehow, hearing the words "normal" put her at ease.

"If you give me a few moments to wrap up here, perhaps I can accompany you back to the SpeedCircuit? We can even stop for a drink and some dinner first if you're up for it?" *A proper date night,* he thought. One that didn't involve being stuck on the Vessel with Cepheus and Roman hiding out. He laid his clipboard on the desk and then proceeded to cross and uncross his arms as if trying to figure out what to do with them now that they were unoccupied.

"Oh," Lucene was surprised. This was awkward. "I would...but I sort of have a date tonight."

Tanager was both surprised and disappointed and was somewhat unsuccessful at hiding both emotions. "Really? May I be so bold as to ask with whom?"

"Dallen asked me to accompany him to the animal lab this evening after we had dinner." Somehow, she could feel Tanager's stomach all jumbled up. It surprised her because she had assumed that following how she had behaved lately and aboard the Vessel, that any thought of romance between them was clearly off the table. "But, some other time?" she offered.

"Of course," he forced a smile. There was something else that bothered him beyond jealousy. He didn't exactly trust Dallen but wasn't sure if it was because Dallen was Vitruvian if he was merely concerned over Lucene's safety, or something else. "Have a good time. And remember, we went through a lot of tests today. If you have questions or don't feel well over the weekend, please call me." This was Tanager's way of letting her know that if something went amiss in her date with Dallen, he was just a phone alert away. He looked down at her wrist, sighing when he noticed she wasn't wearing her watch.

"I will," Lucene promised. "Don't worry, it's in my bag." She smiled. She still didn't entirely trust phones and computers but had conceded to carrying the alert watch with her at Tanager's constant reminders. She still couldn't get used to wearing it, though, for more than an hour or two at a time before it irritated her, and she had to remove it.

At that moment, she was overcome with emotion again. Without thinking, she rushed over to Tanager and wrapped her arms around his torso and hugged him, resting her head on his chest, just under his chin. He paused for a moment in surprise, his arms dangling until he figured out what to do with them. Eventually, he wrapped his arms around her, hugging her back, and a strange energy passed between them heart-to-heart.

At that moment, there were sounds from the hallway outside, and they quickly broke from their embrace. Lucene haphazardly gathered her belongings and left without another word, leaving Tanager to watch her go, more confused than ever.

CHAPTER 13
MARZIPAN AND THE EMBASSY CLUB
OCTOBER. THREE MONTHS BEFORE THE NEW ASSEMBLY.

Lucene had little time to prepare for her date with Dallen and quickly darted into one of the school's private bathrooms to freshen up. Cursing herself for not having the foresight to bring a change of clothes, she dug through her large black backpack, searching for a comb and face powder. It wasn't until she leaned over the sink to splash cool water on her cheeks that she noticed a knit red dress in the mirror, hanging on the door of one of the private stalls. It was Neroni's dress. She glanced down at her own white blouse and burgundy cardigan sweater. *Guess it couldn't hurt to try it on.*

Minutes later, she emerged from one of the stalls, the long-sleeved dress forming snuggly around her arms and hips, accentuating her shape and stopping just at her calf. It was not her usual style, but she had to admit that it fit her well. Her eyes fell to her unfortunate black slip-on flats. *Ah well,* she thought. *They'll have to do. At least they are a step above boots.*

She stuffed her blouse, cardigan, and jeans into her oversized backpack, quickly combed her hair straight, and dabbed some neutral powder on her nose. Not ten minutes later, she emerged from the bathroom transformed into dinner attire, slinging her backpack over her shoulder. Lucene thought perhaps she should leave it at the school to retrieve tomorrow morning before the next round of exams, but then remembering that she needed her pass for the SpeedCircuit and the key to her cottage, she opted to drag it with her instead.

Dallen was waiting for her at the end of the stairs as she descended from the labs on the second floor. He looked up with a mix of pleasant surprise and confusion, both at the same time.

"You look beautiful," he said, reaching over to comb a few bits of stray hair on her head and patting them down awkwardly. She was surprised by the gesture and put her own hand on her head after he was done as if to assess the damage. "Not to worry. It's better now." He smiled.

Somehow, she expected him to look less formal; but there he stood in a similar suit as what he had worn at both the meeting at the League and on their visit to the Makerspace earlier that week. The only difference is that this one was a washed-out navy, and instead of a formal sash, he wore a gold medallion pinned on front of his left shoulder. She assumed it was either an award or a sign of rank but did not question him about it.

"You seem tired," he observed, taking her hand and guiding her toward the front doors that led out to the street. This also surprised her, but since she knew nothing about his customs nor that of Erde's yet, she closed her hand around his politely. "Your eyes have these unpleasant dark circles under them."

Lucene let out a sigh, "I am tired. I was the test subject in a long series of examinations today, and I didn't expect it to take so much out of me."

Dallen paused for a moment and nodded in understanding. "Do you want me to escort you home?" he asked.

"Oh, no," she forced a smile. "I'll be fine. I probably just need to get some food in me, and I'll wake back up." In truth, going straight home and climbing under the covers seemed preferable to her right now, but she didn't want to be rude. Not only that, but it had been so long since she'd actually gone out on a proper date that she'd almost forgotten what it was like. There was still that huge memory gap from New York to the time Tanager arrived to rescue her when her utility vehicle broke down in front of the grocery store, in what now seemed like a lifetime ago. She remembered the New Moon celebration some eight months ago when they were still on Earth. But that wasn't really a date, was it? She shuddered at the memory as a chill tickled her arms. Before that, however, she couldn't remember when she'd dated anyone else. *That just couldn't be,* she reasoned. But she'd been hard-pressed to come up with any name at all.

"I have just the place in mind," he led the way, interrupting her thoughts. "It's only two blocks away. They serve a rice and vegetable dish much like we have back on Vitruvia. You will love it."

In truth, she felt more like a burger, but not just any burger. The kind that Fatima used to make with lamb and eggplant. Lucene didn't even think she liked eggplant, but Fatima had a way of sneaking vegetables into her food without her noticing. "Here we are," Dallen pulled her attention back from Fatima's burger, just as she began to imagine the taste of fontina cheese being melted over the top of it. She held back a sigh as she looked up.

They were standing in front of the Embassy Club. Unlike the understated buildings along the rest of the street, the embassy stood out like a beacon of red brick with gold-trimmed windows and doors. She wasn't entirely sure what this place was, but it looked expensive.

And, unlike many of the other buildings she'd been in lately, this one did not have automatic doors, and someone dressed in a red uniform with large black buttons down the front and a top hat on his head opened an ornate gold door for them as they approached. The doorman averted his gaze so as not to make eye contact. The whole image felt wrong, somehow. Dallen dropped Lucene's hand, turning his back on her as he walked in first. She paused for a moment, confused, but then followed once he glanced back, wondering why she had not followed him. "Thanks," she said to the guard, who said nothing.

In the lobby, there was an actual cloakroom with a young woman checking people's capes, jackets and purses. At least, Lucene assumed she was female. She was very slender with an unusually long neck and face, and a nose that was rounded like an aardvark. Her skin had a blue hue to it, and she had bits of black hairs that protruded out around her ears and chin. Dallen stopped there, eyeing Lucene's backpack distastefully. She had no idea what he expected until the woman behind the counter offered, "May I register your purse for you, Earth woman?"

"Sure," Lucene answered, reluctantly handing her backpack to the woman. She knew that Erde was supposed to be a peaceful planet with little to no crime, but old habits die hard and she still found it difficult handing over her possessions to a stranger. "What gave me away?" she asked.

"I do not understand," the woman answered. "Please explain."

"How did you know I was from Earth?"

"Oh," she nodded in understanding. "Your smell," she smiled.

"What do I smell like?" Lucene had to know.

"Earth skin smells slightly sweeter than people from Erde. Erde people are more citrusy." She smiled proudly. "But don't worry," she reassured Lucene. "After a few months, your chemistry will change, and no one will be able to tell the difference." She tapped her nose, knowingly. "Enjoy your refection."

"Uh, thanks," Lucene answered as Dallen, somewhat impatiently, let out a loud sigh before beckoning her to follow him into the dining area.

The main dining room was unlike anything Lucene had ever seen in real life, the main floor resplendent with high-backed, thrown-like mustard-colored chairs curved like private cocoons surrounding gold-trimmed ebony carved tables with protective glass tops in place of tablecloths. At the center of each table were vases that were at least three feet tall, slender at the bottom to avoid obstructing the diner's views from one another and branching out at the top. Each one was filled with tall yellow and white elderflowers. At least, that's what Lucene assumed they were, but she couldn't be sure as she didn't detect a scent. *Maybe I should ask scent-girl at the front to tell me,* she thought.

As they walked through the high arched entrance, Lucene noticed that there were two balconies surrounding the main room with private dining areas overlooking the main floor. A man with golden hair almost as bright as Dallen's quickly rushed toward him, stopping three feet in front of him and just off-center, presumably not to block his path. He averted his eyes as the guard had done. "Representative Dallen," the man greeted him. He was wearing a similarly uncomfortable-looking red uniform, slightly more form-fitting than that of the guard, and minus the hat. "We are honored to welcome you again. Would you prefer your usual seat?" Dallen didn't answer, merely flicked two fingers at him. It seemed very rude to Lucene, but she admitted she wasn't entirely sure of the customs here. The man nodded and led the way toward a small glass elevator that led to the second balcony. Unlike Dallen, who repeatedly walked in front of Lucene, the host put out an arm indicating that Lucene should enter the lift first. The man followed suit and cranked an old lever that closed the doors and began its short ascent to the second level.

"Cute," Lucene commented. It was as if she stepped back in time—Earth in the 1920s, if you had enough money and the right sort of connections. Dallen cleared his throat but said nothing. The host smiled politely and seemed embarrassed for her.

Once at their table, one female server pulled the chair out for Dallen, another put a cloth dinner napkin on his lap, while a third poured him a glass of water. Once they were assured that he was settled in place, the servers repeated the ritual for Lucene, who grabbed the napkin before it could be placed on her lap. "I've got it," she told the young waitress, "thanks."

The women retreated. It was only after they left that Dallen finally spoke for the first time since they had walked into the restaurant. "Do you like it?" He gestured in a way that suggested he already knew the answer.

"It's beautiful," Lucene acknowledged. "It seems very…fancy." Dallen let out a chortle.

"Yes, I suppose it is," he answered. "The Embassy Club was built several years ago as the central meeting place for dignitaries visiting Erde. There are separate conversation rooms and lounges, and, of course, this common area."

"Common area?"

"Anyone may dine here provided they are accompanied by a member of the club, but the other rooms are for members only."

"Seems rather exclusive for a club that's supposed to be inclusive."

"What do you mean?"

"I mean, if it's a meeting place for people from visiting planets, you would think it would feel slightly more…welcoming."

"It works for most of us," he answered simply, and not without a hint of annoyance. He continued, "It has evolved within the last year as Erde is difficult to reach and doesn't have many visitors. Vitruvia and Earth are the closest neighbors and your people don't have the technology to get here. Therefore, this club mainly caters to Vitruvian dignitaries."

It was only then that Lucene noticed that everyone appeared, well, human-like. There were no blue butterflies or mermaids. "Is there a shapeshifting code, kinda like a dress code?" Lucene wanted to know.

"You confuse me," Dallen eyed her with curiosity as a server brought over a pungent tea, pouring a small resin cup, first for him and then Lucene.

"Thanks," she told the server as the server set it down in front of Lucene. Lucene went to lift the cup to her nose to smell it when the server's eyes grew wide, and she shook her head, motioning toward Dallen. He, in turn, took a sip, nodded thoughtfully, and set it back down without a word. It was only then that the server nodded toward Lucene's cup. Apparently, the rules here were pretty straightforward. Dallen walks in first, gets seated first, drinks first, and does not speak to the staff. "What I was saying is that I've met two other Vitruvians." She recalled her brief interactions with Odessa and Morphinae. "They seemed to take on different forms, but everyone here seems pretty, well, human."

"We're nothing like humans," Dallen was quick to point out. It was funny, his tone was eloquent and soft-spoken, his demeanor calm, and yet she could almost feel every nuance of his emotions. And, to be honest, they lacked depth. She assumed that she simply wasn't used to the cultural differences and that he was harder to read beyond anything but surface-level emotions. This one was easy, however, *disdain*.

"You don't like humans?" Lucene questioned as the servers returned, this time with bowls of rice, vegetables, salts and sauces that they laid out very specifically on the table. Dallen stopped talking. Lucene followed suit. It was only after the servers left the private area that she added, "I don't remember ordering anything." She went to reach over to lift the lid on one of the sauces to see what was inside but noticed his disapproving glance. *Oh, right. He goes first. Was this a man thing or a dignitary thing?*

"I like humans, but you must be aware that they are distinctly more primitive than Vitruvians."

"Do I?" Lucene made it a point to never answer a question with a question, but somehow it popped out of her mouth before she could stop it.

"And, to answer your other questions, in the order asked, shapeshifters are a very limited race on our planet, and few rise to the order of a dignitary."

"Being able to shape-shift doesn't seem limiting," Lucene blurted out. She was tired and couldn't seem to put the brakes on her comments.

"I meant, in other ways," he replied curtly. "I like to think that what we true Vitruvians lack in morphing abilities, we make up for in intellect."

Lucene forgot her second question and was about to ask what he meant by "true Vitruvians" when Dallen started dipping into the various rice and vegetables on the table. Lucene counted three different types of rice, as many sauces, and at least four varieties of vegetables, none of which she had ever seen before. Once he had filled his plate, he did that finger flick, as he had done to the host, indicating that she was free to fill her plate as well. Suddenly, she wasn't feeling very hungry but politely took a modest sample of everything, laying it out in the same way Dallen did.

"To your second question," he answered between bites, "it's Friday evening."

"I'm afraid you've lost me."

"Whenever I am on Erde, I dine here. The staff knows my preferences. I always eat this very dish on Fridays." He smiled proudly as if this were something to be proud of.

An announcement over a loudspeaker prohibited Lucene from answering, *but what if I wanted a burger?*

Lucene was too short to see over the balcony, so she peered between the balcony rails at the host below, who now stood in the center of the room, commanding everyone's attention. The round platform in which he stood suddenly lifted, not only bringing him into greater view but revealing an entire orchestra of men and women that were one level below him. They were circled around him with a variety of brass, string and other instruments—similar to those on Earth, but their shapes and styles were different, some having a combination of metal, strings and mouthpieces as if they were three instruments in one. All in all, there were about twelve members of the band, the entirety dressed in that red uniform, like the host. The only difference was that the host had a different sort of pin on his shoulder. She hadn't noticed it before. Unlike Dallen's, the host's pin was round and silver. The ones that the band members wore were boxlike and light blue.

The host, who now appeared to be the emcee, welcomed everyone in attendance. Lucene didn't notice a microphone, and yet, she could hear him clearly. His presentation was brief. After introducing the orchestra, his platform descended while theirs remained in place, and he quickly exited the center of the room. Without thinking, Lucene began to clap. Dallen shot her a look, shaking his head vigorously. She stopped clapping, but not before several people looked in her direction. She expected a lot of whispering, but no one seemed to say anything at all, returning to their meals as the band played what seemed to be an awfully somber and somewhat off-key melody. Dallen leaned back in his chair and smiled. "Just like home," he said.

"I have a question for you," Lucene asked between bites, jolting him out of his reverie. Even that seemed to unnerve Dallen as he gazed at her hand. It was then that she realized from watching him that she had to finish her bite of food and actually put her spatula-like utensil down before continuing. This dinner appeared to have a lot of rules of which she was unaware. He flicked his fingers for her to continue. She resisted the urge to fling some rice at his forehead. "If you're visiting someone else's world for such a brief period of time, wouldn't you want to experience something other than what you would find on your planet?"

"What a silly question," he chided as if she were a small child. "Why would I want to experience anything less than perfection?"

And yet, she thought. *You are on a date with me. How did that happen?*

She was saved from further comment when the server returned to replace the tea with a cold beverage in a tall flute-shaped glass. It was only then that she realized that he'd finished his tea. She had not, but the server took hers away anyway. Lucene made a mental note to eat and drink faster, just in case. It seemed when he was done eating, everyone was done eating.

"I'm curious," he said. He seemed curious about a lot of things where she was concerned. He kept eyeing her like she was a strange puzzle he was trying to solve. "What powers do you have?"

And here, I thought he was interested in my winning personality.

"We don't know yet," Lucene answered honestly. "That's what today was about. I've got tests over the next couple of weeks to figure that out."

"But surely you have a clue?"

Perhaps it was the cool drink or the food, but somehow her mental filter returned, and she quickly sorted through how much she should say and how much she should keep to herself. There was something...a thought in the back of her brain...that reminded her of someone on Earth. *No,* she told herself firmly. *He's not at all like Drake Cushing. You just get nervous around attractive men in authority, and you feel out of place in this environment.* Still, she finished her thought, it was probably best to exercise caution.

He peered at her, impatiently, over his beverage. At least, he felt impatient to her, even though he appeared very calm on the outside. "I am a little bit empathic," she finally answered simply.

"What does that mean?" he demanded, quickly sitting back in silence as the servers approached. He motioned for them to clear the table, and they all but forced the spatula out of Lucene's hand, eyeing at her offending utensil so she that she put it on her plate so they could take it away. One server looked at her almost apologetically. *I'm sorry,* Lucene read her thoughts. She pushed them away. She wasn't going to open any floodgates accidentally during dinner and embarrass herself any further than she already appeared to have done.

"It means I'm just a little more sensitive to the feelings of others."

"How is that a superpower?"

"I've been asking myself that for months," she joked.

Suddenly, he burst out laughing. An honest laugh. She had done something right, it seemed.

"You're delightful," he decided. "Come, let's skip dessert and visit the animal lab before it gets too late."

Lucene eyed the dessert tray lovingly, but she felt too out of place and fatigued to argue. Plus, she had it in her mind that the animal lab would be like a visit to the zoo and was secretly hoping to discover some adorable alien animals. She got up and followed him to the elevation platform, being careful to stay several paces behind him and refrain from talking to, or making eye contact with, anyone. *Less is more,* she told herself.

Once through the archway, the coat check woman made a loud "hmmm," clearing her throat. Lucene was relieved. Apparently, past the archway was when women were allowed to speak again without permission.

"Oh, yes." Lucene remembered her backpack. "I almost forgot."

The woman set a forced smile at Dallen, the kind that didn't reach one's eyes, as she handed Lucene her backpack. She leaned in quietly, lifting her chin as if sniffing the air and letting Lucene in on secret, "Smells a little briny on the inside, don't you think?"

"I hadn't noticed," Lucene was confused. *What was the matter with her bag?* The woman held her gaze a moment longer. "Thank you," Lucene replied. She knew she was trying to tell her something, but she had no idea what. Dallen handed the woman a gold coin. She bowed her head and retreated into the back of the coatroom, glancing over her shoulder once more as Lucene and Dallen exited the Embassy Club.

Once outside, Dallen took her hand again. *Oh, we're back to the hand-holding thing again.*

The lab was closed for the evening, but the overnight attendant had been apprised of his visit. "Representative Dallen," the small round man acknowledged pleasantly. "Nice to meet you. Name's Mateo, but you can call me Mati. Hey…Lucene, right?" He pointed at her as if to confirm his guess.

"Right," Lucene smiled. *Thank God, a person whose external expression matched their internal feelings.* This man, whatever his name, was actually happy to see them.

"Would you like a tour?"

"This late?" Lucene was surprised.

"Aww, I don't mind. My night shift is jest gettin' started," he answered in a thick accent. His "started" sounded more like "staw-ted." She thought he might be from New York but quickly retracted that thought when she noticed a long rat-like tail waving out the back of his uniform. There was actually a hole for it. He lumbered to a section labeled Area 1. "Follow me." She waited for Dallen to go first, but apparently, those rules only apply at the Embassy Club. Here, he actually held onto her hand as the main doors slid open and what's-his-name led the way.

"Thank you—" *He just said his name!* Lucene tapped the side of her temple, annoyed with herself.

"Mateo," he reminded her. "Don't worry," he winked at Lucene. "It's an odd name. Just cawl me Mati, like the way my hair is always matted down on my head," he patted the top of his head for reference. He was right, his tightly wound hair stuck closely to his head as if afraid of abandonment. She smiled back, gratefully.

"Thanks, Mati," she smiled. *I like him. He's nice…and authentic.*

They made their way through Area 1, visiting habitat to habitat. Some were very large and expansive, others small and condensed. Several appeared to have snow on the ground, and the windows were frosted over, while others appeared barren, with the glass enclosure steamed over. Like Earth, not all animals here appeared to have the same needs.

Lucene stopped abruptly in front of one habitat, a ten by ten room that looked like someone's living room from the 1950s, complete with a green velvet couch, floral wallpaper and rotary phone sitting on top of a chrome-legged end table.

"What is it?" Dallen asked.

"It's a cat," she pointed to a thick tabby curled up on the couch. The room was closed off with a plexiglass shield poked full of small holes.

"Of course, it's a cat," Mati laughed. "What else would it be?"

"But, don't they just live….you know, in houses, here?"

"Well, technically, they are an invasive species," Mati explained. "People need permits to have one in their homes."

"Has this one not been adopted yet?"

"Oh, she has a home," Mati explained. The cat's ears suddenly perked up as she lifted her head, sniffed the air, yawned, stretched and repositioned herself on the couch. She quickly fell back to sleep. "She's under quarantine for another couple of weeks before we can release her into our environment. I sneak a scratch behind her ears on occasion, but I always wear a glove and mask when I do. Can't be too careful."

Lucene couldn't see the harm in a simple house cat, but then, she reasoned, she didn't know what other species were here yet and how their presence might affect them. She, herself, had to go through a rigorous decontamination routine upon arrival.

"My friend, Fatima, is on her way to Erde," Lucene offered happily. "She's bringing our cat Bagheera from Earth. I suppose he'll have to spend a little time here when he arrives."

"At least two weeks, for sure, unless they approve him quarantining along with your friends. Though, usually, if something is up, we know within the first few days." Mati thought a minute. "Hmmm, but maybe he can become a breedin' cat. My gal Tabby," he pointed to the cat behind the glass, "is rare here. If it works out, maybe your boy cat can get together with our girl cat—if her caretakers agree—of course. They are kinda cute as home companions."

"Well," Lucene lamented, "sadly, our boy cat is in no position to bring kittens in the world." Mati paused for a moment, confused, before breaking out into a thunderous laugh. "Oh, I get it now. Poor fella. C'mon, let's hit Area 2. There are some pretty unique creatures in there."

Unique was an understatement. There were mammals that were a cross between koalas and sloths that slept upside down in trees and only ventured out at night, aquatic creatures that were a hybrid between a squid and an octopus, worm-like invertebrates the size of a five-foot snake, and even a cuddly marsupial wombat that made its way into the mix, alongside the very average house cat named Tabby, which wasn't so average on Erde.

For someone not big on trying cuisine that wasn't from his home planet, by contrast, Dallen seemed overly enthusiastic about the unique animal collection at the lab.

"Tell me, Mateo," he asked. "Do you have any special animals here?"

Mati looked horrified and somewhat offended. "They are awl special," he proclaimed.

"Yes, of course they are," Dallen backpedaled. "But, I mean, do any possess any unique talents?"

"Talents?"

"Yes, like having a special poison that paralyzes people, or ones that can glide through treetops, that sort of thing. I'm fascinated by odd creatures." Lucene felt a strange bitterness in the pit of her stomach. *Must have been that weird vegetable sauce,* she reasoned. *A burger wouldn't have done that.* She found herself pulling her hand away from Dallen, who released it without seeming to care.

Mati thought for a moment. "Oh, not so much here," he explained. "Most of our collection houses either ones in quarantine or ones that need our help because they can't make do on our planet—temporarily or permanently."

"I see," Dallen was visibly disappointed.

After about an hour, they had reached the end of their tour, having circled back to the entrance. But, as they did so, Lucene heard a strange sound…almost like a small voice that was humming.

They passed a room with a small wooden door that was partially open to reveal what Lucene at first thought was an aquarium. Then she saw a small cot in the corner, a desk and a tiny screen that may have been their version of a television. Something in the aquarium fluttered.

"What's in here?" she asked.

"This is just my office and rest area when I'm working," Mati explained. "Though, to tell ya the trute (truth), I spend more time here than I do at home." He laughed. "I got eight little ones runnin' around the house at home and hanging from the rafters, and they're not as quiet as those we got here in the animal lab."

"Wow, that's quite a…collection," Lucene acknowledged. *And it sounds horrifying.*

"That's nothin'," he replied. "My wife's sister has fifteen. The missus wants to keep pace, but I've told her eight is plenty."

"Hi," a little voice called from the aquarium. Lucene looked closely to see a small figure that had fluttered to the front of his small glass tank.

"Hi," Lucene answered curiously, pushing the wooden door open slightly wider. "May I?" she asked Mati.

"Aw, sure," Mati agreed, motioning for her to enter. "Go right ahead. That's my best buddy over there."

There, in what appeared to be a miniature wooded area within the aquarium, a small insect with a human-like face pressed his nose and two arched, furry legs against the glass. His face was round and pale green, his neck was skin toned and formed like layers of rolled dough. His round back was the shape of a ladybug's, and dark blue with little black dots. His wings were a luminescent turquoise like that of a butterfly, with six legs to match—the front two being shorter, working more like arms. He couldn't have been more than four inches tall and wide, and he was gorgeous.

Lucene leaned toward the glass. "You can talk!" she seemed surprised.

"Why wouldn't I be able to talk?" he answered, curiously.

"My goodness," Mati chimed in. "Does he ever talk! You can't shut him up."

"What's your name, little one?" Dallen finally spoke up.

"Marzipan!" The little bug puffed his chest up proudly.

"You're named after food? That seems odd," Dallen answered.

"Marzipan is a noble name," the little bug defended. "What's your name?"

"I am Representative Dallen," he replied, as if this should have meaning to Marzipan.

"And you think my name is odd," Marzipan leaped around his habitat, miniature tree stumps to branches, flittering through the leaves and dipping his hind legs in a tiny pond at its center. He seemed quite content in his little grotto.

"Oh, you mentioned scary animals earlier. Well, that's how Marzipan and I became buddies," Mati offered. "I found him in the Southern Cross on expedition and rescued him from a desert glider."

"A desert glider," Dallen was intrigued.

"Mean suckers, if you ask me," Mati answered. "They are about a foot long with the body of a gray lizard, but when they're irritated, their wings open up and fan out in every direction, and they have a lot of 'em. They have three sets of wings that span more than a foot high. They're like peacock feathers, except dark brown, flag-shaped, and not nearly as pretty." Mati opened his arms wide to illustrate.

"Yeah, if Mati hadn't found me, I would have been his dinner," Marzipan added.

"So, where did you come from, originally?" Dallen asked.

"Not sure," Marzipan rubbed his chin. "As far as I know, I'm the only one of my kind here. I used to have an old caretaker. He was kind of a hermit and very lonely. He used to say that he imagined me to life because he needed someone to talk to." Marzipan thought a minute. "That was before the preserves and before Erde was populated like it is today. At least, that's what I'm told from Mati and the World Viewer."

"He means like your TV," Mati whispered to Lucene. She nodded, understanding.

"Even as Erde grew, my caretaker insisted on staying in the Southern Cross anyway, even though it's a very isolated and undeveloped terrain. He's gone now," Marzipan crinkled his lips, deep in thought.

"I'm sorry," Lucene felt his sadness.

"Aw, it's alright. He was very old. But he was the one that used to make me homemade marzipan. And boy, was that delicious!"

"Marzipan has to stay in his habitat because the ratio of carbon dioxide, nitrogen and oxygen is different in his home. He can't be out for more than an hour or two at a time."

"Yeah," Marzipan laughed. "Found that one out the hard way." Marzipan told the tale of his previous caretaker's death. It was simple, really. He sat down at the kitchen table one morning, nodded off and didn't wake up. Marzipan tried to go get help, and almost ended up a desert glider's lunch.

"How long have you lived here with Mati?" Lucene asked.

"Oh, about four years now," he looked at his larger friend for confirmation.

"Don't you get lonely? I mean, being the only one and stuck in a glass cage."

"It's not a cage," Marzipan defended. "It's my home, and I love it."

"Marzipan is the most easygoing buddy a guy could have," Mati nodded. "We talk about everything together."

"Yeah," the little bug added, "and some days, I ask to be relocated to a shelf in different parts of the lab so I can talk to my other roommates and visitors."

"Wait, they can talk too?" Lucene was surprised.

"Of course, they can talk," Marzipan put his fuzzy claw hands on his thick body, tipping his shell backward and standing on his hind four legs. "You just haven't learned to listen…yet."

"Yet?"

"You're Lucene, aren't you?" Marzipan asked. Lucene looked to Mati, surprised. "Oh, I've heard enough about you from the TARA students talking to be able to figure out who you are. They haven't learned to understand my housemates yet. But maybe someday, you'll figure it out."

"Perhaps you will help me," Lucene smiled.

Marzipan thought a moment. "Maybe… I like you," he decided, before fluttering off to an intricate Weaver bird nest, letting out a yawn. "Night, night."

"Goodnight, Marzipan," Lucene answered.

"He's not subtle," Mati laughed. "When he's done talking to ya, he's just done."

"Well, I can take a hint," Lucene yawned herself, remembering, once again how exhausted she was. Her second wind had passed, and her energy was quickly fading. "It's time I made my way home, anyway. Thank you, Mati. I appreciate the tour."

"No problem at all, Lucy… Can I call you Lucy?" Lucene cringed when she heard the name but didn't want to be rude.

"Sure."

Mati showed the two out and they said their goodbyes.

The crisp air was noticeably colder than the lab. Lucene shivered slightly. Dallen took it as his cue to wrap an arm around her; the weight of his arm, coupled with the weight of her backpack, suddenly made her shoulders feel very heavy. "Let me see you to the SpeedCircuit," he offered.

Lucene had mixed feelings about Dallen. A part of him was intelligent and thoughtful. He seemed well-cultured and had this Adonis vibe about him and a chiseled chin that she suspected most Earth women would find attractive. On the other hand, he acted superior, expecting her to understand customs that were foreign to her and fall in line as if she were somehow the lesser of the two. Even sensing this, she had this strange need to prove herself to him and felt insecure in his presence. At that moment, she felt a spark of energy between them when he wrapped his arm around her, and she allowed herself to settle into the comfort of his chest as they walked.

They reached the SpeedCircuit, and Lucene directed them to the platform that led to the Eastern Cross. Oddly, it was dark and nearly barren without any trains, while the platforms leading to the Northern and Western Crosses were bustling.

"Excuse me," Lucene asked one of the attendants standing nearby. "Why is the train not running to the Eastern Cross?"

"I'm not sure," the man answered, apologetically. "I received notification about an hour ago to shut down all connections to the Eastern Cross, including remote locations traveling from the other Crosses back to the Eastern Cross. No one is allowed in or out until further notice."

"Then, how am I supposed to get home?"

"I'm sorry," the man began before a tiny red light flashed near his ear. He was receiving an alert that transferred into a small ear pod that looked like a hearing aid with an extended wire that wrapped around his cheek as if stuck to his skin. "Excuse me for a moment." He touched his ear, instinctively, and listened to the person on the other side for the next few minutes. Dallen tapped his foot impatiently while Lucene folded her arms tighter. It was getting colder out. There were a few more people gathered, waiting for information.

"I understand," he said finally, before signing off. He turned his attention back to Lucene and Dallen. "Well, you're not going to like this," he told them, including his address to the small group that had gathered near them. "The Circuit to the Eastern Cross is not reopening until morning."

"What? Why?" people protested. The attendant raised his hand, motioning for silence.

"I am not permitted to say more at this time, other than to inform you that if you have friends in the city or at one of the other crosses, you may want to stay with them this evening. If you have any pets or people you need to check on at home, I can have a local constable check in on your residence."

"What if someone has no place to go?" Lucene wanted to know. The attendant looked at her oddly, as if it were a strange thing to say. Why wouldn't someone have friends with whom they could stay with in an emergency? Lucene had only been on Erde for a little over a month, and most of that was in quarantine, followed by self-isolation. She hadn't done a great job at connecting with anyone aside from occasional visits from Roman or check-ins from Cepheus and Tanager. "Oh, are you a visiting ambassador staying with a host family in the Eastern Cross, because maybe I can see if we can put you up in a hotel here until morning?"

"That won't be necessary," Dallen replied on Lucene's behalf. "Thank you, sir. I'm sure we can make other arrangements." The attendant wiped his brow and nodded, turning his attention to the other travelers who seemed disturbed by the news. *The SpeedCircuit has never shut down before. Why was this happening?*

Dallen steered Lucene back toward the main road. "My hotel is only a few blocks away, and my suite, while small, has an extra fold-out, efficiency bed. You can stay with me."

"Oh, I couldn't do that," Lucene protested. "Maybe I can phone Tanager, and he can open the school's lounge. I could sleep on the couch there, or something." Lucene removed her backpack and set it on the ground. Leaning over, she began to rifle through it. "That's weird. I can't find my watch. Hmmm, maybe I left it at home?"

"Don't be silly, Lucene," Dallen took her arm, gently pulling her to stand. "It's late. Why wake him to have to come down here and open the school? And, why sleep on an uncomfortable couch in a public lounge when I have a perfectly good arrangement for you?"

She eyed him uncomfortably.

"I promise you," he flashed an Adonis smile. "I will be a perfect gentleman."

CHAPTER 14
DEATH AT THE EASTERN CROSS
OCTOBER. BEFORE THE NEW ASSEMBLY.

Lucene finally arrived home at the Earth equivalent of 9 o'clock the next morning, having returned to wearing yesterday's jeans and white blouse. Neroni's dress was wrapped neatly and stored in her backpack, which was now bulging and threatening to burst. She was surprised to find Tanager there, pacing back and forth the length of her cottage. His eyes looked red, and his curly hair was a disheveled mop as if he hadn't slept all night. When he saw her, his eyes grew wide. "Lucene," was all he said, throwing his arms around her and hugging her tight to his chest. Lucene was baffled, but enjoyed the hug, so she wrapped her arms around his waist and hugged back, the side of her face being ever-so-slightly squished between his shoulder and cheek. She didn't mind.

Finally, he took her by the shoulders, pushing her at arm's length to get a good look at her. "What happened to you? Are you okay? I tried phoning you a thousand times."

"I'm fine," she responded calmly. "The SpeedCircuit shut down last night, and I couldn't get home."

"Why didn't you call me?"

"I couldn't. I thought I had my communication watch in my bag, but it wasn't there when I went to look for it. I must have left it home."

"This is why you should wear it at all times." He drew his thumb and forefinger to his forehead in frustration. "Why don't you ever listen?"

"I'm not a child, Tanager. And everything worked out fine."

"If you couldn't get home, where did you sleep last night?"

"I stayed in Dallen's hotel room." She could both see and feel his frazzled reaction. "I slept on a fold-out couch. Geez! Not that it's any of your business."

"You're right," he answered, with growing annoyance. "It is none of my business where you sleep."

"Well, that was rude."

Tanager wasn't finished complaining. "It's also none of my business if you're safe or not, who you date, where you go at night. None of it is my business."

"Could we get back to the part where you were hugging me? I liked you better then." He resumed pacing. "Don't you think you're over-reacting, just a little?"

"A man was murdered at the Eastern Cross last night." He stopped pacing, waiting for her reaction.

"What? Who? But how is that possible? I thought you were the Peace-Keepers…100 years of no conflict, and all that?"

"Well, somehow, that's changed." He eyed her, cautiously. "Mallory, the costume maker was found stabbed to death in his shop right before closing last night."

Lucene paused for a moment as she let the news sink in. "What? No! That's awful!" Lucene furrowed her brow and fought back tears. She didn't know him well but had become fond of him during their brief interaction. "I was just there last week. I can't believe it." It was only then that she became aware that Tanager was staring at her. "Why are you looking at me like that?"

"The only thing that's changed in the past month is our arrival from Earth with you and Roman."

"Wait, you think I had something to do with this?"

"No, I don't. But others might."

"Listen, I'm really, *really* exhausted," Lucene complained. "I didn't sleep well last night—" Tanager raised an eyebrow. "On the couch!" she reminded him. "I'd really just like to take a bath and nap for an hour. Can I have a little time to process this and maybe get some rest?"

As he was speaking, Neroni, Cluseladek and Xeni arrived.

Cluseladek's toga-like garb was replaced with brown linen pants and a burlap-sack-like top. The sun was coming up, and even in the winter, it was relatively temperate. He wiped a bit of perspiration from his brow. "Good morning, Lucene."

Xeni was dressed in a brown trench coat and hat and had a notepad and pencil clearly tucked in her pocket. The coat was long and dragged slightly on the ground as she walked, kicking up dust. Neroni was the only one dressed sensibly, it seemed, wearing cargo pants and a cotton t-shirt with the sleeves rolled up to her elbows. They all stood a respectful distance away as Tanager and Lucene talked.

"Okay, why are *they* here?" Lucene started walking toward her front door, swinging her backpack down to fish through it, before remembering something. "Oh, great, how am I supposed to unlock the door without that stupid watch?"

"Oh, here," Tanager moved his fingers in front of the door as if inserting an invisible key. She heard it unlatch, and the door swung open.

"What's the point of having a lock, then?" She pushed past him with Tanager close at her heels. He paused momentarily to give a nod to the three standing outside, and they knowingly hung back.

"Well, to my knowledge, you're the only one who actually uses a lock on Erde. No one else has felt the need for one."

"Yeah, tell that to Mallory." Tanager looked pained. "So, what do I need to do to get you, the three musketeers outside, and the police to leave me alone?"

Tanager was exhausted, and even through his own sleep deprivation, he could feel that she, too, was burnt out.

"Why don't I take the team to the Western Cross for investigations while you get some rest. Perhaps we could come back later this afternoon to speak with you?"

"Investigation?" Lucene's interest was piqued. "Doesn't your military and police have guys for that?"

"We have constables, not police. As for our military, they haven't had much to do over the years except monitor for potential outside threats. And, until Erde started trying to help Earth, their jobs were pretty uneventful."

"So, what you're saying is, they have no training or experience investigating a murder?"

"I'm afraid not. The one woman we had with this level of skill died last year at the age of 152. We have some of her recorded techniques for inquiry, but that's all."

A lightbulb went off in Lucene's brain. "Did one of the constables from the crosses ask your A-team to use their Data Collection superpowers to see what they could figure out?"

It took Tanager a moment to process what she had said. "Uh, as a matter of fact, yes."

"This is surreal."

"How so?"

"Well, you are so much more advanced than Earth in some ways, and yet so primitive in others."

"Lucene," Tanager responded calmly. "You may not be aware of this, but at one point in our species' history, one-third of our population was wiped out by a pandemic. Even more were lost when they were unable to adapt to a changing climate. Erde, as a planet, is much smaller than Earth, still undeveloped in many areas and with far fewer people. We've lost a lot over the past century, which is why we work so hard to preserve what we have."

"Is that why you were so interested in helping Earth?" Lucene responded groggily, feeling a little guilty about her cranky responses. "You saw us following your same trajectory?"

"Exactly, and—if I'm being honest—some of it was self-serving. We help Earth in the hopes that some of the skills we've lost on our planet could be re-learned."

Lucene paused for a moment before unfolding her arms, making her way to her front door. "C'mon in," she motioned to Xeni, Cluseladek and Neroni. "Do what you need to do."

"Are you sure?" Tanager touched her sleeve.

"I'm sure."

"We won't be very long," Xeni assured her, shivering as she bounced through the threshold.

"Are you cold?" Lucene asked. "I can turn the heat up."

"It's not that," Xeni's eyes grew wide.

"What is it then?"

"Someone else has been in here while you were gone."

Constable Melokuhle had questioned every possible witness and suspect in the Eastern Cross. So far, Lucene was the only odd one out, as she was one of the last people to see Mallory alive. She remained a suspect. Witnesses also reported seeing a strange man wearing a monk's robe wandering in the shadows of Achel. This same monk had also been spotted at the Western, Eastern and Northern Crosses. At least, it was assumed that it was the same monk. Even in the city, the population was small, and yet, no one could identify the young man. Those in the crosses reported that he always appeared to be lurking around corners, but when they turned to get a closer look, or even to speak to him, he was gone. Curious, Constable Melokuhle traced him back to Roman's high-home near TARA. This was no easy feat, as the man moved like a ghost.

For the first time in the history of his career, he was hesitant to knock on someone's door unarmed, particularly someone who was new to Achel and no one seemed to know very well. All he knew about Roman was that he was studying up on Erde culture and humans from other Earth-like planets, so he could competently teach incoming students anthropology blended with sociology as it related to other species.

"Can I help you?" Roman stood at the door wearing a white terry cloth bathrobe and nothing else. He gazed at the constable with visible discontent. Roman was typically a more affable man, but he'd had enough run-ins with investigators back on Earth that he immediately had his guard up. That, and he and Far had been enjoying breakfast together on the veranda overlooking the city.

"Uh, yeah," Constable Melokuhle took off his hat and tucked it under his arm. "I apologize for the interruption. It's just that we had an unfortunate incident last night, and we're just doing some routine questioning, is all."

"And the human was at the top of your list, is that it?"

"Well, even though you are new to arrive here and are still relatively unknown, you already have a good reputation among students and faculty at TARA." For a moment, Roman's expression brightened. "Actually, it's him I need to talk to," he pointed a finger toward Far, who had crept up behind Roman and was now peering over his shoulder, wearing his usual brown robe.

"Why? What cause do you have to come here and accost my partner in our home?" Roman's mood dropped as quickly as it had begun to rise.

Far touched his arm. "It's okay," he said gently, barely above a whisper. "You should invite him in."

Roman stepped back and flung the door open wider than what was probably needed, gesturing a welcoming (but not really) arm for the constable to enter. Constable Melokuhle slid past him, somewhat sheepishly. This was difficult to do, as the constable was not a small man. In fact, he would have been considered intimidating if he didn't slink around in such a mild way. It was as if he were trying to minimize his presence. This whole confrontation made him entirely uncomfortable. When the constable came within close proximity to Far, the constable backed away slightly. The man seemed so frail that the constable was worried that if he so much as breathed on him too hard, Far would actually fall over.

"How can we be of service, honorable sir," Far whispered as if it were an effort to speak.

"We have had the misfortune of discovering a death at the Eastern Cross," Constable Melokuhle paused to gauge their reactions.

"Might I assume from the fact that you have recently arrived on our doorstep that this death was not accidental or of natural causes?"

"No. Not accidental," the constable confirmed. "Murder."

Roman let out a sigh that sounded as if a car tire had been punctured. It was a sigh that was mixed with both relief and frustration. *On the one hand,* he thought to himself, *I've had no communication with anyone at the Eastern Cross except for Lucene. On the other hand, here we are again with rude questioning as a result of my close proximity to Data Collectors.* He then had another thought, a disturbing thought.

"Who was it?" Roman's eyes grew wide. *Please don't say 'Lucene.'*

"Mallory, the costume designer."

Roman let out a nervous laugh.

"Is something funny, Mr. Aurelius?"

"Not at all," Roman regained composure. "While I'm sorry to hear about this woman's death, I'm relieved that it wasn't someone I knew personally. I know, that sounds terrible."

Constable Melokuhle paused for a moment, adjusting his hat to fit under his arm, as it had shifted during their conversation. He chose not to correct Roman's assumption that Mallory was a woman but made a mental note of it.

"Would you care to sit down, honorable sir," Far asked, motioning toward the couch. Roman cringed. He didn't want this man in their home any longer than was absolutely necessary.

"That won't be necessary, and" he turned his attention to Roman, "you don't sound like a terrible person. Sadly, I did know Mallory, and am saddened by the news." The constable paused to size up Far. Since no one seemed to have gotten a very good look at him, he was taking advantage of the close proximity—thin blonde hair that appeared to have been self-cut and the palest green eyes he'd ever seen on another person. If he weighed more than 100 pounds, the constable would have been surprised. Roman appeared to tower over him, but then, Roman was on the tall side. So, Far was probably about average height. "So," the constable continued, turning back toward Far. "We're a pretty small community, and I've not had the pleasure of meeting you. What's your name?"

"Far," the frail man answered.

"Far," the constable repeated. "Is that your first or last name?

"It's my only name," he replied simply.

"I see," Constable Melokuhle regretted not having a notepad and pen with him. In his research into investigative inquiry, that was one of the first things he found. *If you're not a Data Collector able to transmit information easily back to a scribe ready to document observations, always have a notepad and pen with you.*

That was investigation 101. But then, this was the first time the constable had ever had to actually investigate anything. Unless you count the one time a pet walleye went missing from his neighbor's pond, only to be later discovered (it's bones, anyway) sticking to the side of a gum tree. Presumably, it jumped too far and landed in the tree and later became a condor's dinner. At least, that was the best conclusion he could come up with. His neighbors were confident that this was, in fact, what happened, and provided a simple but important ritual burial for their walleye.

"You mentioned 'our home,'" the constable pointed out. "Far, with all due respect, no one around here knows you. At what point did you come to reside here?"

"What does that have to do with anything?" Roman wanted to know.

"It's okay, my love," Far touched his arm. Constable Melokuhle cringed inadvertently at the touch. "One month ago," Far answered.

"Where did you live prior?"

"Elsewhere," Far answered simply.

"I'm afraid I'm going to need a bit more information than that."

"I was a prisoner in Section 3, near the Royal Training Grounds." Roman put his arm around Far in support.

"I'm sorry to hear that," the constable acknowledged. "How did you escape?"

"What makes you think I escaped?" Far was confused.

"Because you're standing here in front of me," the constable reasoned. "The Royals are not known for mercy. I can assume that they did not actually *let* you go." Constable Melokuhle raised an eyebrow.

Far thought a moment. "You are correct. They did not let me go. Someone helped me."

"Who?"

"Does it matter?"

"You tell me."

Far was quiet for a moment more. "No," he answered finally. "That doesn't matter. But the point of the matter is, I am here." Looking at Far, it appeared as if he were sifting through his mind, trying to determine the right thing to say among lots of options. Finally, he settled on, "...

with my love." Roman's face crumbled as he fought back tears, while Far seemed to have adopted a neutral expression.

"Mister...Far," the constable continued, awkwardly. "You have been spotted in all of the occupied Crosses: the Northern, Eastern and Western regions of our planet. If the Southern Cross wasn't so barren and under-populated, I suspect you might have been seen there, too."

"What are you suggesting, constable?" Roman demanded.

"I'm not suggesting anything. There's just one more curious thing that keeps bugging me, on top of all that."

"And what is that?" Far asked, calmly.

"How is it that you were spotted in most of the Crosses, but I don't recall your name, or any unknown name, for that matter, showing up in the SpeedCircuit registry? If you didn't use the SpeedCircuit, how did you travel?"

Far turned to Roman for support. His partner picked up the cue immediately.

"As you know," Roman replied, "we can retain the rental of hover cars in emergencies and for official business, yes?"

"Yes, and what of it?"

"Well, as a new professor at TARA, as well as a new resident of Erde, I am required to research the culture and behaviors of all inhabitants here."

The constable was busy connecting the dots. It didn't take him long. "And, is there a reason your research requires the use of hover car versus the use of our highly equipped and efficient SpeedCircuit?"

"Constable, is it not a fact that the Circuit was down last night?"

"Yes, but that is very rare."

"But still. Some of us have little time to get up to speed on Erde culture. So, the use of a faster transportation system in order to research the Crosses was essential to me. Far often accompanies me, so I'm assuming that when people spotted him in their town, he was merely exploring while I was doing my appointed research."

"I see," the constable was unconvinced. "And, do you have records of your hover car rentals?"

Roman grit his teeth. His words were half-truths. He did, in fact, make use of the rentals, but he thus far had only re-visited the Western

Cross. *Would they be able to map where he'd actually gone with the rental car?* He wasn't sure. "Of course," Roman flashed a confident smile. "I don't have them handy, but I can request the receipts I submitted to TARA for reimbursement. I'm afraid I neglected to retain my own copies after that."

"Well, if you can get those for me, I would appreciate it," Constable Melokuhle's face began to take on a reddish hue, and his face felt hot.

"Of course," Roman spat out his reply, becoming increasingly agitated. After an uncomfortably long pause, Roman asked, "May I ask you a question, Constable?"

"Certainly, Mr. Aurelius. What is it?"

"You seem to be uncomfortable with, well, us." He pointed back and forth between he and Far. Far remained silent. "Is there a problem?"

"No," the constable adjusted his collar nervously before repositioning his hat on his head. "It's just that..."

"Yes," Roman persisted.

"I'm an old-fashioned man."

"And—" Roman's agitation grew.

"I'm just surprised that two men are, well..."

"Well, what? Living together?"

"No, that's not it."

Roman was taken aback. "From different planets?" He was confused.

"No, I'm used to seeing inter-species relationships all the time. It's just that..." Constable Melokuhle was clearly at odds with himself.

"Just that, what?" Roman couldn't let it go.

"Well, as I said, I'm a little more old fashioned. You said you lived together. With no disrespect, but Far here appears to be a monk. So, I'm guessing you two are not married?"

"Married?" Roman's face broke into a big smile. "That's what you're worried about?" Far also let out a small laugh.

"I know. I know." the constable held his hands up. "It's just the way I was raised."

"Well, honorable sir," Far spoke up, clasping Roman's hand for emphasis. "It just so happens that we *are* married."

"Really?" The constable was surprised.

"Yes," Far explained. "On my planet, Macar, monks marry all the time.

Roman and I are in a committed relationship, so you needn't worry." Far reached around his neck and produced a small pendant attached to a cord hanging from his neck. Likewise, Roman lifted his arm to display a chord with the same circular pendent that he had wrapped around his wrist.

"Oh, well. I get it," the constable was too embarrassed to remember that he was conducting an investigation. "I didn't mean to offend."

"No offense taken," Roman assured him. *Except that you seem awful judgy,* he thought. "And, if that will be all?"

"Yes," Constable Melokuhle backed away. "Nothing more from me. You enjoy your weekend."

With that, the constable left. Roman slowly closed the door behind him, relieved. Far watched everything with an oddly smug satisfaction.

CHAPTER 15
HOUSE ARREST
OCTOBER. BEFORE THE NEW ASSEMBLY.

Cepheus was, once again, making the rounds at the Crosses. Typically, he did this bi-monthly. But given his recent return to Erde, he thought it prudent to be extra attentive to the humans who were currently living on the preserves and that they were sworn to protect. It wasn't an excuse to see Moksha again. He was far too practical for that. At least, that's what he told himself.

He arrived at her purple cottage in time to see Commander Royce and two of her military guards surrounding Moksha. One was placing a tracking band around the Moksha's exposed ankle.

"What is going on here?" he asked, baffled.

"Isn't it obvious?" Moksha's expression was sour. "I'm a former Royal assassin. So, clearly, I was the one responsible."

It took Cepheus a moment to make the connection.

Moments later, Neroni appeared from around the side of Moksha's vineyard, along with Xeni, Cluseladeck and Tanager. Neroni hung her head in a combination of shame and confusion. Cepheus looked to Tanager and thought, *what is happening here?*

Mallory, Tanager answered simply. Cepheus shook his head. This couldn't be.

"Neroni was able to use her remote viewing skills to witness Moksha at the costume shop the night of Mallory's murder. She was even able to confirm the location of the weapon used to kill him. It was stashed in his refrigerator, no blood or fingerprints, but the blade marks match those found..." Commander Royce let out a cough. Talking about blood and murder left her queasy.

"Neroni," Cepheus asked quietly. "Is this true?"

Neroni couldn't bring herself to look at him or Moksha allowing her eyes to drop toward the ground, instead. "It is, but..."

"But what?"

"Can I speak with you and Professor Tanager privately for a moment?" Her eyes were pleading. Cepheus glanced at Commander Royce, who nodded in reply.

"Of course," he answered. He, Tanager and Neroni began walking the dirt trail leading back into town. When they were out of earshot, she spoke. "I don't understand it," she confessed. "I didn't pick up any images in the costume shop, and yet, when doing a routine scan of the Western Cross, I suddenly had a strong but vivid image of Moksha. She was..." Neroni hugged herself, her eyes welling up. "I didn't want to see that. It was awful!" Cepheus touched her shoulder. While his heart was in the right place, he no longer knew quite how to offer comfort. But she was empathic enough to understand. "Thank you," she said quietly.

"Here's the really odd thing," Tanager added. "Xeni reported feeling a cold, ghost-like energy both at the costume shop and again at Lucene's cottage, but nothing in Moksha's home. And Cluseladek scanned the crime scene in its entirety. He claims that there was nothing in the refrigerator except a half of a pomegranate. And yet, the constable later retrieved a knife. I think it was a set-up."

"Set-up?"

"Sorry, it's an Earth term Xeni recently taught me. It means that someone is trying to make it look like Moksha is guilty." Neroni wrapped her arms around herself as if to self-soothe.

"And what do you think, Neroni?" Neroni looked up timidly and whispered, "I only know what I saw."

Cepheus's chest tightened. He trusted both Neroni's skills and honesty. His mood darkened. Perhaps he was foolish to entertain the ideas that a former Royal assassin could actually be a good person. The ground swayed momentarily as he lost focus.

"No, not, not this…not now," Tanager grabbed his one elbow, Neroni the other. Cepheus pulled back from the episode.

"Perhaps we should rejoin the group," Cepheus suggested in a voice that sounded not quite like his own. Tanager and Neroni exchanged looks and nodded.

When they did, Commander Royce was busy giving Moksha strict orders. She was not to leave the borders of her small property until further notice. A constable would be stationed at the Western Cross at all times, making the rounds throughout the day, while military guards would be assigned to watch the house at varying intervals—day and night, in the event she attempted to leave.

"Nice going, Neroni," Clusaledek muttered under his breath, once she had rejoined the group. She gazed up at him, surprised at the comment.

"Whatever do you mean?"

"Nothing you saw matches what Xeni and I saw—just an observation."

"I'm not making it up," Neroni defended, but in her heart, even she had doubts about her own abilities.

"Hmmm," was all Cluseladek said. Xeni peered up at him and then back at Neroni but said nothing. She didn't remember Cluseladek ever being snarky before. This whole thing had everyone on edge.

"So, I've left one home, only to become a prisoner in another," Moksha became indignant. "How then am I to get supplies for my vineyard and food and staples for myself?"

"Should have thought of that before you murdered Mallory," an angry voice called from the road. There stood Abe and his wife, and at least two dozen people living in the Western Cross. Many were holding shovels, brooms and pitchforks in what could only be assumed was a pathetic protest with feeble weapons—pitchforks aside.

"Stand down, Abe," Commander Royce stood in front of the man—an odd sight given her size compared to his. "We don't know for certain that Moksha had anything to do with his death. That's why we conduct investigations."

"This is bullshit," Abe raised an arm overhead in an odd show of protest. There were several cheers and "here, here's" behind him. "Where I come from, we don't stand for outsiders coming in and hurting one of our own."

"May I remind you, all of you," Commander Royce's voice increased in volume, seeming completely out of proportion with the rest of her small frame, "that we were once all outsiders."

There was a mumbling amid the crowd as Cluseladek glared at Neroni, as if to say, "see what you did?"

Cepheus had come to a decision. He snuck up, snakelike, beside Moksha so quietly no one noticed, no one except an assassin trained to notice everything. "Do not be alarmed," he whispered. "I will make certain that you have whatever you need."

CHAPTER 16
CONGREGATION

OCTOBER. THREE WEEKS AFTER THE DEATH AT THE EASTERN CROSS.

Odessa was not exaggerating when she spoke of Reverend Isabella's ability to build a congregation and bring people together. In the three short weeks since Odessa first approached Isabella at the museum, the priestess had managed to pack her Sanctuary with followers and even set up two new satellite churches, one in France and one in Germany. They now joined Dallen on a remote call from the negotiation room at the PDL on Erde. Dallen was joined by Commander Royce, Cepheus, Tanager, and the ever-reluctant Lucene. Once again, Lucene was to stand in place of Roman as the official Earth representative on Erde. Roman had been promptly uninvited given his connection to Far. Lucene had been cleared, for now at least, as no evidence was found to suggest that she had a connection to Mallory's death. Though, given the strange energy that Xeni felt in Lucene's home, there was still some concern about her safety, mostly from Tanager, who had taken to checking in on her, either by calling or stopping in almost daily. Lucene didn't mind the gesture. Dallen did.

"Before I introduce our esteemed Representative Dallen," Isabella addressed the crowd, the amphitheater-styled Sanctuary filled, as she spoke from the small podium at its center. "I would like to remind us of why we are here." Her larger-than-life holographic image hung in the center of the theater, providing a clearer view to those tuning in from remote locations. She was dressed in her formal ceremonial garb, a long white robe with a string of flowers that formed a stole that was wrapped around her neck and hung down each side of her robe. On her feet were simple tan sandals with little material.

Members leaned in with bated breath, hanging onto Isabella's every word. Odessa watched from one of the stained-glass windows near the ceiling, fluttering at the light, in her orange butterfly form, smiling to herself. Suddenly aware of how she might appear to onlookers, she relaxed her wings, glancing at Morphinae, who was in the window at the opposite end of the Sanctuary. Even though he also was in a blue butterfly state (and difficult to see), she could sense his usual lack of emotional commitment to the entire exchange. She wondered to herself if there were some way to make her butterfly form larger, more noticeable, perhaps. But she dared not attempt it today of all days, in case she goofed and enlarged herself into a human butterfly size.

"We are here because we love our planet." There were cheers from the audience. "We are here because Earth is our home." More cheers. "We are here because our voices need to be heard." The crowd erupted while Isabella surveyed the room, nodding. After a moment, she patted her hand in the air, and the crowd settled.

From the Negotiation room, Lucene sent a message to Cepheus. *How come we don't have a crowd of Erde supporters here?* she wanted to know.

Well, Cepheus answered, *we don't really do that.*

Why not?

Because we don't have to.

Lucene was not entirely sure she understood this answer. She leaned over toward Dallen and whispered, "Why are there no Vitruvian supporters present?"

"Oh," he whispered back, "there are."

"Really, but..."

"Please, Lucene. This isn't the time. And, you should not even be addressing a Vitruvian Ambassador so informally in meetings such as this."

Tanager overheard the exchange but said nothing.

Lucene sat back, deflated. They had been dating for several weeks now, and she still hadn't gotten a handle on how she was "supposed" to behave. It seemed to her that in formal settings or when at the Embassy Club (the only place they ever seemed to dine), she was expected to follow Vitruvian protocol, whatever that was; but when visiting places such as art galleries, outdoor botanical gardens or simple sightseeing, she could be herself, sort of. The only sign that she could see that made the true distinction was whether or not they were alone or interacting with other people. Having little dating experience, and only having Fatima's misguided relationships to go by, Lucene assumed that this was normal. She thought that maybe she could ask Neroni about this, but given the current murder investigation, and the fact that she really didn't know the woman all that well, she dismissed the idea.

"Please join me," Isabella finished her speech, "in welcoming Representative Dallen from Vitruvia in Section 2 as he shares with us his bold initiative for uniting Earth, Vitruvia and Erde for the good of our world." Whatever Isabella had said or done over the past few weeks to win over Earth supporters, it had clearly worked because everyone cheered and clapped in unison, without hesitation.

Dallen was pleased, shooting Lucene a smug, "this is just as it should be" look. She smiled back encouragingly, but something twisted in her stomach.

"Thank you, Reverend Isabella," Dallen acknowledged. "As you know, we are on a very important mission, one that few Earthlings are worthy of supporting."

Worthy? Cepheus, Tanager and Lucene exchanged looks.

"You are the chosen…" Dallen continued.

Had Commander Royce and Reverend Isabella been in the same room (on the same planet, even), people would have observed an identical, manufactured expression. Without words, they shared a mutual understanding that sometimes you have to play along with the facade in order to support the greater good. They both adopted a small smile that included nodding, encouragingly, at strategic moments and glancing around the room to gauge the acceptance of the message.

"Sadly," Dallen puffed his chest, his hologram now taking center stage on three locations on Earth. "Virtruvia and Erde are prohibited from the

International Peace Project's Assembly, ironically, in spite of their attempts to help Earth."

Tanager let out a nervous cough. Dallen peered at him with disapproval. Tanager waved a slight apology. Until recently, he wasn't aware that he had any nervous behaviors. The discovery annoyed him.

"What we are proposing," Dallen continued, "is re-uniting Virtruvia and Erde with the Assembly, explaining our position of peace, reconciliation and mutual respect." Dallen paused in all the right places, speaking between applause. "But there's an even more pressing matter than that." The crowd grew silent. "The Earth is in grave danger." There were murmurs in the crowd. "I'm sure you have heard of the Royals…" There were frightened nods from the crowd. "And the Null…" A gasp could be heard. "Then you understand that unless we work together alongside the IPP, the Royals will send the Null to destroy us all—Earth, Vitruvia and Erde."

Something about this didn't sit quite right with Lucene. The knot in her stomach grew tighter. Tanager was also confused, but for a different reason. *That's not accurate.* He directed his energy and emotion toward Cepheus. *Our intelligence suggests that Royals want the Null to avoid Earth so that they can claim it as their new Training Grounds. Is it possible that if the Null avoids Earth, then the Royals plan to offer up Virtruvia and Erde as 'consolation' prizes?"*

I'm not sure, Cepheus replied in thought, *but I don't think so.*

What is he up to? Tanager thought, without thinking. Then, when he realized what he had just said, he was, momentarily, proud of his newly developed Earth lexicon. Somehow, it seemed appropriate at a time like this.

Once again, Cepheus replied, ignoring Tanager's misplaced pride, *I'm not sure.*

"You may be asking yourself," Dallen finished his speech, "what can I do? I'm just a mere mortal." Lucene had to admit that she asked herself this very question quite regularly. "But I assure you, you are much more than that. You are the chosen."

As if on cue, Isabella asked, "Honorable Ambassador Dallen, what can we do to support your mission?"

"I like to think of it as *our* mission," Dallen smiled. The knot in

Lucene's stomach now felt like a rock. At the same time, Tanager put his hand on his belly. *Must have been something I ate,* he thought to himself, reciting, yet another Earth phrase he'd learned from a recent movie. "Our voices need to be heard. And for that to happen, you need to protest the Assembly's removal of Vitruvia and Erde from the IPP."

"But, why now," Isabella followed the script. "Why so many years later?"

"What a great question, Reverend Isabella. That's a great question," Dallen flashed a pearly smile. "Our intelligence has learned that there is a contract in play, in which the Royals plan to overtake Sections 0, Sections 1 and Sections 2 this year, with the help of the Null." The hologram could be seen walking back and forth. Interesting, as Dallen remained seated at the table in the Negotiation Room, although his mouth and head moved in unison in reality and as a projection. "If you proclaim the injustice, Earth leaders will hear you and vote in favor of our reinstatement. Only then can we help you."

"What do you say, chosen ones?" Isabella raised her arms overhead in a natural yet rehearsed manner. The crowd erupted in cheers and applause.

"Just one more thing," Dallen added, as the sound died down.

"What is that, Representative Dallen?"

"We believe there is a baby."

"A baby?" Isabella's eyes flew open in feigned surprise.

"Yes," Dallen shook his head forlornly. "We have reason to believe that there is a baby, a hybrid between the Royals and the Null, a spawn of pure evil."

What the hell is he talking about?! Lucene wanted to know.

Nulls and Royals can't produce a baby, can they? Tanager asked.

No, Cepheus answered abruptly. *This makes no sense.*

"And what will happen if we don't act now?" Isabella's eyes widened.

"Then, the baby will grow up to represent evil in its purest form and destroy the entire universe. And we are the only ones who can stop it. Who is with me?" From all corners of the Earth where Isabella's influence reached, the congregations stood in unison, cheering, yelling affirmations of support, clapping, and even weeping hysterically. Dallen held his fist to his chest in what could only be assumed was a strange symbol of unity.

Commander Royce stood and held her fist over her heart, glaring at Lucene, Tanager and Cepheus that they should rise and do the same. Instead, Lucene folded her arms, Tanager clasped his hands together and rested them on the desk in front of him, and Cepheus held the sides of his chair, trying not to fall into a dizzy spell. Fortunately, one of Commander Royce's attendants was quick to react, turning off the single camera that put them in view of Earth attendees. Instead, all cameras pointed to Dallen, who waved and smiled regally to the masses. But in the back of everyone's mind in the Negotiation Room (save for Dallen's) was the incessant question*: what baby?*

"What the hell was that about?" Lucene demanded when they were outside, crossing the bridge to the SpeedCircuit. Dallen peered around him, embarrassed by her outburst, especially considering he was still in uniform.

Tanager and Cepheus stayed behind to speak with Commander Royce, while Lucene angrily followed Dallen—at his insistence—after the call.

"You need to calm down," Dallen demanded. "Your manner is not befitting the companion of an Ambassador."

"Hate to break it to you, Ambassador," Lucene spat angrily, "but I don't give a rat's ass about how I appear to others or to you!" Lucene marched across the bridge, fists balled, taking fierce little steps. He followed her with a mix of arrogance, curiosity and a small bit of amusement.

"Clearly," he answered, offhandedly. This only made Lucene angrier.

"And furthermore," Lucene spat, "while you may be *an* ambassador, you're not *my* ambassador. In case you hadn't noticed, I'm not Vitruvian."

"Again," Dallen answered calmly, "clearly."

Lucene stopped in her tracks. "What's that supposed to mean?"

Dallen smiled, knowing he had won.

"It means," Dallen took her by the arms and drew her in closer, "that I recognize that you are a strong, independent hybrid."

"Hybrid?"

"Yes, an Erdeling with special powers having grown up on Earth. I can't imagine that had been easy on you," Dallen offered sympathetically.

"No," Lucene was suspicious. "But why are you suddenly being nice to me?"

Dallen looked offended. "Have I not been nice to you?"

"Intermittently."

Dallen pulled her into his chest and hugged her, as he'd imagine Tanager would have done if he had the opportunity. "I will do better," he promised, kissing her gently on the top of her head, noticing her mix of blonde and brown hair with some disappointment. "So, what made you so angry at me today?"

"Well," Lucene confessed. "I may not know politics very well, but I know bullshit when I hear it."

"And, what 'bullshit' did you hear?"

"All that about being worthy, and chosen, and the Royals destroying Earth?" That didn't seem quite right.

Dallen let out a sigh. "My dear Lucene, while you are a very smart girl, you are right—you don't understand the intricate inner workings of politics. Sometimes, you have to—as you would say on Earth—fudge the truth a little for the greater good."

Lucene's mind went back to that time in New York, sitting in the office of Drake Cushing, her boss and sometimes crush, where he spoke about 'forces at work.' Somehow, this felt wrong, in the same way that it had back then.

"But, Isabella…"

"She's been around for centuries. She understands."

"What are you talking about? Earthlings don't live for centuries," Lucene chuckled. "What you know about politics is on par with what you *don't* know about human lifespan," Lucene was amused.

Dallen chuckled. "Of course, you are right." They walked in silence for a few minutes, hand-in-hand (something that Lucene had only recently become accustomed to). "Forgive me?"

"I suppose." Lucene smiled to herself. "So, what have you got planned for us this afternoon?"

"Well," Dallen was cautious about his words. "Your hair."

"What about it?" Lucene grew defensive again.

"It's beautiful," he lied. "I just thought it would be nice to treat you to a...'spa day.'"

"I don't know what you mean." It was true. Lucene had heard about spa days and shopping days and gal's nights out, but these were all just fun ideas in her head.

"You've always dyed your hair brown to protect your identity, correct?"

"I guess. I didn't really know that at the time, though."

"Well, what if you picked one?"

"One what?"

"One color, Lucene." Dallen sighed. "Don't be daft."

"I thought you were going to be nicer to me."

"I'm sorry."

"You don't like the brown with blonde roots look?"

"It's not that," Dallen sighed again. "It's just that...and, please don't take this the wrong way, but, if you are to be on the arm of a Vitruvian Ambassador, there are certain...expectations."

"Such as?"

"Your hair, for one, should be one color. I'm flexible about which one."

"Well, thank you for your flexibility," Lucene answered sarcastically.

"Try to think of things from my culture and my perspective," he pleaded. "Virtruvia is not as...relaxed as Earth...specifically, where you come from."

"Thanks for being specific."

"What I mean is, there are certain standards."

"Which I don't meet."

"But you could...with a little work."

Lucene thought about this a moment. How much was this relationship worth to her? How important was it to fit in? And, most important, in her mind, what was she willing to sacrifice? After all, when all is said and done, he lives on Vitruvia, and she now lives on Erde. "What do I need to do," she asked, finally.

As Lucene would come to find out, meeting certain standards turned out to be more superficial than she expected. It involved dying her hair all brown, which Dallen paid for. He'd wondered why she hadn't picked blonde since that was actually her natural color. "I guess I'm just not quite ready to be me yet," she explained.

She'd also been forced to give up the wardrobe that Mallory had picked out for her in favor of uncomfortable attire, not unlike 'business casual' on Earth. It was constricting and did little to make her feel attractive. The wardrobe included close-toed shoes with pointy heels, ugly and stiff polyester-like pants with a matching blazer (a blazer!), and a long-sleeved starched shirt. Lucene hated it. Dallen seemed pleased.

By the end of the day, Dallen had created the perfect companion, and Lucene had convinced herself that all was as it should be, and the reality of this made her perfectly miserable.

CHAPTER 17
B-612
NOVEMBER. BEFORE THE NEW ASSEMBLY.

"I am sorry I could not be there to meet you in person, my friends," Cepheus's hologram floated in the air in front of a flat communication screen. "But I have matters of urgency to attend to here, and —" he paused, "I am still under watch."

"Ahh, think nothing of it," Ivan sucked in his breath. The air was a bit thinner on B-612, but he was adapting well, provided he didn't move or speak too rapidly. The gravity also felt mildly off. That, or he had lost an awful lot of weight in a short period of time without actually appearing any thinner. He felt physically unstable, but not abnormally so. "I am jest grateful fer yer assistance."

Ivan and Fatima arrived at the way station between Earth and Erde just a few days prior after a somewhat harrowing journey. Neither had any experience with space travel nor had they time to actually test their human-made vessel before takeoff. To make matters worse, Fatima had been having more regular episodes, where her heart would beat abnormally, causing dizziness and a weird cramping in her belly and mid-back. They have been traveling for three months, mostly alone, save for semi-regular communications with Cepheus, on what they hoped was a private connection.

The attendants who met them on B-612 were three third-year nursing students from TARA, accompanied by one flight surgeon and two pilots. Rescuing refugees from Earth was not unusual for them. Still, sending a team out by special request from a lead professor to gather up Earth-traveling, non-astronaut humans, was.

The humor was not lost on the well-read Ivan. B-612 was the asteroid that the famed *Little Prince* lived on in Antoine de Saint-Exupéry's children's tale. Erdelings had a funny sense of humor, he decided, since they named their small and relatively new planet the German word for "Earth" (Erde), and the way station after asteroid B-612. *Adult humans are not the only ones who are funny,* Ivan thought.

"Did you both arrive safely, without incident?"

"Er," Ivan scratched his ear. "Not entirely without incident, no. But we are here, and your team has been jest grrrreat."

"I am glad. Communication has been spotty today, but I do want to hear more details once your vessel is back on track and closer to Erde."

"Aye," Ivan answered. "We have much to catch up on."

"Hi, Cepheus!" Fatima called from her sleep station in the next portal over. "We can't wait to see you, and Tanager and my favorite gal pal, Lucene!" She was courteous enough to leave Roman off that list, and while Ivan liked to think their relationship had moved past any cause for jealousy, he still had to admit that hearing Roman's name set off a weird flame-like reaction in his head. Then she added, "We love you!"

Cepheus's abnormal pallor turned pink. It wasn't that he didn't feel warmth and affection—in truth, he felt it more deeply than most. But since he'd lost his family due to the Royals waging a personal war against him, he had trouble expressing and accepting it, even in its most innocent form. Ivan, who started out as not the most empathic of people, began to pick up cues from his time spent with Fatima. "Don't ye worry, me friend," he confided, "we understand."

Cepheus and Ivan ended their conversation with Cepheus's image floating back into the screen and vanishing. An attendant quickly silenced the connection. "Can't be too careful as to who's listening," she explained.

"Aye," Ivan nodded solemnly. Sometimes, he wished for the days when he could hole up in his garage, work on his inventions, and not talk to a soul for nearly a week. But he had to admit, the tradeoff had been worth it. Life was decidedly better with Fatima in it then not. For her, it was worth the sacrifice.

"Everything okay?" Fatima smiled up at Ivan when he entered her portal. She was under ordered bed rest while they monitored her condition closely. Ivan leaned over to give her a kiss.

"Aye," he answered. "Everything is jest fine." They still had nearly two to three months of travel to get to Erde, but Fatima had to be cleared first.

"Excuse me," the flight surgeon stood in the doorway. She was unusually small by human standards, less than four feet tall and incredibly thin. Her skin was glossy with an energetic glow about it. "May I enter?"

"Of course, Dr. Wilah," Fatima smiled. "I wish Earth doctors were as polite as you are."

Wilah smiled shyly. "I am only here to serve," she answered, "and you don't need to call me 'doctor.' Wilah is just fine." She scanned Fatima's resting body with what looked like the check-out scanner at a supermarket. "Vitals are good for you and—" she paused.

"And what, doc—er, Wilah?" Ivan asked, concerned.

Wilah took a careful breath. "Vitals are good for you and...your baby."

"Say what now?" Ivan's ears were burning. He must have misheard.

"Your baby," Wilah repeated calmly. Fatima looked as if someone just slapped her in the face. "Were you not trying to conceive?"

"Well," Ivan stammered. Discussing this with someone other than Fatima made him rather uncomfortable. "We weren't exactly trying, but we weren't exactly *not* trying, either. How the hell did this happen?" Wilah eyed him curiously. "I mean," he continued to trip over his words, "I know how it happens, as it were, but we're jest, uh..."

"Pleasantly surprised," Fatima's face glowed. "I believe the words my partner is looking for is "pleasantly surprised."

Ivan looked at Fatima with concern. "I'm sorry, Fatima," he apologized. "I wouldn't have dragged ye out here on some crazy scheme and put yer life in danger had I known ye were...ya know—"

"Actually," Wilah hooked a small monitor to the scanner so she could read the results more clearly. "This is fairly new." She slid her finger over the monitor carefully. "From what I can see, Fatima has been pregnant for nearly two months."

Ivan's face turned red. "Well, we were alone in space fer quite some time." He tugged at his ear nervously.

"There's no need to explain yourself to me, Ivan," Wilah offered. "I'm just happy that Fatima and the baby are healthy."

"So, the weird pains?"

"More related to the pregnancy than your heart condition," Wilah validated. "That said, I'd like to monitor you for a day or two more before clearing you to continue your journey to Erde. In fact," she gave a knowing glance toward two of her students. "Given this new information, it may be prudent if we hitch our two vessels together and accompany you the rest of the way home—if you are amenable to that?"

"Of course," Fatima was overcome with emotion. "But we don't want to put you out."

"We have to travel home, regardless," Wilah explained. "I will confirm with our pilots to make certain, but I suspect that with a few modifications to our vessel, we should be able to travel in tandem."

"Aye, and I am happy to help yer crew as well," Ivan offered.

Wilah nodded. "For now, I'll leave the two of you to," she paused, "process what I've just told you." With that, Wilah left the portal, closing the thin sliding panel that served as a privacy door.

Ivan's head began racing. *A child? Really? I mean, I guess I sorta thought it could happen someday, but I'm not exactly young. And, I don't know the first thing about children, let alone raising one on a foreign planet. Hell, I don't even know yet how I'll support us. And..."*

"Hey," Fatima reached out and took Ivan's hand in hers. He stood over her, smiling sheepishly with a mix of overwhelm, love and confusion. "Don't worry," she told him, "we've got this."

CHAPTER 18
TESTS GONE BAD
NOVEMBER. BEFORE THE NEW ASSEMBLY.

Lucene was already in a bad mood when she arrived at TARA that Wednesday for a class gathering, and she didn't know why. It just felt as if her skin were alive, and she was aware of every tiny sensation. The latest outfit that Dallen picked out for her was not helping. It was a combination of a stiff, high-collared course blouse and equally restrictive polyester-like pants. She reflected again on how the clothes Mallory had chosen turned out to have been much more comfortable. Hopefully, Lucene thought, they were still in her closet, and Dallen hadn't had one of his attendants get rid of them. Lucene paused for a moment of reflection about Mallory, saddened by the loss of someone she had hoped would have become a new friend. Her eyes welled up slightly before she pushed the thought away.

"Are you okay?" Xeni asked in her typical, wide-eyed fashion. She was so focused on Lucene that she almost deleted the entire virtual genetic coding that she was creating on her computer. She frantically adjusted the image using eye movements, averting them away and back again as she virtually commanded the screen to move.

Tanager looked up from his desk, saw Lucene's demeanor, and promptly dropped the paperback book he was reading. He'd seen this before on the Vessel, and he knew the signs.

Lucene tossed her backpack on the floor. "I'm fine," she answered abruptly, plopping into her seat at the head of the class. "Why wouldn't I be?"

"No reason," Xeni replied in a whisper and drew her attention back to her project.

Neroni was next to arrive, along with several other classmates. She opened her mouth to speak, saw Lucene's expression, and closed it again. She took her seat, silently. The person sitting next to Neroni moved over a few inches as if her visions were contagious. Or, perhaps, they thought, she had made them up for some reason.

"*Lucene,*" Tanager sent her a mental message. "*If you are not up to today, we can reschedule.*"

"I'm fine; stay out of my head," she answered rather loudly. The class fell silent. "Could we just get started already?" *The only thing worse than being in a bad mood is everyone around you making it evident that they are aware that you are in a bad mood.*

Tanager thought a moment. He was aware of the efforts involved in running today's experiments—not to mention the money TARA invested in the project and in covering Lucene's expenses. Granted, some of the money came from a trust left behind from her parents, but that had long since run out in the efforts of bringing Lucene home.

In spite of his otherwise best judgement, he decided to press on. A few students appeared visibly surprised at Lucene's seeming lack of respect for their teacher, but many could clearly feel the energy she was kicking off. For Cluseladek's part, he silently performed a kindness meditation, sending positive energy in Lucene's direction and attempting to mentally ask students on a similar wavelength to do the same. Given that Lucene's arms were crossed, and she slumped down in her seat like a spoiled brat, he assumed she wasn't feeling it. He continued, nonetheless.

Tanager called the class to attention. Today's first experiment was to re-test the levels of Lucene's telekinetic powers and see how modifications might dial up her powers in this area. The initial baseline tests revealed that this was an area of potential for her. Yet, she presently exhibited little to no skill at moving objects with her mind.

With several objects of varying weights and sizes in place, carefully lined up across the workspace that had been set up in front of Tanager's desk, they began.

First, Lucene sat in front of the table and was asked to focus her attention on the smallest of objects—a vanadium coin that was poised on the edge of the table. Then, Tanager handed her a blindfold and asked her to tie it around her eyes.

"I'd like you to imagine you are still seeing the coin in front of you," Tanager instructed. "Try to knock it off the table and onto the floor by mentally imagining you were moving it with your mind."

Blindfolded? Mentally commanding the coin to move? It seemed rudimentary and outright silly. She tried. Nothing happened.

"Try again, imagining you are actually pushing it with your hand."

Still nothing.

After several more attempts, Tanager asked her to remove the blindfold and rest for a moment. Finally, they continued. "Why don't we try again without the blindfold? How about tracking its intended movement with your eyes?"

At one point, the other objects on the table began to move: a sharpened pencil, a glass of water, a stone, a ceramic plate—but the coin remained adamantly stuck. Tanager recommended she attempt to funnel her energy in one direction.

Lucene let out a loud sigh. *What a ridiculous waste of time.*

This is when the class was called in to assist, with those rated high in telekinesis offering tips that worked for them, to include asking the coin politely to move, blowing in its direction (like a strong wind), and pushing outward with the palm of her hand and imagining energy was pouring out of it and rushing toward the small coin.

"Parlor tricks," Lucene crossed her arms angrily.

"What?" Tanager asked.

"There is no purpose to this. You're just asking me to perform parlor tricks."

Tanager didn't understand.

At that moment, the door burst open as two young children rushed toward Neroni in a loud frenzy. The little boy had a tangle of coiled black hair, while the girl had a long, blue-green mane that ran the length of her back. Both wrapped their arms around their mother, seated at the back of the classroom.

"I'm so sorry, Professor Tanager," Neroni's husband stood at the door. "I only meant to bring my wife her lunch today." He held up a small container as evidence. "She forgot it. But the kids were beside themselves —worried about their mother and insisting on coming along."

"I see," Tanager wrinkled his forehead. "Why were they worried?"

Neroni shook her head toward her husband and he fell silent.

"Because they think she made that stuff up about the wine lady just for attention," the little boy supplied.

"Shhh, hush now," Neroni told her son.

"Who are 'they'?" Tanager wanted to know.

Neroni let out a sigh, "I'm not sure," she confessed. "We've gotten a few notes, threatening me, saying that I am prejudiced against a Royal living among us, even though the leader of TARA is a..." She stopped herself, knowing full well that Cepheus renounced his lineage a long time ago. "But there were other messages coming in on my phone, calling me a hero for drawing out 'the outsider,' their words, and uncovering a killer."

There were murmurs across the class.

"Neroni, this is terrible," Tanager sympathized. "Have you contacted your local constable?"

"No," she hugged herself as her little boy continued to hang on her arm. Her husband now stood behind her, rubbing her shoulders lightly in support. "I didn't want to cause any more trouble."

"Too late for that," Cluseladek chimed in, while several other classmates let out a chortle.

"That was inappropriate," Tanager chastised. "In this class, we will treat one another with respect."

Cluseladek fell silent, a scornful frown replacing the earlier serenity that had accompanied his kindness meditation. Even he was having an internal battle with his emotions, and he was typically one of the most balanced among them.

The scene had distracted Lucene, who failed to notice that Neroni's little girl was now standing beside her. Even with Lucene sitting, the girl, at full height, barely reached her chin. The girl tugged at Lucene's sleeve. "Hey," she whispered.

Lucene smiled in spite of her souring mood. "What is it?"

"I know how you can make that little coin move," she offered.

"Really? How?" Lucene was amused. *Maybe she can take my place, and I can go home.*

"It's easy. You just have to pretend you *are* the coin and ask yourself why you might want to fall on the floor."

"Hmmm," Lucene was skeptical. "I suppose it's worth a try."

While the class was busy discussing Neroni's dilemma, Lucene focused on the coin. Then, she pretended she was the coin—feeling heavy, lethargic, and very warm. There was an uncomfortableness of laying halfway on the table and halfway in mid-air in such a precarious way. The floor, she reasoned, was cool and comfortable. So why not just—"

The coin fell to the floor and rolled toward Xeni's foot. Everyone fell silent at the clatter.

"See, I told you," Neroni's daughter beamed proudly.

"Well done," Lucene whispered, tweaking the girl's nose playfully.

"Your daughter has more skill than any of us," Cluseladek observed. "I thought we weren't supposed to teach anyone else unless under the supervision of TARA."

"My daughter is just naturally curious," Neroni grit her teeth.

"This is very strange," Xeni commented, furrowing her brows as she picked up the coin.

"What is?" Lucene asked.

"This coin," Xeni closed her palm around it and stared into the distance. "It came from the cash register at Mallory's costume shop. How did it get here?"

"I read that his store was robbed," one student offered. "Is that one of the stolen coins?"

"Maybe," Xeni replied. "I'm not sure."

"Some psychometrist you are," another student commented.

"I'm still learning," Xeni pouted.

"Students, please be still," Tanager attempted in vain to regain control of his classroom, but the students wouldn't be silenced.

Neroni motioned to her daughter, who immediately left Lucene's side to join her mother. Neroni quickly gathered up her children as she and her husband attempted to make a rapid exit through the open classroom door.

"What's the hurry?" another student asked, lifting his arm in the air and motioning toward the door, laughing as it slammed wildly in the family's face. To Lucene, he smiled. "Child's play."

"I said, be still!" Tanager called out angrily. A few students fell silent, never having seen their teacher visibly lose his temper before.

Neroni fought with the door, but her classmate held it shut through sheer will.

"That's enough, Louis. Release the door."

Louis was having too much fun now and called for two of his classmates to force Neroni and her family back to their seats for "questioning."

"Yeah," a young woman in class with a misshapen head, chimed in. "It seems like quite a coincidence that Neroni happened to see that wine lady at the preserve, and now money from Mallory's shop turns up here!"

Lucene caught a glimpse of Neroni's face as she hugged her kids to her. She was afraid. *What is she seeing?*

Lucene didn't have to wonder for long as the pencil, water glass, stone and plate went flying through the air as students either jumped to avoid getting struck or attempted to re-direct them away from other classmates. The water glass shattered against the wall, the plate against the floor. The pencil made a rapid beeline toward Tanager's left eye, but he managed to deflect it. The stone was nearly at Neroni's head when Lucene mentally connected with the stone, calling to mind the lake outside that the stone came from (and longed to go back to), which, coincidentally, happened to be right behind the window where Louis now stood.

What Lucene hadn't realized was just how sentient the stone was. It not only wanted to return to the lake, but it also felt Lucene's anger. After all, Neroni had always been kind to her, and now this arrogant student was threatening her, her family, and other classmates and convincing others to join his battle. She glanced down at her arms, briefly. For the first time ever, the tree-like patterns on her arm were glowing a blood red, and she could actually feel the heat coming from the thin lines as if they were tiny embers burning through coal.

Before she could reign the energy back in, the stone turned, making a beeline for Louis's head, striking the boy so hard that blood spilled as he fell to the floor. The stone dropped with a loud thud, cracking one of the floor tiles. Somehow, all that Lucene could feel was the stone's desperation to escape after it realized what it had done. Lucene lunged for the stone, throwing it through the window. Glass fragments flew. Wasting no time, Lucene climbed through the window, feeling shards of glass as they embedded into her hands and knees. Outside, she found the blood-covered stone and rescued it from a tangle of grass on the ground. She leaned over to grab the rock, hugging it to her chest as she turned to see the commotion behind her as several students watched from the window. The sounds of an ambulance could be heard.

"Lucene, wait!" someone called, but the voice sounded a million miles away.

Without a moment's thought, she, and the stone, descended into the lake.

SECTION TWO

"I want you to send me to another dimension, where I can hide out for a bit, see how my other selves are doing. S-s-ee what chaos we can s-s-tir up… The multiverse is a petri dish of possibilities."

CHAPTER 19
THE OTHER FOUNDLING
57 YEARS AGO. BEFORE EVERYTHING.

Tanager Blackletter had been left on the steps of the Dragoste healing center in Achel when he was no more than a month old, with no information other than a note that read, *My name is Tanager Blackletter. My mother loves me very much but is not in the right emotional place right now to care for a child. Please find me a good home. I'm a good baby. I hardly ever cry. Lentils and split-pea formulas are my favorite.* Tanager's mother, Wren, accidentally signed her name to the note before catching her mistake, scribbling out the name and writing "Tanager" overtop of it, drawing the outline of a bird next it.

Neither his mother nor father could be found, and with traffic to and from Erde being heavy that week on account of the approaching Peacock Spider holiday, it was assumed that she visited from a neighboring planet in Section 1 merely for the purpose of dropping him off.

In later years, Tanager would always be left with that subtle feeling of unworthiness mixed with abandonment, coupled with doubt. After all, the Peace-Keepers on Erde would naturally feel it their duty to look after a foundling, but did they truly love him or was it obligation?

"Are you still working, my love? It's late," Petrichor greeted Cepheus at his office door at TARA while wearing a jumpsuit with strawberry patterns all over it. She was carrying a basket. "I brought you dinner, just in case."

Cepheus looked up from his schematics with a look of wonder and surprise. It wasn't as if Petrichor never brought him dinner when he was working late. In fact, she did so quite often, usually when he forgot to meet her at their favorite restaurant on "date night." It's just that he often became so engrossed in his work that he momentarily forgot there were other people in the world; therefore, each time she arrived with a basket of food, it was as if he were seeing her for the first time. This was why she never got angry sitting alone at a table for two sipping blackberry wine and counting the minutes until she knew that he had officially forgotten—again. It was all worth it for that look.

Cepheus glanced at his watch. "Petrichor, I am so sorry." He stood from his desk, moving toward the door. He took her by the shoulders and planted a soft kiss on her lips. "How is it that you put up with me?"

As was custom, Cepheus abandoned his work, and the two walked hand-in-hand to the university's outdoor dining area. They had been dating for a year, and while they were considered very young by Erde standards, both were convinced that they were meant to be together. This was not without a few raised eyebrows as he was technically a nomadic Royal while she was born on Erde. They weren't even sure if they could have children should they wish to marry and start a family—an answer they would get some eighteen years later.

Petrichor set the basket on the table furthest from the school but closest to the stars, and pulled out a canteen of soup, a cold vegetable salad, bread and a chilled container of tea. Cepheus reached in and retrieved cups, bowls and dinnerware.

Petrichor poured him a cup of tea. "Dandelion tea," she explained. "I assume you are still working?"

Cepheus nodded. "I am very close to discovering something," he paused. "I'm just not sure what it is."

"Well, that sounds intriguing," Petrichor acknowledged, setting a bowl of beet and turmeric soup out for each of them.

"Yes, I will have to spend a good bit of time at the Makerspace this weekend." Petrichor raised an eyebrow. Cepheus reached out and took her hand. "I will make it up to you, I promise."

"Hmmph," Petrichor wrinkled her nose at him, taking a sip of the soup. "Guess I'll just have to find another date for the festival this weekend."

"You wouldn't dare."

"Wouldn't I, though?" She wiggled a shoulder seductively. "You're right." She dropped her shoulder. "I wouldn't. Guess I'll have to drag my sister instead."

"I won't be working the entire time. Maybe I can sneak away for a few hours and join you."

"I suppose that would be all right," Petrichor teased. The two sat in silence for a few minutes while they ate. It had been a challenge adapting to Petrichor's mostly-vegetable diet, coming from a more carnivorous species by nature. Petrichor tried to meet him halfway by occasionally adding bits of beef to his dinner plate when he came to her apartment for dinner. When he thought she wasn't looking, he would add a bit more. "I heard something that might interest you today."

"What is it?" Cepheus was curious.

"They discovered a baby boy on the steps of the healing center today."

"Really? Was he okay?"

"He's fine. Chubby little thing from what I've seen in the news."

"Who would abandon their own child? Particularly since it is within every new mother's right to surrender their newborn, without repercussions, if they do so in person."

"Someone unfamiliar with our laws and very overwhelmed, it would seem."

Cepheus's eyes grew dark for a minute, "He's better off." Petrichor took his hand once again.

"I didn't mean to upset you," she replied. "I just thought you would find it interesting since that's where they found you as a young child."

"But I fled my family of my own volition. I wasn't abandoned."

"True. And they could have sent you back."

"But they didn't."

"I'm glad for that."

"As am I," Cepheus put a hand over Petrichor's. "As am I."

---

31 Years Ago. In the Underground Prisons.

Cepheus awoke from his dream of Petrichor, remembering where he was. And, with a sunken heart, he also remembered how violently the Royals had attacked, killing his wife and three children and dragging him back to the Royal Training Grounds for sentencing. He was deemed a traitor for abandoning his throne years earlier and then in establishing the Data Collectors on Erde to help save Earth.

So, there he laid in a fragile heap, perched up against a stone wall, barely breathing and trying to keep warm under a small tattered cloth blanket. It became abundantly clear that he wasn't going to divulge anything that went on at TARA, nor how many Data Collectors were currently on Earth and where they were located. It also became clear to him that he was going to die, if not from cold and starvation, and not from the wounds of torture, then his parents would have him killed. Therefore, when he heard a gentle breathing outside of his cell, he didn't bother to move. He assumed it was his time. He didn't care.

"Get up, vermin," a young female voice yelled from outside the door.

He lifted his head slightly, in a haze of exhaustion and confusion. *Why were they yelling at him from outside the door?*

Moments later, the cell swung open, and in walked a woman dressed in all black, wheeling a small cart. "That's right, on your feet!" She slammed the door behind her.

What was right? He hadn't even moved.

Suddenly, her voice was in his ear. "I'm sorry, my Sovereign. I would never normally speak to you this way."

Cepheus rolled over, peering up at the small but formidable-looking young woman, with a shaved head and rugged arms who was now down on one knee looking at him almost sympathetically.

"Aren't you an assassin?"

"I am," she whispered back.

"Are you here to kill me?"

"I'm supposed to kill you. But what I'm actually going to do, is set you free. But you need to do exactly as I say."

The assassin helped Cepheus to his feet, with her doing most of the lifting. She half-dragged him to the cart, which should have contained shelving filled with an assortment of fun tools of the trade under a curtain. It was empty. "In here," she explained hastily. "Curl up as small as you can."

Cepheus obeyed, not knowing if she spoke the truth or if this was the most sadistic form of torture yet. His skin was battered and torn, and every muscle ached as he folded his tall frame into the cart's hub. She quickly covered him up beneath the curtain.

With that, she wheeled him down a long hallway, the cart bumping up and down along the uneven floor. His cell door remained open.

"That him?" A guard caught her off guard, motioning to the bulging curtain. Cepheus held his already tight breath and tried not to move.

"Pieces of him," the assassin answered, smirking.

"Can I see?" He went to life the curtain.

"Back off," she barked, blocking his arm and delivering a non-lethal under-the-chin strike to the side of his neck. The guard choked and took a few steps back. He let out a few expletives.

"What was that for?"

"I doubt you have the stomach for what's under here. Back away and let me finish disposing of this traitor."

The guard, while twice her size, backed down. He lacked both the skill and the rank. And, if he were being honest with himself, he wasn't sure he had the stomach for what he imagined was underneath the cart, either.

The guard watched her, curiously, as she made a left-hand turn at the end of the hall. "Where are you going?" he asked. "The river's that way," he pointed. She was new to her post. Perhaps she didn't know that.

"I'm well aware of that," she answered sternly. "This one is getting sent, special delivery, back to where he came from."

The guard laughed. What a fine warning that would be, indeed, the bloody remains of Cepheus Baruch being sent, special delivery, back to Erde. He gagged a little as he imagined exactly what the recipient would see when they opened a single-pod vessel to find their favorite professor in a dismembered heap across the control panel.

The assassin had little time left. Once she reached the launch site, she lifted the curtain and helped him stand, and then half-dragged him to a small pod. "The coordinates are set," she said as she lifted the hatch. "Once you're out of the atmosphere, it will put you in auto-hibernation. Let's hope your Erdeling brethren can lock in on you and pull you in once you reach Section 1."

"Let's hope I don't die first," Cepheus half-joked.

"Yes, let's hope that," she answered. Someone was coming. She hit the launch codes and ran from the site before Cepheus could thank her.

The assassin dove behind an armored defense shield and covered her head. When the thunder of the vessel finally died down, she realized that someone was crouched behind the shield with her, and he was not happy.

"Moksha, what have you done," her father asked angrily.

"I sent the traitor back to his planet in pieces, as a warning to all who dare get in our way," she declared with false bravado.

"Those weren't our orders," he stood, motioning for her to do the same. "And besides, no one will believe that you, of all people, took the initiative to do something so violent yourself."

"Why not? We're assassins. Isn't that what we do?"

"That's what *I* do. That's what your mother does. That's even what your brother does. But you, Moksha? You're about as intimidating as a house plant."

"Then why did Sovereign Hamish send me to kill his son?"

"Sovereign Sabrina probably demanded it, and Sovereign Hamish, not really wanting to see his son die, sent the weakest among us in the hopes that what just happened…happened!"

"So, will you turn me in and have them imprison and kill me next?"

"No," Moksha's father thought a minute. "Time to craft a different story." She looked at him questioningly. "Cepheus overtook you, tried to murder you with one of your own tools. He succeeded in rendering you unconscious. I found him trying to escape in one of our pods. Thinking he had killed you, I ripped him limb from limb in a fit of rage, shooting him off into space as a message to those who would betray us. I wasn't thinking of protocol. I was angry."

Moksha nodded. This could work. "But if they don't believe you, then you will suffer my fate."

"Moksha, you are my daughter. I trained you. I will be blamed, regardless." Her heart sank. She hadn't considered how her insubordination would impact her family. "Quickly, we must make this look convincing." She understood.

Her father proceeded to go on the attack, slamming his young daughter in the armored shield and making non-lethal stabs with her own blade under her rib cage and arm. She cried out in pain but did little to fight back. He delivered a blow to her stomach and kidneys, making the movements seem uncalibrated. After all, Cepheus was a Royal, not a member of the military. It had to appear organic. Finally, he grabbed her by the neck, squeezing until he rendered her unconscious, where he dropped her unceremoniously to the ground.

CHAPTER 20
COLLAPSE OF REASON
NOVEMBER. BEFORE THE NEW ASSEMBLY. LUCENE'S COTTAGE.

"May I come in?" Tanager knocked softly on the door. When there was no response, he thought, *please, Lucene, don't shut me out.*

"Stay out of my head," Lucene groused back. But then relented with a sigh, "yes, you can come in."

Tanager tentatively opened the door, somewhat afraid of what he might find. His heart sank a little. Lucene was still in her white linen pajamas, curled up in a ball on her bed, arms covering her head as if protecting herself from falling matter.

He scanned the room. She had taken great pains to move all potted plants and other greenery to one corner of the room, piling them haphazardly under a window, as if they offended her in some way but she didn't want to kill them. Therefore, she still offered them light. On the other side of the room, a closet door was bulging, half-open, where he presumed Lucene had stuffed all trinkets and belongings. In front of the closet, she had managed to push a heavy dresser, stacking the now-empty drawers on top of it. The only evidence remaining that this room was used at all was the small bed in which she was laying and a green nightstand. Its drawer had also been removed and now lived with the other drawers in front of the closet.

"Close the door," she mumbled. "The whole world doesn't need to see the mess that I've become."

Tanager's forehead wrinkled in pain. Even when feeling her emotions deeply, he still wasn't sure what to do. As requested, he shut the door.

"Bet you're sorry you took all that time to journey to Earth for your protege, only to be later disappointed for the wasted effort."

"You are not a wasted effort," Tanager replied. "And my only disappointment is in myself. I should have recognized that you were stressed and canceled class the other day."

"You are not responsible for shielding me from myself," Lucene answered miserably.

Tanager let out a sigh. "If only I could make you see how special you are."

"Special?" Lucene rolled over, allowing him to see her with pink, tear-stained eyes. Her hair on one side of her head wrapped in a tangled mess around her neck, the other side chopped short from when she'd attempted to cut it earlier that day with a pair of nail scissors, the only sharp objects they'd left in her home. "I'm following the same pattern as all the children born of genetically altered Data Collectors, aren't I? We start off appearing as some rare breed with unique gifts. And then, after enough time has passed, we begin to unravel…slowly at first…and then it snowballs. Isn't that what happened to Jim Sparks, Cluseladek and many of the others?"

"This whole process is new," Tanager tried to explain. "We gave you extreme empathy without ensuring that your biological makeup could handle the change. We are to blame."

"You didn't give me anything," Lucene interrupted. "I was an accident. My parents didn't plan on me."

"But they were grateful for you."

"A lot of good that did for any of us," Lucene sat up, staring at Tanager directly in the eyes, daring him to disagree with her. Tanager put his hand over one of Lucene's. She quickly pulled it away, holding it with her other hand as if it burned. Tanager's heart sank a little more. "My energy made them worse, didn't it? The class short-circuited because I shifted the vibration in the room."

"What happened today…wasn't your fault."

"I almost killed one of your students."

"It was an accident."

"That almost resulted in death."

"Louis will be fine," Tanager reassured her. "Turns out, he has a very thick skull. Several students joined me at the hospital to perform an energy healing on him after the doctors had finished treating him." He paused for a reaction that didn't come. He tried again. "He and all our students understand the risks involved with their training."

"Their risks should be the Royals! The outsiders…the enemies…not one of their own. Not someone sent to teach them."

"It wasn't your fault."

"I am a liability." With that, Lucene flopped back on her pillow and pulled the blankets up over her head.

"You know, there were more people in the room than just you."

"What is that supposed to mean?"

"It means that Louis, and several other students, were acting out in anger. They would have likely hurt Neroni and her family, myself and others had you not intervened. While your energy was misdirected, your intention was to help Neroni. Therefore, I refuse to believe that your vibration caused any of this." Tanager thought about this for a moment. "In fact, I don't know what caused this. It was something…something else."

Lucene replayed the part of the story where she struck Louis with the stone, continuing until she was deep in the lake. It was Xeni that ran and called to her, and Tanager, who after handing Louis off to the medical team, dove in and fished her out of the lake. In no part of her story was she in any way a hero. "Please leave now."

"Just one moment more…please?"

Lucene let out a sigh. "What do you want?"

In spite of her resistance, in spite of her pain, he could feel her reaching toward him. How was it possible for him to be so close to someone and so far at the same time?

"It's about Dallen…"

"What about him? You don't like him, do you?" Lucene got defensive. *Is it because he's a Vitruvian? Is that why you hate him?*

"I don't hate him," Tanager replied.

"Stay out of my head," Lucene mumbled.

"Sorry," Tanager sat on the edge of her bed. She recoiled a little but didn't stop him. Instead, she moved her legs aside so that he would have room.

"I'm concerned about the way he treats you."

"The way he *treats* me. What the hell is that supposed to mean?"

Tanager bristled at the thought of Dallen. "On the rare times I've seen you two together, I've witnessed him chastise you publicly and diminish your ideas, calling them childish," Tanager was on a proverbial role. "He dismantles your creativity—"

"He's just being honest…that's the Vitruvian way."

"Brashness and honesty are not the same thing." Tanager was beginning to feel slightly unhinged and couldn't stop himself. "In fact, whenever it is that you are your most brilliant, he manages to put out the flame as if smothering it with a damp sponge."

Lucene paused and then looked at Tanager with renewed understanding.

"I know what's going on here," she whispered.

"What?" Tanager tugged uncomfortably at the hem of his shirt. He waited for the words: *jealousy, envy, possessiveness, resentment…*

"You're worried that his honesty will further damage me," Lucene was matter of fact.

Tanager's face dropped as his heart sank even deeper. He didn't that was possible.

"No, Lucene," Tanager brushed a stray piece of her hair away from her eye. This time, Lucene didn't flinch. She didn't even move, only gazed back at him. "There is nothing wrong with you."

"Hah—" Lucene laughed, her eyes dropping to her bed…to the entire scene.

"Lucene," he called her attention back. He took her face in his hands and looked directly into her eyes. She didn't resist. "There is nothing wrong with you. And when you come to realize that, you may also realize that Dallen is not what you deserve."

"And what do I deserve?" Lucene asked, her voice clipped.

Tanager could feel the skin on his cheeks become hot. Lucene's face contorted, confused. "I feel that you are somehow punishing yourself by courting someone who knowingly mistreats you. You deserve someone who treasures all that you are."

"And, who would that be?" Lucene's voice challenged.

Instead of answering, Tanager moved toward her. Lucene braced herself for a kiss. At least, if it were Dallen, that's what she could expect. Instead, Tanager pressed his forehead to hers—a sign of respect, and one that says, *we are one.*

Lucene sucked in her breath.

"Thank you," she whispered, biting back more tears. "But I don't deserve your kindness. And I certainly don't deserve you. Please leave."

CHAPTER 21
FAR'S MEETING WITH JASPER
AUGUST. BEFORE THE DEATH AT THE EASTERN CROSS.

"By Segue, you were a difficult bastard to find," Jasper Set landed, butt-first on the hard ground. "Ouch, that smarts," he rubbed his hip. He'd never had trouble with varying gravities before, and Jasper couldn't fathom why his entrance had been anything less than stellar.

Far looked up from his fire in surprise. He had been roasting two dessert lizards on a stick when the demon decided to join him. It seemed that Jasper wasn't the only one who had missed his mark. Far was supposed to land at the Western Cross and seek out Moksha, but instead, now sat in the mostly barren and undeveloped Northern Cross. He'd laid his robe temporarily across a nearby boulder and sat in his underwear, bare-chested and pale.

"Have you come to take me back to Section 3?" Far asked softly. He seemed rather indifferent to Jasper's sudden appearance, yet another anomaly in what was turning out to be a very unusual day.

"No, why would you think that?"

"I sense that you know Sovereign Hamish and have some business with him."

"Ah, yes. The prophet. Tell me," Jasper fluttered his wings and stood with some difficulty, "how did you end up way out here?"

"I'm not sure," Far answered quietly. "There's something odd about the energy here. It took me several tries just to make it to Erde at all. I will attempt to move again after I've had something to eat and a little rest." Far offered his stick up to Jasper. "Want some?"

"Nah, you go ahead," Jasper waved his hand. "I've a Data Collector to eat for lunch if the day goes as planned. Wouldn't want to waste my appetite."

Far was silent for a moment as he sized up Jasper. Finally, it clicked. "What is it that you want, demon?"

Jasper circled the frail man several times, in part to try and figure out the best approach but also to adjust to the gravity of this unusual planet. "Hamish sent me to help you reach your objective," Jasper said.

"How can you know my objective when I'm not even sure what it is?" Far asked, innocently.

"Well, tell me what you know, and I'll fill in the rest," Jasper offered.

"Could you stop circling around me," Far requested. "You're making me dizzy."

Jasper let out a laugh. He was amused by the fact that this monk knew he was a demon and yet seemed completely unafraid or disturbed by him. *The Royals must have done a number on him,* he reasoned. He plopped on a tree stump near the fire and watched as Far took a bite of crispy lizard and chewed vigorously. Jasper wondered if the boy were starving or if he simply didn't absorb the food he'd actually eaten. "Certainly," Jasper replied. "Go on, then."

"My instructions are to reunite with Moksha and get her to trust me. Find out what she knows about the Data Collectors. Discover any additional weaknesses the people of Erde might have and return home with intel."

"Interesting," Jasper reflected. "Collecting data on the Data Collectors."

"Did you not already know this?" Far asked, guardedly.

"Course I did," he mocked. "It just sounds funny when you say it out loud.

Far thought for a moment and nodded. It did.

"But Sovereign Hamish didn't tell me how much data to collect, how long to stay, and when I should return."

A light went off in Jasper's scheming little mind.

"Well, you're in luck. That's why I'm here! Hamish sent me to guide you, and guide you, I shall."

"Why would my Sovereign send a demon?"

"A *reformed* demon," Jasper offered. "We're not all what people make us out to be."

"I hope that's true," Far answered, peering at him as if staring into his soul deeply. "Because it doesn't look good for you if you are not."

"Eh, not what?" Jasper had already lost the train of thought.

"Reformed."

"Oh, I see."

"Now, about guidance," Far asked, "what am I to do next?"

"Well," Jasper thought a moment. "Slight change of plan. It is no longer advisable for you to seek out Moksha."

"No?"

"No."

"What, then?"

"Well," Jasper formed his words carefully and with feigned remorse. "Unfortunately, my dear boy. We're gonna need you to kill someone for us."

CHAPTER 22
FUGITIVE
NOVEMBER. BEFORE THE NEW ASSEMBLY.

"I can't help but notice my love," Roman commented, handing Far the book he'd requested, which was, curiously enough, about the art of rhetoric. "That you seem more—"

"More what?" Far had his legs folded beneath him on the couch with several notepads and books strewn around him. He held a simple pencil and journal in his lap.

Roman looked around his typically pristine living quarters. Now there were signs of Far everywhere. For a monk with few worldly possessions, he sure seemed to leave scattered belongings everywhere. One issue at a time, Roman thought.

"More distant, somehow, than before," Roman confessed, sitting on the arm of a chair. Far looked at him, hurt almost. "I'm not complaining, mind you. Just wondering what happened to you…to us, really."

Far thought for a moment, calculating his options. After what felt like a painful silence for Roman, Far reached a handout to him. "Come here, my beloved."

Roman took it, gratefully. Maybe things were okay, after all. He took a seat beside Far on the couch as Far wrapped an arm around him.

"It has been a stressful few years," Far began.

"I know, and I don't mean to pressure you."

"Shhh. Hush," Far patted Roman's shoulder. "There are some things I should tell you."

Roman was relieved. He didn't want to pressure Far to share with him what has happened over the past couple of years, particularly since he wasn't terribly eager to share how he'd lost his mind for a time and thought he was a womanizing Data Collector sent to Earth on a special mission. But Far had been home for several weeks now, and both seemed to be avoiding discussing anything more serious than, "You drink your tea without sugar, now? Me too."

Ever since Constable Melokuhle's visit, Roman had questions he was afraid to ask, lest his partner decide to run again. And, he didn't want that.

"What is it?" Roman asked, hopefully.

Far paused, thoughtfully. "The Assembly, members of the IPP, have got it all wrong," he began.

"What do you mean?"

Far chose his words carefully. "They make the Royals out to be terrible, violent people, but that's not the case at all. A recent encounter made me realize that."

"What are you talking about?" Roman was aghast. "They tortured Cepheus and killed his family. They were responsible for the deaths of an untold number of Data Collectors, and they held you prisoner."

"How do you know they actually tortured Cepheus and killed his family?"

"How do I—" Roman was confused. "Cepheus told us. Tanager was there!"

"Were they?"

"What are you suggesting?"

"Have you ever seen the records of the supposed 'missing' Data Collectors? You would think if they were so important, there would be records somewhere."

"I'm sure that there are," Roman was flustered.

"And as for me, they cured me."

"Did you not tell me upon arrival that you were a prisoner there? That you had been mistreated?"

"I did," Far confessed. "And that part was true. But what I didn't realize—" Far paused, staring off into space as if he were putting together the puzzle pieces at this very moment. "Was that it was part of my healing."

"Your healing?"

"Yes, don't you see?"

"I'm afraid I don't."

"Had they coddled me, I wouldn't have developed resilience. I am now free of cancer."

Roman peered down at his love skeptically. While Far may have been cured of cancer, there was nothing about him that screamed health and resilience.

"So, lack of food, routine beatings—that all…helped you?"

"I'm sure I was exaggerating my training."

"Oh, it was training now?"

"You're mocking me," Far was hurt.

"I'm not mocking you. I just think you may be a little—confused."

"You weren't there," Far grumbled.

"No, I wasn't," Roman put his arm on Far's knee and rubbed it affectionately.

"But this whole thing of perception has me thinking."

"About what?"

"Well, for example, the Data Collectors."

"What about them?"

"If they are trained in powers of the mind, are they more or less susceptible to conditioning than regular people?"

"Regular people?" This line of questioning had Roman very concerned.

"I mean because they are more empathic, does that make them emotionally more malleable? Or, because they spend so much time in meditation and training, their minds are stronger against outside influences? Who is easier to influence, the common man or the Data Collectors?"

Roman thought about this for a moment, remembering Dr. Ennis's concern over the mental health of a group of people being given special empathic skills without the accompanying tools to harness the newly associated emotions properly. He shared his concerns with Far. "I guess it depends on the person and the circumstance," Roman reasoned, the anthropology studies teacher surfacing. "You could argue that some have stronger mental capabilities because they've developed their higher brain to separate emotions from reason and know when to utilize which one successfully. I guess it could go either way."

"That's what I thought," Far smiled, satisfactorily.

"Why all these strange questions?"

"No reason. It just helps me settle a debate I had with a demon recently."

"A demon? What demon?"

Far stood and leaned over to kiss Roman on the forehead. "Don't worry about it, my love. I'm just being ecumenical." Far dropped his robe on the floor. "I'm in need of a bath. Be back shortly."

"I've been meaning to ask you—"

"Yes, my love." Far turned to look at him, hoping his naked form might distract Roman from his questions. For once, it didn't.

"About Constable Melokuhle's recent visit—"

"Not that, again."

"I'm just trying to understand why he would have traced Mallory's death back to you."

"As you pointed out at the time, I was the only anomaly in this town, save for you and Lucene—both of whom could be accounted for. People are afraid of outsiders. I understand that."

"I suppose you are right."

"I know that I am," Far concluded. "Enough talking for one day. After my bath, let's relax and watch a movie."

Cepheus was awakened by a gentle breath that he heard outside of his office door. Ever since his...encounter...with his parents all those years back, the one that resulted in the Royals murdering his family, sleep had been sketchy at best, and every sound sent him on high alert. Therefore, when he sensed movement in the hallway, he grabbed the only weapon he could find on such short notice—a potted plant.

There was a knock at his door. He answered, holding the plant overhead with one long, outstretched arm.

There stood Moksha, much smaller and yet, far more formidable than him. She was wearing a brown linen top that wrapped tightly around her torso and gaucho pants that were fluid. Her feet were bound with gray sandals that laced up around the ankles and calf. In her hand, she carried a teak walking stick that somehow seemed appropriate, given her attire. She glanced at the potted plant, now held ominously over her head by a cautious Cepheus, who was wearing a black pajama set of pants and a top that looked absolutely absurd on a vampire-like half-man and half-lizard.

"Are you planning on killing me with a jade plant?" she asked flatly. "May I remind you that I'm an assassin. Death by jade plant is covered on day one."

Her deadpan expression gave Cepheus cause to pause before he conceded to lower his weapon.

"Moksha," he whispered, leaning past her to scan the hallway for other people, silly since it was in the middle of the night on a weekend. "Why are you here? You are under house arrest. If anyone catches you…"

"Might be easier if you let me in for a moment."

Cepheus backed away from the door, permitting Moksha to enter his den. She paused to survey the room. His office was about the size of single-car garage and consisted of a wooden desk and chair, both covered with books and stacks of paper. Floor space was limited, as books covered nearly all of its surface, and walking through the room was like skipping rocks in a lake. Model planes and other contraptions hung from the ceiling. Against the side wall was a long, thinly cushioned bench covered with a single wool blanket and thin pillow.

Moksha had no psychic skills, and yet it was relatively easy for her to put two and two together. "You live here," she stated. It was not a question.

"For now," Cepheus wrinkled his brow uncomfortably. He set the jade plant on his desk.

Moksha didn't need to ask what happened to Cepheus's home and family. She already knew. What surprised her was that, this many years later, he chose to live in his work office at TARA.

"May I ask," Moksha inquired, "where you eat and shower?"

"TARA has a fully equipped kitchen, including several large refrigerators and stoves. There are also bathrooms with showers on-premises because of the athletic classes we offer." Cepheus stared at her. "But you didn't come here to discuss my living quarters, did you?"

"No," she looked up at him painfully. "I did not."

"Why, then?"

"They burned my house to the ground."

"What? Who?" Cepheus took her hands in his, concerned. He quickly released them, however, once it occurred to him that he was touching another woman—one that was not his late wife.

"The villagers, I assume. My house is gone," she stated stoically. "My vineyard is gone." Tears started welling in her eyes. "I have nowhere to go, and if I turn myself in to the constable, I suspect they will send me to the underground prison at the Defense League, which, as you know, is worse than death itself." She looked into his eyes. Indeed, he did know all about underground prisons in isolation. While the people of Erde tried to manage their rehabilitation centers with more humanity than most, it was still a frightening proposition. Perhaps that is why the cells had remained empty all these years—no one wanted to actually experience them.

"Who knows you are here? Wasn't there a guard stationed at your house?"

"If there was, I don't know what happened to him. All I know is that I awoke in the middle of the night with smoke and fire all around me," she paused, fighting back emotion. "They tried to kill me. I don't mean to sound pathetic, given my former profession, but I came here to seek redemption and find peace. I didn't expect this."

Cepheus thought a moment. "What would you have me do?" he asked calmly.

"Let me stay with you," she pleaded. "Just until the murder is solved, and we can catch whomever destroyed my home."

"But you are a fugitive."

"I know that," she paused. "I need you to keep my whereabouts a secret."

"How," he was confused. "You see where I work and live. How can I possibly hide you in my office, with one picnic bench that I sleep on and a communal kitchen, bathroom, and recreation area that I share with more than 200 other students?"

"They don't even give you a faculty bathroom?" Moksha was surprised.

"If you mean the tree outside my office window, then yes," Cepheus joked.

"Ah, well. I'm used to blending. What time are school hours? I can be sure to lay low during the day until the building locks up at night."

"But where will you sleep?"

She looked disappointingly at the bench. "The floor?" For an assassin, she seemed awfully sensitive, her eyes welling up with tears again.

"It's okay," Cepheus conceded to put his arms around her in an awkward hug. "They'll find who really killed Mallory and who destroyed your home."

"It's more than that," Moksha sobbed.

"What is it?"

"Don't take this the wrong way because I feel terrible that a man was murdered. But…"

"Yes?"

"I am grieving my poor rossenberry plants!" Having been married to a woman who treated her vines as carefully and with as much love, it seemed, as she did her children, he understood. In spite of himself, he found himself hugging her more tightly.

"You can stay with me. We will find a way."

CHAPTER 23
REMOTE CALL
NOVEMBER. BEFORE THE NEW ASSEMBLY.

"You sure picked a crap-tastic time to arrive on Erde," Lucene greeted her friend after not seeing or speaking to one-another for nearly nine months. Some of that was for security reasons, but mainly it involved slowly desensitizing the recently *re-sensitized* Lucene to computers and technology.

"Well it's nice to see you, too," Fatima bubbled, her form appearing in front of Lucene. Fatima was still in bed on the ship, her belly a little larger. "Is that any way to greet your best friend? Wait, you didn't replace me with a new best friend, did you?" Fatima appeared momentarily concerned.

"That would never happen," Lucene answered from her own bed, the school laptop that Tanager lent her, balanced on her knees. "You're the only one who would ever put up with me."

"High praise from you, indeed," Fatima replied, flatly, but then brightened. "I should be there by the first week in February, at latest. I can't wait to see you!"

Lucene couldn't help but feel that Fatima would be sorely disappointed. Still, she mustered a smile. She did, in fact, miss her friend—terribly. "You're not going to try and sneak vegetables in my food again, are you? Because I'll have you know I've been eating fruits and veggies all on my own, thank you very much."

"Wow! The new world must agree with you," Fatima was impressed.

"Not too sure about that."

"What do you mean?"

Lucene got Fatima up to speed, including filling her in on Mallory's murder, Moksha's arrest and later disappearance, and the incident at TARA with a nod to the concern over her sanity. She left out any discussion about the assembly, or Dallen, as she couldn't be certain how easily it could be to intercept their conversation given Ivan and Fatima's present location in space. Her details were sketchy at best, and she replaced all names with aliases. Fortunately, Fatima was good at reading between the lines.

"Well, that's just silly," Fatima offered.

"What is?"

"Well, that part where you said that Dr—" Fatima caught herself. "That part about being concerned that the genetic modification scrambled your brain."

"Why is that silly?" Had anyone else said this to Lucene, she would have gotten defensive. But she gave Fatima lots of free passes, understanding that her friend was always coming from a place of compassion.

"Because empathy is a heart thing, not a head thing."

"There are many neurologists who might disagree with you," Lucene was skeptical.

"My point is," Fatima thought a moment, "everyone is affected by their environment, their internal and external ones. You put someone under stress, and they will react. It's that simple. So, maybe you wouldn't have been able to sling a rock at that dumbass kid. But, splicing or not, you would have jumped in to help your friend. Not your fault that in the *very first test* of your telekinetic powers, it was a little clunky."

"I ended up in a lake," Lucene reminded her.

"Congratulations on being a human, living on an alien planet, and being imbued with supernatural powers that your teachers don't even quite understand yet. I'm more annoyed with their having messed with your parents to begin with—but that's a different story. Don't get me started!"

"I won't," Lucene smiled, feeling lighter for the first time in a long time. "But listen to me babbling on while you are traveling in a new ship to a new planet, and preggers on top of it. Tell me how you are."

This time, it was Fatima's turn to catch Lucene up—the constant questioning by the government, Ivan being accused of helping "enemies of the IPP," their never-ended surveillance when they left their home, the threats. It had gotten to the point where Fatima dared not visit her family, even in secret. Ivan started seeing knock-off versions of his inventions online, but the modifications were dangerous. Those were attributed to him, giving him the reputation of not caring who got hurt in the production of one of his stolen ideas. The government began treating inventors, scientists and registered aliens as threats, with many inventors offering to willingly turn over their creations to their leader in exchange for protection for themselves and their family—forcing them to give up the rights to their products, along with the money it might garner them.

"Has the world gone insane?" Lucene asked when Fatima had finished.

"Yes, my dear," Fatima answered. "Yes, it has. So, you see what I mean? Doesn't matter who you are; people are a product of their environment."

"Perhaps you and Ivan escaped at the perfect time, after all."

"I would say so," Fatima smiled, patting her belly.

"Got a name picked out yet?" Lucene asked.

"We've got a couple we're tossing around, but we'll wait until he or she decides to tell us, in their own special way.

"How very Bohemian of you," Lucene joked. "Are you happy?"

"Very," Fatima smiled. "I may have made some questionable choices in men early on, but it seems to have worked out in the end. And what about you and Tanager?"

"Oh, just friends."

"How is that possible?" Fatima demanded.

"It's a long story…and, I'm sorta seeing someone else."

"What?! How is it that you've waited an hour into the conversation to tell me that?" It was at that point that the connection started to go fuzzy, with the holograms becoming grainy and the audio difficult to hear.

Fatima wasn't entirely sure that this was the technology and not Lucene using her powers to avoid the question.

"It's new, and it's not a big deal. Anyway, the connection is bad. We should probably reconnect another day."

"Hmmph," was all that Fatima had to say.

"What was that for?" Lucene demanded.

"A new romance that you're not shouting from the rooftops, or at least telling your closest friend? I already don't trust him."

Fatima had good reason not to trust Dallen. After the incident at the school, he did the Earth equivalent of "ghosting." There was one awkward visit where he stood the entire time, peering down at Lucene, who, to her credit, had at least made an effort to look presentable. She was dressed in an ugly blue rayon-like blouse that hugged under her arms uncomfortably, matched with a gray, straight cut pair of pants, both of which he had chosen for her during her "spa day." Her hair was now dyed a single shade of dark brown, and she'd even made an attempt at combing it and applying a ghastly shade of pink powder to her cheekbones and a peach gloss to her lips. Still, she could tell from his demeanor that he was displeased.

"You can sit down if you like," she offered from her seat at the kitchen table. A long silence ensued. "What is it?" she finally asked, uncomfortably, tugging the sleeves of her blouse to ensure that her lighting-stricken arms were covered up, something he decidedly did not like.

"I heard what happened at the school," he answered, like a disappointed parent.

"Of course, you did," Lucene bit her lip awkwardly. "Everyone did."

"Are you better?"

Lucene paused before answering. Somehow, *are you better* did not feel the same as *are you okay,* to her.

"Better than I was. I'm taking it day by day," she answered, honestly.

"Are you well enough for dinner at the Embassy Club?"

Lucene's face dropped slightly. She was sick of the Embassy Club. She hated the food, the way she was expected to behave while there, and she particularly hated pretending to be something she was not. Fortunately, she had an out.

"I can't go," she explained. "They asked me to stay here for at least another two weeks under Watch until we make sure I'm better."

"I see," he answered distastefully.

"But I can make us something to eat...or... I can order a meal delivery..." Lucene's cooking skills were nothing short of disastrous, but she could at least assemble a decent sandwich.

"That won't be necessary," Dallen answered. "Perhaps I should have thought to ask before making the journey out here." He noticed her facial expression and realized that this was not an appropriate answer. Dallen softened a little. "What I mean is, I could have had one of my attendants prepare a meal for us, and we could have had one of those picnic-things that you like so much."

"That would have been nice," Lucene smiled. "Maybe next time?"

"Yes," he answered politely, pausing for far too long. "Next time."

But there wouldn't be a next time. Dallen was too worried about his reputation and how it would appear having a mentally ill, Earth-born Erdeling on his arm. She was already a little too free-spirited for his taste, anyway. While he found her ways somewhat charming, he was forced to admit that she would never fit in with his culture. And, he simply didn't have the time to waste grooming her to become an appropriate future mate. *No,* he decided, *this will never work.*

Unfortunately, he never bothered to tell Lucene.

CHAPTER 24
THE PRESENT
DECEMBER. TWO WEEKS BEFORE THE NEW ASSEMBLY.

"We come with good news," Cepheus announced. Even at full volume, his voice was low, but somehow, Lucene noticed, a little brighter than usual. He stood at the door wearing his traveling cape over a surprising red sweater, and...*was he wearing jeans*? Tanager had on the same trench coat and fedora that he had worn when he first met her in the grocery store parking lot on Earth earlier that year.

"For old time's sake," he smiled, referring to the coat and his growing knowledge of Earth slang. They had recently begun a monthly dinner ritual, a reunion of sorts, for the four people who traveled, for good and for bad, seven months together on their journey to Erde. Roman had only attended one of their gatherings.

"No Roman, again?"

Tanager shook his head. "He said he misses you but is busy this evening."

"Disappointing, but I get it," Lucene offered, graciously. "If I'd thought I'd lost the love of my life forever and he suddenly returned, I'd probably want to bask in the glow of just being together for a while." Tanager let out a nervous cough. Cepheus patted him on the back, encouragingly. Lucene didn't notice.

She had the table in her modest kitchen set simply for four, but quickly removed the extra setting. "Sorry, I don't have any fancy dinnerware, but I made us sandwiches."

"Oh, lovely," Tanager answered in a polite way that suggested that the idea was not at all lovely. *Why is everyone so opposed to my sandwiches,* Lucene wondered. "We've also brought nourishment." He motioned to Cepheus. With that, Cepheus produced a picnic basket from beneath his cape. In it, lived several meat and vegetable pies from Marcy's cafe in the Western Cross, as well as assorted fruit, cheeses, and crackers from the shop next door to Marcy's.

"Hmmm," Lucene sniffed approvingly as she accepted the basket. "But you shouldn't have gone through so much trouble as to travel to the Western Cross just to bring me dinner."

"Tonight isn't just about a dinner," Tanager explained, clearing his throat in nervous anticipation. "It's a special occasion." With that, he produced a bottle of wine from beneath his trench coat. It was then that she noticed he had on a green sweater and khaki pants.

"Do you two go around wearing capes and trench coats just for the great reveal?"

Tanager's face turned red. It was probably the first time ever that he understood her risqué sense of humor. "Very funny," he answered. Cepheus did not get the joke.

"Really, do tell...and sit. Sit!" Lucene ordered. "Here, give me that. I may not be able to cook worth a damn, but I can manage opening a bottle of wine." She grabbed the bottle before Tanager could protest. He was about to share that the bottle was one of the few remaining in his collection from Petrichor's old vineyard, once upon a time. He had been saving it for a special occasion. *Still as impulsive as ever,* he thought, smiling to himself.

The gentlemen removed their traveling gear, wrapping coats and capes around the backs of their chairs, and sat. Tanager, suddenly remembering, removed his hat and let it hang on the corner of his seat-back. Within minutes, Lucene had filled their goblets with wine and set a plate full of dinner pies and cheeses at the center of the table. She decided to leave her sandwiches in the mini-refrigerator for now. Finally, she took her seat across from Tanager. Cepheus sat at the head of the table. "So, what's the special occasion?"

Cepheus lifted his goblet in tribute. "First, I am no longer under Watch."

Lucene gasped. Cepheus lost his family after the Royals invaded Erde nearly 31 years ago. They caught him, dragged him back to the Military Training Grounds in Section 3, tortured him and threw him in an underground prison with little to no food or water. And he was Hamish and Sabrina's son. They weren't as nice to those who weren't direct descendants. All because he helped establish the Data Collectors to save Earth inhabitants and because he abdicated his birthright and throne. The Royals didn't want to save the planet. They wanted everything to die off so they could have it for themselves. They were running out of time and needed a place to relocate. In their mind, Cepheus was a threat to their very survival. Why did he care about these weak humans more than his own people, the Royals questioned.

"That's wonderful!" Lucene and Tanager raised their goblets to tap against his.

"There's more," Cepheus continued, pausing for dramatic effect, "neither are you."

"Really," Lucene let out a disbelieving sigh. She had only been under "suggested home stay" for a little over a month, but she was starting to feel the same sense of confinement as she had both when on the Vessel and when in quarantine after arriving on Erde. She was secretly worried that the self-isolation would conflict with her recovery. Apparently, so was everyone else, as Cepheus, Roman, Tanager, Xeni and Neroni did regular check-ins on her.

Cluseladek was asked to stay away, at least for the time being. They were concerned he might set something off in her brain. For Cluseladek, this was a wise move. Even he couldn't understand his behavior and spent the last several weeks apologizing profusely to Neroni. Louis was released from the hospital with nothing but a small scar on his forehead. He, along with several other students, were expelled from TARA and were no longer permitted to study there. They exhibited no remorse. However, no formal arrests were made, probably because they still had trouble working out a punishment system on their planet.

When Cepheus returned home after escaping from the Royals that second time, all those years ago, he refused to let the Defense League take military action. In fact, he suggested the opposite. Instead of going on the offensive, he pleaded with Commander Royce to use their skills to shore up planetary borders against future attacks, but not to wage war on the Royals. He was certain that meeting anger with anger would only lead to more bloodshed.

The smell of meat pies brought Lucene out of her mind-wander. The three ate in pleasant silence for a few minutes. Finally, Tanager spoke.

"We've decided to keep the school closed until after the assembly, though students with ongoing projects in the Makerspace are free to continue their work. Perhaps, after the assembly, we can decide whether it is advisable to resume classes and our research." Tanager didn't have to be a mind reader to know what Lucene was thinking. "You passed all psychological evaluations. It is safe. And," he added, "the school will continue to cover your and Roman's housing during the break."

That last part was a lie, something Tanager had never done before. Therefore, he was surprised that it rolled off his tongue with such ease. The truth was all funding for the Data Collector program was now on hold until it could be determined if the students were experiencing distress from the genetic mutation. It also hinged on the IPP granting Erde re-entry. The human preserves, thankfully, were now self-sustaining; but Roman and Lucene had not established themselves. And, given recent events between Mallory's death and the incident at the school, they were unlikely candidates for hiring in the workforce.

Cepheus and Tanager pooled their resources to continue paying their mortgages. Cepheus had also begun working out the details for ensuring that Ivan would be able to access his funds on Earth once he and Fatima arrived. This was no easy task as Ivan was considered a threat to the government on Earth, and they had temporarily seized his funds. With his recent departure, Ivan and Cepheus had to work quickly to move Ivan's money before they realized he and Fatima had fled, or else they would have no doubt frozen his accounts a second time. And, converting Earth money in the Universal Marketplace was tricky, as is. *Still,* Tanager thought to himself, *one battle at a time.*

They had moved on to the cheeses: pule, tilsit, and raclette. While

Lucene was not as food savvy as Fatima, she'd been around her friend long enough to appreciate the varied flavors and textures. The texture of these cheeses suggested "expensive," and she was not unaware that her newfound Erde family was spoiling her. For once, instead of feeling guilty about the attention, she savored it. Lucene began to feel a warm glow in her heart, something she didn't remember ever feeling before.

"There's one more thing," Cepheus told her, finally.

"More?" Lucene was pretty content with how the evening was going so far.

Cepheus produced a small box. "A little token to celebrate our return to civilization and in anticipation of a successful assembly." He pushed it across the table toward Lucene.

Curious, she opened it. Inside sat yellow-toned palladium earrings and a matching necklace. Suddenly, she was struck by a series of images—a red-haired woman, two small boys and a baby girl, smells from the kitchen and flowers from the den... She took it all in. "These belonged to Petrichor." It was not a question.

"Yes," Cepheus smiled sadly. "Remarkably, one of the few things remaining after our house was destroyed. We had originally intended to pass them on to our daughter, but..." He didn't finish the statement.

"And you're giving them to me?" Lucene's eyes began to well up as she choked out the words.

"Yes," Cepheus answered, his voice cracking a little.

After a long pause, Lucene leapt from the table and threw her arms around Cepheus in a hug. He patted her back, gently, at first, but then hugged her more tightly. Tanager was surprised. Cepheus, while a very kind soul, was not given to affection, at least not in recent years.

"Thank you," she whispered.

Outside, the men headed toward the SpeedCircuit to make their way back to Achel.

"That was a lovely gesture," Tanager remarked to Cepheus. Cepheus merely nodded and kept walking. "All around great evening, I would say." Cepheus nodded again. After a moment, Tanager asked, "Just one question."

"Yes?" Cepheus paused on the desolate and dusty trail in which they traversed. Tanager looked around to be certain no one was listening, out of habit, and then remembered and sent a thought, *why didn't you tell me about Moksha?*

Cepheus was surprised. He was being so careful to keep her whereabouts a secret. Many even assumed she'd fled the planet, a seed that he himself had planted in Commander Royce's brain.

I had to keep my mind as clear as possible, so even our students wouldn't intuit it. I didn't want you to have the responsibility of knowing. "How did you figure it out?" Cepheus asked aloud, pausing before they'd reached the SpeedCircuit platform, currently bustling with travelers.

"My skills may not be as powerful as yours, but I am observant."

You saw her?!

No, my friend, Tanager thought back. *I saw YOU. There's a lightness of being about you that I haven't observed in a very long time. And a red sweater and jeans…really?*

CHAPTER 25
PARIS SKIES
JANUARY. ONE WEEK BEFORE THE NEW ASSEMBLY.

Tanager offered to meet Lucene at her small cottage in the Eastern Cross, but she insisted that she was fine taking the SpeedCircuit alone. He stood nervously at the edge of the Achelian version of the "Eiffel Tower," tapping one of its side anchors with a toe. "You're fine. She's fine," he told himself aloud, but the internal dialogue continued with a very different conversation.

"Who are you talking to?" Lucene asked.

Tanager looked up with a mix of embarrassment and awe. Lucene stood there wearing a blue and white horizontal striped cotton sweater top and a black flared skirt that was asymmetrical, short on one side and long on the other. It almost matched her hair, now all one color but still exhibiting short patches that stuck out in random spikes. She covered it with a lopsided red beret and had a matching silk scarf wrapped around her neck. *She's a mess,* he thought. *An adorable mess.*

He caught himself. "Stay out of my head," he teased.

"I wasn't in your head," she put her hands on her hips. "You were talking out loud."

"Oh," he realized. "Was I saying anything important?"

"I don't know," Lucene confessed. She was busy trying to shut off the random noise in her head. It was if there was a short circuit somewhere, and periodic flashes of images, lights, sounds, tastes, and smells were all vying for her attention. She looked up and noticed that Tanager was smiling at her. The noise stopped. She smiled back.

"I like your hat and neck thing," he motioned to her neck. "It's very… French…I think?"

"Yeah, one of Mallory's clothiers made it, back before—" she paused.

"I know," Tanager nodded in understanding. He, too, had recently visited the costume shop asking for something more Earth-like and current. He left with two pairs of denim jeans and a white, long-sleeved polo shirt, the latter of which he was wearing, along with one pair of faded blue jeans. The pants felt stiff, and he wasn't certain he felt entirely comfortable in them. Both wondered momentarily what would happen to that little shop now that Mallory was gone. An awkward silence ensued.

"So, how have I never noticed this before?" she pointed to the tower. "It's not exactly subtle."

"Perhaps you had other things on your mind?" Tanager suggested. He refrained from pointing out that Lucene's observation skills were low-ranking, at least, they were according to her baseline exams.

"Why?" Lucene shrugged her shoulders. "Why the Eiffel tower?"

"When we set up the preserves, we did our best to make the habitats as Earth-like as possible. One of the new residents happened to be an architect and suggested we have some of the current Earthlings suggest landmarks that reminded them of home. Most are still in production, but we have, as you can see, the Eiffel Tower in our Central area. Big Ben is on the other side of the Makerspace—"

"Are you kidding me?" Lucene blurted out, contorting her face. Tanager's expression suggested that he was not. "How did I miss that, too?" *Really, Lucene,* she told herself, *you need to get out of your head more often and look around.*

Tanager waited patiently for her to return to the conversation. No snapping of fingers like Dallen used to do.

"Sorry, I'm back," she apologized. "You were saying?"

"Well, there's the Taj Mahal under construction in the Western Cross and Pisa at the Eastern Cross. Once the Northern and Southern Crosses become slightly more habitable, we're planning a Stonehenge and a Sydney-style Opera House, but they are a ways off yet."

"Seems like an awful lot of work for a temporary living space," Lucene commented. *Maybe her observations skills aren't so bad,* Tanager thought, careful to guard them so Lucene couldn't get in. *Perhaps she only pays attention when she thinks something is important.*

"Well, for some of us, this will become a permanent home. And, we have to accept the reality of the fact that Earthlings probably only have a decade or two left on their planet to reverse climate change, evolve or..."

"Die," Lucene finished. Lucene absentmindedly kicked a stone pebble on the ground, deciding that death was probably not the best direction to go in while on a date.

"So, where to?" Lucene asked brightly, changing the subject. "Can we ride the tower to the top?" She was hopeful. It was something she'd always wanted to see back home but had never made it past the Eastern United States, much less out of the country.

"Unfortunately, not yet," he answered, watching as her face dropped slightly in disappointment. "But soon," he lifted her chin with his hand before catching himself and withdrawing it. "If you look," he offered, pointing to its center, "an elevation lift is being built. Right now, it's mainly for show, but can you see about three-quarters of the way up." She turned and looked up. Tanager stood behind her, placing one hand on her shoulder and moving his outstretched arm upward. She shuddered slightly and followed his gaze. "It's currently being used as a communications tower. Give it another six months or so, and it will be open for people to ride the elevator to the top." He rested his hand on her other shoulder, and she instinctively leaned into his chest. His chest felt warm and solid, and it was only then that she noticed he smelled faintly of orange...or was it tangerines? Either way, she smiled and decided she liked it.

"It's much nicer pretending we're in Paris than thinking about murder, and the Royals and my nervous breakdown," Lucene confessed. The noise threatened to start up again, but she quickly silenced it. She knew she had to let Tanager know about this new little quirk...but maybe some other night.

"I have a thought," Tanager answered. He stepped back and offered her his elbow like he'd seen on many boring romantic Earth movies he'd forced himself to watch, so he had a better idea as to how best to behave on a date. So far, real life, he was finding out, was not boring at all. In fact, he kind of liked how the evening was playing out so far. Grinning slightly, Lucene took his arm and let him lead the way. "How about, just for tonight, we forget about everything else and just focus on the now."

"That sounds like a great plan." They walked arm-in-arm until they reached the bridge. It was only then that Lucene clued in. She stopped abruptly. Tanager paused, scanning her face questioningly. The Beaux-Art architecture and ornate cherub lamps. "Pont Alexandre Bridge," she exclaimed, her eyes lighting up. "Geez, Lucene," she said aloud, throwing her hands in the air. "Open your eyes!"

Tanager smiled proudly. "Yes, except you can see that this one connects TARA and Achel's commerce district with residential homes and the SpeedCircuit."

The first passerby they'd encountered all evening overheard them. It was an older woman with big, curly gray hair. She wore a wool jacket and had a long, thick black scarf wrapped around her neck. "This one's better," she offered. "No tourists and smog." She let out a laugh and shuffled away.

The two laughed and continued their slow stroll across the bridge. "The French district is pretty small," Tanager admitted, "but I thought maybe we could take the open-air water taxi down to the end of the line. The last stop drops us at a small bistro on the water."

"That sounds lovely," Lucene answered. "I just wish I had Fatima's palate. I'm afraid fine dining might be wasted on me."

"Don't worry," Tanager reassured her. "No pork rinds and ginger beer, I'm afraid. But they do make an excellent crispy duck, clean, of course. Reverend Isabella would be proud. And, I was told to tell you that they have pistachio macarons, but I have no idea what those are. Are they any good?"

"Wow," Lucene was impressed. "You really did your homework." Tanager wasn't entirely sure what she meant by that but assumed it was a compliment. Lucene was trying hard not to compare her short time with Dallen to her current date, but it was easy to see the stark contrast.

To her surprise, the water taxi arrived just as they made it to the wait station platform. The small white river boat looked like one you'd find on Earth, except that it hovered over the water and was completely open on top. The side of the boat aligned with their feet, a small ramp suddenly branching out and locking onto the platform. The driver nodded. "Bonsoir," he greeted pleasantly. "That's the only French I know," he confessed, reverting to his usual Erde tongue.

"Still more than I," Lucene nodded pleasantly. Tanager stepped into the boat first, and then to Lucene's surprise, he put his hands on her waist and hoisted her over the ledge and into the boat. Lucene instinctively grabbed his shoulders for balance. She felt heavier than he'd expected. The men in the movies he'd watched seemed to have no trouble with this. Although, the women in those movies were arguably much thinner than any Earth women he'd ever met in real life. He was secretly beginning to think that they were either a special breed of human or they were aliens in disguise.

"Don't break your back on my account," Lucene sympathized, once he'd set her down. She took a seat on one of the long benches. Tanager sat beside her. There was room for about a dozen passengers total, and one other couple sat with arms wrapped around each other in the back.

"L'amour," the driver fluttered his eyes before retracting the lift and setting the boat in motion.

"That's two words you know," Lucene called to the driver. Without even thinking, Lucene folded her hands over Tanager's, resting them on his knee. A chill went up his spine. He decided it was on account of it being a cool evening.

The driver nodded pleasantly, glancing back at Lucene in the rearview mirror at his side. "So it is," he answered. "So it is."

CHAPTER 26
THE NEW ASSEMBLY
TODAY. JANUARY.

"Order and dignity, please," Kunz Malaya addressed the crowd from his home planet in Section 5. There was a little more gray in his blue-gray fur, but otherwise, little had changed in the Monarch's appearance from when Lucene saw his hologram at the assembly in New York many years ago. He still wore the same silver uniform he had back then, appearing before them as if standing on a platform situated at the end of the table where they now sat. Empathically, Lucene could feel his mixed feelings of nostalgia, remorse and hope. He was a kind soul, she could tell, and secretly hoped she could meet him one day outside of the assembly.

Lucene arrived at the League's Negotiation Room wearing a long-sleeved green winter dress that she formalized with the yellow-toned palladium earrings and a necklace that Cepheus had given her prior to the meeting. She moved her toes freely in the open-toed sandals on her feet and smiled luxuriously to herself before deciding to pop them off altogether by scraping one foot, then the other, across the back of her heels. No one at the assembly could see her feet underneath the table, anyway. *It's nice to decide on one's own attire,* she thought.

Cepheus sat at her right, wearing his usual winter garb, a pull-over cotton sweater and black dress slacks. Tanager stood behind her, wearing his over-worn, retro-style tan tweed jacket and brown pants that she just couldn't talk him out of. Upon arrival, Dallen attempted to sit beside her, only to be blocked by Tanager, who slipped beside Lucene and not-so-discreetly offered him the seat at his side. Dallen took it, reluctantly, before Commander Royce took the next seat over, beside him. Roman sheepishly slid through the Negotiation Room doors just prior to them being closed by an attendant. The Monarch was just beginning his formal welcome. Commander Royce eyed Roman with mild annoyance but nodded for him to take a seat beside Cepheus. The right side of Roman's face was an odd purplish-red as if bruised from an altercation.

Lucene shot him a "what happened to your face" questioning look, accompanied with a physical pointing to her own face.

His downcast look suggested, "Tell you later." Lucene sat back, concerned. And yet, somehow, she had intuited it had something to do with Far. Odd, as the fragile man didn't give off the impression of being remotely violent, and yet, she wondered...

"It has been six years since the Intergalactic Peace Project has met, and I am honored and overjoyed for the privilege you've bestowed on me by allowing me to preside over today's meeting," Kunz Malaya continued. "We currently have six planets in attendance with two who are petitioning for re-entry into the IPP. As is custom, before we hear their petition, we will begin with that stating of intentions..."

Lucene tried not to cry, but in hearing the intentions—upholding peace, working for the good of all, making open communication among different species a priority—it made her heart sink. Six years later, and they seemed no closer to reaching these noble goals. There were several attendants in the Negotiation Room, each pulling the red and gray tapestries aside to reveal flat projection screens providing a window into the other five groups in attendance, including Earth. She was saddened at the sight. When last she attended, there were more than 200 other members there with her. But now, following the explosion and the degradation of the IPP, she saw only about 30 or so members, old and new. And, she could feel their uneasiness. Given the fate of the last group that attended, she couldn't blame them.

It was then that she caught a glimpse of someone familiar—*Reverend Isabella.* As if on cue, the white-haired woman lifted her chin and smiled, seeming to look right at Lucene with her violet eyes. Overjoyed to see her Earth mentor, she was still confused at her presence, even more so when she saw who sat directly beside her—Odessa and Morphinae. *The worlds we live in are strange, indeed.*

"We will now move on to the petitions," the Monarch announced. Each party will have five minutes to speak their position. Given the unusual nature of their requests, we will hear from both parties first, and the IPP will then vote. If one or both parties are accepted, they are welcome to attend the remainder of today's proceedings and will be re-admitted into the IPP." He paused to glance around the room, making sure everyone heard and understood. "However," he continued, "if they are not, then they are to leave the premises immediately, and will not be permitted to re-apply until our next meeting, whenever that may be."

Hopefully, not another six years, Lucene thought. But, to be fair, prior to the assembly explosion all those years ago, the IPP had been meeting annually.

"It has come to my attention that both the Vitruvians and the Erdelings are working in partnership. It is uncustomary for two Sections, with varied species, to petition together. But I will allow it. It has also been brought to my attention that we have an Earthling who is attempting to register on behalf of Vitruvia versus Earth. Is this true?" He looked toward the Earth representatives for confirmation.

"It is Monarch," Isabella spoke. "I am the Earthling making such a petition."

"And, has the Earth council agreed to this most unusual request?"

Bryce Cushing stood, sitting several seats away from Isabella. "We have, Monarch. We support Reverend Isabella's request because we believe it may be in the best interest for all parties in our peace efforts."

"If the Earth council has agreed, then I will allow it." Kunz Malaya turned his attention to the Planetary Defense League on Erde. "I also understand that you have a Vitruvian petitioning alongside of your team. Is that true?"

Dallen stood, "It is, Monarch. I represent Vitruvia and also the best interests of Erde."

"And, does the Erde council agree to this?"

Lucene could feel Tanager cringe and looked down to see him clamping two balled fists together and laying them on the table. Instinctively, she took his hand, a gesture that did not go unnoticed by Dallen. *This is for the best,* she thought. *It will be okay.* Tanager nodded slightly and released the grip on his hands, relaxing them on the table. Lucene, feeling that her gesture may be seen as inappropriate for such proceedings, quickly retracted her hand, letting them sit in her lap beneath the table. But then again, while Dallen might have minded this, Tanager did not.

"We do, Monarch," Commander Royce answered.

"Then, I will also allow this. Reverend Isabella, I grant you the floor first."

With the grace of a swan, Isabella spoke, sharing how she had gathered a team of Earth supporters willing to work with her and Vitruvia to ensure that proper measures were taken to preserve and replenish Earth's natural resources and wildlife, while also restoring air and water quality so that humans could thrive. "I also have the support of two Vitruvians currently living on Earth," she motioned to Odessa and Morphinae. They will work with both Earth and Erde, as needed, to bring these changes. We are also grateful for the support from Representative Dallen, temporarily stationed on Erde, to further support collaboration between Earth, Vitruvia, and Erde. Before I turn my remaining time over to the Erde council, I would like to remind everyone present that we have at least the required 50% of support from the Earth council, and I am sure that once they hear more, they will be more than willing to accept Vitruvia and Erde back into the IPP." Isabella turned her eyes toward the Erde council. "Representative Dallen, I yield the remainder of my time to you."

"Thank you, Reverend Isabella," Dallen bowed. "Given our brief time here, I must be abrupt. Within the last year, we have discovered that, beyond Earth, the human species has been struggling on several never-before-registered planets within Section 0 and Section 1."

"Other humans?" Kunz was surprised. "Living in places other than Earth?"

"Yes, Monarch," Dallen confirmed. "The oxygen, gravity, temperature and other elements have caused them to adapt in different ways than

Earthlings—their appearances evolving over time—but they are, in fact, human."

"May I ask how you came to discover this?" Whispers and the sounds of shuffling could be heard from the varying attendees from all Sections. Some were visibly indignant.

"Actually," Commander Royce answered, standing, "they sought us out after they learned that we were working on Earth's behalf. Most were fleeing their own dying planets. So, you see, if we work together, we're saving more than just Earth and learning to ensure we don't make the same mistakes as they have in the past."

"And, there is more," Dallen looked at Royce, who nodded for him to continue. Cepheus's expression was blank, his posture as rigid as a stone-cold statue. It was the only way he could keep from having an episode at this moment. *Not now,* he told himself. *You've just been cleared and are no longer under Watch.*

"It seems that the Royals in Section 3 have a new alliance." The whispers grew louder. Lucene, Roman and Tanager peered around the room at the projection screens. Section 4 attendees stood behind Kunz Malaya, muttering to one another. One member actually tapped him on the shoulder and began emphatically asking the Monarch questions, something considered the height of impropriety during a meeting of this magnitude. Kunz put his hand up for the man to be silent but nodded that he'd heard him.

"What new alliance?" Kunz Malaya asked calmly. He knew the answer. He, and one representative from each planet, were given the opportunity to read the petitions prior to the assembly. His question was both to inform the IPP and follow assembly guidelines.

"The Royals are working with the Null of Section 4," Dallen paused while his words sank in. "The void dwellers."

The Null were the reason the IPP was first formed. While the Royals made an insincere attempt to join the IPP while continuing their pattern of destruction, the void dwellers had no interest in forming an alliance with anyone. The most violent species in the known multiverse, the void dwellers, lived and migrated through black holes. No one could catch them because no other species could follow them without getting sucked in, never to resurface. Their sole purpose was to destroy, in honor of their mighty Segue.

"We believe that this alliance will put all of us in danger of being destroyed and our planets re-populated with Royals, while we quickly go extinct thanks to the Null. The only solution is for Vitruvia and Erde to be re-admitted into the IPP and that we all form necessary defenses to protect ourselves. In summary, our goals are two-fold: one, to continue our efforts to restore the human species and Earth-like environments and two, to—"

"I am afraid you are out of time," the Monarch proclaimed suddenly. "We will hear from IPP representatives and then take a vote."

"But, Monarch," Dallen protested, surprised at his sudden abruptness. He looked at the clock. They still had two minutes to finish their petition.

"You are out of time," Kunz Malaya repeated, with a hostility in his voice that was so uncustomary that even he seemed surprised at himself. He touched his hand to his forehead. "We will now hear questions and comments from the IPP and cast our votes."

Dallen searched the faces of the team behind him, but all were as baffled as he. He caught Lucene's gaze. She knew what he was thinking simply from his expression. *Aren't you supposed to be special? Do something!*

Lucene's head began to hurt. Something was wrong.

"Reques-s-s-sting the floor next, Monarch," Jasper Set hissed from a seat behind Isabella. Isabella's eyes grew wide. She knew this dark energy but couldn't even bring herself to turn around and face him. Jasper Set had stuffed himself into a traditional suit and tie, his translucent face and red eyes popping out of the top of it. Those around him did not seem to notice that he was decidedly *not* human.

The Monarch acknowledged him, in spite of the fact that Jasper Set wasn't a registered member of the IPP, something that seemed to also escape everyone's attention. The other planets in attendance watched at a distance. They did not recognize him either, and yet, the hair on the back of Tanager's neck stood up. Lucene felt a bitter knot of discomfort in her belly, and Cepheus grew anxious, no one understanding why.

Lucene flashed back to the first assembly she had attended where Drake Cushing lost his temper, going into an angry rant that inspired the same sentiment in those around them. But this man was different. He was calm. He was quiet. He sucked the energy right out of the room.

"I have a few ques-s-stions for our would-be IPP members," his slithery voice addressed the assembly. "The first is for the Rev...the Rev..." He couldn't bring himself to say "Reverend."

"The first is for Mis-s-s-s Is-s-s-sabella S-s-s-simone." Finally, she turned to face him, as fearless as she could be, gathering up strength from the depths of her being.

I know what you are, demon. Isabella thought. She wasn't even trying. But she knew he could hear her. He smiled back. Then, he seemed to remember himself, clearing his throat and contorting and stretching his face as if doing a facial warm-up.

"These supporters you mention. Would they be your cult followers?" The exaggerated "Ssss" were gone. The audience grew restless. Odessa looked at Morphinae, but Morphinae shook his head. It wasn't their place to interfere. Odessa crossed her arms and sat back in a huff, shooting an angry glare at her fellow Vitruvian and uncompromising Balance-Keeper.

"My supporters are fine, loving people," Isabella's violet eyes clouded over in a stormy haze.

"And these fine, loving people will escape with you to Erde to begin a new life in Shangri-La. Is that it?"

"That is *not* it, at all. As we have mentioned, Erde is a sanctuary for humans who are there of their own volition while—"

"Silence!" the Monarch growled at Isabella. "You no longer have the floor."

"But I was asked a question!" she protested.

"Silence, or your petition will be immediately denied." Tanager and Cepheus sat upright, searching the faces of those from Section 5 sitting behind the Monarch, but there were no signs that they viewed his behavior in any way inappropriate or uncustomary. They scanned the Earth audience and found nothing but a strange sense of angry camaraderie.

"How do you expect the members of the IPP to believe your intentions when you sound no more reputable than a cult leader promising to take the flock to another planet and be saved by a special alien race."

"You know as well as I do that the difference is that we have proof that Erde exists. We have records as to their actions, and—"

"Enough!" the Monarch interjected. "There will be no more from you, Rev...Rev...Isabella Simone." Her eyes grew wide. There was nothing she could do at that moment except sit down, close her eyes and pray. Jasper Set let out a chuckle.

"But I'm hogging the floor," Jasper announced pleasantly. "Perhaps someone else would care to speak?"

Odessa stood to request the floor, but Morphinae grabbed her arm—hard. "Ow," she winced. "What the hell is wrong with you?" she asked him.

"I'm not sure," he answered honestly.

He's controlling them. Lucene sent an urgent mental message to Tanager and Cepheus. *I don't think I can stop him. But maybe together we can?*

Manipulating people's thoughts is wrong, Cepheus protested. *No matter how noble the cause.*

Then why have these gifts if we're not to use them in defense? Tanager shot an angry message to Cepheus. Cepheus's eyes began to roll back in his head. His body began to lurch forward. Dallen and Commander Royce jumped to his aid.

"He's all right," Tanager snapped, searching his jacket. "I have his medication." He almost didn't bring it, given that Cepheus was cleared. Perhaps Tanager's intuition had served him well.

Jasper smiled at the screen, the entire IPP now watching the episode as Tanager delivered an anti-psychotic puff of serum into Cepheus's ear.

"Requesting the floor next, Monarch." Director Sutton stood from the Earth's council. Roman took notice. He hadn't seen him in a year, but he still remembered being grilled by Sutton and his men on several occasions about his knowledge of the Data Collectors. This couldn't be good. His presence was also somewhat surprising. It wasn't long after Hamish and his Royal fleet left Earth that the gruesome discovery was made that a casino explosion took out the last of the remaining IPP members on Earth, except for Drake Cushing, whose body washed up on the Gulf shores one day, presumably from a drowning accident. Sutton, who was saved from getting taken out by the Royals on two occasions, where at the first assembly an irritable bowel kept him from making the annual conference on time, and in the second, his ex-wife phoned and told him she'd had a change of heart. He ditched the casino meeting in favor of a possible reconciliation. The fact that he was brave enough to be present today showed either tremendous courage or a deep-seated death wish.

Kunz Malaya acknowledged him.

"Your man up there," he motioned to Cepheus. "You sure he's all right?" There was a look of genuine concern on his face before he seemed to remember that he was supposed to be confrontational.

"He will be fine," Tanager explained, removing his jacket. By now, Commander Royce and Dallen had successfully moved Cepheus to the floor. The rest of the IPP couldn't see him lying stretched out with Tanager's crumpled up jacket under his head.

"Why is he like that?" Sutton wanted to know.

"He suffered traumatic injuries," Tanager explained.

"Hmmm..." Sutton touched his finger to his chin as if in thought. "Nothing to do with the DNA splicing you're doing?"

"What?" Tanager responded. "No."

"Really? Because I have it on good authority from an expert that the Data Collectors have been having some psychotic episodes as a result of the genetic coding. Would this be such an example?"

"Unrelated," Tanager was curt.

"If I brought Dr. Archibald Ennis in here, would he share your opinion?" Tanager's face turned pale. Dr. Ennis was a good man, that he knew. But he would be honest in his assessment, even if it hurt the Data Collectors. More importantly, however, is how they knew about Dr. Ennis. He had always been good at staying under-the-radar in his assistance of the Data Collectors.

"Obviously, I cannot speak for anyone else."

"Hmm. Obviously." Director Sutton sank his chin to chest and turned his ear to one side as if hearing something. "I'm curious," he continued. "What other powers do the Data Collectors have? More specifically, what powers does *that one* have?" He pointed at the screen, and all turned their gaze to Lucene.

Uh oh, Lucene heard a voice. Except, it wasn't from Tanager or Cepheus, and it wasn't from inside her head like the way she usually received messages. This one sounded as if someone were whispering in her ear. She could even feel the breath from his voice. It sounded like...Jasper.

"The same as the others," Commander Royce intervened. "She can transmit messages without interception, a valuable tool when trying to avoid sensitive information being gathered by the Royals or the void dwellers." Commander Royce thought it prudent to leave out the running list of other skills they had recently discovered at the Terrestrial Academy of Research and Awareness (TARA).

"I see," Sutton replied, his voice becoming hollow. "No mind control or altering reality?"

Tanager appeared as if someone struck him in the face. He turned his attention to Roman, who at this moment was trying to shrivel into his chair. Tanager felt the heat rush to his head. *You told Far about our research, didn't you?"* Roman had no empathic capabilities, but it wasn't difficult to determine what Tanager's icy stare meant.

At this point, the IPP erupted, much like the assembly of the past. Multiple beings from the other neighboring planets tried to take the floor. Kunz held his hand to his head.

"Silence!" he yelled. "Order and dignity, please!"

But there was neither in that room. All he heard were accusations that the Vitruvians couldn't be trusted after their deal with the Royals and questions as to why the Data Collectors needed to move in secret if their presence was known. Shouldn't their information be public knowledge?

Jasper Set closed his eyes as if soaking in sunshine and sipping on a smooth cocktail. He took his seat, his work here nearly complete. As if on cue, the entire IPP fell silent as he settled into his chair.

Kunz rubbed his head again and wiped a small bit of drool from the side of his jaw. "We will now take our votes." He moved back, wobbling slightly. Two men behind him grabbed hold of his arms and guided him to his chair, concerned. He waved them away and took a deep breath.

Odessa reached out and took Isabella's hand on one side and Morphinae's on the other. For once, there was no flirtatiousness in her gesture. It was one of fear, comfort and solidarity. Isabella squeezed her hand back. And, to Odessa's surprise, so did Morphinae. Morphinae was still trying to make sense of what was happening, not given to emotion or confusion, he was left with an enormous feeling as if a piece of his mental processing were missing somehow.

The voting commenced, each remote location able to log in and make their decision, one to allow Virtruvia back into the IPP and the other to allow Erde in…or not. Cepheus was still unconscious. The remainder of his team, Royce, Dallen, Lucene, Roman and Tanager, waited with bated breath as the IPP votes were cast.

After what seemed like an eternity, Kunz Malaya struggled to stand. Once again, the men behind him guided him back to his podium. He peered down at the small screen in front of him.

"It would seem," he said sorrowfully, "that we have reached a decision. Overwhelmingly the consensus supports that we all adhere to our creed. That is, to uphold peace at all costs. To band together against the Royals and the Null of Sections 3 and 4 would mean that we are preparing for war, not peace. It seems that the Vitruvians and Erdelings have forgotten what the IPP stands for, as have some Earthlings," he targeted a disapproving glance at Reverend Isabella, who shook her head. She was one of the few people in the room who knew exactly what was happening, yet she lacked the power to do anything.

Wait for it, the voice whispered in Lucene's ear. She jumped in her seat, rubbing her earlobe nervously. Tanager tried to send her a message to see if she was okay. When that didn't get through, he touched her shoulder and looked into her eyes. *What's going on?* he asked. She jumped at his touch and shrugged his hand off of her. Dallen, who missed nothing, was surprised by this. *Stop it,* she yelled at the voice, forcing her attention back on the Monarch who was about to render the IPP's decision.

"Between your questionable religious practices, your irresponsible genetic modifications, the deceptive means by which you gather and manipulate data, and your warlike tendencies, it is the decision of the International Peace Project and members of this assembly that the petitions of Virtruvia and Erde are denied. You must leave this assembly immediately, along with your Earth supporter." Kunz paused for a moment as if there were an internal conflict in his head. "I'm sorry," he looked directly at Lucene, "but your team does not have the support of the IPP. I'm afraid you are on your own."

"What the hell did you tell your boyfriend?" Tanager demanded of Roman as the group, minus Commander Royce, left the Negotiation Room and was now making their way out into the bright light of day. Roman looked surprised. So did Lucene and Cepheus. Tanager was polite. He never swore. He never lost his temper. The meaning of this was lost on Dallen, who shared Tanager's frustration.

"Hear me out," Roman held up in hands as if to tell Tanager to calm down and back off.

"He means that he wants to explain what happened," Lucene supplied, assuming Tanager didn't yet know that Earth expression.

"I know what 'hear me out' means," Tanager barked.

"Look," Roman continued. "I'm sorry. The Far I met at the preserve was not the man I once knew. He was sick and under the influence of the Royals. And now he's just…confused."

"Did it not occur to you, Roman, that sharing confidential information about the IPP and the Assembly with those not working directly with TARA or the Defense League was a bad idea?"

Roman touched his black eye and winced as the group began crossing the long Pont Alexandre Bridge. He wasn't really in pain and Tanager knew it. It was merely a cry for sympathy.

"You asked me to study the culture here."

"I asked you to study *humans* here. What you may or may not have learned about the Data Collectors from our private, personal conversations among friends was just that—private and personal!"

"I don't mean to be critical," Roman defended, somewhat sheepishly, ducking his head at Tanager's glare as if it somehow packed a punch. "But back home we have non-disclosure and other privacy agreements for just this reason. I didn't realize I was giving out sensitive information any more than I realized that Far was…is…mentally ill."

"Maybe you need those agreements on your planet," Tanager complained. "But these things are typically self-explanatory here."

"How was I supposed to know the difference? The four of us are friends. We traveled together. We share information. Far is my partner… why wouldn't I share with him?"

Cepheus felt the need to intervene. "What is done is done," he spoke calmly. Tanager opened his mouth to protest, but Cepheus held up a hand. "Perhaps you and I could discuss this privately," Cepheus suggested. They had reached the midway point on the bridge, and Cepheus's soft words were difficult to hear above the water that ran rapidly beneath it. Cepheus repeated his request, mentally. Tanager shook his head as if annoyed but then reluctantly offered a slight nod.

Roman's apartment complex was closest to the water. "Probably best if I go," he bowed his head. "If and when TARA reopens, I'm available. Just let me know." He glanced furtively between Cepheus and Tanager and offered a quick nod toward Dallen and Lucene before jockeying his way between a few other pedestrians, his lanky frame making as quick an exit as possible.

Cepheus and Tanager slowed their pace. Lucene took the hint. "C'mon," she told Dallen, "walk an old friend to the SpeedCircuit?" She forced a smile that she didn't really feel. She didn't consider Dallen an old friend or even a friend at all. He disappeared without so much as a goodbye. But she wasn't thinking of him at that moment. She was trying to help Tanager.

"With pleasure," Dallen answered thoughtfully. While he may have been lighting up on the inside at escorting Lucene to the Circuit, his expression and the way in which he lengthened his neck and spine suggested that it was more of a moral duty. Lucene quickened her pace, with Dallen falling into step beside her.

"Allow me to explain my somewhat rapid departure..." Dallen said to her.

"No need," Lucene replied. "I get it."

"But don't you see?" Dallen took her arm. "You're better now, and my obligation to this pact between Vitruvia and Erde has been settled. We can be together now."

"No, it is you who do not see." She freed her arm from his grasp. "I have no interest in spending my days pretending to be someone I'm not to fulfill some cultural requirement I would need to adopt in order to be worthy of hanging on your arm." Dallen looked hurt. "Furthermore, can you honestly tell me that if I became...unwell again, that you could handle it?"

Dallen's face dropped. "But, you're fine now," he reasoned.

"And tomorrow, I could be not fine. That's the way mental illness works."

"But, you're not ill," he protested.

"We don't know that," Lucene reasoned. "I've already been abandoned by you once. I don't plan on letting that happen again."

Dallen tried to reason with her. "But I miss you," he protested. "I feel lonely without you." Frankly, it was the first emotional moment she'd ever witnessed from Dallen, and yet, it was somehow not enough.

"I'm sorry," she answered, pausing for a moment. "But I am not responsible for how you *feel*." She turned and continued on to the Speed-Circuit. "No need to accompany me if you've changed your mind."

"Have you?" Dallen stopped suddenly.

"Have I what?" Lucene was confused.

"Changed your mind?"

"You're not making any sense. About what?"

"Is it that you have grown tired of me or that you've grown fonder of someone else?"

"I have no idea what you're talking about," she retorted, tiredly. "You left me, remember?" Even as she was saying it, there was something about it that didn't ring true. And yet, she couldn't quite figure out what it was.

Meanwhile, when they were a safe distance from the others, Cepheus and Tanager resumed their conversation.

"Stay out of my head," Tanager said aloud.

"What?" Cepheus was surprised.

"Stay out of my head," he repeated. "Now, I understand why Lucene found this so irritating when we first met. It's more intrusive than I realized."

Cepheus wanted to protest. He wanted to reiterate that he wasn't attempting to read Tanager's mind and that the skill was only used when confidentiality was needed or when they were seeking to empathically understand the other person. But, in his mind's eye, he could see a red curtain drop as if to signify the end of a theater production. Cepheus was being shut out.

Representative Dallen, once again, ghosted them. He and his attendants left Erde the very next morning after the Assembly rejected their re-entry into the IPP. He put calls in to Morphinae and Odessa, alerting them that their service on Earth was no longer required, and that they were to return to Vitruvia immediately. Odessa cried in protest, begging him to reconsider. But empathy was never one of his strong suits.

"You are a Shapeshifter," he reminded her on a remote call to Earth. "And while your class has certain skills that are important to our people, let's not forget where your kind ranks."

Odessa's nostril's flared. Morphinae realized she was about to lose her temper and say something that would likely get them both killed. "We understand, your Excellence," he replied politely, in his male form—one that Dallen was more likely to respect.

"Who will explain this to Reverend Isabella?" Odessa asked, tears running down her face in what Dallen considered to be a weak and unsavory response.

"No need to say anything," he reasoned. "She will understand when the two of you have left the Sanctuary and returned home.

That was the Vitruvian way, avoid confrontation and leave—leaving everyone else to pick up the pieces after you've gone.

CHAPTER 27
SANCTUARY
FEBRUARY. ONE MONTH AFTER THE NEW ASSEMBLY.

"This is Moira Sugg, signing off. But, please join us at 8 CT for our special series, *Contemporary Cults: The Dangerous Underworld*." Isabella switched off the television.

"I know it's wrong to hate, but I'm beginning to intensely dislike that woman," Isabella mumbled under her breath.

"Bad day?" Odessa flew in through the Sanctuary window accompanied by Morphinae. The two transformed from butterflies into their human form, now standing in the living room of Isabella's private quarters. Isabella grabbed her shawl and pulled it tightly around her nightgown. It was 7:34 a.m.

"We need to have a conversation one day about boundaries," Isabella shot Odessa an annoyed glance. "But yes, bad day. Bad year."

Odessa exchanged glances with Morphinae. Neither were particularly touchy-feely by nature, but Isabella was among the nicest humans they'd encountered, and after spending considerable time with her over the past few months, they had to admit that they had grown rather fond of her. Odessa felt a little pang in the center of her chest. She thought it might be compassion, but she hadn't felt it often enough to know for certain.

"Because of that stupid reporter?" Odessa motioned to the blank television screen. She followed Isabella from her quarters to the main Sanctuary, watching as Isabella began opening the shades and turning on the fountains. Trying to make himself useful, Morphinae filled a pitcher with water from the kitchen and poured it carefully into one of the fountains after noticing that in the Florida heat, some of it evaporated.

Isabella seemed surprised. "Thank you, Morphinae." Morphinae nodded slightly but said nothing.

Odessa continued, "Don't worry about her or what happened at the assembly. We'll find another way." Odessa didn't have the heart to tell her that the two of them were supposed to have returned to Vitruvia immediately following the assembly. Instead, Odessa told Dallen and her superiors what she considered to be a tiny fib—she wasn't feeling well, and it wasn't safe for her to return to Vitruvia until she could be cleared. After all, she could infect the lot of them. To her surprise, Morphinae, who was incapable of lying, backed her story. He didn't consider it a lie. Knowing how much Odessa loved Earth, he knew for a fact that she wasn't feeling well—at the thought of leaving.

Isabella stopped, interrupting Odessa's thoughts. "Don't you understand?" She searched the Vitruvian's defiant eyes. "Since the assembly, and since that news report, more than two-thirds of my congregation have left."

That Sunday following the Assembly, Moira Sugg and her camera team descended on the church as attendees were leaving services, making wild claims that Isabella was operating a cult. She drew references to the recent assembly, asking if she had plans to take the congregation to Erde or worse—to have them commit suicide in a secret alliance with the Null. It was all nonsense, but enough of her members were harassed and ridiculed that, week after week, the size of her congregation dropped. Among those loyal followers, there were several that seemed almost embarrassed to be there, making excuses to their families that they were really going someplace else that morning—anywhere but to the Sanctuary for services.

Odessa's face contorted as her lower lip began to quiver. It was almost as if she were going to cry. "We can fix this," she stammered.

Isabella was too tired to argue. She pulled the chords of the final set of blinds from one of the windows by the alter and recoiled with a start.

There, with his face plastered against the window, was the grotesque Jasper Set.

"Mis-s-ss me?" he hissed, turning into a puff of smoke and permeating through the window. He reformed at the altar, wearing a white suit and red tie. Jasper walked over to one of the fountains and, ignoring Morphinae's slight shaking of his head, dipped his hands in, and proceeded to splash water on his face. "What brand of Holy water is this, again?"

"In the name of all that is Holy, I command you to leave this Sanctuary," Isabella's eyes narrowed. She pointed an outstretched arm to the door.

Jasper bowed as if defeated, unfurling his wings, which somehow protruded out from his suit jacket, and flew to the door. He swung it open as he made his dramatic exit, a strong wind slamming it behind him.

"What just happened here?" Odessa stood beside Isabella, confused.

"No unholy creature can remain in a place such as this. The same is true of your personal abode. If you ever encounter a dark energy and you command it to leave, it must obey."

"Really? Why?" Odessa was legitimately curious.

"It is the Universal law," Isabella answered, simply, explaining to Odessa the ritual of placing an energetic circle of protection around one's home and place of worship and expelling darkness. She nodded with fascination. Morphinae remained unconvinced.

The doors to the Sanctuary flew open once more. "I'm jus-s-s-st kidding!" Jasper flew back in, stopping inches from Isabella's face. "Seriously? I'm an all-powerful demon. What makes you think you can just command me to leave. Me!"

Morphinae tried to help, reciting the Lord's prayer, calling on God, Jesus, Allah, Kwan Yin, Shiva, Zeus, Jupiter, and so on. He was running out of ideas.

"Nope, try again. No. No. No!" Jasper covered his ears, his body growing visibly larger by the moment. With an angry swipe of his arm, he sent the altar crashing into the fountain, its wooden frame breaking to pieces as water from the fountain began spraying across the seats.

Morphinae, a Balance-Keeper, determined that there was an imbalance in this place, and that gave him the right to intervene. He grabbed Jasper by the throat and squeezed just enough so that the demon's eyes bulged. He lifted the demon off the ground.

"Oh, no," Jasper mocked. "What will I do?" Getting stronger by the minute, he flicked his long-nailed finger at Morphinae, and the shapeshifting Vitruvian went sailing through one of the windows, smashing through to the outside. Odessa let out a scream and ran through the front door to Morphinae's aid. "Run, little girl. Run," Jasper laughed. The swirling cloud around him grew bigger, and Isabella could make out the faintest of auras—one was anger. The other was fear. Suddenly, she had an idea.

"Wait!" She put a hand up as Morphinae (scratched, but mostly uninjured) and Odessa burst through the door and headed with full force toward Jasper. They stopped in their tracks. Even Jasper paused, looking at her with confusion.

She smiled at Jasper. "We must treat this being with compassion."

"Huh," Odessa wrinkled her nose.

"What? No, you don't," Jasper responded hastily.

Isabella began walking slowly toward the demon. "Everyone is deserving of love. Clearly, you didn't receive enough of it from the Null. That's why you are the way you are. It isn't your fault," she smiled lovingly.

Jasper Jet began to shrink. "Stop it, witch. I'll destroy you," he yelled, but his energy felt suddenly drained.

"Odessa. Morphinae," Isabella called. "Let's send as much love in Jasper's direction as we can, shall we?"

Morphinae's eyes lit up. Why hadn't he thought of that? He took Odessa's hand gently. Odessa looked down at the hand and back up at Morphinae, confused. But she would try. She tried to think of loving thoughts. Odessa thought of the Gulf of Mexico and how those little silvery fish tickled her toes when they swam by. She loved that. She smiled as she conjured up images of a perfect sunset and the sound of dolphins. Odessa redirected that energy toward Jasper. *Maybe if he got to see a perfect sunset,"* she reasoned. *He wouldn't be so angry all the time.*

Jasper shrank a little further.

Odessa closed her eyes and called up other things she loved: The smell of the earth after it rained, the taste of brie and honey on toast, the feel of the wind on her face...an image of Morphinae suddenly floated before her eyes. *Oh shit.* The discovery hit her like a ton of bricks. She opened her eyes and threw all of that love in Jasper's direction. Isabella took her other hand, and the three stood in solidarity.

Jasper Set let out a few expletives and then vanished. Their greatest weapon wasn't strength, or anger, or calling for help from a supreme being. It was love.

Morphinae accompanied Odessa back to the docks. "Finally," Odessa sighed, transforming into her mermaid-like form and diving happily into the water. "I've missed you," she cooed at the water.

"I don't understand your obsession with water," Morphinae observed. "What is it that you admire about it so much?"

"It's not an obsession," Odessa protested. "It's just peaceful. And it feels nice on my skin." Morphinae nodded. He felt the same way as a butterfly feeling the wind as it breezed past his wings. "You should try it," Odessa encouraged, patting the water as if asking Morphinae to take a seat on a couch beside her.

"I've never been a mermaid before," Morphinae pondered.

"I'm not a mermaid," Odessa grew impatient. "Mermaids aren't real. I am...I just prefer the fishtail for swimming."

"Then why not become the whole fish?"

"Because I really like being a woman. The legs are just not practical for sea."

"So, you're a mer-fish?"

"No," Odessa explained. "I'm simply a woman with a tail."

"Oh," Morphinae did not follow the logic, but he'd come to realize that Odessa was nothing if not illogical.

"Well?"

"Well, what?"

"Are you coming in?"

Morphinae paused for a moment. "I don't really know how to swim," he confessed. He remembered trying it once during a storm and ended up clumsily treading water until he'd had to rescue Drake and Bryce Cushing as boys during a storm. It hadn't ended well.

"You'll be fine; the water's shallow," Odessa encouraged. Morphinae thought a moment before stepping into the Gulf stream. It was warmer than he remembered. Once he was waist-deep, he allowed his lower half to adopt a tail, his upper form still masculine. "Hmmm," Odessa commented.

"What, hmmm?"

"It's just that, well, I've noticed that I often take the shape of a woman, whereas you are more likely to take the shape of a man."

"So, what? We are the privileged few Vitruvian who can shapeshift. Did you know that only 10% of our kind can do that? It's rarer than being a double-jointed human."

"I am aware. I'm not stupid," Odessa put her hands on her hips, akimbo.

"I didn't say that you were."

"But you implied it."

"I think you inferred it based on what you think I meant versus what I actually said." Morphine crossed his arms in front, thrashing his tail awkwardly to stay afloat. Odessa looked at him sternly before taking her tail and splashing the water so hard that a large wave smacked Morphinae in the face. "What did you do that for?"

"You were being too male," she answered simply.

"What does *that* mean?"

Odessa let out a sigh. Morphinae was being impossible. She didn't answer, preferring instead to swim in circles around him. He observed with interest, occasionally trying to swim as well. He'd attempted to match her arm movements but found his gestures were not as smooth as hers. Most likely, he assumed, because she'd had much more practice being in the water. That, and he was convinced, her breasts helped keep her afloat. Finally, he got the hang of it, and stopped swimming, in favor of gently wading in the water, his arms and hands moving in and out and his curled-up tail helping him relax. Odessa lifted her tail up, distributing her weight across the top of the water and lying her head back. He tried it, too. *Why hadn't she led with that,* he wondered. *Floating on top of the water was much easier.*

"Can I ask you a question?" Odessa tried again.

"You just did," Morphinae observed. Odessa splashed him again. Really, he did not understand her very well.

"Do you prefer being male to female?"

Morphinae thought for a moment. "This form does feel more *me,*" he confessed. "Why?"

"Just curious," Odessa answered, thinking for a moment. "I definitely feel more me as—"

"A mermaid," Morphinae finished.

"I am not a mermaid!" Odessa whined. "I was going to say, before you interrupted me, that I feel more natural as a female."

"You look good as a female."

Odessa blushed, as much as a Vitruvian could blush with a blue-green complexion.

"Can I ask another question?"

Morphinae was about to answer again with, "You just did," but remembered that the last time he tried that, he'd gotten splashed in the eyes with brackish water. "Of course," he answered instead.

"If you were married and decided to have a baby, would you be the female carrying it, or would you be the male and let your partner give birth?"

"What kind of a question is that?" Morphinae was surprised.

"A perfectly normal one," Odessa defended. "Don't you ever think about things like that?"

"Marriage and babies?" Morphinae considered the question. "I'm a Balance-Keeper."

"So, does that mean you're not allowed to marry?"

"No, it's just that it's not often…done. We're pretty focused on, well, you know."

"Keeping the universe balanced," Odessa waved her hand tiredly. "I get it. But, it's not against your code, or whatever."

"No, it is not against our code." Morphinae stopped swimming, transforming his legs into human form and digging his bare feet into the sand beneath him, standing upright. "Why are you asking all of these unusual questions?"

Odessa stopped swimming, also transforming her tail into legs, female ones, and standing upright. She bent her knees slightly so that her breasts stayed out of sight, beneath the water. Morphinae was surprised by this since Odessa was not known for her modesty.

Odessa bit her lip and thought for a moment. "Because," she answered finally, "I like you." She paused to gauge Morphinae's reaction. It was blank. She assumed this meant that he didn't feel the same. Without waiting for a further reply, she transformed into a full fish and swam quickly away.

Morphinae watched her as she disappeared into the distance. She surprised him, and he wasn't easily surprised. Even more bewildering to him was a strange pang at the center of his chest. "I like you, too," he whispered back. But Odessa was too far away to hear him.

CHAPTER 28
IVAN AND FATIMA'S ARRIVAL
FEBRUARY. ONE MONTH AFTER THE NEW ASSEMBLY.

Once Ivan and Fatima finally reached Erde, they, along with Wilah and the nursing students who had seen them home, were quickly put into quarantine. They were shown to one of the only remaining available cottages in any of the crosses, in the Western Cross, next door to Moksha's now-burned out residence. They were assigned an attendant who identified herself simply as Iris. However, other than a form that would mildly suggest that "she" was a female, they couldn't be sure. Iris wore a form-fitting black garment with matching gloves and a helmet that masked her face—assuming she had one. There were vents where a mouth would be.

Her voice was sympathetic but direct, and since Wilah did little more than briefly introduce Iris, they felt funny asking whether or not she was a life-form or an android. Ivan and Fatima decided to assume she was a life-form so as not to accidentally offend anyone.

As Iris prepared to escort them to their cottage, Ivan looked for clues.

"So, where are ye originally from, Iris?" he inquired. "Been doin' this work long?"

"Here and now," Iris answered simply.

"So, is that some sort of protective gear you wear because of new arrivals—while we're in quarantine, I mean," Fatima chimed in as a hover vehicle approached the steps of the Dragoste healing center, where they had originally been deposited upon arrival. It was small with a dome-shaped pod that could seat up to four. The entire top half was made of glass.

"Yes," Iris answered. Without another word, she flipped a lever on the hover craft, and the glass retracted accordion-style, opening the space into a car-like convertible. Except, this convertible flew.

"This is amazing," Ivan proclaimed as he surveyed the vehicle. "What does this run on? Hydrogen? Helium? Are those magnetic plates on the top?"

"A hybrid. No, somewhat, and yes," Iris answered. "You should not be out in the open longer than necessary. Please, climb inside."

"With pleasure," Ivan answered, with all the glee of a small child at an amusement park. He held out a hand to help the now five-month pregnant Fatima in.

"Okay, wow," she replied. "I assumed you would have forgotten all about us. I'm touched." She had taken to referring to her and their unborn baby as 'us.' Fatima patted her belly.

"Nothing could make me forget about you," he touched her belly with the palm of his hand. "Although," he added. "This hovercraft is a sweet girl," he admired.

"It is called an air transporter," Iris corrected. "And, it is not a life-form. Therefore, it is neither male nor female, androgynous, nor shape-shifting."

"My mistake," Ivan grinned, lifting the carrier that housed a very unhappy Bagheera and handing him to Iris, who settled the carrier into the passenger seat in front. He climbed into the seat beside Fatima in the back while Iris slid into the driver's seat with ease.

"Please keep arms, heads, and legs inside the vehicle," she requested just moments before hitting a button, causing the dome-like structure to close over the top of them. Some vents looked like gills in the upper sides of the pod, ensuring plenty of airflow.

Fatima tucked in her thick arms, feeling slightly claustrophobic, but she didn't want to complain.

The craft was surprisingly fast and equally quiet as it sailed effortlessly above the ground, gaining altitude at a slow and steady pace. Soon, they were just above the city of Achel and the treetops.

"I feel like Peter Pan," Fatima whispered, hugging Ivan's arm. He placed his hand lovingly on her knee. That was all the words she could manage to form as she surveyed their new world from above.

From their vantage point, they could make out the four quadrants of Achel. They could see the city skyline with greenery built into the architecture so that the buildings themselves housed birds and butterflies and provided homes for a variety of plants and animals. They could barely make out the SpeedCircuit that connected TARA and the wellness center with the platform running to the four Crosses. The city itself was circular, with a grid system to easily link the city with suburban areas and business centers with parks and preserves. They were so well integrated that it was difficult to see where the one ended, and the other began, were it not for the fact that Fatima could have sworn she spotted several gray foxes in what she thought was a semi-urban area.

"What the—" Fatima spotted the Eiffel Tower in one quadrant and the Taj Mahal in another. "Am I seeing things?"

Iris paused for a moment. "Yes," she observed. "You are seeing things."

"No, I meant—"

Bagheera began whining from his crate in the front seat. He had finally adjusted to his new home on the vessel when they were moved again. His pitiful meows grew louder.

"It's okay, kitty," Fatima cooed. "We'll be at our new home soon."

The meows persisted. Apparently, Bagheera had asked a question, but Fatima's answer made no sense. Iris tilted her head questioningly, then nodded as if figuring something out. She purred to Bagheera in a very specific, purposeful manner. He immediately calmed down.

"What did you say to him?" Fatima was amazed.

"I told him not to worry. His mom and dad are not going to leave him, and that they love him very much."

"Why would he think that?" Ivan was surprised, more so than the fact that Iris seemed to speak cat.

"Because the last time you left in a hurry, his other mother went away," Iris explained.

Fatima's face dropped. He meant Lucene. "Can you give Bagheera a message for me?"

"Yes."

"Can you tell him that he'll get to see his other mom very soon and that she also loves him very much?"

Iris gave him the message. They heard a soft purr from the crate.

Fatima sank back in her seat, happily, while Ivan craned his neck in every direction, trying to figure out the air transporter's design technology. He didn't want to keep bombarding Iris with questions.

"May I offer you a suggestion," Iris asked in the manner of a GPS voice-assistant, as if she were saying, "In three miles, turn left on Valhalla Drive."

"Sure," Ivan answered.

"You should consider learning how to speak feline."

One Week Later…

Jasper Set viewed Ivan and Fatima's arrival with growing interest. The incident at the Sanctuary left a bad taste in the chronic bad taste that was already in Jasper's mouth. Reverend Isabella caught him off guard, and he was never caught off guard. *What's with all this love shit?* he wondered. More specifically, why was he so annoyed by it?

Somehow, the answer dropped him at Ivan and Fatima's front door, not three weeks after their arrival on Erde. Quarantine had been hard on Fatima, as she had gone from hiding from the government on Earth, to being isolated on the vessel with Ivan, to finally being in the home stretch on a new planet far away from her family. Extroverted by nature, she was finally feeling the strain of being so close to freedom and reconnection, only to be thwarted again.

At five months pregnant, with a pre-existing heart condition and being in a high-risk group by Earth's standards based on Fatima's age, Dr. Wilah had Fatima admitted to the health center, not a week after she and Ivan had arrived at their new cottage. Because she was both high risk and under quarantine, she was left to the care of the technically helpful but otherwise seemingly unfeeling Iris and no one else. Suddenly, her new home felt, once again, like her old home—a prison.

Ivan was fit to be tied. "Why can't I see her?" His face grew as red as his beard as he yelled at Cepheus over the online visu-phone from the kitchen of his new cottage. He slammed the table with his fist.

"It is for everyone's protection," Cepheus tried to explain.

"I don't git it," Ivan retorted. "Yer supposed to be an advanced species that's used to traveling to and from Earth. Ye really think Fatima is a health threat?"

Cepheus let out a long sigh. He missed Petrichor. He missed his family, and he certainly empathized with Ivan now. "It's just for another week," Cepheus tried again. Ivan sucked in his breath. After being with Fatima, and almost exclusively with Fatima, for the past year, it suddenly felt as if someone had cut his arm off, and he had been expected to suddenly go on as usual. "Dr. Wilah is more concerned about how Fatima and the baby are adapting to this world and how the germs and viruses that live here, along with our atmosphere, might impact them. I'm telling you, my friend, it is for Fatima's safety and for that of your child."

Ivan wiped back a tear and nodded, hanging his head slightly. "I suppose," he finally whispered.

"In one more week," Cepheus tried to cheer his friend up, "we will give you a tour of the Makerspace and begin to discuss your new role in Invention and Development. Fatima will be home, and everything will be as it should be." Something began gnawing in the pit of Cepheus's stomach, but he pushed it aside. Instead, he said, "Don't lose heart, friend."

Jasper listened to the exchange from the cottage window, devising a plan. He asked himself how he could have grown so weak at Isabella's show of lovingkindness, and he had suddenly been transported here. And frankly, witnessing this Earthling's unsuppressed expression of regard for his female friend and unborn baby was sickening. *I mean, really,* Jasper said to himself. *The thing growing in her belly isn't even a person yet.* And yet, here he was, outside their door. Why?

He thought for a moment about love, but he didn't really understand it. According to the textbook definition, it had something to do with extreme affection and concern for someone or something. Those with the love emotion seemed to care about making the recipient happy. He suspected the Null loved him in their own special way, and Jasper had the sense that they, even in their destruction of the universe, were doing it out of wanting what was best for him, to protect him from a worse fate, somehow. Jasper mulled on this for a moment. *Whom do I have extreme affection and concern for? Whose best interested do I have in mind? Whom do I want to protect and make happy?*

Suddenly, an idea struck him that left him physically jiggling up and down as it sank in. In order to combat the love bombs that Isabella, Odessa and Morphinae tossed at him the other day, he had to destroy love in its purest form. To do that, the solution was simple. He had to focus on the one creature that he suspected he truly loved...himself.

CHAPTER 29
GOING OUT WITH A BANG
FEBRUARY. ONE MONTH AFTER THE NEW ASSEMBLY.

"Well, I must s-s-s-say. This is the most fun I've had s-s-since, well, ever!" Jasper Set surveyed his work with pride. There, on the edge of the bridge just outside the main entrance to the Makerspace, the seven of them sat in a circle with legs folded beneath them: Ivan, Roman, Far, Lucene, Tanager, Moksha and Cepheus, each wrapped in a tight-fitting bomb vest, each connected to one-another by a frequency that communicated between the vests, making it deadly for anyone to leave the circle. At the center of each vest was a small red button, the detonator.

He couldn't get at Fatima, somehow, and assumed that it had to do with some strange added superpower that came with motherhood. And so, Fatima lay safety in an isolated room at the health center.

But as for the other lovebirds, it took no more than a flick of his wrist to round the group up from all the corners of Erde and bring them together. *If it was love bombs they liked to toss around,* he reasoned, *then they're gonna love this!*

"I confes-s-s-s, I'm used to using s-s-s-upernatural powers instead of antiquated contraptions. This-s-s was more fun than I thought it would be. I used a few knickknacks from your tech department. Hope you don't mind."

"I'm sorry, my love," Far whispered to Roman. Far wasn't entirely sure he meant it, but it seemed like the right thing to say in this circumstance.

"It's okay," Roman forced a smile. "You were brainwashed with that demon controlling your thoughts. It's not your fault." Roman's entire body was quivering, sweat pouring down his face. He was trying not to move. While he had been clouded by love, it didn't take long to realize that it was Far who was responsible for Mallory's death, not Moksha. An injustice he had planned on remedying when and if he got out of this situation alive.

If ever there were a time that Lucene could summon the power to shift reality, this would be it. She tried to mentally connect with Tanager and Cepheus, but fear was making it difficult to concentrate. The three sat in the circle with disjointed thoughts floating between them.

Deactivate the bombs? How? I have no idea how bombs work, Lucene answered Tanager.

Make them disappear? I tried that. I don't think I can remove energy from a space without replacing it with an equal energy, she explained to Cepheus.

How's it going, guys? Jasper Set's voice interrupted their thought circle, and just like that, their connection was broken.

"What is happening?" Moksha asked Cepheus after he opened his eyes. She'd witnessed the three of them with eyes closed, and an unresponsive Ivan, who stared directly in front of him, eyes open and fixated on a spot on the ground. He twitched, visibly distracted by her question. He tuned her out.

"Jasper has gotten into our heads," Cepheus replied, fighting back what felt like the beginning of an episode.

"That's right," Jasper smiled proudly, walking around the circle, occasionally patting one of them on the head, saying, "Duck, duck...who will be the goose?"

All this time, Jasper had been bored. Using his powers was far too easy. This required work, and he was proud that after all these centuries, his mind was still sharp. He didn't need to explain to them why he was doing this—that much was clear. They were a threat. They fell too easily under his radar for him to let them get away again. With them out of the way, the Royals would have no real opposition left, except for the Null, which he controlled.

Last chance to switch to Team Jasper, Jasper whispered in Lucene's ear. Lucene mentally gave him the finger. Disappointing. He was hoping to have a major battle with her—to see what she was truly capable of. If she were a worthy opponent, then she might actually be useful to him after all. And yet, it had been so easy to pull her in. This surprised him because, on the surface, Lucene didn't give much away, at least not where deep emotions were concerned.

"Now, it wouldn't be any fun for me to just blow you and half of Achel up without adding an element of s-s-s-us-s-s-pens-s-s-e," Jasper explained to them. It occurred to him that his stuttering was somehow lessening the impact of his artfully thought out presentation. He decided to slow his speech, carefully and controlled. Jasper took a deep breath before continuing.

"Let me briefly tell you how this works." He stopped pacing and flew up in the air and landed delicately in the center of their circle. He paused to wave at the crowds that had formed on the Pont Alexandre Bridge with Commander Royce's military barricading what they could of the commerce district on the Northern end, as well as the residential area on the Southern end. Meanwhile, the Defense League was attempting in vain to push the crowds back, not knowing exactly how big of an explosion they were in for, but also not wanting to cause massive chaos with people trampling over one another in a rapid escape. Little by little, the masses shifted further away from the bridge and the Makerspace. "Aww, they're so cute," he pressed his lips together. He seemed to remember himself. "Now, where was I…oh, yes. Each of you has a bomb strapped across your chest…obviously. If anyone leaves this circle right now, all bombs explode at once. If no one leaves the circle, time will run out, and one bomb will explode first, and the others will follow in sequence."

"So, we're dead either way," Lucene grumbled.

"Not necessarily. There is exactly one solution in which s-s-s-six of you get to live. One will die, I'm afraid. Sorry." He pulled a small revolver out of his jacket pocket. "If anyone decides they can't take the pressure and wants to end themselves early, here you go." He placed the gun at his feet, an arm's reach from everyone within the circle. "Otherwise, you have ninety-seconds to figure it out. Ready...go!" With that, Jasper vanished.

They all began chattering at once with Moksha at the helm, cycling through everything she knew about bombs and military tactics.

"If they explode in sequence, and are not connected by wires, then they are on a similar frequency," Moksha offered.

"Maybe we can change the frequency," Lucene added.

"Or break the connection?" Tanager suggested.

"Breaking the connection will just make them all go off at once," Cepheus reminded him.

Far sat in silence, holding Roman's hand. Roman was busy professing his love, having already resigned himself to death.

"What special combination of powers do we have that can work for us?"

A loud beeping erupted. No one needed an explanation as to what this meant. They were almost out of time.

Ivan's brain went into overdrive. Flashing before his eyes were seemingly random images: the compressor of a car's air-conditioning unit, crossing the finish line of a race, fifth-grade geometry class, an elephant with three blind men around it, a string of Christmas lights with one bulb missing. The others went dark. He opened his eyes.

"I've got it!" Everyone stopped chattering. He looked directly at Far and picked up the gun. "Ye have to run," he pointed the gun at Far's chest, its sight on the red detonator.

"No!" Roman protested, putting an arm instinctively in front of Far's body as if to protect him. Far pushed his arm away. Roman recoiled in surprise. Far's face turned to one of smug satisfaction. "Nope," he answered simply.

"Then, I'm sorry," Ivan replied, firing a shot. As the bullet hit, Far disappeared. Ivan sprang for the vest before it hit the ground, only to be tackled by Roman. Lucene locked in on Ivan's thoughts, grabbing the vest before it hit the ground and tossing it over the bridge into the water below. With Roman still strapped to Ivan's back as he clumsily tried a chokehold that wasn't working, his long legs flailing in every direction, Ivan turned his entire body to Moksha. "Run, that way," he pointed in the direction of Big Ben. She nodded and took off at lightning speed, transitioning into her lizard self along the way. She forced her way through the military blockade, apologizing as she shoved any bystanders who were in the way. She didn't know exactly how far she had to go; she just kept running toward the clock tower.

Cepheus also locked in as Ivan nodded a head toward the top of the Eiffel tower at the Southern end of the bridge. He took off in the opposite direction, leaping across the bridge, using the shoulders and heads of onlookers as if they were stepping stones in the middle of a stream. He climbed the tower in the same anole lizard fashion as he'd once scaled the walls of a warehouse one year ago to rescue Lucene.

"Git off of me, ye idiot!" Ivan wrestled with Roman, finally having migrated toward he edge of the bridge, flipping Roman off of him and onto the concrete. Roman let out a moan as his spine connected with the bridge floor.

"Get off the bridge," Tanager ordered them. He, too, had mentally locked in on the plan, albeit later than he would have preferred. "Now!" He grabbed Lucene's hand. With as much energy as she could muster, Lucene began to focus on holding the bridge together. *Hold together. Hold together.* She kept repeating in her mind. Tanager joined her in focusing on the bridge.

Ivan helped Roman to his feet. "C'mon, man. I'll explain later." There was a quake beneath their feet as Far's bomb vest exploded under water, followed by rumbling as the bridge's supports began to crumble.

Hold together. Hold together. Both were tired. Neither was strong enough. And yet…something happened. It was as if another power source had suddenly joined them. Lucene looked up. There, in the crowd behind Commander Royce and her League, stood Clusaladek, Xeni and Neroni, holding hands in solidarity. Calusaladek nodded. *We're here for you,* he thought.

Roman followed Ivan as they ran toward the Southern end. By this time, Commander Royce, while not knowing exactly what was happening, knew enough to clear a path for the two men as they sailed by with the bomb vests beeping wildly.

"Oye!" Ivan called to Royce, struggling to catch his breath. It had been long time since he'd had to move at that speed. "Air…" he gasped. "Support." Commander Royce watched as the bridge began to split apart, with Lucene and Tanager at its center.

"Air support for two rescues on the bridge," Commander Royce yelled above the thunder into the communication watch on her wrist.

Hold together. Hold together. They were beginning to lose footing as the floor crumbled beneath them, the rubble from each half of the bridge threatening to fall in on them as they began their descent into the icy water below.

Suddenly, Lucene and Tanager felt themselves being hoisted into the air by something that had hooked itself to the straps of the bomb vest. As they lurched forward, the beeping stopped, and the world went silent. For a moment, Lucene thought she might be dead and closed her eyes. When she re-opened them, she gazed down her vest. The detonator had turned blue momentarily before going dark.

Ivan's plan had worked.

No one was sure what to do following the day's events. After all, how does one defeat an all-powerful demon? After hours, in the Negotiation Room at the PDL, Ivan, Roman, Tanager, Cepheus, and Lucene were all permitted to return home, each paired with two military guards from the League. Moksha, while she hadn't been officially cleared by the legal counsel, was free to leave but under Watch. And while Commander Royce was smart enough to have figured out where she had been hiding, under the circumstances, she pretended not to notice. After all, there was still the ongoing investigation to see who burned Moksha's house down. There was also the slight possibility that they had also attempted to kill her. Thus far, all signs pointed toward the townspeople. But after the mishap with Moksha the first go-around, Cluseladek, Xeni and Neroni refused to lend their powers to the investigation. They were afraid of making a mistake that would cause the chaos they had already experienced. *One emergency at a time,* Commander Royce reasoned.

Just on duty, the guards were to watch for any unnatural events, calling for backup should the need arise. Meanwhile, scholars at TARA were researching everything they could about mythology, philosophy and the occult, trying to figure out what to do about Jasper Set.

"Hey, wait up," Lucene called after Ivan as he hastily made his way toward the Dragoste Healing Center. He knew they wouldn't let him in the room with Fatima yet, but maybe he could convince them to at least let him peek through the window to her room, maybe make a few funny faces to lighten Fatima's mood?

Ivan slowed his pace, but only slightly. "Now's not the best time, Lucene," he pointed toward the center.

"Real quick, though," she stopped him. He was visibly annoyed but pushed it back. They'd all been through a lot lately.

"Okay, shoot," he said. Then he remembered the bomb and the revolver on the bridge and rubbed his beard uncomfortably. "Eh, sorry. Poor choice of words."

"Never mind that," Lucene continued. "I didn't understand what you explained to Commander Royce. How did you figure out how to disable the bombs?"

"Pretty simple, actually." It wasn't simple; Lucene would come to learn. Ivan was just very smart. "We knew they were synchronized by a signal in some way and that if one went off, the others would follow in short order. So, we had to trigger one and then break the signal before the others would go off. Since I remembered that Far had that weird power of transporting himself over long distances, I figured I could shoot his vest just as he disappeared, assuming he moved fast enough. But then some of us needed to move at great speed, something only two lizard people could do, which is why I sent Cepheus and Moksha in different directions. It would break the triangulation."

"Triangulation?"

"Aye, I figured the bomb sequence was triangulated to balance the signal, so at least three of us had to be out of range in three different directions."

"How on Earth could you possibly know about the triangulation of bombs?" Lucene was curious.

Ivan suddenly turned as red as his beard, tugging at his ear nervously. "Eh, no reason. Listen, I got to git—"

"Understood," Lucene leaned in for a quick hug. "Give Fatima one of these for me." Ivan hugged her back, pausing for an extra moment. It was then that he realized that with all that isolation, Fatima was the only other person to show him affection. He missed hugging friends and smiled at the gesture.

Tanager cleared his throat, uncomfortably, in the distance. He had been mentally trying to connect with Lucene for several minutes now so they wouldn't miss the SpeedCircuit. Beside him were four guards, two for him and two for Lucene. He insisted on accompanying Lucene home. He wasn't sure what he would do if Jasper Set returned but felt surer about his empathic powers than in the guards, who'd never been in an altercation in their life. He couldn't see them being useful at all.

Lucene made her way over to him. *Couldn't you hear me?* Tanager thought. Lucene threw her hands up and asked. "What? Aren't you going to say something?"

I'm trying to. Tanager thought.

Nothing.

It wasn't until they had reached her cottage, and Tanager mentally attempted to unlock her door for her and couldn't, that a frightening thought crossed his mind. *Did they all short circuit on the bridge?* Their combined energies might have been enough to hold the bridge together and temporarily banish Jasper Set, but now it seemed as if their powers might be gone-altogether. He attempted to keep this thought to himself as Lucene fumbled with her communication watch to unlock the door.

What's wrong? she thought, looking at him. It was then that she noticed it—the nothingness. She had no idea how he felt nor what he was thinking. There were no glitchy flashes of sights and sounds in her head. In fact, everything was suspiciously…quiet.

CHAPTER 30
THE WARNING
FEBRUARY. ONE MONTH AFTER THE NEW ASSEMBLY.

"They may have bailed on you, but we have not," Isabella's hologram spoke to all those who now gathered in the negotiation room: Commander Royce, Lucene, Tanager, Cepheus, Moksha, Ivan, Constable Melokuhl and a handful of other military personnel.

Fatima remained in the health center, unaware, but with growing concern at Ivan's lack of communication over the past twenty-four hours. Usually, Ivan visu-phoned Fatima every few hours but had been silent ever since his funny little visit to the center, where the two spoke through an intercom as he told her jokes and made faces at her through the glass. It was short because as soon as Iris realized he was there, she quickly escorted him out.

Now, Fatima was alarmed. *Was something wrong? Was that a goodbye of some sort?* She pushed the thought away. "No, Fatima," she told herself. "Don't worry until you're given something to worry about." She laid back and tried to get some rest. Difficult, as the baby seemed very active that day. "You better not be inventing something dangerous in there, future tinkerer," she joked, wondering if the baby would follow after her and take up cooking and steampunk cosplay. Or, if it would be more like Ivan, creating virtual engines that don't really exist.

Meanwhile, back in the negotiation room, the team was notified that Roman had been *uninvited* from the IPP meeting. Not only was he now considered a security risk, but his Watch status had now been elevated, and his teaching credentials had been temporarily revoked until he faced further evaluation. They needed to know how much Far had told him, how much he'd told his partner, and what, if anything, he was covering up.

"But there's only three of you," Commander Royce stated the obvious to the remaining members of the group. "Without the support of the IPP, Earth and Vitruvia, that leaves the people in this room and you—and you have no means by which to support us."

"Let us try," a new voice said as Odessa stepped out from behind Isabella. "We may be living on Earth—" She paused to glance at Morphinae, who was also dialed in from the Sanctuary, along with Odessa and Isabella. In truth, they didn't know how long they could stall their return. "But Morphinae and I are still Vitruvian. Let us try and use our influence to garner support…if in secret."

"In secret?" Commander Royce echoed her statement. "And what happens under your government if you are discovered helping us?"

Odessa didn't answer. Morphinae did, with his usual calmness. "They would immediately assassinate us and possibly seek vengeance on the Balance-Keepers, and your people as well."

"I see," Commander Royce turned to her team, all highly ill-equipped and completely unqualified for the task at hand. "Save for the one invasion from the Royals, where we were asked not to intervene," she glanced at Cepheus, who cleared his throat uncomfortably. Moksha touched his arm slightly in support. "There has been no other invasion from outsiders, and we've enjoyed 100 years of peace. What happens if we don't intervene?"

"Then Hamish's new order of Royals will take over Earth, killing off the human race on their planet."

"I'm beginning to think that we have overextended our support to Earthlings, and now Erdelings are getting caught in a vicious crossfire," Commander Royce offered, but not maliciously.

"Do you think they will stop there?" Isabella asked. "Erde would be next. And if not the Royals, then what's to stop the demon from sending the Null to roll over and destroy your planet and Vitruvia? We can't be completely certain of the deal Sovereign Hamish made with Jasper Set. We can only speculate given our sources."

Commander Royce looked toward Cepheus and Moksha in hopes of some insight. "I'm sorry," Moksha understood her silent question. "I was merely a soldier and know nothing of Sovereign Hamish's plan." Her gaze fell to the floor in failure. This time, it was Cepheus who lightly touched her hand. She smiled back, gratefully.

Cepheus cleared his throat with some discomfort. "I haven't been immersed in Royal culture for some time, but it is my belief that my fa—," he caught himself. "That Sovereign Hamish is power-hungry." He paused for a moment. "No, that's not entirely fair. My mo—" he caught himself again. "The now-deceased Sovereign Sabrina was the power-hungry one. Sovereign Hamish wanted to please her and—in spite of his cruelty— actually does care about the survival of those under his guard. At least," he paused, "I *think* he does."

"What does that mean to us?" Commander Royce asked.

"It means that if he's making a deal with the Null to wipe out Earth, it's not for power but to save his own military brigade."

"That's what I don't understand," Constable Melokuhl piped up. "Begging your pardon, Commander Royce." He bowed his head in respect.

"No need," Commander Royce answered calmly. "In this space, you may speak freely."

"Thank you, Commander," Constable Melokuhl answered. "What I want to know is..." he peered closely at Cepheus and Moksha. "Who is above your Sovereign? I mean, we were all led to believe that they were in charge. But...that's not right, is it?"

Cepheus and Moksha exchanged nervous glances. Cepheus answered cautiously, "I was a young boy when I left," he explained. "But while under the tutelage of my caretakers, it was taught to me that those above my parents (the word got a little caught in his throat) were kept secret until I was of age, in the same way that the youngers are kept secret until they fulfilled their rite of passage. We did not speak the names of the elders or youngers."

"So," Constable Melokuhl tapped his fingers on the table, his mouth twisted to one corner as he thought. "You don't know."

Cepheus let out a sigh. "Correct. I do not know."

"What about you?" Constable Melokuhl addressed Moksha. "You got anything?"

Moksha seemed surprised before remembering that non-Royals would have no way of knowing the way of things. "I was a lesser Royal, high in the military, but low in our caste system. If *he* does not know," she gestured toward Cepheus. "Then I most certainly would not have been privy to that information."

"Pity," Constable Melokuhl said, then had a thought. "But if Sovereign Hamish *were* power-hungry…"

"Yes?" Commander Royce encouraged.

"Well then, maybe he wouldn't just take over Earth, but you'd think he'd want the Null to take out his superiors. Wouldn't you think?"

From lightyears away, Isabella was suddenly struck by a thought. "Representative Dallen mentioned a baby."

"What?" Commander Royce asked.

"A baby," Isabella thought a moment. "I thought it was curious, and while I know that our presentation to the congregation was…embellished…for effect, I have come to learn that someone selling a false idea will always insert a nugget of truth."

Commander Royce thought a moment before turning back to the group. "Okay, so we've got the Royals who most definitely want to take over Earth and possibly the surrounding planets, to include Erde and Vitruvia. We have a Royal Sovereign who wants to protect his military brigade and potentially overthrow his own leaders." She paused to look at Cepheus. "There's a chance that there is a new Royal baby. And, as you mentioned earlier, it would be kept secret until the rite of passage."

Cepheus shuddered at the thought. *Could his parents have had another child? A sibling?* He pushed the thought away. For the baby's sake, he hoped not.

"Okay, Let's discuss some alternate options," Commander Royce continued. "Given this new information, what happens if we *do* intervene? I need some pros and cons."

In the end, Commander Royce and the Planetary Defense League made the determination that this matter had to be escalated. It was being presented to their superiors—the Elders. This was something that hadn't happened in more than a century, and Commander Royce was not the slightest bit happy about one of her last acts as Commander before retirement: having to awaken the Elders to ask for their intervention. Even more unsettling was their calm response once she had filled them in on the situation.

The answer was clear. After one hundred years of peace, the Peace-Makers were now preparing…for war.

CHAPTER 31
A TEAR IN SPACE
MARCH. TWO MONTHS AFTER THE ASSEMBLY.

"I have good news and bad news," Dr. Ennis shared when Tanager and Lucene were finally able to connect with him via the glitchy online account at Lucene's cottage.

"How about the bad news first?" Tanager and Lucene answered simultaneously before glancing at each other with nervous smiles. They were sitting in a makeshift living room that Lucene had partitioned off from her bedroom. It wasn't much, but the curtain made it feel as if she actually had a one-bedroom house with a proper living room and kitchen versus a studio-like apartment with everything but the bathroom in one space. The two leaned forward on the couch, peering at the small computer screen expectantly.

"The bad news is—" he paused for a moment to look back and forth at the couple, grinning nervously. "It might be permanent." He remembered himself and dropped his expression into one of supreme thoughtfulness.

The two let out a sigh. It was an understatement, they knew, but it was the most that they could muster. Decades of research, extreme financial loss, not to mention the irreplaceable lives sacrificed in the interest of helping Earth.

"It was almost as if a lightning strike blew the electrical circuits out of an entire house. Only, in this case, it was people."

In their efforts to take down Jasper Set and save their lives, the Makerspace and whomever bystanders happened to be near the bridge that day, they had managed to short circuit their abilities. It created a ripple effect, and Cepheus, Xeni, Cluseladek, Neroni and all other Data Collectors failed to have retained any of their genetically modified powers. And, from what they could tell so far, neither did Lucene. After all, she was a bit of an anomaly. For the first time in a long time, they were all...*normal.*

"Can we get some good news?" Tanager finally asked.

"Of course," Dr. Ennis brightened. "None of you appear to have any residual physical or psychological damage. I consulted with Dr. Wilah, and it appears that you and your students are..."

"Normal," Tanager and Lucene answered flatly. Somehow, this news didn't make them feel any better.

Thirty Minutes Later

Tanager took his leave, and Lucene paused a moment to survey her surroundings with an odd curiosity. Months after the odd energy that Xeni felt at Lucene's cottage, Lucene began to feel it, too. Only, she felt it in the pit of her stomach, like she'd eaten something that didn't agree with her. Sometimes it felt bitter, sometimes sour. She made a mental note to ask Tanager about it the next time she saw him. After all, it was assumed she had no special powers anymore. Of course, this wasn't taking into consideration the empathy that many species might have, all on their own. She brushed the feeling aside for the time being.

In the meantime, she'd taken to cleaning her home from top to bottom on a weekly basis, in a ritual that some would call obsessive. She just thought it was common sense. She also began smudging with white sage each week, something she used to do when she worked at the Sanctuary back on Earth. Lucene wasn't entirely sure that it worked in keeping out negative energy, but at least she knew of its antiviral properties, so that was something. And it made her house smell good.

"Ahh, what a s-s-s-weet s-s-s-mell," Jasper Set appeared suddenly behind Lucene, causing her to drop the smoking sage and abalone shell on the stone floor, sending dirty ash everywhere in a swirl of dust. Fortunately, nothing caught fire. Lucene held out the only thing still left in her hand, the feather she used to guide the smoke around the room.

"What are you doing here?" she demanded, wielding the feather like a knife. Jasper put his hands up in mock fear.

"Oh no, please don't attack me with that menacing feather," he laughed. Then sniffed the air once more, pretending to swirl an imaginary glass of wine and sniff it. "What is-s-s- that delightful aroma? Palo S-s-s-anto? No. Copal? No. Ah, white s-s-sage. I should have gues-s-s-ed it."

"What do you want, demon?" Lucene asked again. Her stomach growled with a bitterness she'd never experienced before.

"Isn't it obvious?" He looked at her like an amused puppy. He leaned in as if telling her a secret. Lucene backed away uncomfortably, only to have Jasper vanish and reappear over her shoulder. "You," he whispered in her ear.

"Then why didn't you take me at the Makerspace, instead of strapping us to bombs and making us your hostages?"

"Honestly, I wanted to see just how powerful you were," Jasper snorted. "Actually, you should probably not believe anything I say, or anyone, for that matter, who begins a sentence with 'honestly.'"

"Still waiting," Lucene's heart beat faster.

"I wanted to see your collective power."

"I don't follow."

"If I kept you and then helped Hamish fulfill his plan to overthrow the Royals currently in command, he could take over the Earth, and contract fulfilled." He wiped his hands as if cleaning them. "I just wanted to be s-s-sure it wouldn't come back to bite me in the proverbial ass-s-s-, s-s-o to s-s-speak."

"How so?"

"My Null mamas and papas might feel betrayed if they discovered I purposely led them away from the Divine purpose of the Segue."

"Why do you only hiss sometimes, but not all the time?" Lucene asked.

"I don't s-s-e-e how that is relevant to the convers-s-s-as-ion," Jasper become flustered.

"Oh, I get it,"

"What do you get?" Jasper spat angrily as he spoke.

"You're afraid of the Null, too."

"Don't be s-s-illy, child. I'm a demon. I fear nothing." Jasper quickly recovered, making circles around Lucene until she began feeling dizzy. "That being said," he continued, "I do find it prudent of me to disappear for a while, just in case."

"Where could you go that the Null couldn't find you?"

"Aha, that is the million-dollar ques-s-tion," he shook his finger in her face. "That's what I need you for."

"Still not following."

"Another dimension, s-s-illy," he giggled as if he'd just taken a long whiff of helium. "I want you to send me to another dimension, where I can hide out for a bit, see how my other selves are doing. S-s-ee what chaos we can s-s-tir up."

"Even if I could do that, which I can't, I'm not following the logic. Say you take me with you, why even bother fulfilling the rest of your agreement with the Royals?"

"I may be a demon, but I have a code. I always keep my contracts," he seemed offended at the suggestion that he'd actually go back on his word.

"And the collective power?"

"I thought I might take one or two of you as backup. For instance, that Cluseladek is quite powerful and easy to influence. And, Ivan, I must say, that boy s-s-urpri-s-sed me. No powers, but an awful lot of s-s-smarts. I assumed you would simply use your skills to deactivate the bombs, but it seems that thought never occurred to you… Why didn't that thought occur to you?" He paused.

"It did," she answered. "I couldn't. And if I couldn't then, I most certainly can't now."

Jasper ignored her. "Hmm, I guess I was mistaken. There were two solutions. Clever boy, that Ivan. But I digress," he circled her once more.

"I'm als-s-so banking on their being another *you* on each of the planes, should I go multidimensional hopping. Maybe they have powers that even you don't, who knows?"

"Could you please stop circling me like a shark and sit down," Lucene motioned to a chair. The lunacy of a young woman offering a demon a seat at her table was not lost on Jasper, who sat with a smile, putting his tiny feet, now clad in soot-covered boots, on her kitchen table. She ignored that part.

"The multiverse is a petri dish of possibilities," Jasper smiled, his "Ssss" staying in place for once.

"Has it occurred to you that there are at least two major flaws to your theory?"

"Hypothesis," he corrected.

"What?"

"Hypothesis. Unless we have evidence to support our theory, it is merely a hypothesis."

"Whatever, the point is, all of the Data Collectors lost their powers following your little bomb experiment. We fizzled out. Second, if parallel-universe hopping is a thing, why haven't other Jasper Sets graced this planet?"

Jasper's face grew dark. "I'll s-s-tart with the latter," he spat. "I s-s-sus-s-s-pect that I am the s-s-martest, Jas-s-s-per S-s-s-et."

"Wow, when you get angry, you can't even s-s-say your own name," Lucene mocked.

Without another word, Jasper swept his arm across the table, sending it flying in Lucene's direction. The table sent her sailing backward, threatening to land on top of her. Dishes from her cupboards began flying about, smashing into tiny pieces in every direction. Lucene's mind went back to her childhood, in the back seat of a car with glass shattering all around her. She opened her mouth to scream, but nothing came out as she braced for the hard floor beneath her. Her back and spine landed first, searing pain shooting through her. Lucene attempted in vain to lift her head, but she couldn't. Just as her head was about to smack on the stone ground beneath her, she suddenly felt something soft…a hand.

Light poured in through what Lucene thought were the cottage windows, and she squinted to see. What she hadn't realized at that moment was that the light was not from the windows at all, but from outside, as Jasper, in his anger, had blown the entire roof from her cottage. Someone was kneeling over her.

"My dear," Reverend Isabella addressed Lucene, gently lifting her hand, which was still beneath Lucene's head, and guiding her to a seated position, putting her arm around Lucene's shoulders for support. "Remind me to talk to you later about not always saying the first thing that comes into your head."

"Isabella, what…how?" Lucene was shocked.

"Later," she held up a hand, releasing Lucene's shoulders only when she was certain the young woman could remain seated on her own.

Jasper was so caught up in his own commotion that he neglected to notice Isabella's presence. Outside, the sounds of townspeople could be heard coming to inspect the damage.

"Lucene!" Tanager's voice could be heard yelling in the distance. Moments later, he was at the doorway—the actual door to the kitchen having been blown off. It had flown into the distance, landing in a nearby field. Fortunately, no one besides Lucene was hurt.

"You're jus-s-s-t in time for the show," Jasper squealed gleefully. "Wait? Where did you come from?" He finally noticed Isabella.

"Irrelevant," she answered calmly, standing upright, her arms rigidly at her side.

"Oh, don't try s-s-s-ending those love bombs again," Jasper mocked. "I was caught off guard before, but I'm prepared now."

Tanager ran to Lucene's side, leaning over to help her to her feet. "Are you okay?" He brushed rubble and dust from her hair and hugged her close.

"Not sure," Lucene answered groggily. "I think I'm hallucinating. I just saw…" She stopped mid-sentence as she saw that Isabella was actually in the room.

Cepheus slinked through the doorway, as silent as a cat. "Not again," he said, seeing Jasper, now swirling triumphantly in mid-air. As he swirled, bits of furniture, utensils, and broken dinnerware began to get caught up in a funnel like a tornado. As the wind grew stronger, Tanager tucked his head and pulled Lucene's face into his chest to avoid broken glass from flying into their eyes. A few bits scratched across his back and neck, slicing through his shirt. He winced from the pain.

"You can make all this s-s-s-s-top, Luc—" Jasper had trouble saying Lucene's name. "S-s-s-send me to another dimension, and everything will be fine."

"If I do, do you promise to leave everyone here alone?" The swirling stopped and debris settled on the floor around them, some landing on their feet, weighing them down heavily as Tanager, Cepheus and Lucene attempted to step around it. Cepheus fared the best, gracefully side-stepping most of the damage. "No taking anyone else with you—just me," Lucene offered.

Jasper thought for a moment. "Take the deal," Isabella finally spoke, calmly. "It's the best you're going to get." Jasper felt the hairs on the back of his neck stand up. There was something about her that unnerved him, which was crazy, wasn't it?

"Fine," Jasper answered simply. "Hit me," he closed his eyes and held his arms out.

Lucene looked pleadingly at Isabella. That was as far as she had gotten with her bluff. She really had no idea how she was supposed to do what she promised. *You forget s-s-s-somthing, little girl,"* Jasper spoke from inside her head. *You may have lost your empathic abilities, but I have not. You're lying to me."*

"What's going on?" Tanager asked as Lucene grabbed her ears, shaking her head as if trying to shake water out of them.

"He's in her head," Cepheus replied calmly. "Leave her be, demon!" Like a flying bat, Cepheus sent himself sailing toward Jasper, tackling the demon to the floor before Jasper, in a rage, tossed Cepheus into the open air, following the front door's trajectory and landing him in the open field behind the house.

To Lucene, Jasper spat. "You're useless! How can that be?"

"I told you, I short-circuited," Lucene replied. "I wish I could give you what you want, so you'll leave us alone. But I can't!"

"Pity," Jasper answered simply. The wind began to pick up again—stronger this time, and Lucene, Tanager, and Isabella felt themselves being lifted into the air. The remainder of the cottage suddenly crumbled to the ground. A few shocked townspeople attempted to rush in to intervene, but Jasper quickly caught them in his tornado, now getting wider and wider as it pulled more in with it.

Lucene was ripped from Tanager's arms, feeling herself violently spinning as the outer pressure from the world seemed to collapse in on her body. She could no longer breathe and was becoming dizzy and lightheaded. Storm clouds gathered low to the ground, enveloping her.

In a moment of surprise, she saw something glowing, like lightning rays coming through the storm clouds. Her arms…they were glowing again, the patterns becoming a blood-red and cracking through her skin like growing and expanding embers on a log…just like that day in class when she'd almost accidentally killed someone.

"Stop, demon," Isabella commanded. "I can give you what you want."

The winds died down, Jasper setting his small feet on the floor and leaning forward eagerly. "How?" Lucene landed butt-first on the floor behind him with a thud.

"Ooof," she said, rubbing her hip as she struggled to stand. Tanager landed in the yard and awkwardly struggled to walk through what now appeared to be a war zone. He'd have to check on Cepheus later.

"Stand up straight, Lucene," Isabella commanded. "And don't move."

"How—"

"And don't talk."

For once, Lucene obeyed. Her arms hurt; they felt as if they were burning as the branches continued to grow. Isabella held her arms out, palms facing Lucene. She closed her eyes and began chanting. The branches continued to grow, and light began streaming from them like illuminated beams. Lucene let out a scream as the light enveloped her.

"Stop it! What are you doing to her?" Tanager went to grab Isabella's arms, but he was too late. Lucene vanished, and a giant red swirling doorway appeared. "Go now, demon!" Isabella commanded.

"Where am I going, exactly?" Jasper suddenly appeared nervous.

"I have no idea. It's another dimension, as promised. I have no idea which one."

"Fair enough," Jasper grinned, excitedly, swallowing his fear. "An adventure!" The doorway grew smaller.

"Go now, before it closes!"

Jasper gave one final survey of his surroundings before he took to the air like a tornado and sailed through the portal. As soon as he had, the portal began funneling inward. Lucene reappeared, falling to the floor in a heap as the branches on her arm went dark again—like a light that had gone out.

After a moment of silence, Lucene spoke. "I'm sensing a theme," she joked. This was the third time she landed on the floor in fewer than ten minutes. Tanager went to help her up but winced as he touched her hand as a shock went through him.

"Easy, lover boy," Isabella lowered her arms. "Give it a few minutes before you touch her again. She's still charged up."

"What the hell just happened?" Lucene demanded.

Isabella let out a sigh. "The demon assumed that you had the power to open up a portal to another dimension for him. But he was only half right."

"Half right?"

"Yes," she nodded. "You couldn't open the portal because…you *are* the portal."

"I'm the reason Far's powers inspired fear among the people of Macar," Isabella later explained to Lucene, Cepheus and Tanager. They were at the healing center, being tended to by Dr. Wilah and her team. Isabella had suffered no injuries, but the other three had all been examined and were in the lobby, awaiting final clearance to return to their homes. Had Tanager and Cepheus not met up to tour the preserves and check on the emotional states of the townspeople following Jasper Set's damaging mind control, they wouldn't have been there for Jasper's return.

"I too had the gift of prophecy but used it for my own gain," Isabella continued. "I was forced out because I betrayed the tribe." She shook her head, ashamed. "I am a different person now, but unfortunately, the damage was done. Even though Far was born nearly a century later, he came from my family's lineage. So naturally, they feared him."

"We didn't even know you had met Far," Lucene commented. "Does Roman know this?"

"Aside from the New Moon Celebration last year on Earth, I have had no communication with your friend, Roman. And," she added. "I have never met Far. I have only heard the rumors of his existence and," she laughed, "his terrible sense of direction."

"Fascinating," Tanager rubbed his head, thinking excitedly. "What is the extent of your abilities? Can you teleport yourself anywhere you want to go? What about time travel? Can you truly see the future, or is it that you actually visit the future and then go back in time to report what you saw?"

Isabella eyed Tanager up and down for a moment as if sizing him up. She then glanced at Lucene and Cepheus as if making mental calculations in her mind.

"Soon, I will answer all of your questions...but not today."

CHAPTER 32
MAYBE JUST THIS ONCE...
JUNE. FIVE MONTHS AFTER THE NEW ASSEMBLY.

"My memory is faulty," Cepheus confessed, as he walked with Moksha through her vineyard as she finally returned to assess the damage. In their anger, the townspeople had destroyed everything—her house, her property, her vineyard. Then, when they realized that she was innocent, they returned to try and fix it. They had been successful in re-building her cottage, or at least a version of it, even going so far as to replace the stained-glass windows and painting the house purple. They also cleared the rubble around her front door and added a pathway lined with multicolored chrysanthemums leading from her house to the main dirt road.

Unfortunately, few in the Western Cross knew what to do about the actual vineyard and enlisted the help of those living in the Eastern Cross and even a few remote growers in the Southern Cross. The prognosis wasn't good. It would likely be several years before the vineyard returned to what it once was if ever, leaving her with nothing. She was going to need to find a new way to support herself, and soon. But this wasn't what Cepheus was thinking about at that moment.

"I am quite aware of that," Moksha finally muttered with regards to Cepheus's comment about his memory. She let out a sigh as she gingerly touched a burnt rossenberry branch and fought back a tear. *Some warrior*

I turned out to be, she thought to herself. *Crying over a few dead plants as if they were my children.*

Moksha continued to walk the rows of vines, most blackened by fire and still smelling of smoke even months later, or maybe that was just her imagination. "Did I ever tell you how it was that I escaped my family?" Cepheus lurked over her shoulder.

Moksha paused. "No," she answered cautiously. "How?" Did he know? She wondered to herself.

"A young soldier smuggled me out of the underground prisons and set me on course for Erde by hijacking one of the Royal's pilot vessels."

"Is that so?" Moksha answered with a calmness that she didn't feel. The sleeve of her blouse caught on a branch, and she paused to unhook it with one hand. Cepheus reached out and carefully unwound the threads for her, gently touching her arm as he freed her from the branch. Moksha stood there, looking up at him, curiously. He pulled his hands back once she was free, but her gaze was constant.

"You were younger then, but your voice…" He paused.

"What about my voice?" she demanded as if there were something wrong with it.

"You don't forget the voice of the person who saved your life," he touched the side of her face with several fingers, carefully. "I may have pushed that memory back for a time, but I know it was you."

"Well," she brought her hand to cover his. "You gave me shelter when I was a fugitive, so I'd say we're even."

A long silence ensued. "I'm not very good at this," Cepheus explained.

"You're doing just fine," Moksha smiled.

Cepheus cleared his throat. "There has been no one since Petrichor," he felt a lurch in his stomach as if he were somehow being unfaithful to his late wife.

"I understand," Moksha comforted. "And I'm not in any hurry. Perhaps, when you're up to it, a day trip to some of the natural waterfalls in the Southern Cross? I promise I'll leave my staff and my sword behind," she laughed.

Cepheus thought a moment and smiled back, his saw-like teeth seeming almost normal for a change. "I've never actually been to the falls," he answered quietly, thinking. "Maybe, just this once..."

They continued ceremoniously walking through the fields, one row at a time. Cepheus reached out and touched a burnt berry, and suddenly he had a flash of Petrichor's vineyard, and then the wine at Lucene's cottage during their reunion dinner. His face lit up.

"What is it? Are you okay?" Moksha was concerned he was about to have an episode.

"I have a crazy idea," Cepheus answered.

"You? You seem far too practical to have crazy ideas."

"Tanager saved several bottles of wine that Petrichor and I had gifted him over the years—pomegranate, blackberry, rossenberry, you name it."

"Yes?"

"After Petrichor's death, a few growers tried to recreate the depth and complexity but couldn't. I wonder..."

"What?" Moksha was not the impatient sort, but curiosity was getting the better of her.

"I still own my land," Cepheus confessed. "I just haven't tended to it since..." Moksha touched his shoulder in understanding. He paused for a moment before continuing. "What if we took the DNA from a few sample bottles of wine like we do to create our clean meats?"

"Yes?" Moksha's eyes grew excited.

"We could recreate her exact grapes and grow it on the exact land she did. Her crops always succeeded even in times of great drought when others did not. And," he finished, "she loved them so much they grew in half the time. Just like you, she tended to those vines as if they were members of the family."

"What are you saying?" Moksha couldn't believe what she was hearing.

"I'm saying that while your land is recovering, you should continue making your wine on mine. It wouldn't take years, maybe only months."

It took Far several months to find his way back to the Military Training Grounds. After which, he immediately sought out Fredo to ask for a meeting with Sovereign Hamish. Normally, Fredo would have been outraged at the audacity of the request. But then, nothing was as it once was anymore. And so, he forwarded the request.

"What is it you are trying to tell me, you weak little man?" Hamish asked Far. While Far was technically taller than Hamish, he hunched his shoulders in such a way that he appeared more like a withered and shrunken vine in front of his new master.

"What I'm saying," Far answered in a whisper, as if it hurt him to speak, "is that after I escaped, I tried to return and find the demon, Jasper Set, but he was gone. I've spent months looking for him."

"Really," Hamish was unconvinced. "With your sense of direction, I thought you just kept getting lost on your return."

"Well, that was part of it," Far confessed. "But I'm telling you, the demon is gone."

Hamish thought of this for a moment, wondering what this would mean for their agreement. Would he then still be under the reign of his superiors? Would the Null still threaten to roll over his world? And, most important to him at present, would Earth ever be his to reside on and rule over? He took none of this lightly as, according to his best estimation, his planet only had a few years left before it became completely uninhabitable. At least with Earth, he stood a chance at reversing the damage.

Maybe a little bit of Jasper Set had rubbed off on Far after all because the young man was suddenly struck by an idea. "You are forgetting something very important, my Sovereign."

"And what is that?" Hamish spat impatiently, rubbing his forehead tiredly.

"I am a prophet," Far reminded him. "Even your Royal army couldn't beat that out of me."

"What are you saying?" Hamish was suddenly intrigued.

"What I'm saying is that I see you in a position of great power."

"What's that supposed to mean?" Hamish waved a hand through the air, gesturing wildly. "I'm already in a position of great power."

Far took a chance. "This?" He motioned around the room, matching Hamish's movements. "This is not power."

"Careful," Fredo stood guard at his station in front of the door to Hamish's private chambers, gritting his teeth.

"Whatever do you mean?" Hamish was in the young man's face now. Far could smell the remnants of leftover rodent from Hamish's earlier dinner.

"I see you ruling the entire Royal clan across the galaxy," and then he added for emphasis, "with the Child at your side."

Hamish's eyes lit up. *But is he telling the truth,* he asked himself.

"Is that so?"

"It is so."

"Then answer me this," Hamish challenged, "what is its name."

Far had his Sovereign exactly where he wanted him. You didn't need to be a prophet to figure that one out. Far leaned over and whispered into Hamish's ear, Fredo lurching forward as if to protect Hamish. Hamish waved Fredo away as his eyes grew wide.

"How do you recommend that we proceed, Prophet Far?"

Fredo was taken aback. Was this frail nothing of a man suddenly replacing him at his Sovereign's side? He remembered the last time that this happened to him, and he felt betrayed, yet again.

"I predict that the demon Jasper Set will return. But in the meantime, perhaps we have had our sights on the wrong planet?"

"The wrong planet?" Hamish was incredulous.

"Yes, Earth may be much larger and with more resources, but—as you have noticed—their resources are running out. Why not, as they like to say on Earth, 'go for the low-hanging fruit.'"

Hamish nodded in understanding. "Erde?"

"Erde," Far nodded back.

"How? My superiors will wonder why I am disobeying orders if we attack Erde."

"Not if it's in self-defense," Far reasoned.

Hamish let out a chortle as if it had been choked back in his throat and finally broke free. "You think they will ever believe that the Peace-Keepers will attack first?"

"Give me time, Sovereign," Far smiled. His thoughts went to Roman. "Give me time."

CHAPTER 33
LAVENDER FIELDS
JUNE. FIVE MONTHS AFTER THE NEW ASSEMBLY.

Ivan arrived at their cottage at dusk. He looked down at the old pocket watch Fatima had gifted him while back on Earth at a time when they were merely neighbors and smiled. Not bad. Thanks to his upgrades, the SpeedCircuit was now transporting people from Achel to the Crosses in half the time, cutting his commute to only ten minutes each way by train, plus the ten-minute walk from the station home. He could further cut his travel time five minutes if he adopted a brisk jog, but he wasn't feeling that ambitious.

He felt the little box in his pocket to ensure he hadn't lost it en route. It hadn't moved from when he checked just two minutes prior.

Moksha and Fatima were out front planting purple salvia plants around the border of the home, the two having become fast friends and good neighbors over the course of only a few short months.

"Are ye sure ye should be doing that?" Ivan was concerned, watching a very round Fatima with a very round belly down on one knee with her hands in the soil. Moksha found Ivan's concern endearing but unnecessary. *Humans worry far too much,* she thought. Fatima leaned on her knee for support as she hoisted herself from the ground and slapped her hands together to shake the dirt off. She reached for a cup on the windowsill and took a sip. "Moksha," she praised. "I consider my pallet rather refined, and this iced dandelion tea is the best I've ever tasted."

Ivan's eyes widened, "And, are ye sure ye should be drinking *that*?" He'd never actually had dandelion tea, mind you. He was just concerned about Fatima consuming anything he deemed as not "normal" during her pregnancy.

Moksha, sensing a longer conversation coming, decided to take her leave. "Well, I'm just down the path if you need anything." Moksha took a moment to gather up a basket with a canteen of tea, some fruit bread and gardening gloves that she didn't think twice about throwing on top of the leftover bread. She turned to Ivan as she passed, "Nice to see you again, Ivan." Ivan still wasn't sure what to make of Moksha. She was difficult to read. Fatima had instantly befriended her, but that was Fatima's way. Cepheus had seemed to take a shine to her, and since he was the toughest critic of all, Ivan decided to give her a fair shake.

"Nice to see ye too, Mowk-shah." He still couldn't say her name without making it sound more like an "ouch" and an "ah" versus an "oh" and an "uh." She smirked, having long since given up on trying to correct him. Without further word, she made her way down the dirt path to her home, humming to herself.

Ivan turned his attention back to Fatima, who was now standing directly under his chin, waiting for a kiss. "Welcome home," she gave him a peck on the lips. She took her fingers and tried to smooth out the worry lines on his forehead. "Relax," she told him. "I've been following the doctor's orders. I'm supposed to keep up with physical activity as long as I don't get out of breath and keep the Talk-Sing ratio."

"What the hell is thah?" Ivan wanted to know. He didn't do well with change, and this planet has offered nothing but that since they arrived.

"C'mon inside," Fatima motioned, taking his hand as they walked toward the cottage. "I'm supposed to get my heart rate up enough where I can still talk but not sing, for just a few minutes, and then slow down. I can keep gardening as long as I can work and sing for prolonged periods of time."

"Aye," Ivan nodded. "What if yer someone who doesn't like singing?"

"Honey, I believe you're overthinking it." She paused to grab her beverage cup.

"And what does the doctor say about that?" He pointed to the cup. "I thought pregnant women weren't supposed to drink weird teas and wine and stuff."

"According to Wilah, dandelion tea has medicinal properties, like polyphenols, that are actually good for me. I'm okay having it twice a day as long as I space them out a few hours."

Ivan thought a moment, opening the door to the cottage and waiting for Fatima to enter first. She put the cup down in the kitchen sink. "Okay," he decided. "I was skeptical with the whole Talk-Sing thing, but once ye started throwing around fancy words like polyphenols, you had me."

Fatima moved toward Ivan, wrapping her arms around his waist, turning her hips to one side, so her belly wasn't in the way, and looked up at him, playfully. "I know the quickest way to your heart is when I use big fancy words like—" she released her grasp and backed away seductively, running to the other end of the kitchen table. "Para-virtualization."

"You vixen," he laughed, faking a move to the left to chase her around the table and then doubling back and catching her on the right. He planted a kiss on her lips. She pulled away slightly and whispered, "Axial compressor," and giggled so hard that she grabbed her belly to stop it from jiggling so much.

"So, uh," Ivan tugged nervously at his ear. "Unrelated to fancy words, I kinda wanted to talk to ye about something."

"Everything okay?" Fatima looked concerned.

"Everything's fine. More than fine even." He pulled a chair out for her. "I sorta have to ask ye something, and I think ye should sit down fer it."

Fatima shot him a quizzical look but sat, with some effort. Ivan made a mental note to re-design their kitchen chairs to be more ergonomically friendly.

He pulled out the chair next to her and set it across from her and sat down. He took her hands in his and looked into her eyes, letting out a deep sigh. "So, I know yer not as traditional as some, er, obviously," he eyed her large belly. Fatima stifled a laugh. "I mean, we're a bit older than some—"

"Not here," Fatima interrupted. "Some start families even into their seventies."

"Yeah, but that's here, and we're not from here. There's no guarantee we'll ever evolve to live as long as they. So, from our timeline, we're a little later to the game."

"Not too late," Fatima replied gently.

"No," Ivan agreed. "Not too late." He paused. "But we also went right from the love to the baby carriage things, which is okay if that's how you want it, but—" Ivan tripped over his words.

"Ivan?"

"Yes?"

"Are you trying to ask me to marry you?"

"Er…Maybe?"

"Maybe? Or, yes. They are two very distinct words," Fatima was adamant.

"I'm nah good at this sort of thing," Ivan complained. "You're the better communicator. Ye should ask me."

"Nah, ah," Fatima shook her head. "I'm not letting you off the hook that easily." She took time for a long, pregnant pause, laughing to herself at her mental joke.

"Ah, fine," Ivan released her hand and reached into his pocket. He pulled out a little box and opened it. Inside was an adjustable rose gold ring with a bright purple gemstone that had what appeared to be a vibrant orange flame sparkling from its center. Fatima was mesmerized by it. It was unlike anything she'd ever seen. "Fatima Fortunata, will you be my wife?" He held his breath.

"Of course, I will, silly." She giggled. "Did you really think I would set you up for failure?" She grabbed his face in her hands and kissed him. She turned her attention back to the ring. "This is so beautiful. What is it?"

"Ah," Ivan beamed proudly. "It's a combination of purple musgravite and orange clinohumite, they're pretty rare around here."

"I didn't think it was possible to have a hybrid of two gems within a single stone." She peered at it closely, watching the sparkles of light bounce off the kitchen walls.

"It isn't, at least not in nature so far," he explained. He tugged on his ear. "I made it fer ya in me new lab at the Makerspace."

Fatima was speechless, putting out her left hand so he could put it on her ring finger. Ivan slid it over her finger, and it auto-adjusted to the right size. "What the heck?" Fatima stared at it in awe.

"Yeah, it's adjustable. Figured that once you had the baby, your fingers might get smaller…not that they have to," he quickly explained.

"It's the most beautiful thing I've ever seen," she gushed.

"So far," he answered, touching her belly.

"So far," she nodded, covering her hand with his.

Two days later, Cepheus knocked on the Fortunata house's front door (Fatima insisted on naming their cottage, and since the name meant "fortunate," Ivan lobbied for her surname as the official name of their residence).

Ivan threw open the door, "Cepheus, buddy. Git in here." Ivan and Fatima hugged him as if they hadn't seen him in months, even though it had only been a few days. Fatima's zest for life and affectionate nature was slowly starting to rub off on Ivan, but only for certain people.

Cepheus was not evolving that quickly and lightly tapped them each on the back, gently. But he appreciated the sentiment.

"I come bearing good news," Cepheus explained.

"Please, sit," Ivan motioned toward the kitchen table.

Fatima moved toward the cupboard. "Can I offer you water, juice, or Moksha left us some of her dandelion tea? It's wonderful."

"I know it is; I just came from—" Cepheus stopped mid-sentence. Ivan's eyebrow shot up, but he said nothing. "I'm familiar with Moksha's teas." That didn't come out as intended, and the normally pale face of Cepheus suddenly gave off a pink glow. "Nothing for me, thank you," he finished in his deep voice.

"So, what is it, man?" Ivan took a seat. Fatima opted to stand. Her back was hurting, and she actually preferred it. She leaned into the kitchen counter for support.

"It took some time, but I was able to successfully sponsor you both as temporary residents of Erde," he paused, waiting for Ivan to pick up on its meaning, "with nearly all the benefits of citizenship."

Ivan's face lit up, hopefully, "Even the Monetary Exchange within the Universal Marketplace?"

"Exactly," Cepheus nodded.

Fatima was clueless, watching the men exchange knowing glances. All this time, Ivan had been worried. Earth had been inhospitable, but at least he'd made a decent fortune. He'd abandoned it all coming to Erde, his own funds having been temporarily frozen when Earth officials had him under investigation, leading to lots of hoop-jumping while attempting to transfer money at the Exchange. He had no clear idea how he and Fatima would support themselves, let alone a baby, if they weren't successful in petitioning to take up residency.

"What's going on? What am I missing?"

"It means that we are financially secure again, love," Ivan let out a sigh of relief. "Assuming," he continued, "that my funds aren't on lock-down again because the government has, on multiple occasions, accused me of treason."

"Ah, yes," Cepheus nodded knowingly. "That brings us to matter number two."

"What's that?" Ivan leaned an elbow on the table.

"You're technically under the protection of this preserve. We can further petition you as permanent citizens of Erde, if you are willing to renounce your Earth residency and claim Erde, and its surrounding planetary regions as your home."

"Wait," Fatima questioned. "So, we'd be giving up Earth, but we'd gain citizenship on Erde…and several other planets, too?"

"Yes," Cepheus answered. "Our domain currently consists of five planets, Erde being the youngest and smallest."

Fatima thought carefully. "Does this mean that I'd never be able to return to see my family again?" She felt a deep sorrow in her heart. She longed for her parents, siblings, and extended relatives to be able to be there for the birth of her first, and probably only, child.

"Not forever," Cepheus answered, with some doubt. "At least, I hope not. But Ivan is considered a threat. So, until his name is cleared by the current governing bodies, you won't be traveling to Earth in the foreseeable future."

Fatima's face dropped. She crinkled her face as she fought back tears. Ivan rushed to wrap his arm around her shoulder in comfort.

Cepheus suppressed the grieving in his own heart. He understood. "You don't have to decide right away, but it is the best option for your safety and security. If you are a citizen, then Erde cannot be forced to return Ivan to Earth by government order, and Earth will have no claims to his finances. He'll be able to reclaim his wealth.

"It would be a better life for us," Ivan reasoned, "if we had the money." For some time, he'd had this minute inkling of fear that Fatima may have only seen him as a good catch because of his financial security. When he'd lost that in their escape, he began to doubt himself, and his overall worth.

"Do you not know me at all?" Fatima chastised Ivan. "I don't give a rat's ass about the money. It's *you* that I'm worried about. So, if becoming citizens means you'll be safe, then that's what we'll have to do!" Ivan felt a little tug in his heart and a sense of something. *What was it? Relief?*

"Cepheus," Ivan asked, "Does Fatima have to renounce citizenship as well, seeing as she's done nothing wrong? Won't it hurt her chances of reconnecting with her family?"

"As of right now," Cepheus explained. "She considered an accomplice. So, she is in as much danger as you. It may not matter in a few years, but in dealing with the situation in front of us, the PDL believes that this is your best option."

Fatima and Ivan exchanged glances. "Then," Fatima answered, "that's what we need to do."

Cepheus reached into his jacket and pulled out a rolled document. "Here is more information. You can access the PDL database at TARA to fill out the necessary documentation. I've printed out the guidelines for you." Cepheus laid it out on the table. Ivan was about to laugh and tell Cepheus about the remote computer he had stashed in the basement and that he could tap into the PDL database for that information anytime he wanted, but then he figured it wasn't the best idea, seeing as he was still a fugitive from another planet. It might, he reasoned, hurt his chances of being made a citizen.

"Thank ye, Cepheus. We'll look it over."

"We're about to have dinner. Would you care to join us?" Fatima offered.

"You are very kind," Cepheus answered. "But I already—" The pink glow returned. Fatima sucked in a laugh and pursed her lips. "But I have to get back to Achel on other business matters." Cepheus was about to stand.

"Er," Ivan began. "Do ye have jest a minute more fer us?"

"Of course," Cepheus settled back into his chair, his long legs stretched out in front of him. Ivan made a mental note to, in addition to making the chairs ergonomically more sound, making them adjustable to accommodate varied heights as well.

"We were jest wondering—" Ivan eyed Fatima. She nodded for him to continue. "Not sure how ye feel about this, but ye have been a friend for a long time and have been so helpful to us. We were thinking that, with yer permission, of course, we could name our baby after yer baby."

Cepheus was confused. "My baby?"

"What he means to say," Fatima put a hand on Ivan's shoulder, "is that we just learned that our baby is going to be a girl," she let out a snort. "One of Dr. Wilah's nursing students accidentally let it slip."

"So much fer surprises," Ivan laughed.

"Anyway," Fatima continued. "We were hoping we might name her after your daughter—"

"Tallulah," Ivan finished. He sat at the ready, watching for any signs of Cepheus retreating into himself for an episode. Cepheus sat for a moment, deep in thought.

"No," Cepheus shook his head, to Ivan and Fatima's disappointment.

"Okay, man," Ivan acknowledged. "We understand."

"No," Cepheus repeated. "I mean, yes." The couple was understandably confused. "What I mean to say is," Cepheus paused to frame his words. "I would be honored if you would name your baby after Petrichor and my daughter, Tallulah. But," he cautioned, "you have to change the spelling of the name."

"Why?" Fatima and Ivan asked in unison.

"It's a custom," Cepheus answered. "If a child grows and leads a good life, then you honor them by naming another after them. But, if a child has a bad life, such as—" he welled up in tears. He didn't need to explain. *Such as being killed in childhood.* "If," he recovered, "the child fell on misfortune, then you don't want to pass on that misfortune. In this case, you honor them by naming a new child after them but changing the spelling."

"Like, taking one of the "l"s out of her name, for example." Fatima reasoned.

"Exactly," Cepheus agreed. "My Tallulah had three "l"s in her name. If you took out an "l" or even an "h," that would be acceptable."

"I think we can manage that," Ivan reached his hand up and touched Fatima's hand, which was still resting on his shoulder.

Cepheus's eyes turned bloodshot as he fought back tears.

"I'm not sure what to do here," Fatima's voice stammered. "May we hug you?" Cepheus nodded, and the couple wrapped their arms around him in a tight embrace.

"I am honored," Cepheus finally answered. "As are the spirits of Petrichor and little Tallulah."

"And, if we have any more kids—" Fatima socked Ivan in the arm and shot him a don't even go there look. After he thought it through, he realized she was right; it would have been inappropriate. He was going to say that if they had two more kids, boys, in particular, he would also name them after Cepheus's lost family. Ivan meant to be respectful but realized that this was one of those social oddities where he threatened to say the wrong thing. Fortunately, he now had Fatima to cover for him.

"We can't wait to introduce you to Talula, T-a-l-u-l-a, when she arrives," Fatima smiled. Cepheus looked at Fatima as if seeing her for the first time. His eyes floated back and forth between the two, and for the first time, he realized something. Like Tanager and Lucene, they were now a part of his family.

CHAPTER 34
HOME
JULY. SIX MONTHS AFTER THE NEW ASSEMBLY.

"Go on ahead of me," Tanager advised Lucene as he held a small satchel of groceries in each arm. Lucene laughed over her shoulder as she opened the door.

"Kinda like when we first met," she smiled.

"Sorry, I don't have a window that would be reasonable to climb through," he joked, remembering her aversion to red doors, so much so that she'd sooner climb through an open window versus crossing the door's threshold.

"Very funny—" The words caught in her throat as she stepped inside. Lucene scanned the rectangular-shaped room curiously as Tanager followed behind her, setting the two bags on the kitchen counter to the left of the door, then kicking it closed with his foot.

"It looks like home…I mean, not exactly like Fatima's house, but very…"

"Suburban Earth-like?" Tanager finished. "That one was rather difficult to explain to the designer when I bought this place.

Lucene wandered through the kitchen, unable to find the words. In front of her were labradorite countertops wrapped in a rectangular shape and kitchen appliances that appeared to resemble something found in an ancient department store catalog from several decades ago aligning the wall...a stove, a dishwasher, a refrigerator...even an old-fashioned microwave. Unique to this kitchen, however, were herbs hanging from hydroponic containers above the counter.

"They look old...the appliances, I mean. It was the best they could come up with to look the part but still be functional. If you open the oven, you'll see that it's much more advanced than at first glance." Tanager quickly unpacked the food, stuffing things haphazardly into the refrigerator before slamming it shut. It didn't close right the first time. Agitated, he smacked the door a second time.

Lucene noticed this, curiously, as Tanager was typically pretty meticulous about keeping items organized. He wasn't the type to toss things into a refrigerator absentmindedly. She pushed the thought away, more interested in seeing the rest of his high-home.

Lucene moved on to the dining area where a long wooden table and chairs sat lengthwise along a wall-to-wall panel of sliding glass doors, giving the most spectacular view of the cityscape at sunset.

"It's breathtaking," she was awestruck.

"Yes, well—" Tanager tugged behind his ear nervously. "The designer was skeptical when I told him I wanted the apartment to have a suburban cottage feel, and he said, 'with this view...'" Tanager imitated the rough voice of the designer. "'Listen,'" he continued gruffly, "'I can give you urban Earth, more or less, but *Suburban* Earth in an *Urban* Achelian setting? That's a big ask.'"

"Those sound like challenging Earth colloquialisms to me," Lucene smiled.

"Yes, he's a gentleman I hired who currently lives on one of the preserves."

Lucene nodded in approval. "But he did a good job."

"I thought so..."

By then, Lucene had made her way to the sunken living room with water running down the walls, flowing into a small stream that flowed beneath them, visible through the glass tile.

"That," Tanager wrinkled his forehead, remembering Cepheus's old house, "had a slightly different inspiration."

"I see," Lucene hugged herself. "I assume the bedroom is through there," she pointed to an opening to one side of the living room.

"Ah, yes. Two bedrooms and bathrooms, actually, one that way," he pointed past the kitchen, "and the other behind this wall." He motioned to the living room. "There's also what you would refer to as a laundry room next to the bathroom and—"

"Where it was in Fatima's old house!"

"More or less. It was one of the only houses I got to actually visit while I was on Earth, and Ivan's looked more like an extension of his garage, so I knew that wouldn't work. As I said, I couldn't get it exactly right, so it's more of a hybrid."

"It's amazing, but...why?" Lucene stood by the window, watching as lights from varying hi-rise buildings began to light up in a soft multicolored glow that somehow didn't detract from the stars above. She folded her arms, taking it all in, including the view of the Eiffel Tower in the distance.

"Well," Tanager stood beside her, at first trying to lean casually on the table. That felt too conspicuous, so he adopted her crossed arms position and stood next to her, shoulder-to-shoulder. He could feel the intense buzzing of energy between them and was hoping she could figure it out without him explaining it.

"But I want you to say it," Lucene whispered.

"Hey," Tanager joked. "Stay out of my head."

"That's just it," Lucene responded quietly. "I'm not in your head. I made some assumptions based on observation."

"Really?"

"Don't act so surprised," she answered flatly. "A gal can learn."

"But, the energy," he was confused.

"Chemistry?" Lucene offered. It was disconcerting, not being sure how he felt and what he thought. What she knew of him was no longer based on some kind of other-worldly superpower; but time learning how to understand one another, what each micro expression meant and how to define a slight shift in vocal tone. "You still haven't answered my question. Why did you design your high-home in this very specific way?"

Tanager cleared his throat before making a motion in the air so that the lights in the room came on, adjusting to a dim glow. "It's getting dark, so..." He was avoiding the question.

"I see—" Lucene looked at him, then the floor, then briefly for someplace to retreat in fear. But, she discovered, she didn't really want to retreat. Instead, she moved around the table and toward the kitchen. "Perhaps I can open some wine for us?" She started rifling through the cabinets, having no idea where anything might actually be.

"I did it with you in mind, Lucene," Tanager finally blurted out. "Perhaps misguided, but I somehow thought that maybe someday…you might want to live here…with…me."

Lucene touched the countertop lightly with her fingers. "You know I can't cook worth a damn, right?" She laughed nervously.

"Yes, I am well aware," he blushed. "That's why the kitchen only looks Earth-like but is functional so that *I* can actually use it." He joined her in the kitchen, reaching under the counter for a rossenberry sparkling port he'd been saving from a neighboring town, in the hopes he'd eventually have a reason to open it. After all, as far as he knew, it was a beverage unique to Erde. He set the bottle down when he noticed Lucene wringing her fingers and fidgeting in place, gazing at the floor.

"I'm sorry," he took her by the shoulders and tried to meet her gaze. "I'm not suggesting any of this needs to happen. It was an impulsive gesture, I understand."

After a pause that seemed like an eternity, Lucene answered, "You know, it's not that I'm opposed to learning how to cook," she glanced up at him, hopefully. "Though, truth be told, I'd do much better at repairing that glitchy light." She pointed up at one of the hanging tear-drop shaped bulbs that hung from the ceiling. Technology, she had come to learn, was not nearly as terrifying as she once thought.

"Then, I promise to leave all electrical work to you," he grinned sheepishly and took a step toward her.

Lucene leaned back slightly, only to discover the high bar-top counter at her back. There was nowhere else for her to go.

"I feel it my duty to warn you that unless you tell me not to, I'm going to kiss you right now."

"Well," she answered with more bravado than she actually felt. "It's about damn time."

Tanager touched one hand to the side of her face, wrapping it around her ear and behind her head. With his other hand, he circled her waist and pulled her toward him. Lucene instinctively wrapped her arms around him as he leaned forward to kiss her, vaguely noticing that the patterns on her arm were glowing again.

Truth be told, neither could be completely sure exactly when the kiss began, as the energy between them was so intense that it was as if both were swallowed by a burst of sunlight, and now they floated in a continuous pool of white light flowing in all directions.

CHAPTER 35
HYSECHIA AND MARZIPAN
NOW.

Something caught the corner of Marzipan's eye from his habitat. He unrolled from a leaf he had been sleeping on with a start. There it was again, outside the door of Mati's bedroom. He could make out a low growl and a long tail. Marzipan tried to call for his caretaker but then remembered he had taken the night off to visit his family in the Eastern Cross and wouldn't be back until morning.

"Looking for me?" the tiger-like figure pressed her face up to Marzipan's case. The firefly-like boy backed up, tripping over a small pebble and landing backward into the small pond in his habitat.

"What are you?" Marzipan asked in terror. Its face was white and black striped with flecks of yellow in it, but it had a distinctly human-like mouth and eyes.

"You mean, you don't know?" The cat's paws had digits on the thumb and forefinger that allowed it to easily lift the lid on the habitat and clasp the firefly's delicate wings, lifting him out of his home. "Look again." It pulled Marzipan in so that the little insect actually swayed back and forth with the tiger's breath.

Suddenly, Marzipan's eyes grew wide. "Tabby?" It was the small house cat that had been in quarantine in the next habitat over. "But how—"

Tabby let out a laugh. "Actually, it's Hysechia," she corrected. "Tabby is such an overused name for a cat, don't you think?"

"Uh, I guess so?"

"But how did you get so...big?"

Hysechia bared her teeth in an ominous grin. "A high-protein diet," she answered, "which includes vitamins and minerals."

"Oh," Marzipan was unconvinced. "That makes sense."

"From snacking on little fireflies." Marzipan froze. Hysechia was just about to drop Marzipan in her mouth when she heard a voice.

"Put him down," Isabella commanded from the doorway.

"Well, well, well, what a surprise," Hysechia grinned. "Or what?"

"Or you'll have to answer to me," Isabella held her stance. Hysechia considered this for a moment and dropped Marzipan back into the pond with a splash. He went under water for a moment but quickly floated to the surface, choking out water and wiping it off of his wings.

The feline began pacing around Isabella, who was now fully in the room. There wasn't much space, and Isabella could feel the tail of the cat as it repeatedly circled her.

"Come to clean up your mess, bruja?" Hysechia growled.

"I am no witch," Isabella responded indignantly.

"Oh, forgive me," Hysechia purred as if she found this funny. "That's right. You're a Shaman...same difference."

"They are nothing alike," Isabella was annoyed in the same way that Odessa became irritated when she was confused for a mermaid. It wasn't that she had anything against the occult. She practiced it for many centuries. Isabella just hated labels and being confined to them. "And I claim no faith whatsoever."

"Really?" Hysechia was surprised. "You who have run religious institutions all over Earth have no allegiance?"

"My allegiance is to support those in need. That is all."

"Well, if you hadn't noticed, I am in *need* of a snack," Hysechia gestured toward Marzipan's habitat.

"How did you escape your form?" Isabella demanded.

Hysechia began her guttural laugh, pausing for a moment to lick her paw and preen the side of her ear. Finally, she answered, "I have you to thank for that."

"What are you talking about?"

"The portal, bruja." Isabella's eyes grew wide. "Aha," Hysechia continued. "Now, you get it. When you sent Jasper Set in, you let other spirits out and voila! I had the resources to remove the binds that kept me in the form of a simple house cat."

"What other spirits? I sent him to another dimension. How can this be?"

"No, bruja. You didn't." Hysechia found the whole thing entirely amusing. "Jasper Set isn't in another dimension. He's simply *between the layers*." For the first time in a long time, Isabella was afraid. Her eyes grew wide. "I see that you understand," the feline continued. "When you stuffed him in the middle world, you may have temporarily contained him, but he will get out, just like the other spirits you set free. And when he does, he's going to be sooooo cross with you! Good going, bruja."

The news of her mistake sank in deeply. Jasper Set was still here, between the layers. And, perhaps even more importantly. *What else was there? What had she let out?*

Stay tuned for *The Data Collectors Book Three, Between the Layers,* for the conclusion of this trilogy.

BETWEEN THE LAYERS

THE DATA COLLECTORS BOOK THREE

SECTION ONE

"What I want is revenge. I'd like to see you trapped between the layers where you left me for a hundred years. Do you know what it's like to constantly present myself to the world as a simple domestic cat, lifetime after lifetime, all the while ignorant beings thinking that I was the primitive one, petting me and giving me kibble, calling me stupid names like Tabby, Fluff and Whiskers?"

DRAMATIS PERSONAE

Amy: Erde-born female (Section 1), small-framed, red hair and green eyes.

Roman Aurelius: Human male (Section 0); wavy black hair, green eyes, tall and slender.

The Baby: Born of Sabrina and Fredo (Section 3), now adopted by Hamish.

Bagheera: Male cat (Section 0), black short hair with yellow eyes, very handsome.

Cepheus Baruch: Royal male (Section 1, Section 3), stringy gray hair, yellow eyes; tall and lanky, shapeshifter (lizard/human).

Petrichor Baruch: Erde-born female (Section 1), the late wife of Cepheus, long auburn hair, pale blue eyes.

Tanager Blackletter: Erde-born male (Section 1), curly blonde hair, brown eyes, average height and weight.

Clusaladek: Erde-Born male (Section 1), tall and thin, blonde hair, pale blue-gray eyes.

Constable Melokuhle: Erde-born male (Section 1), bulky with dark skin, curly black hair and brown eyes.

Commander Royce: Erde-born female (Section 1), walnut and gray hair, coal eyes, small and athletic frame with deep wrinkles.

Bryce Cushing: Human male (Section 0), brown hair, blue eyes, medium height and build.

Dallen: Vitruvian male (Section 2), non-shapeshifter, gold hair and blue eyes, tall with strong build.

Far: Macar-born male (Unsectioned by the IPP), blonde hair and green eyes, pale and thin.

Dr. Archibald Ennis: Human male (Section 0), bald, brown eyes, tall and thin.

Fatima Fortunata: Human female (Section 0), purple hair, gray eyes, short and Rubenesque.

Fredo: Lesser Royal male (Section 3), red body and black eyes, large and thick, salamander-like with no noticeable shapeshifting abilities.

Hamish: Royal male (Section 3), brown hair and gold eyes, short and slightly overweight, shapeshifter (lizard / human-like).

Hysechia: Unknown origin, female (Section 1), striped black and white tiger with golden eyes, human-like features.

Ivan (the Tinkerer): Human male (Section 0), red hair and green eyes, medium height and stocky.

Lucene (Lucy) Jones: Earth-born female (Section 0), blonde or brown hair, hazel eyes, average height and weight, toned form.

Kiki: Vitruvian (Section 2), shapeshifter (varied gender, prefers female form), aardvark-like nose and blue coloring.

Mallory: Erde-born male (Section 1), heavyset, dark hair with multi-colored eyes.

Mateo: Unknown origin (Section 1), short and heavy, little hair, has a long tail.

Marzipan: Unknown origin, male (Section 1), firefly and ladybug-like features, multicolored with wings.

Moksha: Royal (Section 3) assassin, black hair, yellow eyes, petite but athletic build.

Morphinae: Vitruvian (Section 2), shapeshifter (gender, species, coloring), Balance-Keeper, often prefers doll-like and butterfly-like forms.

Neroni: Erde-born female (Section 1), olive complexion, slightly heavyset, red-green hair and brown eyes.

Not Christopher: Unknown origin, male, chestnut wavy hair, brown eyes, youthful.

Odessa: Vitruvian (Section 2), shapeshifter (gender, species, coloring), prefers mermaid-like form the most.

Olly: Between-the-layers troll; male, small with large hands and feet.

Pelimar: Erie-born male (Section 1), pale skin with bright red hair and purposefully goth-like features.

Renenet: Unknown origin, female (Section 5), red/brown fur and fire agate eyes, tall and broad, bulky stature, shapeshifter (lion/hu- man-like).

Sabrina: Royal woman (Section 3), black hair and yellow eyes, tall with average shape, shapeshifter (lizard/human-like form).

Jasper Set: Demon male (Section 4), red eyes, bald, thin legs and barrel-like body, small wings.

Reverend Isabella Simone: Female (Section 0), spiritual advisor, white hair, violet eyes, tall and thin.

Wilah: Erde-born female doctor (Section 1), tiny and thin, translucent glow.

Xeni: Unknown origin (Section 1), pink eyes, heart-shaped face, blue-black hair.

LOCALES / SPECIAL GROUPS

Achel: Main province on Erde.

The Assembly: Intergalactic gathering for the Intergalactic Peace Project (IPP).

Balance-Keepers: Special interest group in Section 2, Vitruvians. Will intervene to ensure all forces remain in balance.

Between the Layers: Alternate realms of reality on this plane of existence.

Data Collectors: Specialized team from Section 1, collecting data on Earth to save species.

The Crosses: Preservation sites and residential homes on Erde comprised of four quadrants.

The Elders: Erde's version of Gods. Wise souls who guide the leaders of Erde and their ancestors.

Erde: Planet in Section 1 known for setting up preserves to rescue and protect humans.

Erdelings: Species from the Erde planet in Section 1.

Global Environmental Agency (GEA): Earth organization for environmental concerns.

Intergalactic Peace Project (IPP): Formed to create and maintain peace among intergalactic species.

International Registry of Alien Residency (IRAR): Created by the United Commonwealth (UC) to record and track aliens living on Earth.

The Null: Crustacean-like species in Section 4 trying to destroy the universe in order to serve the mighty Segue.

Peace-Keepers: Nickname given to all inhabitants of Section 2, in particular, those living on Erde.

Planetary Defense League (PDL): Government entity on Erde for protection.

Royals: Nickname given to all inhabitants of Section 3, no specific planet-base, nomads.

Section 0: Earth and planets from common and neighboring galaxies.

Section 1: Erde and planets from common and neighboring galaxies.

Section 2: Vitruvia and planets from common and neighboring galaxies.

Section 3: Royal landscape and planets from common and neighboring galaxies. Galaxy boundaries change regularly.

Section 4: Home of the Null. Limited communication with neighboring species, located in a section of the universe with multiple black holes.

Section 5: Silva and Trappist solar system as well as planets from common and nearby galaxies.

Singulari: The Null people in Section 4. They bow to their God, Segue and refer to themselves as Singulari (which represents their religion).

Terrestrial Academy of Research and Awareness (TARA): A major university in Achel where the Data Collectors are trained.

United Commonwealth (UC): Earth subdivision of the IPP to keep and maintain peace.

Universal Marketplace: A place where money and goods are exchanged.

Vitruvia: Planet in Section 2 known for its renegade band of Balance-Keepers.

Vitruvians: Species from the Vitruvia planet in Section 2.

PRELUDE: THE CURRENT STATE OF ERDE

The threat from the Royals has worsened after Sovereign Hamish strikes a deal with the demon, Jasper Set, sending the Null to do what they do best—destroy worlds in the name of their god, Segue. To make matters worse, Erdelings have lost the support of the Vitruvians and all Sections within the Intergalactic Peace Project (IPP), including Earth, the very reason they are now in danger.

Meanwhile, after the Data Collectors intervened to help support Tanager and Lucene overcome Jasper Set, the Data Collectors appeared to have lost all of their genetically enhanced powers. Under orders from Commander Royce, Cepheus and Tanager have now been instructed to redistribute the students from the Data Collector training program to other areas of study and create new programming that everyone is less-than-enthusiastic about.

The Terrestrial Academy of Research and Awareness (TARA) and its Makerspace is now being converted to accommodate warcraft, combat training, psychological warfare, espionage, and interrogation and has abandoned its efforts to save Earth from environmental destruction and hostile takeover.

This means that after 100 years of peace, Erde must prepare for war for the first time in over a century. The only problem is, they don't know how. Because they are small in number, they are forced to learn and become experts in things they know nothing about and fast. They don't realize quite how much the odds are stacked against them.

To save Lucene from Jasper Set, Reverend Isabella was forced to open a portal that she thought was to another dimension. Unfortunately, what she actually did was to create a tear in the fabric of reality, whereby beings from other Shamanic realms can come and go in and out of their reality, and not all of them are peaceful.

CHAPTER 1
CEPHEUS AND PETRICHOR
THREE WEEKS BEFORE THE END.

"It's unbearable being close enough to touch you, but not being able to." Tears streamed down Cepheus's face as he stood in the living room of his cottage wearing a black pajama set and slippers on his feet—the one's that Moksha bought for him.

"I know, my love," Petrichor answered. Her ghost-like appearance stood before him wearing a gossamer red sundress with strawberries on it, her favorite. There was a yellow daisy in her hair. "Perhaps I shouldn't have come?"

"Of course, you should have," Cepheus moved toward her before remembering that it would do no good. He couldn't hug her fiercely. All he could do was...talk. "You're my wife, and I love you."

Since Reverend Isabella had accidentally ripped a tear between the layers of reality, creatures such as the feline, Hysechia, were released into this plane in their true forms, while others—such as the demon, Jasper Set—were sucked in. Those with unfinished business seemed to be trapped, too. Or, in the case of Petrichor, had chosen to stay and look after those left behind until they were ready to move on. But until the portal was opened, she couldn't seem to break through the barrier in order to get through to Cepheus aside from the occasional dream. She had even had thoughts of using the Data Collectors' intuitive skills to relay messages for her. Still, since Cepheus never specifically asked for this from any of the students, she decided against it—respecting their free will. Without permission, it would be a form of psychic attack and Petrichor was far too kind to do something like that. But when the doorway opened, Cepheus's late wife leaped at the opportunity.

"I don't know how long we'll have the opportunity to keep meeting like this," Petrichor explained, "but I have exciting news." She smiled.

"What is it?" Cepheus brightened a little. "Is it about the children?"

"Two of them, yes." Petrichor reached a hand out. She, too, longed to embrace her husband but could not. "It seems that Tallulah and Cephi have returned."

"You mean—reincarnated?"

"In a manner of speaking, yes," she smiled. "I don't know where they've gone, just that they've moved on."

"And Seth?"

"Not yet," she answered. "But don't worry. Time is different here. And, if I understand the process correctly, he may choose not to return."

"What process? I don't understand." Cepheus was confused.

"I haven't worked it out entirely because—" Petrichor confessed but caught herself. She might have very well worked it out entirely had she not been overseeing Cepheus for the past few decades. "Well, from what I can tell, a soul can return to live again or stay on the higher realms in some other form. Others voluntarily come back as helping spirits."

"Is that what you are, my dear Petrichor?" Cepheus smiled weakly. "You have the kindest heart of anyone I know. That seems like something you would do."

"Not exactly, my love." She smiled lovingly at her husband. "It is true that I have always been here looking out for you. I just haven't exactly...moved on."

"Why not?" Cepheus was concerned. "Are you trapped?"

"No," Petrichor answered. "I don't think so. I just feel as if I'm in a sort of in limbo. I can't move on...until you do."

Cepheus's face contorted in anguish. He couldn't have possibly known how his actions, or lack of them, could have affected his late wife, but that didn't stop the jab of guilt he was now feeling in his heart.

"How am I to ever truly move on from you?" he sobbed softly. "You are the love of my life."

"And you are mine. Yet, I'm asking you to be open to loving again—truly loving again." She eyed him with a knowing gaze. "I'm not asking you to stop loving me, but your heart is so wide, it has room for another."

"If I move forward then, will you be free from limbo?"

"I believe so, my love. But I'm not asking for me."

Cepheus gazed at his wife from head to toe as if memorizing every bit of her features—as he'd done the three other times she'd visited since the tear in the fabric of space—as if it would once again be the last time.

"Cephi," Petrichor called softly. "You are not being unfaithful to my memory. And I am not so selfish as to lay claim to you for all eternity. What I want most for you, my love, is to be happy. That's all I've ever wanted for you." With that, Petrichor's image began to float in and out before disappearing—as she had done so many times before.

He wiped his eyes with the palms of his hands.

"Everything okay out here?" Moksha called softly from the bedroom door, standing there in a long white nightgown that flowed around her ankles. "I thought I heard you talking to someone."

"I'm sorry, Moksha," Cepheus replied. "I had a fitful dream and was working it out by talking to myself again. Give me a moment and I'll come back to bed."

Moksha nodded and retreated into the bedroom, giving him the space she knew he needed. She realized that he felt guilty about their relationship, as if he were somehow being unfaithful to his late wife. Moksha, while sympathetic, had no idea how to help him.

Cepheus looked around the empty living room before returning to the bedroom. He didn't want to lie to Moksha. But what could he tell her? After all, how do you tell your current partner that you were having conversations with your dead wife?

CHAPTER 2
THE ROLL OVER
THREE WEEKS BEFORE THE END.

Jasper Set's disappearance unnerved Hamish. He walked the Royal training grounds in Section 3, watching the military regiments with growing disinterest. They always seemed to be training, he mused, but they hadn't actually fought a healthy battle in years. Somehow, just knowing of their existence had been enough of a threat. He took a vague interest in the newly established Poison Patrol, one of Far's more sadistic ideas, and something of which he thought was an odd suggestion…coming from a monk.

"Becoming a great leader," Far reasoned, "means thinking of the survival of your species as a whole. Sometimes, sacrifices have to be made."

Hamish agreed, though he did question why the poisons had to come with cruel side effects (such as gut-wrenching pain or someone's tongue swelling so much that they could no longer breathe). As a Royal who had never been known for mercy, it struck him as odd that his chief advisor had even less compassion than he did.

"I'm only thinking of you, my Sovereign," Far smiled. "And the Great Gods will reward all who have fallen in the afterlife—more so those who have suffered."

Well, I suppose that makes sense, Hamish conceded. But somehow, even he couldn't bring himself to believe this. *There has to be a better way,* he thought, pausing to witness a young soldier watering a small cyrtostachys renda palm that was drying out. He smiled to himself. *Can things be different?* He wondered.

"My Sovereign," Fredo interrupted his thoughts, calling from the palace steps. "I have news. Permission to approach?"

"Granted," Hamish motioned tiredly. While Fredo had turned into an overgrown lapdog, the one thing he never questioned was his loyalty. Granted, Fredo had had an affair with his wife, Sabrina, but that wasn't exactly disloyal as much as it was poor impulse control. And frankly, him sleeping with Sabrina meant that Hamish hardly ever had to. Perhaps that's why he had turned a blind eye to it for all those years, even though a part of him secretly knew.

"It's the Null, my Sovereign," Fredo appeared breathless from the exertion of running.

"What about the Null?" Hamish was concerned.

"It seems that the deal you made with Jasper Set..." he began, loudly, before Hamish shot him a look and motioned for him to keep his voice down. Fredo dropped his tone into a low whisper. "It seems that the demon has kept his word."

"How so? Jasper Set hasn't been seen in months."

"No, my Sovereign. And yet..."

"Yes?"

"The Null people have rolled over nearly all of the Royal hubs across the galaxy. We're the only of our kind left, it would seem."

As they spoke, a hush fell over the training grounds. All training drills came to a halt as they gazed into the distance.

Over the red horizon, a wave of crustacean-like creatures, with their hissing and popping, rolled past them like an ocean during stormy weather. There was nothing that could be done, despite their training, and they knew it. And so, they watched with a combination of awe and terror. Was this the day that all Royals would die?

Instinctively, Fredo bolted toward the palace steps, bounding them two at a time. He was heading for the nursery to check on the baby. Hamish didn't notice. His eyes were transfixed on the Null.

As quickly as they had arrived, the noisy wave rushed past their planet, as if the Null were blind and didn't even know that the planet existed. Sometime later, the noise died down. The Null had vanished.

At that moment, Hamish began to doubt Far's skills as a prophet since he had assured him that targeting Erde was their best plan of attack. Far had planned to manipulate Roman to gain Erde's trust. He would then ensure that the Royals in high command would view the attempt as self-defense. And yet, none of that now appeared to be necessary.

From what he could observe, Jasper Set had kept up his end of the bargain—wherever he was. Was it that Far was mistaken? That Far hadn't anticipated the demon actually having a strange code of ethics? Or, had something changed?

Thanks to Isabella's mistake, strange beings from another realm had been unleashed on Erde, causing an unnatural shift in time and energy that now rippled across the rest of the universe. But Hamish didn't know about that. If he did, perhaps then he would have understood.

CHAPTER 3
JASPER'S RETURN (SORT OF)
THREE WEEKS BEFORE THE END.

"There's the princess-s-s sleeping high in her palac-c-c-e." Jasper's voice was right up against Lucene's ear, so close that she could feel the breath, and a bit of spit, in her ear. She jumped up in bed.

"What is it?" Tanager asked groggily. He didn't wait for an answer before he rolled over and quickly fell back to sleep. Lucene admired the fact that Tanager was, what she would call, a 'power sleeper.' There was little that woke him of late, possibly because he was putting in so many hours at work. Unfortunately, in Lucene's case, there was little that *didn't* wake her, and Jasper Set was definitely in the 'things that wake Lucene up' category.

Lucene strained her eyes, waiting impatiently as they adjusted to the darkness. "Where are you, demon?" she whispered.

"Right here," Jasper whispered back. This time, the voice moved from directly behind her to her opposite ear. Lucene quickly climbed out of bed, adjusting her pajamas while turning in circles. He wasn't there. Or, if he was, she couldn't see him.

"No, princes-s-s," he laughed. "You can't see me. I'm right here, between the layers." His voice seemed to bounce off of the surrounding walls.

"Tanager," Lucene tried to call out. Somehow, her voice was caught in her throat. She tried to scream but she couldn't.

"I'm afraid it's just you and me," he grinned, his red eyes, beaked nose, and narrow jaw suddenly appearing like a ghost, flying toward her face. She backed up to avoid him until her shoulder blades banged against the wall. She winced in pain.

"What do you want?" Lucene managed to choke out.

"What do you think I want, princes-s-s?" The demon appeared almost offended. "I want you…to set me free."

"I thought we had," Lucene protested. "Reverend Isabella sent you to another dimension. What happened?"

"You know what happened, damn it!" he growled before composing himself. "Rev…Rev," he couldn't bring himself to say her name. "Isabella's a hack! Instead of sending me to another dimension all she did was trap me between the layers of this one. Even Olly can flit about between parallel worlds and loop his way back and forth in time, but not me!"

"Who's Olly?" Lucene asked. There was something at the core of her being that felt as if she should know, but she didn't.

"Never mind. The point is that he's a nothing of a creature and can do it. Why can't I?"

"Well, how is that Reverend Isabella's fault?" Lucene reasoned. "If this Olly person can, and you can't, maybe it has nothing to do with her. Maybe you don't have that capability."

He flew in like a flame, touching his nose to her nose. "I'm an all-powerful demon! How is this not in my skillset?"

"Don't know, but you also couldn't reach Erde for the longest of times because of our frequency. Maybe you're just not…good enough? I mean, from a kindness standpoint?" Oddly enough, Lucene felt mildly sorry for the demon.

Jasper paused and thought on this a moment. What if he were good? He wasn't even sure what a good deed looked like. He quickly dismissed the idea as ludicrous.

"And, what exactly are you talking about…*between the layers*?" Lucene was confused. She hadn't spoken to Reverend Isabella in months. In fact, she was beginning to worry that something had happened to her. Lucene wasn't even sure that Isabella was on Erde anymore.

"Arrogant girl!" Jasper chastised. "Just wait until I signal my Null mamas and papas and let them know I'm stuck here. See how your mangy planet will survive then!"

Something jolted Lucene out of the fog...an alarm. Tanager's alarm. The entire scenario had been a lucid dream. She awoke with a start, but not before hearing Jasper's words in her head, "I'm going to get out soon, with or without your help," he promised. "And when I do, I'm coming for you."

CHAPTER 4
XENI WANTS A DATE
TWENTY DAYS BEFORE THE END.

Xeni arrived at Lucene's high-home a good fifteen minutes ahead of schedule. She had taken to wearing a trench coat and hat dipped over her eye like Humphrey Bogart in Casablanca. She even had an old canvas courier bag strung across her shoulder. The young woman knocked loudly on the door.

"Hi Xeni," Lucene called from the other side. "Come on inside. Door's open!"

Lucene was spooning batter into small muffin tins. Flour covered her arms, and well, most of the rest of her, too.

Fatima eyed her friend from the other end of the kitchen counter, giggling. "Oh, you poor thing. Remind me to buy you an apron for your next birthday."

"How is it that you are spotless?" Lucene looked Fatima's large frame over, but there was not a speck of flour on her.

Fatima ignored her, instead, systematically relocating soiled bowls and baking utensils to the sink to be washed. "Hi Xeni," she noticed the young woman at the doorway. "Nice get-up."

Xeni beamed proudly. Fatima seemed the only one who "got" Xeni. "Thanks!" She smiled widely, bouncing into Lucene and Tanager's high-home before remembering and going back to shut the door behind her.

Since TARA shut down the Data Collector training program, all students on the training path were advised to pick a different course of study—or withdraw from TARA. For Xeni's parents this was not an option and so, they encouraged her interest in criminal justice studies—which also happened to be a field where there was a definite need on Erde. Unfortunately, because there only existed a few past video logs of former, now deceased, detectives, TARA had to rely on the research that came out from planets living in Sections 0, 1, 2 and 5. Xeni, however, chose her inspiration from old Earth detective movies and from the few techniques she'd learn in her Data Collection training about 'blending in.'

"We're in the home stretch," Lucene told her young friend. "Let us just pop these in the oven and we can move on to more exciting things."

Xeni nodded, excitedly, silently clapping her hands together and mouthing the word "yay!" Xeni planted herself on a chair at the dining room table by the long window and removed her portable computer from her bag. Meanwhile, Fatima opened the oven and Lucene slid the tray of lemon poppy muffin batter inside.

Fatima was teaching Lucene how to bake, something that somehow, never happened on Earth. But then, ever since Lucene moved into Tanager's high-home, she had been making a conscious effort to learn how to bake and cook—not that Tanager lacked this skill, mind you. It's just that she felt it somehow unfair that he'd had to do all of the cooking himself, particularly when his workload, at least for now, seemed to surpass her own. So, Lucene set out to learn basic cooking skills, and reached out to the only person she knew with such talent—Fatima.

After last evening's disturbing nightmare of Jasper Set, she was relieved to have the company of her friends to take her mind off things. Tanager reassured her that morning that given the trauma surrounding her last encounter with the demon, it made sense that she'd have some post-traumatic nightmares. And, if they continued, they would talk to Cepheus or Dr. Wilah about it.

At that moment, Tanager surfaced from the master bedroom, dressed in casual attire for a Saturday spent working when he would rather be doing something else.

"Oh, hello, ladies," he smiled pleasantly. "I'm just heading to TARA now and will be out of the way." He gathered a few papers from the dining room table, stuffing them haphazardly into his briefcase. Tanager had gotten so used to living alone that having three women in his high-home, even if one of them was his romantic partner, felt odd to him. And yet, he embraced the pleasant uncomfortableness of it all because it meant that Lucene had become a part of his life—something that he had once been afraid to even wish for.

"You're never in the way," Lucene wrinkled her nose and grinned, shaking her head from side-to-side. "And, if all goes well, I'll have dinner waiting for you when you get home."

Tanager's eyed widened in mock terror.

"Very funny, smart ass," Lucene wrapped her arm around Tanager's shoulders and kissed him, playfully. "But don't worry, I have Fatima supervising."

Tanager double-backed for another kiss, smiling at Lucene as if the world belonged to only them…at least, for that moment.

"Thank you, Fatima," Tanager offered, hugging Lucene close and never losing her gaze. "It's nice to have the reassurance that I can return home without our kitchen being on fire with a burnt Mongolian Beef recipe on the stove."

Lucene swatted his arm. "Don't make me smack you in front of my friends," she laughed, pleasantly. "That was one time! And only because the burner settings were different from what they typically are on Earth."

"Yes," Tanager dared, "*that* was clearly the reason."

"Get out," Lucene demanded, grabbing a wooden spoon and threatening to smack his bottom with it. He went in for another daring peck on the lips, then paused to dust off the flour that had found his way onto his shirt, before making his exit.

"You guys are so adorable," Xeni cooed, letting out a sigh. "That's what I want…real *romance*."

"Xeni, how old are you?" Lucene asked.

"What does that matter?" She seemed almost indignant. If Lucene had to guess, she would have placed her at eighteen or nineteen, and that was being generous. Xeni had all the energy, but none of the angst and drama that Lucene had had more than a decade ago. And while the circumstances were far different, she was hoping that she, Neroni and

Fatima might guide Xeni so that she would not make some of the same horrid mistakes that they had, at least when it came to dating.

"Knock, knock," Neroni called out from the door. A sneeze could be heard from the hallway outside. "May you be absolved of illness," Neroni called out to the sneezer.

"Thank you," Tanager answered in the distance. "Damn cat." As it so happened, Tanager discovered not long after Lucene moved in with him that Bagheera was going to be a problem. Before then, he had no idea that he was greatly allergic to cats. And so, Fatima and Ivan became the proud, adopted parents of the black panther-like cat. And while Fatima did her best to de-fur before visiting Tanager and Lucene's high-home, sometimes remnants of Bagheera became apparent.

"Door's open," the other three women called in unison.

"Good morning," Neroni sang pleasantly. "I hope I didn't keep everyone waiting on me."

"Nope," Lucene wiped a bit of flour off her nose with her arm which only succeeded in making it worse. "You're right on time."

Neroni looked Lucene up and down. "Did you lose a fight with a bag of flour?"

"Very funny," Lucene wrinkled her nose at Neroni. "Why don't you three get started while I change into something less...powdery."

Fatima nodded from behind the kitchen counter where she was wiping it with a dish towel.

A few minutes later, Lucene returned wearing denim shorts and a red t-shirt. Neroni and Fatima were standing behind Xeni, the only one who was seated, all peering with interest at the computer screen that sat in front of the young woman. Lucene took a seat next to the Xeni and craned her neck to see.

"What about him?" Xeni stared dreamily at the computer. She was on Achel's version of a dating site. She clicked on the screen and her potential match popped up above the keyboard as a hologram of the head and shoulders version of the real person. His name was Brad. Brad had brown hair that dipped over his left eye and a pointed chin like Xeni. His eyes were an intense brown—so much so that they almost appeared black. "Hi there," Brad flashed a toothy smile with teeth so white they looked painted on. Xeni's pale face turned a beet red as if he could see her (he couldn't). "I'm Brad, and I'm looking for my dream girl. Could you be the one? I like long walks on the beach and candlelight dinners. I love snuggling up by the fire with a cup of warm cocoa. I'm tired of the bar scene and just want to settle down with the right girl. To tell you the truth, I'm starting to think you're not out there. Prove me wrong."

Xeni was about to hit the "approve" button, which would put Brad in the "maybe" category and push him up the tier of potential suitors.

"Hang on," Fatima grabbed Xeni's arm. "You sure about that?" Fatima had always been the open-minded one, giving everyone the benefit of the doubt, and yet even her bullshit-o-meter was triggered.

"What's wrong with Brad?" Xeni pouted.

"Well, for one thing," Fatima began, "he may very well enjoy walks on the beach and candlelight dinners, but he lost me at the cup of cocoa."

"What's wrong with cocoa?" Xeni protested.

"There's nothing wrong with cocoa," Fatima's voice grew louder and more agitated. "I love cocoa! But leading with that seems like bait to me."

"And furthermore," Lucene added, "that whole 'prove me wrong' line? You don't have to prove shit to him." Lucene noticed Xeni's crest-fallen face. "Tell you what," she softened, "invariably, it's up to you. But maybe a few more profiles before you decide."

Xeni nodded. She clicked on the next profile. This one's name was Morris. Morris had bright-blue curly hair tied back in a ponytail. He had a rough-around-the-edges sort of face that was intriguing to look at. Xeni smiled. She evidently thought so, too.

"Hey, hey," he sang out. "My name is Morris. I'm fun-loving. I like to bash and have a good time and am looking for a gal who likes adventure. She should be funny, sexy and smart. No drugs. No tragedy. Glitter diggers need not apply."

Xeni was about to hit the "approve" button.

"Xeni!" Fatima and Lucene called out in unison. Neroni remained oddly silent, seemingly fascinated by the exchange.

"What?" Xeni complained. "I'm fun-loving and like adventure. I'm smart and can learn to be funny. And I'm definitely not into drugs or obsessed with money."

"Xeni," Lucene explained. "This isn't a job posting where you have to qualify for the position. Of course, you're all those wonderful things. I just find it oddly suspicious that he has to specify all the traits he doesn't want—particularly for a 'no tragedy' kinda guy. And then he talks at length about what *he* wants. What's *he* bringing to the relationship?"

"Well, he did say fun-loving," Neroni pointed out, literally gesturing at the screen. "Look...right there...fun-loving."

She stopped when Lucene and Fatima shot her a "are-you-kidding-me?" look.

They moved on.

There was Franklin who had a very close relationship with his mother—enough to include that in his profile. There was Tommy who wanted to be friends first and didn't want to be pressured into marriage. And there was Bob who was a movie producer in the middle of casting for his next film and...well, never mind about Bob.

Xeni had taken to pausing her hand over the "approve" button as if she expected the women to smack it. "You guys don't like any of my matches," she whined. "I'm going to be alone *forever!*"

"Well, that's a surprise," Neroni pointed at the screen. They all turned to look. There, on Xeni's matches, was none other than her classmate and friend, Clusaladek. Xeni's eyes grew wide.

"Should I click on his profile?" Xeni asked, nervously.

"You know this boy?" Fatima asked, having never met him.

Xeni nodded. "He was one of the Data Collectors in training, also an assistant instructor at TARA."

"How interesting." Fatima eyed Xeni, encouragingly.

Xeni cautiously clicked on his profile. And there, the Adonis-like Clusaladek appeared with his blonde hair and chiseled chin. While he typically oozed confidence in class, it was clear that this was out of his comfort zone. "Uh, hi. I'm Clusaladek. I'm a senior student at TARA and work part-time as an assistant instructor. My friends tell me I spend too much time in my books and not enough time getting 'out there,' so...uh. This is me getting 'out there.'"

"Aw," Fatima gushed. "He seems sweet."

Neroni remembered a time when he was not so sweet, but they had since made amends. And, there was a possibility that he had been under the influence of Jasper Set at the time. She decided to give him the benefit of the doubt.

"I like hiking in the mountains and star-gazing. I'm not too big on sports, but I enjoy a good tennis match once in a while. I'm honest and loyal and would like to meet a woman with similar interests and values. Uh...yeah...thanks for listening."

"Okay," Fatima declared. "If you don't go out with him, I will!"

"But you're *married*...with a *baby* and kinda...*older-ish*." Xeni was confused.

"I'm joking, my dear," Fatima laughed. "I just mean, he seems nice."

"Err," Lucene noticed Xeni's expression. It was one of surprise and a little...fear. "Xeni?"

"Yes?"

"Do you have a crush on Clusaladek?"

"No!" she protested. "Shut up." She caught herself. "I'm sorry, I didn't mean to tell you to shut up."

Lucene held her hands up. "It's okay," she laughed. Lucene wasn't exactly sure how to advise Xeni at this point. Clusaladek was a little older and more mature than Xeni, and in observing them together, it always appeared as if he treated Xeni more like a little sister. She wasn't sure about this match. "What do you think?" Lucene asked Neroni, who knew the two better than anyone.

"I'm probably the worst one to ask," Neroni offered. "I've never actually dated. My marriage was arranged."

"What?" Fatima was surprised. "People still do that...*here*?"

"Well, it's not mandatory, like in some cultures," Neroni explained. "I wasn't forced to marry my husband. We were just told we were of the same vibration and a matchmaker contacted our families and suggested we meet. We met, decided we liked each other well enough, spent time at family gatherings for a bit, and eventually got married."

"But what about love, and romance?" Xeni seemed disappointed.

"I wouldn't have gotten married if I didn't love my husband," Neroni explained. "At any time, we could have chosen to walk away, but neither of us wanted to." She smiled at the simplicity of it all.

"Huh," was all Fatima could say after a long pause, bewildered.

"Look, one more match," Lucene pointed at the screen.

Xeni forcefully clicked the "approve" button on Clusaladek and clicked on the final profile with some reluctance.

"Hi, I'm Christopher," said the boy with wavy short-brown hair and hazel eyes. He had a pleasant sort of face that seemed gentle. "I'm happy to be here and really looking forward to meeting you...whomever you may turn out to be. I think I have a lot to offer. I'm a nice person, and pretty easy-going. I like to think I'm fairly well-educated and cultured. I try to keep myself healthy and in good shape. I really like music, and while I know it's not a popular thing to say, I actually like going to art museums and plays. My ideal partner is patient and kind. She knows who she is and is comfortable in her own skin. She's happy and looks at the world with the same sense of wonder that I do. I look forward to meeting you." Christopher looked directly into the camera and smiled sheepishly with a lop-sided grin.

"I've changed my mind," Fatima announced. "He's the one."

"You're still married *with a baby*," Lucene joked.

But Xeni hadn't been paying attention. Her mind was still on Clusaladek.

CHAPTER 5
"I HATE AMY"
NINETEEN DAYS BEFORE THE END.

There were manuals...lots and lots of manuals and holographic videos from past Erdelings skilled in the areas of combat, psychological warfare, investigation, defense, espionage and interrogation.

Commander Royce checked in with the Elders, a group of ancient spirits that were the closest that Erde had to gods and religion. They were the spirits of ancestors from long ago of which Commander Royce was believed to have descended. Since Erde was a relatively young planet, no one knew exactly how that lineage came to be.

Which is what brought Cepheus, Moksha, Tanager, and Lucene to the Makerspace that Sunday morning when they would have much preferred to be sleeping in. For Tanager, it was his fourteenth straight workday without a break and tomorrow began a fresh week of school.

Commander Royce had given them specific instructions as to what resource materials in the library to study and, so the for now, they worked regularly integrating what they learned and also worked to develop new curricula for the former Data Collectors and other students at TARA. It was also made it abundantly clear that Cepheus and Tanager no longer represented the Intergalactic Peace Project (IPP) as Erde was no longer a member. Instead, their new assignment was to serve the Planetary Defense League (PDL). Therefore, they no longer checked on humans and those claiming sanctuary at the preserves. That duty was now given to Constable Melokuhle and a few of his assistants.

"I never thought I would live to see the day when TARA would go from being the Terrestrial Academy of Research and Awareness to the Terrestrial Academy of Response to Aggression." Tanager rubbed his forehead, tiredly. He sat around a small table in the library with his colleagues in what was now referred to as their private Resource Room. No one else was admitted there, unless one of them were present. The trusted group now included Moksha, who protested to Commander Royce up and down that she was no longer an assassin. However, it was deemed that she had the most knowledge of combat and defense of anyone, and if she wanted to maintain her residence on Erde, she was "encouraged" to use her knowledge to help get the PDL up to speed.

And there was Lucene. No one really knew what she was capable of since all the Data Collectors seemed to short circuit when trying to outmaneuver Jasper Set on the bridge that day, when he threatened to blow them up and half the city of Achel in the process. And yet, somehow, while all of the other Data Collectors went back to "normal," Lucene had these glitchy re-awakenings where like a faulty electrical system, the lights would blink off and on again. For this reason, Commander Royce added her to the list of PDL "agents," citing her ability as "special skills" even though no one knew what they were anymore.

And poor Roman, he was not entirely trusted after he divulged far too much info to his lover, Far (sorry for the pun). Since Far was working on behalf of the Royals and Jasper Set, Roman was no longer privy to PDL knowledge nor was he permitted to teach at TARA. However, given his skills in anthropology and psychology, the PDL hired him as a consultant on psychological warfare. Therefore, he could enter the Resource Room, but only to provide information to the team. For this, they paid him a small stipend which was enough to keep him in his high-home and well fed (or so they thought). And while Roman still got an invitation to Cepheus, Tanager and Lucene's monthly "reunion" gatherings (since the four of them traveled from Earth to Erde together), he was distinctly out of place—none more aware of it than he.

The one vital person missing from this equation was Ivan. His knowledge of virtual technology, artificial intelligence, machine learning and remote sequencing outweighed some of the most skilled technicians at TARA. His contribution to the new TARA training modalities would have gone a long way to help fill in the gaps of knowledge that the academy now faced. There was just one problem...Ivan was still on maternity leave with Fatima. He didn't officially start back until Monday.

"Perhaps we should take a break," Cepheus suggested, rubbing his yellow eyes which now had tired red circles around them like a sunset before a storm. "We've been at this for three hours now, and I've had about all I can stomach on how to teach our students 'ethical interrogation.' I mean really, 'ethical interrogation?' In the end, it's still violence. We're simply justifying the means."

The four stood and stretched. Moksha nodded. "Now you have some understanding as to why I fled from the Royals." Cepheus took her hand gently, rubbing the back of it affectionately with his thumb. She squeezed his hand in return. Unlike the others, Moksha was wearing a green uniform with pants and a wrap-around top that changed colors and allowed it to blend into its environment as if a hybrid of a green screen and a chameleon. Funny, given that she and Cepheus were of lizard descent.

No one liked the new arrangement but they didn't really have a choice. After all, the Royals were still a threat. So were the Null who were now keenly aware of Erde's existence. There was also the strange phenomena that seemed to be happening lately where odd new species of animals began appearing on the planet, while others disappeared.

Not limited to creatures, the team also noticed random objects from the Makerspace disappearing and resurfacing someplace else. This wouldn't typically be cause for alarm were it not for the fact that the "someplace else" often turned out to be a random location where it shouldn't be, such us under the kitchen sink of someone's residence or mixed with a batch of tomatoes at the grocery store.

Plus, they kept hearing about news reports of supernatural events occurring all around them, of the flying saucer and ghost variety, stories not unlike what one might hear on Earth. The best guess from experts was that it had something to do with the conjunction between Jupiter and Saturn while Saturn was in retrograde. It reportedly sent out a ripple effect across the universe.

What they didn't understand (mainly because Reverend Isabella wasn't around to explain it to them) was that there was a little matter of a semi-open portal between this dimension and others, where Isabella had accidentally unleashed trapped spirits who hadn't moved on to their next life or who had been sentenced there as a form of prison. It was like a sink plug that didn't seal properly. And now, there were beings who were trying desperately to get out and back *to* or *at* the people who put them there. There were also beings who were simply born in the other realm who were kicked out accidentally or reacted like curious cats when a door is suddenly opened, and they felt an instinctive need to dash. Yes, there were a few odd beasts on this plane of existence who dove between the layers just for the experience of it. But all this was lost on the group.

"Here's what I don't understand," Lucene offered as she locked up the Resource Room after them (another new phenomenon, locks!) using a wireless sequence that emitted from her communication watch. "While I get that we need to defend ourselves from outside threats, I thought the whole reason that Erde flew under-the-radar of the Null and other beings was because of its vibration—being peaceful and all."

"Quite," Tanager answered, holding her hand as they made their way back to the Makerspace's main work stations. He had wondered the same thing. What had suddenly changed within Erde's energy field? Was it Jasper Set's presence, the shifting consciousness of Erde's current inhabitants, or something (or someone) else? He really didn't have an answer and that bothered him.

Once at the Transporter, Tanager sent a request for the group to be picked up as the Makerspace was far too large for the team to make the rounds on foot unless they planned on several miles of walking—which they weren't. Or, more specifically, Tanager wasn't. Moments later, Renenet arrived, the usual scowl on her face and her lion-like mane looking particularly aggressive that day.

"Oh, Director Renenet," Tanager greeted her hesitantly. "I didn't expect you to be the one escorting us today. If you would rather I run the Transporter, I can..."

"That won't be necessary, Professor Tanager," she answered. "Given our new protocol, I am most qualified to escort you. And, for security reasons, no one in the work areas can travel from section to section using the transporter unless accompanied by an official PDL director, which I am."

"But I thought we were agents of the PDL, too," Lucene whispered to Tanager.

"An agent is lower than a director," Renenet barked at Lucene, before remembering herself. "You do not have authorization," she smiled sweetly. "Please take a seat."

Take a seat. Take a seat. That's all Renenet ever commands me to do. Take a seat. Lucene thought, annoyed. But there wasn't time to argue. There wasn't time for much of anything anymore, at least not for Tanager, who spent far too many nights working late and long weekends away from home.

Once everyone was aboard, the Transporter made its slow spiral up through the Fibonacci-like tunnels of the Makerspace, making routine stops at sections including the Welding Room which had been renamed the Weapons Room; the Robotics Lab which was now the AI and Military Robotics Lab; and the Transportation Shop which had become the Warcraft Shop. In fact, nearly every area of the Makerspace had been converted to support some military purpose. The only exception to this were the few local businesses who rented out rooms to build products they were unable to produce in their own factories. They had special permits (AKA a lot of money), which was deemed acceptable as they helped support the financial upkeep of the Makerspace and TARA.

There was a bitterness in Lucene's stomach as they made the rounds. It seemed as if overnight the Makerspace went from being a vibrant inventor and artist hub to becoming a military base. This wasn't what she expected when she'd left Earth. Tanager witnessed her crumbled expression, noting a tear forming in her left eye. He brushed it away with his fingers. "Don't lose hope," he reassured her, "this is temporary."

"How can you be sure?"

"Because," Tanager reasoned, as if trying to convince himself, "it *has* to be."

———

The last stop on the list was the Model Room which had somehow escaped being renamed the Military Model Room. This was their main agenda for the day since it was on their checklist from Commander Royce with the purpose to see how the new architectural defense designs were coming along. This included creating a dome-like defense shield around Erde, as well as additional on-the-ground defense stations and putting protective barriers around their high-risk structures. "High-risk" were the PDL's main offices, Achel as a whole, the SpeedCircuit, entries and exits to and from the crosses, and national landmarks.

Cepheus and Moksha broke off from the group, exiting the Transporter and making their way to the opposite end of an enormously large and bustling room. They were to survey the air defense shield blueprints and models.

Meanwhile, Tanager and Lucene headed toward an expansive model of Achel, the SpeedCircuit and the Crosses which resembled a miniature train set and tiny village that you might buy for your kids on Earth during Christmas. This one was extremely detailed with small plastic figurines distinct enough to identify TARA, Tanager and Lucene's high-home building and even Lucene's former personal cottage in the Eastern Cross. Oddly enough, Lucene could have sworn her old cottage was a little too accurate, making her wonder how it was they were able to see things like a dish sponge, on a sink, by the kitchen window, just from drone footage (if that's, indeed, what they used to collect their images), or the misshapen shingle on the back end of her roof (she didn't even know it was like that).

Renenet waited by the Transporter eyeing Tanager and Lucene with extreme interest.

"Oh, it's you," a small woman with red hair and green eyes popped out from a back-storage room. She looked wide-eyed at Tanager, surprised to see him. It was the same women Lucene had witnessed on her first trip to the Makerspace several months ago, the one Tanager oddly described as "a mistake" with no further explanation. She seemed to like green as she was once again wearing jeans and a green t-shirt that clung rather tightly around her chest.

"Amy," Tanager coughed, "nice to see you again." He dropped Lucene's hand, something that only Lucene was keenly aware of.

Lucene's eyes darted between Tanager and Amy, but the two merely gazed at one-another with a mixture of nervous energy and anticipation. "I didn't expect to see you here on a weekend."

"Well, I'm usually off today, but Renenet let me know that someone called in sick, so...here I am." She waved her hands as if to say *ta-da!* Lucene peered over her shoulder at Renenet, who started at the mention of her name, quickly averting her gaze and then pretending to plug in coordinates on the Transporter as if to fix some inexplicable malfunction.

"And this is—" Amy turned her bright green and obscenely beautiful (in an irritating sort of way) eyes toward Lucene.

"Ah, this is Lucene..." Tanager paused, awkwardly. "She's recently arrived from Earth, is an agent of the PDL, and is..." He lost his words.

"His lover," Lucene smiled, offering her hand. Tanager choked back an uncomfortable cough. "We work and live together."

"Oh," Amy seemed surprised. "I hadn't realized..."

"It's a new arrangement," Tanager offered.

Why is he explaining this to her? Lucene wanted to know. "So, Amy," Lucene assumed control of the conversation before Amy and Tanager tripped over their own tongues. "Can you give us an update on this defense model so we can make our report for the PDL?" Lucene wasn't generally good at being assertive in situations such as this one, so she channeled her inner Drake and Dallen—two men who were terrible people, but great when it came to negotiation and business.

"Of course," Amy answered, dropping her gaze to the ground momentarily, her head slinking downward as she collected herself before retreating behind the model. "So, if you look here," she pointed to a few visible barricades set up at strategic points along the Crosses, "you can see where we have mapped out areas most vulnerable to air and land attack and set up defense systems to support those areas. These would be a combination of energetic barriers and real fortified structures. We've taken into account technologies that outside species might possess that we lack and have planned work-arounds to prevent attack."

Tanager was impressed. "Beautifully done, Amy." Amy smiled proudly at the praise. And there it was again...that look between them, that distinctly did not include Lucene. In fact, she felt as if she were intruding, somehow.

Lucene was forced to endure this odd back-and-forth for a good fifteen minutes before Cepheus and Moksha could be seen returning to the transporter—their cue to return as well. "Well, thank you, Amy," Lucene spoke forcefully. "You've been most helpful."

"Of course," Amy smiled, uncertainly.

Lucene took Tanager by the forearm and all but steered him back to the Transporter.

"Hey," Amy called before they'd left. "I don't suppose the two of you would like to hear a song from my performance next week?"

"What performance?" Tanager asked.

"We're doing a fundraiser for the Dragoste Healing Center. So, I'm playing a classical Earth piece I know." To Lucene, she added, "The Music Hall is just through there, as you know." She pointed to a small door at the other end of the room. "A quick detour…if it wouldn't be a bother?"

"I'm afraid we…" Lucene started to decline.

"We'd love to," Tanager said with a bit too much enthusiasm.

"Great," Amy smiled, hopefully.

"Lucene, would you go invite Moksha and Cepheus? And tell Renenet we will just be a few minutes more."

Wait, what? Have I just been dismissed? Lucene thought to herself. Apparently, she had, as Tanager and Amy resumed a conversation in hushed voices.

Cepheus saw the look on Lucene's face as she approached the Transporter. He didn't have to guess what this was about—Amy. He let out a frustrated sigh as Lucene made the request. He reluctantly agreed, taking Moksha by the hand and escorting her, with some speed, over to where Tanager and Amy stood, presumably laughing at some inside joke that only the two of them knew about.

Lucene paused, filled with a mixture of confusion, jealousy, anger, and bewilderment. Who the hell was this Amy and why was Tanager so taken with her? And more importantly, why had he not told her about this woman before? Lucene leaned against the wall of the Transporter, thinking, before finally conceding to join the rest of the group.

"Nice couple, aren't they?" Renenet seemed to challenge, speaking sweetly over Lucene's shoulder.

"I hadn't noticed," Lucene retorted. "And you seem to be forgetting that Tanager and I are living together now."

"Oh," Renenet feigned surprise. "I hadn't known that. Curious..."

"What's curious?" Lucene demanded.

"Well," Renenet paused. "I really shouldn't say anything."

"Oh, yes you should," Lucene replied curtly. "You think I don't recognize a set up when I see one? Amy was supposed to be off duty today."

"So, she was." Renenet smiled at her cleverness.

"Ahem," Lucene cleared her throat.

Renenet's fire agate eyes turned and bored into Lucene's. "Tanager and Amy were supposed to be married."

"Oh," Lucene felt as if she'd been slapped in the face. "What happened?"

Renenet narrowed her eyes. "*You* happened."

"What? How is that possible? Tanager and I have only known each other for a little over a year. Were they a couple while he and I were traveling back to Erde?"

Renenet paused for an unbearably long time, giving Lucene enough of an opportunity to run all kinds of horrific scenarios through her head, of Tanager's infidelity (of the heart, if not in actuality) as he awkwardly wooed her on Earth, their trip home... *Oh, God.* Lucene thought, *He didn't actually break up with her after I'd gotten here, did he?"*

"No," Renenet finally answered. Lucene let out a sigh so loud that it sounded as if a helium balloon were rapidly deflating. Renenet eyed her curiously and not without a minor hint of annoyance. "They were over long before you arrived." Renenet looked over Lucene, distastefully.

"Then why is your bitch-o-meter set to annihilate?" Lucene challenged. Sometimes, Lucene couldn't put the brakes on her mouth.

Renenet was about to remind Lucene that she was a director and she shouldn't be spoken to in such a manner, but decided against it, instead, choosing the woman-to-woman assault. "Make no mistake," Renenet peered at her, angrily. "They were *supposed* to be married. But Cepheus kept going on and on about the *Earth-born Data Collector, one of Dora and Zan* who was of the same *vibration* as Tanager," Renenet mocked. "Tanager just fell in love with the *idea* of you," she gave Lucene another disgusted once over, "without actually having met you." That last bit dripped off her tongue in a way that suggested, not so subtly, that Lucene in no way lived up to all that was Amy.

I hate Amy, Lucene thought.

"Lucene, are you coming?" Moksha called, waving for Lucene to join them.

"I'll wait here," Renenet announced, smiling to herself.

Lucene joined the rest of the group, Moksha and Cepheus walking hand-in-hand, while Tanager seemed to follow at Amy's heels like a lost puppy. He almost forgot that Lucene was behind him, until she took his arm, just above the elbow, squeezing it a little harder than necessary.

Down the hallway they went, until they'd arrived at the Music Hall which was essentially a large theater with an ornate concert grand piano sitting on the left of the stage. The group climbed the stage steps and gathered around as Amy sat, shaking her hands nervously before beginning to play Chopin's Fantaisie Impromptu, Op. 66. And there, Amy was transported into another dimension as her fingers flew easily over the keys, leaving Tanager mesmerized. Lucene dropped his arm and retreated into the shadows behind a curtain.

"Isn't she wonderful?" Tanager whispered to Cepheus, who in turn, jabbed Tanager in the ribs with his elbow.

"What was that for?" Tanager whispered in surprise. Cepheus shot him a look and nodded his head over his shoulder.

Lucene, Tanager realized, standing there in the corner of the stage, arms wrapped around herself as if giving herself a hug for comfort. *I'm a complete idiot,* he thought. He walked over to Lucene and wrapped his arms around her. She smiled at him, appreciatively, thinking to herself, *I still hate Amy.*

CHAPTER 6
THE ARGUMENT
NINETEEN DAYS BEFORE THE END.

"Lucene, don't you think you're overreacting, just a little?" Tanager asked as Lucene blew past him into their high-home, all but slamming the door in his face.

She began rifling through the cabinet, clanking pots and pans together before settling on a simple sauté pan and dropping it on the stovetop. Tanager cringed, hoping that wouldn't leave a scratch. She then moved on to the leftovers in the refrigerator. Being a mostly unskilled cook, Tanager couldn't help but wonder if this was in some way part of her protest, forcing him to eat something she made by herself without supervision.

"I saw the way you looked at each other," she replied, unwrapping a parsnip and fennel dish that Fatima helped her make the night before and plopping it in the pan.

"Might want to…" he was about to say, "add olive oil to the pan first," but he was too late. She turned the heat up to high. Instead he asked, "How exactly did we look at each other?" He moved around the kitchen counter and lowered the dial on the stove. Lucene ignored him, as she was now on to the utensil drawer where she rummaged for a wooden spoon. "Lucene," he stopped her, taking her by the arm. "Please, talk to me."

"You both had this shared look of...oh, I don't know. I can't read anyone anymore. But it was something that resembled...*affection*."

"And that's a bad thing?"

"Yes, that's a bad thing!" Lucene whined. "You're supposed to be with me now!"

Tanager tilted his head, forcing Lucene to meet his gaze. "I am with you now. And, I love being with you, although, I must admit, this moment isn't one of the best..."

"The point is," Lucene pulled away, crossing her arms. "It was as if you *missed* each other."

"It's not that," Tanager tried in vain to explain. "But Amy and I were almost married. Just because it didn't work out doesn't mean that I suddenly hate her."

"Hmmph," was all Lucene could say, returning to the stew and stirring it violently.

"Lucene, I know we age differently here, but I am still more than two decades older than you..."

"So you keep reminding me."

"You're acting like a child," Tanager's face began to contort in annoyance.

"Again, thanks for pointing out how you are so much older and wiser than I am."

At this point, the stew was clumping to the spoon as if hanging on for dear life. Tanager retrieved if from her, before turning off the stove and moving the pan to an unheated burner. "Can we please just sit down and talk about this?"

Lucene nodded, tearfully, so they went into the living room and sat.

"What I was trying to say, was that because I've been around for a while, it stands to reason that there were relationships pre-*us*. That doesn't diminish how I feel about you now."

"What about the girl at the bistro?"

Tanager was confused. "What girl?"

"When we went to dinner the other night, you smiled at our server."

"You don't want me smiling at people?"

"No," Lucene let out a frustrated sigh. "It wasn't just a smile it was like you were...flirting."

"I don't flirt," Tanager was offended. "Which is not to say that Brie wasn't attractive but—"

"See! That's what I'm talking about!" Lucene pointed at him triumphantly. *I didn't even know her name was Brie.*

Tanager eyed Lucene calmly and tried again. "Lucene, do you think that being in love means you never get a pang in the center of your chest when you remember a pleasant moment from your past that involved another person, or that you never get crushes or never find someone else even remotely attractive?"

"Yes," she answered simply.

"Well, forgive me for saying so, but I think you're being a little naive."

"Again, with the reflection on my age and lack of worldly experience."

"You never think about Dallen, not in a *what if* sort of way, but remembering some of the good times?"

"There weren't many good times with Dallen, and no."

"What about other people?"

In truth, Lucene couldn't really remember *other people* aside from her former crush on Drake Cushing and her brief dating experience with Dallen. And, as far as she knew, she was immune to crushes. "No, Tanager," she answered finally, "I don't think about other people, and you're the only person I want to be with."

Tanager smiled, wrapping his arms around her. "Well, then we agree on something. You're the only person I want to be with as well. For the record, I don't intend to leave you and I will never be unfaithful."

Lucene hugged him back with all her might, sniffling as a few teardrops landed on Tanager's shirt. *Stupid emotions,* she chastised herself. "I didn't think her playing the piano was all that good," she whimpered.

Tanager's grin grew wider. He took the cue. "I agree, not very good. And, you know what else?" He leaned back, craning his neck as Lucene looked up at him.

"What?"

"I happen to know that's one of only three songs she knows how to play on the piano. She learned them really well to impress people, but really, that's it."

Lucene buried her face in his chest again, slightly relieved. "Tanager?"

"Yes?"

"I think I killed the parsnip and fennel stew."

"I'm pretty sure you did, too. Dinner out?"

"Okay, but not the bistro."

"No." Tanager thought a moment about Brie, the server. "Not the bistro."

CHAPTER 7
NOT CHRISTOPHER
EIGHTEEN DAYS BEFORE THE END.

"Oh, hello. I didn't realize anyone else was here," Lucene shielded her eyes from the sun as she squinted to observe the young man standing over her. She had been lying on a blanket at the water's edge of Tranquil Beach, a small patch of sand and sea located at the farthermost corner of the Eastern Cross. Very few seemed to take the time to visit as it required an intricate connection from the SpeedCircuit to renting a hovercraft and then walking an additional mile and a half from the rental lot.

Most times, Lucene was alone to enjoy the sun, white sand and gentle tepid water as she swam laps, combed the beach, and otherwise did her best thinking about life in general.

Today, however, was not going to be one of those days.

"Lucene, it's nice to finally meet you," the young man said.

Lucene could make out little of his features against the sun's glare, except that he appeared to be of average height and weight, had a thick head of perfectly combed chestnut hair and a clean-shaven light complexion. He was wearing a light blue guayabera shirt and white linen pants. He was tan and his arms were toned. What was most odd to Lucene was that he gave the immediate impression of being…flawless.

"I'm sorry, do I know you?" Lucene was confused. There was something about him that seemed very familiar, but her memory was sketchy, and she couldn't be sure.

He stepped in front of the sun, casting a shadow over Lucene's face. "Does this help, now that you can see me better?"

Lucene wrinkled her nose at him. "Not really," she confessed.

"Oh well, you'll figure it out." He plopped down beside her, bending his knees and planting his feet in the sand. He leaned forward and wrapped his long arms around his shins for support.

"Oh," Lucene suddenly realized (or at least, she thought she did). "Are you Xeni's Christopher? The one she met online?"

"No, not Christopher," he answered.

"Then, who are you?"

"That's for me to know and you to find out."

"You sound like a twelve-year-old," Lucene retorted. Not Christopher had to have been in his early twenties, at least.

"Exactly," he answered calmly, not in the least bit offended.

"What do you want, Not Christopher?" Lucene asked flatly. After all, she was there to sort out the mess that was in her head about Tanager and their relationship, and his former fiancé Amy who Lucene decided she hated, even though she didn't exactly have a reason to.

"I thought you might want to work through some stuff about Tanager and needed a sounding board."

"How on Earth could you possibly know about that?"

"I know everything you know," he answered simply.

Since the portal had closed incorrectly, somehow leaving a tear and the layers of reality became intermingled, nothing quite made sense. Less so, since Lucene was unaware of this. *Hmm,* Lucene thought. *Another Jupiter-Saturn conjunction?* Somehow, that explanation made less sense each time she relied on it. And yet, here was a neutral stranger willing to listen.

"I think he still has feelings for his ex," she finally told him.

"Is that terrible?"

"Yes, Not Christopher," Lucene whined. "It's awful."

"Why?"

"Because, he's supposed to only have feelings for me."

"Hmm..."

"What, *hmm*?" Lucene demanded.

"Are you sure its current feelings versus a reflection of past feelings?"

"Does it matter?"

"I don't know," Not Christopher answered. "Does it?"

"The point is, we have very different ideas about relationships, and mine don't seem to matter because I'm 'naive'." Lucene put the word "naïve" in air quotes before pausing as the waves of the ocean rolled in and out, a little stronger this time, making it difficult to talk without yelling above the roar.

"Well, if you feel that way—" Not Christopher finally answered when the waves died down, inching back from the water's edge as the foam reached his sandals. They slipped off as the water tugged at them, and the two watched as Not Christopher's sandals floated out to sea.

"That's terrible for the environment," Lucene commented.

"Not to worry," Not Christopher answered. "They'll be back."

"Anyway, you were saying..."

"If you feel he's not taking you seriously enough, or discounting what you say because you are younger and less experienced at life—"

"Hey," Lucene interrupted again. "Whose side are you on, anyway?"

"I'm on your side, Lucene," Not Christopher answered. "I've always been on your side."

"Sorry, continue."

"I was just going to suggest that you should talk about it. Isn't that what couples do? Talk about things they need to work through?"

"I've complained about it often enough."

"That's not the same thing, though, is it?"

"Perhaps not," Lucene admitted. She hated that Not Christopher was probably right.

"Hey" Fatima's voice suddenly called. "Who are you talking to?"

Lucene looked up in surprise to see Fatima making her way toward her. She was waddling a little and huffing a little more. Lucene ran to greet her, at least, as fast as she could run on sand (which wasn't very). She noticed her friend struggling to carry a tote bag and had an umbrella dragging behind her leaving a line in the sand. "Here," Lucene said. "Give me those." She grabbed the tote and threw it over her left shoulder and tucked the umbrella awkwardly under her arm. Lucene offered her left arm which Fatima gratefully accepted.

"Thanks, Chica," Fatima huffed. "I guess I'm still not a hundred percent after giving birth."

"Well, it's still quite a walk from the lot. What are you doing here?"

"What do you think I'm doing here?" Fatima smiled. "I wanted to see my best friend."

"Fatimaaaa?" Lucene questioned in a way that suggested she didn't believe her.

"Okay, well I stopped to drop off a loaf of banana bread I baked for you guys and Tanager said you went to your favorite think spot to sort some stuff out. This was the only spot I could think of."

"Good guess," Lucene praised. "Did he encourage you to come out here?"

"He ever-so-gently hinted that you would probably appreciate a chat."

"Well, I've been getting that," Lucene answered when they finally arrived at the blanket Lucene had laid out. "Fatima, let me introduce you to…" Lucene stopped. There was no one there, not even footprints in the sand or an impression of Not Christopher's weight from where he sat on the beach. Lucene surveyed her surroundings.

"What are you looking for?"

"Did you not see the young man I was talking to just now?"

"No, actually, I thought you were talking to yourself…or rehearsing a play."

"Curious," Lucene answered. Not wanting to stress her friend out any more than necessary given her heart condition and the fact that she had recently given birth, she changed the subject. "And how is baby Talula today?"

"As adorable as ever," Fatima bragged. "Ivan took her to the Makerspace for the first time to introduce her to everyone on his first day back. He's already made her a matching baby-sized hard hat." She motioned on her own head and continued, "Which is really just a soft yellow hat for show."

"Is that a safe space for a baby?" Lucene wasn't so sure.

"He just wanted to show her off to his colleagues. And," Fatima giggled, "he also wanted to give her a tour!"

"But she's a *baby*." Lucene doubted that the baby would retain any of that knowledge. She set the tote down on her blanket.

"I know that, silly. May I remind you that I was there when she arrived," Fatima chided, laughing. "But you know what? Dr. Wilah said that she predicted with 100% accuracy the occupation of all three of her kids based on her sure-fire game."

"What kind of game?" Lucene asked as she fought to dig the long rail of the umbrella into the sand.

Fatima pulled a towel from the tote. "Well, she puts out a series of toys in front of her newborn and see which he or she picks."

"That's it?"

"That's it." Fatima grinned. "And guess what?"

"What?"

"Talula sailed right past the plastic spatula and the yarn and went straight for the adjustable wrench. Ivan was beside himself with joy. 'That's my girl,' he said."

"Good Lord, Fatima," Lucene laughed. "Not one, but *two* tinkerers in the house. Better buy some extra fire extinguishers and flame-retardant baby clothes."

CHAPTER 8
FAR'S RETURN
EIGHTEEN DAYS BEFORE THE END.

Roman didn't hear Far enter his high-home early in the morning, but to be fair, Far was waif-like and moved like a silent ninja. And...Roman was one bottle past the point of drunk. It would have taken an army of soldiers to wake him from his current "sprawled-out-on-the-balcony with his bare bottom in plain view to anyone with a decent pair of binoculars and voyeuristic tendencies" state.

The room was disheveled, Far noticed. This was not like Roman at all, who was a perfectionist, minimalist, and mild germaphobe. Yet the living room was cluttered with gin bottles, sushi-style takeout boxes, empty cigarette cartons, and a heap of dirty laundry. In fact, the room smelled of full-strength smoke, nicotine, and unwashed anthropology professor.

Far paused at the wave of feeling that overtook him, allowing it to pass through him before making his way to the balcony. The Royals had done a fair job of de-conditioning emotions out of him but Roman was still his weakness. After all, their love had been real. At least, that's what he believed before the Royals beat it out of him that romantic love and compassion were anything more than false realities. True love came from banding together for the common good of the species, no matter the cost.

Emotions had no place. The Royals were much like the Null in this aspect.

Far tip-toed past the mess, careful not to startle his former beloved. Once he'd reached Roman who was lying face-down on the concrete with a tattered robe wrapped haphazardly around him, he leaned over and gently rubbed Roman's back with one hand–just behind the heart.

After what seemed like an eternity, Roman lifted his nose into the air. With eyes still closed he asked, "Far?"

"Yes, my love," Far answered. "I am here."

Roman rolled over as a smile crossed his lips. It was temporary, as if he were waking from a dream and suddenly remembered that in the real world, Far was a large contributor to Roman and his friends almost getting blown up, and that he was now lying on the balcony in the most embarrassing state imaginable.

Roman held his palm to his forehead and groaned. "No," he muttered. "This is not at all how I imagined our reunion to be. I'm afraid I am in an awful state."

"Nonsense," Far smiled, reverting to a version of his old self, removing Roman's hand and staring deeply into his eyes. "Your state is just a testament to how much you've missed me. And while I would never wish this on you, I would be lying if I said that I wasn't a little bit...touched." Far leaned over to help Roman to his feet and nearly fell on top of him, instead. Far was about as strong as a feather.

Eventually, Roman wobbled his way to the couch, flopping into the cushions. The full weight of his body caused the couch to move slightly. Far settled in next to him, crossing his legs and settling his arms on top of them. Roman rubbed his head and winced at the pain. His brain fog had cleared just enough for him to remember a few things from their last encounter. "Why are you here?" he finally asked.

"Isn't it obvious?" Far answered. When Roman's face indicated that it was not—in fact— all that obvious, he continued. "I missed you. And, sensed that you needed me."

"May I remind you that you were going to let Jasper Set blow us to kingdom come."

Far rolled his eyes as if this were insignificant.

Roman leaned forward, his voice becoming more agitated. "Not to mention that on more than one occasion your fist found it necessary to make its way to my face!"

"Oh, you've over-reacted, my love," Far answered. "Look at me. It's not as if I'm a large man. You know I could never truly hurt you."

"Over-reacting?!" Roman shook his head in disbelief. He began ticking off a bulleted list to support his argument, touching one finger of his right hand at a time for emphasis. "Bomb…fist…emotional distress… abandonment." Roman let out a sigh. "I can't believe I've actually been pining over you! Oh, oh…" Roman remembered. "That woman shop-keeper…what was her name? Mallory? Everyone assumed you murdered her!"

Far caught himself before correcting Roman. It was a man that had been killed, not a woman.

"Oh, come now," Far's voice remained calm. "I'm not a killer. Everyone just blamed me because I was the outsider. Be fair. I'm not the only reason for your current state."

"What are you talking about?"

"Here, let me make you a cup of vegetable broth with garlic. It will help you feel better. We can talk after that."

This was Far's method of operation, Roman had learned. When he didn't want to argue, or he wanted to give Roman a chance to calm down, or he simply needed time to reframe his argument, suddenly it was time to make a cup of broth, take a bath, or get some fresh air.

"No, thank you," Roman growled. "I would like you to explain yourself."

Far ignored him. "How's work going at the Terrestrial Academy?" he asked.

Roman grit his teeth. "It seems I am no longer employed at TARA. But somehow, I expect that you already knew that."

Far glanced at the coffee table where several eviction notices sat in plain sight. "And, they're kicking you out, it would seem."

"When one is not working and unable to pay the mortgage, things like that happen."

"Did your new friends not offer to help?"

Roman's face grew red but he wasn't entirely certain if his anger was misplaced or not. After all, TARA had covered the mortgage on his high-home for months after his dismissal. (It was Cepheus and Tanager that pooled their resources to pay his debts, but Roman didn't know that). There was the small stipend that came in from his "consultant" work at TARA, but that wasn't nearly enough to cover both home expenses, and food and drink that matched his typically high culinary standards. Lucene made every attempt to help him find work and stopped to check in on him regularly. But after months of Cepheus, Tanager and Lucene pleading with him to seek out help and offering what support they could, their visits became increasingly sparser. In reality, Erde was low on qualified emotional counselors, and the team had been working overtime as TARA began transitioning its Makerspace and training modules to become more military-focused. Roman was unaware of this and was a bit too self-absorbed in his current state to actually ask how anyone else was doing. He took their distance as abandonment–they had given up on him.

Far waited patiently for Roman to draw his own misguided conclusions and did nothing to convince him otherwise.

Roman flinched as Far put his hand gently on his shoulder. "I never abandoned you," Far explained. "I was merely preparing something better for us."

"Better?" This made no sense to Roman.

"I would never have let Jasper Set harm you. But since he made a deal with the Royals, I had to make it look convincing. And as for your face..." He stroked the side of Roman's face lovingly. "Well, I'm sorry about that. You're much bigger than I, and I lashed out in fear."

"Fear? You were afraid of...me?" Roman whispered, eyes growing wide. It had never occurred to him that Far's angry outbursts may have been a fear response. But it made perfect sense now that he thought about it.

"Let's not talk about all of that unpleasantness." Far waved his hand. "Water under the bridge. What I'd like to talk about is our future."

"What future?" Roman snorted. "What kind of future can I possible provide for us?"

"Come back to the Royal training grounds with me."

"What? Are you insane? The Royals are blood-thirsty monsters. I can't believe you still support them."

"They are not what they seem, my love." Far balled a fist and took a deep breath. He quickly released his clenched hand and ran it through his fair hair before Roman had a chance to notice. "Most of their decision-making is self-preservation."

"So, you support destroying species living on other planets if it means the survival of your own species."

"If it's self-defense, I most certainly do."

"Self-defense and self-preservation are a bit different," Roman argued. "What are you getting at?"

"Why do you think the Intergalactic Peace Project really kicked the Vitruvians and Erdelings out?"

Roman thought back to the past two IPP Assemblies. "First, because the Vitruvians were allegedly working with the Royals to take over Earth, Erde was wrongly accused of kidnapping Earthlings for the purposes of experimentation and having their own designs of inhabiting the Earth. And, at the second Assembly, Jasper Set clouded everyone's minds into believing that Vitruvians and Erdelings were only interested in war."

"But what if none of that were true?" Far questioned.

"Not true?" Roman was incredulous. "I think you've been brainwashed."

Far took a deep breath. "Don't take my word for it," Far suggested. "Why don't you clean yourself up and go see what's happening at TARA? After that, make some of the rounds at the Preserves and see what they've got in place. When you're done, come and find me."

"And why would I do that?" Roman challenged.

"Because you need me," Far answered. And, after witnessing Roman's unconvinced expression, he added, "And, you will soon learn that I am right."

"How shall I find you?" Roman asked.

"Take the only SpeedCircuit that stops at the Northern Cross and try to be inconspicuous. I'll be waiting for you there."

"That barren wasteland? Is that where you've been all this time?"

"To you, it's a barren wasteland. But for the adventurous, it is ripe for exploring. Crispy dessert gliders cooked on an open fire are rather tasty."

Roman wrinkled his nose.

"But no, my love." Fare finally answered. "I have not been in the Northern Cross for the entire time. "Rather, I have been preparing a place for us at the helm of a kingdom."

"There you go again. What are you talking about, you beautiful, crazy man?" Roman was certain Far was delusional. But then, he himself once thought he was an alien Data Collector sent to Earth instead of a washed-up anthology professor and was put on probation for psychotic episodes once Far received his Cancer diagnosis and had fled to another planet seeking help. There was plenty of evidence to make him question his own sense of reality.

"I am now second in command to Sovereign Hamish, having been named the official Prophet of the Court. I have a very comfortable living arrangement planned for us, my love...if you still want to be with me." Far pouted a little, letting his eyes fall sheepishly to the floor.

Roman pulled Far over to him on the couch, wrapped his arms around the monk and prophet and hugged him tightly. He buried his head in Far's neck. Far sniffed to avoid a sneeze at Roman's rather unsavory aroma. Roman thought his beloved was crying and merely hugged him more tightly. "Of course, I still want to be with you," Roman sobbed. "You're all I've ever wanted." After a long pause, he added, "Let me make the rounds, as you've suggested, and see for myself."

With his head burrowed into Far's neck, he couldn't see Far's sideways grin. Roman was like putty in Far's hands and Far knew it. In a single conversation, Far had managed to manipulate every concrete truth that Roman held dear.

CHAPTER 9
KIKI "THE NOSE"
SEVENTEEN DAYS BEFORE THE END.

Lucene once again found herself on Tranquil Beach for the second day in a row, walking along the water's edge as the sea foam rolled in and out, tickling her toes. She thought about what Fatima said to her the day before, on that very beach, a sentiment that she later learned was also shared by Neroni–that it all came down to trust. Of course, she trusted Tanager, he was the most honest and noble man she'd ever met. What she wasn't so sure about, was whether even *he* could trust his emotions. What if he discovered one day that it was Amy that he really wanted all along, and that Lucene *did* get in the way of destiny? And what Lucene also didn't trust, was herself. She didn't trust that she'd remain stable of mind. She didn't trust that her social anxiety and insecurities wouldn't flare up, and she certainly didn't trust that she was ...well...good enough.

And then there was Amy, who she would come to learn, spoke three languages, was a skilled artist, played classical music (at least three songs), and was an expert chef.

I hate Amy, Lucene thought to herself.

Just then, she caught sight of something flitting in the water. Not Christopher? *No, the thing was distinctly fish-like.* A dolphin? *No, too big for a dolphin. Wait, it has a blue and green torso resembling the Northern Lights. Was it…?*

"Odessa?" Lucene was surprised.

Odessa stopped swimming for a moment, treading water as she tried to make out the image of the woman in front of her on the beach. Finally, she nodded and swam over.

"Lucene," she acknowledged simply. "What are you doing here?"

"I *live* here," Luçene was surprised. "The larger question is, what are *you* doing here?" Even more surprising to Lucene, was that the Vitruvian shapeshifter, while still adopting her mermaid-like tail for swimming also seemed to be wearing…a bra?

"Something the matter?" Odessa made a face at Lucene's glance, transforming her lower half into legs. She wore a wrap skirt around her waist. Somehow, she felt more awkward covering up than she did being uncovered, and was feeling very…conspicuous.

"No, just surprised to see you."

"Well," Odessa explained. "After the last Assembly, we were ordered home; but somehow it got out that I was helping Erde against the wishes of my superiors, and now I am somewhat of a fugitive."

Odessa had become an unlikely ally. Originally an informant for the Vitruvians, she claimed to have no allegiances whatsoever, and was simply doing her job. Yet, she had helped Lucene on more than one occasion: once when Tanager was trying to rescue her from the Royals, once when the Peace-Keepers were fleeing Earth, and again when The Vitruvians and Erdelings attempted to form an alliance and return to the Intergalactic Peace Project (IPP). When the Assembly denied their re-admittance into the IPP, Vitruvians demanded that Odessa return to Section 2—her mission was over and she was being re-assigned. However, instead of returning, she hid out on Earth as long as she could, and then escaped to Erde.

Morphinae, a Vitruvian and a member of an elite group of Balance-Keepers went against his better judgment, and supported her escape. But he didn't go with her.

Lucene and Odessa began walking the length of the beach, Odessa dripping from sea water, Lucene in the same simple yellow sun dress that she'd worn far too often for the better part of a year. It was now faded and had noticeable holes in several places. Her feet were covered in white sand that would get washed away every time the water reached the shoreline and then replaced moments later with a fresh batch as they walked.

"Does anyone know you're here?"

"Yes," Odessa answered. "Commander Royce granted me sanctuary since I'm helpful to Erde and supportive of its mission to help Earth."

"Where do you live?"

"Up there," Odessa pointed to a tiny shack, strung together with what appeared to be palm fronds.

"You live on the beach?" While it sounded lovely in theory, it didn't seem terribly practical.

"I love the water," Odessa sighed. "Aside from being close to it, I don't need much and I was able to build my home quickly."

"But, what do you do for income?"

"You sure ask a lot of questions," Odessa commented. "I'll tell you... but only because I'm bored and I haven't talked to a single person in days. I don't mind, but I'm told that socialization is 'important.'" Odessa put air quotes around the 'important.'

Lucene waited.

Odessa seemed to lose her train of thought. "Oh, right, so I'm sort of a part-time undercover investigator reporting back on any activity that may be construed as subversive to the Erde government."

"Like...a spy?" Lucene was curious. "If that's true, should you be telling me that?"

"Good point," Odessa answered. "Forget I said anything."

"Well, now that you've dropped that bomb, you have to tell me more!" Lucene reasoned. Lucene doubted Odessa's undercover skills, given her propensity for wanting attention, but was dying of curiosity.

"Okay, fine," Odessa relented. "Back on Earth, I was sent on behalf of Vitruvia to collect information on Earthlings and the Royals, and... well...*you*. Kinda like the Data Collectors, only using shapeshifting talents and good old-fashioned detective work. Something, which I might add, that Erde severely lacks. Hence why Commander Royce thought my services would be invaluable."

"Agreed, but..." Lucene pointed to the rickety shack. "Surely they pay you better than this."

"Don't be rude," Odessa whined. "Look at this view!" Odessa pointed. "No one is allowed to build here, but I got special permission, so long as I avoid the sand dunes and cover my windows at night so the light doesn't affect the sea turtles when they're nesting. This is million-dollar property back on Earth!" It was clear that Odessa was very proud of her misshapen hovel.

A shadow passed over Odessa's form as a cloud floated by, only to reveal the bright sun moments later making her Northern-lights-skin flicker.

Lucene was suddenly struck by a thought.

"What?" Odessa stopped. "What is that look for?"

"I was just thinking about something...something that has been bugging me for a long time. Recent happenings have brought it to the top of my mind again." Lucene was momentarily lost in thought.

"Please," Odessa waived her hand in mild annoyance. "Sometime in this lifetime?"

"You just gave me an idea," Lucene was cautiously optimistic.

"About what?"

"There was a girl at the Embassy Club. She had a long aardvark-like nose. Told me I smelled sweet."

"You do," Odessa nodded, as if this were common knowledge.

Lucene paused for a moment, not sure what to make of that assessment, but then continued. "Anyway, the one time I was there last year, she mentioned that my backpack smelled briny."

"What does that mean?"

"I don't know. I didn't think about it at the time, but my watch was missing when I got my bag back. I later found it in my cottage, but I was sure I had brought it with me. And...Xeni said that she was certain someone had been in my cottage. Xeni is–" Lucene started to explain.

"I know who Xeni is." Odessa crossed her arms, gesturing to herself with her hands, "Spy, remember?"

"So, the same thing has started happening again, with things vanishing and resurfacing later. I thought it was some weird energetic reaction to the whole Jupiter-Venus thing."

"Saturn," Odessa corrected.

"Whatever. The point is, what if it's not? What if..." Lucene cringed, her mind going to Jasper Set, to Dallen, to Drake, to Sabrina and the Royals. They all began flashing in front of her as if on a movie screen.

Odessa clapped her hands in front of Lucene's face. "Stop that!" she commanded. "Right now!"

"Right," Lucene blinked, awkwardly. "What if someone was following me then? What if someone is following me now?"

Odessa wrapped one arm around her waist, resting her elbow on it and tapping her fingers under her chin, thoughtfully.

"What? You think I'm paranoid, don't you?"

After what felt like an eternity, Odessa finally answered, "No. I honestly don't."

Lucene wasn't entirely sure why she needed Odessa's reassurance, but it felt good, nonetheless.

"So, who do you think was following me?"

"Well, clearly, I wasn't here at the time but, if I had to guess, a Vitruvian."

"One of your people?"

"*Not* my people...anymore. Their claims of non-interference have always been somewhat murky."

"Does Morphinae know this? Where is he, anyway?"

Odessa's face contorted and Lucene realized she must have said something wrong. "He left the Balance-Keepers, but wouldn't say why. And, from what I've heard, he is no longer in communication with our former superiors. I haven't seen him in over a month, but I suspect he became disenchanted when he realized that the Vitruvians weren't much better than the Royals. They wouldn't out-and-out kill Earthlings, mind you, but they certainly wouldn't mind helping things along."

"But I thought they were on Earth's side...eventually."

Odessa let out an uncomfortable cough. "I'm probably saying more than I should, but their interest in aligning with Erde and Earth was simply self-preservation against the Royals and the Null. Not entirely sure how long-lasting that friendship would have been even if the IPP did agree to let Sections 1 and 2 back into the IPP."

"What about now?" Lucene asked. "Now that they have abandoned Erde and their help was rejected by Earth, what will they do now?"

Odessa thought a moment, shuffling through information in her head as if passing it through a filtering system. "Lucene," she answered finally. "I suggest you go about your life and don't worry about things that are out of your control."

Lucene hadn't been listening. She was lost in her own thoughts. "Well, there's one thing I know for certain," she exclaimed suddenly, not really taking in much of what Odessa had just told her. She was fixated on finding out who had been spying on her and why. She suspected that the girl at the Embassy Club may be able to shed light on the subject.

"What's that?"

"Come on," Lucene said while, not-so-gently, grabbing Odessa's arm. "We need your morphing skills and we need her nose!"

That evening…

Xeni met Lucene and Odessa around the corner from the Embassy Club, wearing her usual trench coat and hat, despite Lucene advising her to wear something more…neutral. Odessa had shape-shifted into the coat-check woman at the club, at least, according to Lucene's sketchy description. After all, Lucene wasn't always the most observant of people; she was tired that night and her memory was not the best. But for some reason, the woman leaning over and telling her, "smells a little briny, don't you think?" in reference to her backpack, left her with questions—particularly after her watch went missing. Therefore, her recollection of the woman turned out to be reasonably clear. She had a blue, aardvark-like nose and patches of dark hair protruding from around her ears. She was thin and tall, her nose excessively large by comparison to the rest of her. And yet, she carried herself with a sense of grace. After a few transitions, Odessa morphed into what Lucene deemed as passable.

"Perfect." Lucene surveyed Odessa's transformation. She turned her attention to Xeni and let out a long sigh. "Xeni, I thought we talked about this," Lucene protested, gesturing to her coat and hat.

"What?" Xeni appeared hurt. "You said to dress neutral. These colors are super neutral!"

Lucene rubbed her forehead with her thumb and forefinger. "That's not what I meant."

"Heh," Xeni let out a chortle. "You looked just like Professor Tanager just then. He does the same thing."

Odessa noticed Lucene's cheeks turn a visible shade of pink and bit her lip to stifle back a laugh. She was well aware of Lucene's burgeoning relationship with Tanager. However, it was one thing to have people be aware of it, quite another to have it pointed out.

To Odessa, Xeni turned and said, "Nice to meet you. I'm Xeni," she held out her hand like a bona fide human.

"I know who you are," Odessa bragged, taking her hand in an overly gentle manner. "I'm Odessa, nice to officially meet you."

Xeni wasn't surprised by this, but mainly because she couldn't help but keep looking at Odessa's very large aardvark-like nose. It bobbed up and down as Odessa shook her hand and Xeni was mesmerized by it.

"I'm usually much more beautiful than this," Odessa commented, which confused Xeni. "Shapeshifter, right?" Odessa explained, making a large, sweeping gesture over her body.

"Oh, yeah," Xeni nodded, putting the pieces together. She'd met a few shapeshifters in her young life, but they were always just one...well, shape. Come to think of it, she hadn't recalled witnessing them ever shift into something else before now.

"Xeni was in the animal lab the other day and smelled something that she described as 'briny,' a weird saltwater smell that she'd never noticed before. And, she had also felt the energy of something in my old cottage. So, unless you have any ideas as to who or what we're dealing with—"

"I don't," Odessa answered curtly. "Frankly, I think you're grasping at straws...on a wild goose chase...making a mountain out of a molehill..."

Xeni's eyes grew wide with fascination at Odessa's use of Earth lingo. She grabbed a notepad from her pocket and began jotting them all down, feverishly.

But there was something in the pit of Lucene's stomach that told her that something big was about to happen. "We need to investigate," she proclaimed, defiantly.

"Yes," Xeni made a fist and drew her elbow toward her in victory.

"Except you, Xeni."

"What?" Xeni pouted.

"Don't get me wrong, you have a beautiful heart-shaped face and pink eyes, but between your striking features and your trench coat, you're a bit..."

"Obvious," Odessa finished.

Xeni sulked.

"But," Lucene offered, "you gave me a great idea, and we will need your super-sleuthing skills when we're back."

"Back from where?" Xeni wanted to know.

Lucene pointed to the Embassy Club and explained their plan. Lucene was not a Vitruvian and wouldn't be allowed in unless accompanied by a dignitary, or, she reasoned, someone who worked at the club. She was hoping the coat-check woman would be working that evening since it was a Friday and about the same time she'd worked when Lucene had had her first date with Dallen, in what now seemed like ages ago. If Odessa could make the guard out front think Odessa was an employee, then they might have a way in.

"Ready?" Lucene asked.

"I was born ready," Odessa winked.

To Xeni, she said, "Wait here." Xeni sulked a little, but nodded agreeably.

At the door, the guard eyed Odessa curiously. "Kiki," he stammered. "I almost didn't recognize you. You look...ahem...taller," he finished. Something was wrong with Kiki, but he couldn't exactly point at what. "You're here a bit early for your shift."

Odessa dropped her voice to sound sugary and snakelike, as Lucene had instructed. "This Earth woman accidentally forgot her purse the other night. I thought I would retrieve it for her before guests arrive for their refection. I just need her to confirm which one is hers. There are several in our lost-and-found."

The guard looked Lucene over, distastefully.

"Well," he was uncomfortable. "It's highly uncustomary for a non-Vitruvian to be allowed inside unaccompanied by a dignitary. Most uncustomary." He shook his head. "I will need approval from my superiors."

"This is no ordinary human," Odessa smiled at him, seductively. Unfortunately, this maneuver did little to entice the guard as she still looked like an aardvark. "This," she leaned in and whispered, "is a special friend of Representative Dallen." Lucene cringed at the name. And, what did she mean by "special friend?"

"Oh, I see," the guard gave this some thought. "Didn't know he was on Erde...haven't seen him in quite some time. But I have been working odd hours lately, so maybe I missed him." He paused. "Alright, Kiki, but be quick about it, else both of us will be looking for new jobs soon." He held the door open and motioned for them to go inside.

Odessa and Lucene quickly made their way to the coatroom. "Okay," Odessa stated and then asked, "now what?"

"We lay low and wait for the real Kiki to arrive."

"How is she going to get inside without the guard being suspicious?" Odessa whispered from the back of the coatroom. "And, what if she isn't even on duty today?"

"Hmm, I hadn't thought of that," Lucene pondered. Maybe she should have asked for Xeni's detecting expertise after all.

Their questions were answered moments later, as the real Kiki arrived at the door, seemingly perplexed at the guard's asking her what happened to the *distasteful mistress of Representative Dallen?* And, *you'd think someone of his stature could have done better."* Suddenly, Kiki sniffed the air suspiciously, turned her head toward the window and smiled.

Can she smell us from out there? Lucene wondered.

Kiki appeared to have made some joke and the guard finally laughed, letting her inside. She made her way behind the counter and to the coatroom, pulling the cloth drapes that separated the coats and purses from the main counter closed. "Okay," she said quietly. "I know there are at least two of you here. Show yourselves."

Lucene appeared from behind a furry coat that tickled her nose. She had been fighting back a sneeze. Odessa, on the other hand, who had turned herself into a tiny moth, transformed back into her standard female form. "Oh, a fellow shapeshifter," Kiki acknowledged. "I like your shape," she complimented. This was not a sexual reference. It seemed almost standard behavior among Vitruvians, not unlike, "I like your dress," or "I like your new hairdo."

"Thank you, and..." Odessa was trying to think of something nice to say, but was coming up short.

"I know," Kiki sighed. "Shapeshifting mishap."

"Whatever do you mean?" Odessa was curious.

"Well, you know how on Earth," she eyed Lucene, "they tell kids not to make ugly faces at people or else they might freeze that way?"

"Yes," Odessa answered.

Lucene nodded in agreement.

"Well, mine did." Her face fell to the floor. "I shifted one day and couldn't manage to shift back."

"Oh, you poor thing," Odessa was not typically known for her empathy, but she found herself putting her arm around Kiki, encouragingly.

"It's not so bad," she answered. "On the plus side, I've got this killer nose. I knew, even from outside, that there were two different species in my closet and I was right!" After pausing for a moment she asked. "And, what are you doing in my closet?"

"We need your nose," Lucene answered, catching herself when Kiki gave her a quizzical look. "I mean, we need your help in identifying scents. It's..." Lucene tried to think of something that might warrant her buy-in, and continued with, "a matter of national security!" This made no sense, but she lifted her chin and puffed out her chest and as they would say on Earth, "owned it."

"Oh, how intriguing," Kiki's eyes lit up.

"I don't suppose you remember the night I came here with Representative Dallen about six months ago?"

"No," Kiki shook her head. "But I've only been working here for a month."

"Oh, but..." Lucene paused. "Is there another girl who works here who..." she pointed to the nose. "Looks like you?"

"Fortunately, no," Kiki answered.

"How odd. Well, okay, but whomever it was had told me that I smelled sweet and she knew I was a human."

"You do." Odessa and Kiki chimed in, in unison. Lucene looked from one to the other, wrinkling her forehead, perplexed. "Well, when you, or whomever it was, told me my bag smelled briny...I was wondering if someone had somehow gotten into my bag while I was at dinner an... left a scent?"

"I honestly don't remember this," Kiki confessed, "if it was even me working that night. But a briny smell could be any one of three: a lower class shapeshifting Vitruvian—"

"I resent that," Odessa interrupted. "I don't smell briny."

"No," Kiki smiled. "You are much saltier...mid-west?"

"Hmmph," Odessa crossed her arms. Kiki knew she was right.

"You were saying?" Lucene coaxed Kiki into continuing.

"Or a rare type of fish found in the ponds in the Western Crosses, which doesn't make sense because they're not edible and they're found in brackish water that most people wouldn't want to swim in. So, the other option could be—" Kiki thought a moment.

"What?" Lucene asked.

"Well, I'm not sure you believe in such things, but there are species from other realms that tend to leave odd scents behind...flowers, oaky smells, and bitter food smells—such as olive brine."

"I vote for Vitruvian," Odessa was convinced.

At that moment, Kiki sniffed the air. She furrowed her eyebrows in a very confused manner. "You two need to stay here. I'll sneak you out in a moment."

With that, she lifted her chin, pulled her shoulders back and emerged to the front counter in time to see an alternate Lucene, dressed in a form-fitting red dress appear behind an impatient Representative Dallen. Her eyes grew wide, but ever the professional, she quickly covered it up. "May I take your purse, Earth woman?"

Lucene peered through a crack in the curtain. She almost let out a yelp until Odessa put her hand over Lucene's mouth. She was witnessing her arrival and her first date with Dallen, months ago. But how was this possible? Her heart seemed to take a up a place in her throat as she forced a gulp of air. When Odessa was confident that Lucene had her emotions under control, she removed her hand. The two retreated behind rows of coats, capes and purses, hiding until receiving new information from Kiki.

Minutes later (which felt like an eternity to Lucene), Kiki made her way to the back with Lucene's backpack. "Is this yours?" she asked.

"Yes," Lucene whispered. "Can I see it?" Kiki handed it over. There, buried beneath her day clothes, lay her communication watch. She passed it back to Kiki. "Kiki, I need you to tell me what happens this evening. Please. How can we reach you after tonight?"

Kiki thought a moment. "Here," she handed her a business card that showed a glam shot of Kiki with a microphone. "I'm sort of a singer on the side. Either call me on this number," she pointed to the card, "or, if you ladies are free tonight, I've got a singing gig at The Beacon."

"Thanks," Lucene accepted the card. "I know Odessa will have no trouble morphing her way out of here, but how can I leave?"

"Easy," Kiki answered. "Dignitaries are always smuggling mistresses in and out of this place." Lucene took offense. It made her wonder exactly how many "special friends" Dallen actually had. Kiki pulled aside a throw rug, revealing a handle that was folded down on a hinge, fitting neatly into a trap door. She lifted it and gave a tug. "This will drop you on the street, the backend of the club."

"Thanks, Kiki, you're a champ."

"No problem, Earth woman." After Lucene climbed in, Odessa followed suit, choosing the moth form again for simplicity. Kiki closed the door behind them and covered it with the carpet...and waited.

That night, Kiki was called from her station exactly one time—a guest needed to be lent proper attire that evening, and so it was requested that Kiki hand-deliver the garment to a private club room. She hadn't been gone more than a few minutes. But when she returned, she checked Lucene's bag, curiously. Sure enough, the watch was missing.

Then, she smelled it...sweetness. It was the alternate Lucene passing her counter. Lucene was about to leave *with* Representative Dallen but *without* her backpack. When she remembered, Kiki leaned in, knowingly, warning her new Earth friend, "Smells sort of briny, don't you think?"

"So, what happened?" Xeni asked eagerly when Odessa (now back to her most human-like form) and Lucene met her a block from the Embassy Club.

"I'm not sure," Lucene filled her in on the weird time warp.

Xeni's eyes grew wide. "Oh my gosh! But I thought that two of you couldn't occupy the same space at the same time. How could you have been there at the same time that last year's "you" was there?"

"Who told you that?" Odessa challenged.

"Just every science fiction movie ever," Xeni explained.

"Well, that explains it," Odessa remained unconvinced. "If it's a rule from a science fiction movie, it has to be true."

"You don't have to be rude," Xeni pouted. "Hey," she had a thought, "were there any other duplicates, I mean, aside from you?"

"No, come to think of it." Lucene thought a moment. "At least, not that I could tell."

"So, what do we do now?" Xeni wanted to know.

Lucene flipped Kiki's card over and over in her hand. "Xeni, since you're new to the dating scene, maybe it's time for a gal's night out."

Xenia's eyes grew wide. "Yessss," the young woman did that annoying thing where she made a fist and pulled her elbow in with excitement. "We should invite Neroni and Fatima, too." Xeni paused for a moment. "How about you, Des? Will you come with us, too?"

It took Odessa a moment to realize that Xeni had just given her a nickname, and was about to protest, until it occurred to her that no one had ever done that before. And, she rather liked it. After all, that was a term of affection and friendliness, wasn't it? She hadn't really done a great job of maintaining friendships, the closest being Morphinae, but he seemed to be avoiding her.

"Oh, I'm sure you'll see me there," Odessa winked. "If I remember correctly, Kiki's got a regular spot at 10 o'clock."

Lucene tried to remember the last time she'd been out anywhere where things were just getting started at ten in the evening. In fact, she was usually asleep by then.

"Okay," Xeni decided. "Meet you out front of The Beacon by 9:30. If you call Fatima, I'll call Neroni, deal?"

Lucene nodded. *Right after I take a nap,* she thought.

"Catch you later, alligator." Xeni waited for a response that Lucene absolutely refused to give her.

"In a while, crocodile," Odessa offered. It was the least she could do now that she had been given a nickname. Xeni smiled before darting toward the bridge connecting Achel with the SpeedCircuit. Odessa morphed into a little bluebird and flew away, leaving Lucene to walk home alone and wonder how she was going to explain all of this to Tanager.

CHAPTER 10
THE BEACON
SEVENTEEN DAYS BEFORE THE END.

Lucene could hear The Beacon before the nightclub actually came into view. Multicolored strobe lights marked the entryway in a light stream that scanned High Street from the top of The Beacon's outdoor signage. The Beacon had a glass, pentagonal prism roof, making the light waves brighter and more wave-like. The club was a stone's throw from Big Ben (one of Achel's many Earth-like replicas) which, sadly, began to chime at that very moment.

Xeni stood next to Lucene wearing a bright red sequined party dress with an unfortunate tulle fabric at one side of her neck that fanned out in front of the right side of her face, making her pink eyes seem almost fluorescent. (*Maybe that was on purpose?*) On her feet, were high-heeled, cuffed sandals as white as snow. For the briefest of moments, Lucene missed the trench coat that the girl usually wore when she was "detecting."

The chimes, the music, and the sounds of people crowding around the club grew louder. Lucene clasped her hands over her ears but it was too late. There were flashes of light in all directions, the street appeared to be wobbling up and down around her, and more and more sounds manifested in her mind as if her brain were cycling through a radio dial. She began to lose her balance.

Xeni grabbed her arm. "Are you okay?" she all but yelled, concerned.

Suddenly, someone grabbed her other arm for support. "Don't worry, we got you," Fatima smiled. The two women stood flanked at Lucene's side until the spinning slowed to a stop. A moment later, Big Ben had finished chiming and the rest of the world seemed to return to a normal level. It was still too loud for Lucene's taste but at least it was...bearable. Lucene opened her eyes.

"Sorry," Lucene apologized.

"No need to apologize," Fatima shook her head. "I know crowds aren't exactly your thing, but it's for the greater good."

In this case, the *greater good* was Fatima getting a reprieve from mommy-duty for the evening and, possibly, helping Xeni get a date. Or at least, making sure she didn't do anything stupid her first night out on the scene. Lucene had a different agenda in mind. She wanted to seek out Kiki to find out what happened after she and Odessa fled the Embassy Club.

It was then that Lucene noticed Fatima's outfit. She was wearing a dark brown steampunk corset dress with a hem that poofed at the bottom, and knee-high boots that laced all the way to the top. With her hair newly died a deep frosted purple, she was quite a sight to behold. It was then that Lucene realized that maybe she was the one who was out of place, wearing the simplest of black cocktail dresses with no lace, sequins or anything remotely interesting about it other than it made her look as if she actually had cleavage. She looked down at her dress. *(Cleavage! Who knew?)* On her feet were black ballet flats. To her, these seemed the most practical for dancing.

"Where's Neroni?" Fatima asked.

"She bailed," Xeni explained as the three made their way to the front door of The Beacon, where they gathered in line for admission. "She said it was family game night at her house. But I think it was more that this really isn't her scene."

Not my scene either, Lucene thought. *And yet, here I am.*

The guard at the door stopped them with a smile. "Hi Xeni, how many in your party?" he asked.

"Uh, three," Xeni answered, counting again as if she were somehow unsure. Lucene was surprised that the guard actually knew Xeni enough to call her by name. Lucene shot Fatima a questioning look, who merely shrugged her shoulders.

"300 Units," he called out.

"I got it," Fatima electronically transferred the money from her watch.

"Thanks," Lucene responded.

"Likewise. That's really good of you," Xeni offered.

"Enjoy your evening, ladies," the guard admitted them.

It took a moment to adjust to the dark lighting as the women found their way inside and headed to the bar nearest the entrance. "How come they didn't ID Xeni?" Lucene wanted to know.

"That's an Earth thing," Xeni waved her hand as if she were someone now an Earth expert. She took a seat on a pub stool and pounded the bar top with her fist to get the bartender's attention. A seven-foot-tall thin man wearing a paisley shirt and lime green tie walked over to them from behind the counter. It was almost as if his top half hadn't figured out how to balance on top of his bottom half, so his torso swayed awkwardly as he approached.

"Refection?" he asked.

"Yeah," Xeni answered. "I'll have a chilled Corsica Slam with a splash of vermouth and a sprig of thyme; don't forget the thyme," she cautioned.

The bartended laughed. "Don't worry, Xeni, I won't."

"Wait!" Lucene pointed her finger between the two of them. "He knows your name. How does he know your name, and how did the guard know your name, if you've never been here before?"

"It was a ruse," Xeni flashed an open palm across her face as if to dazzle. "You need to get out more, and I knew the only way to do it was to make it seem like I needed protecting. Besides, we've got some detecting to do!"

"No," Lucene corrected. "*I've* got some detecting to do. *You* are going to dance and have fun and...whatever it is that people do in places like this."

The bartender cleared his throat. "So, what'll you guys have?"

Lucene thought a moment. "Red wine?" she said it more like a question. The bartender nodded. Apparently, they only had one kind, and that was what she was getting. He looked at Fatima.

"I'll just have an unsweetened iced tea," Fatima answered. "I'm the designated pedestrian," she joked. No one was driving. They were walking. Also, no one but Fatima got the joke. She didn't care, she began laughing, giggling up and down as she did.

The bartender nodded and wobbled away.

"So, what was all that about needing help on the dating site then?" Fatima asked Xeni, as the three huddled in one corner of the counter awaiting their drinks.

"Oh, that part is true." Xeni sighed. "Just because I go clubbing and do the whole 'bar scene' doesn't mean I'm any good tracking down a boyfriend…at least, not a good one."

"Maybe it's your approach?" Fatima offered. "*Tracking?*"

Just then, a haunting voice filled the room. A woman was singing. While the Erde tongue was songlike and beautiful all on its own, that wasn't the language. It wasn't one that Fatima or Lucene had ever heard before. The notes were off-pitch by many musical standards, and yet they somehow worked in this context. The crowd became entranced as they gazed toward the singer on the main stage.

It was Kiki. She was accompanied by an electric violin, a harpsichord and some other wind instrument that Lucene could not identify. The stage, itself, was simple enough, a black backdrop with those awful multicolored strobe lights floating across them.

Kiki was wearing a long yellow evening gown that hugged her slim waist and billowed out all around her on the floor. The yellow offset her blue skin. She was still a sight to behold with her overgrown aardvark nose. But in that moment, she didn't care. And neither did anyone else.

It was then that Lucene noticed something. She peered around the room. There were exceptionally tall and thin people, small and wide people, dancers on the floor with wolf-like faces similar to those living in Section 5, a few baboon-shaped beings, and even several shapeshifting Vitruvians who seemed to change form every time the rhythm of a song changed. But they all stopped dancing when Kiki began singing. Lucene realized that while most of the time she was surrounded by many people who looked largely like herself, a human, in this place, she was as much a rarity as they were…if not more. It seemed as if The Beacon was one of those unusual places where everyone could be exactly who they were, and no one else seemed to care.

After the song, which went on for an unprecedented fifteen minutes or more, Kiki belted out a final high note, holding it for what seemed like an eternity while the room stood frozen. It was followed by a moment of silence as Kiki took a majestic bow. The room erupted in applause, along with some weird clicking noise that people seemed to produce from the depths of their throats. Xeni exaggerated the sound and motioned for Fatima and Lucene to follow her lead, which they did with some difficulty. Clapping was, by far, easier.

"You finally made it, Earth woman" Kiki squealed, all but leaping from the stage. She climbed down and untangled her dress, heading straight toward Lucene. She embraced her in an unexpected bear hug, as if they were old friends. Without waiting for a response, Kiki did the same to Xeni and Fatima. While Lucene was flummoxed, Xeni and Fatima automatically hugged her back with all the zeal of people who'd known each other for years. This was not at all the reserved version of Kiki Lucene observed at the Embassy Club. This one, was noticeably more animated.

"Oh, sorry," Kiki remembered herself. "I'm Kiki," she introduced herself to Fatima. "I've been told I'm not great at boundaries but after being bound and gagged and on my best behavior at the Embassy Club all day, I tend to go a little overboard."

Xeni looked wide-eyed with glee at Kiki's use of Earth lingo. Fatima resonated with Kiki's warmth; it reminded her of the family she'd left behind when moving too Erde. There was this strange moment of familial love between them that, sadly, was lost on Lucene who watched the scene with a minor amount of confusion.

After all, she had been imbued with empathic powers that had been stripped away when they short-circuited trying to banish the demon Jasper Set before he could destroy her and her closest allies. But they seemed to be returning at oddly inappropriate and uncontrolled times, a fact that she'd been hiding from Tanager until...actually, she couldn't even articulate to herself what exactly she was waiting for. He knew about some of it, of course, but not the severity at which it was starting to flood back into her being. All Lucene knew was at this particular moment, she wasn't feeling the love...or much of anything, for that matter.

"I see you've found your watch," Kiki motioned to Lucene's communication watch on her wrist. "Or, at least that someone returned it to you."

"Yes, the day after it disappeared. That's why I'm here. I wanted to ask what happened today after we left."

"Today?" Kiki was confused. "Honey, have you hit your head? That happened more than six months ago. I was wondering why you never came in to ask about what happened."

"Kiki," Lucene answered, confused "In our timeline, it happened earlier today."

Xeni nodded in agreement.

"Hmm," Kiki considered this. "Maybe I'm the one who's hit her head." She felt her skull as if this could be a possibility.

"Given that there were two of me at the Club, I'm going to guess it was something else...some weird time warp," Lucene offered.

Another fact that she'd kept from Tanager when she mentioned going out with the ladies that evening. She knew he'd want to come along and act as chaperone to protect her. Or, he might talk her out of going altogether. And while she appreciated the fact that he cared enough to worry about her, she didn't feel as if she needed protecting.

Fatima stared in wide-eyed fascination as Kiki and Xeni swapped stories about what transpired at the Embassy Club following Lucene and Odessa's visit. Kiki's memory had become a bit faultier as more time had passed. For example, she remembered that the watch had disappeared, but had no recollection of how, when, or who had taken it. So, the hunt led to a dead end. The only memory blazing in her mind from that night was another Vitruvian who had taken on her form. *It's unnerving to run into another you,* Kiki decided.

Lucene wandered from the group. She didn't know where she was going, exactly, but with the loud house music, flashing lights, and dancing, which resumed immediately after Kiki's number, she moved in a hazy, dreamlike fashion. People moved past her, appearing in odd shapes and colors. She stopped after almost walking directly into what appeared to be a human-sized metal birdcage. Except, inside, there wasn't a bird; there was a woman dancing. There were several rings hanging from the top and a bar at its center which she expertly maneuvered in both a seductive and yet artistic manor. Frankly, Lucene hadn't ever seen a person able to contort that way. The woman looked up with one leg somehow flipped over her shoulder.

"Lucene." Odessa dropped from the bar at the center of the cage and fell expertly to the floor, landing like a cat ready to pounce. "Somehow, I didn't think you'd actually show up here."

"Kiki invited us, remember?" Lucene reminded her. "Why would you think I wouldn't show up?"

Odessa thought a moment. "No reason." She held her hands on her hips as if trying to blend in with the scenery. It wasn't working. "You did figure out the time glitch though, right?"

"Just caught on," Lucene acknowledged. Odessa merely nodded.

"Yeah, I remember when I first met her months back, she seemed to know me and was surprised that I didn't remember her. Seemed almost hurt, actually." For a moment Odessa was lost in thought over the incident.

"Um," Lucene finally commented, pulling Odessa back from her daydream. "What are you doing in a cage?" At that moment, a surly looking man with brown fur that framed his entire face and head walked by.

"I gotta get back to work." Odessa nodded to the man. "This is sort of my expressive…outlet."

"Oh, I see." (Lucene really didn't.)

"Listen, if you happen to see him, don't tell Morphinae you saw me here, okay?"

"Morphinae?" Lucene was confused. "I thought you hadn't seen him in months, the last place being back on Earth. Has he contacted you?"

Odessa's face actually turned slightly pink. "No," she confessed. "But he and I have spent so much time together in the past that I, sort of, well, *feel* his energy in the distance. And, I don't know how he'd feel about my dancing. So, just between us?"

"Sure," Lucene furrowed her lips in confusion. Why would Morphinae care about her dancing? More to the point, why would Odessa care what anyone thought of anything she did? She never had before. It was then that Lucene made the connection. *Boy, am I oblivious sometimes,* Lucene thought to herself.

"There you are!" Fatima yelled above the music, waving as she, Xeni, and Kiki made their way over to the cage where Odessa was resetting for the next dance number. Kiki sniffed the air.

"Oh, I didn't realize you were working tonight," Kiki said to Odessa. "I smelled something salty and figured it must have been you."

"I do not smell salty," Odessa protested. "And I work here most nights. I just shift forms regularly. The boss said it makes it more interesting for people."

"Ah," Kiki nodded. "You're the kind that changes scent with each form. I guess I hadn't smelled you enough to realize that."

"You really need to stop saying weird stuff like that," Odessa advised.

"Sorry," Kiki smiled. (She really wasn't sorry.) Modesty was not a particularly strong trait among shapeshifters.

"Now, shoo," Odessa shooed them away. "I am an artiste, and I have to get back to work."

"Me, too," Kiki nodded. To Lucene, Fatima and Xeni she said, "Thanks so much for coming out tonight to hear me sing. It means a lot to me. Please come back again soon." With that, she went back to the hugging thing. When she hugged Lucene, she rubbed her arms and her back a little, awkwardly. No, boundaries did not appear to be a thing among Vitruvian shapeshifters, either. This was quite a bit different from the dignitaries and high-ranking officials from Vitruvia, Lucene noted.

"Time for my next set," Kiki announced. As she returned to the stage, Fatima's eyes turned to Xeni. The young girl seemed to be staring absent-mindedly into space. Fatima waved her hand in front of Xeni's face. "What's wrong with you? Are you okay?"

There, in the distance, working his way through the crowd, was none other than Clusaladek. It only took Lucene a few seconds to realize the real reason Xeni frequented The Beacon…it was Clusaladek's favorite hangout.

Today, he had replaced the toga-like garb he frequently wore in class with black spandex pants and a burnt orange tunic. "Lucene, Xeni, so nice to see you here," he smiled as if they were visiting him at his home. "I'm sorry, we've not met," he said as he turned to Fatima.

"Oh, but I know you," Fatima giggled. Clusaladek seemed confused. "I'm Fatima," she offered her hand.

He shook it, hesitantly. "You must originally be from Earth," he surmised.

"What gave me away?" Fatima asked. Between her heavy Brooklyn-inspired accent and handshake, it really wasn't all that hard to guess.

"Just a hunch," he answered, with that same sheepish, lopsided grin that he had shown in his dating profile. Fatima actually blushed a little.

"Hi, Clusaladek," Xeni greeted, her eyes even wider than normal with a stupid grin plastered across her face. The gauze around her neck somehow seemed to poof up so that it covered the entire side of her face. Clusaladek reached over and attempted to push it down for her in an effort to be helpful, but it just sprang back into place. Xeni couldn't take her eyes off of him.

At that moment, Kiki launched into her next number—a slow ballad.

"Why don't you kids dance?" Fatima suggested, pushing Xeni toward her classmate.

"Of course," Clusaladek flashed an Adonis smile. "Xeni, would you honor me with a dance?"

Xeni nodded, letting out this strange gurgle from the back of her throat as she accompanied him to the dance floor.

As they were walking away, Lucene could hear him whisper to Xeni, "Why are you acting so weird?"

"Young love," Fatima sighed. "Isn't it romantic?"

"What they have isn't romantic," Lucene shook her head. "What they have is a friendship. He sees her like a little sister. And once Xeni figures that out, it's not going to be pretty."

"Oh," Fatima's face dropped. "You're probably right. Poor thing. I guess I shouldn't have pushed the two of them together."

"It's a dance," Lucene reasoned. "There's no harm in that."

Lucene had barely gotten the words out when a loud crash erupted. The glass ceiling shattered as a large, cat-like frame landed on the floor and on top of the two unfortunate shapeshifters who were dancing at that moment. Had Lucene been in contact with Isabella, she would have recognized the creature as Hysechia, the cat formerly known as Tabby, the house cat from the animal lab, now in full lion form.

Much like candy glass, the ceiling's properties changed when shattered. While bits of the glass would have normally cut into the flesh of those in its wake, it was simply a minor annoyance to those covered in it, not unlike people covered in glitter or confetti.

But for Lucene, it brought back memories. Suddenly, she was a little girl in the back of a green SUV as her father fought to stay on the road during a storm. The glass had shattered around her, embedding into her arms as the car toppled over and over repeatedly, with her hanging helplessly upside-down from her seatbelt, and then falling unconscious until days later when she awoke in the hospital. That was where she met her lifetime friend, Fatima, and learned of her parent's death. Lucene crawled under one of the nightclub's tables and wrapped her arms around her head, fearfully.

"Snap out of it, Lucene," Fatima commanded with uncustomary harshness, leaning under the table and slapping her friend's face lightly with the back of her fingers. "We need you."

Lucene's eyes fluttered open as she fought to adjust to the incoming stream of lights. For once, she wasn't fighting the sights and sounds in her head. They were actually coming from the world around her.

There, in the center of room, Hysechia had downed a Vitruvian shapeshifter who had unfortunately chosen the shape of a lamb. Hysechia was now feasting on its flesh while the lamb's dance partner had shifted into a flying black dragon, belching a hot flame onto Hysechia's back. The feline's eyes grew wide in pain and fear. At that moment, she resembled Henri Rousseau's "Tiger in a Storm" painting. The flame-ridden cat began rolling on the floor. Someone thought to open The Beacon's main doors and Hysechia sprang through it, setting a few tables and chairs ablaze along the way— not to mention a few bystanders who dropped to the ground as several bar servers pointed flame suppressors at them, dampening the fires in a coat of white snow.

Now, the dragon shifted back into its preferred form—a woman, as she held her lamb-shaped partner in her arms, bloodied and nearly dead.

"Don't just hide like a mouse. Use your powers and do something!" Odessa commanded of Lucene, leaning over to peer under the table where Lucene was crouched. Lucene let out a relieved sigh. While she had just been talking to her friend, she had had a momentary mental glitch, *was that Vitruvian Odessa? Was the other Morphinae?* Odessa all but dragged the woman out from under the table as Fatima helped steady her friend. The two flanked Lucene and guided her clumsily to the dance floor.

"But I don't know how," Lucene protested.

"Of course, you do," Odessa barked. "The only other person I've witnessed with your level of empathic healing power is Morphinae." Her face crumbled. "And he's not here right now." She pushed Lucene toward the fallen man.

Lucene reluctantly knelt at his side, blood pooling around him with bits of his neck hanging out. Lucene fought back the queasiness in her stomach and focused on the task. Holding her hands over the man, she attempted to imbue her hands with loving energy, sending it his direction. She looked down at the branch-like patterns of her arms, but they were dark…nothing.

The crowd grew restless. The Vitruvian woman stood over her love, hopefully. She may not have had the powers that some other Balance-Keepers on her planet had, but she recognized the ability in others.

Xeni pushed her way through the spectators. "Excuse me!" she called loudly. Behind her, she clasped Clusaladek's hand and dragged his tall frame after her.

"What are you doing?" Clusaladek was embarrassed. "We lost our powers, remember?"

Xeni's body shook as if she were bubbling up energy from the soles of her feet. "I don't believe that," she tucked her head, determined. "Let's go. Lucene needs us."

Clusaladek caught sight of the body and gagged.

"Focus," Xeni, punched him in the arm.

"Ouch!" He recoiled slightly, annoyed. She motioned for him to kneel on the other side of Lucene. He had never seen Xeni quite so determined and obeyed. Odessa and Fatima stood behind Lucene for moral support.

"Medical help is on the way," Fatima told her friend, just as the strobe lights and music stopped. The room fell silent and dark.

Lucene held her hand over the man's neck, being careful not to actually touch him. This time, Xeni and Cluseladek did the same, just as she, Cepheus and Morphinae had done back when Fredo, Sovereign

Hamish's guard, had almost killed Tanager on Earth when he was attempting to rescue Lucene from the Royals.

Lucene remembered, of all things, the words that Neroni's young child had told her recently when trying to use telekinetic powers to make a coin slide off the table and onto the floor, *just think why the coin would want to fall on the floor.*

Why would healing energy want to flow through my arms? Lucene asked herself. It was then that she realized that this had nothing to do with her, her ability, or lack of it. The Universe didn't really care who she was as a person and whether her life was purposeful or not, whether she was a good person or a bad person. Once she took herself out of the equation it was easy…it was simply convincing the energy that life and love were the most important things in the universe and then…

The patterns on her arms began to turn a deep brown and then a red. This time, however, the red seemed to give off smoke and the heat hurt her arms. She bit her lip and fought back the pain as light began streaming directly from her arms and flowing into the fallen Vitruvian.

Seconds later, he coughed up a little blood and then turned his head slowly and smiled groggily at his partner. The medics arrived and hoisted him onto a hover unit that transported him to the Dragoste Healing Center with his partner at his heels. She turned to shoot Lucene a grateful look before disappearing through the front doors.

"We did it!" Xenia's eyes grew wide. "We really did it!"

Xeni stood between Clusaladek and Lucene as the other two stumbled to their feet. Xeni wrapped one arm around Clusaladek, the other around Lucene, pulling them in for a group hug. "We're not broken, after all," she smiled proudly.

Fatima knew she wasn't exactly a part of this healing trio but was still overcome with emotion. She wrapped her big arms around the three of them, "Of course you're not," she whispered, blinking back tears.

Odessa stood behind them and crossed her arms, curiously. "Hmmm…" was all she said.

CHAPTER 11
THE RESEARCH CONTINUES
SIXTEEN DAYS BEFORE THE END.

At Commander Royce's insistence, following a long night of questioning by Constable Melokule and his men about what transpired at The Beacon, Xeni, Clusaladek, Lucene, Tanager, Cepheus and Moksha were "requested" at the Planetary Defense League (PDL) for further interrogation.

"This is not an interrogation," Commander Royce assured them upon arrival. (But it really was.)

Xeni clutched Clusaladeks's arm with both hands, nervously, her pink eyes wide. She shivered like a nervous chihuahua and was beginning to think whether she was cut out to be a detective after all. Here she was, crumbling at the first sign of potential trouble. Clusaladek put a hand over hers. "It'll be okay," he told her. She sucked in a deep breath and held it. "Breathe," he whispered to her. Remembering, she exhaled like a tire losing its air pressure all at once.

"Sit," Royce commanded, and then, as if remembering she added, "please."

They sat.

She nodded for an attendant to go around the room offering water to those she had summoned. Lucene, Tanager, Moksha and Cepheus were used to Commander Royce at this point, but Tanager's students were not.

Xeni accepted the water, her hands still shaking nervously. So much so that she was worried she might accidentally dump the contents of the glass all over herself. Clusaladek retrieved it for her and set it on the table.

"Quite the evening the three of you seemed to have had," Royce singled out Lucene, Clusaladek, and Xeni.

To be clear, Lucene was operating on about three hours of sleep, and it showed. After a long silence, she answered, "We didn't expect a large tiger to come crashing through the ceiling of a night club and trying to feast on one of the attendees, that's for sure."

"No," Royce answered, "I expect you didn't. I'm growing tired of these weird anomalies from Erde's reaction to the conjunction between the Jupiter-Saturn shift. Frankly, I never believed in such things before now. But I have it on good authority that the shift will end in another two weeks or so. Until then, my men have been scrambling to manage unusual emergencies, such as this one."

"May I ask," Tanager interjected, "why you called us here?"

Lucene shrank into her seat. She was so tired when she finally arrived at their high-home that she gave him the briefest of explanations about the evening, none of which included that she and two of his former students used powers they were no longer supposed to have, to save a shapeshifter's life.

Commander Royce was surprised, until she caught a glance at Lucene's expression. "Oh, she hasn't told you?" Both Tanager and Cepheus looked at Lucene, questioningly. The hairs on the back of Moksha's neck bristled. She suspected she already knew where this conversation was going, and it wasn't good.

All eyes were on Lucene for an explanation. Finally, she relented. "The tiger mauled someone on the dance floor," she began.

"Yes," Tanager answered impatiently, "you told me that last night."

"But what I didn't get around to telling you was…that the three of us," she pointed to Xeni and Clusaladek, "combined our energy to keep him alive long enough for the medics to arrive."

Tanager bit the back of his fist, fighting back anger.

"Lucene," Cepheus interjected calmly. "Why didn't you tell us?"

"I didn't get a chance to," she defended. "This just happened last night, and here we are at the butt-crack of dawn at the PDL after only a few hours of sleep!" (It should be noted here that Lucene didn't function well when sleep-deprived.)

"But," Xeni gathered the courage to speak up. "How did you know about it?" she asked Commander Royce.

"There were hundreds of witnesses at the club," Royce explained as if the girl were daft, "all saying that there was a woman with 'lightening flowing from her arms' with two 'regulars' at The Beacon helping her. It didn't take much effort to determine who those 'regulars' might be."

"Are we in trouble?" Xeni asked weakly.

"No," Royce softened, just a little. "But what I want to know is…have your other powers returned? We assumed you lost them permanently." No one answered her. She resorted to a grade-school inquiry. "Show of hands," she demanded. "Who has noticed signs that your Data Collection powers are returning? Not just the glitches that Lucene has experienced…I mean, full-on power?"

Xeni, Clusaladek, and Lucene all nervously raised their hands.

"Why didn't we hear of this sooner?" She glared at Tanager and Cepheus as if they had been hiding something from them all.

"To be honest," Clusaladek spoke. "My memory was shot for about a month after the incident on the bridge. But then it began to sharpen again." He smiled, proudly. "I just thought it was because I'm very smart."

Royce resisted the urge to slap the grin off his stupid face. Commander Royce used to be a patient woman, but now that she was working past when she was originally set to retire at the behest of The Elders, she had grown irritable.

"What about you?" Royce pointed to Xeni.

"I…" Xeni paused, peering down at the table. "I didn't want to say anything until I was sure, and…" Her eyes teared up a little.

"It's okay, Xeni," Tanager offered gently. He may have been angry at Lucene's omission but Xeni, he reasoned, was an innocent bystander with far less life experience than Lucene.

"I don't like what TARA has become," she finally blurted out. "It used to be fun, and creative, and a place where we could learn and develop our skills in a supportive environment. Now, it's just a military school and I didn't want my powers to be exploited as...a weapon."

Tanager's heart sank. He understood. He and Cepheus had been feeling the exact same way. In their case, it was their livelihood and much harder to walk away from the financial security TARA provided. It wasn't until that moment that he fully appreciated what his former students must have been going through—suddenly shuffled into different courses of study with minimal psychological support to address the emotional affects they must be feeling from having initially lost their powers. Tanager and Cepheus adapted to the change easily, but for their students, who had never gone through this type of trauma before, it must have felt as if they'd suddenly lost a limb. The emptiness of not having one's powers must have been devastating for them. At that moment, there was no one that Tanager disliked more than himself.

"I'm sorry you feel that way," Commander Royce answered, matter-of-factly. "I hope one day you can learn to appreciate how your services have become vital assets to the government of Erde."

"What are you talking about?" Lucene demanded. Moksha's face felt flushed. She already knew what was coming.

"I am requesting the re-assembly of all the Data Collectors. Training will resume immediately with you, Professors Tanager and Cepheus at the helm."

"But many students dropped out of school when this happened," Tanager protested. "And others, including Xeni and Clusaladek, have already chosen other fields of study."

"I am requesting that they switch back," Commander Royce made it abundantly clear that this was not a request. "These classes will resume Monday morning and I'm putting in a medical request that all three of you have a full battery of bloodwork and tests to see if there's any other reason why you should have lost your powers to begin with."

Tanager left Dr. Ennis' name out of it and addressed only Erde's most respected physician, Dr. Wilah. "Dr. Wilah confirmed that they, in essence, short-circuited from an explosion of energy. Perhaps they just needed time to recharge and heal," Tanager reasoned.

"Let's reconfirm that, shall we?" Commander Royce eyed him coldly.

She stood, her hair much grayer then even a month ago—possibly from stress—and her gate a little more unstable.

"And those who have dropped out of school altogether?" Tanager asked.

"I suggest you convince them to return," Royce answered simply.

Tanager started to belt out an angry reply but Cepheus stopped him.

"We will do our best," Cepheus answered calmly.

Xeni shot Lucene a furtive glance. *Should we tell them?* she thought. Surprised, Lucene heard her. *No*, Lucene answered. *Not yet. I don't trust her.* Xeni nodded. She was, of course, referring to the fact that she and Lucene were the only ones in the room who knew about the strange time shift at the Embassy Club.

The group stood to leave.

"Be happy, Professor Tanager," Royce finished. "TARA will receive full funding and I will see to it that you and Professor Cepheus are well compensated for your efforts. As for your students," she smiled, "they have long, bright careers ahead of them."

Somehow, at this moment, the future didn't seem very bright at all.

CHAPTER 12
HYSECHIA CONFRONTS ISABELLA

FIFTEEN DAYS BEFORE THE END.

Mateo (or "Mati" as he preferred to be called) was in a state. He searched every corner of the animal habitats at TARA, sweeping his own office and scouring the hallways with the diligence of a curious ferret. But his friend, Marzipan, was nowhere to be found. Marzipan, his longtime tiny friend with the face of a young boy, body of a ladybug and legs like a firefly, was missing from the small cage that served as his habitat. He knew the little bug couldn't last long outside of a carefully balanced atmosphere, and Mati became so desperate, he called his wife and eight children to help him search.

This was the second animal he'd lost from the lab within the past few months—the last being Tabby, an ordinary house cat that caretakers recently brought from a neighboring ally planet in Section 1. They left her at TARA for the planet's required quarantine period. He apologized profusely to her heart-broken adoptive parents. But what else could he do? She'd vanished.

Mati had no way of knowing that when Isabella accidentally sent Jasper Set between the layers of ordinary and non-ordinary realities, that she had managed to unlock Tabby's true form—a very large tiger that went by the name of Hysechia. Hysechia was not nearly as docile as her house cat form. What Mati feared was that maybe little Tabby hadn't gone that far after all. Perhaps she lived as a feral on the streets of Achel, and somehow found her way to his office, where Marzipan lived and ate Mati's friend as a snack. Mati wiped back a tear as his wife patted him gently on the back, trying to console him. His long, rat-like tail swished mournfully.

He was on the right track, as it turned out. Had Reverend Isabella not interfered, Hysechia would have eaten Marzipan straight away, which would have provided about as must sustenance to a tiger as a human eating a rice cake. Really, it was hardly worth the effort.

But when Hysechia wasn't busy losing her temper, and actually took time to think things through, she was then able to devise a cunning plan. It was a plan that took her several months to figure out, but then, it wasn't every day that one had to research how to close the gap between realities, now was it? And to think, she almost ate the little bug that was the key to Isabella's undoing.

"It's about time, bruja," Hysechia greeted Isabella at a remote location in the Northern Cross, a barren land with unpredictable weather and few inhabitants. Strapped to her back was a little self-contained travel cage where the air circulated enough to keep one little Marzipan safe…for now. Today, the weather at the Northern Cross was pleasant and the winds were calm.

"I'd like to say that it's nice to see you, Hysechia," Isabella offered, "but we both know that's not true." Isabella had created a large circle of pebbles around herself, wide enough for her to lay down and stretch her arms and legs out like angel's wings if she wanted to. Inside, sat her hand drum, a small medicine bag of copal, a feather, an iron bowl, a mortar and pestle, a canteen of water, and an assortment of dried herbs in a tied linen bag.

"On the contrary," Hysechia's voice had a sexy, slithery quality that few felines could match (not that many tried). Several tiny orange hairs that Hysechia had on her otherwise black and white body stood up excitedly. "I, for one, am thrilled to see you. And, as you can see," she motioned her eyes up toward Marzipan, "I have something of value to you."

Isabella knelt in the center of the circle and added herbs to the mortar bowl as if adding a pinch of salt, a sprig of thyme, and a dash of pepper to a recipe. She then used the pestle to furiously grind them together. "What use could I have for a firefly?" Isabella glanced at Marzipan out of the corner of her eye.

"You and I both know that you can't seal the tear between the realms without him," Hysechia began pacing back and forth, tracing the outer circle of the pebbles, pawing at them lightly but not crossing them.

"Do we know that?" Isabella's mind worked quickly. Her calm exterior didn't match the jumble of anxiety she felt. She thought she merely sent the demon Jasper Set to another dimension. Instead, she trapped him between the layers of this reality, and in doing so, somehow let Hysechia out. Once free, the feline had immediately transformed into her true form, still feline, but decidedly larger and more aggressive.

Isabella heard other news reports of animals being snatched from a local sanctuary, only to have their carcasses turn up later, having been eaten by what could only be assumed were of canine or feline origin. She suspected this was Hysechia's doing, but the number of dead animals found seemed out of sync with Hysechia's slender form. Did she really eat that much?

There was also a new breed of insect fluttering around. They resembled flying ticks. They didn't carry disease from what scientists could tell so far, but they liked to burrow under the skin and leave an itchy rash, leaving its host little option but to submerge their body under water until the nasty insect gave up and floated away. It was no use to only submerge an arm or a leg because the tick simply moved to another part of the host. So, it became a battle between host and bug to see who could hold their breath the longest.

This is only what she knew about. She shuddered at what else she may have trapped or let out.

"What is it that you want, Hysechia?" Isabella finally asked.

Hysechia now made full circles around Isabella, as if searching for a way in and sizing up her opponent. Her tail twitched irritably. "What I want is revenge," Hysechia answered, honestly. "I'd like to see you trapped between the layers where you left me for a hundred years. Do you know what it's like to constantly present myself to the world as a simple domestic cat, lifetime after lifetime, all the while ignorant beings thinking that I was the primitive one, petting me and giving me kibble, calling me stupid names like Tabby, Fluff and Whiskers?"

"Would you have rather I killed you?" Isabella asked, curiously, looking up from her work, where she was now adding a few pieces of copal to the iron bowl. "I thought what I did was more merciful."

"Merciful!" Hysechia choked. "That's like forcing a rich man to live as a pauper, a god to be trapped as a powerless human, a piranha that only knows how to jump in the air like a directionless mullet, a—"

"I get it," Isabella interrupted the verbal diatribe before it became personal. "So…no?"

"No," Hysechia growled under her breath. "As I was saying before I was rudely interrupted, I would love to see you thrown into an open portal where you'll be stuck between the layers forever, but that's an impractical goal." Hysechia was rather proud of her turn of phrase. She thought she was setting up a suspenseful tale, only to look over her shoulder and find that Isabella was all but ignoring her. "Fine, I'll just eat the firefly now and be done with it."

Hysechia, while mostly feline, seemed to move the digits on her paws with the same agility as a human. She unlatched the leather-like strap that held Marzipan's travel cage in place. Then, she sat on her haunches while the cage fell to the ground with poor Marzipan tumbling around and narrowly missing hitting his head on a rock in his habitat. Somehow, the cage landed right-side-up.

Instinctively, Isabella leapt over her circle of protection to go to the little bug's aid. She immediately realized her mistake, but it was too late.

Hysechia pounced, and the two rolled on the ground, Isabella no match for the tigress. Hysechia pinned Isabella's shoulders, pausing for a moment of self-satisfaction and victory before moving toward the vein in Isabella's neck.

Isabella reached an arm across her makeshift circle of pebbles and grabbed the first thing she could—the hand drum—sandwiching its smooth white, round surface between she and Hysechia's mouth. The feline was surprised for a moment as one saber tooth pierced the drum.

Hysechia backed away, annoyed, flicking her head violently back and forth as she tried to free the drum from where her tooth clung to it before realizing she had paws for that. She tossed the damaged drum aside and leapt.

Isabella had just enough time to roll over the pebbles, replacing a few that scattered in the shuffle. Hysechia flew through the air, but then, as if an invisible force-field blocked her path, smacked into something that sparked a few blue bolts of light as she fell backward, letting out a howl in pain. Hysechia rolled over and sat up, her fur slightly singed.

Both Hysechia and Isabella were out of breath. Marzipan sat up, helplessly.

"Excuse me," he finally asked. "Do I get a say in any of this? I mean, whether I get eaten or not or help stitch tears in the fabric of reality and such? Seems awfully unfair of you."

"What do you propose, little one?" Isabella asked.

"Well, let me clarify a few things first." Marzipan stood and began pacing around his little grotto, which didn't last long as the cage wasn't very big. He finally settled one foot on the roots of a tiny tree, his other foot firmly on the ground. "A portal gets opened and stuff gets in and stuff gets out, right?"

"Correct," Isabella indulged his questions.

Hysechia huffed. *What a waste of time,* she thought.

"And sometimes, it's like a seam on a pair of pants that fit too tightly. It doesn't close exactly right, and when the owner of the pants bends over, it splits, revealing his undies, right?"

"That's the general idea," Isabella answered.

"So, when you seal it, does stuff that's out stay out and stuff that's in stay in? Or is there some…flexibility?"

Isabella thought about this simple question. Her eyes suddenly lit up. *Marzipan, you brilliant little bug,* she thought.

"What?" Hysechia saw the exchange between Marzipan, outside the protective circle, and Isabella, still within the circle. "What am I missing?"

"It means, my dear Hysechia, that things *born* between the layers will eventually return there, all on their own once this realm is sealed. Whereas, things that have been *placed* there, such as a tiger wanting revenge or an evil demon trying to wreak havoc on the universe, would have to be *re-placed* since they were born in *this* realm. So you see, you are not automatically going to return to the other realm when I seal the doorway between worlds. You are free!"

Hysechia let that information sink in. This still didn't solve her problem of wanting Isabella dead.

"So, if I hand the bug over to you and let you close the portal with me on the outside, how do I know you won't open up another one someplace else in the future?"

"Hysechia, we don't even know that Lucene's powers are strong enough to open a portal a second time. So, once it's sealed, it's sealed. Secondly, I would have to find the Crossroads, which I have yet to locate."

"The Crossroads?" This was news to the feline.

"Surely you stumbled upon this in your research when you discovered that little Marzipan is a necessary ingredient for sealing the leak between worlds."

"Apparently not," Hysechia spat.

"Think of the entryway as a moving target. I have to find it again to seal the damage. I am told that this is at what is known as the 'Crossroads,' a strange intersection where time and space behave differently."

"Why not return to where you were when you opened it in the first place and track it?" Hysechia sniffed the ground to demonstrate.

"I'm not certain that a portal to another realm has a scent," Isabella grumbled at Hysechia's suggestion. Though, to be fair, it was as reasonable a hypothesis as any.

"In that case, how do you plan on finding it again?" Hysechia was curious, although her motives were primarily self-serving.

"As I mentioned, I need to find an anomaly of time and space. Everything at Lucene's old cottage where it was first opened, appears normal. The timeline makes sense. I need to find the place where it *doesn't* make sense. That's why I'm here attempting to meditate and get answers from the Great Spirits, before you interrupted me with your vendetta."

"If you had left me alone a century ago—"

"Hysechia, you single-handedly wiped out an entire village! *My* village. It was the first time in history I had a home with people I actually cared about, who cared about me, too!" Isabella fought back the emotion.

Hysechia thought a moment. "I was hungry," she answered simply.

Isabella was too enraged to speak.

"Why didn't you just go back in time and warn them about me. I would have gone about my business and you'd still have your precious village. Aren't you a time traveler?"

Isabella let out a sigh, followed by a pause that lasted for an eternity. "I can only go forward in leaps and bounds," she finally confessed. It was a confession that she'd never shared with anyone, and yet somehow, the words rolled off her tongue easily. Suddenly, her heart felt as if a weight had lifted. She'd never worked out how to go backward and actually save people from dying, thinking that maybe it was punishment from the Great Spirit for having betrayed her people all those centuries ago. So, while she could spring herself through time like hitting the fast forward button on a video, she had no way to get back once she did.

Hysechia let out a laugh so hard she spat a little.

"What's so funny?" Isabella demanded.

"Your family is a joke," she said between bouts of laughter. "Your descendent, Far, can't tell how to get from point A to point B. You can't work out traveling backward and forward in time—you can't even locate the Crossroads. Your cousin Nettle couldn't transport herself more than ten feet in any direction, and as for the gift of prophesy, your own father couldn't predict more than five minutes into the future!"

Isabella's anger bubbled over. She would have transported herself away from this conversation were it not for the fact that she had to ensure that Marzipan was safe first. It would have been irresponsible of her to abandon him.

"Excuse me," Marzipan chimed in, "I don't mean to complain, but all the water splashed everywhere when I fell from Hysechia's back. It's really hot out here and I'm ever so thirsty."

"A dead bug won't be of use to either of us," Isabella commented. She placed her canteen of water which she had intended for her own use, outside the circle. Hysechia relented, dragging the canteen over to the cage, flipping the lid and pouring a spot of it into a watering hole.

"Thank you," Marzipan acknowledged, diving face-first into it and drinking thirstily. "Now, about your dilemma," he offered, wiping his mouth.

"Yes?" Isabella answered.

"What if we pinky swear that once we find the Crossroads and seal the tear, that no one attempts to open a portal or seek revenge on Hysechia again? After all, as a priestess, Reverend Isabella, you do have a code to keep your word. Everything that's supposed to go back, goes back, and everyone's happy." Marzipan rubbed his furry front legs together as if dusting them off.

"Or," Hysechia reasoned, "we leave it open on the off-chance you are lying to me. I kill the bug, and everyone's happy…except him, of course. Sorry," she nodded to Marzipan. She didn't seem sorry.

"But then Jasper Set might eventually free himself. I have no idea how a demon might adapt. He could already be out for all I know. Plus, we still have things that don't belong here wreaking havoc on this world. How is this a solution?" Isabella demanded.

Hysechia had been waiting for this, not very long, as she'd only just thought of it. Her intention was simply to kill her nemesis for sealing her up for so many years—deservedly or not. But maybe she could have her wish after all?

"I have a new proposal," Hysechia offered.

"Yes," Isabella asked.

"You deliberately open the portal again assuming your precious pupil Lucene can manage it. But *you* go through it. I use firefly boy over there to seal you in—poetic justice."

"There's a bit more to it than that," Isabella answered flatly. "Do you actually know anything about the ceremony involved in making sure the worlds are separated?"

Hysechia flashed a smile. "Of course, I know. I knew what you did before you even did…except for the Crossroads. That was new. And…" she paused dramatically, "I'm pretty sure I won't make the same mistakes you did in sealing it." Hysechia paused for Isabella to digest the situation. "Bruja, this is the only way you can be held accountable for what you did to me and for what you unleashed on this world in the first place. Not to mention all of those pesky regrets you've had about your abuse of power in the past. Consider this—redemption."

Hysechia was right, Isabella thought to herself. This could be what she deserved. But she'd have to find a way to warn Lucene and the others what Hysechia's being on the loose would mean for Erde. She needed more time to muddle through this, but time was something she didn't have in this very moment.

"I agree to your terms," Isabella said, finally. "Now hand over Marzipan."

"Not so fast," Hysechia answered. "Why don't I just hold onto him for safekeeping and you let me know when you've found the Crossroads."

Isabella looked at Marzipan who merely held his chin up bravely and nodded. With that, Hysechia strapped Marzipan to her back once more; this time being a little more careful with him, because now she had a reason to keep him safe. Her day was turning out much better than she had anticipated.

CHAPTER 13
EMBASSY VISIT
FIFTEEN DAYS BEFORE THE END.

"I don't understand why you didn't tell me sooner," Tanager stated as they approached the front of the Embassy Club.

"It just happened two days ago," Lucene protested.

"But an overlap of time and space where you literally saw yourself walking into the club with Dallen? This is rather a big deal, wouldn't you say?"

Lucene had lots to say, actually, but she wasn't sure where to begin anymore. She knew Not Christopher was right. She needed to communicate better, but she wasn't entirely sure how to do that. Honestly, it was easier at the beginning when they were empathically connected. Now, it was only Lucene that seemed to be regaining her skills, another factor that she felt bothered Tanager, but he would never admit it. She felt it every time he was disappointed in her, when he thought she was acting immature, and when he disapproved of her decisions, like now.

Unfortunately, he couldn't feel anything that she was feeling. And she wasn't great at explaining it to him.

"Could we just focus on the task at hand, please?" Lucene changed the subject, the one thing she *was* becoming increasingly good at.

Tanager let out a sigh.

"Excuse me," a guard dressed in a regal red uniform blocked the two from entering the club. He held a hand up for emphasis.

"Yes?" Tanager eyed the guard quizzically. "Is there a problem?"

"Unfortunately, we only allow members of the club admittance. And you are clearly *not* members of the Embassy Club." Lucene remembered this guard from two days ago when the fake Kiki helped her get inside to retrieve her purse. Apparently, he remembered her as well. "You sure are popular, aren't you?" He eyed her distastefully.

Lucene was indignant. *Who*, or more specifically, *what* did he think she was anyway?

Tanager ignored the statement. "This is highly irregular. I know of no culinary establishment on Achel, or anywhere in Section 1 for that matter, where exclusive membership is enforced."

The guard puffed up his shoulders. "Well, then you are apparently unaware of Vitruvian customs."

"Perhaps I am mistaken," Tanager grit his teeth. "But we're not on Vitruvia, now, are we?"

The guard was about to respond when Constable Melokuhle passed by. "May I be of assistance?" he asked quietly. It was always odd to the outside observer just how timid the constable was given his height and girth. It was as if he were trying to overcompensate for his profound presence by speaking as gently as possible.

"Constable Melokuhle, so nice to see you again. I believe we haven't spoken since our last meeting with Commander Royce." Tanager eyed the guard for a reaction but received none. "We were just about to have dinner at the Club. Care to join us?"

"No, thank you," Constable Melokuhle answered. "Gotta get back home myself. The missus has dinner on the table and little Charlemar needs help with his schooling tonight." He thought a moment. Constable Melokuhle wasn't the quickest of studies, but given a moment of reflection, he was eventually able to put two and two together. After a momentary glance at the guard, he told Tanager and Lucene, "Enjoy your dinner. I'm certain that agents of the PDL will be treated extra special at the Embassy Club. They are well known for their…hospitality."

The constable tipped his hat and moved along. The guard wrinkled his nose but conceded to open the door. "Enjoy your dinner," he murmured in a way that clearly indicated that he didn't mean it. They had barely made their way inside when the guard could be heard contacting the inside host, speaking into his communication watch in hushed tones.

"May I take your purse or jacket, Earth woman and Erde man?" Kiki asked politely.

"Hi Kiki," Lucene answered pleasantly. "Can I just say, you were awesome the other night?"

Kiki blinked for a moment. "I'm sorry," she answered politely, barely above a whisper. "You seem to know me, but I'm not sure I know you."

The back of Lucene's neck tingled as the hairs on it stood up. She really didn't remember. "Oh, I'm sorry," Lucene spoke in a hushed voice. "I heard you sing at The Beacon. You have no reason to know me. I'm just a fan."

The corners of Kiki's eyes turned upward and a few tears formed, but she fought them back. This wasn't the place for emotions. At that moment, the host arrived. Kiki resumed her duties, looking expectantly at the couple.

Tanager jumped in, taking off his cardigan even though he thought it was rather chilly. He offered it to Kiki. "Thank you," he answered. "I believe my companion would prefer to keep her purse with her."

Lucene didn't have a purse. She had a little black backpack slung across her shoulders. But she didn't argue; it was true. After the last time, she wasn't willing to let it out of her sight.

"Very well," Kiki smiled, accepting the cardigan. "Enjoy your refection."

The host was just as Lucene remembered, wearing the same dull uniform as before, using as few words as possible. "Welcome," he coughed. "I have a table that I believe will be most agreeable for you this evening." He paused. An awkward silence ensued.

Lucene leaned over to Tanager and whispered. "I think you have to flick your first two fingers at him."

"Really?" Tanager whispered back. "Like this?" He motioned slightly, not really sure that that was right at all, but the host nodded his head and quickly directed the two to a small table in the furthermost corner of the club—in the shadows and largely away from everyone. Lucene was slightly disappointed that she didn't get to ride up the old-fashioned elevator again.

Lucene had time to forget parts of her last visit, either willfully because of the company, or because of her sleep deprivation at the time. Yet, it was slowly coming back to her as three female attendants seated Tanager first and seemed almost appalled that he paused to pull the chair out to enable Lucene to take a seat at the table before he did. He then raised his arms, uncomfortably, as one attendant placed a cloth table napkin in his lap before eventually doing the same for Lucene. This time, she didn't protest, having learned the drill.

They offered Tanager a beverage to start and handed him a menu. "Just water for me," he fumbled over his words. "And you?" he turned his attention to Lucene. "What would you like, my darling?" If the servers could turn a shade whiter, they would have. This was highly uncustomary. She tried to remember the bubbly beverage she had the only time she'd been there with Dallen, but she couldn't. "What have you got that's fizzy?" she finally asked. The server closest to her seemed confused, but finally offered, "A peach effervescence?"

"That sounds perfect," Lucene smiled, resting an elbow on the table, knowing full well that they, and probably Fatima, would take issue with this. But she didn't care and she was certain that Tanager didn't either.

"Excuse me," Tanager asked. "But do you have a second menu for my companion?" He did the finger and wrist flick thing again, stumping the servers for the second time in only a few minutes.

One server leaned in helpfully. "It is usually customary for the male to order for the female in this establishment," she whispered.

Tanager nodded, before whispering back, "But I have no idea what my lovely date would care for this evening. And without seeing the menu, I'm sure she doesn't know yet, either." He smiled politely. Therefore, for the first time in the history of the Embassy Club's existence, a woman received a menu.

Unfortunately, the descriptions were written in a foreign language. Therefore, when the servers returned to take their orders, Lucene asked candidly, "Any specials this evening?"

"Specials?" the server was confused. To be fair, the three looked identical, so Lucene was never quite sure which one they were addressing when.

She tried again, "What is the most popular dish on the menu?"

The server thought a moment. "Many guests find the mutton and vegetable stew delightful."

"Okay, I'd like that please."

The server eyed Tanager as if seeking his approval. After a long pause, he finally answered, "I shall have the same, thank you."

The attendants took the menus and returned a moment later with beverages, always serving Tanager first and then Lucene. And when dinner arrived, they gasped in horror as Lucene immediately took a bite of her food without waiting for Tanager to sample his meal first (she was *very* hungry). They peered anxiously at Tanager for a reaction that didn't come. He merely smiled pleasantly and asked, "How is it?"

"Delightful," Lucene smiled at he and the attendants with an over-abundance of enthusiasm. At that moment, Lucene noticed something that caused her face to drop in concern.

"What is it?" Tanager asked, touching her wrist from across the table. She couldn't find the words, so she just motioned.

There, across the restaurant on the balcony level, she witnessed herself on her first date with Dallen. He had just received the vegetable dish with assorted chutneys and sauces. He flicked his wrist at her indicating that she was permitted to eat.

At that moment, the console at the center of the room shifted and the band emerged from the floor as the host stood to announce them—just as it had been when she was there with Dallen.

"It's happening again," Lucene choked. "Yesterday, I watched as I walked past the coatroom. Now, this. It's the same event from a different angle."

Tanager resisted the urge to pay too much attention to the *other* Lucene and her date with a man he had been somewhat jealous of at the time. Instead, he answered, "I don't know of any planetary alignments that would cause a shift of this magnitude."

"Then, what do you think it is?"

"I don't know. All I can tell you for certain is that these inconsistencies in reality, and the odd occurrences all began after Isabella used you to send Jasper Set into another dimension."

"And now, Isabella is missing," Lucene was concerned. "Do you think she is in danger or trapped somewhere? Or do you think she returned to Earth?"

"I don't know," Tanager confessed. "But I would wager that she is the only one who can shed light on this subject."

The two became quiet as the band started to play. Afterward, exactly two people started clapping, Tanager, and old Lucene from the balcony. Lucene grabbed Tanager's wrist. "I don't think clapping is done here," she smiled.

"Is it stuffy in here or is it just me?" he asked.

"Definitely stuffy," she confessed. "But I'm not leaving until I've finished my stew. Eat up, because you know damn well, you're not going to get this at home from me."

"Good point," he nodded, digging into his plate.

They eyed Dallen and the other Lucene curiously. Today's Lucene had to put it out of her mind that she was watching herself, trying to observe the situation objectively. She found that as she watched her other self, she had a strange empathy coupled with the realization that after only a short period of time, she wasn't that woman anymore.

Just then, something bumped into her leg as it shot past them.

"What the—" Tanager started.

Lucene squinted her eyes in order to see what just flew by. Actually, she smelled him first, a little elf that gave off the scent of a dry martini.

How odd is that? Lucene wondered to herself.

"Look, they're leaving," Tanager noticed.

Lucene was distracted from the elf. "Oh, then we should lay low," Lucene offered. "They're going to come down the elevator behind us at any moment."

"I don't think we can lay any lower," Tanager retorted. "They've got us in a shadowy corner closest to the kitchen."

Nonetheless, Lucene found herself ducking her head, shielding her face by resting her palm across it, as the old version of herself and Dallen walked by, not three feet from their table.

After they had gone, Tanager let out a loud and long sigh. The two smiled at one another, relieved. Moments of connection seemed harder to come by lately and they both appreciated when they did.

Finally, the check arrived. One of the servers slipped a notice on the table closest to Tanager's arm.

"Oh, I've got it," Lucene snatched the check before Tanager could respond. Once again, the three attendants turned a whiter shade of pale. Lucene was even worried that one might actually pass out. "It's okay," she explained. "It's not as if we're on Vitruvia now, is it?"

One of the server's eyes twitched, ever-so-slightly, as if she wanted to smile but knew that wasn't permitted.

"There," Lucene smiled pleasantly, "all set." The attendants didn't move. "Oh, please don't make me flick my fingers at you. That's just so condescending."

Still nothing.

"We're all finished here," Tanager finally chimed in. They nodded and retreated, but not before one of them recited, "Thank you for your visit to the Embassy Club, an exclusive club on Erde that caters only to the highest ranking of Vitruvian dignitaries. We would be delighted to serve you again soon." With that, they bowed and made their exit.

Tanager pulled out Lucene's chair as she stood, offering his arm as a few diners at neighboring tables eyed the exchange with a mix of discomfort and curiosity.

Tanager had forgotten all about his cardigan until Kiki whispered loudly, "Don't forget your sweater, Erde man." She held it out for him.

"Thank you," he paused. "I don't know your way of doing things here," he confessed. "Tell me, is tipping customary?"

"Yes," Kiki whispered back, "and I have one for you." This time, she peered deeply into Tanager's eyes. "There are times when fear is good," she said. "It must keep its watchful place at the heart's controls."

Tanager looked at her quizzically, having no idea why she was spouting Earthen Greek literature at him. Still, he smiled, finally noticing a collection bowl filled with traditional Erde coins. He dropped a few in. Kiki bowed her head politely and retreated dramatically into the coatroom.

Outside, the air was crisp and had the scent of fallen rain.

"I don't remember hearing the rain from inside, do you?" Tanager asked.

"No, but it wasn't raining the night I accompanied Dallen to the club. It may have been raining here, today. But I don't think we were having dinner in the 'now,' if that makes any sense at all."

"Not really," Tanager admitted, putting his arm around her as they walked home. Had he given it a moment's thought, it *would* have made sense. It's just that his mind was elsewhere. "But there's one thing that I am sure of."

"Yeah? What's that?" She wrapped her arm around his waist.

"I'm sure of how much I love you," he looked down at her, with an odd mix of hope and expectation.

Something in Lucene's chest tightened a little. "I know," she smiled up at him. It wasn't as if she didn't feel the same. It was just that those words didn't come to her easily.

Tanager kissed the top of her head. "Let's go home," he said.

CHAPTER 14
VIRUS
FOURTEEN DAYS BEFORE THE END.

Lucene was busy smudging their high-home with sage the next morning when the computer sitting on their living room table lit up. There was an incoming message from Dr. Archibald Ennis from Earth. It was not typically safe for him to phone these days, and so she summoned Tanager hastily from the bedroom where he'd just emerged from the shower, clean-shaven and struggling to pull his trousers over still-damp legs.

Lucene accepted the call on the last ring, sitting at the table with Tanager hanging over her shoulder, towel-drying his hair.

Dr. Ennis, who was normally much more cordial, didn't wait to exchange pleasantries.

"You should be getting a call from Dr. Wilah shortly about your test results, Lucene." he explained quickly, occasionally glancing over his shoulder.

Tanager was surprised. Those tests were conducted only two days prior at the Dragoste Healing Center on Erde. How did Dr. Ennis know about them? More specifically, how did he know about them before they did?

"I only have a moment," Dr. Ennis explained hastily. "But here's what you need to know." He leaned in toward the screen, causing his holographic image to emerge directly in front of Lucene's nose. "It was a virus."

"What?" Tanager asked.

"You may recall that over a year ago several students became ill but quickly recovered?"

Tanager did remember. He and Cepheus had been discussing that very topic when traveling back to Earth with Roman and Lucene.

"We didn't know if it had to do with the genetic splicing or an odd bacterial infection. But know we now. It was a virus, likely carried back from Earth at some point in our early Data Collection stages when we brought Earthlings to the preserves."

"But there have been no unusual illnesses on the preserves over the past few years," Tanager reasoned.

"Just because they have built an immunity to it, doesn't mean *we* have. Given the general constitution of our Data Collectors, we might hypothesize that they would recover more quickly than the average Erdeling. On the other hand, no one outside of the Data Collectors appears to have been affected by it. We don't know whether it's simply that the virus infected the general Erdeling population but caused no noticeable side effects, or if the genetic splicing made the Data Collectors more sensitive. However, more tests on the entire Data Collection class will likely be required until we know for sure. They will also likely want to test all students at TARA to check for the presence of a virus in their systems."

"Will Dr. Wilah force us to quarantine?" Tanager asked the next logical question.

"I don't know. Not likely at this time since months have passed since any reported incidents. However—"

"Yes," Tanager persisted.

"I suspect that Commander Royce will use it as an excuse to ban any travels to and from Erde and Earth."

"I don't understand," Lucene interjected. "Why would she need an excuse?"

"I've already said more than I should." Dr. Ennis cleared his throat. "I should be going."

He didn't wait for them to say goodbye before cancelling his call. The computer screen went dark.

"Now what?" Lucene asked, staring at the blank screen.

"Now," Tanager rubbed her shoulders, "we wait for Dr. Wilah's call and pretend nothing has happened." Tanager appeared calm, but on the inside, his mind was racing. *Were the odd outbursts and mental health issues they'd witnessed that day in class because of the demon Jasper Set's influence, genetic splicing, or some odd virus? Or worse, was it that he had simply done a terrible job at helping students mentally and emotionally adjust to their new abilities?*

Lucene put her hand on his shoulder, sympathetically. *You are a great teacher,* she thought. *Clearly, it's not that.* But Tanager couldn't hear her.

The phone rang a second time, pulling him out of his thoughts. The first notification hadn't even finished before Lucene accepted it. It was Dr. Wilah.

They acted appropriately surprised at her news. But Dr. Wilah filled in some gaps that Dr. Ennis missed. It seems that Xeni, Clusaladek, Cepheus, Tanager, and Neroni had a larger viral load than Lucene, which might explain why her powers never went away completely and she seemed to be getting them back at a faster rate. Otherwise, how could Reverend Isabella have opened the portal to send Jasper Set into another dimension?

"Is it the odd smudging that Lucene insists on doing each week?" Tanager asked, wrinkling his nose at the realization that Lucene had set the burning sage stick and abalone shell on the table, and it was now smoking up the entire room. Lucene quickly went to extinguish it, opening the sliding glass doors to air the place out. "We live together now, but Lucene spent the better part of last year living alone."

Dr. Wilah smiled politely. "I am a medical doctor, not a witch doctor, Professor Tanager. While there is some evidence to suggest that smudging kills airborne bacteria and viruses, I'm afraid I couldn't tell you for certain if that is what has made a difference."

"Fair enough," Tanager offered, one of the newest Earth expressions he had come to start using. "But how does this explain the short circuit, all at the same time, on the bridge earlier this year? Did Jasper Set have something to do with it?"

"Again, I'm not a witch doctor, and I know nothing about the supernatural. I don't know what influence a demon may have on the situation, or if a combination of factors might be at play. But what I can tell you is that stress puts significant pressure on one's immune system. I can definitely see where the threat of a bomb explosion and death could trigger such an extreme stress response in our Data Collectors, particularly if they are more empathic."

When Lucene returned, Dr. Wilah explained the next steps of the protocol. Since the test results all came back post-virus, and no one was currently sick, the school testing was more to collect data of her own—to see if anyone was currently sick and who had antibodies in their system. The same protocol was to be put in place for all Earthlings living at the preserves. Since the only noticeable symptoms were a lack of extra sensory skills, there appeared to be no logical way to test the general public unless they collected a random sample, which they weren't prepared to do…yet.

"What if they refuse?" Tanager asked.

"We lost more than a third of our population a century ago due to an uncontrolled pandemic," Dr. Wilah answered calmly. "While I don't anticipate anything of that magnitude here, I'm afraid that Commander Royce will insist upon compulsory testing."

Tanager was of mixed mind as he reflected on how the villagers burned Moksha's house to the ground and threatened to kill her. Was it fear? Frustration? Or, as Dr. Wilah may be suggesting, exposure to a virus that affected their otherwise sound judgement? Clearly, they were lacking empathy, the main trait noticeably missing with those infected. His thoughts also went to Clusaladek and the classroom all those months ago, where students became borderline angry and violent—completely out of character with their normal personalities.

Dr. Wilah interrupted Tanager's mind chatter by politely ending the call, leaving Tanager and Lucene left with more questions than answers.

"Why did Dr. Ennis bother to phone us at all?" Lucene wanted to know. "He told us essentially the same thing except for—"

Tanager nodded. "Exactly," he finished her thought, "except for the fact that Commander Royce will be closing the borders between Earth and Erde travel. He wasn't just imparting information; he was trying to warn us."

As expected, Commander Royce declared the borders closed until further notice, leaving those on the preserves, including Fatima, who was already concerned about when she might get to see her family again, to wonder if that would ever happen.

Fatima rubbed Talula's back gently as she bounced her little girl up and down in the baby carrier that was wrapped around her waist.

"It will be okay," Lucene tried to comfort her friend after having told her the news. Ivan was at the lab—his home away from home—and Fatima was about to head to Cepheus's home to help Moksha with an old grape-treading ritual. It seems that stomping on grapes, barefoot, was not limited to wine growers on Earth.

"How do you know?" Fatima whined, sniffing back tears. Usually infused with unbridled optimism, Fatima was being uncharacteristically morose. "It's easy for you to say it will be okay. You didn't leave family behind. Everyone you love is here."

Lucene thought a moment. *Not everyone.*

Fatima read Lucene's facial expression. She had the luxury of growing up with both parents. Lucene lost both of hers at a young age.

"I'm so sorry," Fatima touched her friend's arm. "That was rude."

"It's okay." Lucene leaned over to roll the hems of her linen pants up and use a threaded strap to secure them in place. "Before you and my makeshift family here on Erde, I've never had anyone like you did with aunt Keti, Tai and your family. It couldn't have been easy not having them around at Talula's birth and being isolated on an alien planet."

"Eh, forget about me. It's no big deal. I'm just being melodramatic." Fatima started down the path to Cepheus's house where Moksha was waiting for them. While she was taking off weight since giving birth, her movements were still a little stiff.

"No," Lucene stopped her. "You're not. How you feel is how you feel. And, that *is* a big deal." She wrapped her arm around her friend, reaching out a hand to pat a very bouncy little Talula on the head. The baby gurgled bubbles and then giggled as if they were the funniest thing ever. She and Lucene exchanged bright smiles.

Just then, something in the distance caught their eyes. They could barely make out the shape of a dog-like creature bounding toward them from across the desert planes, kicking dust up everywhere in its wake. Logically, an animal couldn't possible move that fast and yet, in a matter of moments, it descended on them. And, it was much larger than they realized.

Before them, stood a snarling black dire wolf with flame-tipped ears, red eyes and foam and saliva dripping from its mouth.

Fatima let out a scream.

Instinctively, Lucene jumped in front of her friend and baby, her arms outright as if to shield them. They had just reached the front door of Moksha and Cepheus's cottage.

"Get inside," she ordered Fatima.

CHAPTER 15

DESERT GLIDERS AND DIRE WOLVES

THIRTEEN DAYS BEFORE THE END.

Before Fatima had time to react, the dire wolf leapt at them with Lucene in its most immediate path. Its jaws went right for her throat. Lucene leaned as far back as she could but kept her stance. She had to until she was certain that Fatima and Talula were out of harm's way. Lucene crossed her arms in front of her, helplessly as the wolf descended.

Suddenly, she heard a loud thunk. The wolf still landed on her, but it was so stunned it did little more than topple Lucene onto her back, drooling on her arms as its weight landed on her. It regained its wits quickly and stood, its front paws pinning Lucene's shoulders to the ground, its back paws balancing on her thighs. It was about to attack again when a second whack came. This time, Lucene could see where it had come from. The wolf's eyes widened in surprise as it toppled sideways.

Over them stood Moksha, bloodied staff in hand from the aggressive strikes to the wolf.

Fortunately, Fatima sidestepped before Lucene and the wolf could land on them. Ordinarily, Fatima wouldn't have run, were it not for the fact that her baby was strapped to her chest and needed to be out of harm's way. She darted away from the altercation, heading up the lined path to the cottage, fumbling with the doorknob as a confused Talula, now pressed lightly against the door, began to cry. "Shhhh, it's okay, baby," Fatima whispered, her hands shaking as she was finally able to open it. She slammed it behind her instinctively, and quickly began unwrapping Talula from her chest, looking around for a safe space she might be able to deposit the infant until she returned. She finally settled on the only container she could think of that Talula, who had not yet learned to crawl or roll over, would be safe...the deep-basin that was the kitchen sink. She grabbed the first cushion she could find, Cepheus's black cape that was hanging by the front door, pillowing it onto the bottom of the sink. She rotated the faucet out of the way and gently laid Talula down, who immediately began staring at the faucet, curiously. Something about it amused her and she began giggling. Ordinarily, Fatima would have cherished this moment, but she had other things on her mind.

She searched for a weapon, but the closest thing she could find was an iron skillet. "That'll have to do," she exclaimed out loud and bounded back outside.

Moksha did a good job at keeping the beast at bay, but it was relentless. It ducked back and forth, as if looking for an opening between Moksha's staff and her flesh. It snarled; its red eyes almost reading Moksha's movements. It was beginning to predict her next moves, darting out of the way before she could strike and then lunging immediately after.

Lucene had no weapon and did the only thing she could think of. As the beast's teeth connected with Moksha's calf, Moksha let out a painful wail. Lucene leapt onto the wolf's back, reaching around to pry its jaws from Moksha's legs, cutting her hands in the process. Then she rolled onto her back, using all of her might to keep the jaws from closing.

From beyond the hills a team of desert gliders on high alert scattered, their wings fanning out to make themselves appear larger and more aggressive, and to warn their clan of danger. Behind them, two more dire wolves appeared, an amber-colored one with longer and thicker fur, and a gray one with mangled patches of white around his back and head.

Lucene heard the noise but couldn't see the turmoil. Instead, she thought a moment. *It worked on humans sometimes,* she reasoned, *maybe...*

She tried to command the wolf to stop the attack and to retreat. Nothing happened. Her powers hadn't fully returned yet, and who knows how well her methods affected animals?

So, when that didn't work, she tried to tuck her legs to propel him away from her, adding in the intention that he should sail backward. But he followed her movements as if he knew exactly what she was going to do next. Her arms were getting tired and the jaws were beginning to bite into the backs of her fingers which were now sandwiched together in the beast's mouth. Finally, she attempted to give the illusion that she was much bigger and scare him away...all of this happening in less than a minute. At that moment, she could have sworn she heard the wolf in her head saying, *you're pitiful.*

It bared its teeth as if to smile at her. From her look of surprise, he knew that she had heard him.

What the beast didn't see coming, was Fatima, wildly swinging an iron skillet. It connected with the top of the wolf's head. He fell to one side, long enough for Lucene to roll over and rush to her feet. It was then she witnessed an injured Moksha trying to fight off the other two wolves with her staff.

Had their lives not been in danger, it would have been comical to witness Fatima now coming to Moksha's aid, skillet clenched in both hands as she swung it like a tennis racket at the amber wolf. It caught the edge of it in its mouth and somehow managed to bite into the pan and rip a piece off of the front of it as if it were nothing more than a thin piece of cloth. Fatima's face went pale. *What the hell kind of wolves were these?*

In a last-ditch effort, Lucene did the only remaining thing she could think of. She focused all of her intention on the desert gliders. *What will inspire them to fight instead of retreat? Ah,* she thought, *hunger.* She sent the message of immense hunger, allowing herself to feel that starvation deep within her. As she did, she also imagined that the women in her group were very thin, while the wolves were very large and meaty...but feeble.

Suddenly, the gliders began arriving en masse, rolling across the desert like a dust bowl. They began biting at the red and gray wolves' legs and then climbing up their backs.

"Head for the house!" Lucene ordered Moksha and Fatima, trying not to lose focus.

"Are you sure?" Moksha backed away. She wobbled slightly from the effects of the blood loss in her leg. Fatima caught her arm and steadied her.

"I'm very sure," Lucene was determined. The scene that followed was grotesque. As Moksha and Fatima headed for safety, Lucene kept her stance as the gliders devoured the wolves, leaving disgusting bits of bone and fur on the ground. Two gliders climbed up her back, one even making eye contact with her. She visualized herself as nothing but a raw, upright skeleton. The glider sniffed her ear and then signaled his friend. They leapt from her body, gliding through the air, as their name implied. Unfortunately, since they had just eaten, their landing was not delicate. They both plopped on the ground with a loud thud.

There were now at least two dozen overstuffed gliders waddling off into the sunset like penguins. When they were finally gone, she peered down at the wolves' remains, stepping away from them, queasy. It was then that exhaustion overtook her and she fell to the ground and quickly lost consciousness.

Lucene woke to find herself laying on a long couch in the Baruch house, a pillow beneath her head and a blanket covering her. She had a splitting headache.

"How are you feeling?" Tanager asked gently, touching her shins. He was sitting upright at the end of the couch, Lucene's legs strewn across his lap.

Once she'd opened her eyes, the bright lights blinded her, and the searing pain returned. She quickly shut them. The only problem was, it was now night, and there was nothing but low lights, not much brighter than candles illuminating the room.

"Fine," she answered in a way that suggested that she was not fine. "As long as I don't open my eyes, move, or breathe too hard."

Tanager smiled, sympathetically, trying to think what might help. *Magnesium tablets? A cold pack for her head?*

"Here," Fatima brought over a ceramic cup. "I've mixed you a tincture of magnesium, feverfew, butterbur and vinegar. It'll help." She guided her friend's head forward to take a sip.

"Bleh," Lucene coughed. "It tastes awful." She scrunched her face at the bitterness.

"Don't be such a baby. Drink," Fatima commanded.

Lucene drank it, before falling back onto the pillow. It seemed to help almost immediately. Within a few minutes, she could open her eyes and keep them open. She surveyed the room.

Moksha sat on a recliner in the corner of the room, her injured leg propped up, having been wrapped tightly in gauze. Cepheus had just returned from the healing center with an antibiotic—highly uncustomary for them to provide one without actually seeing the patient. But it seemed they were overwhelmed with calls of strange wild animals randomly attacking pedestrians throughout the Western Cross. Oddly enough, as night fell, the incidents stopped altogether. From the glass door overlooking the room, the waxing half-moon shone brightly with a small and full pink moon floating just behind it.

Ivan was busy entertaining Talula, who seemed to like being in the sink so much that he stood over her rotating the copper faucet back and forth while she gleefully clapped her hands. Just to mix it up, he occasionally rattled a set of metal measuring spoons and threatened to steal her nose with an oven mitt. Oblivious to what happened hours earlier, Talula seemed to be having the best evening of all.

"Constable Melokuhle should be here shortly to make a report and photograph the scene before the remains can be removed," Tanager explained, putting his hand over his mouth and fighting back a gag reflex. He refocused on Lucene and put the wolf carcasses out of his mind. "Are you up to speaking with him?"

"I guess so," Lucene sighed. All she wanted to do was go home, climb under the covers, and sleep for the next 48 hours. *Why am I so exhausted?*

Tanager jolted in surprise. For the first time since the short circuit on the bridge, he *heard* her. As training at TARA resumed and the effects of the virus wore off, it seemed that his own skills were finally returning. At least, he hoped that was the case and it wasn't a fluke. He kept this to himself because he was also becoming increasingly aware of the searing pain in Lucene's head. He had to mentally block it out to avoid becoming overcome with pain and exhaustion himself. "Moksha and Fatima said the gliders suddenly attacked the wolves," Tanager commented. "Do you remember?"

"Yeah," Fatima chimed in, looking at Lucene. "We were gonna try and nab you but then we saw your arms were glowing. Figured we had to let you finish doing your thing."

"We rushed to pull you inside after the desert gliders retreated. Well," Moksha pointed out, "Fatima did most of the pulling." She looked down at her leg.

"Don't let her fool you," Fatima commented. "Now I get why Moksha has the reputation of being a badass. By the way, your arms shocked me, *literally*! It was a hundred times worse than the shock of static electricity when you drag your feet across a carpet."

"Sorry," Lucene moaned.

Moksha considered herself the gentle sort, former Royal assassin or not. She wasn't sure she really wanted to be known as a 'badass.' But the thought gave her an idea.

"You know what?" she exclaimed. "This world isn't safe anymore. I need to train you how to fight—all of you."

"How often do you plan on having to defend yourselves against wolves?" Tanager wanted to know.

"Sadly, a stun gun is still the best option for that. Don't know that we can procure something like that around here though."

"Weapons are typically frowned upon on Erde," Tanager said while dropping his lips in a down-turned expression, not for emphasis, just to express his disapproval as he considered all manner of weaponry that was likely already in production at TARA these days. "Though," he looked sadly at Lucene's current state and continued, "we've never had to deal with wild and formerly extinct wolves before."

"Well, never mind that," Moksha continued. "There's a lot we can't seem to defend well against—chaos-loving demons, wolves, neighbors who burn your house down…" She paused for a moment, thinking about her old cottage with a minor level of nostalgia. The original plan was to grow new vines on Cepheus's land while hers recovered, but since the relationship blossomed, Moksha moved in with Cepheus and gave up her cottage to someone else who might need it. "And, as much as I hate violence, Erde hasn't been able to shut other worlds out. I just think that on this point, Commander Royce may be right. Self-defense should be taught in school, but not limited to students. I'm offering this to you, my friends." Moksha almost teared up a little as she said it. It took her a long time to establish any place that she'd call *home* and she'd become rather protective of it. "It may not be the best against wild animals, but it can certainly help in hand-to-hand combat. And really, what else have you got?"

"Moksha," Cepheus protested calmly, "while I appreciate the sentiment, that's not something I would choose for myself."

Tanager nodded. "And I am working insane hours as it is. When would I have the time?"

"I'll train with you," Fatima piped up. "Lucene will, too."

"Wait, why are you volunteering me?" Lucene protested, rubbing her head.

"Aww, c'mon," Fatima smiled. "Remember all the new stuff we tried on Earth? Bocce ball? Yoga? Sailing? It'll be fun."

Moksha hadn't intended on making it *fun,* but if it got her buy-ins, she was all for it.

"What about you, Ivan?" Fatima called into the kitchen. "You wanna train with Moksha and learn how to defend yourself?" She bit back a smile as if the only one in on a joke.

Ivan's face became flushed. Baby Talula wondered why he stopped clapping the plastic oven mitt together and reached up to touch his face, curious. There were a few things from his younger years that he hadn't gotten around to telling Fatima.

"Nah," he answered. "I'm good. But ye go ahead. I think the training will be good fer ye. Wouldn't want another incident like this to ever happen again."

SECTION TWO

"There you go, questioning again. The Netherworld is the opposite of the Hitherworld, which is where we are now. In the Netherworld, a finely-dressed bloke by the name of Jasper Ssset—lots of esses in his last name, it would seem. He let on that you might be able to use someone of my skillset."

CHAPTER 16
ISABELLA'S CONFESSION
ELEVEN DAYS BEFORE THE END.

Classes weren't due to start for another hour, but there were still a handful of students wandering the campus at TARA. The newly appointed "agents" of the PDL were surprised to find Reverend Isabella waiting on a picnic bench outside of the Makerspace Monday morning, none more so than Lucene.

"Isabella," Lucene called, running up to her mentor and friend. "Are you okay? Where have you been?" While Isabella was a kind soul, one thing she wasn't was a hugger—something Lucene had become aware of in the short time living on Erde. She lifted up her arms, noticed Isabella's expression, and then dropped them at her side.

"I am fine, my dear," Isabella answered with her usual calmness. While she often wore colorful, flowing jumpsuits and scarves that caused many to mistake her for a supermodel, today her outfit was surprisingly subdued. She wore an amber-colored wrap-around tunic and matching headpiece. On her feet were what appeared to be recycled plastic brown flats. Make no mistake that Isabella still stood out. It was impossible for her not to. "What I want to know is, how are *you*?" She eyed Lucene's hands and arms, covered with several small bandages where she had fought off the dire wolves not a day earlier.

"I'm okay," Lucene glanced at her arms, self-consciously. The branch-like tree patterns on her arms kept routinely glowing on and off all evening. They would become uncomfortably warm for a few minutes and then stop, which did little to help her sleep, but seemed to do wonders for her injuries. One would have assumed that her attack had been several weeks ago as most of the marks on her hands were starting to scar.

"Fighting off dire wolves with your bare hands," Isabella commented. "That was pretty brave of you."

"How did you know that?"

"I know many things," Isabella answered calmly as Tanager, Cepheus and Moksha gathered at Lucene's side. "Perhaps we could talk...somewhere private?"

"Of course," Tanager responded. "The Resource Room would be most appropriate."

The guard at the new security station didn't think so. "I'm afraid this woman does not have authority to be on school property," he answered gruffly.

Cepheus began protest when Isabella spoke up. "*This woman*?" she was incredulous, mocking the guard. "Is that any way to speak to the spiritual advisor who delivered two of your babies last year in a large tub of water while you cowered in the bathroom because you couldn't take the site of blood?" The guard paused for a moment. "How are Verny and Zachery by the way?"

The guard awkwardly cleared his throat, reaching to adjust his belt uncomfortably as if he'd just finished eating a large meal. "Growing up fast," he laughed. "They've even started talking a little, just a few simple words here and there."

Isabella nodded and smiled encouragingly. She had been a temporary resident of Erde since she opened the portal to save Lucene and banish Jasper Set last year, though that didn't seem to stop her from flitting from one planet to the other when it suited her.

"Surely," Cepheus seized the opportunity, "there could be no issue with Reverend Isabella, our spiritual advisor, meeting with us on official business. You can clear it with Commander Royce if you care to phone her this early in the morning."

"Er," the guard rocked back and forth on his heels. Behind them, several faculty and students began to line up, impatiently. "I suppose it would be all right." He finally agreed to let them pass.

"Ridiculous," Tanager mumbled under his breath. "We've never had to go through such measures before just to walk into a damn building."

Lucene rubbed his back with one hand, supportively. "It will get better," she said. She wasn't sure she believed that, exactly, though she did hope that it was true.

Once they'd reached the library, Cepheus opened the door to the Resource Room which, to an onlooker, was camouflaged to look like a wall mural.

"The Knights Templar," Isabella remarked as she walked inside, eyeing the room in front of her.

"Please," Tanager offered her a chair.

"Thank you," she replied, winking at Lucene as if to commend her on her choice in partners. Lucene sat to her left, Moksha to her right, with Tanager sitting at Lucene's other side and Cepheus taking his place at the still unoccupied seat beside Moksha around the table.

"Reverend Isabella," Cepheus began, cautiously. "We have been searching for you for quite some time. We need to ask you some questions, but are curious as to what brought you to us today?" Cepheus drummed his fingers nervously on the table, while Tanager cleared his throat several times before Lucene eyed him oddly. Moksha sat calmly with her hands resting in her lap, a neutral expression on her face.

Isabella let out a sigh. "I confess," she declared suddenly, her face dropping shamefully, her eyes downcast. This was an uncharacteristic display of emotion from the woman. *There is no point prolonging the inevitable,* she thought.

"What?" Tanager sat upright, confused. "Confess to what, exactly?"

"To opening the portal, of course!" Isabella thought this was obvious. "The strange happenings all over town—a tiger-like feline terrorizing the zoo, dire wolves back from extinction, dead men walking, subtle and inexplicable distortions of reality—surely you had noticed these things?"

"We did," Tanager answered, cautiously, "But we assumed these were strange anomalies because of the conjunction between Jupiter and Saturn sending out ripples to neighboring planets. We just thought these oddities were…celestial."

"Celestial?!" Isabella couldn't believe what she was hearing. Though, to be fair, when Lucene had questioned her about the portal that seemed to evaporate when closed (becoming nothing more than the burning embers on her arms), Isabella explained it away as simply a metaphysical side effect of being an Erdeling born on Earth, imbued with special empathic powers. When Lucene had been struck by lightning, it triggered an anomaly in time and space. So, sending Jasper Set into an alternate plane of existence was simply an expression of that anomaly. That last part was a lie, though she hadn't realized that she had been lying at the time. Now, she had to come clean.

"I was wrong," Isabella blurted out. "As a time bender and a descendent of a prophet, I should have known better, but I made a mistake. Seems to be a family trait," she grumbled, thinking of Far's bumbling about the universe, making one miscalculation after another.

"What, exactly, do you think you were wrong about?" Tanager wanted to know.

What, exactly, is a time bender, Lucene wanted to know. That seemed to her the more interesting question.

"I didn't send Jasper Set into a parallel world," she sighed. "I sent him between the layers."

"What does that mean?" Moksha asked.

"In Shamanic culture, they talk about our reality and the non-ordinary realms," Isabella explained. "It would seem that he is still here, just between the layers."

"Oh," was all Tanager could think to say.

Isabella eyed him, questioningly.

Cepheus spoke up, "We were actually going to ask about something completely different," he said hesitantly. "We wanted to know if you were aware of any special arrangement between the Vitruvians and Commander Royce?"

Isabella was confused. "I don't know what you're talking about. I may be a prophet, but I'm not omnipotent and I certainly can't see and know everything. I only get bits and pieces of insight through prayers and meditation." People always seemed to believe she had special knowledge regarding just about everything. Being a prophet was hard.

"But you were supporting Representative Dallen, Odessa, and Morphinae at the last IPP assembly."

Isabella eyed him cautiously. "That was at the behest of Odessa who thought it the only way to help preserve Earth and Erde." She paused. "What is all this about?"

What this was about were some odd internal anomalies at TARA, particularly in the animal lab and the aerospace lab. Items went missing, only to return later in the exact space in which they vanished…random items like reamers and parts of a winglet kit, skin scrapings from the exotics room, and in one case, a missing litter box. (It should be noted that the litter box was one of the few items that never actually returned.) This was an improvement from two weeks prior, where items resurfaced in remote locations. It was as if whatever (or whoever) took them figured out how to recalculate and return them to their original location.

When they shared this information with Commander Royce, letting her know that they suspected someone was pilfering bits of information from TARA, she dismissed it. She even went as far as to suggest that one of the local businesses who rented the Makerspace for production were simply trying to get a leg up on the competition. "I'll have Constable Melokuhle look into it," she promised. But this answer made no sense, given the lockdown of the Makerspace. You needed to ask permission to use the bathroom these days.

"While we have no proof," Cepheus explained. "I have reason to believe that Commander Royce has been selling secrets to an outside source, perhaps the Vitruvians. Technology that could, essentially, be used to destroy us."

Suddenly a light bulb went off in Isabella's brain. She smiled, knowingly.

"So, you did know?" Tanager asked.

"No," she shook her head at her own ignorance. "I did not know. But it makes sense. How else could all of this," she motioned to the library around her, "be here."

The reality sank in their collective chests like the end of a movie where the dog dies and everyone is grieving. But in this case, it was as if they were, in part, responsible for the animal's passing.

"So," Moksha finally interjected, "if it turns out that TARA has been funded by the Vitruvians this whole time on the pretense of helping Earth, you mean to say that not one of you were even remotely suspicious of this before now?"

"No!" Tanager fought back anger. "Certainly not!" He shot Moksha a look of betrayal. Whose side was she on, anyway?

"Sorry," Moksha's voice softened. "Didn't mean that to sound quite so confrontational." Sometimes, her automatic defenses went up when she didn't intend for them to.

"Don't worry about it," Tanager grumbled.

Cepheus smirked, in spite of the current situation. Tanager was sounding more and more Earth-like the longer he was around Lucene which, these days, was all the time.

Isabella thought a moment. "I am not sure what to do with the information I have just been given, but about the portal I mentioned, the other realms?" This, to Isabella, was a far more immediate danger.

"What is it, Reverend Isabella?" Lucene asked, concerned.

"We have to seal it," she declared. "Unnatural spirits are getting in and out because it didn't fully close properly. Or, perhaps that *I* didn't close it properly."

Cepheus cringed. He didn't think of his visitations of Petrichor as *an unnatural spirit* at all.

"Jasper Set will get out," she continued. "And when he does, I have no idea how he will retaliate. Plus, we can suspect, but can't be entirely certain, that those vanishing items are being snatched by something else, or simply floating in and out between the realms all on their own," Isabella reasoned.

"Why haven't you told anyone of this sooner?" Tanager challenged.

"I did," Isabella answered, deflated. "I just told the wrong person."

"Commander Royce?" Moksha put the pieces together.

"Commander Royce," Isabella confirmed. "She asked me to keep this information to myself for now, but after the dire wolves—" For the first time ever, Isabella's eyes began to well up.

Lucene touched her arm gently. "It's okay," Lucene told her friend. "We're okay."

"What do we do now?" Moksha asked.

"I've been searching all my resources and everything I know about portals. From what I have found, we need to close it, but to do that, I will likely need to re-open it altogether to reset it. But to do *that,* we need to find a glitch in time and space."

"A glitch?" Tanager asked. "What does that mean?"

"It means that in the everyday realm, we have a timeline—a past, present and future. Whereas, in other Shamanic worlds, such as the upper and lower realms, time does not exist in the way it does here. We can, theoretically, float between time and space. In the non-ordinary middle world, however, there is a timeline. But..."

The group leaned in, eagerly.

"There is a vortex at the Crossroads of the non-ordinary realm where time and space can be manipulated. It doesn't follow an ordinary timeline. That's what we need to find...the Crossroads. Only then can we re-seal it."

"How in the world are we to figure out where that is?" Moksha asked.

"That, my dear," Isabella answered, "is the million-dollar question."

"Well, prepare to open your checkbooks," Lucene joked as she and Tanager exchanged knowing glances. "Tanager and I know *exactly* where it is."

Unfortunately, knowing the exact location of the Crossroads wasn't the only impediment. According to Isabella, they had to wait until sometime between a full moon and the *waning gibbous* (her words). It also had to coincide with the end of the Saturn and Jupiter conjunction or at least the energy it was kicking off. No one particularly understood what this meant aside from Isabella. But no one else had a better solution. She made the mess. She had to fix it.

And so, they waited.

CHAPTER 17
TRAINING
TEN DAYS BEFORE THE END.

"How's this?" Fatima jabbed the air clumsily a few times and followed up with a full-on punch with an energy that sprang from her back heel to her hips and out through her right fist. Her face had the seriousness of someone who just passed a kidney stone.

"Wonderful," Moksha answered flatly, limping slightly over to Fatima, who smiled proudly, "if you want to break your wrist."

Fatima's facial expression sank.

"Here," Moksha reached out and adjusted her fist so that it aligned with her wrist and forearm. "Think of it as a kink in a garden hose. You have to keep it straight for water flow. The same is true of energy. "

The women began training at Moksha and Cepheus's house, oddly enough, on a small patch of grass surrounded by rows of grapes. They still had grape smashing on the agenda, a plan that got discarded the other day because of the wolves. Moksha was leaving that for last because it was the most fun and the messiest.

It would also give her a chance to demonstrate on the grapes how to smash someone's instep, break a knee, or scrape someone's shin with one's heel. The repeated movement would build muscle memory, and she'd end up with crushed grapes for a first season of wine—greatly enhanced by science, of course. Thanks to Cepheus's idea of using the same technology on grapes as they do lab-grown clean meats, production was fast.

They replicated grape vines from a sample of Petrichor's bottled wine, grew parts in a lab and transplanted them to the vineyard. They also discovered that as Lucene's skills were returning, she seemed to be able to influence the vines. As she moved throughout the vineyard, the vines actually bowed toward her as she passed. And, Lucene couldn't help but speak to them lovingly as one might speak to their children. This was another reason why Moksha insisted on training in the vineyard. She believed Lucene's energy helped them grow faster and heartier.

That wasn't all. Lucene's own wounds healed at such a rapid rate that she began hovering her palms over Moksha's injured leg, and in two days, Moksha was able to walk on it again and the wound had sealed as if the injury were several weeks old. Like most things, it was a power that became stronger with practice.

After a few more rounds of straight and reverse punches, upward jabs, and backhand *hammers* and elbow strikes, they moved on to wrist and shoulder locks.

"Is this it?" Lucene asked, standing in front of Fatima and attempting to peel her friend's hand off, which was grasped firmly around her own wrist, and then lock her 'opponent' in a new, reversed wrist lock.

Moksha let out a sigh. Somehow, Royals seemed to understand combat instinctively. This did not appear to be the case with humans. And they hadn't even gotten to defending against species with more than four limbs yet.

To Fatima, Moksha asked, "How do you feel, Fatima?"

"Fine, thanks," Fatima smiled, not really understanding where Moksha was going with this.

"Here, Lucene. Try it on me," Moksha instructed as Fatima released her grasp and took a step back. Moksha grabbed Lucene's wrist enough to make her wince.

Lucene reached her left hand across her body and tried to peel Moksha's hand free. Moksha let out a fake yawn. "My turn," she said. "Grab my wrist."

Lucene obliged, and within a split second found herself kneeling on the ground crying *uncle*. Moksha had taken Lucene down with a simple but effective lock that forced her to contort her body just to avoid the pain. There were many counters to this maneuver, of course, but Lucene didn't know any of them yet.

Moksha was curious how a combination of Lucene's powers with training would serve her in the long run, but that was a discussion for another day. The only stipulation in her training was that she didn't attempt to use any telekinetic or mind-altering skills during basic training, at least not until they could be sure that she wouldn't accidentally hurt anyone, including herself. Lucene made a mental note to talk to Tanager about this. The Data Collectors might do well with these skills, but only when they could be trusted. And after the incident at the school last year, when the students became violent, this type to study may have been a long way off.

"Sorry." Moksha released her grasp and helped Lucene to her feet. "I know you want to be careful not to hurt Fatima, but you need to develop better speed, pressure and accuracy, unless you simply plan on holding hands with the enemy."

"Very funny," Lucene rubbed her sore wrist.

"All right, shake it out, ladies." Moksha rapidly shook her hands and wrists in the air as if trying to shake something off that had gotten stuck on them. This was followed by a few cool-down shoulder, hip, knee and ankle rolls and some light stretches. "I think it's time we take a break before the last part of today's training."

Fatima groaned. "I'm not sure my sore body can handle any more of this."

"Oh, don't worry," Moksha assured her. "We're moving to the lower body, which tends to be easier since we typically have more power in our legs."

"Still—"

"Humor me for fifteen more minutes." She led Fatima and Lucene to a large outdoor basin. "It begins with smashing and it ends with wine."

"That fast?" Fatima wrinkled her nose, curiously.

"No," Moksha smiled. "I cheated and bought a bottle from the market for us. It was the least I could do after torturing you both all day."

"So, how long does this training last, exactly?" Lucene wanted to know.

Moksha wanted to answer that the training never stops but given the deflated look they both had on their faces, she decided to side-step the issue altogether.

"Let's mash some grapes, shall we? We can discuss it later."

CHAPTER 18
WAR
TEN DAYS BEFORE THE END.

"Cepheus, old boy," Ivan knocked on the closed door of his friend's office at TARA.

Cepheus, who was presently napping on the bench that had been his bed for a number of years, groggily lifted his head. He'd been having trouble sleeping ever since Petrichor's ghostly nighttime visits. Mainly because he eagerly awaited for her to return and was afraid he might miss her. And then after, there was that dreaded mix of sorrow, grief and guilt.

Plus, after years of sleeping on a hard bench with little back support, he'd actually gotten used to it. Therefore, when at home with Moksha who insisted on purchasing one of those cushy, form-adapting mattresses, he slept on something unnaturally comfortable. Whether this was some type of suppressed self-flagellation, he didn't know. All he knew was, these days he needed a nap to fill in the gaps of restless nights if he was going to continue to function well at his job. Cepheus finally made his way to the office door, accidentally hitting his forehead on the door's edge after not backing away quickly enough after opening it.

"Ye okay?" Ivan questioned. "Ye seem a little...stressed."

Cepheus rubbed his forehead, surprised. After all, Ivan was typically so hung up on the thoughts in his head that he often paid little attention to people's emotions unless someone else pointed them out. He did, however, miss the part where Cepheus smacked his head on the door.

"I am a little stressed, yes," Cepheus confessed.

"What's stressing ye, if you don't mind my asking?" Ivan suspected it might be the very thing that had been stressing him out, too.

"I question everything that's happening at TARA and the Makerspace of late. And, after a lifetime here, I am also starting to question my role… if I should even be here."

"I hear ye," Ivan nodded. "Been asking meself the same questions lately." The two were silent for a moment while Ivan carefully formed his words. He rubbed his earlobe with his thumb and forefinger nervously. "Er," he finally continued, "not to add to yer stress, but—"

"What is it, my friend? You can speak freely."

"Well, when I first arrived, it was all about building out technology for efficiencies, like transportation, growing food, clean energy. Now, I'm just back a week and suddenly it's…"

"What?" Cepheus knew the answer but somehow needed the perspective of someone outside of he and Tanager, both of whom had been tied to the school for decades and possibly lacked objectivity.

"Well, pardon me fer saying so, but now it seems to be for war." Cepheus's face dropped. "I don't mean to upset ye," Ivan continued. He wished Fatima were here right now. She was the better communicator.

At that moment, a member of Renenet's security team passed the office. He was wearing a crisp, tan uniform with brown boots and a distinctive, government-issued hat. The officer's manner suggested a clearly defined purpose of surveying the halls for anything that shouldn't be. He didn't walk, exactly. He marched.

"Perhaps we should take this conversation in my office," Cepheus stepped back to leave room for Ivan's bulky frame to slide past him before shutting the door.

It was only after the sound of the officer's footsteps had passed that they resumed communication. "I get that they want to be proactive about defending Erde from the neighboring Sections, particularly since they no longer have the support of the Intergalactic Peace Project nor the Vitruvians, but some of these precautions seem less defense and more offense. It's making me a wee bit uncomfortable," Ivan confessed.

"What have you been asked to do?" Cepheus was curious. It was his understanding that Ivan and his team were to outfit some of the newer vessels with defensive armory against attack, along with non-lethal micro-bullets that shot out tiny signal disruptors, thereby throwing an assailant's spacecraft off course and cutting off communication with similar vessels. But that was all that he was aware of. Apparently, there was more.

"Well," Ivan let out a sigh, "it started off all normal-sounding to me, making sure our security team, the military and our local constables had upgraded uniforms to protect against most of the lethal weapons used in hand-to-hand combat. Things like that. But then it started to enter gray areas. My first day back at the lab, Renenet asked our team what it would involve to take a concoction created in the chemical lab and stuff it into a small handheld device. So that, when released into the atmosphere, it could specifically target certain species and make them ill."

Cepheus's sallow complexion grew even more yellow. This sounded like something the Royals would do and even what Earthlings would do, but certainly not peace-loving Erdelings.

Ivan pressed on. "Then, a few days ago, she asked for small, explosive-like devices that could be deployed from multiple-sized vessels at any moving or non-moving target."

"You mean, she asked you to create a bomb," Cepheus confirmed.

"Yeah, she tried very hard not to use that exact word but I knew whah she meant. I told her flat-out that I know nothing about explosives but she was quick to point out how I diffused a network of them months back when Jasper Set tried to kill us all. Hard to deny when hundreds of people were around to witness it."

"Where did you leave it?" Cepheus asked.

"I requested a meeting with Commander Royce and the PDL so they could tell me the *exact* purpose of said explosives and what *exact* specs it should have. She was none too happy but I figured it would stall them a bit. I can't create what they are reluctant to talk about."

"Let me know if you need my support or Tanager's," Cepheus answered. "I know we'd both be happy to offer our thoughts on these new…requests."

"Thanks, man. And ye know," Ivan continued, "it's not as if I'm not grateful for all ye have done for Fatima and me, getting us safety to Erde and securing my finances in the universal marketplace, but if these requests keep coming in, I'm tellin' ye right now—I'm out."

"I understand, my friend." Cepheus was saddened. "And I'm telling you, you won't be alone."

A loud murmur erupted down the hallway. Moments later, their conversation was interrupted by someone banging loudly on the office door. "Everyone out," the officer who had recently passed the hall flung the door open. "We're under attack. Achel needs to go on lockdown. Follow me to the basement."

They weren't alone. TARA was bustling that day. They met Tanager in the hall who paused to try and reach Lucene using his communication watch.

"Damn it," he swore out loud as a few more guards shuffled him onto a transporter where he was sandwiched in between Ivan and Cepheus, followed by at least a dozen other students and faculty members. "Lucene," he muttered to himself, "why don't you ever keep your damn watch on so I can reach you?"

"Hang on," the officer commanded, setting the transporter in motion with everyone struggling not to lose their footing. Fortunately, the sheer volume of people in the transporter meant they were packed in like sardines, so falling over was not really an issue.

Once on the underground level, the masses were shuffled into a newly developed safety shelter. There were cameras set up in the bunker, where outside, at least three diamond-shaped spacecrafts flew past the outside of the Makerspace and TARA and made a beeline for the Dragoste Healing Center a few blocks down.

"What the—" Ivan's face turned white. He recognized the markings on the side of one of the crafts—a bright orange stripe that contained a panel for sending an energy field around the craft enough to deflect sonic particles and assault from incoming fire power. It was one they recently developed in the transportation lab, with one major difference. This one wasn't surrounding itself with an energy field. Instead, the panel opened up and opened fire, directly at the medical center.

Ivan's watch began to receive an alert—Fatima.

"Hallo, my—"

"Where are you? Are you okay? I'm watching the news and freaking out!" Ivan could hear little Talula in the background beginning to cry as she picked up on her mom's stress.

"I'm okay. We're safe. What about you? What's happening there?"

Cepheus hung over Ivan's shoulder. He neglected to remember his watch that morning and had no way of checking on Moksha or Roman or anyone.

"I'm home. Moksha's here with us, too," Fatima answered. Cepheus let out a relieved sigh, overhearing Fatima through the small speaker. "There's nothing happening at the Crosses, at least not from what we've heard, but there were three vessels spotted entering the atmosphere about twenty minutes ago. Have you heard from Lucene or Roman? Lucene left our training session over an hour ago, but I haven't been able to get in touch with her since—"

With that, all communication devices went silent and the cameras went blank.

"They've blocked the signal," Ivan yelled. "We need to get out of here and do something!" He ran to the doorway of the shelter. A rather small officer blocked him. Oddly, he was carrying a billy club. Ivan had never witnessed any of the security, nor the local constables for that matter, carrying a weapon before.

"Stand down, man!" the officer commanded. "I've heard from Commander Royce. The situation is being contained."

Ivan felt helpless. Were it not for the fact that he knew his family was safe, he wouldn't have left it alone. He would have fought his way out of the room, insisting that he had to do…something. Instead, he clenched his fists until they hurt. It was then that he noticed Tanager pacing back and forth, agitated.

"No Lucene?" he asked.

"No." Tanager ran his hand through his curly hair. He suspected Lucene may have gone to her usual meditation spot at the Eastern Cross but suspecting and knowing were two different things.

Ivan put a supportive hand on Tanager's shoulder but really didn't know what to say outside of that. An "I'm sure she's fine," didn't seem like a sensible response at that moment, as he had no idea if she really *was* fine.

From his high-home balcony, Roman watched as three vessels descended from the sky. At first, they flew directly toward the Makerspace at TARA. He held his breath but did not move. It was almost as if he were frozen in place and the world was slowing down and beginning to move at half speed. At the last moment, the three vessels shifted. They darted past his building at such close proximity that Roman could actually see that there were at least three people aboard one of the crafts. They all looked distinctly…human.

The crafts then formed a V-shape, the two blue ones in back following the leader. This one was white and had orange stripes. Roman didn't understand the distinction. Suddenly the one in front opened fire in front of the healing center. It let out three blasts at the front steps, demolishing the grand entranceway but leaving the hospital itself, intact. Then, as quickly as they arrived, they pointed their noses upward and shot out of the atmosphere.

Roman could see soldiers storming the healing center, ensuring everyone inside was safe and blocking off the scene. Most passersby ran for shelter as soon as they saw the vessels and heard the shots. But a few quickly began gathering around the now-demolished concrete steps of the building, in shock.

"Far was right," Roman muttered to himself. He looked down at his watch. *No one is calling to check on me,* he thought. In that moment of self-pity, it hadn't occurred to him to check on anyone else.

CHAPTER 19
MALLORY'S RETURN (SORT OF)
TEN DAYS BEFORE THE END.

Mallory's Costume Shop remained closed until it could be determined what was to be done with it. Since he had no heirs, it would naturally go to the government to auction off. One of his clothiers, named Pelimar, offered to buy the shop, even drawing up a very precise business plan to apply for a bank loan. This, it would so happen, was the same man who designed Lucene's favorite French off-the-mannequin outfit that she found an excuse to wear at least once a week.

But Commander Royce had other plans, insisting that Pelimar's request would only be met if he agreed to use the shop to create military uniforms first. Only after those needs were met could he use the shop for his own clothing designs. While Pelimar was an artist first and businessman second, he had to admit that having the steady stream of commissioned uniforms would help get the business up and running quickly. So, with some reluctance, he agreed.

As Lucene passed the window, after a slight detour returning home from Moksha's training session at the Western Cross, she saw the sign *Re-opening Soon as Mallory and Pelimar's Costume Shop*. It would seem that Pelimar was sentimental, leaving Mallory's name on the door in respect to his mentor and former employer.

Lucene had no real reason to be there. And yet, every two weeks she found an excuse to visit the Eastern Cross, usually for specific herbs and pantry items that only the grocery store there stocked. This excuse would have been much more believable had it come from Fatima instead of Lucene.

In truth, there was a grocer not two blocks from the high-home that she now shared with Tanager but she had grown fond of the older couple who helped her in the Eastern Cross, and so she would make a special trip on the SpeedCircuit as often as she could. And each time she did, she would make it a point of stopping by the darkened doorsteps of Mallory's old shop which was just down the block from the food store.

She was saddened at the loss of one her first friends in this new world as she had entertained the idea that he would eventually become a confidant and person she could always count on, like Fatima, only jollier (if that was even possible).

Lucene strained to see through the darkened window, placing the edges of her palms against the glass to block out the streetlights and see more closely.

Suddenly, a ghostly face appeared in the window...Mallory's. Despite his gossamer form, his eyes still sparkled like multicolored prisms.

She sucked in her breath, blinked, and looked again.

Mallory was motioning her inside.

Lucene looked around but saw no one else on the street. She set her groceries on the ground before carefully reaching for the door handle. In true Erdeling form, it was unlocked. Lucene stepped inside, cautiously closing the door behind her.

"Mallory?" she asked quietly. "Tell me I'm not seeing things."

She heard a distant giggle. "Okay, you're not seeing things," the boisterous voice of Mallory called. He sounded far away as if he were speaking through a telephone.

"Where the heck are you?" Lucene was filled with both excitement and apprehension.

Nothing...there was only silence. She called out several more times but still she heard...nothing.

Lucene carefully wandered through the shop. While the racks of clothing remained, the walls were no longer covered with prom dresses and flashy costumes. Instead, they displayed military uniforms of varied ranks, along with non-military personnel support garb she had started seeing at TARA. Frankly, it was depressing. A sprawl of gray polyester-like pants with matching jackets was laying across the counter as if waiting to be sized and sorted.

Lucene crept into the sewing room in the back. *Odd*, she noticed, all of the sewing machines were upright and staggered across each side of the table, just as Mallory had wanted it so that seamstresses could talk to one another as they worked, without craning their necks. He thought this would be good for morale. But one sewing machine had been turned on its side. Lucene walked over to it and ran her hand across it.

She turned it upright and pressed the power button. It whirred loudly and vibrated as if agitated. But that was all. Lucene turned the power off and took a closer look. She didn't know a thing about sewing. Therefore, she couldn't have explained the problem she saw with the bobbin as she poked around, nor that the hook assembly was wonky, and that the thread uptake was locked. Yet, somehow, she knew how to fix this.

"Might want to unplug it first." Mallory appeared before her in gossamer form. "Just so you don't accidentally sew your fingers together or electrocute yourself. One of us dead is quite enough."

"Holy crap, Mallory. You scared the shit out of me!"

Mallory's ghost laughed heartily. "Oh my gosh, if you could see the look on your face, child."

"Wait, how?" Lucene pointed at him.

"Don't you know it's rude to point," he reprimanded. "I've been trying to connect with you for the past month, every time you walked back and forth in front of the shop window. I would have thought you were daft, but thus far, you are the only person who is able to see me!"

"What happened to you?" Lucene asked. "I mean, I sort of know. But where are you now?"

"Well, *A*...I was murdered. That part we all know. And *B*...some sort of limbo? I've always said that this shop is my life. Apparently, it's my death also!" He giggled some more. But then it turned into a sob as he put his hand over his face. Lucene tried to hug him but her hand merely felt cold air as it went through him.

"Cut that out," he complained. "It tickles."

"Sorry," Lucene apologized, pulling her hand back. Instead, she unplugged the machine.

"Why are you here, child?" Mallory asked.

Lucene's eyes grew red. "Well, I sort of missed you," she confessed.

"Aw," he pouted, "that's sweet. Now tell me the truth."

"That is the truth," she whined.

"And?" Mallory pressed her.

Lucene let out a sigh. "And, I have no discernible skills," Lucene explained as she—without thinking—took apart the hook assembly, used a cloth lying nearby to clean it—and then reassembled it. She also snapped the loose bobbin back in place, re-threaded the machine and adjusted the thread tension. "Unlike Amy," she wrinkled her nose, "I can't cook. I can't play the piano. I'm not an artist. I'm not a scholar. And, any special powers I had are now as uncontrollable as the weather, though they are, admittedly, getting a little better. Still, my ability to grow plants and magically re-energize broken car batteries are still in question." Lucene was in full-on self-pity mode. "But I thought maybe…"

"Yes?" Mallory was interested.

"Maybe I could learn to sew?" She looked up at Mallory who had his elbow resting on his forearm with a hand to his mouth as he tried not to laugh.

"Is that so funny?"

"No, my child. What's so funny is that you repaired the machine in five minutes that Pelimar has been fighting with for weeks.

"Are you sure?"

"See for yourself," Mallory challenged.

Lucene plugged it back in and picked up a piece of remnant fabric, looking up at Mallory, questioningly.

"Go ahead," he urged, "but keep your fingers on each side of the cloth and be mindful of the needle."

Lucene obeyed, turned it on and hesitantly placed the cloth under the feed dog. The machine appeared to have a clear display panel on the side of it where she tapped in instructions. It began to whir, and within moments, she had created a simple but effective straight stitch.

"Voila!" Mallory smiled.

Lucene smiled but then remembered the very important fact that Mallory was, in fact, dead. "Mallory, as happy as I am to see you, you can't stay here forever."

"Well, obviously," he chastised. "I was only planning on hanging around until I was sure this place was up and running again, and now I'm hanging around until these grotesque uniforms go away and this shop returns to its former glory."

"You may not have that kind of time," she explained. Even as she did so, his image began floating in and out.

"Whatever do you mean?"

"My friend, Isabella, accidentally created a leak of sorts, making it possible for lifeforms on different layers within this plane of existence to pass back and forth. That's probably why I can see you now."

"Well, what's so bad about that?"

"It's distorting reality and letting some beings out who are not as nice as you."

"Oh," Mallory thought for a minute. "That explains a few unsavory characters I've run into lately."

"The point is," Lucene continued, "once she seals the leak, I'm afraid you may be stuck in that realm with those entities, forever. I mean, I don't really know for sure—even Reverend Isabella isn't certain. But I worry…isn't there a different…better realm for you?"

"You mean like heaven?"

"I dunno, maybe?" Lucene wasn't sure herself. "Maybe it's that unfinished business idea. And when you're ready to let the shop go, you'll move on. Only, I'm afraid, you're short on time."

"My, my, aren't we morbid?" Mallory tsk-ed at her.

"What are you doing in my shop?" a male voice asked. Lucene jumped with a start, nearly sewing her fingers together in the process.

"I warned you," Mallory said.

Lucene quickly turned the power off and unplugged the machine.

"Uh," she looked down at the square of fabric. "I was, uh, fixing your machine?"

The young man standing in front of her had the brightest blood-red hair she had ever seen. It was molded to his head like one of those old troll dolls that they used to sell on the end of pencils, whose hair went wild when you spun the pencil between your palms. His face was narrow, oval shaped, and powder white. He was wearing black lipstick. In his hand was a metal hanger. He wielded it like a weapon.

"You broke into my shop to fix one of my damaged machines?" After he thought a moment, he realized the hanger wasn't going to be of much use to him, so he set it on the table and then crossed his arms, impatiently, waiting for an explanation.

"Just tell Pelimar the truth," Mallory encouraged.

"He won't believe me," she replied, looking at Mallory's hazy image as it floated behind the young man.

Pelimar looked over his shoulder, quizzically. "Who are you talking to?"

"Uh, listen, Pelimar—"

"How did you know my name?"

"Well, aside from it being on the shop sign," Lucene began, letting out a sigh, "Mallory told me."

"Oh, did he?" Pelimar laughed. "And when did you last talk to our old buddy Mallory?"

"Who are you calling old, red-headed Goth-i-mar!" Mallory retorted.

"About two seconds ago," she pointed.

Pelimar looked. He saw nothing. "You do know he's dead."

"I am aware of that, yes."

"So, you talk to dead people?"

"Apparently?" She wrinkled her nose. She was as confused about it as he was.

"Get out of my shop before I call the constable."

Lucene thought a moment, coming up with only one possible response. She pulled up a voice from her belly and answered jovially, "Who are you calling old, red-headed Goth-i-mar!" Lucene's impression was quite extraordinary.

"How did you know he used to call me that…as much as I asked him not to?" Pelimar furrowed his brow with a mix of suspicion and annoyance.

"Because he's still here."

"And I suppose he taught you how to fix my machine, is that it?"

"Don't be gauche, Goth-i-mar. I am an artiste. I don't fix machines.

That's what I had *you* for." Mallory waved his hand for Lucene to relay the message.

"Don't be gauche, Goth-i-mar," Lucene imitated, "I am an artiste. I don't fix machines. That's what I had *you* for."

Pelimar let out a laugh. "You know, you've got him spot on. I just wish I believed in ghosts but I don't." Mallory stuck his tongue out at him. Lucene let out a laugh. "What's so funny?" Pelimar demanded.

"He just stuck his tongue out at you."

"Look, could you lose the whole 'Mallory is a ghost thing' and tell me what you want."

Mallory shot her a *well, go on* look.

"I want you to take me on as an apprentice and teach me how to sew." The words flowed with surprising ease because, up until that very moment, she wasn't entirely sure what, exactly, she wanted.

Mallory's eyes beat into Pelimar's brain. "Just agree, silly boy," he mumbled.

"Wouldn't there have been easier ways to ask for a job than to break into my shop?" Pelimar reasoned.

"I didn't break in," Lucene defended. "The door was open. And I came in because I thought I saw something…or…someone."

Pelimar waived a hand in the air. "I know, a ghost." It was clear from his expression that he had no intention of entertaining this idea.

"So?"

"So, what?"

"About my request?" Lucene scrunched up her face like a small child not entirely certain whether her parents were going to agree to her request or chastise her for even asking.

"Just agree, silly boy," Mallory tried again. "You could use the help, you know?" He looked toward Lucene to support her own cause. And so she did. *Just agree…agree.* Lucene focused her intentions as hard as she could.

"I can't believe I'm saying this," Pelimar poked a finger in his ear as if there were a fly buzzing around in it. "But I agree. I mean, what I'm saying is, okay, I will take you on as an apprentice. Uh, what's your name?"

"Lucene," she and Mallory answered in unison. Pelimar flicked at his ear again and looked in Mallory's direction, squinting in a confused manner.

"Okay, Lucene." He turned to face her. "I can't pay you much, but if a standard apprentice wage works for you, we can start there. If you prove useful, then we can negotiate a raise in three months. How does that sound?"

"That sounds perfect." Lucene put her hand out to shake Pelimar's, but he shook his head. Earth customs were clearly not his thing. He peered at her hand as if it carried with it a severe rash (it didn't). Lucene retracted her hand, awkwardly.

"When can you start?"

Lucene suddenly felt a chill and looked over Pelimar's shoulder. Mallory was gone.

Lucene returned home that evening to find Tanager pacing back and forth across the living room, muttering to himself.

"What's going on?" Lucene asked, surprised. She set her small bag of groceries on the table.

"Where have you been?" Tanager spat out before pulling her toward him in a bear hug.

"Okay, I'm confused. Getting really mixed messages here." Lucene returned the embrace with some hesitation.

"Fatima said you left the training with Moksha hours ago." He backed away, searching her face for an answer.

"I didn't know I had to check in with you as to my whereabouts," Lucene answered defensively. "If you must know, I made a side trip to the Eastern Cross to pick up red curry paste and dried ancho chili peppers…and a few other things."

"We have a store two blocks away."

"I like the store I used to go to," Lucene began raising her voice.

"Since when did you become picky about gourmet ingredients?" Tanager raised his voice to match hers.

Lucene angrily unpacked her tote bag, holding up the curry paste and chili peppers as evidence. "In case you thought I was lying to you."

"When have I ever accused you of lying to me?"

"I don't know. You seem awfully concerned about my whereabouts. I hadn't realized you were so suspicious."

"Suspicious?" Tanager was incredulous.

"Or controlling. Maybe both. I don't know." Lucene was flustered, her face becoming flushed.

"And now I'm controlling too?" Tanager ran a hand through his hair and then held his arm out as if he were about to give a speech. "Did it ever occur to you that I may have been worried about you?" His eyes widened as he searched her face for understanding. "That maybe a phone call to let me know you were running late might be a good idea so that I wouldn't pace the floor thinking something bad had happened to you? Oh, that's right," he continued, frustrated, "you never take your communication device with you."

Actually, it *hadn't* occurred to Lucene. This whole 'checking in with another person' concept was new to her. She felt a pang of guilt for her outburst. "I hadn't intended on staying that long, but then I stopped and talked to Mallory and time got away from me. And, why were you worried about me, anyway?"

"Just a moment," Tanager circled a finger in the air. "Back up...you talked to Mallory?"

Lucene let out a sigh. "Yes, but—"

"You know he's dead, right?"

"Clearly, I do, but—"

"Then, how exactly did you talk to him?"

"If you'd stop interrupting me, I'll tell you."

Lucene stopped to grab a pitcher from their refrigerator and a glass from the cupboard to pour herself a glass of iced turmeric tea. She motioned the glass toward him in case he wanted one as well. He shook his head. They sat at the dining room table for the next ten minutes as Lucene recounted her interaction with Mallory's ghost and Pelimar, including the part about the apprenticeship. She finally concluded with, "I'm sorry I worried you. I'll call next time if I'm running late or at least have someone else call if I forget my watch."

But Tanager's mind was buzzing. He was already on to the next issue. "But you already have a job," he protested. "You are an agent of the PDL and you're my research assistant. I need you." Lucene placed a hand on his forearm. Before she could respond, he kept rambling on, "Assuming we can even return to TARA after today's attack..."

"Wait, what?" Lucene's grip on Tanager's arm grew stronger. "What attack?"

"Three fighter vessels entered the atmosphere as if targeting the Makerspace, but at the last moment, they veered off course and ended up destroying the steps of the healing center before vanishing."

"Holy crap. Was anyone hurt?"

"No, but now you know why I was so worried about you. Lucene, I thought something happened to you," his eyes were rimmed with red as he fought back tears.

With that, she wrapped her arms around his shoulders and hugged him fiercely.

CHAPTER 20
CEPHEUS AND LUCENE
EIGHT DAYS BEFORE THE END.

For all the times that Commander Royce called the PDL agents together for one or her many meetings, she was surprisingly silent about the attack on the Dragoste Healing Center. When Ivan and Tanager requested a meeting with her to explain that the vessels the attackers were using had a striking resemblance to those Ivan and his team were building in the Makerspace (fitted with weapons to match) she dismissed them, citing that a top-secret investigation was underway and that she would reach out to them should she require their assistance.

This was a far different Commander Royce from the one who, just six months ago, gave them an open invitation to meet with her and speak freely about any concerning issues. In fact, this new version of Royce went so far as to tell them that given her current responsibilities, any requests for future face-to-face interactions should be made through Director Renenet.

Suspicious, Lucene decided to employ Kiki's sniffing skills to determine if Commander Royce, was in fact, Royce at all, instead of a shapeshifter posing as the commander. But the verdict came back with disappointing news. After Kiki had diligently tracked Royce at the PDL headquarters to her high-home in Achel, she determined that Royce was most likely an Erdeling. To be fair, Kiki hadn't actually smelled Royce prior, but she had the varied Vitruvian scents in her nasal directory, not to mention the sweet smell of Earthlings and the citrusy aroma of Erdelings. Royce was, decidedly, more citrusy. This left Lucene with more questions than answers, the main question being, was Commander Royce somehow involved with the latest attack? Or, at the very least, was she covering up for someone? Perhaps their suspicions were correct about her working with the Vitruvians...or someone else. The sourness in the pit of her stomach returned, a feeling that had been happening far too often lately.

Between the wolf onslaught, the attack on the healing center, the supernatural interactions spurred by the tear between the layers, her on again, off again empathic powers, not to mention her strained relationship with Tanager lately, Lucene's nerves were frayed. So she thought of the one person who might be able to help her gain clarity.

"Lucene, how nice to see you," Moksha greeted her at the door.

"Hi, Moksha. Sorry to bug you guys so close to dinner." Lucene was ushered inside Cepheus and Moksha's cottage. Lucene, who had taken to carrying a staff with her in case the wolves returned, set it by the front door. She had also come equipped with an ultrasonic wave handheld contraption that Ivan assured her was a high frequency that would irritate dogs, and would most certainly work on wolves. It was the best he could come up with on short notice, though he couldn't be sure if the irritation would make them more violent or send them running in pain. Therefore, the staff seemed like a good back-up plan. She unzipped her backpack and tucked away the contraption.

"He's expecting you," Moksha continued, "his study is just through there."

Of all the times Lucene had been to their cottage, she hadn't recalled ever seeing Cepheus's study. She expected it to be like his office at TARA—cluttered with books, models of flying vessels, blueprints and all manner of gadgets thrown in disarray. But to her surprise, when she knocked lightly on the door, it opened to reveal a wall-to-wall bookshelf with a sturdy cherrywood desk in front of it. On the opposite wall were framed maps of Earth, Erde, and several neighboring planets in Section 1 of which she was still unaware. Unlike his office, this room was distinctly organized and minimalistic. Lucene suspected that Moksha had something to do with the present state of his study and his home.

"Lucene," Cepheus spoke softly, a warm glow crossing his face. "It's always nice to hear from you outside of work. Is this a social visit or is there something I can help you with?"

Lucene felt a pang of guilt, as aside from their monthly reunion dinner which now included Moksha but almost never included Roman, she'd been lax in her social visits. But to be fair, there seemed to have been one situation after another since her arrival on Erde.

"I wish it were merely social but I've come partially for advice and partially to ask a favor."

"Of course," he answered sincerely, "whatever you need. Please," he motioned to a club chair next to his desk, "make yourself comfortable. Would you care for a beverage? Moksha's just brewed a batch of reishi mushroom tea."

"No, I'm fine, thanks." Lucene fought to fit the words together in her mind.

"What's troubling you?" Cepheus asked calmly. "You know you can tell me anything."

"I know," Lucene sat down, hesitantly. "So, I've been thinking...you know how we stopped my meditation training on the vessel because I became a little...unstable...for a bit?" That was putting it mildly. She had to be put in hibernation for the remainder of the trip after becoming mentally unwell.

"Yes, of course," Cepheus confirmed.

"And then we started back up again at TARA with Tanager's class and then I sort of flaked out a second time?"

"I remember," Cepheus nodded calmly. Cepheus fought back the urge to defend her instability on the amount of stress she was under, the trauma she'd endured, genetic splicing, Jasper Set's influence and now, a confirmed virus. In fact, he thought she had recovered and adjusted remarkably well these past few months despite everything she'd been through. Instead, he paused and said nothing, giving her time to find the right words.

"Well, I've been afraid of resuming a meditation practice or developing any of my skills because I have been worried about short-circuiting again."

"What makes you think you would, as you say, 'short circuit' again?"

"Let's just say, my track record hasn't been all that great," Lucene admitted.

"But Lucene, you're a different person now than you were even a few months ago. And now you have the support of those of us who love you and understand what you're going through. Back on Earth, you knew you were in danger but didn't know why or from whom. Now, you've faced your demons—in some cases, quite literally, and look at the woman you've become."

Lucene wasn't sure who started tearing up first, but both were wiping their eyes. She knew Cepheus loved her and that he had become a part of her new family on Erde, but it was still nice to hear. "I wish I could see myself as you see me," she answered honestly, "because what I see in myself isn't all that great." Lucene sniffed as a few stray tears ran down her face.

"I wish you could, too," he answered in earnest, "because what I see is a pretty courageous woman." Lucene averted her gaze. After another awkward pause, Cepheus asked, "Do you *want* to continue your training?"

"I think so," Lucene replied quietly. "I mean, I think part of the problem before was that I became overwhelmed and lost my filtering system. All the sensory stuff came in at once and I lost the ability to let it in a little at a time."

"I know exactly what you mean." And he did, having spent a number of years *under watch* because of his own episodes, which fortunately, were now under control.

"But the thing is—"

"Yes?"

"Stuff is coming back, whether I like it or not—little things like manipulating energy for healing, telepathy, some telekinesis—"

"These are not little things, Lucene," Cepheus reasoned.

"Yeah, I guess not. And there's the ethical mind control, though, in recent use, it was more a matter of survival."

"The mind manipulation of the dessert gliders to overrun the dire wolves was quite impressive," Cepheus acknowledged.

"Thanks. And, you know, my memory is still a little fuzzy, but even that's getting better as I work through stuff. So, I guess if it's going to be there, like it as not, I should start training again. Otherwise, it's going to be erratic and unpredictable."

"That makes sense," Cepheus agreed.

"On the other hand," Lucene reasoned. "What *if* I go off balance again and become erratic and unpredictable?"

"I suppose that is always a risk."

"What should I do?"

"You know my immediate go-to is meditation, but since that's what we're talking about, perhaps begin by asking yourself four questions."

"What questions?"

"First, what do you have to lose by doing nothing?"

"Myself," Lucene answered without thinking.

Cepheus paused a moment at her revelation before continuing. "Second, what do you have to gain by doing nothing?"

"Nothing…it's just status quo."

"Third, what do you stand to lose by training your powers?"

"Myself."

There it was again. Cepheus persisted.

"And last, what do you stand to gain by training your powers?"

"The greatest potential of myself."

"So, what will you do?"

Lucene paused a moment, grinning. "That was five questions."

Cepheus let out a chuckle. "So it was. Still, what will you do?"

"If I decide to start meditating again—slowly, of course, just to see how it goes…will you work with me again?"

Cepheus tilted his head sideways forming a lopsided grin, his canine teeth sparkling. Anyone who didn't know Cepheus might have been frightened by it, but not Lucene.

Finally, he answered, "I thought you'd never ask."

Moksha insisted that Lucene stay for dinner and as the three of them sat, a strange howling began. At first, they thought it was the wind as a storm had begun brewing outside. But then they heard it—more wolves. Just then, an advisory notice began flashing on Lucene's watch. She hit play for those at the table to hear.

"Warning! Several packs of wolf and tiger-like creatures have been spotted in the Western Cross," the announcer said. "The PDL and all security units have issued a mandatory lockdown. Secure your outdoor farm animals as much as possible to prevent a possible feral attack and bring all pets inside. Furthermore, residents are required to stay inside until further notice."

Lucene was about to shut her watch off when a second alert came in. "Warning! A severe thunderstorm warning is in place across all the Crosses and the City of Achel. For your security, the PDL recommends that all residents take shelter until further notice."

Lucene turned off the alerts, looking at Moksha and Cepheus whose hands seemed frozen in space, hovering over the noodle bowls Moksha had prepared.

"I sure picked a craptastic time to visit, huh? Want me to try and catch the next SpeedCircuit out before it's shut down? Otherwise, you'll be stuck with me for a while."

"Nonsense," Moksha answered. "The couch in the living room folds into a bed and we have extra blankets and pillows. You can sleep here tonight and catch the Circuit when it opens back up in the morning—providing the lockdown has been lifted by then, of course."

"I'm sorry," Lucene sighed. "I didn't mean to burden you."

Cepheus reached out a hand and took Lucene's supportively, giving it a father-like squeeze. "You are never a burden to us. Besides, we have work to do after dinner," he smiled.

Apparently, training was to resume sooner rather than later. Lucene squeezed his in return before remembering. "Oh, I almost forgot. Excuse me one second…"

To her host's surprise, Lucene dropped his hand and left the dinner table. She hit a button on her watch one more time.

"Lucene, where are you? Did you get the alerts about the storm and the ferals on the loose?" Tanager asked on the other end, fear clearly audible in his voice.

"I did," Lucene answered. "I just sat down to dinner with Moksha and Cepheus. I was planning on heading home right after but—"

Tanager let out a loud sigh. "You need to stay where you are, of course."

"I know. Sorry about that. But at least I remembered to call this time!"

"There's nothing to be sorry about. I'm just glad you are safe. All three of you, please be careful."

To emphasize his point, the howling resumed outside, closer this time. The storm became much stronger and rain began to beat down on the roof.

She could hear as Tanager sucked in his breath, having clearly heard the sounds from across the miles. Lucene watched as Moksha and Cepheus began triggering locks on the cottage that lowered see-through shields that barricaded the windows as if preparing for a hurricane.

"Don't worry, my friend," Cepheus called over Lucene's shoulder. "We won't let anything bad happen to her."

Lucene's stomach began to growl. After all, they hadn't had a chance to eat yet.

"Have you spoken to Fatima and Ivan yet?" Tanager asked.

"No, you're the first person I called. I suppose I should check on them."

"Go have dinner, Lucene. I'll give them a call. I promise to let you know if anything has happened."

"Okay, thanks. And, weather and circumstance permitting, I'll be home at first light."

"Take your time. Just be safe," Tanager spoke softly.

In the kitchen, Moksha and Cepheus had returned to the table, waiting politely for Lucene to join them again.

"I will be. Sleep well," Lucene's heart sank a little. It was then that she realized that she hadn't been away from Tanager for a single night since they'd moved in together. She hadn't expected the sudden hole she felt in the center of her heart. It wasn't so much that she couldn't bear a night apart. It was the fact that she had no choice in the matter. She was, for all intents and purposes, stuck.

"You, too, and Lucene..."

"Yes?"

"I love you."

She almost blurted out her usual, "I know" as the right words always got stuck in her throat. Perhaps it was the thunderstorm outside, the howling of the wolves and the realization that tomorrow was never really a given. So, instead she answered softly, "I love you, too."

CHAPTER 21
THE WIND AND THE WOLVES
EIGHT DAYS BEFORE THE END.

Lucene and Cepheus sat on the floor of the study facing one another, several feet apart. Both were sitting cross-legged with eyes closed. Outside, the wind and the wolves were still howling.

Moksha assumed the role of security guard, telling the two to focus on their meditation; she would alert them if anything happened. So, with the windows and doors secure, Moksha sat in the living room, staff at the ready, just in case. At one point, she witnessed a tiger-like creature steaming up the window as it peered inside. But the hurricane-proof shutters worked against the strength of a supernatural wild animal as it pawed at the window in vain.

Instinctively, she touched her leg where the dire wolf had attacked her. Thanks to Lucene's energy healing and her own constitution, nothing was left but a scar where the wolves' teeth had broken the skin. This was not particularly interesting to Moksha who had a series of scars from her short time as a Royal assassin before escaping to Erde. In fact, most of the remaining scars she did retain were a result of her father beating her so that the Royals didn't learn that she had helped Cepheus escape. Oddly enough, she didn't look at these wounds as abuse—

according to their dysfunctional culture, he was protecting her. Sadly, she didn't know what happened to him, or any of her family, for that matter.

Occasionally, Fatima would send a short message alert from their nearby home. Moksha smiled and sent an, "All is fine here. How about there?" message back. After her not-so-warm greeting from humans living on the preserves when she had first arrived, she was grateful for Fatima's friendship. Of course, those on the preserve had been there for quite some time and seem to have forgotten that they were once outsiders, too. But Fatima was new and hadn't forgotten. And, given her nature, Moksha was fairly certain that she never would.

"And Lucene?" Fatima asked.

"Meditating," Moksha messaged back.

"Oh, cool. But don't freak out if she starts screaming from sensory overload. She does that sometimes."

Moksha grinned, "Thanks for the warning."

Inside the study, Cepheus began with simple reviews, not unlike what they would practice when she was a young child and he was contacting her remotely from Erde. The same exercises that her own father would work with her on, as well. For example, he would think of a color, a shape or an object, and she would relay what it was. Then, she would send messages back. Then, they moved on to words and sentences. It seemed juvenile, at first, but it was almost as if they were re-calibrating her intuitive skills.

And as they did so, memories began flooding back. Lucene remembered calling out to Cepheus for help the night her parents died. But at the time, she thought of him more as an angel that could miraculously save her. As an adult, she now understood that while his skill level was much more advanced than the average human, he wasn't an angel or a deity. But he did try to help her. In fact, he had been looking after her for her entire life.

Finally, Lucene moved into the void, that is, a meditation that shifted from a place of breath awareness to that blissful space of nothingness. In there, it was quiet and peaceful. There, nothing unpleasant could get in.

"Did you miss-s-s- me, princes-s-s?"

"What the hell are you doing here?" Lucene spoke aloud, unnerved. This time, she wasn't even dreaming.

"What is it?" Cepheus opened his eyes, concerned. "Who's there?"

Lucene kept her eyes closed.

"Go ahead," Jasper encouraged. "Tell him."

"It's Jasper Set," Lucene whispered. She was becoming increasingly agitated.

"Lucene," Cepheus reminded her. "You control what experiences you let in. If you don't want to see him, block him out."

"You can do that...if you want," Jasper whispered back. "But then you won't be in on my little s-s-s-ecret."

"What secret?"

Jasper's image flew into view, more clearly than the last time, wearing an outdated three-piece tweed suit over his barrel-like body. His skinny legs were adorned with what could best be described as brown stockings. How his wings protruded from the suit she couldn't tell, but there he was, hovering in midair with a mixture of anger and absurdity.

"I've discovered a way out," he spat. "I couldn't seem to squeeze in and out between the layers like other beings, but then it occurred to me." He paused for dramatic effect. Lucene said nothing. She merely waited. "Go on! Ask me 'what?'!" he yelled, agitated.

Lucene felt a mixture of fear, anger, annoyance, and confusion all at once. She emotionally distanced herself as if the emotions floated all around her but could not attach themselves to her. Finally, in a moment of calm she asked, "What has occurred to you?"

"My energy is too big to fit through the tear unless the tear is bigger or the portal is opened altogether. My greatness-s-s was getting in my way!"

"Yeah," Lucene answered sarcastically, "that's always been the problem."

"Lucene," Cepheus whispered. "Talk to me. Are you okay?"

Jasper was confused for a moment. "Is that the guy I tossed into the field?"

Lucene ignored him. "I'll ask the same question I've asked you before. What do you want?"

"I want what I've always wanted...you, for starters. I still believe there's lots of dimension-hopping to be had, s-s-seeing what havoc I can wreak on other realms. See what my doppelgängers are doing. Your powers are returning, are they not?"

"How did you—"

"I know lots of things," he spat angrily. "I see everything from here. I jus-s-s-t can't always-s-s do anything about it…yet!"

"Couldn't we just try again?" Lucene reasoned. "Have Isabella send you into another dimension and you can see what the other Lucenes in their alternate lives are up to?"

"Rather irresponsible of you, isn't it?" Jasper offered. "To sic me on your other selves?"

Lucene had to admit that he had a point. Still, the *other* Lucenes—if parallel dimensions were actually a thing—hadn't exactly sent any new Jaspers to this realm, so perhaps they were better equipped to deal with him than she was.

"Besides," Jasper continued. "I've got issues with Rev…Rev…" he choked, "Is-s-abella. She trapped me like she trapped the kitty Hys-s-echia. The prieste-s-s-s seems to be making lots of enemies these days, don't you think?"

"So your grand plan is that I simply go with you to other dimensions, which we don't know how to get to and—"

"You're not a quick study, are you Lucene?" Jasper barked.

"Enlighten me," she answered flatly.

"The whole arms burning, ring of fire…*you* are the portal to other worlds. Is-s-s-abella may have had the coordinates off, but the concept is s-s-s-olid. You just need to figure out how to get us there."

"Where, exactly? You're not making any sense."

"Anywhere that isn't here!" he bellowed. Jasper's nerves were frazzled and he was even less coherent than usual.

"So, if I go with you, what's in it for me?"

"For you?" He thought a moment. "Not much, if I'm being honest. But in exchange, I will call my Null mamas and papas off. They're still looking for me, you know. You'd be saving your precious planet."

Lucene opened her eyes, momentarily. Cepheus was there at the ready. "What is it?" he asked, concerned.

"Jasper says if I go with him, he'll call the Null off from destroying Erde. Would your—" she stopped herself before saying 'father.' Instead, she reframed it. "Would Hamish have made a deal with Jasper without protecting Erde, given that you reside here?"

"Excuse me," Jasper flew into Cepheus's face, but Cepheus was unable to see him. "This is a private conversation." He turned to Lucene. "But I can answer that." He began bouncing up and down hysterically, like a small child. "I found a loopty-doopty-hole, as it were."

"A loophole?"

"That's what I just said! Stop repeating me." For a moment, he lost his train of thought. "That's right. I was permitted to do whatever I wanted on Erde, but not harm his precious Cepheus unless abs-s-solutly necess-s-sary. I suppose he assumed I would 'take the girl and run' so-to-speak. But then the plan changed."

"How did the plan change?"

Jasper knew he should have kept it to himself, he really did. But he was a braggart, and being stuck between the layers, he was left bragging to beings who didn't seem to adequately admire his capabilities. This annoyed him. "Hamish decided that Erde might be a better option for the Royals than Earth."

"Well, that makes sense," Lucene answered. "That's why Dallen and the Vitruvians were trying to work with Erde…to help protect it from the Royal invasion."

Jasper shook his head. "Oh, you poor, stupid girl." Lucene didn't react, she merely waited, knowing he couldn't help but tell her why. "The Vitruvians have no interest in helping Erde survive…quite the contrary. And I will keep my contract with Hamish and not harm his precious Cepheus…unless absolutely necessary."

"So, if I go with you—"

"Then I will redirect the Null."

"I don't understand."

"Of course, you don't. You're an idiot."

"Explain it to me," Lucene was not the least bit moved by the demon's insults.

"I will call the Null and redirect them to the space between the layers…Erde remains intact."

"But the other realms of reality? Won't they be in danger of being destroyed?"

"Who cares, so long as your friends are okay?"

"But that would be irresponsible, don't you think?"

"That's your deal, not mine." Jasper crossed his arms in front of him like a defiant teenager.

"One more question," Lucene thought a moment.

"What?"

"Why is it that you'd want to trap your surrogate family in an alternate reality?"

If it were possible for Jasper's face to become any more translucent, it would have. Instead, he merely looked dazed as if someone had slapped him hard across his jaw.

Lucene's empathic powers may still be under repair, but this one was obvious. "Oh," she answered, "I see. You're still afraid of them. In fact," she continued, "you're not calling them to rescue you. You're trying to bait them…so you can plan your permanent escape."

Jasper didn't answer. Instead, he began spinning like a cyclone, disappearing into a cloud of smoke.

CHAPTER 22
MORPHINAE'S REALIZATION
SEVEN DAYS BEFORE THE END.

"You knew." Morphinae flew in as a falcon, transitioning into his male form once he reached the sands of Tranquil Beach, appearing to be anything but tranquil. In fact, he appeared angry—a rare emotion for Morphinae.

"You're back," Odessa's eyes lit up before she remembered that she was mad at him for disappearing on her after she'd made her declaration of love. Okay, she reasoned with herself. It was less of a declaration, and more of a simple, "I like you," but she hadn't expected him to run away like that and not contact her for months.

Morphinae ignored her. "How could you lie to me?" he demanded. "After I covered for you back on Earth?" He was referring to the time she stalled in returning to Vitruvia, claiming to be ill, giving herself time to escape to Erde and claim sanctuary.

"What are you talking about?" she squeaked out, nervously. His eyes seemed almost flame-like. He'd never gotten angry with her before.

"I'm talking about how Representative Dallen and other Vitruvian dignitaries made a side deal with Drake Cushing in exchange for Lucene and for dibs on Earth, should it become uninhabitable by humans—"

"That's old news. They were trying to protect Lucene from the Royals. And, it was self-defense. If the Royals got her powers—"

"The Royals were never interested in Lucene's powers for themselves. They were just handing her off to Jasper Set in exchange for Earth. And later, protection from the Null."

"Again, old news—"

"Let me finish," Morphinae growled. Odessa fell silent.

"The Vitruvians *claim* non-interference, except in self-defense. Therefore, I thought it odd when they reached out to me, a member of the Balance-Keepers and asked for my help. Dallen said he feared for the safety of the Vitruvian people if the Royals took over Earth and spread to Erde. How long before they got to Vitruvia? And he *knew*!" Morphinae's voice grew louder before he remembered himself. "He knew that if he gained the extra support from the Balance-Keepers, that you would do anything to support the mission."

"What are you talking about?!" Odessa's eyes grew red. "Why would he assume that?" How could Dallen have known how Odessa felt about Morphinae, when she didn't even know it herself until recently? "As you can see, I abandoned my position. If I go back to Vitruvia now, they'll likely kill me."

"No, they wouldn't. This is exactly what Dallen wanted you to do."

"Oh, c'mon. You're not making any sense."

"The Vitruvians interfere and they interfere on a regular basis. They have every intention of occupying Earth and Erde and killing off the Royals—something which will become infinitely easier now that the Null has rolled over all Royal domains except for the training grounds. Sovereign Hamish was rather short-sighted in his planning when he made a deal with Jasper Set."

"Really? I had no idea—"

"Stop!" Morphine grit his teeth. "Stop lying to me. The only reason the Vitruvians wanted to make an alliance with Earth and Erde was when they thought they might have the protection of the IPP and surrounding Sections to guard against a Royal attack. Once that plan failed, they returned to the original plan, with one major difference."

Morphinae eyed Odessa, as if giving her the opportunity to confess. She opened her mouth to speak, but then shook her head.

"I can't," she whispered.

"How long have you been giving intel on Makerspace technology and the happenings on TARA and the preserves to Representative Dallen?"

Odessa thought about denying it, but she knew it was useless. And, she didn't want to lie to Morphinae. In a way, she was somewhat relieved. He turned away in disgust. All of his suspicions were true. "I never want to see you again, Odessa," he grumbled.

"They said they'd kill me," Odessa pleaded. Morphinae stopped, standing with his back to her. "I disobeyed orders by fleeing to Erde. Commander Royce was ready to send me home in a body bag until Representative Dallen thought I might be useful here after all."

"Commander Royce?" This surprised Morphinae. "Why would she do that?"

"Where do you think all the money came from to fund TARA and the Data Collector initiative to start with? This is a small and rather poor planet with lots of smart people but no funds to do anything. And yet, look at how advanced the Makerspace is. Who do you think privately funded all that?"

"Disappointing," Morphinae answered. "And here I thought the Erdelings were the only honest people among us…wrong again." With that, Morphinae transformed into a Peregrine Falcon and flew away.

Odessa stood there, numb. Of all the beings in the multiverse, she'd just lost the one she had expected to be by her side forever. And he had left her, not once, but twice. And this time, she feared, it was permanent.

She didn't have much time to wallow in self-pity. For there, in the distance, making their way toward her hut was none other than Lucene and Reverend Isabella. Lucene didn't wait to ask Odessa why she was crying, nor did she tap into the shapeshifter's emotion and realize that she was in the middle of heartbreak. She was on a mission and so was Isabella.

Instead, Lucene looked directly into Odessa's eyes and announced, "We need to talk."

CHAPTER 23
OLLY
LAST OCTOBER, BEFORE THE NEW ASSEMBLY.

"Beggin' your pardon, my Liege, my Viceroy, my Marquess, my Baron, my Dauphin," the thick, elf-like being bowed, gesturing with his hands as his head nearly hit the floor.

"Who are you? How did you get in here?" Dallen asked, jumping from his high-backed chair that looked suspiciously like a throne…in a hotel room. He nearly knocked over the long-stem fluted glass he was holding, as he was sipping a fine Vitruvian port. "Guards!"

"Now, now," the elf answered. "Let's nah be hasty." He held his palms out as if to calm the ambassador down.

Dallen wasn't prone to yelling. In fact, when he wanted his guards, or a servant of any kind, he'd flick his fingers and they'd come running. If they weren't in the room, all he had to do was tap his lapel pin and a minimum of three attendants would appear. Realizing that his yelling hadn't worked, he began tapping the pin, fervently.

"Now, now," the elf tried again. "That won't not be necess'ry. I just wanna talk is all. I gave your serfs the night off just sos we can talk."

"You…what? How?" Dallen sniffed the air, distastefully. There was a strange aroma that wafted off the visitor, almost like olives…no, that wasn't it. Olive brine. He smelled like olive brine.

The elf-like creature stood there dressed in layers of dirty cloth and wore large boots that made a floppy sound as the sole of his left foot hung loose, while the toes of the right boot had a hole in it, revealing a hairy toe. The creature's face was large and round and seemed about two sizes too big for his torso and one size too small for his feet.

"I said, I gave 'em the night off sos we can talk. Mind if I sit down, my Liege, my Viceroy, my —"

"Ambassador or Representative Dallen is fine," Dallen interrupted. "Either of those titles are acceptable." Dallen really wasn't sure that he wanted the aromatic elf to sit down. He didn't even like having him in the otherwise immaculate room.

The elf plopped down on the carpet and crossed his legs under him, leaving Dallen to return to his chair-that-looked-like-a-throne and sit down. He looked down at the odd creature, expectantly. In his mind, he was cycling through all the neighboring Sections he knew. The elf certainly wasn't from Sections 0, 1 or 2, that was for certain. Unless the Royals were hiding a rare species, he couldn't be from Section 3. Could he be from one of the Trappist planets in Section 5?"

"I knows what you're thinking my Liege—" The elf caught himself. "Er, my Ambassador Dallen." He scratched an itch under his chin and flakes of skin floated to the carpet. Dallen's stomach turned, just a little. "But I'm not from any of those places."

"How did you—"

"Oh, I knows lots of things. But don't worry, I'm here to help you."

"Help me? Help me do what?"

"The way I sees it, is you want three things," the elf began ticking them off his thick hands. "You want the power. You want allegiance. And, you want the girl."

"What girl would that be?" Dallen began grinding his teeth.

"Why, Lucy," he answered.

"You mean, Lucene."

"Something like that," the elf waived his hands. "By the way, since you never bothered to ask, my name's Olly. Nice to meetcha, finally."

"Finally?"

"Are you always so...questioning?" Olly wanted to know. "Er, never mind. As I was saying, I was talking to this fine gent the other night. Goes by the name of Jasper. Ever heard of him?"

Dallen threw his hands in the air, frustrated. "No, of course I've never heard of him. And even if I did know a Jasper, it wouldn't likely be the same Jasper that you know, would it? The universe is a pretty big place, don't you think?"

"Now, now," Olly put his palms out to appease Dallen. "Don't get testy. I'm still getting caught up after being stuck in the Netherworld for so long."

"The Netherworld?"

Olly let out a snort. "There you go, questioning again." He laughed. "The Netherworld is the opposite of the Hitherworld, which is where we are now. In the Netherworld, a finely-dressed bloke by the name of Jasper Ssset—lots of esses in his last name, it would seem. He let on that you might be able to use someone of my skillset."

"So, you're looking for a job?"

"In a manner of speaking," Olly answered, lying on his side and leaning on a propped-up elbow. Dallen mimicked the movement by leaning his forearm on the arm of his high-backed, red not-a-throne. "You see, unlike my new friend, Jasper, I have only just recently discovered this kitschy new power whereby I can easily float between the Netherworld and the Hitherworld."

"And how does this help me?"

"I can bring you things."

"What sort of things?"

"For example," Olly held up Lucene's communication watch. "This here belongs to your lady friend. Only, she doesn't know it's missing yet, cuz it isn't. I snagged it at the dinner you haven't gone to yet."

"How did you know we were going to dinner?"

"I told you my Ambassador, my Representative Dallen, I knows a lot of things."

"You are very confusing."

"Thank you for not asking another question," Olly praised. "The thing of it is, the last time, I was a bit late and had to plant that watch in her home when she wasn't around."

"The last time? How many times, exactly, have you stolen her watch?"

"Er," Olly counted on his fingers again, only to realize he didn't have enough of them. "Two hundred and seventeen? Two hundred and nineteen times? Not really sure. You see, me and Jasper seem to be in a loop, of sorts. And, it's not just linear. It's sorta, five-dimensional and all."

"That doesn't make sense."

"Ah, but it does my—" Olly thought for a bit. "My Viceroy." He had gotten it wrong again. "The thing of it is, the loop we're stuck in is not just this timeline, but many parallel timelines. I've stolen that there watch hundreds of times, and it most always ends the same way."

"So, you fail every time. Then why would a high-ranking Vitruvian Ambassador, such as myself deign to hire you?"

"Well, my good sir, that's the funniest bit of all. See, I'm stuck. But you're not. Ergo, heretofore, I can bring things of consequence to you. For example, another gift…a trinket, if you like."

Olly handed over a tiny oblong silver box, not much bigger than a matchbox.

"What's this?" Dallen paused, not entirely certain whether or not accepting a gift from such a questionable source was a good idea.

"See for yourself…literally!" Olly's body quivered as he laughed to himself at a joke that only he got.

Dallen accepted it, hesitantly. Inside, lay two round, clear pieces of plastic. "You brought me Earth eyewear? I'm not even sure they use contact lenses anymore. And, my vision is perfect."

"Oh, these are quite different. Give 'em a try."

Dallen considered his options. His guards were not there to protect him. He had no reason to believe anything this little troll had to say and yet…curiosity got the better of him. He placed one of the lenses carefully in his non-dominant eye (making sure he'd at least have the good one if he needed it). Immediately, the vision in his eye began to adjust like a camera lens, in and out and finally focusing on Olly's right earlobe. There was a fly buzzing around it.

"That's not all," Olly smiled. "Blink and pause." He demonstrated.

Dallen blinked and paused for an additional second with his eyes closed. What flashed before him underneath his eyelid was a photo of Olly's ear, just for a moment before it disappeared.

"Now," Olly ordered, "check your fancy pin there."

Dallen didn't know how Olly was privy to that info, but he tapped his lapel pin in a distinct pattern, and images appeared and there it was —Olly's ear.

"You see, you don't need a camera or any special anything. You can snap photos of anything you'd like to remember—anything at all. It's a present for you, from me to you."

Dallen thought for a moment. "I do believe I would like to employ your services after all, Olly. But just answer for me one question, will you?"

"Certainly, my Liege."

"You said that in every parallel universe, 'It almost always ends the same way.'"

"That I did, my Vizier."

"So, thousands of them?"

"At least, my Lord."

"And in how many of them—"

"Yes?" Olly rubbed his hands together, eagerly.

"In how many of them," Dallen paused, "do I get the girl?"

Olly thought a moment, ticking away on his hand. "Only four, I'm afraid. At least, so far."

"That's okay," Dallen reasoned, smiling to himself. "I like a challenge."

CHAPTER 24
MALLORY & PELIMAR'S COSTUME SHOP
SIX DAYS BEFORE THE END.

"Hey Lucene," Xeni called, enthusiastically, as she and Kiki burst through the doors of the newly renovated Mallory & Pelimar's Costume Shop. Pelimar looked up, at first with mild annoyance, but then he became transfixed, somehow.

Xeni smiled bashfully, as she tucked a strand of her hair behind her ear before realizing the cloche hat she was donning got in the way. She repositioned it to prevent it from falling to the carpet. "We were in the area on a class assignment and figured we'd stop in and see your new digs and bring you a sandwich. Here!" She thrust the bag over the counter at Lucene who was, at that moment, adding price tags to new inventory. Pelimar had been busy logging yesterday's sales receipts, yet he hadn't moved since the two women arrived.

"Thanks," Lucene answered. "That was thoughtful of you…and, I like your hat." For the first time, Xeni was actually wearing garb that was flattering, a simple scoop-neck off-white blouse and gray jeans. Oddly, her pink eyes looked blue today. *Contacts?* Lucene wondered.

"We weren't sure what you'd like, or who else was here," Xeni shot a hopeful glance in Pelimar's direction, "so we got one tuna sub and one tempeh avocado roll."

Lucene peeked into the bag. "Which one is which?" The two sandwiches were wrapped in identical paper.

"Let me see," Kiki offered, sniffing. "The one on the right is tuna." Kiki's attire was a little odder than Xeni's, with a high-collared blue button-down shirt that was camouflaged against her skin. The shirt was long, reaching almost to her knees. Underneath, she wore black leggings. This was quite different from what she wore on stage and not nearly as interesting.

"Cool place," Xeni scanned the small shop, approvingly. Once she noticed Lucene's pause, she added, "Oh, you go ahead. We already ate. We're on a mission to—"

Now, it was Kiki's turn to nudge Xeni. They were given explicit instructions not to share what they were doing in the Eastern Cross. It wasn't that they were doing anything particularly interesting, per say. It was more the school's way of teaching them to keep their eyes open and mouths shut.

"Snitches get stitches," Xeni would often say. It didn't make any sense in the context of the conversation. Lucene made a mental note to explain to Xeni one day just what that expression actually meant.

As it would so happen, Xeni opted to stay in the criminal justice training program at TARA. Since Commander Royce required all Data Collectors to resume their training, Xeni had to find a loophole by declaring a "double major." Kiki, who had become a fast friend, thought maybe it was time she went back to school. And, "detective-ing" seemed as good of a course study as any. After all, maybe she could put her nose to good use. Kiki was several years older than Xeni, and as much as she enjoyed singing, working as a coat-check receptionist at the Embassy Club was hardly fulfilling and certainly didn't do much to sustain her financially.

"Hey Pelimar," Lucene called over her shoulder. "Which one do you want?"

"Wha—" Pelimar was jolted from a daydream.

"Which one do you want?" Lucene repeated. "The tempeh or the tuna? Or, do you wanna go halfsies?"

"Which would you pick?" he asked while staring up at Kiki, batting his eyes and leaning one elbow on the counter and resting his chin on his upturned palm. *She was exquisite...her eyes, her voice, her blue skin...her aardvark-shaped nose...*

"Aw," Xeni blushed, sheepishly before it occurred to her that Pelimar wasn't talking to her. He was talking to Kiki. *What the heck am I doing wrong?* Xeni wondered.

"Oh." Kiki's gaze fell to the floor. She wasn't used to many people actually looking her straight in the eyes. Usually, they stared straight at her nose. Or worse, at the floor, to avoid looking at her nose. "I'm more of a tempeh gal, myself," she confessed.

"I'll have the tempeh, then," he smiled, never losing her gaze.

Lucene's eyes went from Pelimar, to Kiki, and back to Pelimar again before an exasperated glance at the ceiling. She shook her head, disbelieving. What is it with young people in love? They were so...obvious.

Xeni was crestfallen. She leaned on the counter and let out a sigh.

"Don't lose heart," Lucene whispered. "Your time will come. Hey, thanks for the sandwich."

Xeni's expression brightened a bit. "Ain't nothing but a chicken wing."

Lucene let out a sigh.

"C'mon Kiki," Xeni finally coaxed. "We have an investigation to finish."

"Call you later?" Pelimar asked Kiki.

"Mmm, hmm," Kiki nodded, shyly.

Wow. They didn't waste any time, Lucene thought.

Outside, Xeni and Kiki resumed their "class project" which was to essentially follow a pre-determined subject for half of the day, collect clues and document anything they could about the subject, all without making contact. It was a lesson in detective training not unlike Xeni's former Data Collecting training, save for two important factors. One, the Data Collectors were gathering as much information as possible on the entire species with the intention of helping the planet's survival as a whole. Whereas, in this case, they were following a mock trail in order to solve a pretend crime set up for training purposes. Second, they lacked their empathic, genetically engineered skills. In Xeni's case, it had been psychometry. And while her old powers floated in and out at random, they weren't reliable, forcing her to actually use the tools she was learning.

Xeni was envious of Kiki, not only for garnering Pelimar's attention, her amazing singing voice, but also for her uncanny tracking skills. There were a lot of reasons for Xeni to envy Kiki, but Kiki was unaware of this, and treated her new friendship as sacred.

"Okay, where did we leave off?" Xeni pulled her notepad out of her back pocket.

"Huh?" Kiki was smiling to herself.

"Snap out of it," Xeni chastised. "We're on assignment, remember?"

"Sorry," Kiki murmured.

Xeni immediately felt bad. After all, it wasn't her friend's fault that Pelimar liked her better. She also now had two very underwhelming dates behind her, all of which only made her even more convinced that Clusaladek was the one for her...he just didn't know it yet.

Xeni stopped at the SpeedCircuit platform and scanned her notes. "Our subject stopped here to meet someone."

"Allegedly," Kiki offered.

"Allegedly," Xeni acknowledged. "Except, that's what the class notes said, so I'm pretty sure that's the scenario we're going with." Xeni continued, "They left a clue behind, but what?" Xeni rested her hand on one of the guideposts designed to direct people toward the correct platform.

All of a sudden, a series of images flashed before her eyes. A drunk man...a monk...the smell of gin and cigarette smoke...war planes...an intense anger.

"What is it?" Kiki's eyes grew wide.

Xeni spotted Roman, dressed in a black coat with matching jeans and a flat cap. He was heading for the platform going to the Northern Cross. And given that the Northern Cross was an undeveloped wilderness, his attire was completely inappropriate.

"Change of plans. C'mon." Xeni took off, keeping a modest distance from Roman, leaving just enough time to catch the Circuit train before it left the station. "Two for the Northern Cross," Xeni declared to the attendant, flashing her watch. It registered two tickets, one for each of the young women.

"You sure about that?" the attendant asked, glancing at their attire.

"Don't worry, we just want to see it. We won't linger."

"Suit yourself." He waived at the train, indicating it should wait a few moments while they boarded.

On the circuit, Roman didn't bother to look up. Instead, he hugged himself, tucking his face low toward his chest. It was only then that they noticed that he had a small suitcase on the chair beside him, strapped in so that it didn't go flying about when the train took off at high speed.

"Last call. Take your seats and strap in," the attendant ordered.

The women obeyed, taking seats several rows behind Roman so they could keep an eye on him.

"What's this all about?" Kiki whispered.

"I'm not sure," Xeni confessed. "But I haven't had psychometric flashes like that since my powers fizzled out last year."

"Wow!" Kiki's eyes grew wide. And then she realized something. "Uh, what powers?"

"Shhh," Xeni hushed her. "Keep your voice down. I'll explain later."

Kiki was intrigued. She didn't know whether Xeni was onto something or should be on something…such as an antipsychotic medication. But truth be told, she was having fun. An adventure! She settled back into her seat while the SpeedCircuit took off.

They arrived at the Northern Cross an hour later. The weather there was unpredictable, cold and blustery one day, and hot and humid the next. Today, the clouds rested over the terrain, casting a continuous dark shadow over the rocky landscape. A few small tumbleweeds rushed past as the winds kicked up, causing the women to cough back dust. They had to stop several times to turn their backs to the wind as it whistled past their ears before taking cover behind a large bolder. There, they discovered, they could safely watch Roman at a distance. At that moment, he sat on his suitcase, facing the boulder where they hid not twenty feet away.

"What are we waiting for?" Kiki whispered, but Xeni couldn't hear her above the wind. She was about to yell louder when Xeni realized this and held a finger to her lips. Kiki fell silent.

Roman grew quickly impatient. He stood, arms outstretched as if on a crucifix. "Okay," he called. "I'm here. Where are you?!"

Xeni peeked around the corner just as a gust of wind blew her hat off, revealing a short mess of blue-black hair underneath. She let out a few expletives.

Kiki wasted no time, pitching her nose out and, literally, sucking the hat toward her like an elephant snatching its food. She grabbed it from her snout. "Got it," she mouthed. Xeni nodded, impressed. By the time she had the courage to look again, there was someone else standing with Roman—the monk from her vision. His back was toward her. The wind settled. She witnessed the monk outstretch his hand, but not before turning his head in her direction and grinning. She darted behind the bolder.

Xeni was afraid to look again, fearing she'd been spotted. Kiki gestured toward the top of the rock and before Xeni could stop her, she had scaled the side of it, peering carefully over the top.

"There's no one there!" she called to Xeni.

"What?" Xeni peered around the corner again. Kiki was right. Roman and the monk had vanished.

Xeni wasn't entirely sure what to do with the new information that she and Kiki had collected. Although, somehow, she understood that it was important. When her current professor dismissed her investigations as trivial, she went to the one teacher she respected most—Professor Tanager.

Unlike his colleague, Tanager was intrigued by the findings. When the young women were done telling their tale, Xeni asked, "But who was he and what does it all mean?"

Tanager cleared his throat, uncomfortably. "I can't tell you more at this time, Xeni." Xeni's face fell, disappointed. "But there's one thing I can tell you," he paused for dramatic effect, "the two of you are going to make fine detectives one day."

Kiki beamed proudly, even sticking her overabundant aardvark nose in the air triumphantly and letting out a strange toot. The two headed for the door in Tanager's office before a flash hit Xeni. The scene was suddenly vivid…not as memories are, but as if a person were reliving the exact moment. She turned to her teacher.

"Professor Tanager?" She asked.

"Yes, Xeni?" Tanager had been jotting down notes from their conversation to share with Lucene, Cepheus and their team.

"It didn't strike me until just this moment but…weren't the two men we saw today the same ones on the bridge with you the day you and Lucene almost got blown up?"

Tanager wasn't hardwired to lie, and he didn't have time to come up with a convenient diversion. Instead, he settled on the truth. "They were," he finally answered.

"Hmmm," Xeni attempted to replay the circumstances of that day in her mind, but there was some confusion. "Were those men the good guys or the bad guys?" Once again, her world was compartmentalized into the frame of the late-night detective movies on Earth, ones where the good guys and bad guys were clearly defined.

"Honestly, Xeni," Tanager answered, "I'm just not sure."

CHAPTER 25
THE END FOR HAMISH
FIVE DAYS BEFORE THE END.

"Why are these doors open?" Hamish demanded of Far, who was at present, standing on the balcony overlooking the training grounds.

"Just breathing a little life into this place," Far explained. "Given how difficult it was getting them to budge, I venture a guess that they've never been opened before.

"No," Hamish stood beside Far, taking a deep breath. He wasn't sure why he hadn't thought of it before. But, he decided, he did enjoy the fresh air. "While I respect you as a prophet and spiritual advisor, Far, you are never to make decisions such as these without asking my permission. Is that clear?"

While Far didn't see why he would need to ask permission for as small a matter as opening a few glass doors, he nodded. "Yes, my Sovereign."

"Where is Fredo?" Hamish asked. "My guard is rarely out of range for any length of time."

"My apologies, Sovereign," Far answered. "I asked him to show Roman the training grounds. And, given that he is not of Royal descent, I was concerned how his presence would be received if he went unattended."

Hamish grew angry. "Once again, you overstep your bounds, Far!" He wasn't even looking at his prophet. Instead, he was staring over the balcony at nothing in particular, his eyes yellow with a sudden rage. "You don't open doors in my chamber without permission. You don't invite humans to this planet without getting it cleared through me. And, you certainly don't give orders to my Royal guard without asking me first! If Sovereign Sabrina were still alive, she would have had you hanged by now for insubordination!"

Far fumbled with something he held behind his back, tumbling its handle over and over as if weighing his options. Finally, he'd reached his decision.

"Yes…my Sovereign," Far answered forcefully, as he shoved a dagger into Hamish's back. Hamish was thicker than he anticipated, and during Hamish's moment of shock, Hamish took it upon himself to tug at the knife, both hands reaching behind his back in an effort to retrieve what was out of reach for his thick arms. Hamish fell face-first to the floor, and Far had to step on him to finally dig the blade out from between his shoulder blades. Far wasn't taking chances; he stabbed Hamish again, using both hands to thrust it in and twist the knife violently. After all, the Royals had fiercely strong regenerative skills. Far's plan had been tougher to execute than what he anticipated. In his mind, he would easily tip the sovereign over the balcony once he'd stabbed him. But that's not what happened, and now he had to figure a way to lift a large man up and toss him over the ledge.

"What are you doing?" Roman yelled in horror as he and Fredo burst into the room.

Another of Far's miscalculations. It's hard to pin Hamish's death on Roman—an angry Earthling who would do anything to protect his planet—when he was caught holding the weapon. Roman was supposed to be surveying the grounds, that part was true, but he wasn't accompanied by Fredo. Instead, Far arranged to have Fredo 'accidentally' locked in the underground prisons. Roman must have heard his screams and let him out.

Far had to think quickly. He dropped the knife and began shaking. "He…" Far stammered, drawing out tears with ease. "He attacked me," Far sobbed. "I had to defend myself."

Fredo's first concern was to his sovereign. He used his transmission watch to call for medics, before gently rolling Hamish onto his back to see if he was still alive.

Roman stood before Far. "He attacked *you*..." Roman put the pieces together. "And yet he was facing away from you. Why, pray tell, was he stabbed in the back?"

"What?" Far appeared helpless. "I don't understand! I was so frightened!" He moved toward Roman as if to hug him. Roman saw the blade, but it was too late as it made its way into Roman's side. Roman yet out a yelp as Far dove again. This time, Roman was prepared, sidestepping Far. With the ease of an ice-skater, Roman spun sideways, tossing Far's frail form over the ledge. He gasped for breath, watching in horror as his beloved hit the stone staircase on the mountain below and kept tumbling toward the ground. Several soldiers saw it, looking up at Far before rushing toward Hamish's chamber.

The medics arrived first. One moved toward Roman.

"Not him!" Fredo grumbled, motioning toward the fallen Hamish.

"That's right," Roman winced, bending over and holding his side as blood soaked his shirt. "Him first," he gestured with his free hand.

Three ran to Hamish. One took pity on Roman.

"Here, let's have a look at that," he said. He was wearing a black wetsuit-like uniform similar to Fredo's. He even had Fredo's red salamander shape but had a much smaller frame and a gentler voice. "I must admit, I'm not experienced at human emergency interventions, but so far, you appear to bleed the same way as we do. I'll see what I can do."

"Thanks," Roman winced again as the guard had him stand fully upright and roughly removed his bloody shirt and then attempted to tightly wrap a tourniquet around him. "I...appreciate...that!" Roman bit his lip in pain.

The solders burst in.

"Get this human to the hospital, immediately," the medic instructed the main soldier. "It can't wait." They paused for a moment, unsure why a non-Royal would be of any consequence to them, but since it came from one of Sovereign Hamish's chief medics, they followed instructions without question.

Hamish was not as lucky. The remaining medics shook their heads. It would only be a few moments now. While the Royals were hearty by nature and could even regrow limbs and were resistant to infection, there was little to be done if the heart had been punctured. Ironic, as it would seem that having a heart really *was* the key to their undoing.

The medics backed away to give Fredo room to speak to his Sovereign. He knelt beside him and for the first time in his life, he began sobbing.

"Why the tears?" Hamish whispered, coughing up a bit of blood. "I thought you hated me?"

"So did I," Fredo confessed. "But I have been sworn to protect you my entire life. Without you, my life has no purpose."

"It most certainly does," Hamish responded. "There is one more in line for the throne. You must continue to protect him with your life."

Fredo was taken aback. Surely his child, the illegitimate one born between he and Sabrina was not now to become the sovereign? Fredo's feeble mind wondered how a baby could rule anything. The most he could do is protect it and guard it until it grew older. But who would rule until that time? (It should be noted that never once did Fredo consider that he could assume a leadership role.)

"I will protect the baby with my life," he swore to Hamish.

Hamish realized he had misunderstood him but merely smiled. "Of course, you will," he answered. With that, his eyes rolled back in his head.

Hamish was gone.

CHAPTER 26
HAMISH AND CEPHEUS
FOUR DAYS BEFORE THE END.

Hamish sat in Cepheus's living area, gazing back with interest at two gray foxes that were peering at him curiously through the glass doors to the back patio. "Ah," Hamish said to them. "So, you can see me, too?" One of the foxes perched his front two paws on the door at the sound of his voice. He was still wearing the robe he was murdered in, but somehow, the bloodstain where he had been stabbed was not visible. Hamish wondered if he had somehow manifested that effect to save Cepheus from seeing him that way. He wasn't sure.

Cepheus awoke from a fitful sleep in his bedroom. While it was getting easier, he still had better luck sleeping on the bench in his office at TARA. He was instantly on his feet, tip-toeing toward the living room at the noise. "Petrichor, is that you?" he asked.

"No, my son," Hamish answered. "It is not. And why would Petrichor be here?" He was curious. It never occurred to him that he shouldn't have even been able to be there, and yet, there he was.

Cepheus was taken aback, eyeing his father's gossamer-like visage with surprise. "Are you—?"

"Dead?" Hamish finished. "Yes, it would appear so."

"What happened?" Cepheus asked, suspiciously. One could not help but be suspicious around his parents, even ones that were dead.

"Far happened."

"Roman's beloved? He...killed you?

"Yes," he nodded solemnly. "Listen, I'd love to stay for a chat, but I seem to have an awareness of some portal closing soon...or, being opened and closed. I don't have the exact details, but your mother has resurfaced and has been clamoring at me nonstop since I arrived. And, I'd rather not be stuck here between the layers when the Null get here."

Cepheus thought a moment. He knew that since Lucene had visited him, that the Null were coming. He just didn't understand how it would affect his dead father.

"Then, why are you here?"

"I came to warn you."

"Warn me about what?"

"The baby."

"So, there is another heir." It was the one piece of the puzzle that Cepheus hadn't quite worked out yet.

"Yes, but with my untimely death, the Royals—what's left of them, that is—are under the rein of Far...unless, of course, Fredo actually gets the courage to overthrow him. But frankly, I don't see that happening, at least not until the boy gets older."

"The baby is a boy?"

"Yes," Hamish nodded sadly. "There was never any rite of passage. No ceremony. I'm not even entirely certain that any of the remaining Royal military brigade even knows of his existence. I suppose Far has a plan for that, too. I clearly underestimated that weak little scrap of a man."

If Far had been occupying the same realm, Hamish wasn't aware of it, just as he was unaware of Far's demise not long after his.

"What have you come to warn me about, exactly? A baby is not exactly intimidating."

"No, but if Far has his way, he will assume control as the boy's guardian...or worse. And, the way I left things..."

"Yes," Cepheus was growing impatient, but not with his father. He was frustrated about how long it was taking him to fit all the pieces of this puzzle together.

"The Royals were planning on taking over Erde first, then the surrounding planets under its jurisdiction, and then Earth—if Earth is still habitable at that time."

"Erde. Why? Earth is much larger than any of the worlds we occupy with much of the terrain and air qualities more easily adaptable by our people."

"True," Hamish agreed. "But with Erde no longer a part of the IPP, it no longer has the protection of surrounding Sections. All on its own, your little planet is an easy target. Frankly, I should have thought of it sooner, but I suppose I had a soft spot because you lived here."

"I didn't think you had any soft spots," Cepheus replied, roughly. But in truth, he didn't mean it. This was not the first time Hamish had attempted redemption for his past treatment of his son.

Hamish let out a sigh. "His name is Cefeus the Second…spelled with an 'f' instead of a 'ph'."

Cepheus ground his teeth anxiously, a bead of sweat forming on his brow as his pupils narrowed angrily. It wasn't just that it was a version of his name. It was more that one of his twins was to bear his name, but the Royals took his family away. His son never got to grow up, and now he's learning that his father dared name the second son after him.

"It was meant to be respectful," Hamish tried. "I realize I'm not good at doing the right thing, but…I missed you."

"You missed me?" Cepheus as aghast.

"Believe me, if I could do it all over again, things would have been different…better."

"You would have spared my family?"

"Yes, and I probably would have murdered your mother earlier on."

"I'm not sure that's better."

Hamish suddenly glanced up as if he heard a sound. "Shut up, my darling. I'm talking to our son." It would seem that his mother, Sabrina, was lurking between the layers as well.

Cepheus realized that he hadn't been visited by Petrichor in quite some time, not since she'd encouraged him to learn how to love again.

"Can you see Petrichor?" Cepheus asked. "It's been quite some time since she's come to see me."

"No," Hamish was confused. "I don't think so. This place is rather murky and quiet. If she's here, I certainly haven't seen her."

Hamish looked down at his arms. They were fading in and out. "We're running out of time, please let me finish."

"Okay," Cepheus finally sat in the chair across from his father. "Finish."

"There was an amendment to the new contract between myself and the demon called Jasper Set." Cepheus waited for Hamish to continue. "Cefeus the Second was next in line to assume control of the Royals should anything happen to me, which—as you can see— it did. Unless—"

"Unless what?"

"Unless Cepheus the Senior returns to reclaim the throne."

"What? Why would you do that?"

"The High Royals are no longer a threat. I made sure of that by having Jasper send the Null to roll over their domains, sending them into oblivion. You could turn the Royal military brigade around, use them to defend yourselves against the Vitruvians."

"The Vitruvians? But they are our allies."

"Are they?" Hamish began fading.

Cepheus thought for a moment. Mistakenly, the Data Collectors were trying to protect Earth from the Royals and potentially Vitruvia. He was furious with himself as everyone's true motives came to light. Somehow, throughout all of the wars and deception, now Earthlings, the Royal clan, and the Vitruvians were all seeking a new target—Erde.

"Just one more thing, Father," Cepheus called. Hamish came back into focus, his face breaking into a smile at his son acknowledging him as 'father.' It was the first time, in a long time, he'd remember him doing so.

"Yes, my son?"

"You didn't need to change the spelling of Cefeus the Second's name."

"Of course, I did. Look at how we destroyed your life."

"No, Father, you didn't. I have a very good life."

With that, Hamish reached out a hand as if to touch his son's face in an uncharacteristic show of affection. "When you find Jasper Set, remember to demand to see a copy of the contract. It was my last Royal act." And with that, Hamish was gone.

Cepheus wasted no time in telling Moksha about the visit, who listened solemnly but said nothing. She put on a brave face, but Cepheus knew what she was thinking. She thought he was going to abandon her on Erde, but that wasn't the case at all.

Instead, he had to put a few things in motion first. Namely, he had to let Tanager, Lucene and Isabella know about the interaction, so that when they opened the portal, and assuming that Hamish was right and Jasper would surface, he had to demand to see the new contract. Given Lucene's recent vision of Jasper, he was fairly certain that this was the case. He also needed to enlist the help of Ivan. After all, the borders were closed after the recent attack from what they came to learn were Earthlings possessing Erde technology. So, if he was going to escape, hopefully taking Moksha with him, a vessel had to be prepared in secret.

While all this weighed heavily on Cepheus's mind, not to mention all the work he'd have to do to change protocol and behaviors at the Training Grounds, somehow, he felt a warm glow at the center of his chest. Something about all of this was...right.

CHAPTER 27
MAKERSPACE REUNION
THREE DAYS BEFORE THE END.

"You know I support any decision you make, but I still don't understand why you chose to work for a minimum apprentice wage at the costume shop," Tanager protested as he and Lucene walked hand-in-hand toward the Makerspace. In his other hand, he carried a small briefcase. As usual, Lucene preferred to carry her notepad and pen in the backpack currently strapped across her shoulders.

Tanager eyed their surroundings, nervously. Given the air attack a few days ago along with the emergence of dire wolves and storms, he had become increasingly protective of Lucene. She wouldn't have been at the Makerspace today were it not for her insistence.

"My serving part-time as an 'advisor' for Commander Royce isn't exactly fulfilling," Lucene complained. "And it certainly doesn't pay as well as she seems to think it does," She paused while the glass doors of the main entrance slid open for them. Tanager waited while Lucene entered first. They paused again while a guard summoned them through a pathway that scanned them for outside weaponry and to confirm that they were who they said they are and not shapeshifters…yet another of the new protocols put in place as the Makerspace attempted to curtail outside threats. "And furthermore, you think I don't know that it's really so that Royce can keep an eye on me as my powers re-emerge? She's not being supportive. She's just using me."

"I don't think that's...exactly true," Tanager replied, walking through the pathway while the scanner confirmed that Tanager was, in fact, Tanager. Lucene's imagery always came through as a swirling circle of red energy, something the guard had been briefed on, since no one else's form looked like that. They simply looked like outlines of, well, people. "I think she values your contribution to our team."

"And what, exactly, do I contribute?"

Tanager let out a sigh once they had reached his office. "My darling..." Tanager set down his briefcase and scanned his communication watch in front of the door to unlock it, something that would not have happened just a few months prior. He paused, placing the palms of his hands on her upper arms, rubbing them affectionately. "You contribute your knowledge and experience. You help with research and lesson plans. You have excellent problem-solving skills. And—" his forehead wrinkled a little.

"What?"

"Nothing?"

"No," Lucene followed him inside his office. "Not nothing. You always wrinkle your forehead when something is bothering you. What is it?"

"It's just that," Tanager framed his words carefully, "do I not provide you with everything you need to be...happy? Is there something missing in our lifestyle that makes you feel the need to earn more money?"

"Honey," Lucene explained. "It has nothing to do with money, per say, but I would like to contribute more to the household and not have you take on the lion's share."

Tanager made a mental note to look up "lion's share" later. He hadn't heard this Earth expression before. He'd only just learned about "honey," a term of affection he decided that he rather liked.

"What I mean is," Lucene continued. "I need to find something I'm good at besides laundry and grocery shopping...and I'm not all that great at those to start with." She thought back to the now-pink shirt of Tanager's that used to be red. He told her that it looked better bleached a blotchy pastel but she knew that he was only being polite.

"But you are excellent at growing herbs and repairing light sockets," Tanager pointed out.

"I think that has more to do with my weird energy and are not necessarily skills," Lucene had to admit. "Why are you so opposed to my part-time job at Mallory's shop when Pelimar was nice enough to take me on as an apprentice, even though I have no experience whatsoever? He's training me and pays me an actual wage as I learn. And, I get to negotiate for a raise in three months. How about that?"

"So," Tanager tumbled the ideas over in his brain like clothes in a drying machine. "It's not that you're unhappy with me," he added carefully, "or us. It's that you want something purposeful so that you can be happy with...yourself."

"Yes," Lucene smiled. "That's it, exactly."

"Well then," Tanager smiled, kissing her forehead. "I support you, wholeheartedly."

Before Lucene could ask why he thought she may have been unhappy with him, there was a knock at the door. Amy peeked her head around the corner. "Oh," she seemed surprised to see Lucene. She was holding a plate of wrapped muffins. "Sorry to interrupt." Amy decided to ignore Lucene altogether, catching Tanager's gaze and holding it. "I was baking last night and I remembered how much you liked my poppyseed muffins. Thought I'd bring you a batch."

Not just poppyseed muffins, Lucene thought bitterly. *Her poppyseed muffins. Specifically. Of course, because Amy bakes.*

A long, awkward pause ensued before Tanager responded. "Thank you, Amy. That was very thoughtful of you." He glanced over at Lucene. "We'll certainly enjoy them at lunch today."

Lucene smiled to herself. *At least he said 'we,'* letting Amy know that she and Tanager were, indeed, a "we."

"Perhaps you'll join us for lunch if you have the time? We can share these together," Tanager finished.

No! No! No! Lucene thought. *Why couldn't you have stopped after the 'we!'* She turned to Tanager. "Well, I'm off to the Crafting room," she explained. "I'll see you at lunch." She forced a smile-less grin, which was quite difficult to manage. She didn't wait for a reply before marching past Amy, wordless. Lucene didn't wait to hear what happened after she left, hopefully, nothing. She quickened her pace toward the Crafting room so she could flip through sewing designs and find something to bring to Pelimar to teach her when she showed up for her apprenticeship again in the morning. Instead of taking the Transporter, she decided to walk the winding Fibonacci ramp several floors as it finally spun her in front of her chosen location. It was surprisingly quiet. She was, as it turned out, the only person there at the moment.

The crafting room had a cozy feel about it, despite the size. The areas were sectioned off with translucent, noise-filtering drapes. Depending on the zone, one would find crochet and knitting materials, traditional watercolor and acrylic paints and easels, or, in the case of the sewing area, a few outdated industrial sewing machines and handmade wooden cabinets filled with cloth-cutting scissors, fabrics and an assortment of needles for hand-made projects. Suddenly, the sparsity of both materials and people made sense. If the Makerspace was now serving a military purpose, one would assume that traditional arts and crafts would slow progress down. And with places such as Mallory and Pelimar's Costume shop providing uniforms, duffel bags and other materials, there was little need for this space. Lucene didn't mind. She could use this as her personal play station, and learn, and mess up, quietly to herself until she'd developed some skills. By then, she reasoned, things might actually return to normal.

Lucene could have easily pulled up designs from the electronic library collection but there was something about the musty smell of old, worn-out books that she loved. Because, also in the cabinet was a collection of tall, faux-leather-bound design books. She found one on women's fashion from a place she had never heard of. She brought it carefully over to a work table and sat down on the end of a long bench and began carefully turning the heavy pages so as not to accidentally free any yellowed sheets from the binding.

One page featured a long, cream-colored chiffon skirt that was long in places and short in others with a lopsided blouse to match. *Maybe not for The Beacon,* she thought. *But this is definitely Bistro material. Eat your heart out, Brie.*

"Not something I would think to choose for you, but striking, nonetheless," a male voice announced over Lucene's shoulder. Lucene shuddered. She remembered that ego-filled accent...Dallen. The Vitruvian ambassador who she dated briefly last year before she realized that, for one thing, she didn't want to change everything about herself to be "worthy" of hanging on his arm. And, for another thing, she did not appreciate his talent for ghosting people. He and his representatives high-tailed it out of Erde when it became clear that an alliance between Erde and Vitruvia to rejoin the Intergalactic Peace Project would not be possible. And that was after he disappeared from her life without warning, only to resurface soon after and assume that their relationship would go on, business as usual.

"How did you get in here?" Lucene asked, candidly.

"Not exactly the greeting I was hoping for," he opened his arms, "no hug for your old friend?"

"We're not friends," Lucene reminded him.

"No," he agreed, "though I wish we were." Once he realized that a hug was not going to happen, he awkwardly lowered his arms, standing there in the exact same uniform with the exact same gold hair that was so bright it reflected light off of it.

"I'll ask again," Lucene was guarded, "how did you get in here without an escort? That was protocol even before the recent security changes."

"You simple girl," Dallen shook his head, "who do you think installed those measures in the first place?"

"So, it's true?" Lucene had been doubtful until this moment. "Commander Royce has been selling you information and technology in exchange for Vitruvians funding the Makerspace."

He leaned forward to run a finger down the side of her face. She grabbed it and bent it backward just as Moksha had taught her to do.

"Ouch!" he yelled, pulling his hand back. It was then that she noticed several men behind the noise-shielding drapes. "It's all right," he called to them. "Stand down." To Lucene, he asked, "What was that for? I thought you liked it when I was affectionate."

"Not anymore," she answered. "Keep your hands to yourself."

"My, we are feisty these days, aren't we?" He smiled, almost approvingly. "I think I like this more aggressive side of you."

Lucene felt a sudden bitterness in the pit of her stomach. She put her hand over her communication watch and twisted the ring around it once to the left and then tugged it upward to set off a silent alarm.

"I'm afraid that won't work," Dallen commented. "My system, remember? That was the first thing I had shut down. Helps that I also had access to your watch for necessary re-programming some time ago." He paused for the information to sink in. It was Dallen who was responsible for confiscating her watch at the Embassy Club that day, and Dallen who had it later returned to her cottage, leaving her to falsely believe that she had forgotten it, somehow. "Yes," he read her facial expressions. "I always know exactly where you are and when."

"And, *what exactly* do you want?" Lucene demanded, grabbing a pair of jagged cloth cutters from the cabinet. One of Dallen's guards immediately came up behind her and wrenched it from her right hand and attempted to wrap her neck in a chokehold. She stepped back, reflexively, scraping her heel against his shin as he let out a howl. She wrapped one arm around his waist and pivoted him across her hip, landing him with a loud thud onto the sewing table. Two more guards emerged but Dallen held his hand up, commanding them to be still.

"What I want," Dallen answered calmly, "is *you*. I thought that was obvious."

"I told you 'no' before and I'm unavailable now."

"Ah, yes," Dallen grinned, "Tanager." The guard on the table rolled over, steadying himself as he stood, shooting an angry glare in Lucene's direction. "While romance would be nice, that's not what I want you for."

"Then what? My powers are gone," she lied. "What use am I to you?"

"Well, you see..." Dallen took a step toward her before she shot him a warning glance. He held his hands up in surrender and took a step backward. "That's not exactly true, is it?"

"What are you talking about?" Lucene demanded.

"That shapeshifter you healed at the dance club..." he said. "What was that about?"

"How did you—" Lucene stopped herself. There were hundreds of people who could have reported it, but at that moment, there was only one who came to mind...Odessa. "Oh." Lucene fell silent.

"She proved to be useful after all," Dallen acknowledged. "I may know where you are but I can't always know what you're up to without informants." He watched her micro-expressions fluctuate between anger, horror and defeat and found it highly amusing. "I also learned about the little portal you opened up. So, you see, you may be the woman I *have* always dreamt about."

"A weapon," she stated flatly.

"A weapon, a healer, a tool—" he paused as her face crumbled. "Oh, don't look so offended. That's all you really are here. Do you think Tanager would be half as interested in you if you weren't fascinatingly damaged with a hint of supernatural possibility? Intellectuals like that love a puzzle. And you, Lucene, are quite the puzzle."

"There are others who have this skill," Lucene caught herself before mentioning Morphinae's name, just in case Dallen didn't already know, or the Data Collectors in training such as Clusaladek, Xeni and Neroni. Though, she assumed that he did. "Why me?"

"Because I don't want them," Dallen stamped his foot like a small child. "I want you." He contorted his face. He thought emotions such as love were primitive and he didn't particularly like the way he felt about Lucene. Though, the emotions seemed less difficult when she was with him then when she was not. Therefore, he assumed that having her by his side was the simplest solution.

There were more guards that emerged from around the room, surrounding her. "Let's not make a scene. I simply want you to accompany me back to Vitruvia where you will become my dutiful companion. I promise you won't want for anything. And in exchange, you will help us in our efforts to occupy Erde."

"Wait…what?" Lucene was confused.

Dallen let out the most rambunctious laugh that she had ever heard. "Oh, you didn't know that part, did you?" He paused. She shook her head. He shook his head, mocking her. "That's the best part. All this time, your Data Collectors have been trying to protect Earth from invasion and environmental destruction, and yet, all this time, Vitruvia has been feeding Earth technology…Erde's technology. So, while you are doing the noble work of saving Earth, it's been trying to destroy you."

"No, that can't be true," Lucene protested. And yet, somewhere in the back of her mind, she feared it might be.

"Look around," Dallen challenged. "Vitruvia *did* want to align with

Erde to defeat the Royals—a little matter that Sovereign Hamish and Jasper Set conveniently settled by having the Null destroy the major Royal clan. Vitruvia is a thriving planet. Erde has the same potential. Well, we couldn't very well offer Earthlings the opportunity to settle in our domain without a few rules in place, now, could we? Therefore, in exchange for jurisdiction and allegiance, we promised them—"

"Erde," Lucene finished, horrified.

"Perhaps you are not so simple after all. But you can be a good girl and accompany me to Vitruvia. If you do, I promise not to harm any of your Erde pals—not a single curly lock on your boyfriend Tanager's lovely little head."

"But there's only one thing I don't understand," Lucene questioned.

"Only one?" Dallen was skeptical. Lucene chose to ignore him.

"Inventors like Ivan were willing to help advance Earth and were shot down and pegged as terrorists before they could even get started. If they already had the technology in house…why?"

"I suppose it's all in the marketing," Dallen reasoned. "*Know your audience.* Isn't that what they say on Earth? *Read the room.* Your friend Ivan was empowering the masses. That's not what leaders want. They want to subdue the masses and empower the sovereigns. A simple truth that your very humanity-conscious friend, Ivan, never understood."

As if on cue, Ivan burst into the room with a Vitruvian guard strapped to his back and three more at his heels. "Lucene, are ye okay? I came as soon as I'd heard." He leaned over and flipped the guard on his back to the ground, seemingly with ease. Two others flanked him on each side.

"How?" Dallen asked, calmly. "I blocked the signal."

"Not from me, ye didn't," Ivan growled. "Workaround," he added in a huff, as it came to fisticuffs with the two men pursuing him. "Aww, c'mon then," he reasoned, "I left this kinda gang life years ago. Vowed never to go back. Don't make me embarrass ye in front of your sovereign, now…"

But Dallen's men were relentless and obviously less genteel with Ivan than with Lucene, as Dallen did nothing to keep them at bay. They pounded on Ivan mercilessly as his thick frame took a beating.

"Stop it!" Lucene wailed, coming to Ivan's aid. She landed a front kick to the side of one assailant's knees, causing a loud crunch as the man crumbled in pain. To the other, she dug an elbow into his spine, assisted by a press from her supporting hand. She followed this by reaching her arm around and digging her fingers under the man's chin, pulling his head back while pivoting her torso away from him and pressing her foot behind his knee. His knee buckled. She assisted his fall with her left hand as her right delivered a punch to his kidneys. He crumpled to the floor.

Moksha, you beautiful assassin, you, Lucene praised in her mind. *Thanks for the training.*

The persistent man rolled over and grabbed her ankle. Lucene was about to dig the heel of her opposite foot into the man's crotch, but by then, Dallen's men resorted to weaponry, now poising a laser gun at Ivan's head. Lucene stopped in her tracks, putting her foot down.

Somehow, Ivan could feel the heat of the laser. He put his hands up in surrender. But in an uncustomary surrender-like way he pleaded, "Look, man. I may have gotten into a wee mess of trouble as a young lad. But thah's not how I am today. I vowed never to kill another. Don't make me start today."

The man behind him found this funny, his finger on the trigger. But instead of aiming it at Ivan's head, he repositioned it to center a bright green beam on Lucene's forehead.

"No!" Ivan yelled, spinning around and knocking the guard's weapon free as it fired, grazing the top of Lucene's hairline. It burned her scalp lightly as it shot into the wall behind her. The man smacked the butt of the gun's handle into Ivan's temple, and it took only moments for the guard to reposition as a bloody Ivan clutched his head, trying to regain his wits enough to react.

"Not the girl," Dallen yelled, angrily at the guard. He didn't jump in front of Lucene to protect her, exactly. More like sidled up next to her and pushed her head down in an attempt to get her to duck. She fell on top of the man holding her ankle, knocking the wind out of him.

Not much of a hero, Lucene realized, rolling off of the guard. Not that she had ever expected that he would be.

Another shot rang out as Ivan tackled the guard that was attacking them. Dallen fell, a dribble of blood leaking from his neck.

"Ah no!" Ivan cried, head in hands. His worst nightmare come true.

He ran over to Lucene first, now sitting up from her spill on the hard floor. "Ye okay?"

Lucene caught her breath and nodded.

Ivan turned his attention to Dallen, now lying in a heap on the floor. Ivan rolled him over as the ambassador's eyes rolled back in his head. Lucene crawled over and felt his pulse...light but steady. "He's alive," Lucene told Ivan, to his relief.

"Of course, he is," a female voice called, just as Commander Royce, Constable Melokuhle, and others rushed in, seizing Dallen's guards and subduing them. The voice belonged to none other than Amy.

It was then that Ivan and Lucene noticed something. There, in the neck of Dallen, was an ever-so-tiny hand-sculpted figurine of a soldier, with the tiniest of metal blades protruding from his head. It was one from the large model that Amy had been showing Lucene and Tanager earlier that month. "Don't worry," Amy reassured, "it's toxic enough to paralyze, but not to kill. He'll be fine in a few hours."

Ivan was relieved. Lucene...surprised. Had Amy not intervened, there was a good chance that she and Ivan would have been dead, or abducted. Either way, she was in the small-framed, red-haired woman's debt.

"Thank you," Lucene told Amy, quietly.

"Don't thank me," Amy answered, the rims of her eyes slightly red. "I didn't do it for you."

No, Lucene thought. *Of course, you didn't.*

Thirty Minutes Prior...in the Military Transportation Lab

Ivan was in the Military Transportation Lab during one of the only times he was confident that the Makerspace would be relatively quiet. Most of the work he did to prepare Cepheus's escape pod, he did in the middle of the night by disabling the tracker on his communication watch. And, on the off chance a security guard noticed his presence, he was able to convince them he was doing firmware updates that could only happen when computer devices were not being used by students or outside vendors renting the space.

He peeked under a black tarp that he used to cover the small vessel. At present, it was about the size of a compact car designed to unfold and enlarge into four times its size once out of Erde's atmosphere. Ivan laughed to himself. All he did was post an, "Out of Order" sign on the outside of the tarp, along with a second sign that read, "Dangerous voltage - Do not touch," and no one messed with his project.

Now, there was just one thing left to check. He had to be able to disable the security system so that no alarms would sound when Cepheus and, hopefully Moksha, made their escape.

He removed the cover of his communication watch using a simple 3-D printed eyeglass toolkit. (Yes, he invented that, too.) But when Ivan lifted the face off the frame of the watch, something was wrong.

"What the—" he took out a magnifying glass and looked closer. The little red beacon inside that was used as their "panic button" to set off the alarms had been disabled. It didn't flash blue periodically to show that it was working. Someone had already disabled it.

"Ivan!" A flushed Amy ran into the room. She was out of breath. "I... me...Transporter...Renenet..." She bent over and placed her hands on her knees to catch her breath. When she couldn't, she pointed. There, slumped over the door to the Transporter was Renenet. Her uniform was blood-soaked, forming a pool on the platform outside. Ivan ran over to her and felt for a pulse, but it was too late. Renenet's face and arms were bruised a deep purple from where she tried to fend off her attackers.

Ivan lost no time in returning to his abandoned watch. With a few split-second adjustments, it lit up and the entire Makerspace began wailing at the sound of the alarm. The Transporter that carried Renenet also sprang back to life.

"C'mon!" He grabbed Amy's hand and pulled her after him toward the vehicle. Amy braced herself, seeing her friend's mangled body.

"I can't!" she cried, pulling back as she fought off nausea.

It was then that the sound of voices and boots on the ground could be heard echoing through the winding halls that led to some of the internal, smaller rooms.

Ivan had no choice. "Sorry," he apologized to the dead Renenet as he dumped her body onto the platform and climbed inside. To Amy, he said, "Ye have to git in. I dunno who we're up against. But ye can't stay here alone!"

Amy sucked in a deep breath and nodded. She didn't even wait for Ivan to unlatch the door and slide it open for her; she put her hands on the door frame and vaulted herself over the wall. It was impressive. Even Ivan paused for a moment.

"Well?" She looked at the controls.

"Right."

They had intended to follow the shortest track to the safety of the outside world and wait for backup. Instead, what happened was an interception of the Transporter's signal, hauling them at great speed swirling down the circle, coming to a stop in front of the Crafting room where the Transporter stopped so abruptly that Amy and Ivan were thrown against the sides of it, and ended up landing on the metal floor in two heaps.

From the floor, Ivan's head spun dizzily. Then he heard people talking... *Lucene!* He realized, *she's in trouble.* As he fought with the door and spilled out onto the platform, two guards descended on him. He peered over his shoulder at the slight frame of Amy, still crumpled in the corner of the Transporter. She was so small; they didn't notice her. He took his foot and kicked at the Transporter's door, slamming it shut with Amy still inside.

The guards dragged him to his feet. It was then that Ivan the tinkerer, middle-aged man, father of Talula and husband of Fatima tapped into something he'd shut away a long time ago...his past. And for the first time since he was a teenager, he picked up fists and started punching.

CHAPTER 28
ROYCE AND DALLEN FACE OFF
THREE DAYS BEFORE THE END.

"What the hell were you thinking?" Commander Royce screamed at Representative Dallen, slamming her fists on the table in the Planetary Defense League's Negotiation Room. He flinched slightly but was otherwise unaffected.

When Royce discovered Dallen in the Makerspace trying to abduct Lucene, she made a show of "arresting" him, though Ivan, Lucene and Amy couldn't help but notice that Constable Melokule and the security guards were awfully gentle with the dignitary. They hadn't even bothered to bind his hands behind his back, and yet he followed her, agreeably. The guards were rougher on Dallen's security team, particularly after they learned of Renenet's death.

"Come now, Commander Royce," Dallen flashed a smile. "Don't you think you're over-reacting?"

"You killed the PDL director who oversees TARA, a very trusted and loyal friend at that!" Royce, who hadn't previously exhibited obvious outbursts seemed about to throw a full-on fit.

"Unfortunately," Dallen replied, emotionless, "we didn't realize just how loyal. And, as a slight correction, I didn't kill her. One of my men did, in self-defense."

"Because they were where they shouldn't be, and she was following protocol to have them arrested!"

"I apologize for the aggressiveness of my men. However," he continued calmly, "they shouldn't have been apprehended. We have every right to be in the Makerspace. After all, Vitruvia pays for it."

"That wasn't part of our arrangement," Royce began grinding her teeth. "And I thought I told you that the girl was hand's off."

Dallen's face crumbled for the shortest of moments before recovering. "But—" he began defensively, before becoming silent.

"What?" Royce put her hands on the table, her gray-black hair spilling all over it. She leaned in ominously, which was no easy feat for a small woman with deep-set eyes and an abundance of wrinkles. And yet, Dallen was taken aback. "You're going to tell me that Vitruvia pays for her, too?"

Dallen slunk back in his chair. In the back of his mind, he wanted to answer, "her training, yes." But then he realized that even that was no longer true. In fact, when he had abandoned her last year, he also cut off funding to TARA's research, her training and the cottage where she lived. In a moment of something that resembles remorse, he had to admit that if Tanager and Cepheus hadn't stepped in to cover her expenses, unbeknownst to Lucene, and Royce hadn't taken pity on the girl making her an honorary "agent" of the PDL, Lucene could have actually become homeless on this planet. He thought for a moment that his actions may have been hasty, but then dismissed them. After all, he was a dignitary of the highest breed. They simply didn't make mistakes like that.

Dallen shrugged his shoulders as a stressed bird might ruffle its feathers. "I don't have time for this, Commander Royce. Just tell me how we can smooth over this little matter." He turned his head away. He wasn't even able to meet her gaze.

Royce took a deep breath, sighing it out heavily. "There is no *smoothing* over this little matter,'" she answered. "I want you and all Vitruvians—" she paused a moment, thinking of Odessa and other shapeshifters who'd sought sanctuary on Erde over the years. "All Vitruvians under your command, and not under the protection of Erde due to sanctuary laws, off of this planet immediately. We will no longer accept your financial support, nor will we turn over any new technological findings to Vitruvia. All new discoveries remain the intellectual property of Erde."

Dallen jumped from his seat. "But that's absurd? That research belongs to us! We paved the way for these discoveries!"

"Please let me finish," Commander Royce continued calmly. "In exchange for this agreement, we will not contact the Vitruvian government and seek to execute charges against you and your men for the death of my esteemed director, Officer Renenet. And we will overlook your attempt to abscond with our PDL agent, Lucene Jones, against her will."

"Agent…really, pshh—" he mocked.

"I assure you," Royce replied curtly, "she is a valued member of our team…and, a *human being*," Royce reminded him.

Dallen's gaze met Royce's. "Do you have any idea what you are doing? Earth already has much of your weaponry. Between Earth and Vitruvia, Erde doesn't stand a chance against us should we decide to occupy. And without our financial support, your economy would be in ruins."

For the first time in her long life, Commander Royce knew exactly what the Elders would have her do without waking them up. It was a gamble, and a leap of faith, but something worthy of the Peace-Keepers. "My offer stands," she answered. "Leave immediately, and we won't file charges against you. Just know that if any Vitruvian sets foot on this planet without express permission from the PDL, they will be arrested immediately."

Two guards who flanked Dallen on either side coughed uneasily. They didn't expect their leader to agree to this. They expected him to threaten immediate occupation of Erde and to hold Royce, herself, as hostage, to force Erde to bend to their will. But somehow… that isn't what happened. Whether this had anything to do with the blurred lines of reality or the sudden image Dallen had of Lucene burning in his brain, encouraging him to 'do the right thing,' he couldn't be sure. But, without any fanfare, he agreed to her terms.

Dallen, his guards, and fellow representatives moved out of Erde the next morning, leaving Erde to, as was always the case when Ambassador Dallen left the planet, pick up the pieces.

CHAPTER 29
AT THE CROSSROADS
THE END. NOW.

If they hadn't realized where the Crossroads had been prior, it had become blatantly obvious now as storm clouds gathered directly over the Embassy Club, a swirling tornado-like funnel swarming slowly on the rooftop. The storms had been increasing each day as they got closer to the pink moon being full. With each swirl, more and more of the rooftop was jarred loose as the thunderous wind picked at pieces of the shingles that had been secured there. The ground shook, and it became challenging to remain upright.

"This way," Reverend Isabella summoned Lucene and Tanager to follow. Isabella had summoned Lucene the evening prior, letting her know that it was time. Tanager was not needed in the process as Isabella had informed him, more than once. But if Isabella's ceremony included using Lucene to close the portal, then he was going to be there…just in case. Just in case…what? He didn't know. But he refused to leave Lucene's side. Each of them carried a separate basket of supplies, the contents of which were unknown to everyone except for the priestess.

It was easy keeping the streets clear that day, as news reports of the strange weather encouraged everyone to stay indoors and take cover until it passed. A few reporters showed up at the Embassy Club with cameras and microphones but were quickly silenced by Commander

Royce's team. Normally, she would not have been moved to do so as Erde had always permitted its people to speak freely. But given the gravity of this situation, coupled with the bull's eye she had now placed on her back, thanks to her sending Dallen and the Vitruvians packing, she wasn't taking chances nor risking sending Erdelings into a panic.

She had some knowledge of the 'other realms' from her meetings with the Elders over the years, much of which she shared with an untrusting Isabella, not that she blamed the priestess. Royce recognized that she had much to be regretful about. She understood what many did not, that if left unsealed, the leak could possibly grow and suck everyone into it…and let a few more beings out, including Jasper Set.

Reverend Isabella eyed the reporters as they were hastened away with disgust. It was half for them and their constant portrayal of her as a charlatan, and half directed toward herself. *How is it that, in spite of my best intentions, I manage to create a scene in lifetime after lifetime? How is it that I always mess up? Is this a testimony to me and my lineage?* She thought of Far and shook her head, sadly.

But enough of that. They had their 'team' in place, and it was show time.

Before entering the building, Isabella spotted Kiki "the nose" around the corner. She purposefully sniffed the air before vanishing, her way of letting them know that Hysechia was just around the bend. The three quickened their steps, making their way past the reception area and into the main dining hall of the Embassy Club. But this time, instead of a central stage for the band, there was a swirling pool of red that seemed to circle the orchestra pit like water circling a drain. If one were to peer over the edge, there was nothing by a turbulent mass of liquid and gas that bubbled up like lava. Tables and chairs surrounding the pit were either tossed on their sides or covered with shards of glass from broken vases and scattered rose petals from last night's dinner seating. Apparently, diners had to be evacuated quickly as this monstrosity of a wormhole opened up suddenly. The only positive note in all this is that the band had been delayed on account of Hysechia managing to tear up tracks on the SpeedCircuit, causing trains to have to divert and find alternate routes—yet another reason why Hysechia had to be stopped.

She would have killed the band, and countless other people, if left to her own devices.

Isabella set to work, thrusting the basket toward Tanager. "You can make yourself useful by placing these stones around the vortex, about a foot apart and two feet away from the opening of the hole." He took the handle and dropped his arm slightly...heavy. He clasped it with both hands. Clearly, Reverend Isabella was as strong as an ox. "And don't fall in...lover-boy," she winked.

He let out a sigh. Tanager wasn't entirely sure that Isabella liked him very much. Or maybe she did but she didn't seem to respect him. *Lover-boy,* he thought to himself. *How demeaning.* Still, his first concern was Lucene. His second concern was everyone else, and...well, that about summed it up. Tanager followed instructions and started his trail of stones around the mouth of the opening. He peered curiously over the edge, sweat beginning to bead around his forehead. The pit was a swirling pool of red, and it kicked off the heat of a thousand suns (or maybe Tanager was exaggerating, but it was pretty damn hot). He could see no end to the abyss, and as the swirling continued, it slowly expanded. He worked more quickly.

"What can I do?" Lucene wanted to know.

"You can sit down and be quiet," Isabella answered. Lucine crinkled her lips and pursed them to one side. *Perhaps I am being a little harsh,* Isabella thought to herself. "You will have plenty to do soon enough. You need to conserve your energy," she softened. For whatever reason, Lucene bypassed actually setting one of the chairs upright and sitting on it, in favor of planting herself directly on the floor and crossing her legs underneath her. Somehow, this felt like the thing to do, although she wasn't sure why. Perhaps she just felt more grounded this way.

"So," Lucene spoke, "I'm confused. I thought we were re-opening the portal using yours truly. But it looks as if it's already open, all by itself," Lucene stated the obvious.

"Yes," Isabella answered, thoughtfully. "Ever have one of those loose flappers inside an old toilet?"

"Yes."

"At first, it stops sealing properly, and so the water never really fills the tank without someone pushing it back in place. Then, it opens up one day when triggered and refuses to close altogether."

"Not sure I follow," Lucene confessed.

"Too many beings able to wheedle their way in and out between the layers triggered a larger problem. I'm hoping you can help fix it."

"Am I the toilet flapper in this scenario?" Lucene wanted to know.

"I'm afraid so," Isabella confessed.

Outside, Hysechia crept cautiously up to the door with Marzipan's travel cage strapped to her back. Marzipan clung helplessly onto a few makeshift branches as the feline lumbered toward the Embassy entrance. Next to her, was another feline. He called himself Odin and he was very handsome. His fur was an odd blend of white mixed with light blue stripes—something that Hysechia had never witnessed before but quickly decided that she loved.

"Are you sure?" Hysechia asked her new partner. She had only met Odin recently, when she serendipitously ran into the fellow feline at a local park. Hysechia was there to feast on a new leash of foxes that had set up residence there. Odin, being rather clumsy, had alerted the foxes of his presence, sending them scattering in all directions. Hysechia would have normally been annoyed by this, given her current state of hunger. But Odin merely bared an innocent grin and flicked his tail with interest at the other feline predator in his midst. He enquired about the little half-boy and half-ladybug strapped to her back, and Hysechia was all too quick to fill him in. She had been between the layers for so long and it was certainly nice to have companionship.

"Most definitely," Odin nodded his thick head. "Given what you've told me about this…Isabella, is it? I'd say she has it coming."

Hysechia nodded. "She most certainly does. But—"

"But what?" Odin asked.

"What if I accidentally get trapped between the layers again? I may, once again, be reduced to a common house cat, unable to stalk and prey as I like."

"Would that be so terrible?" Odin asked. "To be cared for and fed regularly?"

"Of course, it would!" Hysechia hissed. "Would you want the life of a kept cat for yourself?"

"No," Odin had to admit, "I would not."

"Then, tell me why we're doing this again?" Hysechia challenged. She was beginning to doubt her knew partner.

"Because you want revenge on the person who reduced you to a common house cat," Odin reasoned. "Isn't that why you are so cross with Rev…" Odin caught himself. "This revolting human?"

Hysechia nodded. "Yes, it is true. But—"

"But what?" Odin persisted.

"I'm trying to weigh my options here and you're not helping!" Hysechia hissed.

"Forgive me, my lovely Hysechia. I did not mean to make someone as wondrous as yourself so angry."

Hysechia caught herself. Marzipan rolled his eyes and crossed his arms from his travel cage. He even kicked a fake pebble in annoyance. But that merely threw the cage off kilter and he was knocked sideways. Rubbing his hip, he stood.

"I'm not angry," Hysechia bared her teeth in a smile. "And," she relented, "I concur. The only solution is to go inside and toss the revolting Isabella into the vortex. Then, we seal her in it, just as she did to me."

"Purr-fect," Odin rolled his R's luxuriously. "Unless you want to scrap the whole 'revenge' thing and go hunting in the forest again. I support that, too."

"No," Hysechia lifted her upper lip defiantly. "She needs to be punished.

With that, Hysechia, Odin and Marzipan entered the Embassy Club as if they were dignitaries and had actually been invited.

The lobby was dark, but they made their way to the main hall, pausing at the archway, unseen. Tanager had finished putting the circle of stones around the hole and was now on to some strange saging ritual that Isabella had tasked him with. He had a vague notion of what to do after having watched Lucene perform this repeatedly in their high-home. For someone who was of no use, she seemed to be using him quite a lot, he thought. Every few moments, he glanced over at Lucene who was constantly peering around the room with a combination of bewilderment and fear. Occasionally, their eyes met and he would smile and then she would smile. For that micro-moment, everything in the world was okay.

As for the rest of the world, it was silent. Each detail was measured, thought out and protected. And so, Cepheus, Moksha, Ivan, Fatima and everyone else they knew were radio silent because anything might throw their plan off and cause it to fail.

"Mis-s-s-s—s me?" A familiar voice suddenly called. No one could see the infamous demon, Jasper Set, but his voice echoed the halls as vibrantly as an opera singer's final aria.

"Are you friggin' kidding me?" Lucene blurted out. They expected his arrival once the portal was officially re-opened, but not now.

"Nope, nope and...nope!" Jasper's voice sailed around her. "Not friggin' kidding you. Not even plain old kidding you! Just...here!"

"How?" Lucene asked as Tanager and Isabella held still. Even the two felines in the lobby with the poor little Marzipan in tow stopped, cautiously.

There was a loud rumbling sound outside, unlike anything they had ever heard before, almost as if thunderclouds were rolling in slow motion across the sky. This was followed by a cacophony of whistles and pops and an odd chattering that sounded like rattlesnakes.

"Uh oh," Jasper cupped his hand behind his ear, "sounds like the mamas and the papas are here."

"What?" Isabella was incredulous. "You brought the Null people... here? How...when you were trapped between the layers?" They knew his plan because he had not-so-discreetly shared it with Lucene during her meditation. What they couldn't figure out was how he was already out and about.

"Wrong, my dear Rev...Rev..." He still couldn't bring himself to say it. "Is-s-s-s-s-abella," he finished. "You trapped the future me between the layers. Remember, time is a wee bit behind here. In fact, I wonder if I might s-s-s-s-s-top you from s-s-s-s-s-ending me there in the fir-s-s-s-s-t place."

Isabella was at a loss. If she abandoned her efforts, then Jasper Set—the old one—would still be free and it would take only a matter of moments before the Null rolled over their planet and turned it into nothing but empty space.

While Isabella, Tanager and Lucene pondered on the gravity of the situation, Odin was busy unstrapping Marzipan from Hysechia's back.

"What are you doing?" Hysechia whispered.

"I am only getting the annoying little firefly prepared for—"

"I am not a firefly," Marzipan protested.

Odin leaned in closely, so close that when he inhaled, Marzipan almost got sucked into his left nostril. "Quiet, firefly," he warned. "You are hanging on by a wing and a prayer and only because you are useful."

There was a gleam in Odin's eyes, and suddenly, Marzipan saw it. He opened his mouth to speak. "Oh, you're—" but Marzipan caught himself, clasping his own hands over his mouth in case the words escaped, accidentally.

Hysechia became distracted, hunching low to the ground and wiggling her hind quarters like a cat about to pounce on her prey.

"It s-s-s-s-seems we have vis-s-s-itors," Jasper noted.

Isabella looked up in time to see Hysechia's feline form lunging toward her. She pounced…so did Odin. Just as Hysechia reached Isabella, Odin's giant paw stepped on the cat's tail. Hysechia let out a roar.

"You betray me!" Hysechia tugged at her tail with all her might. "Let me go!" Odin hung on tightly as Hysechia kept pulling.

"Very well," Odin answered finally, lifting his paw with the next tug. When he did, Hysechia catapulted past Isabella into the abyss. She reached a paw out and swatted at her nemesis before falling, and Isabella lost her balance. About to fall face-first after the feline who was now spiraling downward into the pit, Isabella felt an arm wrap around her waist and pull her backward. She landed on top of Lucene with a thud, accidentally jamming an elbow into Lucene's ribs.

"Ow!" Lucene whined. "How come all of our encounters end up with me falling on my ass with the wind knocked out of me?"

Lucene and Isabella rolled over and crawled to the edge of the pit in time to see Hysechia disappear moments later with nothing by the echo of a loud wail spiraling back upward. Odin peered over their shoulders. Isabella recoiled with a start. But not Lucene.

"Odessa," Lucene acknowledged, "you look good as a cat."

"Why thank you—" Odin's voice changed into its female counterpart but her cat form remained. "Hang on," Odessa was surprised, "how'd you know it was me?"

"Your smell," Lucene lied.

"Hmph," Odessa actually sat on her hind quarters and crossed her paws as if crossing her arms. "No, really." Lucene didn't answer. But somehow, she saw what little Marzipan had seen. There, deep in her pupils, was her soul. And it was the soul of one Vitruvian "not-a-mermaid."

"Are you all right?" Tanager gasped, having circumvented the pit and was now at Lucene's side, out of breath.

Lucene didn't have time to answer as the wind picked up with a thunderous roar, debris beginning to fall as the roof of the club was ripped off in its entirety. Overhead, the Null began to gather as if looking for someone…their lost son, Jasper.

"Hate to dis-s-s-sturb this s-s-s-s-weet little reunion. But I believe this is the end."

"But if you allow the Null to destroy us, won't you be killed too?" Lucene asked.

"Hmmm…hadn't really thought of that. What do you s-s-s-s-s-uggest?"

"I suggest you send your family into the portal and let us seal them inside," Lucene answered.

"How does this in anyway benefit me?" Jasper wanted to know. The angry sounds of hissing grew louder. His parents were upset with him and he knew it. Though, he wasn't sure if they were angry at the current version of him or the version stuck between the layers. Somehow, as a demon, he was aware of both of his "selves" simultaneously, across time, an awareness that left him with the nastiest of headaches.

Obviously, they were both the same demon, but still…was it that the Null assumed he ran away? That they learned how he diverted them from some planets and directed them toward others? Or had they caught on to his only fear…that they would realize that he wasn't a spawn of the Null nor a gift of the great Segue. He was just an ordinary demon, one that the Null would need to destroy just as they had done to all the others, along with their accompanying worlds.

He shrank his large torso as if a turtle trying to stuff his head back into his suit jacket. He wasn't having much success. "Okay, I s-s-s-s-ee your point," Jasper whispered, even though he was mostly sure the Null couldn't understand them. Perhaps his Null mamas and papas would, in fact, kill him, too. "I'm always up for a good bargain. I tell you what. Gather 'round children." He motioned for Isabella, Lucene, Tanager and Odessa to move closer. They did so with much reluctance, never taking their eyes off the demon. "There's a s-s-s-s-tory about a prophet leading the Null directly to the throne of the Mighty Segue. Perhaps-s-s-s one of you might," he motioned his eyes toward the pit, "take a tumble for the greater good? The Null will follow. I will make sure of that."

"Can't you lead them?" Tanager asked. "Surely, if you direct them, they will follow your direction and you can escape before we seal the portal."

"While I do appreciate your excellent plan," Jasper Set mocked, "pardon the pun, but it's hotter than hell down there…even for a demon! No thanks. I'll pas-s-s-s."

"I'll do it," Marzipan called from the travel cage. They had forgotten about the little firefly. "I can fly overtop and then buzz away really fast at the last minute. My wings are heat-resistant," he announced triumphantly.

Odessa pranced over to retrieve the cage, picking the handle up in her mouth and returning to the group. "I don't think so, little man," she mumbled, putting him down. "That heat will melt your wings in a heartbeat, despite your 'heat resistance.'" Given that his wings were already sticking to the side of his round body, he was forced to admit that she might be right. Still, it was brave of him to offer.

"No," everyone looked up to see Tanager was already perched on the edge of the pit. "I'll do it."

"No!" Lucene protested. "I can't let you do that!"

"Lucene, Isabella can't do it because she is the only one who knows how to seal the portal. You can't do it because she needs you to do it."

Just then, there were confused sounds emanating from the kitchen area. "How?" Lucene began to ask before remembering…time is different here. Commander Royce may have cleared the area of pedestrians in our time, but those at the back door were coming in for their night shift. They were from the past. This world was on a loop.

"Odessa, get them out of here!" Tanager commanded.

"Leave the bug," Isabella cautioned. "We need him." It was then that Lucene clued in to Marzipan's superpower. Why hadn't she realized it sooner? She had the sudden image of Marzipan gorging himself on too much sugary foods and...

Odessa nodded, taking off at tiger speed to chase the would-be workers out of the kitchen. The swift movement jarred Lucene away from her thoughts.

The Null began descending before anyone could argue with him. Lucene moved toward Tanager in an attempt to pull him away from the edge.

"I may not be very strong, or always say and do the right things," Tanager explained, his face dropping sadly, "but I can die for you."

Lucene's heart melted. She opened her mouth, but no sounds came out. It was not that she was at a loss for words. It was that Isabella had begun chanting and her throat was suddenly paralyzed. Within moments, Lucene's arms were glowing as the tree-like embers grew. As she transformed into a swirling pool of light, her energy somehow blended with that of the abyss.

"Will you keep your word, demon?" Tanager asked.

"I always do," Jasper Set giddily jumped up and down like a small child. Isabella's chanting grew louder.

"Then there's just one more thing..."

"And what's that?"

With that, Cepheus emerged from the shadows. He looked at his friend for a moment. "Are you sure? I could—" he motioned toward the abyss.

"Absolutely not," Tanager replied, "you have a planet to rule." He referred to their conversation soon after Hamish's ghost paid a visit to Cepheus. They need you. Erde needs you." Tanager shot a knowing look to Cepheus.

"What is-s-s-s he talking about?" Jasper looked between the two men, a visible mixture of confusion and impatience.

"I demand to see the final contract between you and my father, Sovereign Hamish of the High Royals."

"Oh, that," Jasper seemed almost disappointed. He was hoping it was something much grander. With a flick of his wrist and a snap of his fingers, a scroll appeared. "Here." He floated it over to Cepheus, the edges of it singed from the heat of the abyss. "Seems to have brought me nothing but grief and nothing to show for it to boot." He looked regretfully at Lucene, having failed to secure both her allegiance and the multi-dimensional plane-hopping support from Far. In fact, at this very moment, his world felt almost ... hopeless.

And then something happened...

There was this inexplicable 'thing' that settled all at once in the center of Jasper's chest. What was it? He had watched a small firefly willing to risk his life for his friends. He watched as Tanager was going to unselfishly, and without hesitation, sacrifice his life for the woman he loved. Meanwhile his own Null family was ready to destroy this world and eat him for dinner for having betrayed them. He couldn't think of anyone who would make that kind of sacrifice for him. This thought bothered him.

"Hang on," he told Tanager. "I will give you the signal when it's time to jump." He spoke slowly, cleanly, without a single extra 's' in his words. With that, he winged his way up to meet his family. He waived his arms, hissed and popped, as if explaining something to them...probably that he hadn't betrayed them, that this was the will of the Mighty Segue. He was to deliver the prophet for them to follow, and he had done just that.

Jasper made one final survey of Tanager from the sky. "Oh well," he whispered to himself, "I always did wonder what would happen to a demon in the afterlife."

With that Jasper Set performed his one and only act of love.

He dove...headfirst into the pit with the entire Null following him as he did.

Tanager jumped back in shock, Cepheus grabbing his friend's arm to ensure he didn't accidentally fall into the abyss. After the final crustacean-like creature had flown into the dark portal, it began to close. As it did, the floor turned an ugly shade of gray with soot scattered everywhere. Lucene spun around several times before dropping to the ground in a heap. Tanager lunged to her aid. Isabella grabbed his arm. "Not yet, lover boy. Still charged up, remember?" He did remember from the last time, but instinct was instinct.

Lucene let out a cough. "Okay, Marzipan time to yack up lunch."

"Ew, that's gross," Marzipan protested. "That's not at all—"

"Eat, little bug," Isabella pulled a jar of actual marzipan from her basket. His eyes lit up.

"What is all this about?" Tanager enquired.

"I didn't realize it until now," Lucene explained. "But I got mental flashes from Marzipan's past." Tanager was visibly impressed by this as Lucene had never exhibited any psychic skills that would point to witnessing past events experienced by others. "Marzipan's old friend who rescued him from the desert gliders?" she continued. "He said that he manifested him because he was lonely. And maybe, in a way, he did. But what if—somehow—there was a leak between the layers back then and Marzi over there escaped. Not sure how he figured out he could seal the leak with firefly yack but—"

"I'm not a—" Marzipan's whining was interrupted by the regurgitation of what he had just ingested. And, there was a lot of it. Tanager coughed and turned away, his stomach beginning to cramp and heave. He had a terrible gag reflex.

"Come, help me," Isabella said to Lucene and Cepheus, ignoring Tanager. And for the next hour, the three spread firefly yack all over the blackened areas of the floor. Somehow, the expansion stopped at Isabella's stones, meaning Isabella was either exceptionally good at math or she was exceptionally good at protection spells. Either way, the stones were a guidepost for all the ground they needed to cover.

Meanwhile, Tanager dragged his cold, sweat-soaked body into the lobby and tried not to think about it, his stomach still queasy. "Some hero I turned out to be," he thought miserably. His one act of bravery was outshined by a weak stomach.

"It might take a few days for all of the anomalies to end," Isabella explained to Lucene and Cepheus, "but they will." Lucene thought for a moment about Not-Christopher and let out a somewhat disappointed sigh. Cepheus's mind went to Petrichor. Was she safe? He suspected so, since she hadn't revisited him in some time. Perhaps after her gentle nudge to move on, she was finally able to do so, herself.

And so, the leak between the layers was closed and the embers of Lucene's arms gently faded.

CHAPTER 30
RECLAIMING THE THRONE
NOW...ONE DAY AFTER THE END.

"So, you are leaving?" Moksha watched, fighting back tears, when she arrived at Cepheus's office at TARA, only to find him packing an assortment of contraptions into a small suitcase. The room was still a mess, but somehow, he had no trouble rummaging through drawers and sifting through the piles of books and tools that littered the floor, finding the exact pieces he was searching for.

Cepheus paused, surprised at her presence. "How did you know where to find me?" he asked.

"Where else would you retreat to when you needed an escape...or tools for the journey?" Moksha leaned against the door frame. "Were you at least planning on saying 'good-bye'?" Her skin began to form a red hue as her face grew warm. She wasn't certain whether her feelings were anger or grief, most likely a combination of the two.

"Moksha, I—"

"I understand," she interrupted.

"No," he abandoned his packing to meet her at the door. "I don't think you do. Please, let me explain." He wrapped his arms around her, pulling her into his chest before Moksha's resistance gave out and she began sobbing, tears running down his shirt. "I have to go," Cepheus spoke gently. Moksha wrapped her arms around his waist and held onto Cepheus tightly. He continued, "If I don't, the Royals will continue their mission to take over Erde, and they won't stop there. But if I resume control, I can turn things around, and perhaps the Royals stand a chance at being the official military support of Erde and all of Section 1."

"You're wrong," she sobbed, sniffing between words. "I understand *why* you have to go. I just don't want you to."

Cepheus paused for what felt like an eternity.

"I want you to come with me," he finally said.

"What?" Moksha peered up at him in surprise. "You mean for military protection?" Cepheus paused for a moment before letting out a cat-like laugh. "What's so funny?" Moksha demanded.

"No, Moksha. I am not inviting you to be my personal guard. I'm asking you to become a sovereign—alongside me at the throne."

"Oh, come on," she backed away, socking him in the arm.

"Ow, what was that for?" Cepheus rubbed his arm.

"You shouldn't toy with my emotions like that. Look at me! I'm a former assassin. I know nothing of being…well…sovereignly!"

"Neither did my father when my mo—," he still couldn't get the word 'mother' out. "When Sabrina married my father. He too, was in the lower military caste."

"But I don't know the first thing about ruling."

Cepheus grinned. "Neither do I. But we can learn…together." He reached out and pulled her toward him a second time. "I confess, it won't be as glamorous as it sounds being a sovereign. The training grounds have become a waste-pit and the brigade are not going to be easy to decondition and re-train."

"Well, at least I can offer support in that area," Moksha smiled up at him. "I am a former assassin hell-bent on peace."

"Interesting choice of words," Cepheus's grin grew wider, displaying his saw-like teeth. "Is that your way of saying 'yes'?"

"Of course, it is, my love. Anywhere you are is where I want to be."

"I had another thought. But I must ask that you refrain from punching me in the arm again."

Moksha let out an uncharacteristic giggle. "Okay, I promise. What is it?"

"I was thinking of asking Isabella to accompany us as an advisor to replace Far."

Hamish had died before he got to see Far's death, and it would seem that the monk was not lurking in the other realm with Hamish and Sabrina. He was, presumably, someplace else.

"Are you sure that's wise?" Moksha looked up at him, surprised. "Some of her methods of persuasion have been…questionable," she finished, recounting in her mind the time Reverend Isabella put on a show for her followers, alongside Dallen, in order to garner support.

"While her actions have not always been ideal, her intentions are always with the highest good in mind. I believe we can work with her on, as you mentioned, her methods."

"If you think so, I trust your judgment," Moksha conceded before laughing. "And here I thought you were far too practical for crazy ideas."

"Oh, Moksha," Cepheus kissed the top of her head. "You are in for many more surprises. This, I can promise you."

CHAPTER 31
THE NURSERY
NOW...ONE DAY AFTER THE END.

For as large of a salamander as Fredo was, he still gave the appearance of a small, lost child. He stood by the great window in his former sovereign's chamber, overlooking the training grounds. He even crossed his arms behind him as Hamish had done. And yet, it just wasn't right. Now that Hamish, Far and Sabrina were gone, there was no one left to rule. In this situation, the Royals would have likely sent one of their superiors to oversee the grounds, except that the Null had destroyed the entire race with the exception of those located on their small and dying planet in Section 3.

This meant that, technically, Fredo was now in charge. His subordinates expected it of him. There was just one small problem...while Fredo was built like a formidable beast, he was still dumb as a rock, a fact that he was becoming increasingly aware of as the sweat poured down his bright red salamander face. If he showed weakness, no doubt someone would challenge him, and he was terrified of what would become of their planet if that happened. He would be killed, and so would the baby.

"Excuse me...my Sovereign," a nurse cleared his throat as he peered his head around the large chamber door.

Fredo looked around for a moment, expecting to see Hamish. Then it occurred to him. The nurse was talking to him.

"What is it?" Fredo grumbled from deep in his throat.

"The baby is awake. Usually, our late sovereign would hold it each evening but since…" The nurse's voice trailed off.

Something in the center of Fredo's chest gave the littlest of pangs. *Would it be possible? Of course, it would. Why wouldn't it be?"* With a new flash of hope, his spirits brightened. "I'll be along in just a moment to…cradle it."

The nursery was not what one might expect. Instead of being filled with animal murals on the walls, pastel colors and a floating mobile above the baby's crib, this one was as stark as a sterile hospital room. No wonder the baby was fussy when Fredo arrived. Even a warrior such as himself thought the room could at least use a splash of color.

He approached the crib with caution. When Hamish had been alive, he wasn't allowed to touch the child, his child, born from a short-term affair with the former Sovereign Sabrina. He thought back on the encounter and fought back a tear. To her, he was just a plaything. Fredo, on the other hand, actually had feelings for his former sovereign that were possibly stronger than the man she'd actually chosen to rule with her had for her.

Fredo peered over the bars of the sleep station. The child had distinct lizard eyes and a tail. It likely wouldn't develop legs for several more months. Instead there were two round, leathery stumps where they would later form. Around its eyes and marking its face were peculiar red streaks. If it weren't apparent yet that the child was his, it soon would be.

"Would you like to hold the baby?" the nurse asked with uncustomary sympathy. Perhaps babies had a way of summoning compassion. Fredo nodded nervously. The nurse reached in and gently lifted the swaddled baby. A look of fear crossed the salamander's face. "Don't worry," the nurse reassured, "this one's made of tough stuff and isn't likely to break easily."

Fredo put out his thick arms to accept little Cefeus. It was then that emotion overtook him and he began sobbing for the second time in his still relatively young life. The nurse peered over his shoulder nervously at sounds from the next room. Several soldiers were in the examination room next door being treated from training injuries. They couldn't see this weakness in their new leader. The nurse quickly shut the door.

Fredo's mind began racing. *I know nothing about raising a child. I know even less about ruling an empire. But if I don't, someone else will and my child most definitely will not be allowed to live. He would be considered a threat. What am I to do?*

At that moment, he heard something through the walls. It was coming from the opposite side from where the soldiers were now blustering on about the range and depth of their injuries—of which they were enormously proud. It sounded like…humming. *Ah,* he thought to himself, *the human.* Even thinking about Roman next door left a bitter taste in his mouth. Humans were vermin, and he didn't like them. How could they have bothered to nurse this one back to health and…

A thought crossed his mind. Fredo didn't typically have many of them, and this one he savored for quite some time.

The baby wiggled a little in Fredo's arms, so he rocked it gently, making a little cooing sound that he'd heard Hamish doing around the baby and one that Sabrina had done on occasion when Cepheus had been born so many years ago. Young Cefeus let out a slurping sound and smiled. There it was again, that little pang in the center of Fredo's chest—one that was growing stronger all the time.

Fredo made his way toward the door, baby in arm. The nurse looked questioningly at him. "Stay here," he ordered, "we will return shortly."

The nurse nodded and offered. "Feeding time is in thirty minutes," he reminded Fredo. Fredo grunted that he understood.

Once in the hallway, he stood upright, puffing out his chest proudly as several soldiers passed. They each lowered their gaze deferentially as they did so. Once they were out of sight, he threw open the door that held the human. Roman looked up, surprised, and not without a hint of terror on his face. He opened his mouth to speak but had no idea what to say, so he closed it again.

Several days had passed and his wounds were healing nicely. It still hurt to sit up, and the carnivorous food they offered him did little to help his already sensitive digestive system. What Erde lacked in meat, the Royals made up for a hundred-fold. He was becoming so sickened from nothing but animal protein several times a day that he was certain that he was going to become a vegan as soon as he could get back to Erde. That is, he reasoned, if they let him return. He wasn't sure they would. The nurse had been kind—a rarity from the Royals. He tried to sneak him what he thought were vegetables but the greens he brought were varied palm fronds, grasses and inedible flowers.

Roman eyed the baby, curiously.

"It's a baby," Fredo grunted, as if Roman hadn't guessed.

"I can see that," Roman answered cautiously.

"I know nothing of raising a baby," Fredo spoke quietly to ensure no one else heard their conversation. He shut the door with his free arm. It made a loud thud, causing the baby to begin to wail out in frustration. Fredo tried cooing but it didn't work.

"May I?" Roman offered, putting his arms out.

Fredo eyed him distrustfully. "Don't hurt it," he cautioned.

"I won't," Roman answered, sitting as upright as possible in his bed.

Fredo handed him the bulky little baby. Roman began to purse his lips distastefully. Truth be told, it was the ugliest child he'd ever seen. He caught Fredo's dark expression and shifted into one of his well-practiced wide smiles. Roman started talking to the baby, reciting strange words that Fredo had never heard before, "For in and out, above and below, 'tis nothing but a magic shadow show, played in a box whose candle is the sun, round which we phantom figures come and go."

This all sounded like gibberish to the salamander. He could barely read, and even if he could, *The Rubayait of Omar Khayyam* would not likely have been his first choice. But the baby began cooing once again, soothed by Roman's calm voice. So the salamander let Roman continue with his gibberish.

When Roman had finished, Fredo spoke. "You know things," Fredo announced, gruffly.

"I like to think so," Roman refrained from his usual sarcasm. He valued his life too much.

"I was told you study people," Fredo was having trouble finding his words.

"Yes," Roman confirmed. "I taught anthropology for years on my planet and spent quite a bit of time studying your culture as well."

"Can you help me?" Fredo asked, realizing how weak and pathetic that sounded, and so he added sternly, "Help me understand how to rule the training grounds so there is no mutiny and I will let you live."

Something stirred inside Roman. His heart was still broken—once again—over Far, and with his death came a conclusion that he was somehow not ready for. He had felt abandoned by his friends on Erde, rejected from the school who fired him on Earth after his breakdown. He really couldn't remember the last time he actually felt…useful.

"I will gladly help you," Roman answered, sincerely. "With one small request."

"What's that?" Fredo asked, gruffly.

"Vegetables," he answered.

"Vegetables?" Fredo was confused.

"Beans…whole grains…fruit…seeds, even." Roman continued. "What's a guy got to do to get a meal that hasn't been slaughtered first?"

Fredo's mind circled around the request. Finally, he had an "aha" moment—possibly the first one in his life. Sovereign Sabrina brought back lots of exotic animals from varied planets, usually with no regard as to how they might react in their existing world. He remembered a menagerie of parakeets, conures and cockatoos that she brought from one of her Earth visits to her former Florida casino. They ate fruit and vegetables and seeds. He also remembered a pesky raccoon that kept unlocking chamber doors, and a salt marsh vole that had very poor hygiene and would leave his remains everywhere. Yet, he was pretty certain that they ate beans.

Funny, Fredo thought, *he's asking me to feed him like a Royal house pet.*

"Help me with the baby," Fredo finally answered, "and I will see to it that you have your requested…pet food."

CHAPTER 32
THE SEAHORSE
NOW...ONE DAY AFTER THE END.

"Where are you off to?" Morphinae asked, flying in with wings outspread, still in his falcon form. He then transformed into his usual blue, life-sized crochet-doll frame—bare-chested, wearing tattered jeans. Odessa never did understand where he got the idea for this manifestation, and never really thought to ask. Instead, she turned to face him, grabbing the only weapon she could find—a conch shell she'd found on the beach. She wielded it, hesitantly. "What is that for?" Morphinae was surprised. He took a step toward Odessa, only to notice then that she backed away, her eyes wide. "Do you think that I would ever hurt you?" he asked.

"I dunno," Odessa confessed. "It's not as if you've never killed before. And you did say that you never wanted to see me again," her eyes began welling up with tears. She brushed them aside.

"I've killed a total of three times in my life, and it was only to restore balance," Morphinae explained. "You know as well as I do that the last one was necessary."

Odessa did know. He had mistakenly rescued a boy from drowning, who would grow into Drake Cushing, Lucene's former boss at the United Commonwealth on Earth. Doing so would later result in Drake being involved in thousands of deaths, leaving Morphinae to feel partially responsible. In the end, he did the only thing an admirable Balance-Keeper could do—he drowned Drake in his adulthood, thereby restoring balance. Now, it seems that Drake's brother, Bryce, had taken the reins after his brother's death, and proved no better than his predecessor.

"And," Odessa asked cautiously…is this one of those times? A time where it's necessary?"

Morphinae surveyed the small shack that was Odessa's dream home. She had a bed made of bamboo strung together with reeds. The top of it was a pile of palm fronds where one would expect a mattress to be. On top of that sat a small, hand-woven suitcase that looked about as sturdy as the leaky thatched roof above their head. He eyed her with a mix of confusion as if he were seeing her for the first time.

"I have never and will never harm you," Morphinae told her. "I am surprised that I need to tell you such things." Morphinae wasn't one to get offended, and yet her words bothered him for some reason.

Odessa's face contorted as if it were about to crack as she broke down in tears, and cried between her sobbing, "I've failed my mission with the Vitruvians! I failed Isabella! I outed Lucene's powers and betrayed you! Even when I try to lead with good intentions, I seem to do a spectacular job of messing everything up." She covered her face with her palms, collapsing on the floor in front of the bed and pulling her knees into her chest.

"I don't feel betrayed," Morphinae answered softly.

Odessa looked up, cautiously, sniffling a little. "You don't?"

"No," Morphinae answered. "I'm used to leading with my head. I've always laughed at you for leading with your heart. But it has come to my attention that I could stand to be more…feeling."

"And what brought that to your attention?"

Morphinae put his hand out to help Odessa to her feet. "It was more a 'who.' You, of course."

"You don't hate me?" Odessa was surprised.

"Who could ever hate you?" Morphinae answered with a warmth that Odessa had never heard from him before. He was still holding her hand.

"Lots of people," she answered, wiping the tears from her eyes with the backs of her hands. "I was just packing to escape. But I have no idea where to go. Commander Royce has sealed the borders of Erde—no-one in and no-one out. If the Vitruvians discover my location, they will kill me. And this planet is so God-damned small that I would have to morph my way into an insect and spend the rest of my days as a bug in order to survive." Odessa may have been a bit melodramatic, but there was some truth to what she was saying.

"I have another idea," Morphinae shared.

"Really? What?"

"I don't know if it's possible," Morphinae explained. "But remember when you once asked the question about which of us would carry the baby if we were to have a child?"

"I remember," Odessa was shocked. "But I didn't think you had." Frankly, she thought, Morphinae all but laughed at the idea.

"Well, it got me thinking…about seahorses."

"Seahorses?" Odessa was confused, still bewildered that Morphinae had actually given thought to anything she said, particularly about suggestions about becoming a couple.

"Yes, seahorse males carry the baby to term."

"I'm afraid I'm not following."

"We know that we can shape-shift into male and female forms, and vary our outward appearance—"

"Obviously," Odessa answered, crossing her arms and waiving a hand in the air.

"But what if we could shape-shift and merge into one form?"

"I'm not sure that's possible." Odessa was skeptical.

"There are legends that we shape-shifting Vitruvians can go a step further then changing our personal forms. We can actually combine our energy to become a single new form."

"I've never heard that," Odessa challenged. "Is it true?"

"I'm willing to find out if you are," Morphinae answered, walking from the shadows of the shack and out into the sun while guiding Odessa by the hand.

"Where are we going?" Odessa followed, barefoot in the sand.

"To the sea, of course." They stopped at the water's edge, hand-in-hand and looking out at the setting sun over the water. "There's just one caveat," Morphinae added.

"What's that?"

"Unlike marriage and divorce and shifting from one form to another, I am not sure that, once merged, we could ever separate again."

Odessa paused carefully to think this through. "And," Odessa wanted to clarify, "you're willing to risk being stuck with me—a part of you—for the rest of our lives?" Odessa sucked in her breath.

"I have never been one to take on friends and yet you are my first friend—my best friend. I cannot ever see a time where I wouldn't want to be stuck with you," he answered practically.

"But—" Odessa started to speak.

"What?"

"Do you love me?" She winced, afraid of what the answer might be.

"I'm telling you that I want to spend the rest of my days co-mingled as a single entity." Morphinae grew impatient. "What do you think?"

"Is that a 'yes?'" Odessa grinned out of the corner of her mouth. "I'm gonna need a definitive 'yes'."

"Yes," Morphinae answered, uncomfortably, while averting his gaze. "I've already explained that I'm a thinker not a feeler. Why do you insist on making me say 'feely' things?"

Odessa smiled.

"So, what form are we taking?" she wanted to know, looking down at her female shape for what she assumed might be the last time. She had to admit to herself that a part of her would miss having breasts. There was something fun about them.

"I told you, a giant seahorse."

"No, you gave the seahorse as an example of—" Odessa caught herself. "You know what? Never mind. We are to become a giant seahorse, then?"

"Well, you do love the ocean and we could spend our days in this one," he gestured his long arm over the water as if Odessa couldn't see it.

"Is such a thing possible?" Odessa asked. "I mean, won't Erdelings find it odd?"

"The sea is pretty large. Who is to say that anyone will ever know?"

And with that, Morphinae and Odessa performed one final shape-shift, turning themselves into the most beautiful blue seahorse that any world has ever seen. They swam away together as one, never to be heard from again.

Years later, Fatima would tell her daughter Talula tales about the mythical seahorse. It was right up there with the Loch Ness Monster, Bigfoot and Santa Claus on Earth. And yet, somehow Talula sensed that there was some truth to this story, and often spent her younger years sitting on Tranquility Beach, gazing out over the sea, looking for the mythical seahorse. A few times, she was sure she spotted the united couple, Morphinae and Odessa, but it was always a quick flash out of the corner of her eye. So, she never could confirm it.

Still, without anyone really knowing who documented the story or why, the tale of Morphinae and Odessa became a legend in the Erde storybooks. The tale grew more and more incredible with each telling. It was cited as one of the most romantic stories of all time.

CHAPTER 33
REDEMPTION
NOW...TWO DAYS AFTER THE END.

Commander Royce stood before the elders in a dark, circular dome located in a sectioned-off area of the PDL. They were larger than life as if they had morphed out of the red rocks of Sedona, towering over her in an equally intimidating and mystifying manner. The lead elder was soft-spoken with a long beard and tired eyes. He enjoyed his sleep and wasn't often awakened. And yet, this was the third time in a year. Only this time, Royce had not reached out to the elders. For the first time in her lifetime, they "requested" her presence. Royce was afraid. What vibrational shift had her actions caused that woke them up? Or, was it simply the recent shift as Reverend Isabella struggled to close the portal she'd accidentally left open?

"It seems we are faced with a dilemma," the eldest said. Except, when he spoke, it was as if the others were speaking in unison. They echoed him in hushed voices.

Royce suspected she knew exactly what the problem was (her), but she had to know for sure. "Of what problem do you speak?"

"Amina," he called her by her first name. No one else, except for the elders, actually knew it. She was Commander Royce for as long as anyone could remember. "You come from a long lineage of helpers. You, yourself, have spent a lifetime in service, and yet..." He paused, sadly. "What has happened?"

Amina's face dropped. Erde was a land of peace. But by living according to the morally "best" ways, instead of flourishing, it made them a target for intruders, unwelcome guests for those they wished to help (such as Earth), and financially bankrupt.

"I didn't think I had a choice," she cried softly. It was true. She hadn't intended to provide weaponry and technology to Vitruvia in exchange for financial support and protection. It happened slowly at first, and by the time she realized it, she was neck-high in deceit.

"Why didn't you come to us sooner?" The female elder next to the bearded one asked, softly.

"I thought I could handle it myself. And—" she paused. "I was embarrassed. I didn't want to seem...weak."

"We could have helped you...advised you. That's what we're here for," the old woman said.

"I'm sorry," was all that Royce could muster. After a long pause she asked, "What is my punishment? Is it death?" She assumed that her time had finally come. After all, she was old even by Erde standards, and in all likelihood she probably only had about forty years left of her life. She didn't want to die in disgrace, of course, but she had lived a full life. One hundred and ten years was a pretty good run, wasn't it?

"Death?" another elder, one of indeterminate gender, was surprised. "Do you mean to suggest that you think we'd murder you?" They seemed almost offended.

"Well, I don't know," Amina confessed, "I sold out my people by accepting money in exchange for weaponry and technology to the Vitruvians, knowing full well that they could use those resources against us..."

"And then their selling it to the earthlings?" the first elder questioned.

Amina let out a sigh. "I only learned of that recently."

"And tell us," the female elder asked softly, "what made you decide to make this arrangement with the Vitruvians?"

"I," Amina choked, "I thought it was for the best. As a small planet, less than the size of a country on Earth, without the IPP support, we had nothing. If TARA and the Makerspace shut down, there was little else to help keep the planet sustained and ... relevant. Even if we could grow our own crops and keep ourselves fed and clothed, we had no protection against outside invaders, natural disasters...nothing."

"And, you believed the Vitruvians could provide that?"

"Yes."

There was a collective sigh among the elders. A murmur, as if they were in a back room somewhere discussing her fate, even though their faces were present. Finally, they returned.

"We have a proposal for you," they said in unison.

"A proposal?" Amina was confused.

"Yes, call it redemption, if you like. We have some specific suggestions for you to employ that will help Erdelings, all optional, of course, with the understanding that you will remain at your post for at least one more year."

Amina was surprised. She was due to retire last year and assumed after the mess she'd cause, they would want to be rid of her sooner, rather than later.

"Why are you not punishing me?" she asked.

"While misguided, you were acting according to what you believed was best. By our estimation, you went off track a year ago. Spend the next year correcting it, and all will be forgiven."

Amina thought a moment. "Like...karma?" she suggested.

"Call it as you like," the elders said as they began to fade. "We're very tired. Come back tomorrow, and we'll tell you all about our plan."

CHAPTER 34
RESIGNATION
NOW...THREE DAYS AFTER THE END.

"Why are you here, Professor Tanager?" Commander Royce asked. It was the first time anyone had sought her out in her home. She invited Tanager into her high-home on the outskirts of Achel, which turned out to be walking distance from where he and Lucene currently resided. "And, how is it that you figured out where I lived? No one else has ever attempted to do this before."

"Forgive me, Commander Royce," Tanager apologized, removing the fedora that he wore for the occasion and holding it to his chest. "I didn't mean to intrude upon your personal space." He didn't answer the question about how he'd found her. That was thanks to Kiki's earlier efforts to ensure that Royce was not a shape-shifting imposter. It was the young girl who actually discovered Commander Royce's place of residence.

"Amina," she answered.

"I'm sorry, what?" Tanager was confused.

"Amina," she answered. "I'm not on duty. Therefore, you can call me by my first name.

Being on familiar terms made it more awkward for Tanager, but it did serve one purpose; it humanized Commander Royce, somehow.

"Amina," he repeated, circling the hat in his hands nervously. "Given everything that's happened lately, I thought you should be first to know before I give my official resignation in the morning."

Amina paused for a moment. "I see," she finally answered. "Please, sit down." Amina motioned for Tanager to have a seat on the wrap-around couch that took up most of her living room. "Reishi tea?" she offered, pouring herself a glass from the pitcher that sat on a glass table in front of the couch.

"Eh, no, thank you," he answered, sitting and resting his hat beside him.

Amina took her seat on the farthest corner of the couch, sipping her iced tea. After a moment of silence, Amina finally addressed Tanager's admission, "You are not giving your resignation in the morning."

Tanager was filled with a mixture of disbelief and indignation. Of course, he was. "Yes," he answered, "I am."

Amina let out a sigh. "Before you make your final decision, will you at least allow me to argue my case?"

What case? Tanager was very confused. Amina took his silence as permission to continue.

"I am aware that my decisions this past year have been unconscionable."

Tanager crossed one leg over the other and began tapping his fingers on his knee, uncomfortably.

Amina placed her glass on the table. *No coaster,* Tanager noticed. Lucene would have chastised him for that. He smiled to himself.

"Our entire planet was on the verge of bankruptcy, Professor Tanager," Amina spoke loudly to regain his attention. "I did what I thought I needed to do in order to save our economy and feed our planet."

"And for that, you were willing to sacrifice Lucene?" Tanager was angry. "One small price to pay for the good of the whole. Is that it?" He completely disregarded the fact that her actions also placed very large and lethal weapons into the wrong hands which impacted the entire planet. But at this moment, he had a very singular focus.

"No," Amina answered. "What I tried to do, and failed, was dance a fine line between giving them what they wanted and protecting our people."

"What is that supposed to mean?" Tanager challenged.

"I sold them weaponry—"

"To the Vitruvians—who you knew were going to give it to Earth. The very people we were trying to protect had plans all along to overthrow our planet."

"Yes, but there are pieces of which you are unaware."

"Such as?"

"Such as the fact that I did my best to have technicians at TARA alter some of the final blueprints before any weaponry or technology was given to the Vitruvians."

"Technicians?" Tanager immediately thought of Ivan. "Was my friend, Ivan, involved?"

"No," Amina answered. "I assure you that your friend was not privy to any of this. "And," she continued, "part of the agreement included a special clause."

"What kind of clause."

"Ambassador Dallen was not to lay a hand on Lucene. She was not part of the arrangement."

"You can see how that worked out."

"Yes," Amina sighed. "That was unfortunate."

"But this doesn't change the fact that I cannot support TARA and its current operations. Which is why I need to resign as lead professor of—"

"Stop," Amina said, elements of her 'work-self' creeping into her voice. "Give me three months."

"What?"

"Give me three months to turn TARA around. It won't be exactly what it used to be," Amina confessed. "But I promise you it will be closer to what it should be, and a place in which you can be proud to work."

"How, exactly, are you planning to do that?" Tanager was skeptical.

"Give me until tomorrow morning to make my proposal. I can meet you at TARA to discuss it. Let us just say, I have met with the Elders and I am seeking my redemption."

Tanager sat back on the couch for a moment, more confused than ever.

Amina leaned forward, resting her elbows on her knees for emphasis.

For the first time in the years that he had known Commander Royce, she had tears in her eyes. "I can be better," she whispered regretfully.

The morning talk at TARA included Tanager, Lucene, Cepheus, Moksha, Isabella, Ivan, and for once, Fatima, with baby in tow. They sat around the table in the private Resource Room as Commander Royce established new guidelines for TARA.

She addressed Lucene first. "I know I haven't exactly given you a specific role as a PDL agent," she touched Lucene's arm in what was the only time Royce had shown any type of affection. "I'd like to change that."

"Okay," Lucene answered suspiciously. "What did you have in mind?" She was well aware of Tanager's move to resign yesterday and was still distrustful after Dallen almost succeeded in kidnapping her.

"Your healing ability has not gone unnoticed," Royce replied. "But I think we should officially pay you as a natural energy worker at the Dragoste Healing Center. We still need to see how your skills match up against traditional medicine, but I suspect we'll find that the cost of hiring you is a small investment compared with what they will save in long hospital visits, surgeries, and rehab which may or may not be necessary."

Moksha rubbed her knee, instinctively. She shuddered to think how she would have fared following the wolf attack were it not for Lucene's intervention.

"Is this one of those 'not really a request' requests?" Lucene challenged.

Royce smiled, knowingly. "No, this is an optional request. But I believe you can do a lot of good by accepting. It's only part time, of course, and as you grow into your skills, you can pass that on to students at TARA."

"Gimme a day or two to think on it?" Lucene finally answered.

"Of course," Royce replied.

Commander Royce then turned her attention to Tanager and

Cepheus. "As for my esteemed professors, you will have the opportunity to continue running the Makerspace and TARA as you have done previously, leading the Data Collector training program and developing a self-defense weaponry program which, like it or not, we desperately need right now."

Tanager let out a sigh as if letting out hot air from a bicycle tire.

"Three months," she reminded him. "Give me three months to prove that I can help turn this planet around and make it worth you staying on at TARA." She didn't, however, have any idea how to address the fact that money was tight, and he was likely taking a pay cut.

Cepheus clung to Moksha's hand under the table, neither one letting Royce in on the fact that they had no intention of remaining on Erde for much longer. Still, he reasoned that any one of Tanager's lead students: Xeni, Clusaladek or Neroni would be able to support Tanager with the Data Collector training program.

"May I ask what it is we're training them to do, exactly," Tanager asked pointedly. "It's pointless to continue trying to collect environmental data on Earth—they clearly don't want us."

"I know," Royce explained. "But we still need those skills—not quite as militant as what we've seen in the past year in their training, but more of a…compromise."

"Compromise?" Tanager asked.

"Yes, we can still support neighboring planets in need, but we also need to prepare ourselves for the eventuality of war. And without the Vitruvians financial support and protections, we need to start training now, and training fast."

"Exactly how much 'financial support' are we talkin' about?" Ivan asked.

"I don't have the exact details in front of me but, why—"

"Er," Ivan rubbed his ear. "I might be able to provide modest support to your endeavors provided you're willing to grant me a wee request."

"What kind of request?" Royce wanted to know.

"It's just that, this border-closing thing… While I understand your reasons, there's got to be a way for certain parties to travel back and forth for specific reasons. Seems like planetary suicide to cut ourselves off from all outsiders."

Cepheus leaned forward as if to speak, but remained silent. Fatima reached out to give Ivan's knee a supportive squeeze. At that moment, Fatima and Cepheus exchanged knowing glances. Ivan was, once again, looking out for them.

CHAPTER 35
TRANSITIONS – THREE
NOW...THREE WEEKS AFTER THE END.

"What's bothering you?" Lucene asked when Tanager met her on the steps of the newly refurbished Dragoste Healing Center. For the past week, Tanager had insisted on meeting Lucene for lunch on the days when she was working at the center or the costume shop. He would pace back and forth outside like an insistent cat until her break arrived. Sometimes, he'd bring lunch, like today. At other times, they would dart into a local cafe for a quick bite.

She didn't really need to ask. Even without using any of her telepathic skills, this one was pretty obvious.

"Here," Tanager handed her half of an almond butter and ginger seitan hoagie as she sat on one of the concrete steps. Tanager joined her. Oftentimes, other people on their lunch break sat nearby. But on this particular day, they were alone. He set down a satchel and produced a canteen of water. "Hope you don't mind sharing. I forgot to wash yours, so we'll have to drink out of just the one."

"Why would I mind?" Lucene took the canteen and gulped some of the water. She wiped her face haphazardly with the back of her hand before handing it back to Tanager.

"So," Tanager slid the sole of his foot across the new steps, absentmindedly, noticing how smooth they were. "How does it feel being the breadwinner of the household?" He forced a smile.

"Good one," Lucene acknowledged. She didn't recall having used that Earth expression around him. He must have figured it out all on his own. "But the better question is, why does it bother you so much?"

Tanager let out a sigh and thought a moment. "I don't mean to be old-fashioned. I really don't. But ever since I've known you, I've sort of had to…take care of you, in a way. Please don't take that the wrong way," he paused, awkwardly, waiting for the resentful remark that didn't come.

"I won't," Lucene answered calmly, taking a bite of the hoagie.

"Anyway, I didn't mind. Truth be told, I kinda of…liked it. It made me feel important, as if…you needed me."

"I do need you," Lucene interjected.

"No," Tanager shook his head. "You enjoy being with me. You've chosen to be with me. But you don't *need* me," he paused. "And, that's how it should be, I suppose. But now I feel...less than—"

"Less than what?"

"I think that's it…less than," Tanager finished.

"Is it so awful that I now have two very good careers that happen to support our home?"

Tanager took her hand. "I think it's wonderful. Some people spend their entire lives trying to find themselves and their purpose and you've found yours. It's just that, even with Ivan's generous investment, TARA has lost a great deal without Vitruvian backing. After a lifetime of service to the school, I'm now making about what I did as a teaching apprentice more than thirty years ago."

"But this is temporary—" Lucene objected.

"But what if it's not?" He looked her straight in the eyes. "What if this is the best I can ever do for us from here on out?"

"Do you love your work?" Lucene asked.

"Of course, I do," Tanager answered.

"And, do you love me?"

"More than anything. Why would you even ask that?"

"And between my contribution to the household, and your contribution, do you agree that we can continue to create a good life together?"

"That was never in question—"

Lucene leaned over and kissed him. "Then stop crunching the numbers and realize that this is a team effort that goes well beyond money or one person taking care of the other. We're in this for the long haul, right?"

Tanager's eyes began to well up, but he fought back tears. Instead, he hugged Lucene tightly to his chest and smiled. "I'm not entirely certain I understand what 'the long haul' is," he confessed. "But if it means that you and I are together for an eternity, then I'm all for it."

"There you go," Lucene smiled, hugging him back. "That's exactly what I mean."

At the Fortunata Household

"So, I've been meaning to talk to ya...about stuff you may have heard concerning the incident in the sewing room the other day." Ivan peered over Fatima's shoulder. She was giving Talula a bath in the kitchen sink. For some reason, kitchen sinks were the baby's favorite places—not the bathroom sink, the bathtub or even the deep utility sinks at TARA. No, Talula preferred kitchen sinks. They didn't know whether it was the scents from Fatima's cooking, or the shiny faucet, or the sound of the water running. Whatever it was, she gurgled with glee the entire time she was in there.

Ivan paused a moment to reach over Fatima's shoulder and tickle under Talula's chin, playfully. Talula grabbed his finger, her tiny hand not making it all of the way around it and held on tight.

"The grip of a tigress," he commented. Fatima suddenly got a chill, and shivered for a moment, but wasn't sure why. "So...about the other day."

"You mean where you saved Lucene from being kidnapped or killed and helped uncover Dallen's underhanded dealings with Commander Royce? Is that what you mean?" Fatima carefully rinsed the mild shampoo out of Talula's sparsely covered head.

"Er," Ivan tugged at his ear. "I s'pose you could look at it that way." He coughed.

Fatima grinned out of the corner of her mouth. "Or do you mean the part where you almost killed three of Dallen's guards in the process?"

"Er, yeah. That part."

"Here, hold this," Fatima handed him a large bath towel. "Baby, incoming." Fatima lifted Talula from the bathtub and handed her chubby little body over to Ivan who wrapped her securely in the towel, nice and warm. He felt a little perplexed. Fatima just acknowledged that he almost murdered three men and yet she felt comfortable handing their baby to him. Why?

Fatima went to the kitchen table where she had a cloth diaper and onesie at the ready. Ivan knew the routine and gently placed Talula on the table, still swaddled in the thick towel so that Fatima could put the baby's diaper on.

"You were defending my best friend. I'm glad you were there."

There was something odd about Fatima's voice. Perhaps that it was unusually calm as she proceeded to guide fat little baby arms through the sleeves of the onesie. She was typically more…boisterous.

"Fatima, it's more than what happened at TARA. There's something I have been meaning to discuss with you, fer the past year or so, if I'm being honest."

"Really?" Fatima lifted Talula up and the baby instinctively laid her head on her mother's chest as Fatima bounced her lightly up and down. Talula let out a loud yawn. Apparently, bath time was very tiring. "What is it? Should I be concerned?"

"There's a reason I've spent the better part of my adult life as a hermit, tinkering in my garage."

"You're an inventor. It's kind of your thing."

"But it's more than that," he rubbed the baby's back as Fatima continued to rock Talula gently. "I sort of had a rough time of it in my youth, got in with some not-so-great people. I wanted a different life for myself and I thought, if I could bring just one of my ideas to life, I could escape."

"And you did," Fatima touched the side of Ivan's face, lovingly. "Just look at what you've accomplished in the past few months alone when given access to new technology on this planet."

Ivan let out a sigh. "The reason I was targeted by the police, and the reason you are separated from your family now, is more than their fear of my inventions empowering the masses. They were looking for a reason to come after me." Ivan found himself fighting off becoming overly emotional.

"Hey now, what's this?"

"I haven't raised my fists in over twenty years and I vowed never to again. You should know…"

Fatima leaned over and kissed him lightly on the lips before he could finish his sentence. "Hush. That was a different lifetime."

"But, aren't you worried about me around the baby?"

"Unless our baby grows up and befriends a drug lord or opens a chop shop, I don't think we have anything to worry about."

"Wait," Ivan backed away. "You…knew?" How could she know all about his sordid past, his teenage years scraping by with no family to speak of, an orphan who took to the streets at thirteen, mixing with those he thought were his friends, but weren't.

"Of course, I did, silly," Fatima pulled him out of his daydream. "I may not be as tech savvy as you, but I do know how the Internet works."

Talula began to fuss, making a little sucking sound to indicate she was hungry…again.

"But about your family…" Ivan began.

"Yeah, I hope you don't mind, but they'll end up being in our neighborhood after Moksha and Cepheus abandon their house for a palace." The two were relocating to the Royal Training Grounds, a fact that was still unbelievable to everyone. "Aunt Keti and Tai are going to help me manage the vineyard for Moksha, possibly indefinitely."

"Wait, they're coming …here? To Erde?"

Fatima's eyes grew wide, followed by the largest smile Ivan had ever witnessed.

"Part of the trade negotiations to keep Earth and Erde borders open on a case-by-case basis. Many on the preserves are moving back to Earth, and thanks to your negotiations with Commander Royce, she sanctioned my parents, my brother, and my aunt and uncle to relocate here. I was going to tell you before you decided on this walk down memory lane." Fatima tilted her head back and leaned in closely, seductively (at least, as seductive as you can be while holding a baby). "So you see, my darling. You're not the only one with secrets."

The Animal Lab

"You're back!" Mati squealed, his long tail swishing from side to side. Now that the cat was no longer in quarantine, he could pick her up. Before the cat could protest, he scooped her into his arms and hugged her. "Tabby! Where have you been? Your parents will be so thrilled when I tell them you came back."

Where else was she going to go? Back in her house-cat form, her options were to scrounge for scraps on the street until an animal collector inevitably caught her or return to the animal lab where at least she would be reunited with her adoptive caretakers and be fed and sheltered for the remainder of her days…at least until the next lifetime.

"Put me down, you vermin," Hysechia tried to hiss at Mati. "You smell like a two-week-old sausage that's been left out in the sun!"

Unfortunately, the only thing that came out of her mouth was a pathetic, "Meow?"

CHAPTER 36
GOODBYE, NOT CHRISTOPHER
NOW.

"Hello, Not Christopher," Lucene stood at the water's edge at Tranquil Beach as Not Christopher suddenly appeared beside her. This time, he was wearing a tan guayabera shirt with the same white linen pants. He was barefoot. Lucene wasn't sure why the change of wardrobe.

"Good to see you again, Lucene." He gazed over the horizon.

"I figured out who you are."

"Really?" Not Christopher turned to look at her. "How?"

"I thought you were going to ask, 'who?'"

"My question is far more interesting, don't you think?"

"Perhaps," Lucene smiled at him. "Please, sit a moment, if you don't mind getting sand on your clothes."

"You know I don't."

The two sat, Lucene crossing her legs in front of her and digging her fingers into the cool sand simply because she liked the way it felt.

Not Christopher sat beside her, stretching his legs out in front of him, one over the other and leaning back on his hands.

"The reason why I couldn't remember most of my crushes from the past, except the one who tried to kill Reverend Isabella and hand me over to the Royals..." She waited.

As if reading her thoughts, Not Christopher nodded. "Trauma has a way of sticking," he acknowledged.

"Agreed."

"But the others?"

Lucene nodded her head, peering out over the water, seeking the right words. Of course, he already knew what those were.

"You were my ideal man, Not Christopher," Lucene answered simply. "I must have invented you around the age of twelve. And, once I did, who could live up to you? You were the perfect fantasy boy."

"What gave me away?"

"Aside from your obvious perfectness, I think it was the 'for me to know and you to find out' phrase that tipped me off. Not something most adults would say, is it?"

"I suppose not." Not Christopher blushed slightly at being described as 'perfect.' Of course, he would; Lucene imagined him that way. Humility was built in. "But I'm not so perfect anymore, am I?"

"No," Lucene admitted. "I mean, you are, but there's perfect and there's—"

"Perfect for you," Not Christopher finished.

"Exactly."

"On the one hand, I might never criticize you…never find another woman attractive…never become impatient or misunderstand you—"

"True," Lucene agreed.

"But on the other hand, I would never have imagined sacrificing myself to the Null people to save your life, or designing a high-home to remind you of the only home you'd known on Earth. And I certainly wouldn't have risked hell and high water to retrieve you from Earth, almost getting killed by the Royals in the process."

"No, who could have imagined that? But—"

"But, what?"

"Renenet said that Tanager called it off with Amy because he had this ideal vision of me, being of the same vibration and all."

"But he explained that to you. And, you didn't exactly turn out to be so perfect yourself, now did you?"

"Definitely, not."

"And yet, he didn't suddenly go running back to the arms of his ex-lover, now did he?"

"No," Lucene smiled, hugging herself. "He didn't."

"What did he do?"

Lucene paused. "He loved me even more."

"Flaws and all," Not Christopher agreed. "Though, I don't think Tanager views them as flaws. Frankly, I think he finds them charming. That's not something I would have ever done. Which brings us to the cold hard truth that—"

"I don't need you, anymore, Not Christopher. I'm sorry."

"You don't have to be sorry," he explained, "I'm a figment of your imagination. I could only be offended if you created me that way."

"One thing?"

"Yes?"

"Did I never think to give you a name?"

Not Christopher laughed. "No, I guess you did not. You created me with perfect hair, perfect teeth and skin. And I'm in pretty good shape, if I say so myself. I'm well-read and educated and like all the same things that you do. And yet…no name."

Lucene smiled, placing her hand on Not Christopher's arm. Surprisingly, she could feel it.

"The portal," he explained. "It messes up perceptions a bit. I seem to be flesh and blood, but I'm not. In fact," Not Christopher stood up, brushing sand from the back of his pants, "once the portal finishes closing, I won't be back anymore. Is there anything else you need to say to me before I go?"

"Just, thank you," Lucene's eyes began to turn red, just a little. "I believe I am going to miss you, Not Christopher."

"Goodbye, Lucene," Not Christopher said as his visage began to fade. Just then, his sandals washed in on an ocean wave. He stooped to pick them up. Before completely vanishing, he stood upright and said, "And not to worry. There's someone much better waiting for you at home."

The End … For the Time Being.

ABOUT THE AUTHOR

Danielle Palli is a multi-genre author, Board Certified Positive Psychology & Mindfulness coach, and multimedia content creator & book coach. She lives in Florida with her husband and a plethora of pets. She finds joy in nature, travel, music, theater and the arts, and is known for singing and dancing around the living room at any hour of the day or night. As a free-spirited outlier enamored with life, she finds that life is more exciting when you color outside the lines. Learn more: www.-DaniellePalli.com.

www.ingramcontent.com/pod-product-compliance
Lightning Source LLC
Chambersburg PA
CBHW070824020826
48982CB00014B/451

* 9 7 8 1 7 3 6 7 9 8 2 3 2 *